Derek Nicholls was b̶o̶r̶n̶ ... native Birmingham and at Durham University. After a nomadic existence in the RAF and as a computer consultant, he now lives near Banbury in Oxfordshire. He is the author of three previous novels, as well as the predecessor to *In Her Own Right* in the Boothby-Graffoe saga, *The Dangerous Flood*.

In
Her Own
Right

DEREK NICHOLLS

WARNER BOOKS

A *Warner* Book

First published in Great Britain
by Little, Brown and Company in 1995
This edition published by Warner Books in 1996

A CIP catalogue record for this book
is available from the British Library

ISBN 0 7515 1320 2

Typeset by Solidus (Bristol) Limited
Printed and bound in Great Britain by
Clays Ltd, St Ives plc

Warner Books
A Division of
Little, Brown and Company (UK)
Brettenham House
Lancaster Place
London WC2E 7EN

To my fellow author
and dear friend,
Dinah Lampitt

The Boothby-Graffoe Family
1914–1968

Edmund Boothby-Graffoe
7th Duke of Lincolnshire

William,
8th Duke
(1855–1921)

Ralph,
9th Duke
(1890–1925)

MARRIED

Celia Jameson
(1903–   )

Gerald
(1892–1916)

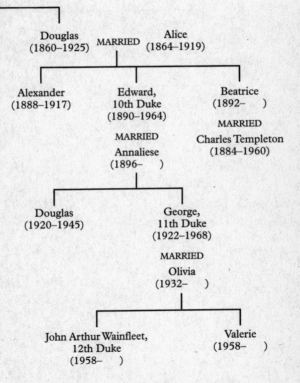

Douglas
(1860–1925) MARRIED Alice
(1864–1919)

Alexander
(1888–1917)

Edward,
10th Duke
(1890–1964)

MARRIED

Annaliese
(1896–)

Beatrice
(1892–)

MARRIED

Charles Templeton
(1884–1960)

Douglas
(1920–1945)

George,
11th Duke
(1922–1968)

MARRIED

Olivia
(1932–)

John Arthur Wainfleet,
12th Duke
(1958–)

Valerie
(1958–)

Author's Note

Like its predecessor, *The Dangerous Flood*, this is a work of fiction and all the principal characters are imaginary. I emphasise this particularly in respect of the Archduchess Annaliese von Habsburg, who is presented as a member of a very real and distinguished family. The Habsburgs ruled Austria uninterruptedly from 1273 until their enforced exile in 1919 and they still exist. The present head of the family, Dr Otto von Habsburg, eldest son of the last Emperor, is a member of the European Parliament and has many living relatives. But Annaliese, her parents Joseph and Elsa, and her brother Leopold are products of my imagination.

However, since the story takes place against the backdrop of events in Europe and Great Britain, my characters do tend to have contact with real people, individuals whose place in history puts them in the public domain.

I owe a debt of gratitude to Alice Wood, my editor at Little, Brown, whose encouragement and suggestions have been invaluable.

Derek Nicholls

Prelude

'He was the sort of man who *would* get himself murdered! You might even say he deserved it.'

Lavinia Torksey's scathing description of Ralph, Ninth Duke of Lincolnshire, met with little dissent. Always seen as a danger to the reputation of the aristocracy, the late Duke had few sincere mourners. In private, even his young widow had come to the conclusion that she was glad to see the back of him. There was a flicker of cynical admiration for the manner of Ralph's death: he had been killed by a jealous husband. But it was no substitute for the sort of sympathy a man of thirty-five ought to have earned – especially since he had inherited from his father only four years previously.

Two days after the murder, the bereaved Duchess had given birth to a baby. Powerful men in the Establishment had spent the intervening period generating doubt as to whether the child – if a son – could or *should* be the heir. In the event, the little boy lived for only a few hours, and Edward Boothby-Graffoe, Ralph's cousin, took the title and a huge fortune.

'He's decent enough,' Lady Torksey assured those who had never heard of the new duke – and they were in the majority. 'Face facts, for heaven's sake. Whatever he does, he must be an improvement on that *creature*, Ralph!'

Unintentionally, the newspapers had damned him with faint praise, painting a picture of a worthy but dull man who was the same age as his ill-fated predecessor. In fact, Edward was probably the brightest intellect any branch of his family had ever produced. Following a brilliant passage through Winchester and Oxford he had entered the Foreign Office and made exceptional progress. He was well on the way to achieving his ambition of being Head of the Diplomatic Service by the time he was fifty-five: indeed, but for the need to wait for the retirements that would unblock his path, the prize might have been within his grasp even sooner. For Edward, the dukedom had started as an unexpected, utterly unwelcome chore: then, after the three worst days in his life, it wrecked his career. Since he was now eligible to sit in the House of Lords and become involved in politics – officially, in contrast to the ill-advised dabblings of 1921 – there was no question of him being allowed to continue in the Civil Service. No one outside his immediate circle knew that he regarded this as a cruel blow: all that mattered was that the Tenth Duke seemed to be a steady, upright chap with the unnecessary luxury of a decent brain.

In any case, the real interest was riveted on his wife.

Lady Torksey again: '*She's* the one that matters and you couldn't have found anyone better in a hundred years. Mark my words, she'll do a magnificent job!'

Following the furore stirred up by Ralph's death, Annaliese, Duchess of Lincolnshire, was a godsend to the press in the news-starved summer of 1925.

Firstly, she was extraordinarily beautiful. Tall, with a mass of lustrous, golden hair, she carried herself with a bearing that inspired admiration and respect even before the amazing, cornflower-blue eyes cast their spell. Later, there was time to take in the broad forehead, firm chin, generous mouth, and wonderful cheek bones.

Next, there was her family background. She had started life twenty-nine years ago as the Archduchess Annaliese von Habsburg of Austria. It was the assassination of her cousin, the Archduke Franz Ferdinand, at Sarajevo on 28 June 1914 that had triggered the events which culminated in the Great War.

How could a man supposedly as dull as Edward Boothby-Graffoe have captured such a marvel?

Her Grace moved swiftly to nip speculation in the bud by granting an interview to Geoffrey Dawson, editor of *The Times*, and Viscount Rothermere, owner of the *Daily Mail*. She began by stating that she had met her future husband in pre-war Vienna, when he was a relatively minor official at the British Embassy. Later, both Dawson and Rothermere suppressed Annaliese's hints that Edward's true occupation had been that of a spy, nor did they dwell on the couple's dismay at being torn apart by the outbreak of war after barely two months of tenuous friendship.

'The difference in our social standing made it impossible for Edward to think of love,' Annaliese said, letting her two confidants see that she was amused by his temerity. 'Although he was the nephew of a duke and well-connected, I was an *Arch*duchess of the Imperial Family. He was frightfully abashed by it.'

Two of Fleet Street's most hardbitten practitioners were bowled over by the mischievous warmth of her smile and effortless, accent-free command of English.

Then, with calm dignity, Annaliese had spoken of the War's dire effects in Vienna and the consequences for the Habsburgs. She recounted the final quarrel with her parents and her subsequent departure to Germany to work as a nurse. 'I went with my maid . . . it would have been impossible without Eva. Oh, I was very determined and headstrong, but she was the one who knew how to *do* things.' They had, Annaliese went on to explain, spent nine months in a field hospital on the Western Front before being transferred to a big infirmary in Berlin. There, on a grim January afternoon in 1919, after a separation of four and a half years, Edward had simply appeared out of nowhere.

'How did he know where you were?' Rothermere asked. 'Had you managed to contact him?'

'No. Edward was a member of the British delegation at the Paris Peace Conference. My brother, Leopold, was also there, playing politics.' She disapproved strongly. 'Edward and Leopold bumped into each other and all was revealed. Edward left for Berlin almost at once.'

'Heading for a blood-bath,' Geoffrey Dawson murmured, recalling the civil war that had raged through the German capital and several provincial cities during the first half of 1919.

Annaliese shuddered at the memory. 'That night, the night Edward reached Berlin, the *Freikorps* murdered Rosa Luxemburg and the big guns hardly stopped. They even shelled the hospital! Many were killed, including my friend, Eva.' She fell silent, her face clouded by remembered grief.

'But you managed to escape?' Viscount Rothermere prompted.

'Yes, we fled to Paris.' Annaliese toyed with the idea of elaborating on the difficult journey, but decided against it. There was no point in resurrecting that day of fear and peril, when the 'dull' Edward had, without a moment's hesitation, shot dead a Spartacist Red Guard who tried to molest her. The romance that had sprung from the danger was a thing of the past, best left undisturbed. Masking her sadness with a disarming gusto, Annaliese completed the tale.

'I hate Paris and refused to stay there a minute longer than was necessary. My parents were exiled in Portugal, but I didn't want anything to do with them. And, like all the Habsburgs, I was banned from Austria, so I was stateless.'

'Difficult,' Geoffrey Dawson murmured.

'Not in the least,' Annaliese sparkled. 'My ambition was to come to England. The easiest way to do that was to marry Edward. By the way, we were very much in love.'

Dawson and Rothermere chuckled indulgently: their assistants had unearthed the details of the hurriedly arranged ceremony at Fontainebleau. Further research had shown that the newly-weds, seeking to spring a colossal surprise on Edward's parents, had arrived in England two days after his mother died, a victim of the terrible 1919 influenza epidemic. No one mentioned that, of course. Instead, Annaliese volunteered a flood of details about her work at Boothby's, the family-owned auction-house in Bond Street, and was disarmingly forthcoming about her friendship with the slightly notorious Nancy Shenstone.

The Times and *Daily Mail* duly printed extensive articles. At once, Annaliese's fame and popularity were assured.

The previous Duke of Lincolnshire seemed destined for a permanent place in the gossip-columns.

From the age of seventeen, he had devoted much of his time and energy to seduction. The tally of his conquests beggared belief, prompting the maxim that no woman was safe from his attentions. In all honesty, there were many ladies who were so smitten by the physical excitement he generated that they had no wish to be safe – quite the contrary, in fact. Forgetting their husbands – the Marquess of Axholme, as he then was, went out of his way to avoid single women – Society's beauties flung themselves at his feet. For sixteen years, Ralph revelled in the uproar caused by his promiscuity. Then, Celia Jameson popped up from nowhere.

In 1923, two years after succeeding to the dukedom, Ralph had married Celia. Since he ranked third in the hierarchy of the peerage, the wedding should have been *the* social event of the year, but was not announced until a month after it had taken place in clandestine privacy. No one knew who Celia was, or when and how she and Ralph could possibly have met. Despite the efforts of Lady Torksey, Nancy Shenstone, and many other dedicated searchers after the truth, the curtain of mystery was to remain impenetrable.

Under Ralph's regime, Allardyce Castle had virtually ceased to be a social focal point and Celia's public appearances were rare. Even so, a few people – including Annaliese and Edward – were able to meet her. They discovered a disturbingly attractive young woman of twenty-one who was painfully ill at ease as the Duchess of Lincolnshire. She did, however, appear to have put a stop to Ralph's compulsive lechery. The men with whom she came into contact saw that, out of her depth though she was, Celia had a potent aura of sexuality. It was obvious that Ralph's apparent fidelity was being achieved by expert gratification of his every whim. He stopped hunting for new conquests and dropped all but one of his established mistresses.

Allardyce Castle, nestling in Wiltshire's idyllic Vale of Pewsey, had the vastness of its 8,000-acre park to act as a barrier to the outside world. Consequently, no one knew about Blanche Hamilton, wife of the estate manager. She had been Ralph's favourite sexual accomplice for eight years, surpassing and outlasting all the others, always there when needed. For the first eighteen months of his marriage, Ralph saw Blanche very infrequently. But, during the latter stages of Celia's pregnancy, the affair was resumed with all its special, furious passion. Blanche's husband knew what was going on and turned a blind eye: the effects of shell-shock in the Great War had left him a pathetic wreck of a man, an object of pity whom most people crossed the road to avoid.

As well as considerable property in the centres of London and Bristol, and 30,000 acres at Glengrantach in Perthshire, the Duchy of Lincolnshire estates included a group of farms in North Devon. Early on the morning of Monday 15 June 1925, Richard Hamilton left Compton Allardyce to carry out a six-monthly inspection of the farms. He told Blanche that he would not be back until Saturday evening.

Ralph returned from a three-week absence in the USA on Wednesday afternoon. He spent less than an hour with Celia before leaving for what he claimed was an evening with friends who lived fifteen miles away. In reality – and Celia, very near the end of what had been a wretched pregnancy, was aware of this – he went to the Hamiltons' house, hidden away in Keeper's Wood on the eastern side of the Park. He was still there at midnight when Richard Hamilton arrived, nearly three days earlier than expected.

Anticipating the unusual, Richard left his car several hundred yards away from the house and approached quietly. Not that Blanche and Ralph were likely to hear much above the noise they were making in a bedroom. After fetching his shotgun from a shed, Richard climbed stealthily upstairs, passed through the wide-open door and committed a double murder. Firing from point-blank range, he blew the heads off Blanche and Ralph as they thrashed in the final throes of intercourse.

Calmly, Richard went downstairs, telephoned the police station in Marlborough, and told the night sergeant what he had done. Then he reloaded the gun, put the muzzle in his mouth, and pulled the trigger again.

Six weeks later, the reverberations of horror and scandal

showed no signs of diminishing. In the midst of shocked confusion, Edward and Annaliese were a beacon of hope, so ideal that Ralph's murder and the tragic death of his posthumous son began to seem like a blessing in disguise. The Tenth Duke and his Duchess were perfect in every way and had two wonderful sons. Douglas, Marquess of Axholme, was five, George, his younger brother, was three. To complete the distinguished family, Edward's sister, Beatrice – *Lady* Beatrice Boothby-Graffoe now that her brother held such lofty rank – was the elegantly attractive head of Boothby's in Bond Street.

Everything had turned out for the best.

But things were not what they seemed.

All too early in her marriage, Annaliese had begun the painful process of discovering that Edward was a rigidly puritanical stuffed shirt, ruled by a bigoted code that was at odds with the beliefs of his parents. Although Annaliese had never known her mother-in-law, it was evident that Lady Alice was at least as broad-minded as her husband. Lord Douglas Boothby-Graffoe, who, after an awkward start, had become Annaliese's first real friend in England, always displayed the most liberal attitudes.

The first bone of contention had been the question of Annaliese working at Boothby's. On this issue, Edward was confronted with a *fait accompli* and gave in with a pretence at good grace. Paul Marks, who also worked at the auction-house, was another matter. The discovery that he was helping Annaliese and, therefore, close to her, threw Edward into a rage. Paul, impeccably mannered and knowledgeable, was a homosexual, a species that Edward detested: being near to one made his flesh creep, he said. For all their sakes, but with Edward's reputation and career at the Foreign Office particularly in mind, Annaliese was *ordered* to have as little as possible to do with Paul. While appearing to accept the harsh judgement, Annaliese found that the first seeds of resentment had been sown.

The quarrels over Nancy Shenstone were far more serious and protracted. An American heiress who had married a much older man, gaining a title in return for bailing him out of a financial mess, Nancy was a stunningly beautiful woman of fiercely independent views. She lived apart from her husband at a house in Upper Belgrave Street. Its exotic name, Martha's Vineyard, hinted at the epicurean lifestyle behind its bland exterior. The snoopers and gossip writers were never able to prove a thing, but Lady Shenstone, and all those lucky enough to be her friends, had a tantalising whiff of wickedness about them. Edward reacted angrily when Annaliese began to visit Martha's Vineyard.

Ignoring his nagging, Annaliese continued to see Nancy. All might have been well but for Franklin, the butler at Lord Douglas's house in Cadogan Square, the place that was effectively home for Edward and Annaliese during the first six years of their marriage. Franklin, who had never bothered to conceal his dislike of Annaliese, spied on her and told Edward that she continued to visit Nancy.

And it was Franklin who started the quarrel that Annaliese immediately felt was dangerously close to the last straw. Beatrice's fiancé had been killed during the War – ludicrously, it always seemed, as a result of an encounter with a back-street thug in Marseilles while on a secret mission with Edward. There had never been any question of Beatrice marrying anyone else, however, she fell deeply in love with Charles Templeton, a merchant banker. To all intents and purposes, Beatrice and Charles lived together, a fact that everyone succeeded in concealing from Edward for an astonishing length of time. Eventually, it was Franklin who let the cat out of the bag, maliciously emphasising the point that Charles Templeton was married.

The ensuing row was appalling in its intensity, driving Beatrice to the brink of a nervous breakdown and outraging Annaliese. Hearing of it, Lord Douglas left Upper Overs, his secluded home in the Ashdown Forest, charged up to London, sacked Franklin and read the riot act to Edward. The peace that was finally restored was all the more uneasy because the rift occurred only two days before Annaliese and Edward, accompanied by their sons, were due to leave for Portugal to see Annaliese's parents – her first contact with them for nearly eight years.

In the end, Annaliese allowed Edward to accompany her and the boys purely to avoid upsetting her mother and father. As things worked out, the visit began well with a chastened Edward at pains to behave and impress. By the end of the first week at the villa on a remote headland above the fishing village of Cascais, there were signs that redemption of the marriage might just be possible. Then, Edward made a blunder that was to put the matter beyond question. Leaving a lunch-party consisting of his father-in-law and two other exiles, Edward walked down through the large, terraced garden in search of Annaliese. She was at the swimming-pool with her mother, the Archduchess Elsa. While Elsa sunbathed, Annaliese was swimming. She was naked and in no great hurry to reach for a robe once she left the water.

Edward's outburst of moral indignation was fearful, baffling Elsa and stirring Annaliese to white-faced fury. His justification was that the grounds were crawling with sentries, members of the old Imperial Regiment whose duty was to safeguard the lives of Annaliese's parents and two neighbours – the Archduke Maximilian and a member of the Russian Royal Family who had escaped the Bolsheviks. Painfully aware that he had made an utter fool of himself, Edward fled to the lane outside the villa, only to be confronted by a young boy who had brought a cablegram from Cascais. Lord Douglas

Boothby-Graffoe had suffered a heart attack. He was alive, but very ill and Edward's immediate return to England was inevitable. There was no question of Annaliese accompanying him and they parted coolly, she relieved that there had been no opportunity to attempt a reconciliation.

Reaching England on 9 June, Edward found his father out of danger and improving. Four days later, a second heart attack killed Lord Douglas. Annaliese decided to let her holiday run its pre-arranged course, insisting that it was pointless attempting to get back in time for the funeral on the 17th. At midday on 19 June, Edward learned of Ralph's murder.

There should have been two other people protecting him from the dukedom. But Ralph's brother, Gerald, and Edward's elder brother, Alexander, had both perished in the Great War. The only hope was Celia's unborn child – which *had* to be a son. The little boy, originally seen by Edward as a gift from the gods, died within hours of delivery on 21 June. The following day, Edward went to Southampton to meet Annaliese.

She, knowing nothing of Ralph's murder, was unaware that she was already Duchess of Lincolnshire. On the short voyage from Lisbon, she had resolved to leave Edward. Weary of his moods and patrician attitude, she was also sick to death of the frustration produced by the ineptitude of his irregular attempts at love-making. She wanted a new life.

Dashing on board the liner the minute it docked, Edward told Annaliese what had happened and discovered her plans. He pleaded with her to stay – not for himself, but to assist with the ordeal of the inheritance that had been thrust upon him. Without her, he would renounce the title.

On her first visit to Allardyce Castle in 1921, Annaliese had fallen head over heels in love with a place that she considered even more beautiful than Schönbrunn. The chance of being its mistress was irresistible. Brazenly honest, she left Edward in no doubt of her reasons for granting his request. And there were conditions.

'You and I will have to live our lives differently,' she said. 'I shall want certain freedoms, Edward.' After staring at him long and hard to ensure they understood one another, she added, 'There will be total secrecy and discretion, of course.'

He accepted the terms, knowing that they were not open to negotiation.

Ralph and his baby son were laid to rest in the family vault beneath the Castle's private chapel on 29 June. Nancy Shenstone was present and, for the first time, was treated with respect by Edward. That afternoon, the smoke from a large fire was seen over Keeper's Wood. The house in which Ralph, together with Richard and Blanche Hamilton, had died so gruesomely was being razed to the ground.

The Duchess of Lincolnshire had ordered it.

1

1925

'My wife is in charge of things here'

Annaliese's patience was near the end of its tether. 'Edward, you've been ready for an hour,' she said. 'At least consider the poor man who's waiting to drive you to London.'

'You want to get rid of me.' The hangdog expression that went with the accusation was unflattering, emphasising the length of Edward's rectangular face. With his sleek, fair hair and pale blue eyes he could look handsome – but not when he was feeling so sorry for himself.

'No, I simply think that you should leave for your holiday and let me get on with putting this place right.'

For the umpteenth time, Edward wandered to one of the deep, mullioned windows. This was the largest of the three sitting-rooms in the suite on the first floor of the West Wing that Annaliese had chosen as their private quarters. Gazing across the Park, Edward registered something akin to distaste before turning to ask, 'Are you sure you won't change your mind and come with me?'

'No. How many more times do I have to tell you that I will not

twiddle my thumbs while you and your friends shoot birds.'
Edward was paying his first visit to Glengrantach, his Scottish
estate. After being driven up to London, he was meeting half a
dozen political associates for the long journey on the sleeper to
Perth. 'None of your colleagues are taking their wives,'
Annaliese went on. 'Why should I be the one to suffer?'

Edward made a growling noise and stared at his shoes.

'Tell me what's bothering you,' Annaliese ordered.

'Celia.' It was an involuntary reaction, not a reply.

'What about Celia?' Annaliese asked wearily. This had been
simmering for six weeks, never quite escaping from Edward's
churlish reticence. 'Spit it out.'

'Are you *sure* we ought to have her living here?'

'I'm absolutely sure.' As ever when she was unyielding,
Annaliese's voice was soft. 'She *is* the Dowager Duchess. You
can hardly put her out on the street.'

'Please don't exaggerate, my dear.' Edward was pompous
now he thought he had the advantage. 'I simply think she'd be
better off living elsewhere.'

'Why?'

'Why?' Edward shook his head in disbelief. 'The place has
the most awful memories for her and things won't improve.'

'That isn't what Celia thinks,' Annaliese said.

'She'll change her mind,' Edward insisted. 'Bound to. It's
not worth having The Chantry done up. For that sort of
money we could buy her a little house in Town.'

The Chantry was the old Dower House, close to the north-
western entrance to the Park. Not used for nearly forty years,
it was badly run down and needed substantial renovation.
Until the work was completed, Celia had rooms in the East
Wing.

'When did you last see her?' Annaliese asked.

'I don't know . . . it must be two weeks . . . that evening
you invited her to dinner.'

There was a cynical twist to Annaliese's smile. Not only had Edward spent most of the last two weeks in London, he would no more dream of visiting the East Wing than flying to the moon. 'Why does Celia irritate you so much?' she asked.

'She doesn't.'

'In that case, stop complaining. When she's settled in The Chantry, she'll be two miles away and you won't see her at all. In any case, she's gone away for a holiday.'

'When?'

'This morning.'

'Where's she gone?'

'She implied that she's visiting a friend.'

'Rubbish!' Edward sneered. 'She has no friends.'

'Don't be ridiculous. Of course the poor girl has friends and she must need them after what she's been through. God knows, *we* haven't been any use to her.'

Edward grunted and returned to the window, scowling at one of the most beautiful views in England. Sensing that there was something else to be raked over, Annaliese waited.

Eventually, after clearing his throat, Edward asked, 'About this wedding.'

'Yes?'

'I'm sorry, Annaliese, but it doesn't seem the done thing to allow servants to marry in our private chapel.'

'You're wrong on several counts,' she said coolly. 'Firstly, I'm encouraging, not *allowing* it. Gwen and Matthew would never have dreamed of suggesting such a thing. Secondly, I don't regard them as servants. They've been loyal to me since I arrived in this country. Remember what happened? We found your mother dead, your father inconsolable, and I was left alone when you had to go back to Paris. I wouldn't have survived without Gwen. Finally, whatever the tradition, I don't see the chapel as "private". I want it to be used by everyone connected with the estate.'

'People will talk,' Edward complained.

'I'd be disappointed if they didn't!' Annaliese's chin had a dangerous tilt, informing Edward that the discussion was over. In all honesty, having made his half-hearted protest, he was as anxious to be away as she was to see the back of him.

'You'll attend to Charles Templeton?' he asked.

'Naturally.' Annaliese appreciated the full significance of the casual question. Angered by their attitude after Ralph's murder, Edward had discharged the bankers and lawyers who had dealt with the Lincolnshire affairs for over two centuries. Having made that one, decidedly contumelious decision, he wanted to be certain that Annaliese was assuming responsibility for bringing order from the resultant chaos. Allowing Charles, his sister's lover, to take over was Edward's idea of a conciliatory gesture.

'We need an estate manager, too,' Annaliese said, moving towards the door. 'Do you want me to look into it?'

'You intend overseeing that side of things?'

'It was what we agreed,' Annaliese reminded him.

'Yes,' Edward nodded absently, concentrating most of his energy on their brisk progress along the wide corridor that ran the whole length of the West Wing. 'You'd better find someone who's up to it.' After a laugh that betrayed his unease, he added, 'Get a chap who won't run amok with a shotgun.'

Annaliese made no response to the flash of tasteless humour. They had reached the head of the Castle's main staircase. Below them, in the entrance-hall, Baskerville and Mrs Pritchard waited, observing the time-honoured rule that the butler and housekeeper would take formal leave of the Duke when he left his main residence for more than two days.

Edward detested it. The man who had fitted effortlessly into the upper levels of the Foreign Office, and whose opinions should have ensured that he welcomed privilege, was rattled by these semi-feudal displays. If anything, Annaliese made it worse by taking his arm as they descended the stairs: the action, intended to boost him, showed how much in command of her status and surroundings *she* was.

'May we wish Your Grace an agreeable stay in the Highlands,' the butler said, handing Edward his hat.

'Thank you, Baskerville,' Edward replied, cursing himself for sounding grateful.

'Come along, Edward,' Annaliese said. 'You've kept Kirby waiting long enough.'

Glancing at the uniformed chauffeur standing rigidly at the open passenger door of the Rolls-Royce, Edward saw that he was one of Annaliese's new acquisitions, staff recruited to replace those she had dismissed within hours of setting foot in the Castle as its chatelaine. In a way, not being honoured with Matthew was an advantage. The po-faced Kirby, still unsure of his position, was unlikely to make any attempt at conversation on the eighty-mile drive to London.

'Enjoy yourself,' Annaliese told Edward. 'Let me know how you are.'

'A postcard, perhaps?'

'Excellent! Small enough to prohibit details of your "sport". Go on.' She kissed him. 'And cheer up.'

Until Kirby had manoeuvred the Rolls away from the gravel circle, Edward looked like a stuffed dummy, waving self-consciously at Annaliese, ignoring Baskerville, Mrs Pritchard, and his sons who were at a window of the Long Gallery with Gwen.

Annaliese remained motionless, watching the motor car disappear towards the south-western entrance of the Park, beyond which lay the village of Compton Allardyce. Why, she wondered yet again, was Edward so disturbed by Celia? He desired her, of course, that much was established fact. But did that *really* explain why he wanted her out of the way? Perhaps if she were living in London an affair might be possible: wasn't there a clause in the unwritten code about not fouling your own doorstep?

There were, however, far more interesting things demanding Annaliese's attention. The social contacts neglected or alienated by Ralph must be resurrected; the Castle needed a great deal of redecoration; less pleasantly, because Ralph had failed to make proper settlement of his father's affairs, *two* lots of death duties had to be paid.

And, most importantly, the Duchess of Lincolnshire intended to take a lover. As yet, the lucky man was unaware of the happiness that awaited him. Hugging herself with glee on his behalf, Annaliese dashed back to the imposing flight of stone steps into her new home.

Late that night, when the only sounds in the great house were its own creaking and whispering, Annaliese went up to the second floor to see Gwen in her room next to the nursery where Douglas and George were asleep. Their evening chats, companionable and frank, were a custom forged in the difficult days at Cadogan Square from 1923 onwards.

Annaliese began by going over the final arrangements for the wedding, now only three days away. In response to a more than usually truculent frown from Gwen, she asked, 'What's wrong?'

'Matthew's getting cold feet,' Gwen said. 'Oh, not about us being wed, he likes that.' Annaliese was relieved. It would be awful if anything came between a couple who had been devoted sweethearts for so long. 'He's afraid of all the nobs you're bringing in.'

'I've been as sparing as I can,' Annaliese protested. 'The fact that both you and Matthew have no family hasn't helped. Mr Templeton is giving you away, Lady Shenstone has volunteered to act as your mother, and Lady Torksey will look after Matthew. What could be simpler than that?'

'Nothing,' Gwen agreed. 'I'll tell Matthew to get a grip on himself. Look on the bright side, it isn't as though we'll have to put up with *him*.'

'Oh, Gwen,' Annaliese sighed, 'it is naughty to talk about Edward like that.'

'I'm only saying what you think,' Gwen retaliated. 'George is getting the same.'

'What can we do about it?' Annaliese asked, seriously worried. Their dark-haired, rather introspective younger son had always been unsure of Edward: sometimes, Annaliese was afraid that George would grow up believing that his father was a bore.

Gwen shrugged. 'Leave it to Douglas.'

The idea seemed sensible. Charmingly complementary, the two boys took it in turns to defer to each other. On matters requiring brain power, George was the one who mattered; when it came to climbing trees, or exploring the Castle's dire cellars, Douglas became leader and protector. The brave, boisterous Douglas worshipped Edward.

There was another worry about George. 'Is he showing any sign of being more settled here?' Annaliese asked.

'He will.' Gwen, like Annaliese, adored Allardyce Castle and was at a loss to understand George's dislike of the place. 'I think it's all too much for him at the moment.' Abruptly, Gwen changed the subject. 'Will you be going back to London with Lady Shenstone?'

Annaliese, who knew where this was leading, tried delaying tactics. 'That depends on you and Matthew. Are you certain you don't want a proper honeymoon?'

The idea offended Gwen. 'Not on your life! What's the point of traipsing off to some strange place when we've got all this?' A grand sweep of an arm denoted the Park and the countryside for miles around. 'We can borrow one of the motors for days out and take the boys with us.'

'In that case, I shall be going to London,' Annaliese said.

'And you'll see Major Brandon?' Gwen's face was alight with an expectancy that verged on the wicked.

'I may bump into him.' Annaliese's stab at lofty indifference lasted only as long as she avoided Gwen's eyes. Once contact was made, they laughed like wayward schoolgirls.

Baskerville and Mrs Pritchard had worked at the Castle since 1905. Ralph's father had set them on, liked them, and, with a nudge of promotion here and there, had lifted them to the top of the staff hierarchy. Sick and tired of Ralph, they had been on the verge of leaving at the time of his murder.

Their quarters were on the top floor of the Central Wing, well away from the other servants. Each had a bedroom and sitting-room and there was a small, shared kitchen. Mrs Pritchard was a war widow; Baskerville, who had never married, had been her late husband's best friend, had risked his life trying to get him out of the barbed wire at Cambrai. More often than not, only one of the bedrooms at the end of the isolated, virtually private passageway was used.

While Annaliese and Gwen chatted, the butler and housekeeper were sharing a pot of tea.

Mrs Pritchard said, 'His Grace seems to have it in for the poor Dowager.'

'He wants rid of her,' Baskerville replied. 'And you know what I think, Doreen. He's right.'

'Oh, Ted!' Although she was no great admirer of Celia, Mrs Pritchard felt sorry for the girl. 'You mustn't blame her on account of her husband.'

'I grant you that.' Baskerville was always at pains to treat his dear friend's opinions with respect. 'The fact is, though, our Dowager is a nobody.'

Mrs Pritchard nodded disconsolate agreement. 'If only we

knew something about her. Where *did* he find her?'

'I reckon there's only one answer to that,' Baskerville said, causing Mrs Pritchard's handsome face to sharpen with curiosity. This was new. He'd always claimed to be as baffled as everyone else.

'What is it, Ted?'

He grimaced, wishing he'd kept his mouth shut. 'You won't like it.'

'That makes no odds. Tell me.'

'Well, you remember the old Duke's funeral?'

Mrs Pritchard shuddered, immediately aware of the event in that distressing day to which he was referring. Towards the end of the buffet after the burial, Ralph had marched into the Long Gallery and announced that his father had expired in the bed of a London whore. Fortunately, all but a handful of guests had left the Castle; Mrs Pritchard – together with Edward and Annaliese – was one of those present and she still felt ill at the thought of it. Soon afterwards, she recalled, the pattern of Ralph's comings and goings had changed as he dropped his established mistresses. Marriage to Celia followed.

'You don't mean you *believe* what he said about the old Duke?' Mrs Pritchard asked.

'I'm afraid I do, Doreen.' Baskerville's face was grave. 'You see, His Grace told me what he used to get up to in London. The silly old gentleman was quite proud of himself. And there was all that performance about bringing the body back.'

'Mmm . . . that was a proper cloak-and-dagger business,' Mrs Pritchard agreed. Then, knowing she was clutching at straws, she asked, 'Surely *he* couldn't have met the woman?'

'I don't see how he could have avoided it,' Baskerville said. 'Look at the facts, Doreen. His Grace, the old Duke, was dead in her flat. Ralph went racing off in the middle of the night to sort it out.'

Mrs Pritchard reflected on the tactics they had always

adopted to avoid giving the Ninth Duke of Lincolnshire his
due: the casual use of his Christian name was the ultimate sign
of contempt. She said, 'I can see what you're getting at, but
isn't this what they call circumstantial evidence?'

'That's what I used to tell myself,' Baskerville conceded.
'Then I got to wondering why our new man hates the sight of
Celia. You mustn't be taken in by His Grace, my love. Some
folks are taking him for a fool, but he's got his head screwed
on. He was a bigwig at the Foreign Office and that means he
has friends in high places. Look at the way the newspapers
took against her.'

'You think he knows she was a prostitute?' Mrs Pritchard
gasped.

'Yes, I do. Explains a lot, doesn't it?'

'What about Her Grace? Does she know?'

Baskerville shook his head. 'I doubt it. It's not the sort of
thing you'd tell a lady of her class.'

'No, I suppose not.' Mrs Pritchard was appalled. Secretly,
she had made her own connection between Celia and the old
Duke's death – only to be ashamed of herself. Now, her most
trusted and respected friend was confirming thoughts she had
dismissed as too awful to contemplate. 'Perhaps it's as well
that poor little boy didn't live,' she murmured.

'I'm sure of it.' Baskerville's conviction made him sound
heartless. 'We might not have got Their Graces if he'd
survived.'

On impulse, Mrs Pritchard asked, 'Do you think they're
happy together?'

He blinked, taken aback by the sheer irrelevance of the
question. 'It's of no consequence, is it? They know where
their duty lies and they'll do it. That's good enough for me.'
As an afterthought, Baskerville said, 'Do you think they're
unhappy?'

'It's hard to tell.' Mrs Pritchard's brow furrowed. 'I don't like them having separate bedrooms.'

'That doesn't mean a thing with people of quality,' Baskerville replied. 'Anyway, mark my words, His Grace will fix that Celia. I reckon he can be a crafty devil when he sets his mind to it.'

He glowed with so much pleasure at the prospect that Mrs Pritchard didn't have the heart to contradict him. From what she had gleaned during the past few weeks, the new Duke of Lincolnshire, clever as he might be, seemed short of common sense.

Nearing the end of her long journey, Celia was beset by doubts. As the train plunged into the last tunnel, blotting out the brilliant scenery that had lifted her spirits, she felt a sense of foreboding. What was the point of going back, trying to recapture what, at a prematurely careworn twenty-three, she already thought of as her youth?

She was doing it for the compellingly simple reason that there was no alternative. However far they had grown apart, Arabella Fenton was the only person on earth who could provide Celia with even a fraction of the comfort and help she needed.

Just as suddenly as it had descended, the darkness of the tunnel was gone, replaced by bright sunlight, palm trees, and white buildings. Brakes grinding, rocking across a maze of points, *Le Train Bleu* drew into Nice. Celia lowered the window and looked out, praying for an early glimpse of Arabella. She was there, attended by two porters, and standing on precisely the right spot to greet Celia through the window when the train finally stopped.

'It's so wonderful to see you, Arabella!' Celia was shocked to find herself close to tears. 'You look marvellous, absolutely marvellous!' It was no more than the truth: did Coco Chanel know that her famous chemise dress could look *this* good?

'Darling, I'm *so* pleased you're here,' Arabella cried, her voice warm with emotion. They kissed and Arabella stood back, frowning. 'Sorry, but you don't look all that clever. Hardly surprising, really. A few days will soon put you right.' She craned her neck, looking up at the luggage-rack. 'Is that all you've brought with you?'

'I didn't want to arouse suspicions,' Celia said.

Arabella made a sympathetic face and turned to the porters, giving them instructions in perfect, idiomatic French. In no time at all, they were making their way down the platform.

'I can't get over how splendid you look,' Celia said. Arabella, who was thirty-seven, had added the sleek gloss of the Côte d'Azur to her svelte beauty. Men engaged in joyous reunions with wives and mistresses managed to grab a few moments to stare longingly at Arabella as she made her serene way towards the exit.

A motor car, sensual and powerful-looking, was waiting for them. There was a man whom Arabella introduced simply as, 'Gaston'. He was about fifty, wiry, fit, with steel-grey hair cropped short, a deeply lined face, and eyes that missed nothing. He glanced only briefly at Celia while saying, '*Enchanté, Madame*,' yet she felt comprehensively scrutinised.

'What sort of car is this?' Celia asked as they pulled away from the station forecourt.

'A Bugatti,' Arabella replied. 'Expensive. Splendid, isn't it?' She was rummaging through her handbag for a pair of sunglasses. 'You'll need these. Until you're used to it, the glare can cause a nasty headache.'

Celia, already screwing her eyes up against the dazzling reflections from the sea and white walls, was grateful. 'It's a shock,' she confessed. 'But I can see why you love it here. Isn't England dull? Look at this fantastic road.'

'This is the *Corniche*,' Arabella said. 'It goes all the way to

Menton – that's beyond Monte Carlo.'

After the restless overnight journey from Paris, there was too much to absorb. However, in all the daze and confusion, there was one certainty: the Côte d'Azur glittered with beauty and wealth. Already, Celia wanted to be part of it.

The Bugatti devoured six miles of the *Corniche* in under five minutes, then Gaston slowed down, veering on to a much narrower road that twisted and turned into the village of St. Jean-Cap-Ferrat. Arabella's house proved to be a mansion set in a large, walled garden on a hillside that gave superb views of the harbour and the sweep of the coast to Monte Carlo.

They alighted from the car in a courtyard whose walls were festooned with bougainvillaea, hibiscus, and dozens of other colourful, sweet-smelling flowers. After gazing round in awed delight, Celia asked, 'Is this yours? Do you own it?'

'Yes. Come along, darling, you look worn out.'

'I am, actually,' Celia said, noticing that Gaston was hurrying indoors with her bags. 'Who's he?' she whispered.

'He looks after me,' Arabella replied airily. 'He's a sort of bodyguard.'

'Is that necessary?' Celia looked round apprehensively.

'It's better to be safe than sorry. What would you say to an early lunch followed by a rest?'

'Heavenly!'

Guiding her up an elegant, plushly carpeted flight of stairs and across a spacious landing, Arabella took Celia to a bedroom that was furnished and decorated in cool pastels, a refreshing contrast to the garish view from the windows. Celia's luggage was at the foot of the bed and Gaston had disappeared. 'He has his own little place at the bottom of the garden,' Arabella said, reading her friend's mind. 'Shall I leave you to your own devices? We'll talk later, when you've recovered.'

Emerging from the bath half an hour later, Celia saw that

the French windows had been opened, giving access to a balcony. Her lunch – a seafood salad, fruit, and a basket of freshly cut *baguette* – was on a table beneath a canvas awning.

As she ate, Celia studied the harbour. Fishing craft were bustling to and fro like a swarm of ants, but they did not hold her attention for long. Much more interesting were the splendid vessels moored alongside a jetty that was obviously fairly new. Although they looked like miniature luxury liners, Celia supposed that the four boats were known as yachts and belonged to men of great wealth. The only signs of activity were a few crew members, immaculate in their uniforms: like all elitists, they were arrogantly proud of themselves. It was association with power and privilege that caused them to be like that and gave Celia a stab of envy and desire.

The delicious food and a glass of wine produced drowsiness. Leaving the balcony, Celia drew the curtains and slipped into bed. She was asleep within minutes.

It was almost 5.00 pm when she woke, aroused by a slight disturbance to the villa's silence. Instantly alert, Celia was sure that it was a man, chuckling. There was a short exchange of conversation in which Arabella was involved: she, too, was amused and speaking what sounded like a foreign language. A door opened, followed by muttering and giggles. There was a gentle slap – a playful palm on buttocks? – then, light footsteps along the landing receded downstairs. Springing out of bed, Celia rushed to peer through a chink in the curtains. A dark-haired, flamboyantly handsome man was making his way through the garden. He was jaunty, had obviously just enjoyed outstanding sex. Passing Gaston's chalet, he was lost in the riotously lush vegetation that seemed to extend down to the harbour. Celia waited and, after a minute or so, was rewarded by the sight of him strolling along the jetty. He boarded one of the yachts to a show of respect from the crew who were on deck. Smiling,

Celia pulled on a peignoir and went in search of Arabella.

She was in the bathroom adjoining her bedroom, lounging sybaritically in warm, perfumed water. 'Good sleep?' she asked Celia.

'I feel much better, thank you.' Celia sat on a cork-topped stool to gaze quizzically at her friend. 'That bed looks as if a hurricane has hit it,' she said, feigning disapproval.

Arabella laughed, throwing back her head. 'That's a good description of Umberto,' she gurgled. 'I must tell him. He'll be pleased.'

'Is this a professional relationship?' Celia asked.

'Darling, be sensible, I beg of you.' Arabella was aggrieved. 'Umberto is quite wonderful, but commercial considerations come first. He wouldn't have it any other way.'

'I thought you were coming here to retire.'

'So did I.' Arabella's beautiful shoulders rose in an expressive shrug. 'That was before I discovered how much in demand I was.'

'Your friend went back to one of the big yachts,' Celia said. 'I watched him.'

Arabella nodded. 'Umberto is a financier . . . and a prince.' She was amused. 'He's also an admirer and close friend of Mussolini.'

'A Fascist?' Celia was dubious.

'There's no need to worry. Prince Umberto Gastaldi's main interest in life is himself. Most of my clients are the same . . . only the best will do for them.' As if to illustrate the point, Arabella raised one of her superb legs clear of the water. 'And the best is *very* expensive on the Côte d'Azur.' She reached out to clasp Celia's hand. 'We can talk about this later. What about *you*, darling? Tell me everything.'

For ten minutes, Celia spoke of Ralph's murder and the death of her child, adding detail to the stark facts she had provided in a letter written two weeks after the double tragedy. Arabella listened in silence, determined not pass judgement, or to remind Celia that she had warned her against marrying Ralph. Not until the story was finished did Arabella ask, 'The new people ... cousin-in-law Edward and the Habsburg woman? Are they kind to you?'

Celia pulled a face. 'There's a problem with Edward,' she said. 'He knows what I was doing before I met Ralph.'

'*He does*?' Arabella's face registered both shock and mischievous curiosity. 'How?'

'In exactly the way you forecast. Remember David Blake?'

'Oh, yes.' Arabella smiled grimly. 'One couldn't forget.'

On the night when Ralph's father had died during intercourse with Celia, Arabella was entertaining David Blake, a barrister, in the next bedroom. At the time, Blake had been a tower of strength in organising a way out of the disaster. Not until several months later, when Celia was considering Ralph's proposal of marriage, did the saviour become a potential threat. Arabella, who always seemed to know everything, discovered that, not only was David Blake a member of the same club as Edward, the two men shared a passion for bridge. It was inevitable, Arabella said, that the way in which Edward's uncle had died would, sooner or later, float to the surface.

'I'm agog to know how the subject cropped up between you and Edward,' Arabella said.

'He told me.' Briefly, Celia was unnerved by the memory. 'He came to see me after Ralph died. The newspapers were saying that Edward would have to be the duke, regardless of my baby, and he was in a shocking state.'

'Why?'

'He didn't want it. I didn't believe him at first. I asked him what the newspapers had against me and he said they probably knew I'd been a whore.'

'Mmm. People in high places,' Arabella mused. 'It's

amazing how stories can get around without ever quite becoming public knowledge. Go on.'

'Edward promised to do his best to see that my son inherited,' Celia continued. 'We both assumed the baby would be a boy. Anyway, I didn't believe him.'

'Why not?' Arabella was surprised.

'It didn't ring true. What man would turn down fifteen million pounds and a title?'

'I'd say that Edward Boothby-Graffoe was a possibility,' Arabella replied. 'He was devoted to the Foreign Office, had visions of being in charge. You could say that becoming a duke has ruined his life.'

'I didn't realise that, not at the time.' Celia's expression was rueful. 'I thought he was after some sort of arrangement, so I offered to sleep with him.'

Arabella whistled at the ceiling. 'How was that received?'

'Badly!'

'I'm not surprised.'

'Don't jump to conclusions,' Celia protested. 'He'd love to. You should see the way he looks at me sometimes.'

'But this wasn't one of those times?' Arabella suggested, faintly mocking.

'No. I should have been more careful. The way I went about it disgusted him.'

'Self-disgust,' Arabella corrected. 'A powerful force with some men. How did you come to make such a hash of it?'

'I was three-parts drunk,' Celia admitted. 'Out of control. He was so annoyed that I imagined he was going to attack me. I fell over myself and got tangled up in a chair.' Celia hesitated, pulled herself together and finished the story. 'Mrs Pritchard – she's the Castle housekeeper – dashed in, the labour pains started and they took me to hospital. You know the rest.'

'How on earth do you and Edward cope with each other after *that*?' Arabella wanted to know.

'We don't. Fortunately, it's a very big place so that I can keep out of his way. He does the same.'

Arabella shook her head sadly. 'Where does all this leave you? What's your position at Allardyce Castle?'

'I don't know,' Celia said wretchedly. 'I haven't the faintest idea how the aristocracy works – Ralph kept me in the dark. I think it depends on Annaliese.'

'Does she know about your "past"?'

'I'm almost sure she doesn't. She goes out of her way to be nice to me.'

'Yes, I can accept that,' Arabella said. 'One doesn't tell the little woman that the Dowager Duchess was a tart!' After they had laughed at the overdone, cut-glass accent Arabella had used to express the sentiment, she asked, 'What's Annaliese like?'

'Baffling,' Celia replied. 'Her background doesn't show *all* that much and she's very ordinary in some ways. Ralph always said that she'd married badly and knew it.'

'Their Graces are alleged to be delightfully happy.' Arabella quoted the English newspapers with an arch smile.

'That's rubbish,' Celia retorted. 'She married in haste and she's repenting at leisure. From what I've seen, they're leading separate lives.'

'Isn't she one of Nancy Shenstone's friends?'

'Very much so.'

'And Nancy's clique *do* have a certain reputation,' Arabella said. 'How fascinating. You say she's good to you?'

'A house on the estate is being done up for me and she's paying me an allowance.'

'With or without Edward's consent?'

'Without,' Celia said. 'I'm sworn to secrecy.'

'Ho hum! It sounds as though she's in charge.' Arabella reached forward to pull the plug from the bath. 'Pass me a towel, darling. So, we come to the burning question: what are you going to do about it all? What are your plans?'

'I don't have any,' Celia admitted.

'Wrong,' Arabella said, stepping out of the bath. 'Totally and utterly wrong! If you don't have plans, other people will foist theirs on you.'

'I appreciate that.'

'Be prepared, then.'

'There was one idea that occurred to me,' Celia said, knowing that her lack of confidence was annoying Arabella. 'I'd rather like to work at Boothby's, their auction-house.'

'Do you know anything about the business?'

'Not a thing. I could learn, though. Annaliese did.'

'How would that help you?'

'Money, of course!' Celia replied. 'I still have what I saved when we worked together, but it's never enough, is it?' After a slight pause, she added, 'And I'd make contacts.'

Arabella studied her friend's expression, suddenly sly and suggestive of their time in St James's. 'Does that mean you want to entertain men again?'

'Why not? I'm like you, Arabella, I enjoy doing it as well as banking the money.'

'Yes, you were good.' Arabella's mind was busy with possibilities, weighing pros and cons. Gently, she asked, 'Did the baby mark you?'

'Not in the least. Look!' Celia stood up and slipped out of her robe.

'Goodness, you're better than ever,' Arabella breathed. 'Tell me, how well-known are you in England?'

'I'm not. Ralph and I had hardly any social life.'

'No pictures in Society magazines?'

'Not as far as I know.' Celia searched her memory. 'The wedding was secret and I don't think the newspapers got a photograph of me after the murder. They were hanging around near the Castle when I came out of hospital, but Annaliese had them shifted.'

'Good.' Arabella nodded, still thinking. 'Even so, you'd be a fool to try anything in London, *especially* using clients of Boothby's. However, things are different here, on the Côte d'Azur. For one thing, I make it a rule to deal only with foreigners, I *never* take Englishmen.' She smiled cynically. 'Apart from anything else, they're mean and incompetent.'

Celia was stunned. 'Could we be partners again?'

'I fail to see why not, darling. At certain times of the year, I can't cope with the demand. Imagine having to turn them away! There are also the gentlemen who need *two* women!'

'We always did rather well with them,' Celia laughed. 'Could we really take up where we left off?'

'I don't see why not. No one's likely to recognise you.'

'When do we start?'

Arabella chuckled at Celia's eagerness. 'We must wait a while, introduce you gently. Look, dear Umberto has asked me to dinner on his yacht this evening – he's expecting friends from Monte Carlo. Come with me.'

'Won't they mind?' Celia asked.

With exaggerated care, Arabella scanned Celia's naked body. 'No, darling, they won't mind in the least,' she murmured.

'I'm going to use the telephone,' Annaliese said. 'And you, dear Nancy, as a reward for your patience, can listen in.'

They were inside the house in Upper Belgrave Street. Although she sensed that something momentous was afoot, Nancy had been as good as gold during the journey up from Wiltshire, content to chatter about the wedding of Gwen and Matthew, which had been a happy success.

It took some time for the operator to make the connection to Sandringham House, the Norfolk home of poor old Queen Alexandra, widowed for fifteen years, as deaf as a post, and rumoured to be in rapidly deteriorating health. When an ossified, male voice answered, Annaliese said, 'Good afternoon. I wish to speak to Major Brandon, please.'

'I doubt whether the Major can be disturbed.' As if toying with irrelevance, the voice asked, 'Who is this calling?'

'The Duchess of Lincolnshire.' Annaliese added a little something to her tone.

The result was pleasing. 'Ah. If Your Grace would be so kind as to hold the line, I will locate Major Brandon at once.'

'Attagirl!' Nancy whispered and winked villainously.

He was slightly out of breath when he reached the phone: later, he was happy to admit that he was 'all of a doodah'. 'This is a nice surprise, Annaliese. How are you?'

'Very well, thank you, John. And you?'

'The same. I'm sorry I never answered your letter, it . . . er . . . well, congratulations on your new status, despite the circumstances etcetera. How are you managing?'

'By the skin of my teeth,' Annaliese laughed. 'The last seven weeks have been hectic, but I've beaten most of it and I'm treating myself to a little holiday.'

'I see. Where are you?'

'In London.'

'Ah . . . er . . . is there any chance of us meeting?'

'That's why I'm calling, John. Can you get up to Town tomorrow?'

'Yes, well, almost certainly. The fact is, what with one thing and another, I haven't taken any leave this summer. I could probably get a few days off – if that would suit you?'

'Ideal,' Annaliese said. 'Could you ask and call me back?'

'Certainly. Where are you?'

'With Nancy Shenstone. Do you have the number?'

'Belgravia one-four-one-two,' John said at once.

Annaliese laughed. 'That knowledge would raise eyebrows, Major.'

'This may take an hour or so,' he said, his sense of humour crippled by anxiety.

Annaliese replaced the receiver to find Nancy gazing at her intently. 'Is this *it*?' Nancy asked.

'I hope so. It depends on John, doesn't it? What if the poor man throws a fit?'

'Be positive!' Nancy said firmly. 'He won't. Hell, he's wanted you for long enough.'

'That might make it worse,' Annaliese said, her courage draining away. Nancy launched into one of her morale-boosting harangues: for ten minutes, she was forceful and very American. Just as Annaliese reached the point of crying, 'Enough! I *will* be positive!' the telephone rang.

'I can have a week off, starting tomorrow,' John announced.

'That was nowhere near an hour,' Annaliese joked.

'I'm sorry.' John sounded huffy. He was nervous.

'Don't be. I'm pleased.'

'Good. I'll get in touch with my usual hotel to see if they have a room.'

Annaliese took a deep breath. 'That won't be necessary, John. You'll be staying here, at Martha's Vineyard.' Driving the point home, she added, 'With me!'

The silence from the other end of the line was terrifying. Nancy, who was doing her best to share the earpiece, drew away to roll her eyes and make a series of frantic, unintelligible signs.

'Are you still there, John?' Annaliese shouted.

'Yes?' Was someone trying to strangle him?

'I thought we'd been cut off.'

'No.' He paused. 'Er . . . does this mean . . . I . . .'

'It does. Is that all right?'

'Yes, of course. Yes.' He *was* being strangled! 'Look, I shan't be able to get away until after lunch tomorrow. Her

Majesty needs me to deal with some chaps from one of her charities.'

'Just get here when you can. Goodbye, John.'

'Oh. Right.'

Having terminated the call so abruptly, Annaliese found that she was shaking.

'That's the ticket,' Nancy crowed, patting her on the back. 'You've done it.'

'Haven't I, though!'

'Hey, I'd give a thousand bucks to see the look on that poor guy's face.'

'I'm trying not to think about it.'

'C'mon, let's get busy.' Nancy was dragging Annaliese out of the chair. 'Stop looking like a dead duck, honey, you've been dreaming of this for long enough.'

'So has he,' Annaliese muttered, attempting to spread the blame. 'It was his idea in the first place.'

Ostentatiously, Nancy said nothing.

Twenty-four hours later, Annaliese was brimming with confidence as she greeted John Brandon after his taxi ride from Liverpool Street station.

He was a tall, distinguished-looking man of forty-seven. Invalided out of the Great War in 1916, John Brandon had been a professional soldier in the Royal Artillery. He returned home to find that his wife had run off to Canada with a man whose main purpose in leaving England was to escape debt. After a year of painful convalescence and emotional misery, his luck changed: the mysterious forces that arranged such things spirited him off to Sandringham as a member of Queen Alexandra's household. One of his duties was the discreet disposal of those works of art that the Queen had never liked, stuff that King Edward VII had accumulated willy-nilly. Boothby's was the chosen outlet.

As a result, Annaliese and John became friends.

Then, after two years, he did an astonishingly brave thing. This reticent, impeccably courteous man sought out Nancy, telling her, in effect, that he desired to be Annaliese's lover. He explained that he had learned two things: firstly, that Annaliese was the victim of an increasingly wretched marriage, secondly, that Nancy, her closest friend and a woman with a certain reputation, was a potential go-between. The meeting, in the Savoy Grill, had taken every last ounce of John's courage and determination.

Because of Annaliese's second pregnancy and the difficulties of George's birth, it was nearly a year before Nancy passed the message on. A week later, popping into Boothby's for a chat, John found himself swept off to lunch at Whitaker's in Cork Street and a conversation even more extraordinary than the one with Nancy.

'Although I am still doing everything in my power to preserve it, my marriage *is* unsatisfactory,' Annaliese had said. 'Particularly in one respect. Nancy Shenstone thinks that I should take a lover. However, for the time being, I cannot bring myself to do that. But I do want us to be friends, very good friends. Can you bear that?'

John had said, yes, he could. At two-weekly intervals they had a meal together then went to a theatre, or a recital at the Wigmore Hall. Revelling in the company of an exceptionally beautiful and intelligent woman, John never forgot those vital words, *for the time being*.

Until the previous afternoon's telephone call, Annaliese's last communication had been a long letter written while she was in Portugal. Unaware of the events lying in wait at Compton Allardyce, she had told John of her decision to leave Edward.

The moment the front door of Martha's Vineyard was closed against prying eyes, Annaliese embraced John and bestowed a warm kiss on his lips.

'Where is your husband?' he asked.

'In Scotland, slaughtering grouse. Plotting, too, I imagine.'

'Plotting?'

'He has *friends* with him.' Annaliese gave the word a coating of sardonic, Viennese mockery. 'They will arrange his entry to the House of Lords and decide the line he will take.'

'He intends being active in politics?'

'He has my total support.'

Nancy, unashamedly hanging round to indulge her curiosity, saw the special smile exchanged by Annaliese and John, a smile of the deepest understanding.

'I shall take John up to our room,' Annaliese told Nancy, supplementing the words with an eloquent look.

Afterwards, secure in the splendour of what they had accomplished, Annaliese and John laughed at the way they had gone about it.

By unspoken consent, they rushed at the first attempt at love-making, desperate to have it out of the way, to be able to say they'd done it, broken the ice. Tight-lipped, standing with their backs to each other, they flung off their clothes and stumbled into bed. It was several minutes before they realised that there was no cause for concern: physically, they were as much to each other's taste as they were mentally.

'Yes, we've done the right thing,' Annaliese said, drawing John into the embrace of her legs. 'Make me happy, John, please make me happy.'

Tenderly and with great skill, he did. Her relief was so immense, that the beautiful whirlwind of orgasm which ended years of frustration reduced her to tears. Cradled in John's arms, she struggled to smile, insisting, 'Don't misunderstand . . . I'm not sad.'

'I know.' He grinned. 'At least, I think I do.'

'Let me tell you.' Her face was taut with intensity. 'I've never felt anything like *that* before. Never!'

John nodded, indicating that he shared the wonder.

'Do you know what I intend to do about my marriage?' The blue of her eyes was suddenly cobalt.

'I think so.'

'What?'

'Thanks to Ralph, the house of Lincolnshire has had enough uproar and scandal to see it through the rest of this century. Your instincts and background dictate that you will do everything in your power to guarantee stability. Therefore, you will not leave your husband.'

'Correct. Besides, I like being a duchess.' Annaliese's eyes were sparkling with mischief.

'That doesn't surprise me. All the right people are saying what a splendid job you'll make of it.'

'Are they?' She was flattered.

'Of course they are. And because you were an archduchess, it's agreed that you're entitled to be a duchess . . . in your own right, as it were.'

'How nice.' Annaliese smiled. 'Continue with your ideas for my future. I shall give every sign of supporting my husband. What else?'

'Well . . .' John faltered, unable to express his hopes.

'What about *us*?' Annaliese prompted.

'Shall we see each other from time to time?'

'You fool,' Annaliese chuckled. 'We shall meet as often as possible – that's very often, by the way – and have lovely sex until it's coming out of our ears. What do you say to that?'

'I may not be able to satisfy your demands.'

'In that case, I shall get rid of you.'

The ensuing days showed that there was no chance of the joke becoming reality. After nights that drained them of energy, they woke late, had breakfast in bed and pottered around until lunch-time. During the afternoon they swam in the indoor pool – one of the house's many exotic attractions – and Annaliese spoke to Gwen on the telephone, checking on the well-being of the boys and the progress of the thousand and one jobs that the Castle staff had been instructed to complete before Her Grace's return. At around seven, Annaliese and John went out to dine at Whitaker's, where they were known and unlikely to cause comment. It was Annaliese's idea to slip away in the evenings, re-entering Martha's Vineyard by a back door and using the service stairs to reach their bedroom.

'You're protecting me,' John said.

'Protecting you?' Annaliese feigned bewilderment. 'What from?'

'Nancy's guests and their activities.'

'I have no idea what you're talking about.'

John appeared to accept her profession of innocence and concentrated on his lamb cutlet. Then, out of the blue, he asked, 'Is Cordelia Milford still a regular at Nancy's?'

Caught off guard, Annaliese gaped at him. Unable to stop herself, she said, 'I'm amazed that you know about *her*.'

'The extent of my knowledge sometimes takes *me* by surprise,' John smiled. 'I believe that she likes an audience for her exploits with young men.'

'I've heard that, too,' Annaliese said.

'Whereas we seem perfectly content with each other,' John murmured.

Annaliese's eyes sparkled as she raised her glass in agreement. The radiance of their love made her look no more than eighteen.

On their last night together, Annaliese introduced the matter that had been occupying her mind for weeks.

'John, I need an estate manager at the Castle. Will you consider it?'

'I've no experience at that sort of thing.'

'You're a man of natural authority, used to telling people what to do. Everyone would respect you. What more could I want?'

He shook his head ruefully. 'You have me at something of a disadvantage.'

He was flat on his back, she was astride him, her jaunty grin concealing the sensual turmoil deep within her. 'I planned it,' she said. 'Just think, we could do this every day. Twice on Tuesdays and Thursdays.'

'Is that wise?' John asked.

'What the devil are you talking about?' Annaliese hooted. 'What's being wise got to do with it? Don't you like it?'

'That isn't what I meant, dearest.' John was deadly earnest, doing his best to ignore the distractions produced by Annaliese's rotating hips. 'If I were to come to Compton Allardyce, we'd virtually be living together. People would gossip. Your husband couldn't ignore it.'

'You have no idea what you're talking about,' Annaliese insisted. 'Listen. The Park is very large and private. I control it. My word is law. Edward *loathes* it. He won't spend a minute longer there than he has to.'

'Where will he live?'

'Cadogan Square. He loves that house.'

John switched to a new line of argument. 'Her Majesty depends on me for so much – I don't know that I could leave her.'

'I appreciate that, my darling. But she's very old and frail. What becomes of you when she dies?'

'There'll be nothing for me to do,' John replied. 'To put none too fine a point on it, "they" will dispense with my services.'

'So, will you promise to consider Compton Allardyce?'

'I promise. Now, shall we enjoy this?'

'Of course,' Annaliese laughed. On the brink of losing control, she welcomed John's desire for activity. As his thrusting took them towards blissful oblivion, she thought how much better than Edward he was at this love-making lark. Should she tell him that? No, not yet: he'd had enough shocks for one week. But her hostess was sure to demand full details and Annaliese looked forward to providing them; perhaps knowledge of John's prowess would stop Nancy bragging about Jack Nesbitt!

Celia stayed at St. Jean-Cap-Ferrat for nearly five weeks, eventually returning to England with reluctance and in the face of her friend's opposition.

'Why bother, for God's sake?' Arabella demanded. 'You've done *tremendously* well here. What *is* the point of going back to people who don't want you?'

'To be honest, I'm not sure,' Celia admitted.

'Well, then!' Arabella was annoyed.

Celia took a turn round the room, stared at the harbour, and said, 'They owe me something.'

'What?'

'*Something*,' Celia shouted. 'I don't know yet.'

Arabella's eyes were piercingly shrewd as she asked, 'Do I smell a desire for revenge?'

'Possibly.'

'That's pointless,' Arabella retorted. 'And dangerous.'

'No it isn't.'

They argued for a whole afternoon and evening, at the end of which Celia remained resolute.

'Very well,' Arabella sighed. 'Have it your own way. Will you accept help?'

'Certainly. What sort of help?'

'Who can you fall back on? Your parents?'

'They don't exist,' Celia snapped. 'You know that, for Christ's sake.'

Arabella shrugged off the rebuke. 'No friends, either.'

'I'll manage,' Celia said.

'Oh?' Arabella was amused. 'What will you tell the Duchess of Lincolnshire, when she asks where you've been? What excuses will you make next time?'

'She won't ask.'

'That's not the impression you've given of her. Hasn't it occurred to you that Edward might get suspicious?' Arabella took a piece of paper from her handbag. 'This is the address of my aunt, Ursula Croft. She has a very nice house in Putney Vale, near Richmond Park. I've written to her about you.'

'What can she do?' Celia asked.

'Ursula will turn you into someone with a respectable past and an alibi for the future,' Arabella said. 'She'll give you a home, a forwarding address, and a justification for everything you want to do. Ursula is my mother's sister, she's quite young — about forty-three, I think — very jolly, and on her own. I recommend you adopt each other.'

'Does she know how you earn a living?' Celia asked, starting to show an interest.

'Darling, she taught me how to set about it,' Arabella laughed. 'She *has* retired. Her past is buried and she's a pillar of local society.'

The following evening, Celia caught the train to Paris. She left behind a wardrobe full of new clothes and lingerie purchased from one of Nice's most exclusive shops. Most of the prodigious bill had been settled with money provided by Karl Nachbaur. A Prussian industrialist, he had spent the summer in Monte Carlo, bolstering the profits of the Casino. He had worshipped Celia on sight, begging her to allow him to prove that he was one of the world's greatest performers in the bedroom. She would cheerfully have indulged him for a quarter of what he insisted on paying her.

'Actually, he isn't bad,' Celia told Arabella. 'But he's a dreadful bore. He goes on and on about Communism.'

'All our men do. They see it as the greatest danger since Lord knows when.'

'I suppose the stories coming out of Russia are rather awful,' Celia replied.

'Mmm . . . blood-curdling.' Arabella smiled wickedly. 'I wonder if the poor take the same view as the stinking-rich?'

'Good point,' Celia agreed. 'Isn't Umberto's chap, Mussolini, a sworn enemy of Communism?'

'True. Hence, *Herr* Nachbaur and his ilk are admirers of *Il Duce*,' Arabella said. 'The Côte d'Azur is packed with Fascists. Actually, your man, Karl, could be a Nazi, something to do with a man called Hitler.'

'What's their game?' Celia asked, not all that interested.

'I believe they're like Fascists, only worse,' Arabella said facetiously.

Upon her early morning arrival in London, Celia telephoned Ursula Croft from a call box in the foyer of the Victoria Hotel.

'Yes, my dear, Arabella has put me in the picture,' was the immediate response. 'Why don't you spend a few days with me before you return to the country? That will give us a chance to arrange things.'

Queen Alexandra passed away on 19 November, two weeks short of her eighty-first birthday. Ten days later, John Brandon caught a train to Wiltshire. He was met at Pewsey by Matthew in a Rolls-Royce. All innocence, Annaliese claimed to have come merely for the ride. 'I've been working frantically hard lately, organising our first Christmas here. I thought it would do me good to get out.'

'It's extremely kind of Your Grace to take the trouble,' John replied, playing the part that he assumed was expected of him.

On a crisp, clear day, the first sight of the Castle's sublime southern aspect affected John powerfully: like all newcomers, he was speechless with admiration.

'Superb, isn't it?' Annaliese said with just the right amount of proprietorial pride. 'Built between 1425 and 1450 to a design by John Craxton.'

'It's like the nave of a great church.'

'Exactly so. Poor old Craxton wanted to do a cathedral, but never got the chance. This is what it would have looked like. It's in the Perpendicular style, you know.'

Smiling gently at her enthusiasm, John said, 'Indeed it is.'

'There are three wings behind the front,' Annaliese went on. 'Eighteenth-century – not nearly so beautiful – decent enough in their own way, I suppose. It's a very big house.' She lowered the partition and leaned forward. 'Will you take us everywhere, please, Matthew? I want Major Brandon to see as much as possible. Go to Gainsborough Wood first.'

'Gainsborough?' John murmured.

'A place in Lincolnshire, isn't it? These links with the title crop up all over the place.'

The wood, two hundred acres of oak and beech trees, was in the north-western corner of the Park. Hidden away at its heart was an attractive house, which, with its outbuildings, showed signs of extensive and tasteful renovation.

'That will be yours if you accept the post, Major Brandon,' Annaliese said. 'Will it do?'

'It seems quite excellent, Your Grace.' John paused nervously. 'Er . . . forgive me for asking . . . that isn't where the previous man lived?'

In deference to Matthew's sensitivities, Annaliese curbed the desire to box her lover's ears: fancy him thinking that she could be so stupid! 'No, his house was in Keeper's Spinney, about a mile away. I had it demolished.'

Ten minutes later, she pointed out another carefully restored house. 'That's The Chantry, where the Dowager Duchess lives.'

'Ah.' John was uncertain of what, if anything, to say. Relying on the partition being sound-proof, he asked, 'Isn't she slightly awkward?'

'Not in the least,' Annaliese replied. 'The poor girl's had a dreadful time and needs looking after.'

'How's she bearing up?'

'Bravely. She's had some luck recently.'

'In what way?'

'A long-lost aunt has turned up. A pleasant woman, I gather.'

John, not sure whether Annaliese was serious, kept quiet.

When the tour of the Park was over, Annaliese took John inside the Castle and up to the Long Gallery, two hundred feet long and eighty feet wide, with fine window tracery making up the whole of the south-facing wall. 'What do you think of *this*?' she asked, her gesture implying that she had been instrumental in its creation.

'Magnificent,' John agreed. 'That's an unusual feature, though.'

He was staring at a trestle table and two folding chairs set by one of the soaring windows. Apart from the few sticks of makeshift furniture, the immense chamber was empty.

'I thought it would be a good place for lunch,' Annaliese said. 'With luck, the sun will be warm enough to stop us freezing.' As they reached the table, she drew his attention to the view, glorious even in winter. 'This place is very special,' she whispered. 'Do you believe in magic? Take this job and I'll show you.'

John was torn between the expression in her eyes and

sympathy for the two servants who trekked back and forth to bring them a four-course meal from a kitchen that was probably half a mile away. The footman and maid were stoical: Edward, who turned up as coffee was being served, was badly put out and wanted to complain.

'I must say, my dear, this is an extraordinary way of having lunch,' he said tetchily.

'Isn't it just.' Annaliese grinned unrepentantly. 'Edward, this is Major Brandon.'

John, already on his feet, shook hands, saying, 'How do you do, Your Grace?'

Edward, gradually learning to live with the title, mumbled something that might have been, 'Good of you to come, Brandon.'

'I'm doing my best to persuade the Major to be your estate manager,' Annaliese said.

'Quite so.' Edward cleared his throat. 'You're the fellow from Sandringham?'

'I am, Your Grace.'

'I was sorry about the old Queen. She was a fine lady.'

'She was.'

Edward shuffled, half turned to glance at the huge expanse of floor separating him from the entrance to the Central Wing, and was unsettled. 'Well, I expect you'll be good enough for us,' he said to John. 'Bound to be, eh? Not that it's my decision. My wife is in charge of things here. I'm far too busy, you understand?'

'Of course, Your Grace.'

'Good. Right.' Edward shuffled again. 'Well, glad to have seen you, Brandon. I hope you like it here. Most people seem to think it's a pleasant spot.' Determined to escape before anyone could utter another word, Edward was off, clattering across the wooden floor, leaving John open-mouthed.

'Do you believe me *now*?' Annaliese said, as the echoes of the retreat died.

'Yes, I suppose I do,' John said weakly.

'And you won't mind us having to be discreet, not spending *too* many nights together?' Annaliese contrived to be both challenging and coquettish.

John's discomfort, generated by Edward's extraordinary behaviour, disappeared. Suddenly, his gaze became shrewd. 'I don't believe I shall, Lady Lincolnshire,' he said, investing the innocuous statement with a wealth of meaning.

Annaliese held out a hand, which he took eagerly, glad of her touch. 'Shall we discuss your salary, Major Brandon?'

After her visit to the nursery that night, Annaliese said to Gwen, 'Now that we have an estate manager, the next job is to find a governess for the boys.'

'A *governess*?' Gwen frowned, fearing infringement of her territory.

'I think I mean a tutor,' Annaliese replied. 'Someone to teach them more than either of us can. I expect the poor creatures will be packed off to some frightful school sooner or later, but I'm going to keep them here as long as possible. I shall look for a woman. They can wait a few years to have their heads filled with nonsense by men. We need a *young* woman, a girl you will like.'

Gwen smiled approvingly.

'Also, I want a bicycle.' Annaliese stretched and yawned.

'A bicycle!' Gwen wondered if she was witnessing early signs of mental breakdown.

'I had one when I was a girl. It was a good way to get round Schönbrunn. I used to ride it down the corridors.' Seeing the expression on Gwen's face, Annaliese said, 'How else am I to get to Gainsborough Wood?'

'Ha!' Gwen smiled knowingly. 'A bike won't be much fun in the rain.'

'You're absolutely right,' Annaliese said. 'When it's wet, Matthew can drive me!'

They both thought it was a tremendous idea.

2

1926
'I think she'd like to be useful'

On a beautiful Saturday afternoon in May, the matter of death duties was being thrashed out in the small sitting-room that had become Annaliese's office. Charles Templeton was there as both banker and legal adviser; Beatrice was accompanying him to represent Boothby's; John Brandon had the necessary ledgers and files to answer questions. Edward himself was eighty miles away, preparing to host a dinner at Cadogan Square for some of his colleagues in the Palace of Westminster.

In respect of Ralph and his father, the Inland Revenue was asking for £1,400,000. Charles had prepared a list of options for raising the money and they were discussing his suggestions. Annaliese wasted no time in throwing out his first two ideas.

'I know we could simply write a cheque, but it goes against the grain,' she said. 'I'd like to keep the money intact. By the way, where is it?'

'I'm holding it on deposit for you,' Charles said.

'Do you have arrangements with a Swiss bank?' Annaliese asked.

'Naturally.'

'In that case, let them have most of it,' Annaliese said. 'Edward is very gloomy about the economic outlook and I fancy he's right. Leave half a million here and move the rest to Switzerland.' Charles made a note. 'I'm sorry to say,' Annaliese continued, 'that there's no chance of selling Glengrantach.'

'I could get two million for it tomorrow,' Charles said.

'Edward will agree to anything but that,' Annaliese said. 'Glengrantach and the House of Lords are the only things that make his life bearable.'

Charles, disregarding the caustic edge on her humour, said, 'In that case, we shall have to do it in bits and pieces.'

'Mmm . . . yes.' Annaliese was preoccupied, considering an option that wasn't on Charles's list.

Shortly after she had settled in the Castle, Matthew had been summoned to fix a loose floor-board in her bedroom. Instead of doing a straightforward job of nailing the wayward timber down, Matthew had found himself constructing a hiding place between the joists. There, wrapped in tissue paper and stout linen, were the precious stones known to the deposed crowned heads and aristocracy of Europe as the Falkenberg emeralds.

They had belonged to Annaliese's mother, handed down through generations of her family, the Wittelsbachs of Bavaria. Elsa had insisted that Annaliese bring them back to England at the end of her holiday, saying that the jewels were no longer safe in Portugal. The sixty stones, most at least as big as a half-crown, had travelled in Gwen's luggage.

Should they be sold to pay the death duties and leave the estate unscathed? No, there was no pressing need and Annaliese suspected that it was too soon to put the emeralds on the market. Grandpapa Wittelsbach had hinted at dark secrets: perhaps it was best to wait thirty or forty years, for certain people and their grudges to go to the grave. In any case, this hardly seemed like the proverbial rainy day for which Elsa had donated the jewels. Briefly, Annaliese experienced a shiver of premonition, as if a time would come when the emeralds would be needed.

Beatrice was saying, 'Annaliese, are you unwell?' She sounded anxious.

'Sorry. I was miles away.' Annaliese smiled reassuringly. 'Come along, Charles, tell me what to do.'

'I think you should get rid of all your property in Bristol.'

Annaliese looked at John. 'I agree,' he said.

'Remind me, what do we have there?' Annaliese asked.

'Four streets containing seven hundred and twenty houses. There are also warehouses and a tannery.'

'Lord above!' Annaliese was astounded. 'How on earth did the family acquire that lot?'

'Mostly with dealings the Fifth Duke had with the Merchant Venturers,' John said. 'One can't say that it was all entirely above-board, but we ended up with the deeds.'

Smiling her appreciation of his research efforts, Annaliese said, 'We shall be selling over seven hundred families, shan't we? I'd want to be sure of the buyer.'

'I have someone who would fit the bill,' Charles replied.

After an amused wait, Annaliese asked, 'May we know who, please?'

'It's the City and Corporation of Bristol,' Charles said. 'They'll give us a fair price, improve the houses, and guarantee the existing rights of the tenants.'

'Good. What can we expect?'

'Two hundred thousand. The warehouses and tannery are worth four hundred thousand.'

Annaliese wrote the figures down. 'So we want eight

hundred thousand for the junk from the attics.'

'It's hardly junk!' Beatrice spluttered. 'There are two Rembrandts for a start.'

'What about the other pictures?' Annaliese asked.

'There are an awful lot of Vermeers and Van Dycks,' Beatrice said.

'This is confirmed, is it?'

'It is.' Beatrice paused. 'If you took them to New York for auction . . .' She left it trailing in the air.

'I wonder if Nancy would like to help?' Annaliese said.

'How would you stop her?' Beatrice asked.

Turning to John, Annaliese said, 'Have you managed to discover what these pictures were doing in that loft?'

'All I can tell you is that it's at least a hundred years since anyone went up there.'

'And you think they'll raise the necessary money?' Annaliese asked Beatrice.

'You'll have some left over,' Beatrice promised.

'In that case, we have no need to sit here any longer,' Annaliese said. 'Charles and John, you have things to discuss, I believe?' They nodded. 'Let's escape, then, Beatrice. It's far too nice an afternoon to be stuck indoors.'

Mrs Pritchard brought tea to the terrace outside the West Wing, an ideal spot in which to enjoy the afternoon sun. Beatrice gazed round, admiring the views. 'Idyllic,' she murmured. 'No wonder you're so happy here.'

'It isn't *all* that much nicer than Upper Overs,' Annaliese pointed out. She had a soft spot for the house in the Ashdown Forest that Beatrice had inherited from her father, Lord Douglas.

'Possibly not,' Beatrice agreed. 'This is bigger and grander, of course. I think it needs someone like you to feel *comfortable* here.'

'Am I that bad?' Annaliese said.

'You know what I mean,' Beatrice laughed. 'You're used to splendid places. Anyone who wasn't brought up at Schönbrunn might find this slightly excessive.'

'Mmm.' Annaliese conceded the point grudgingly. Even with Beatrice, she was unwilling to admit that these lovely surroundings might have influenced her decision to stay with Edward. Fortunately, there was a perfect way out of the difficulty. 'Is it true that Charles is instituting divorce proceedings against his wife?' Annaliese asked.

Beatrice jumped as though stung by a wasp. 'Who told you that?' she cried.

'John Brandon was in London the other day,' Annaliese replied. 'He had lunch at his club. It's a bigger gossip-shop than Martha's Vineyard.'

'Very well-informed,' Beatrice said ruefully.

'I thought what good news it was.' Annaliese was curious to know what, if anything, had changed: because of the risk to his wealth, Charles had always shied away from the question of divorce.

'His wretched wife has decided to be reasonable,' Beatrice replied. 'At last!' She was relieved, confirming that her support of Charles's attitude had involved strain.

'Why?'

'She wants to go to South Africa with a man,' Beatrice said. 'She'll settle for a lump sum that Charles thinks is reasonable.'

'Does this mean we can look forward to a wedding?' Annaliese asked eagerly.

'Probably.' Beatrice was doing her best to give the impression that she wasn't much bothered. 'Nigel wants us to.'

Nigel was Charles's fifteen-year-old son, heir to the bank, and infinitely fonder of Beatrice than he ever had been of his wayward mother.

'What about you and Charles?' Annaliese teased. 'Do *you* want to?'

'I expect so.' Beatrice laughed nervously.

'This is splendid news.' Annaliese was thrilled. 'You can have your own children and I shall be an aunt.'

'Oh, I think I'm much too old for that,' Beatrice said, looking rather frightened.

'Rubbish, you're twenty-eight, Beatrice. No age at all. Speaking for Douglas and George, they'd like a little girl for a cousin.'

'Well, we shall have to see.' Beatrice leaned forward anxiously. 'Don't say anything to Charles yet, Annaliese. He's frightfully cagey about it – worried about scandal.'

'My lips are sealed,' Annaliese promised. 'Stop worrying, Beatrice, look on the bright side. Think how glad Edward will be when you turn into an honest woman.'

Beatrice pulled a gruesome face. 'I'm dreading that.' Serious again, she asked, 'How is he?'

'As well as can be expected. He's making an absolute orgy of disliking this place. His other great interest in life is telling all and sundry how quickly the country is going to the dogs. I feel quite sorry for poor Stanley Baldwin.'

'Isn't Edward supposed to be on his side?' Beatrice asked.

'Officially, yes. In practice, he swears that Baldwin is an incompetent buffoon.'

'Is there anyone he approves of?'

'He likes Churchill,' Annaliese said.

'Isn't he the man who says there might be another war?'

'That's the one.'

'Ridiculous,' Beatrice scoffed.

'Possibly.' Annaliese was uncertain. 'Quite a few people seem to agree with the idea. Edward brought some of his friends down for a weekend last month and they talked about it all the time.'

'Charles thinks that Edward is mixing with a rum crowd,' Beatrice said.

'This bunch *were* pretty outlandish. Do you know, one of them kept giving me come-to-bed looks.' Annaliese exploded into laughter. 'When he wasn't preaching the virtues of Fascism, he was doing his damnedest to seduce me by sheer will-power.'

'Who was that?' Beatrice asked, deeply shocked.

'Some buffoon by the name of Rashleigh. *Lord* Francis Rashleigh, if you please.' Annaliese was shaking with mirth. 'He's offensively rich and I was under orders to be nice to him.' She assumed an air of mock grandeur. 'He's only a *life* peer, a mere upstart. He *reeks* of money, so I suppose he greased Lloyd George's palm. However, according to my dear husband, Lord Francis is a sound chap.' Annaliese let out a shriek of derisory laughter.

'I presume Edward didn't mind this man's interest?' Beatrice said cautiously. 'Not the way things are between you.'

'He wasn't bothered,' Annaliese replied. She had to play a game with Beatrice, pretending that she and John Brandon were not indulging in a deeply passionate affair. Beatrice was ill at ease, teetering on the brink of asking if Annaliese thought it likely that Edward suspected, or was seeking comfort elsewhere. Before she could make up her mind, the cheerful uproar of Douglas's arrival provided total, blessed distraction.

'Auntie Bee! Hurrah!' Douglas hurled himself into Beatrice's lap and hugged her half to death. 'We've been fishing in the lake. George got a shark, but he escaped.'

'Was this the same shark as last year?' Beatrice inquired solemnly.

'I *think* so,' Douglas said, deadly earnest. 'George knows. Where is he?' After looking round crossly, Douglas bawled,

'George, get a move on! Auntie Bee's here.'

In his own good time, and smiling contentedly, George appeared. He was carrying a jam jar full of tadpoles; at his side, and holding his other hand, was a boldly attractive young woman who had obviously been joining in a great deal of fun. While George stood on the tips of his toes beside Beatrice's chair to kiss her, she was studying the girl who was attempting to detach herself from a motley collection of fishing tackle.

'You haven't met Henrietta, have you, Beatrice?' Annaliese was saying.

'No.'

'Well, here she is. Henrietta Timberlake, the ogre we found to teach the boys. She's a demon for mathematics and discipline. Henrietta, this is my sister-in-law, Lady Beatrice Boothby-Graffoe.'

'How d'you do, Lady Beatrice?' Henrietta had an extremely robust handshake and a broad, open smile that displayed big, even teeth. Her manner was a mixture of jolly hockey sticks and wide-eyed curiosity.

'Henry – that's what everybody calls her – was at Cambridge,' Annaliese said. 'Girton College. Graduated last year.'

'How marvellous,' Beatrice said. 'What on earth made you saddle yourself with this pair of hooligans?'

'There was no alternative,' Henrietta said cheerfully. 'No one else would take me on.' Lowering her voice conspiratorially, she added, 'I'm a problem, you see.'

'And we have to put up with it,' Douglas moaned. 'Do you know what she makes us do, Auntie Bee?'

'What?'

'*Latin*.' Douglas was doleful. 'It's *awful*.'

'Impressive, though,' Beatrice said. 'Tell me what you know about Latin.'

George piped up. 'Latin is a language as dead as dead can be, first it killed the Romans, now it's killing me.'

Laughing, Beatrice asked, 'Who taught you that?'

'Henry did,' Douglas said. 'See what we have to put up with, Auntie Bee? It isn't fair, you know. And Mama doesn't take any notice when we complain.'

'It's for your own good,' Beatrice said, dreadfully straight-faced. 'You'll feel the benefit when you grow up.'

'We wouldn't mind some benefit *now*,' Douglas said in a tone so heart-rending that Annaliese and Beatrice were unable to contain their laughter.

Henrietta decided it was time for them to go. 'Come along, you two, let's hand you over to Gwen for disinfecting.'

'Are you staying tonight?' George whispered to Beatrice.

'Yes, I am,' she said and was rewarded with a beatific smile.

Douglas was negotiating with Henrietta for a story after they had been scrubbed and put in clean clothes. 'We'll see,' she said. 'It depends.'

'She means the thirteen times table,' George told Beatrice. 'I can do that, so we'll have a story.'

'*Treasure Island*,' Douglas roared, jumping from Beatrice's lap and racing off to be first into the bath, uttering blood-curdling whoops of joy at the prospect of Long John Silver. George and Henrietta followed at a more sedate pace, collecting fishing nets and rods as they went.

'Your Miss Timberlake looks like a gem,' Beatrice said.

'She is,' Annaliese replied. 'The boys love her, Gwen thinks she's marvellous, and even Edward approves. What more could I want?'

'How did you find her?'

'I advertised in *The Times*.'

'Lots of replies?'

'About three hundred dragons and Henry,' Annaliese said.

'She was the only one I bothered to see and we hit it off at once.'

'Isn't it rather a tinpot job for such a bright girl?' Beatrice suggested.

'Yes. Fortunately, she does seem to have upset one or two people – including her family – so she was glad to come here.'

'What did she do to cause offence?' Beatrice asked.

'Well, being clever isn't good for a girl, is it?' Unsurprisingly, Annaliese was disgusted by the thought. 'To make matters worse, Henry implied that she was slightly unconventional in her relationships with men.'

'In what way?'

'From what I can gather, she makes it plain that she doesn't expect the fun in bed to be one-sided. They have to please.'

'Good gracious.' Trying to look shocked, Beatrice found herself suppressing a giggle. 'So young, too. Where does she come from?'

'She's twenty-two and her parents live in Marlborough. That's full of Timberlakes – they keep racehorses at one of the big stables there. So does our friend, the Duke of Laverstoke.'

'You've met him?' Beatrice was pleased. 'What's he like?'

'Lovely man. And Clementine, his wife, is a hoot. They're at Eaton Mandeville, near Chippenham.'

'I know,' Beatrice said longingly. 'I hear whispers that Hubert Laverstoke has things to sell. I'd love to get in there.'

'Why don't I ask them over for lunch tomorrow?' Annaliese said. 'That should do the trick.'

'Do you think you could?'

'Let's try.'

Leaving the terrace, they returned to Annaliese's office, now deserted. 'I wonder where Charles and John have gone?' Beatrice said.

'Leave them be, wherever they are,' Annaliese said,

reaching for the telephone. 'There's something I want to discuss after this.'

Arranging lunch with the Laverstokes for the following day took no time at all. Settling herself and looking serious, Annaliese said, 'Celia.'

'What about her?' Beatrice was wary.

'She's asked if she could work at Boothby's,' Annaliese said.

'Oh!' Beatrice was unwilling to express an opinion.

'Not full-time, though,' Annaliese went on. 'She was hoping that she could do two lots of three or four months every year.'

'What about the rest of the time?' Beatrice asked.

'She wants to spend it with her aunt. They intend to travel. Miss Croft has connections in the south of France.'

'Oh. I see. We'd all like to go there.' Beatrice sounded uncharacteristically bitter.

'I wouldn't,' Annaliese said. 'It's a beastly place, full of crooks and pimps.'

'Does this aunt exist?' Beatrice was suspicious.

'I've met her.'

'When?'

'About two months ago,' Annaliese replied. 'I was invited to supper at her house.'

'What's she like?'

'Pleasant. Cultured.' Annaliese paused, searching for other attributes. She almost said, 'Convenient', but settled for, 'A good influence, I think.'

Reluctantly, Beatrice grasped the nettle. 'What could Celia do at Boothby's?'

'I've no idea,' Annaliese replied. 'You're dying to say that she knows even less about things than I did when I imposed myself on you. She might add tone and interest, don't you think?'

'I *suppose* so.' Beatrice was far from convinced. 'Why does she want to work?'

'I think she'd like to be useful,' Annaliese said. 'Earn her keep, as it were. Meet people, too.'

'Another husband?'

'There is that.' Annaliese was inscrutable, her eyes fixed on infinity.

'Oh, I don't know,' Beatrice said, breaking an uncomfortable silence. 'What do *you* think, Annaliese? You're the one with the instincts and intuition.'

'And never were they more sorely needed,' Annaliese muttered under her breath.

'Pardon?' Beatrice, not quite catching it, was impatient.

'Oh, it wasn't anything important,' Annaliese said, irritated by her inability to reach a decision. 'I tell you what, Celia can join us for lunch with the Laverstokes.'

'Is she here, actually in residence?' There was a hint of sarcasm in Beatrice's tone.

'Yes, and bored to distraction, if I'm any judge.'

'Will she come?' Beatrice asked. 'She's awfully shy.'

'If she can't conquer that, she's no good for Boothby's,' Annaliese said firmly.

Early the following evening, when Beatrice and Charles were on their way back to London and Celia had returned to The Chantry, Annaliese strolled in the rose garden with Hubert and Clementine, Duke and Duchess of Laverstoke since 1899.

'What's your impression of Celia?' Annaliese asked.

Clementine sniffed portentously, making herself look almost ugly. She was forty-eight, thirteen years younger than her famously handsome husband, and one of Society's great beauties. In terms of her ability to crush knaves and fools, she was rated on a par with Lady Torksey.

'To be honest, Annaliese, I was charmed by the girl. Hadn't expected to be, of course.'

'She was on her best behaviour,' Annaliese replied.

'The poor creature was terrified of me,' the Duchess of Laverstoke chuckled. 'That'll be the ghastly Ralph. No doubt he filled her head with blood-curdling rubbish.'

'But what am I going to *do* with her, Clem?' Annaliese pleaded.

'Is she an embarrassment?'

'No, not really,' Annaliese replied.

'How does the absent lord and master view the problem?' Clementine asked.

'He wants rid of her.'

'No, that won't do at all.' Clementine turned to her husband for confirmation. 'Do you agree, Hubert?'

'Absolutely, m'dear. You see, Annaliese, if you wanted to boot her out, it should have been done when you and Edward took over. It wouldn't look good now.'

'I appreciate that, Hubert. Edward would have preferred her to go, I insisted she stayed.'

'A mistake, perhaps?' Clementine squinted along her slightly aquiline nose at Annaliese.

'Perhaps,' Annaliese admitted. 'Having got this far, my inclination is to absorb her into the family.'

'Keep her out of trouble?' Clementine suggested.

'Something like that.' Annaliese found herself with far too many sentiments from which to choose. She settled for, 'I don't want a revival of interest in Ralph. The newspapers were happy to accept that Blanche Hamilton was the "scarlet woman". It must stay that way.'

'Amen to that,' Clementine said.

'I think the answer's obvious,' Hubert advised. 'She wants to work at Boothby's, let her.'

Clementine nodded sagely. 'Give her plenty to do under

supervision and she'll be as right as rain. She could be popular with some of your clients.'

'Beatrice isn't keen,' Annaliese said. 'And she has my sympathy . . . Celia doesn't know a thing about any sort of fine art.'

Hubert rumbled, cocking an eyebrow at his wife. She nodded. 'Why not send her over to Eaton Mandeville,' Hubert said. 'We've got even more high-class junk than you, Annaliese, and my boy, Desmond, is a bit of an expert . . . got all the books and what not. He could teach her a thing or two.'

Annaliese said, 'I wouldn't like her to be a nuisance.'

'Not a chance of it,' Hubert responded gallantly. 'Desmond will enjoy it.' Clementine's look indicated that she didn't view that possibility with favour. 'Make the girl feel she belongs,' Hubert went on. 'Do her a world of good. As a matter of fact, Desmond was thinking of compiling an inventory of everything . . . can't for the life of me understand why we haven't got one. There is the possibility that we might get rid of a few things, you know.'

'That will please Beatrice,' Annaliese said. 'If you let Boothby's act for you,' she added hurriedly.

'Oh, no question about it, wouldn't dream of trusting any of the others. Anyway, why doesn't Celia help Desmond? She'll learn a devil of a lot.'

'I'll see to it,' Annaliese promised. 'Thank you, both, very much.'

'Don't be too grateful,' Clementine warned. 'We shall be asking you for favours soon.'

'Obligations of class,' Annaliese said.

'*Exactly*!' Clementine was delighted that her new friend and fellow-duchess acknowledged this vital principle. 'Ralph would never have accepted that, not in a million years. That's why he was such an out-and-out menace.'

'It was one of the reasons,' Annaliese smiled.

'True.' Clementine produced another of her sniffs. 'By the way, is Edward ever going to settle here?'

'I doubt it,' Annaliese replied, unfazed by Clementine's frankness. 'At least, not until he's too old for politics.'

'That could take forever,' Hubert laughed. 'There are chaps in the House of Lords who should have been pensioned off twenty years ago. God knows what they think they're doing.'

'Edward intends to exert influence,' Annaliese said.

'Someone needs to. That man Baldwin will bamboozle us into trouble if he isn't stopped.'

Annaliese was surprised. 'Goodness, Hubert, I thought it was only the firebrands who took that line.'

'When it comes to "Uncle Stanley", I'm a firebrand. He's a disaster.'

'Why?' Clementine asked, more to discover her husband's hidden political passions than out of genuine interest in the Prime Minister.

'The only thing he's fit for is telling the public what they want to hear,' Hubert said. 'Nothing else, that's all he can do. It's his version of Lloyd George's "Land fit for Heroes" twaddle and it's going to land us in the soup. The silly devil ought to be facing up to problems, not telling us how good everything is when any fool knows that it isn't.'

'Now see what you've done,' Clementine said to Annaliese. 'Come along, Hubert, old chum, we're going home. If you haven't calmed down by the time we get there, it's a darkened room for you, my lad.'

Throughout June and July, Celia and Lord Desmond Prideaux were almost inseparable as he guided her through the artistic riches of Eaton Mandeville.

Celia had resented the suggestion that she should help catalogue the house's treasures, convinced that she was being fobbed off or patronised. Only Annaliese's subtle insistence that the task, however menial it might seem, was a precondition of a job at Boothby's forced Celia into reluctant agreement. Then, the first meeting with her would-be mentor transformed resentment into boundless enthusiasm.

Lord Desmond, the Duke of Laverstoke's younger son, was twenty-three, the same age as Celia. Unusually for someone in his position, the astounding good looks inherited from his parents were accompanied by a reticent charm. He was the first man who had ever treated Celia as an intelligent equal and she was captivated.

Each morning, Desmond drove fifteen miles to collect Celia from The Chantry and took her to Eaton Mandeville, a Palladian-style mansion in a perfect setting between Chippenham and Melksham. In the early evening, after each absorbing day, Lord Desmond delivered his pupil back to the house in the north-western corner of the Compton Allardyce estate and fled – there was absolutely no other word for it – as if gripped by mortal fear. Celia, who was attracted to her handsome tutor and sensed his need for adventure, became exasperated.

Towards the end of the second week, after encouraging Desmond to extend a dissertation on the Italian Renaissance for nearly two hours past their normal finishing time, Celia floated the idea of stopping for a meal on their way back to Compton Allardyce. 'My treat, of course,' she said, careful to make the offer sound flippant. 'A little reward for your trouble.'

'That's a good idea,' Desmond replied, catching her mood. 'I know a place near Devizes. The food's good and it isn't too far out of our way.'

Afterwards, relaxed and beguiled by Celia's eagerness to review what she had learned during the day, Desmond went into The Chantry. He stayed until midnight, guzzling coffee, driving home the influence of the Medicis, and singing the praises of his particular hero, the flamboyant goldsmith, Benvenuto Cellini. When, after a final rueful look at his watch, Desmond tore himself away, he said, 'We must do this again.'

'I'd like that,' Celia murmured and kissed his cheek.

Although the comparatively chaste gesture sent Desmond perilously close to embarrassment, he was soon spending every evening at The Chantry, often not leaving until the small hours of the following morning. Nevertheless, as informative and entertaining as he was, Celia's hopes of converting him into a temporary lover were doomed to disappointment. There was no doubt that Desmond found her desirable: catching him in unguarded moments, she saw his eyes full of hunger. Once or twice, Celia was certain that he was about to make a move, yet the instant she willed him on, Desmond retreated into boyish confusion, seeking refuge behind a screen of erudite verbosity on a minor point from the day's artistic research.

Baffled and piqued, Celia wondered what on earth was holding Desmond back. She guessed that he was sexually naive: Eton, Oxford, and two years of struggling with his awkward role as the younger son of a duke practically guaranteed his virginity. That being so, he was likely to be in awe of the woman who had managed to satisfy the notorious Ralph until pregnancy impaired her ability to inflame and enslave. Moreover, Desmond's mother, the formidably perceptive Clementine, lurked in the background. Tactfully, she made a point of keeping out of the way when Celia was at Eaton Mandeville, but what instructions had she given her much-loved, idiot son about his association with the Dowager Duchess of Lincolnshire? It was bound to be something like: 'Desmond darling, I want to help Annaliese, so do your best with Celia. But do *not* get involved. If you lay a finger on that blasted woman, I'll strangle you, so help me!'

Shrugging to herself, Celia concluded that it was best to leave Desmond with the innocence that was, quite obviously, proving a trial to him. Renewing her determination to be accepted at Boothby's, she used every minute of their time together to tap Desmond's wealth of knowledge. How many people, Celia wondered with a flash of wry amusement, would believe that she and a rather delectable young man were harmlessly involved in her house until two and three o'clock each morning?

Shortly before the early dawn of a Saturday towards the end of June, the headlights of Desmond's departing car were seen by Annaliese and John Brandon. They were half a mile away on the brow of one of the Park's many undulations. John was walking Annaliese back to the Castle, one hand clasping hers, the other guiding the handlebars of the bicycle on which she had nonchalantly ridden into Gainsborough Wood five hours ago.

'Who's that, at this time of night?' Annaliese asked.

'That'll be Lord Desmond.' After a reflective pause, John added, 'He's later than usual.'

Tilting her chin, Annaliese gave a sniff that was worthy of Gwen at her most disdainful. John waited for the pronouncement.

'Inevitable, I suppose,' Annaliese muttered.

'You're jumping to conclusions,' John accused mildly.

'Of course. She's *bound* to be sleeping with him.'

John was alert to the nuances in Annaliese's tone and choice of words. Blame was being allocated, hinting at mistrust of Celia.

'You could be doing Lord Desmond an injustice,' John said. 'I think he deserves credit for having more sense.'

'Really? Why?' Annaliese was curious.

'As a second son, Desmond will have to marry well,' John

replied. 'For that, he needs a more or less unblemished reputation.'

'So no hanky-panky with Celia?' Annaliese asked.

'I think he's got enough gumption to realise that.'

Chuckling, Annaliese squeezed John's hand and said, 'Don't you like her, either?'

'It's hardly my place to have opinions, is it?' John said, pretending to be deadly earnest. 'Come along, dearest, let's get you back home. It will be light soon.'

'These beastly early mornings are my only quarrel with summer,' she grumbled.

By the end of July, Celia had learned enough to persuade Beatrice that she was worthy of a junior post at Boothby's. Lord Desmond, apparently anxious to watch over his pupil, continued to pop in and out of Compton Allardyce at odd, unexpected times. Not knowing that he always kept well away from The Chantry, Annaliese assumed the worst, but kept her misgivings to herself.

3

1929
'You're a pompous fool, Edward'

Accompanied by the boys and Gwen, Annaliese visited her parents at Easter. When the trip was being planned, Edward had expressed some interest in joining them, but it came as no great surprise when he dropped out two days before the ship sailed. With the air full of talk about a General Election, he insisted on remaining in London, afraid of missing the merest whisper of rumour. His absence was never mentioned during the two weeks in Cascais. Instead, the Archduchess Elsa, who hinted that she continued to enjoy an afternoon in bed with a man half her age, asked Annaliese if she had, as instructed, acquired a lover. Assured that the matter had been taken care of, Elsa smiled and let the subject drop, devoting herself to spoiling Douglas and George. She was fascinated and slightly perturbed by Douglas, who was even more full of himself these days and inclined to be bumptious.

'Blame Moss Close,' Annaliese said.

'What on earth is *that*?' As usual, they were conversing in German and the two English words puzzled Elsa, making her suspect a strange mental disorder.

'A preparatory school in Surrey,' Annaliese replied. 'Edward went there, so did his father. It's a family tradition. Douglas is in his second year.'

'Preparatory for what?' Elsa asked.

'Public school.' Annaliese gave a short, mirthless laugh. 'These places aren't in the least public. A boy has to come from a very special clique to gain entry.'

Elsa, unable to understand, asked, 'And this place is turning Douglas into a self-opinionated toad?'

'Edward says he'll grow out of it,' Annaliese replied, clearly sceptical.

'And will George go there?'

'In September,' Annaliese said grimly.

If anything, Gwen's dread of George's departure was the hardest thing to bear, stemming as it did from her failure to conceive a child after nearly four years of marriage to Matthew. Although neither of them regarded the lack of a child as a particularly bad blow, Annaliese knew that it had sharpened Gwen's affection for George and she hated the prospect of him being away in what she referred to as a 'toffee-nosed orphanage' for twelve weeks at a stretch.

Since it was a subject too painful to discuss, they had evolved a series of looks that spoke volumes.

'Do you *want* George to go away?' was how Gwen would begin, balefully accusing.

'Of course I don't!' was always Annaliese's angry response.

'Are you going to try stopping it?'

'Yes.'

'How?'

'I don't know yet. I'll think of something.'

'Well, you'd best get a move on. There's not much time left.'

'Do you think I don't realise that?'

They indulged in the silent duel on the ship back to Southampton at the end of the holiday. It was late evening and the boys were tucked up in bed. Tired of shilly-shallying, Gwen said, 'You could try a bit of cunning.'

'That's more or less what I've decided,' Annaliese replied.

'You don't sound all that keen.'

'I'm hoping I shall improve,' Annaliese sighed.

The Election, held in May, was preceded by an astonishingly dull campaign in which none of the parties were able to put forward policies that gained the electorate's confidence. The best that the Conservatives could manage was the slogan 'Safety First' plastered all over the country on portraits of Stanley Baldwin. The poll was indecisive, giving Labour 288 seats, while the Conservatives won 260, and the Liberals 59. Baldwin resigned on 4 June, Ramsay Macdonald formed a minority Labour Government, and Edward was so disgusted that he abandoned London in favour of Allardyce Castle. There, much to his surprise, Annaliese was sympathetic to his state of mind.

'I find the public's apathy inexplicable,' she said. 'After all, times aren't easy for most people, are they?'

'Far from it,' Edward replied, pleased by her interest. 'If nothing else, I'd expected unemployment to rouse a few passions. Instead of which . . .' He shrugged hopelessly.

'Peace, too,' Annaliese said. 'Surely, that's an issue?'

'It *should* have been,' Edward said. 'In the end, everyone took it for granted.'

'And you believe that's unwise?'

Edward's smile, the warmest she had seen for a long time, was a compliment to her shrewdness. 'Internationally, things are a mess,' he said. 'Germany is in uproar, most European Governments are weak and obsessed with internal problems, and no one knows what Russia is up to. In my view, there's a great deal of danger just below the surface.' He assumed an expression of mock piety. 'Don't worry, I'm not going to get on my hobby-horse and deliver a lecture about the Peace Treaty.' Everyone knew that he considered the documents signed at Versailles in 1919 to be both iniquitous and stupidly short-sighted, practically certain to cause trouble in one form or another within twenty years.

'What about the League of Nations?' Annaliese asked forlornly.

Edward, good-naturedly declining the invitation to launch into a diatribe, simply said, 'An ineffectual talking-shop, my dear, not worth the paper its high-falutin charter is written on. Look at the mess they made of Palestine.' While Annaliese was wondering whether she should ask for an explanation, his mood changed. Casting off all pretensions at statesmanship, Edward said, 'Look, it's a lovely afternoon, why don't we go into the Park with a picnic tea? George can come, too. Tell Miss Timberlake that he's excused lessons for the rest of the day.'

Baffled by his father's sunny disposition, George took time to adjust. For the best part of a nerve-racking hour, Annaliese was waiting for her bemused son to come out with something like, 'Why are you being so nice, Papa?' Mercifully, the danger passed and they settled down to each other's company. Before tea, they fished in the lake and Annaliese, comfortable in the shade of a tree, saw that father and son were engaged in continuous, earnest conversation. Afterwards, Edward commented on the extent of George's knowledge.

'He's a very clever little boy,' Annaliese said guardedly.

'He certainly is – much brighter than Douglas.' Edward paused thoughtfully. 'Is George your favourite?'

'A mother mustn't have a favourite,' Annaliese replied, wondering if Edward had noticed and deciphered the intricacies of her feelings for the boys.

'I'm impressed by George. If he carries on like this, it will be worth sending him to Oxford. But I'm blessed if I know about Douglas. He's an absolute duffer.'

'These are early days,' Annaliese pointed out. 'And Douglas has other qualities. He'll be an excellent heir.'

'That's vital,' Edward agreed. 'I can't see him being frightened of the job when it's his turn.'

'Aren't you more at ease with it now?'

'Only because you do most of the donkey work.' Edward took her arm. 'I suppose George misses Douglas when he's away?'

'It's only natural,' Annaliese said, persuading herself that she wasn't *quite* lying. In reality, George rather liked having Gwen and Henrietta to himself and was glad when Douglas went back to school at the end of each holiday. Annaliese was torn between admiration and concern that her younger son was becoming a little too self-sufficient.

Not that Edward was bothered with pursuing the subject of George any further. For the remainder of the afternoon and throughout the evening, he was at pains to foster the reborn spirit of intimacy with Annaliese. They had dinner together – a thing they rarely did these days unless compelled to do so by a social occasion – and afterwards, Annaliese invited Edward to spend the night in her bedroom.

It was, she soon discovered, impossible to recall precisely how she used to respond to him. In the end, afraid of betraying signs of her relationship with John Brandon, Annaliese was reduced to inertia while Edward satisfied himself. Having forgotten how inexpert and selfish he could be, she found that simulating pleasure was an ordeal that almost defeated her. Delighted by the turn of events, Edward failed to notice her thinly veiled displeasure. The fear that he would want to do it again evaporated when he smiled, murmured an incomprehensible endearment, and fell fast asleep.

Remembering his fondness for early morning love-making, Annaliese slipped out of bed as soon as she woke at 6.30. An hour later, a drowsy Edward registered a mild complaint when she re-appeared, bathed and dressed, but meekly accepted the statement that she had a busy day ahead of her. More than that, he tagged along when Matthew drove her to the village to inspect progress on the work to improve four of the houses. The Duke of Lincolnshire's presence in Compton Allardyce brought the entire population out to pay their respects. At first worried that Edward would take to his heels, Annaliese was soon amused by the bashful, rather boyish way in which he accepted the deference and esteem of his tenants.

Back in the Rolls-Royce, Annaliese said, 'You're turning into an aristocrat.'

'Am I?' He seemed overawed. 'It's devilish difficult, you know. I'm embarrassed when people fawn on me simply because of who I am. Perhaps I'd do better if I got out and about more?'

'You'll soon learn,' Annaliese said reassuringly. 'I have to see how things are progressing in Keeper's Spinney. Do you want taking home first?'

'Can I come with you?' Eager to please, Edward added, 'I'd like to know what you're doing and I promise not to be squeamish about Ralph.'

In fact, not a vestige of the tragedy remained. After the demolition of the Hamiltons' house and the removal of every last brick and tile, the entire three-acre site had been cleared. Now, a gang of men were felling the trees that had screened the area.

'We shall have enough logs for a lifetime when this is finished,' Annaliese said. 'I'm putting a new plantation in here. When Douglas is fifty, no one will have the faintest idea what this was.'

'Very good.' Edward looked round, nodding at the workmen who paused to doff their caps. 'Could we sell any of this timber?'

'We are doing,' Annaliese replied. 'It's being taken into Marlborough by the lorry-load.' She left him briefly to give instructions to the foreman, returning to suggest that Edward accompanied her on the morning's last task, an inspection of a new drainage scheme on the western boundary of the Park. Edward's admiration for what was being done continued over lunch, which they took on the terrace. Mrs Pritchard, who supervised the serving of the meal, was delighted to see Their Graces in such good form and radiated contentment. Aware of the housekeeper's mood, Annaliese prayed that her optimism was not premature.

Tentatively, attempting to hide his nervousness with a jocularity that was overdone, Edward suggested that they should retire to bed. 'We used to do it in the afternoon,' he said. 'In the old days, before Douglas was born.'

At Annaliese's apparently enthusiastic instigation, they made love twice, with scarcely any interval between the two bursts of activity. Afterwards, while Edward caressed and admired her body, Annaliese decided that he must, surely, be at his most amenable, willing to listen to sense and reason.

'There is one concern I have about George,' she said, careful to sound casual.

'Mmm? What's that, my dear?'

'I can't help wondering whether sending him away to school is the right thing – bearing in mind the sort of child he is.'

'Don't worry, it will be the making of him.' Edward, willing himself to be capable of taking her again, was not paying a great deal of attention to what Annaliese was saying.

'He's going to miss Gwen and me terribly,' she persisted. 'And he still hasn't come to terms with this place. Going somewhere else strange is likely to be upsetting.'

'Don't worry, he'll soon knuckle down,' Edward said, patently not caring.

'Is that what he's supposed to do, "knuckle down"? Isn't he entitled to enjoy himself? Why *does* he have to go?'

'Why?' The realisation that Annaliese had a bee in her bonnet made Edward draw away as he began to take her seriously. 'Because Moss Close is a very good school.'

'It isn't improving Douglas. Quite the contrary, actually.'

'Douglas is never going to be much of a scholar,' Edward said. 'You can't expect miracles.'

'I'm talking about his attitude, *not* his studies.'

'What's wrong with his attitude?' Edward was propping himself up on an elbow, frowning angrily. Annaliese's heart sank: the slim hope that this would be easy was in tatters. With no other alternative, she attacked.

'Your precious Moss Close has turned Douglas into an insufferable little snob!'

'Don't be ridiculous,' Edward fumed. 'He's a grand boy.'

'How do you know? When did you last bother to spend more than five minutes with him?'

'Look here . . .'

'No,' Annaliese cut in, '*you* look here. I won't allow George to go to this place.'

Edward's initial reaction was lofty derision. 'You won't allow . . .' He stopped, scorn being replaced by hard-eyed suspicion. 'This is why you lured me into bed, isn't it? You were hoping to twist me round your little finger.'

Annaliese, too overcome by self-disgust to deny it, watched as Edward sprang out of bed and reached for his clothes. 'My God, how can you sink so low, Annaliese?' he said bitterly.

'I'm trying to protect George,' she shouted.

'Mollycoddle, you mean,' Edward roared. 'It won't wash, do you hear? George goes to Moss Close in September and that is final.' Before Annaliese could begin to think of retaliating, he had slammed out of the room.

Twenty minutes later, Edward returned, wearing one of his 'London' suits. 'I'm going back to Cadogan Square,' he announced. 'It's the best place for me. I shall be safe there.'

Dressed and dispiritedly trying to arrange her hair, Annaliese turned from the dressing-table mirror to give him a look of weary contempt.

'*Safe?*' she asked mockingly.

'That's right.' Realising that it had been a stupid thing to say, he was huffy, standing on his dignity.

'You're a pompous fool, Edward.'

'What, for defending my principles?'

'If your so-called principles are more important than George's happiness, then, yes, you're a pompous fool.'

The issue of Moss Close – and much else – was sealed.

Over tea in the nursery, Annaliese asked George. 'Are you looking forward to going to school with Douglas?'

He gave it a lot of thought before saying, 'Sort of. I shall miss Gwen and Henry – and you, of course – but it sounds fun. Douglas will look after me.'

'I'm sure he will,' Annaliese said. 'And you'll be able to join in the games.'

'I don't think I shall care for games,' George replied. 'Too rough. I shall probably play the piano instead.' Shoving a last wedge of cake into his mouth, he stood up. 'I'd better get on, Henry's given me a ton of homework.'

After he had wandered off, looking comically earnest, Gwen stared long and hard at Annaliese. 'What was all that about, then?'

Tense with irritation, Annaliese replied, 'I tried to talk Edward out of it. I failed. Badly!'

'Is that why he went off to London in such a mood?'

'Yes.' Annaliese slumped, looking defeated.

'You can have another go when he's calmed down,' Gwen said.

'No, I can't,' Annaliese sighed. 'I'm sick to death of it, so don't mention it again, please.'

Gwen's brow furrowed. This was what she and Matthew called 'a touch of Vienna'; Annaliese was turning her back on a problem, walking away from it, and no force on earth would change her mind. Another aspect of the wretched business occurred to Gwen. 'You'll be getting rid of Henry?'

Annaliese was startled. 'Why should I want to do that?'

'She won't have anything to do, not with poor George gone.'

'I'd like her to stay,' Annaliese said on impulse.

'What will she do if there aren't any lessons?'

'I haven't the faintest idea, but I'll think of *something*.' Annaliese paused to assess her spontaneous decision. 'Yes, we need a brainy girl like Henry. Do you think she'll stay?'

Gwen nodded. 'She likes it here. The other day, she told me she was dreading the thought of having to leave.'

'Good.' Annaliese was relieved. 'I'll find her a job, don't you worry.'

'So . . .' Gwen smiled archly. 'With misery-guts out of the way, I suppose you'll be nipping off to see Major Brandon tonight?'

'No. Definitely not!' Annaliese was horrified by the idea. 'I need time to get over the upset.' Lamely, she added, 'And things.'

The truth was that she was riddled with guilt. The escapade with Edward – which had been squalid as well as unsuccessful – was a betrayal of John. It was likely to be some time before Annaliese felt able to face the man who truly loved her.

On the day after his angry departure from Allardyce Castle,

Edward had lunch with Lord Francis Rashleigh in a secluded corner of the House of Lords dining-room. When asked what was wrong with him, Edward talked freely. Although initially surprised by his own willingness to discuss such matters, once started, there was no stopping him. Rashleigh, who had disposed of his own wife once she had given him a son, was outraged.

'Are you telling me that you've had no conjugal rights for five years?'

'Not until this miserable business,' Edward said. 'And it turned out to be a trap. She only did it to persuade me not to send George away to school.'

'That's the younger one, the chap you think needs backbone?'

'Exactly. *She* wants him to stay at home and be pampered.'

Rashleigh shook his head sorrowfully. 'Women are devious creatures when they put their minds to it.' He studied Edward. 'I imagine this puts the kibosh on things?'

'Absolutely. You won't catch me being cheated like that again.' In a moment of rationality, Edward added, 'Not that I shall be given the chance.'

'Your wife obviously doesn't care for the physical side of marriage.'

'No, she doesn't.'

'Shall you divorce her?' Rashleigh asked.

'Good God, no!' The mere idea appalled Edward. 'After my predecessor, we have to avoid scandal at all costs.'

'Ah, yes, *him*,' Rashleigh smirked. 'So, what will you do for comforts?' He winked.

'Go without,' Edward replied. 'I've done it for long enough.' Sounding stoic, he looked miserable.

'There's no need to. Take a leaf out of my book.'

'What's that?'

Rashleigh glanced round to check that no one was within

earshot, then leaned forward, his arrogant features assuming a crafty, Jack-the-lad look. 'When I want a woman – which is pretty often, I don't mind telling you – I *buy* one.'

Automatically, as a result of a reflex action, Edward was shocked. 'I couldn't do that,' he whispered.

'Why not?'

'It doesn't seem right.' The instant the words were out, Edward was painfully aware that he sounded like a prig. He made it worse with, 'I couldn't face a common tart.'

'Do grow up, old man,' Rashleigh said, as though scolding a much-loved but slightly wayward gun dog. 'The sort of girls I'm talking about aren't common.' He chuckled. 'And in case you were thinking it, neither are they cheap.' He held up a hand to stifle Edward's objection. 'Imagine a beautiful woman, very beautiful indeed, who is a complete expert in the noble art of *sex*. She is dedicated to making sure that you experience sensations you never knew existed. As far as you're concerned, that is her sole purpose in life. Additionally, if you want to talk, she will listen to your problems without the slightest sign of boredom or bad temper. Finally, and take note of this, Edward, there's none of the emotional nonsense. When you've had enough, she'll go away until the next time you need her.'

'Such women exist?' Edward asked quietly.

'I know two dozen.'

'What do they cost?'

'About fifty for an evening, a hundred for a whole night.'

Edward blinked. 'That seems expensive.'

'You can get it for ten,' Rashleigh said dismissively. 'But you wouldn't be seen dead with one of *them*. Believe me, the girls I'm recommending are worth every single penny.'

'Er . . .' Groping for words, Edward cleared his throat rather too noisily. 'How does one make contact with these girls?'

'Through me.' Rashleigh was the conceited man of the world.

'Yes, I see. Where?'

'At a *very* nice establishment in Dorset Square.'

'A brothel?' Edward said starkly.

For once, Lord Francis Rashleigh was flummoxed. 'Well, yes, I suppose so,' he admitted grudgingly. 'If you insist on being so damned uncouth.'

'I couldn't possibly visit such a place,' Edward said, a hint of regret in the sanctimony. 'It would have to be far more private. I'd need a categorical guarantee of discretion.'

'Arrangements could be made for the girl to visit you.'

'Not at Cadogan Square!' Edward retorted.

Rashleigh was amused. 'Can't you trust the staff?'

'No.' Edward glowered. 'They're mostly Annaliese's appointees and think the world of her.' Bitterness boiled over. 'They treat her like royalty, which she is, in a way.'

'I thought she never left Allardyce,' Rashleigh said.

'That used to be the case, but she's in Town quite a bit lately. Works part-time at Boothby's, you know.'

'That's in Bond Street,' Rashleigh mused. 'Perhaps I should pop in one day and butter her up.'

'I'd rather you didn't,' Edward replied. 'It would make her suspicious. In any case, she doesn't much care for you.'

'You surprise me,' Rashleigh guffawed. 'Here was I thinking that the poor woman suffered from acid indigestion whenever I appeared.' After enjoying his own joke, he became serious again. 'Would you be happy if I arranged for you to have an evening with one of Helen's treasures in an hotel?'

Edward thought about it, shook his head, and, belatedly, asked, 'Who's Helen?'

'Helen Swann, dear boy. She's in charge of operations, what *you* would call the brothel-keeper.' Having enjoyed Edward's discomfort, Rashleigh heaved a theatrical sigh.

'How *can* we fix this? I know, what about my place?'

Rashleigh's town house was in Bruton Street, Mayfair. It was a hotbed of political intrigue and clandestine liaisons, in the latter respect, Edward suspected, rather like Martha's Vineyard. If nothing else, that implied the servants could be trusted. Rashleigh confirmed it. 'It's perfectly safe. One of Helen's girls often spends the night there. If I'm honest, I'm no more keen to be spotted in a bordello than you are, old man.'

Edward gazed into space, as if contemplating an arcanely intellectual hypothesis. In the end, his verdict was precisely what Rashleigh had guessed it would be. 'I shall have to think about this, Francis. I'll be in touch.'

It took him ten days to make up his mind, after which Rashleigh organised the assignation with astonishing speed. Before Edward had time to change his mind, he found himself dining with a young woman who introduced herself simply as Flora. They were alone at the house in Bruton Street, in a first-floor suite that matched the facilities of a luxury hotel.

Flora neither looked like a prostitute, nor behaved in the way that Edward had feared. Certainly, she was beautiful and the dress from the popular young couturier, Norman Hartnell, suggested a pleasing body, but her manner was fastidiously ladylike. The fact that she had an intelligent grasp of foreign affairs enabled Edward to enjoy dinner in a relatively relaxed frame of mind. But, at the end of the meal, when Flora said, 'Perhaps you would care to make yourself comfortable in the bedroom, Mr Allardyce,' he was alarmed. Her smile was warm and comforting. 'Please don't worry. I know it's your first time. I intend to make sure that you enjoy it.'

She left him to his own devices, not entering the bedroom until his nakedness was hidden under a sheet. Ignoring his trepidation, Flora began to remove her clothes, slowly and artfully revealing a sensationally voluptuous body. When only silk stockings and a minuscule suspender belt remained, she broke the trance-like silence to ask, 'Ought I to keep these on?'

'Yes, I'd like that.' Edward was excited, beginning to believe that he would not make a fool of himself.

'What do you think?' Flora asked, sliding into bed beside him. 'Will I do? Do you think I'm nice? My legs – you like them?'

'God, yes!'

'It's going to be lovely,' Flora murmured, casting off the demure façade as her hands went to work. 'I've been told you need some fun. Let's see what you like best, mmm? My goodness, you're so *hard*.'

When Flora left at midnight, spirited away in a chauffeur-driven car, Edward was both exhausted and flushed with excitement at what she had done to him. Curiously, there was a final perverse thrill: he found that he enjoyed paying her, handing over ten five-pound notes, watching her count them and slip them into her stocking top. The next day, Rashleigh was asked to arrange another meeting with Flora as quickly as possible. Before long, she was spending two nights a week at the house in Bruton Street and was worrying about the possibility that 'Mr Allardyce' might be developing a strange sort of emotional attachment to her. Soon, however, she realised that there was no danger of this. Her client had three totally different states of mind. When they began their evenings with a discussion of foreign policy or politics, he was cool and objective, treating her as an intellectual peer. Then, in bed, submitting to Flora's sensual skills, he thought only of pleasure. Finally, when he was satiated, he became super-cilious as he paid her and fixed their next appointment. To her amusement, Flora found herself flattered on arrival and treated with contempt when she left.

Edward was convinced that, at long last, he had established the ideal relationship with a woman. The cost – up to £10,000 a year if he continued to use Flora twice a week – was insignificant when set against his physical and mental well-being. As the summer progressed, people began to remark that the Duke of Lincolnshire was becoming far more agreeable.

Annaliese couldn't remember a blacker day than the one that took George away to school. Even her war-time experiences paled into insignificance against the trauma of losing the son she had hoped to keep at her side. Afterwards, when the ordeal of parting was over, she wondered if bursting into floods of tears might, in some strange way, have improved the dreadful business. But no one did, of course. George hung on to the bravery that had kept him going through the last week and Annaliese, Gwen, and Henrietta felt that they could not let him down by giving vent to their feelings.

Unfortunately, Douglas was at his brash and know-all worst. While the trunks were being loaded into the car, he proceeded to give his brother yet another lecture on what a twerp he was going to be until he had learned the rituals and pecking order of Moss Close. Just as Annaliese felt that she would murder Douglas if he didn't stop, Edward, who was delivering the boys to school on his way to London, intervened.

'*Do* shut up, Douglas, there's a good chap,' he said, firmly good-natured. 'George is going to cope, so let's not make it sound a hundred times worse than it is, eh?'

'Sorry, Pater,' Douglas said, taking the point.

Pater! Annaliese thought angrily. Was there no end to Moss Close's airs and graces? Ordering herself to stay calm, she stood in line behind Gwen and Henrietta to bid farewell to George.

'Take care of yourself, my darling,' she said, kissing him repeatedly. 'It will be Christmas before you know it. And, George, you will write, won't you? Tell me what it's like.'

'Yes, Mama, I promise.'

Everyone smiled, Edward made a particular point of being affectionate to Annaliese, and they set off.

'He'll be all right,' Gwen told Annaliese as they waved. 'Douglas is a pain in the neck, but he won't let George come to any harm.'

'Are you sure?' Annaliese asked.

'Certain.' Gwen's manner changed to the impudence that was one of her most endearing characteristics. 'What's got into Himself these days? Reckon he's found a woman?'

'Mmm. I think so. Yes.' Baffled by Edward's benign mood since the disaster in her bedroom, Annaliese had reached that same conclusion about a month ago. 'I wouldn't be surprised if he isn't seeing her tonight.'

'I hope he's being careful. We don't want no tittle-tattle.' Gwen was severely proprietorial, taking responsibility for ensuring that Compton Allardyce avoided damaging rumour.

Annaliese's laugh was heavy with irony. 'That's the one thing you can rely on,' she replied. 'Edward will be circumspect. So much so, that I wonder how it's possible for him to have an affair! Come along, let's cheer ourselves up with Viennese coffee.'

They went to the sitting-room office to decide what Henrietta's duties would be now that George had gone. Gratefully, the wayward offshoot of the Timberlakes had accepted the offer to remain at the Castle as Annaliese's social secretary. All that remained was to work out what that entailed.

'Before we start, there's something I simply must tell you,' Henrietta said. She looked surprisingly uncomfortable.

'Oh?' Annaliese gazed at her quizzically, intrigued to know

what was unsettling the normally unflappable young woman.

'Yes. Well . . .' Henrietta very nearly succeeded in tying herself in knots.

'Spit it out, Henry,' Annaliese ordered.

'The fact is, I'm sort of *seeing* Desmond Prideaux — Lord Desmond, that is.' Henrietta paused. 'To be honest, we're having a bit of a canter.'

'My word.' Smiling, Annaliese leaned back in her chair. 'Good for you, Henry. Are you enjoying yourselves?'

'Er, yes. Rather!'

'I don't mind what you get up to in your own time,' Annaliese said. 'Others might, though. Forgive me if I'm treading on delicate ground, but I was under the impression that Desmond was having what you call a canter — and I do like that, by the way — with my cousin-in-law, the Dowager Duchess.'

Bemused, Henrietta said, 'Whatever gave you that idea?'

'Well . . .' Confronted by genuinely blank astonishment, Annaliese was uneasy. 'They were always together. He often stayed late at The Chantry.'

'Nothing happened,' Henrietta replied. 'At least, not in *that* way. Actually, if you ask me, I think our dowager put the fear of God up Desmond.'

'I'm relieved to hear it,' Annaliese said, mentally congratulating John Brandon for his assessment of the relationship. 'Forgive me asking, but does Desmond's mother approve of you?'

'Gosh, no! I doubt if Desmond's said anything about me.' Henrietta, with no wish to meet the formidable Clementine, clearly hoped that her lover's reticence would continue indefinitely.

'Is anything likely to come of this?' Annaliese asked. 'An engagement, perhaps?'

'Who knows?' There was a daredevil bravado about

Henrietta's response that made Annaliese check her curiosity. It looked as though nothing beyond a good time was intended and one had to assume that Henrietta and Desmond knew what they were doing.

'Right, to business,' Annaliese said. 'What on earth does a social secretary do?'

'I've made a list,' Henrietta said, producing a sheaf of papers. 'You'll be amazed.'

On 7 October, Annaliese conducted a sale at Boothby's that was noteworthy on several counts. The 52 lots, all items from a house that was being sold to raise death duties, realised a total of £515,000, the first half-million-pound total to be achieved in a single day's auction. Many of the successful bids came from Americans, both dealers and private collectors, attracted by advertisements in New York magazines and Nancy Shenstone's ceaseless advocacy of Boothby's during her visits to the USA. The admired and much sought-after catalogue had been researched and written by Celia, who now worked without help or supervision.

Less happily, it was Beatrice's first day back after a long absence for illness caused by a devastating depression. Three months previously, she had miscarried for the second time. The earlier misadventure, soon after Beatrice and Charles married in 1927, had been attributed to sheer bad luck and was soon forgotten. Annaliese, a frequent visitor to the house in Regent's Park that Beatrice and Charles had shared almost since the start of their affair, quickly realised that the second mishap was an infinitely more serious blow, demoralising Beatrice and rendering her incapable of dealing with anything outside the safety of the house – not even her beloved Boothby's.

'It's a question of coming to terms with it,' she told Annaliese. 'I simply can't face going through *that* again, so we shall have to give up trying. It's ghastly.'

'Not the end of the world, though,' Annaliese replied.

'It is for Charles.'

'Has he said so?' Annaliese asked. 'Has he even *implied* anything remotely like that?'

'Well, no, he hasn't,' Beatrice admitted. 'But I know what he thinks deep down.'

'I doubt it,' Annaliese said gently. 'What Charles wants is to have you back to normal and loving him. He doesn't care about anything else. He's such a good man.'

'Yes, I know — at least, that's what I keep telling myself.' Beatrice shook her head, miserable at her inability to come to terms with the loss of a second child, blaming herself. 'Sitting around moping isn't any good, is it?'

'Come to the Shifnal sale next week,' Annaliese urged. 'There'll be a good turn-out, lots of people you know, all dying to see you.'

'Yes, I could probably manage that,' Beatrice agreed.

She did, but only by the skin of her teeth. Although her old friends were glad to welcome Beatrice back, those who didn't know her tended to avoid the pale, tense woman who hovered at the back of the auction-room, unable to settle or enjoy the ebb and flow of the sale. The men, especially the Americans, had eyes only for Celia, jostling for the chance of a few words with her. Doing her best to be self-effacing, she spent most of the pauses between lots deflecting compliments and invitations.

At 5.00 pm, when it was all over and the large crowd had dispersed, Annaliese invited Celia to dinner at Cadogan Square. 'As a celebration,' she said. 'Especially of your *marvellous* catalogue.' As if providing an extra incentive, Annaliese added, 'Don't worry about Edward. He's either at the House of Lords or dining at his club.'

Celia smiled at the slightly conspiratorial camaraderie,

often in evidence these days and a sign of her growing value to Boothby's. Tempting though the offer was, she still felt the need to keep her distance, to make herself useful, possibly indispensable, without exposing herself to the risks of over-familiarity. 'That's kind of you,' Celia said. 'I'm afraid I promised to take my aunt to the cinema this evening.'

Before Annaliese could respond, Beatrice was also excusing herself. 'I must go home to Charles. He'll be worried about me. You know how it is, first day back at work . . .'

'Oh, I see.' Clearly annoyed, Annaliese produced her diary. 'You and Celia will be here tomorrow, I presume?'

Beatrice and Celia exchanged looks and nodded.

'In that case, I shall go back to Allardyce now,' Annaliese said. 'I can catch the six-fifteen from Paddington. I must ring Matthew to meet me at Pewsey.'

She swept off abruptly, reminding the two surprised women of her Imperial background and upbringing. It was unnerving, like a sudden shaft of harsh sunlight.

'She adores the Castle,' Beatrice said, feeling a need to apologise for her sister-in-law. 'Doesn't really like London.'

'Who can blame her?' Celia replied, pretending not to have noticed anything out of the ordinary. 'And she did awfully well today, don't you think? The Shifnals weren't expecting more than four hundred thousand.'

'They'll be over the moon,' Beatrice agreed.

After a slightly awkward pause, Celia said, 'I'm sorry about your baby, Beatrice. If ever you want to talk about it, I'll be happy to listen.'

'Thank you.' Briefly, there was a surge of sympathy between them. All too soon, however, as Beatrice found the memory of Celia's son even more painful than her own loss, it faded. They were glad to go their separate ways.

After the cab ride to Putney Vale, Celia collapsed into an armchair and reached for the whisky and soda that was waiting for her.

'How was it?' Ursula Croft asked.

'Very good indeed. More than half a million.'

Ursula whistled. 'How splendid! Was your catalogue appreciated?'

'I earned a star or two.' Celia sipped at the whisky, smacked her lips, and said, 'There were a lot of Americans at the sale.'

'Ah.' Ursula nodded. 'They know how to spend money.'

'Don't they just.' Far away, conjuring up agreeable memories, Celia said, 'They were interesting. Different. I liked them.'

'And the feeling was mutual?'

'Yes, I think it was.'

'One hears good things about American men,' Ursula said. 'They're supposed to make better husbands than Englishmen.'

'*All* of them?' Celia laughed.

'Oh, no, it isn't that simple. You have to compare like with like. I'm talking about the upper crust, the ones with the money and power.'

'I shall bear that in mind,' Celia said, not entirely serious.

'Do,' Ursula urged. 'Marriage to a nice, wealthy American would solve a great many problems.'

Celia was thoughtful. 'You're right.' Her mind returned to the day's events at Boothby's. 'Annaliese knows how to handle them. She was brilliant. Something very funny happened at the end, though. She asked Beatrice and me to have dinner with her. When we said we couldn't she decided to go back to Compton Allardyce.'

'Tonight?'

'Yes.'

'What's wrong with that?' Ursula asked. 'You're always

telling me how much she dislikes that house in Cadogan Square.'

'Yes, she does.' Nevertheless, Celia's curiosity was roused. This was not the first time Annaliese had thrown what seemed to be carefully made plans out of the window in order to make a dash for Wiltshire. When the fancy took her, she was perfectly capable of catching the 9.30 pm train, even though it was non-stop to Westbury, twenty miles beyond Pewsey, putting Matthew to immense trouble when he should have been tucked up in bed with his insolent little wife. These impulsive manifestations of homing instinct surely went beyond Annaliese's well-known affection for the Castle? Celia's instincts told her that more powerful forces were at work. There was a man, but who? For a time, John Brandon had been under suspicion, but Celia's certainty that Annaliese would never allow herself to become involved with an employee ruled against him. 'No, it can't be him,' Celia muttered.

'Sorry, what was that?' Ursula asked.

'Nothing. I was only burbling,' Celia said. 'It wasn't important.'

'I have something that *is*,' Ursula replied, her face alight. 'Let me get you another drink, you'll need it. I had lunch with an old friend today, Helen Swann.'

The name was vaguely familiar to Celia, rang disquieting bells. 'I'm sorry, I can't place her.'

Ursula handed a replenished glass to Celia. 'She runs a really posh place in Dorset Square. Delightful girls, hundred-pound-a-night standard. Helen and I used to be friendly rivals and find it pays to keep in touch. It's amazing how many things we can still do to help each other.'

'Really?' Celia was wary.

'Every month or so we have a meal at a lovely place near Hampton Court.' Ursula settled herself and sipped champagne with exaggerated enjoyment. 'It's hideously wicked of us, but we do tend to gossip on these occasions. I'm afraid cats get let out of the bag.' Seeing Celia's mounting apprehension, Ursula abandoned teasing flippancy. 'Worry not, my dear, *you* weren't mentioned, not even hinted at.'

'Thank God for that.' Celia's laugh was unnaturally loud. 'I worry.'

'That's because you can't tear yourself away from this silly idea that you're getting the best of both worlds,' Ursula chided. 'I do wish that you'd make a choice between Bond Street and Cap Ferrat.'

'I thought you had something to tell me,' Celia said, irritably fending off another lecture.

'Yes.' Ursula drank champagne. 'Three or four months ago, the Duke of Lincolnshire began to avail himself of one of Helen Swann's girls.'

For several long moments, Celia was very still and quiet. Finally, she said, 'Well, well!'

'It's becoming a habit. Twice a week.'

Slightly puzzled, Celia said, 'The only thing that surprises me is that he found the courage.'

'From what I gather, there isn't a lot of that needed,' Ursula said. 'He doesn't go to Dorset Square, the girl visits him at a friend's house.'

Celia was rapt, like a child contemplating the mysteries of a fairy-tale. 'Who is this accommodating friend?'

'Helen didn't say and I didn't ask,' Ursula replied. 'There's no point in forcing these things.'

'But you will find out?'

'All in good time.' Ursula studied Celia. 'What will you do with this knowledge?'

'I've no idea.' Celia's mind was awash with possibilities, many of them misty, needing time to come to fruition. 'It's going to be very useful, though.'

'Nothing as crude as blackmail, I hope?' Ursula viewed the prospect with revulsion. For her, the inviolate secrecy of the relationship between a man and his courtesan had always been a sacred article of faith.

'Oh, no,' Celia replied. 'At least, not directly, and not yet.'

'Don't be silly.' Ursula was exasperated. 'We both know that extortion would be stupid and dangerous, so why pretend otherwise? You *must* make up your mind what you're going to do with your life.' After enduring Celia's sulky silence for a few moments, Ursula said, 'I had a letter from Arabella this morning. Prince Umberto has asked her to marry him.'

'Again?' Celia was disdainful.

'He's proposed before?'

'Last summer. She laughed at him.'

'She may well be doing so this time.' Ursula said. 'But her letter had an awful lot about his *palazzo* in Florence, the house in Milan, and what sounds like a rather splendid villa at Brindisi – where, incidentally, she's thinking of spending Christmas.'

'Oh!' Celia was offended.

'*Please* think things over,' Ursula pleaded. 'Bear in mind that Arabella is a good deal older than you. She'll be forty next year.'

'That doesn't mean a thing,' Celia said. 'With her looks, she could carry on indefinitely.'

Ursula nodded. 'I know that. There's quite a demand for the more mature woman.' She paused. 'At lunch, dear Helen made me an offer that will be difficult to refuse.' She smiled proudly. 'But simply because a woman who's well into her fifties is capable of entertaining a man, that doesn't mean to say she *will* – not if an attractive alternative presents itself. If Arabella decides to become a princess, what will you do?'

'I'll settle for London,' Celia said cheerfully and, Ursula

thought, without a shred of conviction.

On the day before George and the far less important Douglas returned for the Christmas holidays, Annaliese was in a rare old state. Its sheer size and complexity made Allardyce Castle an essentially calm place; it was possible to have several blazing rows, together with what Baskerville called 'a big spit and polish exercise' and still leave most of the huge building slumbering in peace. Frantic to ensure that George was welcomed into a joyous riot of festivity, Annaliese almost succeeded in turning the entire Castle into an upside-down, raving uproar. The resident servants were supplemented by staff borrowed from the Duchess of Laverstoke, no one knew how many Christmas trees there were, and, while John Brandon was growing concerned about the quantities of holly and ivy that were being taken from the woods, Mrs Pritchard despaired of ever cleaning up the mess as the boughs were dragged in and hung.

In the background, flitting from room to room in mounting anxiety, Henrietta resembled the proverbial cat on hot bricks. Dozens of times, nearly tripping both of them up in the process, Henrietta intercepted Annaliese to say that she *must* speak to her. 'Yes, yes, yes, in a minute!' Annaliese snapped and promptly disappeared, tearing off to hurl further confusion into another part of the bedlam. Not until 9.30 in the evening, when nearly thirteen hours of chaos were finally subsiding, did Henrietta get her chance, finding Annaliese collapsed in the nursery, gratefully wolfing dried-up leftovers of the sandwich lunch.

'Yes, Henry, what is it?' Annaliese asked, exhaustion making her sound brusque.

'I'm sorry to be a nuisance, but if I don't get this off my chest today, it could be three weeks before there's another chance and I think you need to know as soon as possible.'

'Sit down, my dear,' Annaliese said, remembering that they had not had a chance to talk since Henrietta's journey into Marlborough the previous evening to see her doctor. 'Are you all right?'

'Oh, yes, I'm fine,' Henrietta grinned. 'Very fit, but pregnant! The little perisher's due next July.'

'I see.' Annaliese recalled Lord Desmond Prideaux's engagement, announced two weeks ago. He was marrying the daughter of a Norfolk farmer, effectively joining a wealthy business based on 15,000 prime acres of arable and dairy activity. Earnestly, half-afraid of the wrong answer, Annaliese asked, 'You aren't considering anything awful, I hope?'

'Get rid of it, you mean?' Henrietta's green eyes flashed with anger. 'Not ruddy likely!'

'Good.' Pleased both by the answer and its vehemence, Annaliese said, 'You'll stay here, with me?'

'If I may.'

'Naturally.'

'I can't see anyone else wanting me.'

Annaliese imagined that an illegitimate child would be the last straw for Henrietta's family. Aloud, she said, 'You have to sympathise with their point of view. You're a trial, Henry.'

'Aren't I?' Henrietta wasn't in the least repentant. 'Perhaps this will quieten me down.'

'I'll believe that the day I see pigs flying over Keeper's Spinney,' Annaliese hooted. 'Are you still seeing Desmond?'

'No. We agreed that he should behave himself after the engagement.' Brushing aside wistfulness, Henrietta said, 'I'd prefer it if no one found out that he was the father.'

'We shall do our best,' Annaliese replied. 'Mind you, I expect the baby will want to know when she's grown up.'

'That's a different matter.' Henrietta paused, smiling. 'She? You think it's a girl?'

'There'll be hell to pay if it isn't,' Annaliese said forcefully.

'Beatrice isn't going to give me a niece, so I'm depending on you, Henry. Don't you dare let me down.'

'I'll do my best,' Henrietta said, laughing. Suddenly serious, she asked, 'Do you think Gwen will mind?'

'Oh, she'll *mind* like anything,' Annaliese replied. 'It will be awful for her. But that won't stop her spoiling the child rotten.'

'That would be lovely for both of us. Er . . . what about His Grace, your husband. What will he say?'

Annaliese sighed, surrendering to the weariness of the frantic day. 'It's more than likely that he'll want you thrown out, but don't worry, Henry, it's simply a question of choosing the right time to tell him. Leave it to me.'

In the event, the opportunity never arose over the Christmas season. During the week that Edward spent at the Castle, his bland amiability was so patently skin-deep and fragile that Annaliese left well alone.

There were, in any case, her concerns for George. Irritatingly, there was nothing tangible. He was brimming with health and energy and claimed to be enjoying Moss Close. He had made friends – dismissed, typically enough by Douglas, as a bunch of weaklings and sissies – and George had brought a glowing report home with him. So what was wrong, Annaliese asked herself, why was she unwilling to accept it all at face value? Perhaps it was the look on George's face in unguarded moments, a distant, oddly perceptive expression that suggested he knew far more than was good for a little boy of eight.

4

1931–1932
'No, Mr McBane didn't ask me to marry him'

Britain was complacent, believing that the repercussions of the 1929 Wall Street Crash and the subsequent depression in America had passed it by. Then, at the end of July 1931, trouble loomed. Unemployment rose to three million and a House of Commons committee produced a report stating that the Government was spending far more than it could afford. There was a flurry of meetings and conferences in London – including one that purported to address itself to Germany's economic catastrophe. Nothing was done, Parliament drifted into its summer recess and Ramsay MacDonald went to Scotland on holiday.

The international money markets disapproved. A run on the pound began, gaining momentum by the hour. To check the drain on its gold reserves, the Bank of England borrowed heavily in Paris and New York. On 11 August, as Edward and his friends travelled north to Glengrantach for the annual grouse slaughter, Ramsay MacDonald dashed back to London in a belated, panic-stricken attempt to head off the crisis. By the 23rd of the month, the Labour Government had come to an end, dissolving into disarray, like the forsaken hopes of the 1920s.

Astonishingly, however, there was no election. In a process that was never explained to the nation, a constitutional conjuring trick that was destined to be an endless source of analysis and acrimony took place. Stanley Baldwin led the Conservative Party into a coalition that became known as the National Government.

*

On the afternoon of 29 August 1931, a Saturday, Annaliese and John Brandon felt bound to discuss the extraordinary state of affairs in Westminster, allowing their embargo on politics to lapse for a while. They were in bed at John's house in Gainsborough Wood, drowsy after making love.

'Some of the papers are saying that it's the King's doing,' Annaliese said. 'He's supposed to have bullied Baldwin and MacDonald into this alliance. Is that likely?'

John took his time. 'Possible, but not likely,' he said eventually. 'His Majesty will have lectured them on their duty and he can be outspoken. On the whole, I'd say it was cowardice.'

'*Cowardice?*' Annaliese propped herself up to peer into John's eyes. 'Explain.'

'Neither Baldwin nor MacDonald has the faintest idea what to do. If there were an election, they'd have to produce a manifesto and people would expect answers. Since they can't do that, they're hiding behind each other.'

'You sound like Edward,' Annaliese spluttered.

Resenting the comparison, John was cold. 'How is your husband? Have you heard from him?'

'No, I have not,' Annaliese said, shaking with laughter, 'and I hope it stays that way. He'll be denouncing Baldwin morning, noon, and night, sending everyone into a coma.'

'I doubt that,' John said drily. 'Don't all his companions share his views?' Not waiting for an answer, he went on. 'This National Government caper *does* worry me.'

'Why?'

'Ah, well, that's it, you see. I don't know.' John smiled ruefully. 'I have this uneasy feeling that compromise isn't what this country needs. This is a time for firm government.'

Annaliese added a worry of her own. 'In the middle of all this dashing around and doing nothing, Germany has been forgotten.'

'Yes.' John was lost for a while, deep in grave thoughts. 'I'm fearful of the mess that Germany has been allowed to get into,' he said at last. 'The worm will turn.'

Annaliese sensed that he was voicing a mere fraction of his misgivings. Setting the sufferings of the German nation since 1918 against what she knew of their proud but dark determination, she too experienced a tremor of foreboding. She clutched at a straw. 'Germany has no leader. They can't do anything without someone to order them around. Their politicians are bigger idiots than ours.'

'Are you saying that they don't have a capable man anywhere?' John asked.

'No, I don't meant that – it's just that they haven't found him yet.'

'He may not be far away,' John suggested. 'Right under their noses, but regarded as a joke?'

Annaliese decided to make light of it. 'Is this Schicklgrüber, the Austrian corporal?' she teased, using what many believed was the real name of Adolf Hitler's father, a name that was easy to mock.

'It's possible,' John said. 'The way things are in Germany, nothing is *impossible*.'

'Oh dear.' Annaliese pulled a face. 'Are we to be serious now? No more fun?'

John laughed. 'I wouldn't be such a brute as to point out that it was you who started this conversation.' Six years close to her had taught him to mirror Annaliese's moods.

'Good.' She wanted to make love again, but had a point to make. 'Actually, I was talking about the mess *this* country is in – no, don't interrupt – and I wanted to tell you what Charles Templeton said the other day.'

'I can guess,' John said, gathering Annaliese into his arms. 'He thinks you were extremely clever to move the family fortune to Switzerland. Am I right?'

'Yes, you beast.' Chuckling, she drew him into her, sighing at the pleasure of penetration. 'Show me how clever you are at *this* so that we can forget the stupid, wicked world.'

That same evening, over dinner at St. Jean-Cap-Ferrat, Arabella told Celia that she had decided to marry Prince Umberto.

'You see, darling, it really *is* time for me to retire now,' Arabella said. 'I've thought and thought and this is what I must do. I hope . . .'

'No, it's quite all right,' Celia said, cutting her short. 'You don't have to explain. I understand.'

Her sharp tone caused Arabella to glance at Umberto for reassurance. He sipped wine and smiled complacently. 'There's something I'd like you to consider,' Arabella said to Celia. 'Obviously, I shall be getting rid of this place and I wondered if you'd like to take it over – live here all the time, find another girl.'

'Goodness, no.' Celia was floored by the proposal. 'I couldn't possibly. For a start, I doubt whether I could afford to pay what this place is worth.'

'Umberto has an idea,' Arabella said, smiling at him encouragingly.

'But of course I do.' As always when he was about to show

off his almost impeccable English, the Prince preened, making sure that Celia was treated to the full splendour of his profile. 'I will purchase this delightful house from my beautiful Arabella and rent it to you, dear Celia, for a *pitiful* amount. Why not have *two* girls and take twenty per cent of what they earn? You will flourish.'

Momentarily snared by his dark eyes, Celia came close to believing and accepting. Only with a great effort of will was she able to say, 'No, Umberto, thank you, but I couldn't.'

'Why not?' He reached for her hands, clasping them in a caress designed to melt hearts. 'I shall send all my friends to visit you and the money will pour in. Better than that, you will find a husband, a great man like me, huh?'

Reclaiming her hands, Celia laughed. 'It's very good of you, Umberto, but, no. Really, I mean it. I think I will marry, but I've rather set my heart on an American.'

Thunderstruck, Umberto turned to Arabella and poured out a tirade of Italian that sounded blood-curdling. She laughed and said, 'I think my aunt Ursula might be to blame for this. She *adores* Americans.'

'Lunacy!' Umberto roared. 'What drives her to it?'

'She says they're the best lovers,' Arabella replied, mischievously aware of the earthquake that would follow.

When he finally calmed down, Umberto flung himself to his knees beside Celia's chair. 'I beg of you, stay here, my lovely one,' he wailed, summoning tears to his eyes. 'If not – and better still – come with us to Italy. *Yes!*' He turned to Arabella. 'That's good, don't you think, *Caro?*'

'Indeed.' Arabella smiled and nodded encouragement to Celia. 'Gaston is coming with us, why not you? Yes, we could have a marvellous time, especially when Umberto disappears with one of his mistresses.'

While the accused was indulging in breast-beating denial, Celia stood up, left the table, and slipped through the French windows into the garden. Shaking, with her mind in turmoil, she was incapable of deciding whether it was anger or sorrow that was overwhelming her. Although unwilling to commit herself to it permanently, Celia loved the Côte d'Azur with a fierce, almost physical passion. In the six years since her first arrival, she had made fourteen visits, each lasting at least a month, adoring the sensuality and frenzied gaiety. It was a place in which almost every man seemed inspired to be nearly as good a lover as Ralph. How dare Arabella bring it all to an end!

Softly, her feet making no sound on the lush lawn, Arabella emerged from the deepening twilight. She was anxious. 'Darling, are you all right? You went off so suddenly. You're upset, aren't you? Do you think I'm doing the wrong thing, making a big mistake?'

'Oh, Arabella, how can I tell?' Celia said dejectedly. 'Perhaps when I get over the shock . . .' Her voice tailed off.

'Sweetheart, you've had plenty of warning.' Arabella put her arms round Celia as though comforting a hurt child. 'All my little hints.'

'I know.' Fighting back tears, Celia pressed her face against Arabella's shoulder until she felt able to continue. 'I just refused to believe it. Silly of me. I'm going to miss you and this house so very much.'

'Don't,' Arabella cried. 'Either come to Italy, or accept Umberto's offer – he's quite serious about it. Imagine, if you took over, I'd be able to visit you, keep my hand in with a little freelance work.' She laughed at the prospect.

Stubbornly, Celia shook her head. 'No, it's London and Boothby's now until I find a husband.'

'Are you sure about marrying an American?' Arabella was deeply sceptical.

'Why shouldn't I?' Celia was defensive. 'The ones I've met are bloody nice, and I'd much rather live in America than Italy.'

'Why?' There was a trace of fear in Arabella's voice. 'What makes you say that?'

'How long will Fascism last?' Celia demanded. 'Isn't it only a sort of fad that's bound to end badly?'

'Don't be silly, Italy's the only country in Europe that's being run properly these days.' Arabella became intense. 'Listen to me, Celia. There was a British politician here on holiday two weeks ago, a Conservative, very senior, he'd be in the cabinet if Baldwin had the guts to form a decent Government. He was frightened to death of what was happening in England. According to him, the country's lost its nerve and sense of direction. But he was full of praise for Mussolini. *Why* won't you see sense? There's nothing to keep you in London, or that miserable place in Wiltshire. Move into this house and bring Aunt Ursula with you. She'd sell up like a flash.'

Celia's tenuous hold on her feelings broke. 'I don't want to be here without you,' she wailed. 'How would I cope? I can't even learn a few phrases of the language – or hadn't you noticed? You have to do everything – order my clothes, deal with waiters, negotiate with new clients. I won't even have Gaston to help me.'

Stunned, Arabella took a pace backwards. 'This is all because of a language problem?' she whispered. 'No, it can't be. You aren't serious, are you?'

'Yes.'

Arabella looked at Celia, who was sulky and embarrassed by her admission. 'Look, this is what we can do,' Arabella said soothingly. 'Gaston will find someone else to look after you. I'm sure he can find a reliable man, he has contacts everywhere.'

'No, no, no!' Celia screamed. 'That's no good.'

Before either of them realised what was happening, Arabella was screaming too and the situation was beyond control. As they both screeched hurtful things they didn't mean and would regret forever, Umberto charged into the garden, waving his arms, pleading for calm and unwittingly making the quarrel ten times worse.

No one had much sleep that night as Arabella and Umberto tried everything they could think of to make Celia change her mind. But it was all to no avail: the following evening, after a day of hysterical argument and tears, a sullen Gaston drove Celia to Nice for the night train to Paris. She was travelling with one small case, having instructed Arabella to dispose of everything that she had accumulated at the villa. Arabella, profoundly upset and mystified by her failure to change Celia's mind, refused to accompany her to the railway station and threatened to make a bonfire of her clothes. They parted under a cloud of overwrought anger and Celia knew that she had burned her boats.

There was a General Election on 27 October. The National Government won 554 of the 615 seats in the House of Commons. Although most of the huge majority was made up of Conservatives, Stanley Baldwin was content to allow Ramsay MacDonald to continue as Prime Minister. MacDonald, reviled as a traitor by the main sections of the Labour movement, and ousted from the Party leadership by George Lansbury, had the support of only seven so-called Labour MPs. That he should head an administration containing over 400 Conservatives was ludicrous, a situation without parallel in British politics. In theory, because of the broad range of opinion it represented, the National Government of 1931 was the strongest ever elected; in fact, subsequent events were to expose it as the most feeble-minded rag-bag ever to occupy the Mother of Parliaments.

Edward, one of a small minority who dissociated themselves from the initial smugness, was disgusted, both by the facts and his inability to influence them. The loss of Flora added to his black humour. She had, Helen Swann regretted to say, given up working and retired to the country. Furious at not receiving advance notice of his deprivation – especially from Flora herself – Edward made a poor fist of selecting a replacement. No less than four of Helen Swann's girls joined 'Mr Allardyce' at Rashleigh's house, but, to their immense relief, all were rejected. Temporarily unable to stomach the atmosphere in the House of Lords and sick of London in general, Edward retreated to Wiltshire.

Annaliese and Gwen braced themselves for trouble. Even Baskerville, who persisted in admiring Edward despite repeated discouragement, told Mrs Pritchard that they were in for a bad time. 'That's the first time His Grace has been what you might call rude, Doreen. He's in a *shocking* mood.'

'It's the Government, I shouldn't wonder,' Mrs Pritchard said, sounding wise yet not understanding why anyone could be upset by Mr MacDonald, Mr Baldwin, and all the other fine gentlemen who were doing such a good job.

Grimly prepared for the worst, no one expected Edward to be enchanted out of his foul mood by a little girl who was sixteen months old – particularly since he had previously gone to great lengths to avoid acknowledging the child's existence.

In July 1930, Henrietta had complied with Annaliese's instructions and given birth to a daughter. From the very start, the infant was a placid, well-behaved delight. She had her mother's green eyes, a remarkably pretty face, and a single tuft of golden-blonde hair. Henrietta decided that her name was to be Athene, the Greek Goddess of Wisdom who was also Patroness of the Arts. However, when informed that the father's name was unknown, the Vicar of Compton Allardyce refused to baptise the child. The Reverend Wright – immediately renamed Wrong by an incandescently angry Annaliese – had been appointed to the living during Ralph's lackadaisical tenure of the dukedom and was a somewhat narrow-minded, curiously idealistic individual to whom Edward attributed Communist sympathies. Whatever his affiliations, the Reverend Wright lacked any perception of where and how his bread was buttered. The speed at which the sky collapsed on him after a single telephone call from Annaliese was to haunt him for the rest of his life – which was spent at a parish in a less than perfect suburb of Swindon. Until a new, more suitable man could be found, the Bishop of Salisbury sent one of his archdeacons to baptise Athene in the Castle Chapel.

Afterwards, the party went to Annaliese's favourite room, the vast Long Gallery, to toast the baby's future in champagne. Picking the right moment, when Henrietta and Annaliese were alone together and some distance from the other guests, Clementine Laverstoke joined them. She gazed at Athene, angelically asleep in her mother's arms, then favoured Henrietta with a searching stare. Eventually, she reached out and Henrietta, mesmerised, dutifully handed the child over. Athene opened her eyes and gurgled at the Duchess of Laverstoke.

'This little sweetheart is my granddaughter, isn't she?' Clementine said quietly, ensuring that only her immediate companions were able to hear.

'I didn't invite you and Hubert just for show,' Annaliese murmured.

The two duchesses exchanged eloquent looks.

'On this occasion, I'd better keep my opinions of Desmond to myself,' Clementine said. She smiled gently at Henrietta. 'You've been an absolute brick over this, my dear. Thank you.'

'Er . . . not at all, Your Grace,' Henrietta stammered.

'I presume Athene will want for nothing?'

'Don't be silly, Clem,' Annaliese said, rescuing a speechless

Henrietta. 'She's one of the family.'

'I thought so. You'll bring her to see me?'

'Naturally. And you must pop in here whenever the fancy takes you.'

Content, Clementine wandered off to deposit herself in one of the Long Gallery's deep window-seats, cradling Athene to her bosom.

'There's a thing,' Annaliese whispered to Henrietta. 'You're an "absolute brick". That's the ultimate accolade.'

'I don't think I shall ever recover,' Henrietta gasped, torn between elation and a nervous breakdown.

Edward, who had absented himself from the christening in an unpleasantly obvious way, was glad of its by-product – the Reverend Wright's disappearance – but was unwilling to credit Athene for her part in bringing it about. His antipathy to the child rapidly became a sour fact of life at the Castle: when Edward was in residence, Athene had to be kept out of his way. Annaliese, assuming that the accident of illegitimacy was at the root of his animosity, was outraged but remained silent.

Then, in November 1931, two days after his flight from London, Edward stumbled across Athene in the library. Half an hour earlier, Henrietta had been consulting reference books in search of information for a speech Annaliese was to make at a charity luncheon. Entering the room, Henrietta had dumped Athene into a heap of Labradors on the hearth to keep her quiet and out of trouble. Sighing and heaving, the dogs adjusted to the newcomer – whom they adored – and went back to sleep. Ten minutes later, excited by a discovery in one of the books, Henrietta dashed off, forgetting Athene.

She was still nestling contentedly among her friends when Edward came into the library. He did not spot her until he had drawn an armchair as close to the fire as the dogs allowed and was about to scan *The Times* in search of fresh nightmares from

Westminster. Their eyes met and Athene said, 'Dukey,' grinning happily. While Edward was wondering what to do, Athene clambered over a dog, swarmed up the side of the chair, and deposited herself in his lap.

On the brink of recoiling, Edward found himself engulfed in the most unexpected feelings. Suddenly, he realised how badly he had always wanted a daughter. Drawing Athene into his arms, he was contemplating the impossibility of achieving his latent ambition when the door burst open and Henrietta, frantic to rectify her carelessness, dashed in.

She stopped in her tracks, horrified. 'Oh, I'm *so* sorry, Your Grace,' she squeaked. 'I was in here, looking a few things up for my lady, and I forgot the little one. Whatever must you think of me?'

'Please don't concern yourself, Miss Timberlake,' Edward said. 'There's no harm done. Quite the contrary, I'd say.'

Athene clapped her hands in gleeful agreement.

Later, Henrietta told Gwen, 'He's quite handsome when he lets himself go. He had a lovely smile.'

Edging nervously towards Edward in his armchair, Henrietta said, 'If I may, Your Grace, I will remove your burden.'

It was an inanely stilted form of expression and Athene, who hardly ever cried, made it worse by bursting into floods of peevish tears when she saw what was afoot.

'Perhaps,' Edward suggested diffidently, 'she'd like to come with me when I exercise this lot.' He prodded a foot at one of the dogs. 'I take them to Keeper's Spinney in a shooting-brake and let them run. I'll take good care of her, Miss Timberlake.'

Athene, grasping the essentials, stopped crying and bawled, 'Yes!'

Grinning stupidly, Henrietta nodded, grabbed her child, and fled.

After breakfast the following day, Edward and Athene went

off with the dogs. When they returned, they were the firmest
of friends, with Athene already showing signs of being the
dominant partner. In less than a week, Edward was promising
to buy her a pony when she was two.

Gwen, watching the Duke of Lincolnshire's metamorphosis
with wry amusement, said, 'This is a turn up for the book,'
to Annaliese. 'What's come over him?'

'Don't ask questions,' Annaliese retorted. 'It's some sort
of miracle, so let's enjoy it while it lasts.' Having a shrewd
idea what lay behind Edward's fascination with Athene, and
with no intention of obliging him, Annaliese refused to be
drawn further.

Soon, she was confronted by the fact that Edward's
persistent good humour was a confounded nuisance, preventing her from seeing John Brandon. Annaliese was loath to visit
Gainsborough Wood while Edward was at the Castle. His
usual flying visits were no hardship, but when he showed no
inclination to leave, Annaliese began to fret. The trying
situation was given an ironic twist when John, invited to
dinner by Edward, came out of his shell to demonstrate an
impressive grasp on politics and international affairs. Thereafter, John was a frequent visitor in the evenings, often helping
Edward put the world to rights. On a miserable morning in
mid-December, at the end of a business meeting in her office,
Annaliese told John, 'This is likely to last until the New Year,
I'm afraid. But I warn you, Major Brandon, when he finally
does clear off to London, you are going to be *furiously* busy.'

Softly, he replied. 'I think about it constantly.'

Christmas brought a compensation for the annoyance of
Edward's presence. George, who had been devoted to Athene
since her birth, found that he had something in common with
his father at long last. Now it was George, not Douglas, who
went to the woods with Edward, Athene, and the dogs, and
it was George who was allowed into that holy of holies, the

library. Badly put out, Douglas muttered darkly about chaps who, not content with befriending a baby, had to choose a *girl*, and began to cultivate Baskerville. The butler admitted to Mrs Pritchard that he was flattered by the young Marquess of Axholme's attentions, especially since it was right and proper. There was, Baskerville said, a tradition in the big houses that the heir should grow up close to his father's butler.

During the Christmas period, Celia flitted in and out of the Castle more or less at will, acting for all the world like a relaxed, fully accepted member of the family. Unobtrusively, Annaliese watched closely, intrigued by the change in her. At the beginning of September, Celia had returned from one of her mysterious absences in a bad, restless frame of mind. When she had declared that she would now like to work full-time at Boothby's, Beatrice objected.

'Have you seen the mood she's in?' she asked Annaliese. 'We can't expect clients to put up with that.'

'She'll get over it,' Annaliese replied. 'I know she's going through a bad patch, but she *is* useful to us and I wish you'd admit it.'

Beatrice, much more her old self now that Charles had succeeded in persuading her that he was perfectly happy with Nigel and didn't need another child, grinned sheepishly. 'You're right,' she said. 'I must be more charitable to her.'

At the end of October, Celia's attitude changed dramatically. For ten days, her cheerfulness threatened to become uncontrollable euphoria. Then, rather than the depression that Annaliese had feared, Celia settled into a state of serenity. Virtually overnight, she seemed to mature, gaining the poise and lustre whose absence had always somehow diminished her beauty.

Annaliese felt certain that Greg McBane was responsible.

On 26 October, the day before the General Election, the

auction at Boothby's had consisted of items from two house clearances. The largely mediocre array of furniture was made interesting by three paintings that many experts believed were the work of Velasquez, rescued from a century of obscurity by Celia's sharp eye and persistence. Greg McBane shared that view and was struck by the excellent condition of the paintings: their disappearance into a wine cellar had been organised by someone who had used blankets and a stout wooden box as a refuge. Consequently, McBane, a dealer from New York, intended to have the pictures come hell or high water and he annihilated all other bidders with a ruthlessness only available to the very wealthy.

After the sale, when he asked Beatrice how the paintings had come to light, she introduced him to Celia. Later, using hindsight for all its was worth, Beatrice claimed that a spark of instant rapport had flashed between Celia and McBane.

That evening, they had dinner at his hotel, The Dorchester. Over cocktails, Celia advanced their friendship considerably by making a confession. 'The grapevine told me that you would attend our sale today, Mr McBane, so I did something slightly naughty.'

'How's that?' he asked, untroubled.

'Since Boothby's haven't had the pleasure of doing business with you before, I made inquiries.' Celia smiled nervously. 'To use an Americanism, I had you checked out.'

'Lady Lincolnshire, that was very, very wise of you.' In a flash, his mock gravity was replaced by a crooked, engaging grin. 'It's good to know that *someone* in this town has a grain of business sense. Can I be frank in return? I can't claim to have been as quick off the mark as you were, but I have spent some time this afternoon discovering as much as I can about you.'

'Oh.' Celia found it impossible to avoid dismay. She struggled to console herself with the thought that McBane wouldn't be here, his grey eyes showing a desire to be her friend, if a million-to-one fluke had taken him anywhere near the truth of her past.

'Hey, don't be scared,' McBane said. 'There's nothing sinister here. We've saved ourselves a whole heap of time.'

'How is that, Mr McBane?'

'The way I see it, Lady Lincolnshire, if we know all the facts, we don't have to bother with all that difficult conversational stuff.' He shuffled and looked earnest. 'Would you permit me to address you as "Celia"?'

'I'd be offended if you didn't – Greg.'

A widower of fifty-two, Gregory H McBane was a compact, fresh-faced man of middle height, an inch or two taller than Celia. His youthful appearance was enhanced by the shortness of his pepper-and-salt hair and simmering energy. His companions invariably had the feeling that something good was going to happen at any minute. There were no children from the marriage that had ended four years ago with his wife's death. While Gabriella had been alive, he hadn't worried too much about that; lately, he'd got to thinking that a couple of kids would be real nice.

For all his easy-going manner, Greg was a scion of one of New York's leading families and, behind the fortune he had made for himself, there was a stack of old money. His sister, married to a Rockefeller, divided her time between Boston and Washington, where she was the most influential woman outside the White House. Greg's elder brother, Jefferson, was a highly respected member of the US State Department, currently occupying the coveted post of Ambassador to Great Britain.

'I *could* stay with Jeff in Grosvenor Square,' Greg told Celia, 'but he's a guy who takes himself a mite too seriously.' His roguish smile drew them closer together. 'He cannot accept that I don't want to sit up half the night getting lectured about democracy being in the melting-pot.'

Greg owned two galleries. The one near the corner of Fifth Avenue and East 49th Street was quite small, little more than an office in which a few treasures were displayed in a way that suggested indifference. It was in a good area, close to St Patrick's Cathedral and the Waldorf Astoria, and it got folks interested. Once they were inside and hooked, they were told of the comprehensive selection of fine art stocked at the much larger showroom at Westhampton on Long Island. For serious customers, there was the offer of lunch at Greg's mansion with its superb views of three exclusive bays. The business method was simple: believing that auctions were a waste of time, Greg gave each item a price and sold it to the first person who was prepared to pay it.

'Is that what you'll do with the Velasquez pictures?' Celia asked as they neared the end of dinner.

'I haven't decided yet,' Greg replied. 'I might keep them for myself. Look, Celia, can we stop the small talk and get down to important things?'

'Certainly.'

'Right.' He marshalled his thoughts. 'From what I hear, you've had a raw deal – your husband being murdered, losing the baby – all that.'

'Things could have been better,' Celia said.

'A little bird tells me that they haven't been too good since.' Greg's eyes were shrewd. 'Seems you don't have the right pedigree to be accepted in the top circles.'

'I was a nonentity before I married Ralph,' Celia replied. After two hours in the company of this man who was old enough to be her father, she was perfectly at ease. 'I'm getting used to it.'

Greg finished his wine and stared at her, assessing, rather as if he were wondering which of his regular clients could be persuaded to buy a particular picture. 'Can I cut the crap and get straight to the point?' he asked.

'Please do.'

'Are you happy with what you've got or would you like something different – better, maybe?'

'I'm not unduly happy,' Celia said in a way that made the understatement plain.

'Would you consider letting me show you an alternative?' Beneath the strong exterior, Celia saw that he was nervous.

'I have a feeling that I would enjoy that very much indeed,' she said.

He seemed dazzled, stupefied by his luck. 'How about that?' he said, grinning from ear to ear. 'Hey, you're not kidding, are you?'

'No, Greg, I am not kidding.' Celia reached for his hand. 'If I'm allowed to cut the crap too, I'd say that this is when our luck changed.'

In the six days before Greg McBane sailed back to New York, he and Celia spent as much time together as their other commitments allowed. Eager for a second, expert opinion, Celia arranged for Ursula to meet the man she already regarded as her saviour. On the way back to Putney Vale after the evening with Greg, Ursula admitted to being bowled over by her 'niece's' American. 'If only I were ten years younger!' she concluded whimsically.

'God help me if you were,' Celia said. 'I saw the way he was looking at you.'

'Mmm. Yes.' Briefly, Ursula permitted herself the luxury of a speculative little smile. Returning to reality, she said, 'It wouldn't do me the least good. He was only being polite to me – it's *you* he's interested in and it seems like a case of hook, line, and sinker.'

'Are you sure?' Celia was excited.

'Yes.' After checking that there was little chance of the cab driver being able to eavesdrop, Ursula became stern. 'A piece of advice, though: stay well away from his bedroom.'

'What, *always*?' Celia was dismayed.

'Don't be ridiculous,' Ursula scolded. 'What I'm saying is, let him make the running when he's ready. Your Mr McBane is a gentleman of the old school who expects certain standards in a woman.'

'A puritan, you mean?' Celia said, annoyed.

'No, I don't mean that at all,' Ursula sighed. 'You must act the lady until he says otherwise.' She smiled knowingly. '*Then* you'll be expected to behave like a whore. And if I'm any judge of these things, Mr McBane will prove to be more than adequate.'

Greg McBane's frequent letters promised that he would return to London for ten days at the end of November. He was as good as his word.

'Is this truly a business trip?' Celia said after he had collected her from Boothby's on the evening of his arrival.

'Why else would a man cross the Atlantic at this time of year?' he teased.

'We have nothing to warrant such courage,' Celia replied. 'It's terribly quiet.'

'Maybe I'll look in at Sotheby's and Christie's, then.'

If he ever did, they were quick, unproductive calls that were never mentioned over dinner or in intervals at the theatres they attended. Convinced that he had travelled 3,000 miles across a stormy ocean to see her, Celia's curiosity forced her to ask, 'Who takes care of the shop while you're globe-trotting?'

'I have assistants,' Greg replied. 'They're paid to be good.' Chuckling, he added. 'They wouldn't dare be any other way with my sister, Phyllis, keeping the eagle eye on them.'

'Is she as formidable as she sounds?' Celia asked nervously.

'She sure is, only even more so. Don't worry, honey, she likes the sound of you.'

'You've told her about me?' Celia's eyes were wide with delight.

'Hell, I had to! Phyllis is a great girl, but she's set herself up as the matriarch.' He smiled at the expression on Celia's face. 'The thing about matriarchs is they *dee-test* surprises — simply cannot abide them. So, being a cunning old devil, I'm preparing her for when you come to visit with us.'

'And when is that likely to be?' Celia asked, skittishly innocent.

'Next summer or fall?' Greg suggested tentatively.

'I'm looking forward to it,' Celia said, wondering what was wrong with spring.

For nearly three weeks after his departure, Ursula kept the secret of the slim, beautifully wrapped package that Greg had deposited with her. On 21 December, the eve of Celia's departure to Wiltshire, she handed it over. 'Mr McBane asked me to give you this.'

For some strange reason, Celia was alarmed. 'What is it?' she asked warily.

'It's a Christmas present, you idiot,' Ursula replied.

'Oh. I see.' Celia took the package, turning it over, shaking it, weighing it. 'Shall I open it now?'

'I'd save it,' Ursula advised. 'Keep it for Christmas morning when you might be feeling lonely.'

Celia did, forcing herself to leave it until she had looked at all her cards and the gifts that Annaliese had sent over from the Castle. The card with the Italian postage stamps was thick and heavy; attempting to make peace, Arabella had written six big pages extolling the joys of life with Umberto. Celia read and reread it carefully, noting the numerous hints that she might like to visit Brindisi for the summer. After resolving to compose a conciliatory reply that explained why she was unable to accept the invitation, Celia opened Greg McBane's present.

As diamond necklaces went, it was a modest piece that had probably cost no more than £2,000. But its unassuming elegance, chosen with immense care to suit her, and the simple message on the card, brought tears of joy to Celia's eyes.

When she was driven to the Castle for Christmas lunch, the necklace remained on her dressing-table, snuggling in its case. Inspired by it and the thought of what she was going to write to Greg McBane, Celia had the air of serene assurance that alerted Annaliese to the possibility of love.

Returning to London in early January 1932, Edward found that Helen Swann had a new girl for his approval.

Her name, she said, was Daphne. She was nineteen, claimed to originate from a good family, and was tall, with the lissome grace of a cat. Her greatest asset in breaking the ice was an inability to take her work seriously. In the manner of a brisk games mistress with a ribald sense of humour, she had mounted Edward and ridden him to a most satisfying conclusion before he was fully aware of what was happening. Although she lacked all knowledge of his interests, she chatted endlessly about what her other clients liked her to do to them. Edward found that he enjoyed vicarious eroticism almost as much as Daphne's practical demonstrations of the techniques she described in such vivid detail.

'He thinks you're the bee's knees, my precious,' Helen told Daphne after talking to Edward on the telephone.

'Gawd help me!' Tossing her mane of straw-coloured hair into wilder disarray, Daphne puffed greedily at a cigarette. 'Does that mean I'm stuck with him on a regular basis?'

'That's the way it looks, dear heart.'

'Heigh ho. Still it's better than walking the streets, I

suppose.' After laughing immoderately at her own joke, Daphne added, 'He's *useless.'*

Philosophically, Helen Swann said, 'Into every life a little sadness must fall.'

'If you say so,' Daphne muttered and went off to bathe in preparation for a much more enjoyable client.

Edward slipped into a routine that enabled him to tolerate the Government's incompetent stupor. On Sunday and Thursday evenings, he was at Rashleigh's house with Daphne; on Monday, Tuesday, Wednesday, and Friday, he dined at Fisk's, his club, collecting political gossip and playing bridge. He spent the days at the House of Lords, speaking regularly and acquiring a reputation as a stern critic of the Government. Early on Saturday morning, Edward was driven to Allardyce Castle, where until the middle of Sunday afternoon, he doted on Athene.

When she was in London, Annaliese's occasional encounters with Edward at Cadogan Square passed off easily, but his presence at the Castle for a significant part of each weekend was a different matter. The main difficulty was conversation: what *could* they talk about? After exhausting the topics of Athene, improvements to the Park, and Clementine Laverstoke's latest exploit, Annaliese found herself starting to mention Celia and Greg McBane.

At first, Edward was unresponsive. Then, at the end of February, having been told that Greg had sailed for New York after two weeks in London, he showed interest.

'Is this a serious relationship?'

'It's looking that way,' Annaliese replied. 'Celia was walking on air while he was here.

'McBane?' Edward was pensive. 'McBane? Isn't he important – has good connections?'

'His brother is the American Ambassador in London and his sister runs Washington.' As an after-thought, Annaliese added, 'Or so Nancy Shenstone tells me.'

Refusing to rise to the bait of the woman whose existence he still preferred to ignore, Edward muttered, 'I wonder if this is wise – letting her associate with a man like that.'

'What *do* you mean?' Annaliese asked sharply.

'Well . . . I . . .' Cursing himself for the blunder, Edward retreated. 'Nothing,' he said curtly. 'Nothing at all.'

'How strange,' Annaliese said, more to herself than Edward.

'I told you, it's nothing,' he repeated. 'I made a mistake, mixed him up with another fellow.'

Only much later did Annaliese come to appreciate what a dreadful state she and her husband had reached: the chasm that divided their marriage even prevented them from discussing matters of great importance.

Flippantly, Annaliese said, 'Celia and Mr McBane are off to Paris for Easter. I wonder what the outcome of *that* will be.'

Approaching the reception counter of the Hotel *George Cinq*, Greg halted, perplexed and bashful.

'What is it?' Celia whispered, afraid that he was feeling unwell.

'I've done something bad, honey,' he said. 'I went ahead and did it instead of asking you. How dumb can you get?'

'Yes?' Celia was smiling. Her instincts told her that she was going to like his revelation.

'Well, it's like this . . . I've booked us into a suite.'

'I see. What's wrong with that?'

'A suite, honey, *one* suite for the two of us.' Greg was whispering, teeth gritted, fists clenched. 'It ain't right, is it? I'll talk to the guy on the desk, he'll fix it. You take a seat over there so's you don't get embarrassed, huh?'

'Whoa! Hold steady.' Celia succeeded in keeping her face straight. 'How many bedrooms does this suite have?'

'Two. Yeah, at least two, maybe three.'

'In that case, I can lock myself away and be perfectly safe?'

'Absolutely! That's *exactly* what I was gonna suggest, except I didn't think you'd believe me.'

'Well, I do,' Celia said.

Exultant, Greg marched towards the desk where he was greeted as if he were royalty. What impressed Celia above all else was his solution to the language barrier. Greg spoke English and every member of the staff did the same, albeit with varying degrees of success.

The suite, consisting of eight rooms, took Celia's breath away. She noticed that Greg seemed to think it wasn't quite as good as he had hoped: what *was* he used to? After dinner, they danced in the ballroom, then, after goodnight kisses that lasted a long time, went their separate ways to sleep off the effects of an exciting, tiring day.

The following morning, over breakfast in the suite, Greg suggested a shopping expedition. 'I'd like to buy you a gown or two,' he said.

'A gown?'

'Hell, frocks, dresses – whatever you British call the darned things.'

'You think I need them?' Celia asked, pretending to be offended.

'No, I think you *deserve* them,' Greg replied. 'You're a very lovely lady, Celia, and this is the place to make you look real good. Where shall we go?'

The designer with the best reputation for ready-to-wear high fashion was the flamboyant Elsa Schiaparelli, whose salon was in the Place Vendôme. Despite the Italian's famously informal hospitality, Celia found the first few minutes a daunting experience and was full of admiration for the way Greg took the place over, making everyone laugh as he winkled out an English-speaking *vendeuse*. Having stipulated that Celia should be fitted up with at least two evening gowns and two dresses for day wear, he accepted an invitation to take coffee in Schiaparelli's office, leaving Celia free to make her choice of the ravishing garments on offer.

Given nearly two hours in which to browse and discover how she looked in the finest *haute couture* products, Celia selected the minimum four dresses, not daring to raise the squalid subject of price. Greg settled the bill with American dollars and the eye-catching packages were delivered to the *George Cinq* during lunch.

After the meal, Greg asked to be excused so that he could make a transatlantic telephone call to check the progress of a big deal. 'It's coming up to nine o'clock on the East Coast, and that's a good time to catch 'em,' he explained. 'I'll be as quick as the operators will let me. Why don't you try on your gowns – make sure they're still OK?'

Guessing that a connection to America would take some time, Celia treated herself to an interlude of pure, selfish hedonism. After showering, she brushed her hair until it gleamed and rolled it into a chignon. Carefully, she applied slightly more make-up than usual, dramatising her eyes and cheeks. Then, she put on Greg's diamond necklace. Finally, dispensing with underwear, she began to try the Schiaparelli dresses, twisting and turning in front of two full-length mirrors, amazed and captivated at what she saw.

She lost track of time until there was a tap on the door and Greg called, 'I'm through, honey. Can I come in?'

'Of course.'

She was wearing an evening dress in brightly patterned silk that showed off every nuance of her body. After taking one step into the room, Greg stopped, very much like a man who has run into a wall. 'That is great!' he breathed. 'You look fabulous, Celia, truly fabulous.'

'Thank you,' she laughed. 'That's for the dress *and* the compliment.'

'Do the others look that good?'

'They certainly do – although this is my favourite.' Showing off, Celia made several turns and struck poses, making Greg fully aware of her supple, animal grace. He was deeply affected, so much so that Celia knew he was dying to take her in his arms with an ardour that was bound to drive them towards the ultimate passion. But, instead of moving closer, he backed away.

'What's wrong?' Celia asked in a small, disappointed voice.

'Sweetheart, forgive me,' Greg said huskily. 'Fact is, I want you – I want you like hell.'

'I don't see anything wrong with that,' Celia replied, her knuckles white with the effort of feigning calmness.

'No.' Looking dazed, Greg repeated the word several times. Then, laughing nervously, he said, 'I'm a regular, old-fashioned sort of guy. It's gonna have to wait until we're married – I couldn't live with myself any other way, Celia.'

Smiling, she nodded. 'OK, Greg, that's fine by me.'

'I warn you, though, when it is right and proper, you'll be working hard to keep me happy.' Greg was absolutely serious.

'Will you be returning the compliment?' Celia asked.

'You can bet your life on it, honey.'

'Good! Now, where shall we go?'

He took her everywhere, including the Easter Monday races at Longchamp. There, while Celia's radiance turned countless heads, they sketched out the first part of their future. The final touches were put to the plan when they returned to England to spend three days with Ursula before Greg sailed to the States.

He would come back in July for a week of business appointments which, he was at great pains to point out, would allow them ample time to be together. Then, he and Celia would go to New York, choose a ring at Tiffany's, and announce their engagement.

'It's the way I want to do it,' Celia told Ursula. 'Why should I worry about what people in this wretched place think? Apart from you, no one's ever cared about me.'

Ursula agreed. She was thrilled by the news and knew that Greg was right in saying that Celia would be the toast of New York. It was a wonderful new beginning for her. 'Will you bother coming back to England after the engagement?' Ursula asked.

'What an interesting idea,' Celia mused. 'I'll ask Greg. I'm sure he could arrange for me to stay over until the wedding.'

'See, you're picking up the language,' Ursula joked.

Publicly, to everyone other than Ursula, Celia was calm: in secret, she bubbled with excitement and counted the days. Because the trip to America entailed over three weeks away from Boothby's, Beatrice had to be informed. Unsurprisingly, she fished for details. Celia admitted that, yes, Greg McBane *was* involved, but poured cold water on Beatrice's assumptions of romance. Nevertheless, when Beatrice passed the news on to Annaliese, her dewy-eyed expectations were undiminished.

'I'm sure he's going to pop the question, ask her to marry him. Isn't it exciting?'

Annaliese gave the impression of disinterest. She was preoccupied with organising a visit to Portugal which was becoming complicated out of all proportion by George's plea that his best friend from school, a boy called Robert Chappell, should go with them. Unwilling to deny George anything, Annaliese was finding that the inclusion of an extra person in the holiday party was making it difficult to book a passage on the dates she wanted. However, even though Beatrice was left feeling that Annaliese hadn't listened to a word she'd said, Nancy Shenstone was told that Celia was going to America with Greg McBane when Annaliese looked into Martha's Vineyard two evenings later.

He arrived on Monday 18 July and installed himself in his usual suite at The Dorchester. Celia joined him for dinner and dancing on the first four nights, but went to Ursula's house at Putney Vale on Friday: as well as needing a full night's sleep, she had to pack for their departure to New York. In any case, Greg was summoned to a reception at the American Embassy on Friday evening. 'I ought to go, honey,' he told Celia. 'I haven't seen Jefferson since I met you.'

'Yes, do your duty,' Celia agreed.

'That's what it is,' he grumbled. 'Duty! I'll bet it's a complete balls-ache.'

'Take care of your balls,' Celia urged. 'They're valuable.'

They laughed and Greg said he was sure the evening would present no threat to his manhood. 'Leastways, I'm assuming not,' he added. 'No one's told *me* what this shindig is in aid of.'

It proved to be a cosmopolitan gathering, whose 250 guests represented a wide range of opinions and professions. Present as one of the Ambassador's most prized social contracts, with a roving commission to 'oil the wheels', Nancy Shenstone observed apparently idle chit-chat, serious business negotiations, fund-raising, and the beginnings of an attempt to entice the great tenor, Martinelli, away from the Metropolitan Opera in favour of Covent Garden.

Undeceived by the urbane veneer, Nancy was alive to the serious undercurrents, mostly of a political nature. The President of the USA, Herbert Hoover, was in deep trouble as the depression worsened and all the smart talk for next year's election revolved around Franklin D Roosevelt, the Democratic Governor of New York. Even so, Nancy saw that the Republicans were out in force, telling everyone how great they were and, behind the façade of bullshit, trying to find out exactly what was going on in Europe.

Although he stayed resolutely on the fringes of the crowd as it ebbed and flowed through the five rooms being used for the reception, Nancy spotted the Chairman of the Senate Foreign Relations Committee, a roughneck from Kansas. He was holding court in a dimly lit corner of an ante-room that was being ignored by the handful of Society photographers in search of glamorous women and their escorts. For over two hours, a steady stream of British politicians went to the table for a five- or ten-minute chat. Since they were all known for their hostility towards the cosy alliance of Baldwin and MacDonald, Nancy had no difficulty in guessing at the nature of the conversations.

Then, at 10.30, there was a surprise: Edward appeared, obviously straight from another engagement. Nancy, deeply fascinated by a young man who was beginning to thrill to the realisation that he *was* going to be taken back to Martha's Vineyard and put through his paces, saw that an aide whisked Edward from the Embassy's entrance to the table in the corner, whereupon the atmosphere became more intense than ever.

While Nancy danced with her splendid new friend, Edward and the American senator talked for nearly an hour. Eventually, it was the Ambassador himself who separated them, saying that he had a whole bunch of folks dying to be introduced to the Duke of Lincolnshire. Nancy, by now as eager as her escort to escape, watched as Edward went through the motions of meeting a dozen gushingly amiable people with whom he had absolutely nothing in common. Suddenly, in one of those strange moments of calm that can fall on a large, packed room, Greg McBane strolled through a gap in the crowd. His brother, the Ambassador, collared him and introduced him to Edward.

'Wait,' Nancy whispered, tugging against the arm that was guiding her away to bed. 'There's something I want to see. Be patient a tiny bit longer.'

Greg McBane, mindful of what Celia had told him about Edward, was polite but cool. Edward, however, was enthralled by his new acquaintance, talking with great animation and pointing to the chairs at the end of the room. Reluctantly, Greg followed him.

'Now what could those two *possibly* have to talk about?' Nancy murmured to herself.

Once the two men were seated, Edward said something that brought a smile to Greg's face. Unfortunately, owing to the swirl of the crowd, Nancy missed the point at which the smile faded. Her next view of Greg showed him to be annoyed, standing, and about to walk away. Catching his sleeve, Edward spoke with tremendous force to regain his attention. Again Nancy was unsighted, this time by a flurry of activity as Viscount and Lady Furness made a rare public appearance together. Thelma, the Prince of Wales's mistress, said to have introduced HRH to an American couple by the name of Simpson, was rumoured to be anxious about the growing friendship between the Prince and Mrs Simpson. The photographers fell over each other to get pictures of Lady Furness, blotting Nancy's view with their flashbulbs and antics. When the mêlée cleared, Greg McBane was on his feet again. This time, there was no detaining him and he stormed off, as angry a man as Nancy had ever seen. In sharp contrast, Edward was pleased with himself. Snapping his fingers at a nearby waiter, he took a glass from the tray and drank contentedly, a sardonic half-smile on his face, unaware that he was being observed.

Puzzled, wondering what she had witnessed, but eager to embark on what was likely to be an excitingly pleasurable night, Nancy smiled at her rugged companion. 'Let's go, lover,' she said.

Soon after lunch the following day, mildly concerned that Greg had not been in touch, Celia took a break from packing to telephone The Dorchester. The response seemed slipshod and confused. Then, after several false starts, it emerged that Mr McBane had left the hotel.

'There must be some mistake,' Celia said.

'No, madam, he went at six-thirty this morning. Urgent business in New York, apparently. I believe he had no sleep last night.'

'Oh.' Celia froze. 'There'll be a message for me. I'm Lady Lincolnshire.'

A check was carried out. 'No, I'm sorry, my lady, Mr McBane left no messages.'

Looking on helplessly, Ursula watched every last trace of colour drain from Celia's face.

An hour later, while Celia was hunched on a chair in her bedroom, too shocked to weep, Ursula was busy on the telephone. Her skills of persuasion finally unearthed the fact that a Mr G McBane had sailed from Southampton at noon on the *Mauretania*, a last-minute transfer from United States Lines, the clerk in the Cunard office said.

Imprisoned in grey-faced shock, Celia refused to believe it. 'This is a mistake,' she said. 'He'll be in touch.'

On Monday, while everyone at Boothby's imagined that she was *en route* to New York, Celia waited impassively. In the middle of the afternoon, a cablegram arrived. Transmitted from mid-Atlantic, it read:

Have discovered what you were before you married Ralph Lincolnshire. I want nothing more to do with you.

McBane.

Celia stared at it for over an hour before asking, 'How?

How did he find out? Who told him?'

'I doub⁺ if we shall ever know,' Ursula replied. She was shaken and profoundly upset by McBane's disappearance and the cable; she'd had him marked down as a considerate, forgiving man, incapable of such venom.

It was time to take a grip on a dreadful situation. 'You're supposed to be on holiday,' Ursula told Celia. 'We're going to Shanklin. I have some good friends there who will look after us.'

Celia made no objection, but before they left the following morning, she cut the Schiaparelli dresses to shreds and dumped the resultant sad mess in the dustbin. The diamond necklace she would sell. Ursula's friends owned one of the finest hotels on the Isle of Wight and did everything in their power to make Celia welcome and comfortable. Sometimes, she was reasonable company, yet she never, as far as Ursula knew, gave herself the solace of a good weep, and she often interrupted a pleasantly mundane conversation with the question, 'How did he find out? *How*?' Beneath an apparently calm surface, Celia was amassing a terrible bitterness.

It was in evidence when she returned to Boothby's and answered the inevitable questions. 'Yes, thank you, Beatrice, I had a lovely time. No, Mr McBane didn't ask me to marry him. Which is just as well, because I wouldn't have him if he were the last man on earth!'

Another two weeks passed before Annaliese put in an appearance after her visit to Portugal and a period clearing up outstanding matters at Allardyce Castle. By then, Celia's moods had come to be regarded as a phenomenon to be suffered in silence.

5

1933
'Don't *ever* think you're in control'

The cricket match against Leacroft at the end of the summer term was one of the highlights of the Moss Close calendar. This year, it was being played at home in magnificent weather and Douglas had shone in his farewell appearance for the First XI.

Batting first, Leacroft had scored 231 for 6, a total that caused many to believe that the visitors had the game in the bag. They reckoned without Douglas and his friend, Lambert. Opening for Moss Close, they put on 182 in an hour and a half of whirlwind stroke play and enterprise that went far beyond the abilities of most thirteen-year-olds. The fact that they were both out rather stupidly in the same over did nothing to dampen the spirits of the spectators: after a record first-wicket partnership, Moss Close were cruising to victory.

Relaxing after their exertions, Douglas and Lambert lounged in deck chairs on the verandah of the pavilion, watching the two fresh batsmen carrying on the good work. None of the other boys dared to approach them: they were exalted beings, prodigious run-scorers, and soon to be departing for illustrious schools, Winchester in Douglas's case, Eton in Lambert's. The two exemplars clapped ostentatiously every time the ball was hit and occasionally deigned to shout, 'Good stroke.'

Presently, Lambert's attention wandered and he was gazing into the trees behind the sight-screen. 'I say, Axholme, isn't that your brother over there?' he asked.

Douglas spotted George. He was sitting on the grass with Robert Chappell. They were sharing a book and a bar of chocolate. 'Yes, that's him,' Douglas said. 'Swotting again.'

'Always with Chappell,' Lambert pointed out.

'Mmm – yes.' Douglas was uncomfortable, never quite sure whether there were hidden allusions in that sort of remark. Obeying his instinct to press on regardless, Douglas said, 'I think Chappell's coming with us to Portugal again. He doesn't hit it off with his stepfather, you know.'

'This is to see the Habsburg grandparents?'

'Yes.'

'Didn't they mind having Chappell foisted on them?'

'They liked him,' Douglas said. 'He and George played duets on the piano.'

'Good God Almighty!' Lambert was appalled. 'Sissy stuff *again*.'

By and large, on the whole, good friend though he was, Douglas was glad that Lambert would not be joining him at Winchester. There were far too many of these nasty little digs about George and Chappell, and Douglas suspected that they weren't for his ears alone. 'They've got over the sissy stuff,' he told Lambert firmly. 'George will win the cross country next term and Chappell should make the First Fifteen – he's a frightfully good three-quarter.'

Lambert, who had been Douglas's vice-captain in both cricket and Rugby, knew that this assessment was right.

However, he wanted the last word. 'They'd do better to take their noses out of books, though.'

'There's no harm in a chap being brainy,' Douglas retorted. Of late, he had begun to feel twinges of unease about his own shortcomings in this respect. Irregular verbs and geometry had been known to get him down and things were supposed to be much worse at Winchester: it was a 'clever' school.

Feigning disinterest, Lambert cast a lordly eye round the boundary. He was in time to see the great unwashed clustered round the score-board make futile attempts to smarten themselves up as the headmaster, the dreaded 'Slasher' Hawkins, appeared. He was accompanied by Edward.

'I say, your guv'nor's arrived,' Lambert said.

'So he has.' Douglas stood up and waved, but failed to obtain a response. Edward and Slasher were engrossed. 'He missed my innings,' Douglas complained, sinking back disconsolately into the deck chair. 'He promised he'd be here for start of play.'

'House of Lords, I expect,' Lambert opined sagaciously. His father, a scrap merchant in Birmingham, who was much taken by his son's friendship with the Marquess of Axholme, was an ardent supporter of Edward's increasingly scathing criticism of the Government.

'It gets worse,' Douglas groaned. 'All we ever hear about these days is that chap, Hitler. I'll bet you ten shillings that he's telling Slasher all about him.'

After looking at the headmaster, who was nodding and performing his habitual hand-washing mime, Lambert asked, 'Who's Hitler?'

'He's the fellow who's running Germany – used to be a corporal.' Douglas paraded his knowledge with great pride. 'He got himself made Chancellor in January. I'm not *exactly* sure how he did that, by the way. Calls himself the Fewrer.'

Lambert was scornful. 'If you ask me, old man, you're the one who needs to leave the books alone,' he drawled.

Even though she appeared to recover from the shock of losing Greg McBane, Celia never stopped torturing herself with that question: 'How did he find out?' The four letters she sent to his Long Island mansion were ignored and, if he ever did visit England again, he did so in the greatest secrecy, creating not a single ripple in the close-knit world of fine-art dealing.

Without once displaying her own anger at the run of events, Ursula's steadfast sympathy sustained both Celia and her bitterness. Despite his final, mean-spirited gesture, Ursula continued to like McBane and believe that he and Celia would have made each other very happy. Whoever had supplied the poison deserved to suffer.

Inevitably, in the full knowledge that it was pointless, Celia and Ursula spent countless hours in speculation, raking through the men who had been Celia's clients during her time with Arabella at both St James's and Cap Ferrat. Nothing suggested itself as remotely possible. Belatedly, and cursing themselves for being so slow on the uptake, they decided that it must have happened during the American Embassy reception – at which, Ursula discovered, there had been 250 invited guests and a large number of semi-official gatecrashers. Even if they could have obtained a list, the culprit's name was unlikely to have suggested itself.

Then, almost a year to the day after Greg McBane disappeared from Celia's life, Ursula visited her dentist and returned with the answer.

'This was in the waiting-room,' she said, taking an eleven-month-old Society magazine from her bag. 'The receptionist let me "borrow" it.'

Celia waited as Ursula flicked through the glossy pages, talking as she went. 'There are lots of photographs of the do at the Embassy on the night in question. One of them tells us all we've been wanting to know. Ah – here it is.' Ursula placed the magazine on the table, stabbing a finger on the relevant illustration.

Celia found herself staring at Viscount and Lady Furness, not particularly happy, either with each other or the sudden appearance of the photographer. Seeing nothing else, Celia glanced up, mystified.

'Look at the background,' Ursula instructed. 'In the shadows to the left of Thelma.'

Doing so, Celia gasped. There were Greg and Edward, apparently having an argument.

'Edward,' Celia whispered. 'Edward. Yes, of course, I should have known it.' Her eyes were burning.

Ursula nodded grimly. 'He's a fool,' she said.

'Why?'

'For putting sheer, downright spite before common sense,' Ursula replied. 'If he'd kept his mouth shut, he would have been rid of you – three thousand miles away and out of his life forever.'

'That's interesting,' Celia said. 'I wonder if he really is that much of a fool, or . . .' She left the sentence unfinished.

'Or what?' Ursula asked.

'Perhaps he has some devious scheme.'

'Pah!' Ursula was contemptuous. 'I doubt if he's capable of it. He saw a chance to wreck your life and grabbed it. What are you going to do about him?'

'I don't know,' Celia said, already deep in thought. 'I need time to work it out.'

In the event, it took less than three hours. As they were eating supper, Celia asked, 'Is he still using Daphne?'

'Yes, twice a week.' Ursula smiled. 'Daphne, it must be said, isn't enjoying it. She thinks he's an incompetent bore. Actually, she's threatening to leave Helen because of him.'

'*Is* she?' Celia smiled into the far distance. 'What does Helen think about that?'

'She's extremely upset,' Ursula replied. 'Apart from your friend, Edward, Daphne has a clutch of good clients. Helen's afraid of losing them if Daphne goes.'

After a long pause, Celia said, 'I'd rather like to change places with Daphne.'

The two women stared at each other, Ursula calculating all the implications. 'You could bring yourself to do it?' Ursula asked.

'Did you never sleep with a man you detested?' Celia retorted.

Smiling wryly, Ursula said, 'Frequently. They paid for this house. I used to charge them double and, do you know, there was an extra fillip of something in it – lying back and watching a man you despise work himself into a lather over next to nothing. Yes, I can see your point, it would put him in a terrible position. But how, for heaven's sake? One has to assume that he'd take an awful lot of persuading.'

'*That* is what we have to work out,' Celia replied. 'I want to talk to Helen Swann and Daphne. Soon. He'll be going to Scotland for the grouse in two weeks and I'd like to have started by then.'

'Started?' Ursula frowned.

'I'm not thinking of a one-night shocker,' Celia said. 'Oh, no! He isn't getting away that easily. I said that I want to change places with Daphne – that means twice a week, *permanently.*'

'He won't put up with it.'

'Ursula, darling, let me worry about that,' Celia said. 'Have words with Helen Swann. *Now*, please.'

Intrigued and eager to have Ursula in her debt, Helen Swann saw them the following afternoon. Although it was Sunday and they were smuggled into the big house in Dorset Square through the servants' entrance, the astute eye and mind could detect that it was a busy time in the luxurious bedrooms on the first and second floors.

'Don't ask me how they manage to escape from their nearest and dearest on the Sabbath, but they do,' Helen Swann burbled as she ushered Celia and Ursula into her parlour. 'It's pandemonium. Do sit down, tea will be here directly.' Once they were settled, Helen, who retained much of the beauty of her youth, abandoned the scatter-brained amiability and became formidable. 'Tell me about it,' she said to Celia. 'Explain yourself.'

Concisely, without displaying a shred of emotion, Celia did so, recounting her transition from prostitute to Duchess of Lincolnshire, then Dowager Duchess, and the way in which she had been prevented from becoming the second Mrs Greg McBane, assured of respect and wealth for the rest of her life.

After listening in attentive silence, Helen exclaimed, 'Bloody hell!' with great feeling, rolling her eyes at Ursula. Leaning back in her armchair, she regarded Celia with respect. 'So, the stories about William Lincolnshire were true,' she said. 'He *did* peg out on the job?'

'I'm afraid so,' Celia replied.

'He was such a nice man,' Helen sighed. 'Arabella pinched him off me, you know.'

Surprised, Ursula asked, 'He was one of your clients?'

'Oh, very much so.' Helen's eyes sparkled. 'I used to look after him personally. He was a real toff, the genuine article.'

'Unlike his successor,' Celia said acidly.

'What *was* Ralph like?' Helen asked.

'Marvellous in bed, awful out of it,' Celia replied. 'I'm interested in the present duke.'

'Daphne thinks he's a pain in the bum,' Helen said. 'She's upset, threatening to leave.'

'I'll take him off your hands,' Celia offered. 'I'll pay your normal commission, of course.'

'Twenty per cent,' Helen said quickly.

Celia nodded. 'Agreed.'

'This is all very well,' Ursula protested, 'but *how* are you going to do this?'

At that moment, a maid came in with the tea. 'Have you seen anything of Daphne?' Helen asked her. 'Is she here?'

'Yes, Mrs Swann. She's been having her hair done.'

'Ask her to pop in, will you, Joyce?' When the maid had gone on her errand, Helen said, 'We have our own hair-dressing and beauty salon – one of the perks of the job.'

Daphne duly appeared, fizzing with curiosity. 'I expect you've heard of Ursula Croft,' Helen said. 'Her friend is Celia. She may choose to tell you more about herself.'

They all said, 'Hello,' and Helen went on, 'Celia wants to replace you in Mr Allardyce's affections, Daphne.'

'Really? How super. When? Straight away?' Daphne's face was a picture of joy.

'Not quite that quickly,' Helen replied, smiling ruefully. 'You see, precious, our client doesn't know about the swap and probably won't like it. We have to find a way of "persuading" him to accept it.' She glanced at Celia for confirmation.

'That's right.'

'Oh.' Daphne was crestfallen. 'That means tonight is still on?'

'I'm afraid so,' Helen said. To Celia, she explained, 'Daphne meets Mr Allardyce twice a week, on Sundays and Thursdays, regular as clockwork.'

'Next Sunday, then – we must do it next Sunday.' Celia's urgency cheered Daphne up.

'Splendid.' Helen beamed, acting as if the whole thing was organised down to the last detail. 'Perhaps you two girls would care to slip away to plot and scheme while I have a few words with my friend, Ursula.'

Daphne took Celia to the beauty salon which was now deserted. 'Are you going to work for Helen?' Daphne asked.

'Sort of,' Celia replied evasively. 'Only part-time. Mr Allardyce is my only interest.'

'Why?'

'Because I hate his guts,' Celia said.

Totally bewildered, Daphne shook her head. 'I haven't come across anything like *this* before.'

'And I don't suppose you will again,' Celia said. 'Can we get on? I want to know all about Mr Allardyce. What happens when you go to him? What does he like?'

For well over an hour, Daphne described the client's sexual foibles and behaviour. Celia was eager to know the layout of Rashleigh's house, especially the suite in which the business was done. Returning to Helen Swann's parlour, they found her and Ursula, their business also complete, giggling like schoolgirls over a French lingerie catalogue.

'All fixed,' Daphne said in response to Helen's questioning look. 'The deed will be done next Sunday.'

To reassure Ursula, Celia added, 'We think we can make it work.' Her thoughts raced on. 'Actually, it can't fail. Whatever happens, he'll be humiliated.'

As they took their leave, Helen gave Ursula a final reminder. 'If you get here for two o'clock on Wednesday, you'll have plenty of time to prepare before I introduce you to the gentleman.'

Celia, pretending not to hear, waited until they were back in Putney Vale before asking, 'And what, pray, happens on Wednesday?'

'Like you, I'm going back to work,' Ursula said.

'This is part of the bargain with Helen Swann – you're doing it for me?'

'I'm afraid so,' Ursula groaned. Then, unable to keep up the pretence of misery, she laughed. 'I'm looking forward to it.'

Not meaning to, Celia found herself saying, 'How old are you, Ursula?'

'Never you mind,' was the robustly good-natured response. 'Helen says I'm in fine fettle and just what Mr X is looking for.'

'I wouldn't dream of denying it,' Celia replied, taking a fresh, admiring look at Ursula. 'You'll give him a grand time.'

'From what Helen says, he might do the same for me,' Ursula chortled. 'He's supposed to be a very decent sort.'

The plan, which began with Celia's arrival in Dorset Square at 7.30 the following Sunday evening, revolved around the strict timetable upon which Edward insisted for his association with Daphne. Since she, unlike her predecessor, Flora, was not worth speaking to, she was required to reach Lord Francis Rashleigh's house at precisely 9.00 pm.

Celia and Daphne ran over the details, adding refinements, agreeing what to do in the event of trouble. They changed into elegant evening dresses – Celia had bought a new one specially – and shared a stiff brandy to settle their nerves. On the dot of 8.50, the cab arrived.

Travelling along Baker Street, Celia reminded herself what they were expecting to find. If all went to plan, the house would be virtually deserted. Daphne had never seen Rashleigh; if he was at home during her visits, he always kept well out of the way. Tonight, he was known to be out of London, staying with friends in Hampshire. They would be admitted by a butler, who, Daphne swore, was unworthy of the title and, at this time on a Sunday, interested only in what he was about to do with one of the maids from a nearby house.

Sure enough, the man was not the type to find employment with the best families. His over-familiar greeting of, 'What ho, Daphne, darling,' was followed by downright impertinence when he spotted Celia. 'What's this, then, eh? Is our Mr Allardyce getting big ideas?'

Not prepared to bandy words with him, Daphne swept towards the stairs with Celia following closely. The butler laughed, closed the front door and hurried away to meet his girl. Nodding at Celia, Daphne led the way to the first floor, turned along a corridor and slipped in through one of the doors. They were in a small dressing-room; it led into a bathroom; beyond that was the bedroom.

'Good evening, Mr Allardyce,' Daphne called in a high, bright voice. There was an answering mumble.

Celia and Daphne undressed, co-ordinating their movements so that, even if the noises did carry to the bedroom, it would sound like one pair of shoes, one dress, and the whisper of only one set of silk underwear. Together, holding hands, they moved into the bathroom. They exchanged a series of 'good luck' gestures, and Daphne went into the bedroom, leaving the door wide open. Standing behind it, Celia heard everything with a clarity that was startling.

Edward said, 'Good evening, Daphne. How are you?' It was heavily polite, the way a man who was unsure of himself would address an inferior.

'I'm very well, thank you, Mr Allardyce,' she replied. 'A pleasant weekend?'

'Yes. I took Athene to Salisbury yesterday.'

'Really? How nice.' Daphne, who had no idea who Athene was, drew back the covers. 'Mmm – you're ready,' she crooned. 'Have you been lying here thinking about it?'

'Yes.'

'Nice. What shall we do first? Would you like me to suck you?'

Edward grunted.

'I thought so.'

As arranged, Daphne went about it with gusto – at least, she made a lot of noise and, to judge by his sighs, gave her client some pleasure. Smiling cynically at the thought of the prudish Edward wallowing in fellation, Celia steadied herself and waited.

Eventually, Daphne paused to speak. 'You're very hard, this evening.'

It was the pre-arranged signal and Celia entered the room, her feet silent on the thick carpet. Edward was flat on his back, his head turned away from the door. Before summoning her accomplice, Daphne had made sure that, as was often the case when she did this to him, his eyes were closed. It was an odd habit, probably designed to shut the woman out, pretend that she did not exist, was not witnessing his depraved abandon.

Daphne was sitting on the edge of the bed, her body bent at the awkward angle needed to perform her lascivious task. All that could go wrong now was that Edward might notice the movement caused by the extra weight on the mattress as Celia pressed against Daphne, ready to replace her. He did not. At the moment of changeover, Daphne said, 'Sorry, Mr Allardyce, you're making me breathless.' Edward smiled, smug at what he regarded as a compliment. Almost at once, an eager mouth closed over the tip of his penis and he let out a moan of contentment.

There was an imperceptible draught of air as Daphne hurried to the bathroom leaving Celia and Edward alone.

Slowly, sensual and snake-like, she eased herself on to the bed, supple enough to keep him in her mouth until she had almost finished straddling him. Edward took the invitation. 'Yes!' he grunted, pushed hard and penetrated.

Celia deployed the talent which gave her most pride. Keeping her body perfectly still, she used her vaginal muscles to stroke and squeeze Edward's shaft. A blissful expression stole over his face. After enjoying it for several minutes, he murmured, 'I'm glad you've learned how to do that, Daphne. It was one of Flora's best tricks.'

Quietly, very matter-of-fact, Celia said, 'I doubt if *any* woman can do this as well as me.'

Edward's eyes snapped open. That, and a momentary look of utter amazement, were to be his only attempts at outrage. Celia watched the process of calculation start. She saw him speculate on the information, collusion, and cunning that must have gone into trapping him, she observed and relished his resigned acceptance of an incredible situation.

The distant sound of the front door closing echoed through the house.

'That's Daphne leaving,' Celia said. 'You won't be seeing her again.'

'You're working for Helen Swann?'

'Not entirely.' Celia smiled at his reaction to the ambiguity. 'You'll be dealing with me in future. Do you want to stick to Sundays and Thursdays?' Seeing that Edward would not answer, Celia went on. 'Not here, though. I don't like that butler and I've no wish to bump into your friend, Rashleigh, who's an idiot, by all accounts. No, *Mr Allardyce*, since I'm one of the family, we can transact our business at Cadogan Square. Or, you could visit me at The Chantry on Saturdays. Don't the evenings get pretty boring after Athene has gone to bed?'

'I suppose it's no use telling you to go to hell?' Edward asked.

'Not a scrap,' Celia said amiably.

They studied each other, he flat on his back, she with the advantage of a dominant position. He could have thrown her off: not much force would have been required, yet Celia knew that Edward was not even considering it. Whatever thoughts were chasing round his head, he remained rock-solid within her. Slowly, she began to tease him. His eyes, the only sign of life in the inscrutable mask of his face, fastened on her breasts.

'You've always wanted me,' Celia said. Her tone, seductive and vindictive, inflamed him.

'Yes!' he shouted. 'Damn you, yes, I have.' As if in a rage, he was thrusting at her.

'*Keep still*,' Celia hissed. Shifting slightly so that she could do so, she gathered Edward's testicles into a painfully restraining grip. 'Don't *ever* think you're in control. From now on, I am.'

Immobilised by fear and discomfort, Edward said, 'Why?', his voice hoarse.

'I've only just found out who told Greg McBane about me,' Celia said, relaxing her hold and savouring the sudden flood of expressions across Edward's face. 'An old copy of *Belgravia Life* turned up in a dentist's waiting-room. It had lots and lots of photos of that reception at the American Embassy. Remember? You were so busy pouring poison into Greg's ear that you didn't notice Marmaduke Furness and his slut of a wife. The photographers fought to get pictures of them and you were in the background.' After giving herself a moment or two to study his expression, Celia added, 'In case you didn't know, Mr McBane left England the following morning and has never been back. Nor has he answered my letters.'

'I . . .' Edward thought better of it.

'No, it's best not to apologise,' Celia said. 'You aren't nearly sorry enough – *yet*.'

The significance of that final, heavily emphasised word was not lost on Edward. There was a more immediate concern, however: Celia was forcing him towards orgasm. It was relentless but slow, offering no hope of a quick end to an ignominy that had to be played out under her malevolent stare. When, at long last, he was carried beyond the point of no return and his features were contorted by an ecstatic agony, his ejaculation was accompanied by Celia's disdainful mocking. 'What a sight! The very soul of respectability turns out to be the same as any other man. Go on, enjoy yourself – it's costing you enough.'

When he had finished, she detached herself. 'Stay there,' she ordered. 'I have to go to the bathroom – my Dutch cap, you know. Shan't be long.'

Returning a few minutes later, Celia got into bed beside Edward, kicking back the sheet he had drawn over himself. 'You've got quite a good body,' she said, trailing a fingertip from his chest to his still-erect penis.

'This is ludicrous,' Edward said, wanting to be angry, but failing miserably because of her insidious fondling.

'Is it? Don't you think we deserve each other? I'm going to make you happy – in your own, strange way.'

'Do I have any alternative?' Edward grumbled.

'No.'

As if thinking aloud, Edward muttered, 'I can hardly denounce you after this.'

'Edward, *dear*, you haven't been in any position to do that since you took over the title. You should have done it then, bundled me up with all the other dirty washing, got me out of the way. The fact that you didn't surely means that you were prepared to overlook my transgressions.'

'Nonsense,' Edward protested.

'It's how people will see it.'

Knowing she was right, Edward said, 'You're a bitch, Celia.'

'Am I?'

'Yes, you're a complete bitch and I want you, so help me.'

'That's why I'm here,' Celia said sweetly. 'Just this once, you can take me.' She rolled onto her back and spread her legs invitingly wide. 'Go on, treat yourself.' Shaking with desire,

Edward fell on her. 'This is a special favour,' she said, driving him mad with the tight embrace of her thighs. 'I meant what I said about being in control. Show me what you can do – faster – harder . . .'

Afterwards, when his body and senses were more or less at peace, Edward said, 'It won't be easy to fix things up at Cadogan Square. You're virtually a stranger there these days – I'll need time to think of reasons for you to stay overnight.'

Celia smiled, untroubled by his exhausted dead weight: his worries about a place to meet betrayed enslavement.

'I appreciate that,' Celia replied. 'What *shall* we do in the meantime, though?'

'God knows,' Edward muttered. 'Can't you think of anything?'

'I'm sure my aunt would be glad to look after us at her house. It's in Putney Vale, near Richmond Park. You'll like it.'

'Is that the best you can do?' Edward complained, anxious to avoid contact with a witness who could easily turn into an extortioner.

'What about hotels?'

'Out of the question!'

'Then it will have to be Putney Vale for the time being,' Celia said. 'Don't worry, Aunt Ursula is the soul of discretion and, believe me, Edward, you'll be paying enough to keep both of us as quiet as church mice.'

Edward struggled out of the embrace that owed nothing to love or kindness and glared at Celia. 'Is this woman *really* your aunt?' he asked. 'I've never known whether to believe it.'

'Haven't you?' Celia's smile was a brazen flaunting of her new-found power. 'That, I regret to say, is your problem, not mine. Does it matter?'

Sullenly silent, torn between self-disgust and a new hunger for the body that surpassed the dreams he had harboured over the years, Edward realised that it didn't.

In his haste to get rid of her, he agreed to telephone Celia on Wednesday evening to confirm the arrangements for their next meeting. Dining at his club with two political allies, Edward was determined that he would do no such thing: having fallen prey to an astounding piece of cunning, there was no earthly reason why he should compound the blunder. Definitely and absolutely not. But shortly before nine o'clock, a few minutes inside the time-limit stipulated by Celia, he excused himself from the table and went to the call-box in the entrance hall.

'Is anything wrong?' Celia asked after Edward had announced himself. 'You sound furtive.'

'I'm at Fisk's,' he replied. 'This booth is supposed to be sound-proof, but one can't be too careful.'

'Indeed one can't.' There was a gurgle of amusement in Celia's response. 'How are you?'

'I'm very well,' Edward said stiffly.

'Good. So am I, by the way. Well, what about tomorrow?'

Edward hesitated. Celia, who could sense the struggle in his mind, held her breath. Eventually, in a strange, harsh voice, he whispered, 'Yes, damn you, I'll be there.'

'You won't regret it.' It sounded like a sensually alluring promise until Celia added, 'Not until afterwards.'

'As I did on Sunday.' Edward was bitter.

Celia laughed and terminated the call.

Leaving the cubicle, Edward leaned against the door, overcome by self-disgust. Agreeing to meet Celia again – and on her terms at Putney Vale – was sheer madness. For a few moments, he told himself that he wouldn't keep the appointment. Yes, it was as simple as that: if he stayed at the House of Lords until midnight, hidden away and incommunicado, there wasn't a thing Celia could do. Thereafter, he could avoid her – just as he had done for the past eight years – and her scheme would be dead.

Then he remembered what had happened on Sunday night and saw a vision of her body, surpassing all his lustful expectations. At once, Edward set about contriving a justification for the folly on which he was about to embark. In its way, it was destined to be one of the most successful intellectual exercises he ever performed. Naturally, his calculations ignored Annaliese.

Celia left Boothby's slightly early on Friday afternoon so that she could call at Dorset Square to see Helen Swann.

'Well, how goes it?' Helen asked eagerly. She knew nothing beyond Daphne's report that the substitution on Sunday night had taken place without a hitch.

'Extremely well.' Celia's smile was triumphant. 'Our Mr Allardyce spent last night at Ursula's.'

'Good gracious.'

'It's the only place at the moment,' Celia explained. 'I refused to have anything more to do with Rashleigh's house and we can't go to Cadogan Square until he's prepared the ground.'

'He agreed?' Helen was astonished.

'He has no choice. By the way, Ursula seems to have got on awfully well with your Mr X. She *did* enjoy herself.'

'So did he,' Helen enthused. 'That's going to be a regular event.'

'Good.' Celia opened her handbag and gave Helen a small bundle of banknotes. 'Your first commission payment.'

Helen counted the money and was baffled. 'There's eighty pounds here – we agreed twenty per cent. You haven't been with him *four* times, surely?'

'No, twice,' Celia said. 'I've doubled the price.'

'My word!' Rapidly, Helen calculated that the Duke of

Lincolnshire's pleasures were going to set him back something like £20,000 a year. 'Didn't he complain?'

'Sort of,' Celia replied. 'But his heart wasn't in it. He's even more of a mess than I thought. Knowing that I hate him, and that I'd shop him at the slightest provocation, seems to get him excited. You should have seen him last night.'

'Some men *are* like that,' Helen sighed, implying that she felt sorry for them. She waved the money. 'Are you sure about this?'

'Totally. I owe you a lot.'

'Thank you. Long may it continue.'

'Oh it will,' Celia said. 'If ever this poor old country gets a Government that's worthy of him, our mutual friend has political ambitions. So you see, Helen, he can't afford the tiniest whisper of scandal.'

6

1935

'That was an accident. Nothing changes'

George had done more than merely survive Moss Close.
Although an abject failure at any team sport, he had lived up
to Douglas's hopes as a cross-country runner, winning the
coveted Sir Osbert Somers trophy in both his last two years.
Scorning his athletic prowess, George said that it was pure
fluke to make up for his incompetence at other games. Deep
down, however, he was aware that his ability to cover four
miles of ploughed fields and bramble thickets faster than
anyone else had saved him from being an object of complete
ridicule.

Watching closely, doing her best to read between the lines
and paying special attention to what George did *not* say,
Annaliese came to a stunning conclusion about the ethos of her
adopted country. Most of George's fellow-pupils vilified him
for being clever. Before moving on to Winchester, Douglas
had allowed the odd revelation to slip out and, yielding to
subtle interrogation, Robert Chappell provided a few illumi-
nating snippets. What it boiled down to was that the British,

despite their voluble protestations to the contrary, mistrusted education and knowledge. Indeed, deep down, they loathed it.

It was, in fact, something of an insult to describe George as 'clever'. At the age of thirteen, his intellectual powers had developed to a quite exceptional extent. Attending the annual ritual of Founder's Day and Prize-Giving at the end of George's last term, Annaliese was drawn to one side by the school's best teacher and told that her younger son was the most gifted boy to pass through Moss Close in thirty years.

George had proved the point with what struck Annaliese as a curiously perverse gesture of bravado. Sitting the Common Entrance Examination for a place at a public school, he had been awarded full marks, a rare if not exactly unheard-of achievement. (Two years earlier, Douglas's decidedly medi-ocre result had called for much string-pulling by Edward to wangle a place at Winchester.) In theory, George's brilliant performance would have opened the door to any school he chose, but he fell in with the unwritten law that Boothby-Graffoe boys went to Winchester.

Constantly growing more perceptive and sensitive, George saw that Annaliese was torn between pride in his academic prowess and dismay at losing him until he was eighteen.

'I'm not looking forward to it any more than you, Mama,' he said. 'But could you have stopped it? *Honestly?*'

Squirming, Annaliese said, 'Perhaps – if you'd done badly in the exam. Your father might not have been willing to use his influence for you.'

'Oh, I'm sure he would,' George replied. 'It's best this way, bowing gracefully to the inevitable with a dash of superiority.'

Heavily laced as it was with George's increasingly ironic precocity, the statement was small comfort.

Had Annaliese but known, George's decision was nowhere

near as simple as that. He had made a pact with Robert Chappell: they would go to Winchester *together*. If, for any reason, Robert was denied admission, the two boys intended running away. Robert's only sympathetic relative, an uncle who farmed in Northumberland, had promised to shelter them if the worst happened. In the event, Robert did sufficiently well in the Common Entrance to be offered Winchester and his stepfather stumped up the fees, hoping to have seen the last of a troublesome millstone.

The fifty-mile expedition on the day before term started made Annaliese aware of what a strange family they had become.

After his third trip to Portugal, where Elsa and Joseph treated him as another grandson, Robert Chappell had spent the remainder of the long summer holiday at Allardyce Castle, now virtually his home.

Politely, but stuffily firm, Douglas declined to travel to Winchester with George and Robert. A chap in his position – embarking on his third year and hoping for a place in the Second XV – simply couldn't afford to be seen associating with new boys, even if one of them was his brother. To Annaliese's amazement, Edward supported Douglas's stand: presumably, only an Old Wykehamist could understand these ridiculously arcane practices!

So, on the day itself, three cars made the journey from the Castle to Winchester College.

First, at 10.00 am, Douglas was driven off by Edward in the newest Rolls-Royce Phantom. At noon, and acting under direly strict instructions not to leave a minute sooner, George and Robert set out. Annaliese travelled with them and their driver was John Brandon, nowadays delegated to carry out all manner of tasks on Edward's behalf – a fact that caused Annaliese much irreverent amusement in view of what John did best of all at his house in Gainsborough Wood. Finally, following close behind in the shooting-brake with Matthew at the wheel, Gwen, Henrietta, and the five-year-old Athene went to inspect the much-vaunted school. The awesome size of the ancient establishment and the attitude of the older boys did nothing to reassure them.

'I don't know how George will cope with this lot,' Gwen muttered.

'It does make you think,' Henrietta agreed, unimpressed by the sight of so much strutting, privileged youth.

Robert, who looked upon Henrietta as a substitute mother, and had stayed close to her instead of following Annaliese and George on a tour of the buildings, was quick to offer reassurance. 'I'll take care of George,' he said. 'Anyone who bothers him will get a black eye.'

Henrietta believed him. Robert was big and strong for his age and had a pugnacious streak that complemented George's far more cerebral outlook. 'All right, but be careful,' she advised. 'This lot could eat you for breakfast if they put their horrible little minds to it.'

'Don't worry, Henry,' Robert said, squeezing her hand. 'We'll manage.'

In the absence of Edward, of whom there was no sign, George's housemaster, quite overwhelmed by Annaliese's beauty, assumed that John Brandon was her husband. To avoid embarrassing the man – and enjoying the expression on John's face – Annaliese refrained from correcting the misapprehension.

However, when Annaliese and John were alone after saying goodbye to George, she became broodingly thoughtful. 'I suppose it was a natural enough mistake to make,' she said. 'I mean, the poor soul took one look at us and jumped to the obvious conclusion – well, *he* thought it was obvious.'

'Can you be sure of that?' John asked, unable to resist a mild joke at his beloved's expense. 'Aren't you wondering if we're starting to look as though we belong to each other?'

'Yes, perhaps I am,' she admitted.

'Does the idea bother you?'

Annaliese searched the sky for an answer. 'I don't believe it does, my darling,' she said eventually. 'The fact is, Edward *must* know about us.'

It was Annaliese's contention that, since becoming her lover ten years ago, John had 'improved'. By this, she meant that his tendency to nervous diffidence had been supplanted by confidence; generally, he no longer gave a hoot what anyone, other than Annaliese, thought of him. Nevertheless, she had expected her offhand remark to give him at least a flutter of concern.

John surprised her. 'Of course he does,' he said calmly. 'In fact, looking back on it, I'd wager that he knew from the start, when you brought me to Allardyce.'

'Mmm. That's interesting.' Annaliese walked a few paces in silence before asking, 'To what, therefore, do you ascribe his acquiescence?'

Smiling at the way she had expressed herself, John said, 'I'm the good fellow who can be trusted to misbehave discreetly. Dash it, he actually *likes* me. Look at the jobs I get given, for heaven's sake. I was acting *in loco parentis* with George.'

'So the housemaster's mistake was understandable?'

'I'd say so.' John paused. 'As to Edward's acquiescence, there is another side to the coin. While I'm taking care of you, he's free to pursue his own interests.'

'Aha, yes.' The fact that her scowl was not meant to be taken seriously did not stop Annaliese putting fearsome effort into it. '*Her*!'

'I wonder if you're right about that,' John said.

Comically cross, Annaliese stamped a foot and went slightly red in the face. 'Of course I'm right, you silly man. Why else do you think Celia . . .'

John interrupted her. 'Hush, dearest, there are Gwen and the others.'

They had reached the courtyard in which those parents who had delivered their sons, instead of packing them off by train, had parked their cars. Gwen and Henrietta seemed happy enough as they gossiped away, but Matthew was looking round anxiously, hoping to catch sight of Annaliese and John.

'Has anyone seen Douglas or my husband recently?' Annaliese asked.

'No, my lady,' Matthew replied. 'The Phantom isn't here, so His Grace must have left.'

Annaliese shrugged. 'Well, what do we think of this place?' she asked expansively.

'Like a prison,' Gwen said.

'Horrid!' was little Athene's considered opinion.

Sensing Annaliese's mood, Henrietta tried to be more optimistic. 'Robert promised to look after George.'

'Oh – good.' Annaliese's vagueness was a sure sign that she was denying the existence of a problem, refuting the notion that George needed protecting. 'Well, we've done our duty,' she said. 'Let's go home.'

As the two cars drew away from the College, Gwen turned for a last, long look. 'You don't care for it one little bit, do you?' Henrietta said.

Gwen sniffed expressively. 'It must suit some. Douglas likes it.'

Henrietta took careful note of what Gwen had omitted to say and looked for ways of entertaining Athene.

Sitting beside John in the other car, Annaliese became brightly cheerful. 'When we get back, shall we slink off to your house?' she said.

'A romp round the bedroom and a quiet dinner some-where?' John replied, detached, pretending that it was nothing to do with him.

'Could you put up with that?'

'I'll do my best.'

They were in one of their favourite haunts, a small hotel on the southern edge of Savernake Forest, an out-of-the-way spot about seven miles from Allardyce Castle. The food was simple but excellent and the owner always made sure that Annaliese and John were afforded total privacy.

'Why do you believe that your husband is having an affair with Celia?' John asked.

Annaliese thought about it. Presently, she said, 'It's the atmosphere they generate when they're together.'

'It's odd,' John agreed. 'I've always put it down to the fact that they can't stand the sight of one another.'

'That used to be the case,' Annaliese said.

'Still is, surely?'

'Well, yes, *sometimes*.' Unsure of her own reasoning and her fleeting, intuitive glimpses of Edward's sexual penchants, Annaliese began to play with lumps of sugar. 'They vary such a lot. One day they seem to be getting along reasonably well, the next time you see them, they look ready to kill each other. And why is she at Cadogan Square so much now?'

'Playing the hostess, from what I can gather,' John said. 'She's very good with your husband's Westminster friends.'

'How good?' Annaliese demanded fretfully.

'Oh, nothing improper.' John, who kept in touch with his old London contacts, was quite certain. 'By all accounts, she's become a political expert. Powerful men confide in her. The downfall of Stanley Baldwin is being plotted.'

'That's ridiculous,' Annaliese snorted. Then, after giving herself time to think, she said, 'Good luck to her. I could never put up with *politics*.'

'In other words, she's relieving you of a chore,' John said. 'You hate Cadogan Square and politics, Celia is dealing with them.'

'What about Sunday evenings?' Annaliese was off on a new tack. 'Edward always used to go back to London on Sunday afternoon. Now, he goes over to Marlborough to have dinner with our MP – you know, Younger, a ghastly individual!'

'Well?' John, who was aware of Sir Andrew Younger's shortcomings, waited.

'I don't think Edward goes anywhere near Younger,' Annaliese said. 'He wouldn't be seen dead with a man like that.'

'What does he do?' John asked patiently.

'He goes to Celia at The Chantry, of course.'

'That should be easy enough to verify,' John said.

'Oh, I can't be bothered.' Annaliese was suddenly pooh-poohing the idea. 'Who would do it? *We* couldn't hide in the woods to keep a look-out and one can't involve servants in a thing like that – not even Matthew. And you can't trust the evidence of your own eyes, can you? I was wrong about Desmond and Celia. In any case, we're hardly in a position to spy on people, are we?'

John watched Annaliese carefully. She had worked herself up into an overwrought, confused frame of mind. 'What's troubling you?' he asked gently.

'Nancy Shenstone swears that Edward might have stopped a man called McBane marrying Celia,' Annaliese said. 'He was a rich American – very rich, extremely nice. I met him at Boothby's.'

'How is your husband supposed to have done this?' John was sceptical.

'Nancy saw Edward talking to McBane during a reception at the American Embassy. The next day, McBane went back to America – suddenly, earlier than he had intended.' Annaliese held up a hand to forestall John's objection. 'Later, we found out that McBane was supposed to be taking Celia to New York to announce their engagement.'

'How much later was this discovery made?' John asked.

'Six months,' Annaliese admitted. 'Yes, I know, it sounds feeble.'

'And when did this business at the American Embassy happen?'

'Three years ago.'

'At which time, your husband definitely did loathe Celia,' John said. 'He used to tell me what a confounded nuisance she was – at great and embarrassing length. Would Celia have lived in America if she'd married this McBane?'

'I assume so,' Annaliese said.

'Your husband should have been overjoyed at the prospect.'

Annaliese nodded.

'In any case, what could he have told McBane that was so bad?' John asked.

'I have no idea.'

Reaching across the table, John clasped Annaliese's hands. 'On balance, I'm inclined to agree with you that they *are* having an affair,' he said. 'In her own way, she's an attractive woman.'

'Edward's always liked her.' Annaliese smiled knowingly. 'In *that* way. I'm sure that he pretended I was Celia the night we conceived George. But I also believe that he has a good reason for hating her.'

John smiled. 'That sounds like a powerful combination. Much too highly flavoured for a simple chap like me.'

'We don't do badly, though.' Annaliese's eyes softened as she remembered their love-making of two hours ago and hoped for more.

'Look, Annaliese,' John coaxed. 'Whatever Celia and your husband are up to, isn't it a sleeping dog that's best left alone? Why risk disturbing the balance?'

'That's a very *Viennese* way of looking at it, Major Brandon,' Annaliese chuckled.

'I thought it would appeal to you.'

'It does.' Annaliese leaned across the table to kiss John's nose. 'Pay the bill, sweetheart, I want to go back to bed.'

From its abnormal inception, the relationship between Edward and Celia had developed into something that was, if anything, even more bizarre than its beginning.

There was a definite, unmistakable point at which the change began, a Sunday evening in June 1934, about ten months after their first encounter at Rashleigh's house. They were at The Chantry and, as the sun set and birds rejoiced in the last chorus of the midsummer day, Celia fell into a hypnotic harmony with Edward's body and experienced orgasm.

Any faint hope that he had not noticed her pleasure faded with the look that came over his face when reality replaced gasping insanity. As the sternly reproachful expression softened and Celia sensed that he was about to say something idiotic, she grabbed the initiative. Coolly offhand, she said, 'That was an accident. Nothing changes.'

'Oh. I see,' Edward said morosely. 'Surely we can be friends, though?'

'Why? What's so special about you? Remember, you're the *third* Duke of Lincolnshire to make me come.' Celia drove the point home with a lopsided, cynical smile.

Edward's response to the rebuff was unexpected. Eagerly, he asked, 'Which one of us was best?'

Without a moment's hesitation, Celia said, 'Ralph, of course. That's why I married him.' Amused by Edward's mortification, she added, 'You have a long way to go.'

'I'm willing to learn,' he said tightly.

'We'll see.' Celia, knowing that she had regained control, was curt.

'I suppose you'll charge extra for lessons?'

Celia met his sarcasm with a mocking smile. 'No, I don't think so. Our present arrangement is satisfactory.'

It had taken Celia no time to spot that Edward positively enjoyed paying for his pleasures, a quirk that experience had taught her was not uncommon. By treating sexual activity as a commercial proposition, a man sealed it into a secret niche that was cut off from the rest of his life, free of everyday worries and complex emotional problems. Understanding Edward's need to isolate the depravity of his lust from his fine brain, Celia occasionally pitied Annaliese, wondering if she had the faintest idea why her marriage was such a mess.

'I'd be grateful for anything you could teach me,' Edward said. It was the entreaty of a man who found that intimidation and blackmail added an extra, biting edge to his gratification.

When the fancy took her, Celia indulged him. Gradually, his skills improved and her climaxes occurred more frequently. Edward developed a prurient curiosity about Celia's experiences with other men – especially Ralph, whose memory he detested. Splendidly inventive though her husband had been as a lover, Celia found that she had to fabricate stories to gratify Edward's craving.

Imperceptibly, they began to talk of other things, broadening their relationship. In politics and international affairs, Celia proved to be Edward's *alter ego*. Her instinctive grasp of the way governments conducted their affairs was Machiavellian, based on cunning and her rapport with the venal. She was, Edward discovered, the perfect foil to his intellectual approach to statesmanship.

In June 1935, Ramsay MacDonald gave up the Prime Ministership, citing ill health as the reason. Seamlessly, without creating a ripple, Stanley Baldwin took his place. A week later, over dinner at Cadogan Square, Celia expressed the opinion that Baldwin would be able to immerse himself in domestic issues, turning his back on the worsening international arena. There were only two guests that evening, a pair of Conservative MPs who shared Edward's view that Europe in general and Britain in particular were sleep-walking towards unmitigated disaster. Their names were Anthony Eden and Leo Amery, both of whom wanted Winston Churchill as Prime Minister.

The debonair Eden smiled at Celia and said, 'Keeping Baldwin busy – you give the impression that you have something specific in mind, Lady Lincolnshire.'

'I do indeed,' Celia replied. 'She's called Wallis Simpson.'

The MPs exchanged uneasy looks. Leo Amery said, 'We are led to believe that His Royal Highness has assured Baldwin that there's nothing in it. He and Mrs Simpson are friends, nothing more.'

'The Prince of Wales was being less than honest,' Celia replied.

'Oh.' Amery was startled, Anthony Eden shuffled, perhaps shocked by Celia's bluntness.

She went on. 'His Royal Highness and Mrs Simpson were at Boothby's last month. We received a request for a private viewing of some rather interesting jewellery we had in from France.'

'Ah, yes. My sister, Beatrice, mentioned this,' Edward said, anxious to make a contribution.

'Go on, Lady Lincolnshire,' Eden prompted.

'They stayed for nearly an hour and I was with them all the time. Never, in all my life, have I seen a man so helplessly besotted with a woman.'

'Well, *if* that's true thank God she's married,' Leo Amery said.

'Oh, it's true enough,' Celia said. 'Rely on it. But not on her husband, Mr Amery. He can be disposed of in half an hour.'

'What are you suggesting, Celia?' Edward, alert to

worrying possibilities, was alarmed.

'Bearing in mind the state of the King's health, I believe that Mr Baldwin could have a constitutional crisis on his hands before any of us are much older. There must be several reasons why a twice-divorced "Queen Wallis" wouldn't be acceptable.'

'Dozens!' Leo Amery spluttered. 'But His Royal Highness knows all this. Dash it, he's no fool.'

'Isn't he?' Celia asked the simple question in a way that rattled both Amery and Eden and, for a few moments, made Edward wonder if she were intimately acquainted with the Prince of Wales.

After a while, the conversation turned to Germany, where Hitler was systematically tearing up the 1919 Peace Treaty. According to one of its clauses, Germany was allowed an army of no more than 100,000. Having introduced conscription, Hitler had openly avowed his intention to have well over 500,000 men under arms by the end of the year. Instead of attempting to enforce the rules, France was taking steps to increase the strength of its own army and Baldwin had announced additional expenditure on munitions – though not by nearly enough to satisfy Churchill. The evening ended on a sombre note after Eden had said that he expected Hitler to march into the Rhineland when he deemed the time to be right.

'And no one will lift a finger to stop him,' Edward declared.

Celia saw that, although they declined to comment, Eden and Amery agreed with him.

On 3 October 1935, Italy attacked Abyssinia. The unprovoked, premeditated onslaught included the dropping of bombs and poison gas on defenceless civilians. The Emperor, Haile Selassie, appealed to the League of Nations and Italy was duly branded as an aggressor. Sanctions were imposed, but coal, oil, iron, and steel were specifically excluded and the Suez Canal was not closed to Italian warships or troop-carriers. In future, no one would be able to claim that the League was anything other than an impotent cipher, precisely what Edward had said from the start.

Celia began to question him closely about the odium being heaped on Italy. 'Is that all that's going to happen?' she asked. 'Is anyone likely to declare war on Mussolini over this?'

'No. Apart from Germany, Europe is in the hands of cowards.' Realising that her unrest went deep, Edward added, 'Why? What's bothering you?'

'My best friend is married to an Italian prince,' Celia said. 'He was – still is, I expect – a great admirer of Mussolini. I'm afraid for her.'

'I'm sure there's no need to worry,' Edward replied. 'What's his name?'

'Umberto Gastaldi.'

Without requesting further details, Edward said, 'I'll make inquiries. It may take time, though. I shall have to wait for the right opportunity.'

The opening that fell into his lap three weeks later eclipsed his wildest hopes.

Still under the banner of National Government, Baldwin won the General Election in November with comfortable ease. But, as he set about pottering on his avuncular way, the government was swamped by public indignation. Early in December, Sir Samuel Hoare, the Foreign Secretary, met Pierre Laval, the French Premier, in Paris. Details of their secret pact to bring an end to the crisis by offering Mussolini two-thirds of Abyssinia became public as soon as the ink was dry. The outrage over a piece of back-door kowtowing to a bully knew no bounds – especially when it was learned that Hoare had been passing through Paris on his way to a holiday. The proposed dismembering of Abyssinia had, to all intents and purposes, been cobbled up over a drink while the Foreign Secretary waited for a train connection.

Stunned into even greater inactivity than usual by the outcry, Baldwin attempted to ride out the storm. After blustering and refusing to recant, Sir Samuel Hoare was forced to resign and was replaced as Foreign Secretary by Anthony Eden. On the evening of his appointment, Eden sent for Edward and asked him to join the government as a junior minister to act as his representative in the House of Lords. Ten years after the enforced departure caused by his inheritance of the dukedom, Edward was back in the Foreign Office.

A week later, as Christmas approached, he was able to tell Celia of a message he had received from Rome. 'Prince Gastaldi is working at Mussolini's Finance Ministry in a senior capacity. His wife is said to be very beautiful and popular. They seem to be having a good time. Being near the top of the pile, they're looked after extremely well – personal guards, that sort of thing.'

'Thank you,' Celia said, genuinely grateful. 'My aunt will be pleased.'

Edward, suddenly aware that he had provided Celia with information she regarded as invaluable, felt entitled to ask, 'By the way, purely as a matter of idle curiosity, what's your connection with the Princess Gastaldi?'

Celia hesitated, then shrugged. 'I can't see it doing any harm,' she said. 'The Princess used to be Arabella Fenton. We worked together before I met Ralph. Actually, she was with me the night your Uncle William died.'

'I see.' Edward rubbed his chin. 'Did Gastaldi know of her background when he married her?'

'Yes, he was like Ralph.' Celia's smile was teasing. 'He wanted an expert.'

'H'm. I suppose I'm beginning to appreciate that,' Edward said wryly.

'You are indeed,' Celia said. Edward's behaviour since Anthony Eden's summons suggested that power *was* an aphrodisiac.

When George and Robert returned to Allardyce Castle for Christmas, there was nothing to suggest that their first term at Winchester had not been an enjoyable success. Questioned by Annaliese, Douglas said that George was doing fine, absolutely fine – although his airily facile manner prompted the suspicion that he hadn't taken the slightest interest in his brother.

On the first morning of the holiday, Henrietta allowed Athene to wake George by scrambling into bed with him, while she went to the room across the corridor on the West Wing's second floor to rouse Robert. She found him sitting up, sorting through a stack of books.

'Hello, Henry,' he said, smiling and tilting his face for her kiss. 'I thought I'd better organise the prep the miserable devils have given us. Look at this lot – they don't believe in Christmas.'

As she pretended to sympathise with him, Henrietta was preoccupied with the state of the boy's torso. Robert, who slept without a pyjama jacket, was covered in bruises about the shoulders, upper arms, and back. 'You've been in the wars,' she said casually.

'Rather a scrappy game of rugger last Saturday,' he replied, grinning jauntily.

Henrietta doubted it. The variegated colours of the contusions – everything from grey to a livid purple – suggested that the blows had been sustained over a period of several days, not in ninety minutes of rough sport.

Reading her mind, Robert said, 'Don't be upset, Henry. They only *look* bad — and George is all right, just like I promised.'

7

1938
'Annaliese and I have gone beyond that sort of thing'

On 12 May 1937, attired in ermine-trimmed robes and with coronets on their heads, Edward and Annaliese had been in the first rank of peers at Westminster Abbey for the coronation of King George VI. Two weeks later, Stanley Baldwin tendered his resignation to the new Sovereign. He was seventy years old and, after piloting the country through the shock of the Abdication Crisis, considered his duty done. His place at 10 Downing Street was taken by Neville Chamberlain, previously Chancellor of the Exchequer.

No British Prime Minister since William Pitt in 1793 had faced such peril abroad. In March 1936, Hitler had occupied the Rhineland without a whisper of protest from anyone; four months later, Spain was plunged into bloody civil war by another Fascist, General Francisco Franco; Europe was full of timid men doing their damnedest not to upset Mussolini and waiting for Hitler's next move like rabbits in the baleful, mesmeric glare of a stoat.

Edward's assessment of Chamberlain's ability to cope with

the challenge was scathing. 'He's nothing more than a jumped-up tradesman with the mentality of a filing clerk,' he told Annaliese over Sunday lunch at the Castle.

'Oh. I've heard people say that he was very effective as Minister of Health.'

'Poppycock,' Edward snorted. 'He spent five years shuffling figures and inventing forms. How much ice will that cut with Hitler and Mussolini?'

Offended by his disagreeable manner, Annaliese made no reply and the attempt at a serious discussion came to an abrupt end.

That evening, after Edward had indulged himself in Celia's bed at The Chantry, she was infinitely more interested, and, he thought, astute.

'Isn't Chamberlain rather a pigheaded individual – thinks he knows it all? Won't be budged once he makes his mind up?'

'That's what they say,' Edward replied. 'Not a champion of collective responsibility.'

'Believes he can do it all himself, ten times better than everybody else put together?' After thinking about it, Celia added, 'And he seems totally reasonable and *bland* – ineffective, some might say.'

'Exactly.'

Celia's eyes narrowed calculatingly. 'What about Eden? How long will he tolerate it?'

'God knows.' Edward was concerned. 'I've tried to talk it over with him, but he clams up.'

Anthony Eden resigned in February 1938, no longer able to stomach the Prime Minister's approach to and interference in foreign affairs. A new word – appeasement – was creeping into the vocabulary of politics. Chamberlain, who detested sanctions against Italy on the grounds that they gave Mussolini an excuse for war, was browbeating the supine League of

Nations into lifting them. Edward, resigning with Eden, said, 'In effect, Chamberlain's line is: "I will take no action against you for murdering my neighbour and stealing his house so that you can have no reason to hate me".'

'The public seems to agree with Chamberlain,' Celia pointed out.

'*That* is the most appalling aspect of it,' Edward sighed. These days, the only joy in his life was the rapport he shared with Celia. Against all the odds and her will, they had become friends. She retained full control of the relationship, but there was an affinity, all the more enjoyable for its conspiratorial nature and the money Edward handed over after sex. In a strangely symbiotic way, they were united against the appeasing majority and Annaliese's indifference.

The Treaty imposed on Germany at the end of the Great War had specifically forbidden union with Austria. Nevertheless it was expected. The *putsch* in January was badly prepared and easily put down. Kurt Schusnigg, Chancellor of Austria, was summoned to Hitler's lair at Berchtesgaden in the Bavarian Alps and ordered to give Artur von Seyss-Inquart, the leader of the Austrian Nazi Party, a Government post. As Minister of Public Security, Seyss-Inquart deployed terror tactics to stir up public unrest and, on 12 March, requested German help to restore order. The *coup*, or *Anschluss* as Berlin was quick to designate it, was completed the following day. Hitler roared into Austria at the head of a convoy of *Waffen SS* limousines and armoured personnel carriers, travelling along roads bedecked with swastikas and crowded with yelling supporters. From Vienna, Hitler went to his birthplace at Braunau and laid a wreath on his parents' grave. That night, 13 March, the Gestapo moved into the back streets of the Austrian capital to hunt down Jews and dissenters.

Hitler's timing was, as usual, impeccable. Great Britain was still in the political turmoil caused by Eden's resignation: his successor, Lord Halifax, saw no reason to comment, let alone interfere in Austria. Meanwhile, in France, yet another Government had collapsed on 10 March and if anyone was aware of events beyond the Brenner Pass, they said nothing. In little more than twenty-four hours, without shedding a drop of blood, seven million Austrian citizens had been absorbed into the sixty million of the German Reich.

Listening to the news on the wireless at lunch-time, Annaliese was horrified. Although she pretended to ignore the country of her birth, she loved it with a fierce, possessive passion. How could such a dreadful thing have befallen her precious Austria? What would Hitler do next? Distraught with worry, she considered telephoning Edward to ask for his opinion. Deterred by his certain bad temper if she bothered him in London, Annaliese roamed aimlessly round the Castle, cursing John Brandon's absence on a visit to the farms in Devon. Gwen and Henrietta looked on, all the more worried by their inability to help.

Then, just after 4.30 pm, the Rolls-Royce Phantom came up the road from the south-eastern gate to the Park, with Rigby driving in a way that suggested great urgency. Edward was grim-faced when he jumped out and began to dash up the steps, but smiled when he saw Annaliese.

'I thought I should come,' he said. 'This awful business about Austria.'

Taking his arm, Annaliese felt ridiculously grateful. 'That's very kind of you, my dear,' she said. 'I've been going out of my mind.' Edward nodded, spotted Baskerville hovering attentively, and ordered tea to be brought to the library where they found Henrietta and Athene poring over an atlas.

'No, please stay,' Edward said. 'There's no need to go, we're all worried about the same thing.' He was knee-deep in dogs, patting sleek heads as they clustered round him, wagging and grunting with joy. Briefly, Annaliese saw a vision of a man happily at ease with what might have been his family – if only Douglas and George could have been there!

Extricating himself from the Labradors, Edward sat down. Athene came to his side and, big girl though she was now, he lifted her on to his knee.

'Tell me the worst,' Annaliese said. 'What does Chamberlain think?'

Edward was grim again. 'Inasmuch as he thinks *anything*, this will probably be dismissed as a valid case of self-determination. Austria has a lot in common with Germany . . . language, culture, *Weltanschauung* . . .' Edward made an eloquent gesture with a hand. 'So, it's perfectly natural that the two countries should merge.'

Annaliese carried on, in tune with his cynically realistic message. 'No doubt there will be a referendum to show that ninety-nine per cent of Austrians approve of Hitler's action.'

'Already in hand, I imagine,' Edward said.

It was Athene, after studying the sombre faces around her, who broke the subsequent silence. 'Is Hitler a *very* wicked man, Uncle Edward?'

'Yes, I'm afraid he is, darling. The big trouble is, too few people realise it. *That's* why he's so dangerous.'

'Does Mr Chamberlain know that Hitler's bad?' Athene asked.

'I'm afraid not,' Edward replied.

'What's Hitler's next move likely to be?' Annaliese asked.

'No more, surely,' Henrietta cried. 'He must have enough by now.'

But Edward was shaking his head. 'He'll go for Czechoslovakia.'

'Why?' Henrietta was aggrieved. 'What have they done to upset him?'

'Nothing at all,' Edward said. 'But if you look at the map,

you'll see that the man who controls Austria *and* Czechoslova-kia controls central Europe. He could strike north into Poland, or south into Rumania.'

'He could go further,' Henrietta said, tracing a finger across the page of the atlas. 'Bulgaria and Greece might be at risk.'

'And Hitler would then join forces with Mussolini to terrorise the Eastern Mediterranean and North Africa,' Edward pointed out.

'What excuse could Hitler *possibly* dream up for a quarrel with Czechoslovakia?' Annaliese asked.

'He doesn't have to, there's one ready-made.'

Guessing at the answer, Annaliese groaned. 'Not that wretched Peace Treaty again?'

'Yes. The wise men of Versailles gave the Sudetenland and three million Germans to Czechoslovakia. Can you think of a better reason for a bust-up?' For once, Edward avoided that faint trace of 'I told you so' that invariably coloured his comments on the failings of the Treaty. It was, Annaliese thought, a sign of his desire to be of comfort to her.

Edward stayed in Wiltshire for ten days. He and Annaliese kept to their separate bedrooms, pretending not to notice each other's visits to Gainsborough Wood and The Chantry. Between these passionate encounters with their lovers, they experienced the beginnings of a new friendship. Annaliese was certainly glad of Edward's presence when one of her mother's letters brought appalling news.

'What is it?' he asked, worried by her expression of dazed disbelief.

After rereading nearly a whole page of Elsa's flowing script to be sure, Annaliese said, 'Mama thinks that Leopold may have been involved with Seyss-Inquart in paving the way for Hitler and the *Anschluss.*'

'The Habsburgs aren't allowed into Austria,' Edward said gently, respectful of the pain this brutal fact caused every member of the great and honourable family. 'So how can this have happened?'

'He signed the documents,' Annaliese replied, near to tears. 'Gave up all claims, said he'd never do this, that, or the other. He's been there for years – since 1920, I imagine.'

Edward tried another course. 'Where does this information come from?'

'Well, according to Mama, the papers in Vienna are saying that Leopold has become *Gauleiter* of Innsbruck.' Annaliese turned to a new page of Elsa's letter. 'Also, one of Max's old friends in Vienna says that it's true. Can this be possible?'

Thoughtful, Edward searched for a kind way of implying that he thought Annaliese's brother was capable of anything.

Correctly interpreting his silence, Annaliese nodded. 'What a pity I can't meet him,' she said.

'On the contrary, it's a blessing,' Edward murmured, slipping a comforting arm round her shoulders. 'I don't want you hauled up on a charge of murder.'

Sure enough, Hitler demanded the Sudetenland.

As with Austria, the Nazis in Czechoslovakia created civil uproar, challenging the Prague Government to take repressive measures. Instead, partial mobilisation of the Czech Army along the German frontier was ordered and, in what was to prove an isolated burst of acumen and bravery, Chamberlain informed Hitler that Britain might become involved if military action were taken against the Czechs. The crisis evaporated.

However, as April wore on, Edward discovered that appearances were extremely deceptive. Terrified by the threat of war, Chamberlain sent Lord Runciman on what was to be the first of several missions to Prague, nominally to act as advisor and conciliator. Behind the scenes, the process of persuading the Czechs to surrender the Sudetenland had begun. Chamberlain, having convinced himself that Hitler's grievances were legitimate and that his demands could be refused by no reasonable man, embarked upon a course of catastrophic self-delusion. And, as Celia had predicted, he did so with an arrogant but reasonable assurance that beguiled the British public until the very last, fatal moment. Summer grew out of spring, and the British went to extraordinary lengths to persuade themselves that all was well.

In July, Douglas left Winchester with a sackful of glowing character testimonials, but academic attainments that were best forgotten – a minor blemish to which no one paid any attention. Now a handsome and beefy youth of eighteen, Douglas was destined for Sandhurst and a career in the Army that was expected to occupy him for about twenty years. There was a nebulous, unspoken plan that, when Edward was seventy, Douglas would come home and prepare himself to become the Eleventh Duke of Lincolnshire.

No sooner had he arrived at the Castle than Douglas was anxious to be off to spend the summer in Dorset with a school-chum who was also entering Sandhurst in September. Among other things, the two young men hoped to join Edward for a week's shooting at Glengrantach but, as Douglas told his confidant, the butler, there was an infinitely more enjoyable game afoot.

'It's the girls, Baskerville. I'm dying to get at 'em. Rupert has a sister and she's invited two of her friends to stay. I intend having a marvellous time.'

Smiling indulgently, Baskerville issued a mild warning. 'His Grace, your father, would recommend prudence, my lord. We do not want a young lady "in trouble", as they say.'

Douglas winked. 'Don't worry. Rupert reckons his sister knows all about that sort of thing. She's dying to meet me.'

'I understand, my lord. In that case, may I wish you an enjoyable holiday.'

Baskerville, anxious to avoid Mrs Pritchard's disapproval,

decided not to breathe a word about the Marquess of Axholme's hell-bent intention to sow a few wild oats. Mrs Pritchard – in common with Her Grace, Baskerville suspected – was not unduly keen on the heir, preferring his quieter brother. By all accounts, Lord George was an exceptionally bright lad, but Baskerville was at a loss to understand why no one seemed concerned about him and Robert Chappell.

George and Robert, looking forward to another visit to Portugal, were preparing a new, much more difficult repertoire of piano duets for Elsa's entertainment. But ten days before they were due to set out, a telegram arrived: Annaliese's father was dead. At seventy-four, he had fallen prey to a massive heart attack.

All thoughts of the holiday were abandoned and Edward took charge. 'I'm arranging for us to fly from Croydon tomorrow,' he told Annaliese.

'*Us?*' She was surprised.

'Don't you want me with you?'

'Of course – especially if we're going in an aeroplane.'

'I wouldn't dream of letting you face this on your own,' Edward replied, rather gallant. 'Besides, I admired your father.'

Stifling the urge to ask why he had allowed thirteen years to pass without a meeting, Annaliese said, 'It's good of you to help. What about the boys? Should we take them?'

'No, your mother will hardly be in the mood. They'll have to do without a trip this year.'

That evening, on the pretext of needing to discuss something urgent with Younger, the local MP, Edward went to The Chantry to tell Celia of the dash to Portugal. Half an hour after his departure, Annaliese went to Gainsborough Wood to see John Brandon: yet again, even in the midst of mounting sadness for her father, the thought crossed Annaliese's mind that the pattern of life at Compton Allardyce was very strange. As usual, however, more pressing matters demanded her attention.

John Brandon was gently comforting. Two miles away, Celia reacted peevishly. 'You're devoting a lot of time to your wife lately. What am I supposed to do while you gallivant off to Portugal?'

Stung by her unwarranted jealousy, Edward became angry. 'Pull your weight at Boothby's, of course. And while you're about it, you might look for another man to help with your savings.'

'Why do you say that?' Celia asked sharply.

'Charles Templeton has been grumbling about my expenditure,' Edward replied tetchily.

'You can afford me.'

'*I* know that and so, unfortunately, do you. Charles, on the other hand, wonders what the hell I'm spending it on.'

'It's nothing to do with him,' Celia shouted. 'Can't you arrange to have a private account with someone who doesn't stick their nose in?'

'Yes, I suppose I shall have to. I don't like it, though.'

After Edward's door-slamming departure, Celia realised that she must watch her tongue in future. Catch him in the wrong mood and Edward was just about capable of making a full confession to Annaliese who, for the sake of family unity, would forgive him. There was no point in forcing the issue so long as the goose was prepared to carry on laying golden eggs. Reassuringly, despite his anger, Edward's eyes had betrayed his continuing need for her.

Feeling stupendously brave after the flight to Lisbon, and admitting that she had enjoyed everything except the landing, Annaliese reached the villa in the hills to find that a huge collection of uncles, aunts, and all sorts of cousins had come to her father's funeral. Mostly from Switzerland and the

Balearic Islands, they packed the three small hotels in Cascais
and the houses belonging to Max and Vassily. Sad though the
occasion was, Annaliese was glad to meet them all, to listen
to their woes and explain what it was like to be an English
duchess. Vassily, who appointed himself Edward's protector,
was mischievously amused by the gathering. 'I'll swear there
are more Habsburgs here than there ever were in Vienna,' he
told Edward. 'In exile, they breed like rabbits. Know why, eh?
They still believe they will go back to rule Austria. Can you
beat that?'

Edward was fascinated by Elsa, still beautiful at sixty-eight.
Already, she had enveloped the loss of her husband in a serene
dignity that removed the need for halting speeches of
condolence. Treating Edward as a valued friend who had been
a frequent visitor, she also demonstrated a shrewd insight into
the state of his marriage to her daughter. In addition to the
double bed in the room that Annaliese and Edward had used
in 1925, there was a divan in the adjoining dressing-room.
Grateful as she was for Edward's company and support,
Annaliese heaved a secret sigh of relief when he made it plain
that he would use the dressing-room.

The day of the funeral was fine and pleasant, a gentle sea
breeze holding the temperature down. Shortly before
11.00 am, they were all gathered in the church at Cascais,
waiting for the service to begin. It was to be conducted by an
Austrian priest from a village near Salzburg, a man who
travelled Europe to baptise, marry, and bury members of the
exiled Imperial Family. The expectant silence was disturbed by
the roar of a powerful motor in the square outside; heavy
footsteps sounded in the porch and someone barged into the
church.

Turning, Annaliese recognised her brother, Leopold – or
thought she did. He had put on a good deal of weight and his
face had a jowly, dissolute look. Elsa, also craning her neck,

nodded. 'I informed him, of course,' she whispered. 'Max knew how to do it. I didn't think he'd come.'

Superciliously, ignoring dozens of curious stares, Leopold strode to the front and made his way towards Elsa, pushing past Max, Vassily, and Edward as though they were nothing more than minor nuisances. He kissed Elsa, said, 'My sympathies, Mama,' favoured Annaliese with a curt nod and knelt to enact a pretence at prayer.

The solemn liturgy began and there was no further attempt at communication between mother and son. At the end of the service, Leopold ostentatiously offered his arm to Elsa, escorting her to the grave, assuming his dead father's mantle. Annaliese saw that Elsa, who was furious, complied with the charade only to avoid a scene. However, when the interment was over and people were moving away, she detached herself from Leopold and demanded, 'Where did you spring from?'

'Lisbon. I arrived yesterday. Naturally, our Embassy looked after me.'

'*Our* Embassy?' Elsa was mocking.

'The German Embassy,' Leopold snapped.

'Quite.' Elsa's amusement was far more effective than disapproval. 'And to what do we owe the pleasure?'

'Papa's death, what else?' Leopold was rattled. 'And I need to know that his affairs are in order.'

'Ah, I understand,' Elsa said quietly. 'You'd better come back to the house. We can find room for you in one of the cars.'

'I have my own vehicle,' Leopold said, puffing himself up. 'The Ambassador put it at my disposal.'

Elsa saw the big, black Mercedes and uniformed driver. 'Follow us, then,' she said. 'By the way, have you nothing to say to your sister and brother-in-law?'

Leopold turned to Annaliese and Edward. Declining to shake his hand, they stared at him coldly.

'You two have done well for yourselves,' Leopold said, continuing to speak German, making no effort to be pleasant.

'I take it that you're referring to the consequences of my cousin's murder,' Edward retorted. 'We did not wish it.'

'I accept that,' Leopold replied. Switching his attention to Annaliese, he became sardonic. 'But what about you, dear sister? I hear that you enjoy being a duchess. All that work for good causes and telling ignorant people which *objets d'art* and trinkets they should buy must make you very important.'

Unable to restrain herself, Annaliese rose to the bait. 'You amaze me, Leopold. Surely, the *Führer*'s dogsbodies have better things to do with their time than study London Society?'

'We have to be prepared. Who knows when Mr Chamberlain will attack us with his umbrella?' Happy with his jibe, Leopold strode off to his car.

'Try to ignore him,' Edward whispered, clasping Annaliese's hand.

'I'll do my best. What I can't stomach is that he's so insufferably *thrilled* with himself.'

'One suspects they all are,' Edward said. 'The man with the umbrella doesn't seem to have noticed.'

At the villa, while the guests sipped drinks, helped themselves from the buffet tables on the terrace, and talked about the old times, Elsa took Leopold to the room that the Archduke Joseph had used as a study. Hovering near the door, Annaliese soon heard voices raised in anger. She put up with it for nearly five minutes, then, pulling an apologetic face at Edward, opened the door and plunged into the argument. Almost immediately, she was out again, admitting that Elsa had ordered her to go away.

'What's going on?' Edward asked.

'Leopold wants his inheritance. It's the only reason he came.'

'That can't surprise you.'

Annaliese shrugged. 'I don't know him any more, of course. Anyway, he's out of luck. Papa's will excludes him – very, very specifically.'

'Your father changed it?' Edward asked.

'No, it's the will he made eighteen years ago when they came to live here. It seems that Papa always knew that Leopold would go to the bad.'

Edward nodded his approval of Joseph's assessment of his son's character and drew Annaliese towards the rooms in which most of the guests were gathered.

The row in the study dragged on for another twenty minutes. When Leopold emerged, finally convinced that there was nothing he could do, he was in a monumentally foul temper. One hundred-odd descendants and relatives of the old Emperor, Franz Joseph, fell silent, staring at Leopold with unconcealed distaste. He stood stock-still, glaring round: several moments passed and the tension became oppressive.

It was as if something inside Leopold snapped. Raising his right arm in a Nazi salute, he shouted, '*Heil* Hitler!' Then, head held ridiculously high, he swaggered through the stupefied crowd and disappeared. In the ghastly silence, everyone heard the engine of the big Mercedes roar into life.

Timid sniggers and grimaces were followed by mild ridicule. Perhaps the strain of travelling had exacerbated Leopold's grief for his father; drink could be involved; he might be heading for a nervous breakdown; whatever the reason, it was bad form to inflict such tawdry histrionics on Elsa. Probably, Leopold would soon come to his senses and feel ashamed of himself.

Studying Edward, Annaliese saw that he, rejecting all the possible excuses, took an extremely serious view of her brother's behaviour. Grimly fearful, Edward suspected that they had been given a glimpse of an attitude that was about to subjugate Europe.

Over breakfast the following morning, Edward attempted to take the initiative in resolving the problem that he and Annaliese felt Joseph's death had created.

'Look here, Elsa, there's something we must thrash out. Not to beat about the bush, will you consider moving to England?'

Unfazed, Elsa asked, 'You think you could smuggle me in?'

'I could have a jolly good go at it. I have influential friends.'

'Really, Edward!' Smiling sadly, Elsa shook her head. 'I'm German by birth and Austrian by marriage. I know England's being run by fools, but even they wouldn't be stupid enough to let *me* in.'

'Mama, we must try,' Annaliese insisted. 'You can't stay here on your own.'

'Why not?' Elsa seemed intrigued, anxious to discover what vital fact had escaped her attention.

'It isn't safe,' Annaliese said.

'It is. You've no idea how much things have improved since Salazar took over. Max says he's a detestable individual, but he's turned Portugal into a peaceful, law-abiding country.'

'How about Spain?' Annaliese protested. 'The civil war might spread.'

'It won't,' Elsa replied, completely sure. 'Salazar's a crafty devil. He won't let us get involved in anything, not even the trouble that Hitler will cause.'

'You think there will be war in Europe?' Annaliese asked.

Elsa looked at Edward. 'Inevitable, don't you think?'

'Not *quite*,' Edward said. 'There are measures that would avert it.' He omitted to point out that no one would take them. 'As to Salazar, I agree with you, Elsa. Portugal will steer clear of trouble. Ultimately, there could be drawbacks to isolationism, but the medium-term advantages look attractive.'

'What do you call medium-term?' Elsa asked.

'Ten years, maybe more.'

Elsa turned to Annaliese triumphantly. 'There you are, it's perfectly safe here. You have no need to worry.'

'But I *shall* worry!' Annaliese wailed.

'Why? Because I'm getting old and likely to be taken ill? Oh, don't look like that, darling, it's what you were thinking.' Annaliese nodded miserably and Elsa continued, totally unruffled. 'Max and Vassily are younger than me and we have plenty of servants, all of whom are trustworthy and devoted to us. We shall manage. Face facts, there isn't anywhere else we can go – apart from Switzerland, and I've never liked the place.'

And that was the end of it. In the two days before she and Edward flew back to England, Annaliese made several attempts to change her mother's mind, forcing Elsa to insist on an end to the nagging.

A tearful parting left Annaliese bereft of words until they were in the air, halfway back to England. Clutching Edward's hand, she whispered, 'I could easily believe that I shall never see Mama again.'

'You know that's silly.' Edward was comforting. 'Here's something that might cheer you up. I made Max promise to drop you a line every month to let you know how your mother is. So you see, she won't be able to get away with white lies in *her* letters.'

'Thank you,' Annaliese murmured, greatly comforted. After a while, she said, 'I wonder what will become of Leopold?'

'That depends on which way the War goes,' Edward replied.

Annaliese twisted in her seat to stare at him with burning

intensity. 'You *really* believe there will be war?'

'I'm afraid so.'

'As bad as the last one?'

'It could be much worse. Our capacity to inflict damage has increased enormously – at least, Germany's has.'

Uneasily aware that she was clutching at straws, Annaliese said, 'Hardly anyone agrees with you.'

'I know.' Edward's smile was ruefully good-natured, making him look boyish again. 'Only the die-hards and warmongers like Churchill.'

'I'm sure you're wrong.' Annaliese smiled cheerfully and squeezed his hand.

'No one hopes that more than I do,' Edward said earnestly.

When they landed at Croydon, an inexplicable and rather sad thing happened. The companionship between them, born at the time of the *Anschluss* five months ago, began to seep away. Matthew, waiting with the Rolls, sensed the change as Annaliese and Edward discussed their immediate plans, suddenly awkward with each other, wanting their own way but wary of causing offence. After a series of false starts that nearly led to a quarrel, it was agreed that Matthew should take Edward to London and then drive Annaliese to Wiltshire. At Cadogan Square, where Annaliese showed no inclination to leave the car, Edward gave her a perfunctory peck on the cheek and went indoors, leaving one of the servants to sort out his luggage.

Unruffled, Annaliese sat in contemplative silence until they were past Chiswick and humming along the Great West Road. 'Have you seen anything of Major Brandon while I was away?' she asked Matthew.

'Bumped into him only this morning, my lady.'

'How was he?'

'Very well. He said he was looking forward to having Your Grace back, safe and sound.'

Annaliese relaxed against the luxurious upholstery, smiling softly.

At Cadogan Square, dinner was late, delayed by Edward's compelling and repeated need for Celia.

'It seems that you didn't take advantage of Portugal to make it up with Her Imperial Highness, the Archduchess,' Celia said.

'Did you think I might?'

'Who can tell?' Celia laughed. Flaunting her nakedness, she watched him start thinking about what they would do after dinner.

'You don't have to worry about that,' Edward said, sounding as though he were reassuring an anxious wife. 'Annaliese and I have gone beyond that sort of thing.'

As Edward turned away to hunt for a clean shirt, Celia shook with silent laughter. *That sort of thing*, indeed. What an ass he was when he put his mind to it!

The crisis over Czechoslovakia re-emerged and gathered momentum. Hitler's demands were relentless and Chamberlain became feverish, always dashing off somewhere to launch a fresh attempt at appeasement. Invariably, he travelled alone without advisors, supremely confident in his own ability.

On 24 September, the Czech government ordered a second mobilisation, France followed suit and held military consultations with Britain. Four days later, the Royal Navy was put on full alert and Chamberlain broadcast to the nation. To Annaliese's astonishment, she heard him say: 'How horrible, fantastic, incredible, it is that we should be digging trenches and trying on gas masks because of a quarrel in a faraway country between people of whom we know nothing.'

John Brandon, seeing Annaliese's mouth drop open in disbelief, shook his head sadly. 'The Birmingham businessman echoing the views of the public,' he said. 'The man in the street neither knows nor cares a fig about Czechoslovakia.'

'Yes, but . . .' Having exploded, Annaliese saw the hope-lessness of it all and shut up.

On 29 September, after an 'invitation' from Hitler, Chamberlain flew to Munich for a last-ditch conference between Britain, France, Germany, and Hitler's ally, Italy. The next day, the Czechs were confronted by Chamberlain and Daladier, the French Premier, and ordered to comply with Hitler's demands. Collective security had been replaced by collective blackmail to achieve peace at an ignominious price.

While German troops marched into the Sudetenland, Chamberlain returned to England. At Heston Airport, near Hounslow, he was met by a crowd of journalists and newsreel cameras. Brandishing a piece of paper signed by Hitler, and with his umbrella clutched firmly in the other hand, Neville Chamberlain proclaimed 'Peace for our time' and stated that Hitler had faithfully promised to make no more demands.

Practically everyone believed him. Alfred Duff Cooper, First Lord of the Admiralty, was one of the rare exceptions and resigned from the Cabinet. Churchill lodged a strong protest at the Munich Agreement, but struggled to make himself heard against the uproar of a hostile House of Commons.

Annaliese, sharing Edward's view that Chamberlain had used a combination of cowardice and arrogance to commit an act of treachery that would come to be seen as one of history's greatest blunders, felt sick to her soul.

As the autumn of 1938 faded into winter, Allardyce Castle seemed to lose much of its unique, atmospheric spirit. Each day, Annaliese scanned *The Times*, anxious for a sign that her fears were groundless. At weekends, Edward related what he had learned from his incessant prowling round the nooks and crannies of Westminster. It was always the same: at best, the news was indifferent, at worst, terrible. With every day that passed a sense of foreboding settled over the great, beautiful house and its surroundings.

It was, Gwen realised, no time to voice her worries: the opportunity for that was long since past. She should, possibly, have had a quiet word with Annaliese at the beginning of September after George and Robert Chappell had returned to Winchester.

In any case, what *was* the problem?

One morning during the summer holidays, Gwen felt sure that George's bed hadn't been slept in, merely rumpled to look as though it had. Then, a few days later, she thought that Robert must be having the most terrible, persistent nightmares to get his bed in such a mess.

Bit by bit, Gwen came to the conclusion that the two boys were spending most of each night in Robert's bed. They were sixteen, did that mean anything? Was it a habit they'd acquired at school?

Several times, Gwen almost raised the matter with Matthew or Henrietta. But she always fought shy of it because of fear of embarrassment or accusations of making a mountain out of a molehill.

Gwen, who recognised her own naivete and tendency to over-anxiety, persuaded herself that she was imagining things and left Annaliese to fret about the menace of Nazi Germany.

8

1939–1945
'This means you'll have to get married'

In January 1919, Annaliese and Edward had escaped from a Germany that was crushed by defeat on the Western Front and riven from within by a catastrophic civil war. The economic woes and internal bickering of the Weimar Republic had reinforced the view that Germany was finished, a third-rate wreck of a country that would never again be capable of causing trouble. While the world's statesmen averted their gaze, or struggled ineptly with domestic issues, Adolf Hitler transformed the Fatherland into the most fearsome fighting machine in the history of mankind. And he took less than six years about it.

At dawn on 1 September 1939, without any formal declaration of hostilities, Hitler launched the *Blitzkrieg* on Poland. Two days later, after the ultimatums from Britain and France had been ignored, Europe was at war again.

Annaliese was forty-three at the outbreak, forty-nine when Germany was finally crushed in 1945. With few exceptions, she loathed every hour of the five years, eight months, and eight days it took to stamp out the Nazi scourge. Times without number, John Brandon urged her to look on the bright side and, just as frequently, Annaliese demanded to know what on earth he thought he was talking about. Always, to her dying day, she regarded what became known as the Second World War to have been the blackest, most futile part of her life.

The initial period, the so-called Phoney War, was the worst. Nothing seemed to be happening – except a never-ending flood of pointless restrictions designed to make those in authority appear usefully busy.

'And another thing,' Annaliese railed at John. 'What's the point of this blackout nonsense? It won't make a scrap of difference to the German bomb-aimers, but it's turning the roads into a death-trap. Do you know how many pedestrians died in London last month?'

'Er – rather a lot?'

Annaliese, who had no idea of the facts, said, 'I wouldn't be surprised if the road deaths exceeded the numbers killed by the *Luftwaffe*. The Government doesn't say a word, of course.'

John, suspecting that Annaliese had a good point, remained judiciously silent.

Petrol rationing was Annaliese's ultimate *bête noir*. Unless she was prepared to put up with smelly, overcrowded trains that paid scant regard to the timetable, she was either trapped in London or marooned at the Castle. A solution, which enabled her to spend time at Boothby's, was to stay with Beatrice and Charles at Upper Overs. The delightful, rambling old house in the Ashdown Forest, twenty miles south of London, had been left to Beatrice by her father, and seemed a perfect place to hide, despite the constant noise of aircraft passing high overhead. Travelling to and from London each day with Beatrice and Charles was the least objectionable way of doing something useful. Government propaganda placed great emphasis on 'business as usual', the way in which mere civilians could show Hitler that he wasn't winning.

According to Beatrice, London's social life, far from being curtailed, positively thrived. During the first winter of the conflict, many people came to the conclusion that they preferred war to peace. 'Making the best of things' meant that there was always an excuse for an all-night party and half a dozen casual affairs. Generally, Annaliese put up with about three weeks of business as usual, then escaped to Wiltshire and John Brandon, staying until her conscience drove her back to the tedium laced with danger that was London.

There was one thing for which Annaliese was profoundly grateful. Unlike many of the country's great houses, the Castle was not requisitioned for military use – or not until the early days of 1944. This was due to Edward's unashamed exploitation of his influence.

Edward had a good war. Unlike many to whom the double-edged phrase was applied, he worked tremendously hard, contributed much, and deserved more than the modest recognition that eventually came his way.

Astonishingly, Neville Chamberlain survived for eight months, despite the daily exposure of his shortcomings. Although he had stumbled into a declaration of war against Germany, Chamberlain thereafter behaved like a man in a trance, lacking any notion of what to do next. Made rash by the inactivity of the Phoney War, Chamberlain told the House of Commons that 'Hitler had missed the boat.' That was on 4 April 1940. Two days later, Germany attacked Norway. By the end of the month, notwithstanding valiant efforts by the Royal Navy, the swastika flew everywhere from Stavanger to Tromsø.

The debate demanded by the Opposition on the situation began on 7 May and rapidly turned into a vote of confidence in the Prime Minister. Leo Amery, speaking from the Government back benches, set the Commons alight in a withering attack on Chamberlain. He concluded by quoting Oliver Cromwell's words to the Long Parliament: 'You have sat too long here for any good you have been doing. Depart, I say, and let us have done with you. In the name of God, go!'

Chamberlain sat tight during the second day of the debate and gained a majority in the vote – albeit with 60 Conservatives abstaining and 30 voting with the Opposition. Then, on the morning of 10 May, the signal traffic at the War and Foreign Offices was clogged with the news of Hitler's long-anticipated attack on Belgium and Holland. Still Chamberlain refused to go. Not until he had accepted the need for a National Coalition Government and had it hammered into him that the Labour and Liberal Parties would not serve under his leadership did he tender his resignation. At 6.30 that evening, Winston Churchill was at Buckingham Palace, kissing King George's hand on his appointment as Prime Minister.

Two days later, Edward entered the Government, as a Minister of State at the War Office, a department headed by Anthony Eden, the man untainted by appeasement and Munich. It was Edward who gave daily reports to the House of Lords on the evacuation of Dunkirk and broke the news of the fall of France to their Lordships. In December, he had a new job. Churchill sent Lord Halifax to Washington to perform the crucial role of British Ambassador and moved Anthony Eden to the Foreign Office as Halifax's replacement. For the second time, Edward followed Eden to the building that had always been the focal point of his ambitions.

In many respects, the ensuing four and a half years were the most fulfilling of Edward's life. He was at the centre of national and political power, contributing to decisions of far-reaching importance, respected by his peers, and much in demand socially whenever he was able to spare a little time. From the summer of 1940, Celia became his constant companion, doing so in circumstances that were free of possible scandal and gave her the prestige for which she had always longed.

The removal of Annaliese from their lives helped enormously.

It came about as a result of a chance visit to Boothby's by the Princess Royal, who, by virtue of her marriage to Henry Lascelles, was also Countess of Harewood. The Princess was dashing round the leading fine-art establishments in search of a birthday present for her mother, Queen Mary. Purely as a passing gesture of courtesy, she said to Annaliese, 'How are you coping with the War, Lady Lincolnshire?'

The reply was forthright. 'Not very well, Your Royal Highness. To tell you the truth, I'm bored and rather ashamed of myself.'

'Oh? Why?' Suddenly Princess Mary was giving Annaliese her full attention.

'Everyone seems to be *doing* something,' Annaliese said. 'But I can't find anyone who wants me.'

'Are you quite serious? You're looking for work?'

'Yes, ma'am.'

The Princess Royal looked Annaliese up and down and liked what she saw. Taking Annaliese's arm, she led them out of earshot of everyone else. 'I'm rushed off my feet,' she said. 'I'm Commandant of the Auxiliary Territorial Services — that's the women's Home Guard, only don't tell anyone I said so, and I'm in charge of the British Red Cross. My engagement book looks like a Chinese puzzle — I have two secretaries trying to make sense of it. Could you help?'

'Doing what?' Annaliese asked eagerly.

'Largely, it's a question of boosting morale. Can you make a decent speech – only a few minutes?'

'I'll have a go.'

'And inspect things?'

Annaliese laughed. 'I'm good at that.'

'You mustn't find faults,' Princess Mary said. 'They work miracles with next to nothing, so you have to turn a blind eye if everything isn't quite right. How are you at organising?'

'A demon.'

Princess Mary took another long look at Annaliese and said, 'Shall we have lunch and talk about this properly?'

A few days after Annaliese's visit to Kensington Palace, an announcement appeared in the Court Circular of *The Times*. HRH The Princess Royal, Countess of Harewood, was to be assisted in her duties with the ATS and Red Cross by Annaliese, Duchess of Lincolnshire.

The press adored her. However remote the location, or obscure the event, there were always at least two photographers waiting when Annaliese arrived. She looked stunning in uniform and proved to be a genius at off-the-cuff remarks. Petrol ceased to be a problem and Annaliese travelled constantly, sometimes spending a day or two at Harewood House in Yorkshire where, among other surprises, the Princess Royal displayed her comprehensive knowledge of cattle breeding and confessed to being painfully shy.

Discreetly aware of Annaliese's need to dash off to Gainsborough Wood whenever she was able to snatch a night at Compton Allardyce, Gwen and Henrietta looked after her. Between them, they mended and washed her clothes, kept her diary, and made whatever excuses were necessary. Matthew did his best to get on with the ATS drivers – generally buxom and boisterously cheerful – who turned up at all hours of the day and night.

Celia observed Annaliese's progress with wry detachment, drawing Edward's attention to what the newspapers were printing.

'Your wife is a celebrity,' she said one morning over breakfast at Cadogan Square. 'Ever the ministering angel!'

Edward gave vent to the strangled 'Harrumph' sound which, as a rule, indicated embarrassment. In this case, it was accompanied by a self-satisfied smile. By some curious quirk, war-time Society had come to believe that there were *two* Duchesses of Lincolnshire, one who rushed here, there, and everywhere, helping the Princess Royal, and another who took care of the Duke. The previous evening, at a Foreign Office reception for Charles de Gaulle and his Free French supporters, Edward had overheard a small group speculating as to whether he and Celia ever shared a bed.

'I'd be surprised if they didn't,' one woman said. 'There must be opportunity and need.'

Her male companion replied, 'He's doing a first-class job, you know.'

Another man went further. 'Bloody good luck to Lincoln-shire, I say. He was always against the appeasers. Deserves a bit of fun – and I'll wager she knows how to provide it.'

Celia was aware of the undercurrents and passed them on to Ursula, with whom she maintained diligently close contact despite her hectic life as the unofficial mistress of Cadogan Square. As well as being genuinely fond of her 'aunt', Celia regarded her as an insurance policy: one day the good times were bound to end and Celia had no intention of reverting to a solitary existence. The link with the elegant house at Putney Vale also held out the faint hope of news from Arabella – although Ursula and Celia were afraid to mention her. The outbreak of war had cut off Arabella's letters and, as 1941 progressed, it became apparent that Italy was in serious trouble.

After supper one evening, Ursula made a tentative attempt to explore the future, asking, 'How long will this go on?'

'Me and Edward?' Celia said, reading her friend's mind.

'Yes.'

'Mmm ... that's a good question. Probably not much beyond the end of the War.'

'Oh.' Ursula was surprised. 'Why do you think that?'

'Politics,' Celia replied. 'There'll be a change of Government — a big one — and Edward will be out on his ear. It could finish him.'

'Surely not,' Ursula protested. 'Churchill will carry on forever.'

'That's what Edward believes,' Celia said. 'He has no idea of what's happening underneath the war effort and the "Britain can take it" claptrap. Did you know that there are more industrial disputes and strikes *now* than ever before?'

'I certainly didn't,' Ursula said, shocked.

'It's perfectly true.' Celia leaned forward, intense and angry. 'Three weeks ago, a convoy — or what was left of it after the U-boats had finished — got to Liverpool. It was carrying food from America. Unfortunately, the port was closed because of a strike. The ships had to wait in the Mersey for five days while the dockers were persuaded to unload it.'

'This sort of thing isn't in the papers,' Ursula said.

'Of course it isn't. Annaliese told me about this gem — she stumbled across it by accident, on one of her ATS jaunts. She was disgusted and who can blame her? No, Ursula, there are some very nasty attitudes going the rounds in dear old England.'

Feeling that it was time to put her head in the sand, Ursula changed the subject. 'You and Edward are getting on well, though?'

'Splendidly.'

'You still control him in bed?'

'More than ever,' Celia said. 'To be honest, I didn't think it would last this long. Most men need something new after a year or two.'

'It's amazing. You're being treated like a duchess at long last *and* paid a small fortune for sleeping with him.'

'Quite a large fortune, actually,' Celia said mischievously. 'Especially since your friend, Helen Swann, decided she didn't want any more commission.' Helen, considering that she had received adequate compensation for the loss of Mr Allardyce's custom, had waived her rights to further payments in 1940.

Ursula raised her glass of whisky in a toast. 'Happy times while it lasts.'

'And so say all of us.' Celia laughed, stretching like a contented cat. She looked so happy that Ursula came close to mentioning Greg McBane, to suggest that everything had turned out for the best. Instinct told her to remain silent: however much she pretended otherwise. Celia clung to a residue of corrosive bitterness. Being Edward's mistress and confidante *was* good, but it was a poor second best to what Celia would have experienced as Mrs Greg McBane, queen of Long Island.

Douglas's war began frustratingly.

In September 1939, he had completed the first of three years at Sandhurst and felt sure that the rest of the course would be abandoned so that he could get to grips with Hitler's *Panzers*. The powers that be dithered. Days, then weeks passed. Finally, in time for Christmas, it was decided that Douglas's entry would have their instruction reduced to two years. So, in the early summer of 1940, Douglas had to read about the evacuation from Dunkirk in the newspapers and attend lectures on the tactics of the Boer War.

There were compensations, the most pleasant of which was Sophie Scott-Thomas, the sister of Douglas's school-friend and fellow-officer cadet. From their very first meeting in the summer of 1938, Douglas and Sophie got on famously. Blessed with a natural talent for bedroom romping, Sophie soon relieved Douglas of his virginity. Bold and adventurous, she encouraged her young, inexperienced lover to take rather more thirty-six hour passes than Sandhurst allowed. Since there was always someone to cover for him and Sophie *was* exceptionally jolly, Douglas played the risky game with gusto and always got away with it.

He never took the affair all that seriously, expecting that Sophie would become a thing of the past once he was commissioned and sent overseas. In August 1940, when Second Lieutenant the Marquess of Axholme was posted to a tank regiment on Salisbury Plain, he assumed that it was a stepping-stone to somewhere interesting like Singapore or the Middle East. If anyone had told Douglas that he was to spend over eighteen months training conscripts in the rudiments of playing soldiers, he would have laughed derisively.

Overnight, Sophie became a necessity. Thanks to Baskerville, she was installed as an almost permanent guest at Allardyce Castle, less than half an hour's drive from Douglas's base. Annaliese, whose frenetic comings and goings meant that she hardly ever saw the girl, tolerated Sophie, never quite displaying hostility. But Edward, having satisfied himself that her family background was beyond reproach, rather approved of Sophie. Douglas was amused by the over-jovial bursts of paternalistic, man-of-the-world support Edward provided on his flying visits to the Castle.

In July 1942, Douglas was posted to North Africa and Sophie went home to Dorset to wait and pray.

Emerging unscathed from the triumph of El Alamein, Douglas joined the Anglo-American invasion of Morocco and Algeria which was designed to kick France's Vichy administration off the fence of neutrality. Douglas's Christmas card, sent from Marrakesh, told of his promotion to captain and recommendation for the Military Cross.

George and Robert left Winchester in the summer of 1940 with places at Oxford: George had won a scholarship to Edward's old College, Robert was accepted by Keble. There were, however, strings attached.

'They'd prefer us not to go up until the War's finished,' Robert said. 'We're expected to do our bit.'

'I can go straight away.' George said. 'I think I will.'

Though prolonged, the subsequent argument was mild. At one point, George considered registering as a conscientious objector, but gave up when Robert pointed out that the last thing he should do was to draw that sort of attention to himself.

'You do realise,' George said, 'that there's next to no chance of us staying together if we join up?'

'Frankly, it's best if we don't,' Robert replied. 'The Army doesn't much care for our sort. And we won't be "joining up". It's conscription; at least, it is for me and I can't see even your father being able to get you out of it.'

'He wouldn't try,' George retorted, displaying a rare glimpse of rancour.

'Look, Georgie, we don't have much choice,' Robert insisted. 'Let's do our duty, get it out of the bloody way and enjoy ourselves at Oxford when it's all over.'

Robert, barred from aircrew duties by the colour blindness discovered at his medical, was nevertheless accepted by the RAF and sent for training on radar, the invention that was believed capable of making aerial warfare much more destructive. To his utter astonishment, George was plucked from a tidal wave of recruits at Aldershot, commissioned in three days, and dispatched to a basement in the War Office to play what looked like an insignificant part in strategic planning. His superior, a wearily cynical major from the retired list, told George that he could expect to be there for the duration. 'You're supposed to be brainy,' the old soldier said, making it glaringly plain that he considered this to be a handicap.

As the hostess of the dinner-party at which Edward had exerted his influence, Celia was curious to know why George had received such exceptional treatment.

'We need people like him in planning,' Edward replied. 'The War Office is full of men who think it's still 1914. Winston's clearing them out, of course, but it takes time.'

Later, hoping to catch Edward off guard, Celia asked, 'Did the Prime Minister have a hand in getting George fixed up?'

'Yes, he did.' Quickly Edward added, 'That's highly confidential, by the way.'

'Of course.'

Celia was often party to conversations that infringed every part of the Official Secrets Act and, therefore, found the reminder suspicious. Subsequently, she watched George closely.

He lived at Cadogan Square, walking to the War Office every morning with a steel helmet and gas mask over his shoulder. At first, he was a potential nuisance, threatening to disrupt the lifestyle which Celia now took for granted. But the War Office proved to be a hard taskmaster, often requiring George to work all night. In any case, it never occurred to Edward that his son's presence in the house should interfere with his need for Celia.

Slowly, as he was given more worthwhile tasks, George began to enjoy his job. He never mentioned Robert Chappell, let alone took him to Cadogan Square. Nor, during the periods of leave that they went to great lengths to share, did they spend much time at Allardyce Castle. Instead, they met at discreet country hotels near the places where Robert was stationed, first in Sussex, then Norfolk, after Robert was transferred to Bomber Command in January 1943.

Their meetings were not always happy. More than most people, George suffered from the disruptive effects of the War, losing his sense of direction and self-confidence. Time and again, he accused Robert of infidelity, always without a shred of evidence.

'There *must* be someone else,' George would say.

'What on earth makes you think that?' Robert was patient and tender.

'I don't know – you come into contact with hundreds of men.'

'So do you.'

'No, I don't. I'm stuck in a rut with has-beens and brass hats.'

'That sounds like a complaint,' Robert replied, introducing a careful note of humour. 'Would you like to be surrounded by glorious youngsters with uncontrollable urges?'

'Don't be ridiculous,' George snapped. 'And even if I were, I'd ignore them.'

'I know that.' Robert was conciliatory. 'So why do you think I'm different? Look, quite apart from the fact that I love you, can you see me prancing round an RAF camp shouting, "I'm a queer, come and get me boys"?'

They both smiled at the accidental *double entendre* in the word 'camp' and George said, 'No, I suppose not, Bobbie.'

'What *is* wrong with you these days?' Robert asked, deeply concerned. 'Why are you always so edgy and crabby?'

'It's the bloody War.' George stopped, thought, and corrected himself. 'No, that's not it – it's the way people are behaving. Good God, even Mother and Father are at it.'

'They have been for some time,' Robert said. 'Didn't you ever notice the funny things that used to happen during school holidays? You can't blame the War for that.'

'They're doing it quite openly now, though,' George

complained. 'I don't mind Mother and John Brandon so much, but Father and *Celia*.'

'You've never liked her, have you?'

Taking time to think, George said, 'There's something bad there. I can't get it out of my head that she has some sort of hold over Father.'

'Try seeing the irony of it all,' Robert suggested. 'These people acting like alley cats would be the first to condemn us. Rich, don't you think?'

'More than condemn – we could be locked up, even though we don't actually indulge in buggery as such.'

'Being slightly fastidious wouldn't save us,' Robert agreed, pulling a mock-solemn face. 'Even so, we must fight to preserve democracy and hypocrisy.'

'What a ghastly mess,' George muttered.

On 9 July 1943, a powerful British and American force invaded Sicily. Within two weeks, when the Allies were poised for an attack on the Italian mainland across the Straits of Messina, hysteria gripped Rome and Mussolini was thrown into prison. The new Government declared its intention of fighting on alongside Germany, but Fascism appeared to have had its day. From intelligence sources, Edward learned that Prince Umberto had disappeared from public view a few days after Mussolini's arrest. There was no definite news, least of all concerning Arabella; Ursula and Celia waited and hoped, refusing to admit that it was hopeless.

To stiffen the notoriously inept Italian forces, Hitler rushed extra troops into the peninsula. Only at Monte Cassino were the Germans able to make an effective stand – and that after wrecking Naples and exposing themselves to revenge attacks by their so-called friends. By February 1944, when only a temporary stalemate was preventing the fall of Rome, Douglas was sent home, unharmed, now a major, and with a bar to his Military Cross. Granted a month's leave and a transit posting back to Salisbury Plain, he had been promised a place in the 'big one'. After talking to Edward and learning something about 'Operation Overlord', Douglas went to collect Sophie Scott-Thomas from her home in Dorset. They spent a week in Cornwall, snug in an hotel that seemed unaware of rationing, then returned to hide themselves at the Castle.

They found the peace and quiet of Compton Allardyce in tatters. The Royal Army Service Corps, with expert help from the Royal Artillery and a detachment of American Marine Gunners, were turning the Park into a vast ammunition dump. Annaliese, accepting that requisition was inevitable and thankful that the interior of her home was to be spared, tried to pretend that she didn't mind as acre after acre of turf, untouched for two hundred years, was ploughed up by the incessant comings and goings of lorries and vehicles with caterpillar tracks.

The main stores were in the woods, where the stacks of shells and metal boxes were covered with tarpaulins, then shrouded by camouflage netting strung between the bare, winter trees. To reach John Brandon's house in mid-March, Annaliese walked through a landscape that was unrecognisable and menacing: was this how it had been behind the lines on the Western Front nearly thirty years ago?

'You realise that we're surrounded by enough high explosive to blow us and most of Wiltshire to kingdom come?' John said as they snuggled into bed.

'Yes, I worked that out for myself,' Annaliese replied. 'Especially when I heard about the ack-ack guns.'

The minor road that ran along the northern boundary of the Park had been closed to all civilian traffic and was now the site of three substantial anti-aircraft batteries.

'Purely a formality,' John said. 'The RAF has such a grip

on things that Jerry would never get an aircraft within five miles of the south coast.'

Annaliese sighed. 'I've trusted you for long enough, so I'd better carry on. But if I lose so much as one single pane of glass, look out!'

John was proved right. The only disturbance came from the RASC who, having packed the woods with ammunition, brought in excavators to dig trenches in the western half of the Park and buried thousands more boxes.

The activity carried on until the evening of 28 May. At midnight, two hours after total silence had descended for the first time in over three months, Douglas asked Matthew to drive Sophie back to her parents and took his leave of Annaliese and Edward.

'We're off to the seaside tomorrow,' Douglas joked. 'I'll send you a postcard from France.'

Not sure what came over her, Annaliese made a fuss of Douglas, telling him to take care of himself.

'Don't be silly, Mother,' he laughed, crushing her in a fierce hug. 'After what I've been through, this will be a doddle. The Germans have given up trying to knock my block off.'

When Douglas had hurtled off in his red MG, Edward said, 'He's probably right. The planning for this has been phenomenal.'

'Is this the invasion of France?' Annaliese asked. 'Dunkirk in reverse?'

'That's the general idea.'

'It doesn't seem possible.'

Edward shrugged. 'We'll see,' he said, strangely enigmatic.

Not surprisingly, neither the wireless nor the newspapers had so much as a whisper of what was about to happen. However, Annaliese received a message from the Princess

Royal to cancel visits she had arranged in the Portsmouth area for 3 and 4 June. All roads were expected to be jammed and train services badly disrupted or suspended. At lunch-time on 5 June, John Brandon returned from a visit to an estate pensioner, who now lived in a village near Shaftesbury, with the news that everything south of a line from Eastleigh, near Southampton, to Yeovil was sealed off.

Next morning, news bulletins announced that the liberation of France was under way. During the night, a mighty armada of 4,000 ships had converged on the beaches of Normandy to land a British and American Army under the overall command of General Eisenhower. Because the Allies had absolute air and naval supremacy in the Channel and had sprung a tremendous surprise on the enemy, the landings were proceeding even better than expected. By nightfall, 130,000 men were ashore: casualties were reported to be exceptionally light for such a dangerous mission. When maps appeared in the newspapers on 7 June, Edward said that the invasion had been launched across the beaches from which William the Conqueror had sailed in 1066. He added that George, who was now in charge of the entire department he had joined as a dogsbody in 1940, had played an important part in the planning. Annaliese was delighted.

On 10 June, a convoy of lorries began to move the stockpiled ammunition from the Park to Swanage. A brigadier arrived to explain what was happening and to thank Annaliese for her forebearance. 'We're loading this stuff onto barges and towing it across,' he said. 'The Channel's like a mill-pond and there's not a German to be seen.'

'It really is going as well as that?' Annaliese asked.

'Absolutely. To be honest, Lady Lincolnshire, we can hardly believe our luck.' The brigadier waved his stick at the mayhem in the Park which they were observing from the Long Gallery. 'In the worst case, we were expecting to shift this lot at night.

As things have worked out, we can do as we please. Makes life much easier, as I'm sure you'll appreciate.'

'I'm glad,' Annaliese said without conviction. She had supposed that clearing the Park of the ammunition would be far less destructive than the original operation. Instead, exuberant haste was causing a great deal of damage. Annaliese was about to ask the brigadier whether it was necessary to uproot trees in order to defeat Hitler when Henrietta brought the telegram.

Douglas's charmed life had ended twelve hours after the first landings, on the evening of D-Day itself.

Almost simultaneously, in London, Edward was contacted by the War Office. It seemed that Douglas's tank, pressing forward to deal with an unexpectedly fierce pocket of enemy resistance, had taken a direct hit and exploded with ghastly consequences for all five men on board. It had happened at Creully, a village to the east of Bayeux.

When Edward telephoned Annaliese, they were like strangers because neither of them knew what to say. Whereas Edward had his emotions under the tight control that he imagined was expected of him, Annaliese was guilty at how very little she felt. Naturally, she was sorry for Douglas, but there was no sign of a mother's grief. Had she really disliked her elder son so much? Probably not – although there had been no question of love since that wretched prep school had transformed Douglas's natural confidence into overweening self-esteem. And there were deeper, more fatalistic forces at work in Annaliese's mind: what did one more death matter after all the misfortune that had befallen Europe and, more importantly, her family since Cousin Franz Ferdinand visited Sarajevo on that June Sunday in 1914?

In one of the awkward pauses, Annaliese asked, 'What will happen to Douglas? Will he be buried in France?'

'I imagine so,' Edward replied. 'It's normal practice. Should I try to get him brought home? It might be possible.'

'No, don't bother,' Annaliese said and was relieved when Edward, apparently not noticing her indifference, blundered into a halting account of what the War Office had told him about the action in which Douglas had died.

Finally, when they had run out of things to say, Annaliese asked, 'What about George? Does he know?'

'I doubt it.' Edward was wary. 'I'll make sure I see him this evening.'

'And Sophie,' Annaliese said. 'She ought to be told.'

'Leave it to me,' Edward volunteered. As they terminated the call, he wondered if Annaliese was glad that George was now the heir. If so, did she have the faintest inkling of the difficulties this was bound to create?

Returning from a boring, uneventful day at Boothby's, Celia was surprised to find Edward at Cadogan Square so early in the evening.

'What are you doing here at this hour?' she asked. 'Is the Foreign Office working part-time now the War's nearly won?'

Seething at her facetiously disagreeable tone, Edward went to the sideboard for a whisky and soda – an exceptionally strong one, Celia noticed. He drank deeply. In a cold, 'official' voice, he said, 'Douglas has been killed in action. We heard this morning.'

Afterwards, Celia wondered whether it was the starkly tragic news that rattled her, or that word *we*, excluding and somehow threatening. She said the first thing that came into her head and it was woefully inadequate. 'When? Where?'

Edward's anger was abrupt and terrible. 'Does it matter?' he roared. 'Is that all you're interested in, the petty, gory details? Aren't you *sorry*?'

Frightened, Celia said, 'Yes, of course I am. Very sorry indeed.'

Ashamed of his outburst, Edward fortified his drink. 'You must forgive me,' he muttered. 'To tell you the truth, Annaliese upset me. Rather badly. She didn't seem to care. Frankly, she was bloody callous. Dash it, the poor boy was her son, too.' Celia walked to a window to gaze into the Square, wondering what to say and do. When she turned back, Edward was in an armchair, hunched forward, elbows on knees. Utterly desolate, he had tears in his eyes. 'I never showed Douglas how much I cared for him,' he said tonelessly. 'He was my pride and joy, yet I couldn't tell him what he meant to me. Oh, we seemed to rub along all right, but it should have been so much better. *My* father always showed his love, why couldn't I?'

Speaking to himself, he was surprised when he looked up to discover Celia staring at him. She, deeply embarrassed and out of her depth, was appalled to see the way grief had aged Edward. Suddenly and shockingly, he looked every one of his fifty-four years – rather more, in fact.

'I'm sorry,' Celia said. 'I really am very sorry.' The words were empty and, rather than attempting to offer comfort, she was backing away from Edward.

'George will be here soon.' With a painful effort, Edward pulled himself together. 'He promised not to be too late.' The resolution went and he was distracted. 'Funny thing was, he never asked why I wanted to see him. Actually, while I was on the telephone, it sounded as if he was in the middle of a party. They were having a beano, I suppose, celebrating the way the invasion's gone.'

'Well, if you have to talk to George, you won't want me in the way.' Celia was edging towards the door.

'That might be best,' Edward said. 'He'll take it badly. He won't like being my heir. You see, he's . . .' As if snapping out of a dream, he shut up, glaring at Celia with renewed hostility.

She, concerned only to escape, failed to realise that Edward had pulled himself back from the brink of a revelation. 'I'll go to Ursula's,' Celia said. 'Perhaps I'll see you tomorrow?'

Edward waved a hand dismissively.

An hour later, after one look at Celia, Ursula asked, 'Whatever has happened?'

'Edward's son, the elder one, Douglas, was killed on D-Day.'

'How awful.' Ursula frowned. 'Shouldn't you be with him? He needs comfort, surely?'

'No.' Celia was tormented, studying herself in the mirror on the hall-stand. 'What can I do? I hardly knew Douglas. I think it's all over, Ursula. It's come sooner than I thought.'

'Did Edward say so?'

'No, there was no need, I could see it. I've lost my hold over him.'

'As easily as that?' Ursula asked.

'If you call losing a son *easy*, then, yes!' Celia snapped. After a pause, she was more controlled. 'The thing is, Ursula, Edward and I both know that I can't expose him now. The War and time have changed everything.'

In fact, her assessment proved to be accurate but pre-mature. After staying away from Cadogan Square for a week, Celia returned with the intention of moving some of her clothes to Putney Vale. Although she had chosen a time when Edward should have been in the House of Lords, he was at home, poring over a stack of official documents. Work was immediately cast aside so that he could bundle Celia into bed and use her with a savage vigour that was at odds with his careworn appearance. Afterwards, when she tried to refuse payment, he became angry. She took the money to silence him, fearful of what an eavesdropping servant might pick up, and fled.

Ten days later, Ursula had a message when Celia came in from work. 'Edward telephoned. He wants you at Cadogan Square this evening. Nine o'clock sharp.'

'How did he sound?' Celia asked apprehensively.

'I'd say you were in for a busy night,' Ursula replied drily.

Robert Chappell went across to Normandy on 25 June with a hand-picked bunch of RAF technicians. They spent two weeks setting up radar stations to protect the Allied advance, then returned to Plymouth courtesy of the Royal Navy. Before catching an early morning train to London, Robert used the military telephone office at Millbay to leave a message at the War Office for George.

He was waiting at Paddington. In a relatively quiet corner of the buffet, Robert learned of Douglas's death. Eventually, when further sympathy was futile, Robert said, 'You're the Marquess of Axholme.'

'Yes.'

'The next Duke of Lincolnshire.'

'Yes.'

They stared at each other uneasily for several moments.

'Father's taken it badly,' George said.

'Bound to. What about your mother?'

'Doesn't seem to care all that much.' George was clearly distressed by Annaliese's lack of feeling. 'She's started harping on about Vienna and what her people – the Habsburgs – had to put up with in the old days.' After shaking his head in bewilderment, George added, 'It looks as though I worry Father. I had a lecture about being *careful*.'

'He knows about us?' Robert asked.

George shook his head, still unsure of what, if anything, Edward had said. 'I don't know. It was a funny do. He was like a chap trying to walk on eggshells – over-subtle hints that didn't get anywhere – never looked me in the eye.'

'Mmm.' Robert rubbed his chin. 'This means you'll have to get married.'

George was aghast. 'Have you gone mad?' he whispered indignantly.

'Not in the least.'

'Why should *I* want to marry?' George asked.

'To provide the next heir, the Duke after you.'

George shook his head vehemently. 'To hell with that. Someone else can have the damned title.'

'Who?'

'I don't know,' George blustered. 'There's bound to be somebody.'

'There isn't,' Robert said quietly. 'I've been close to your family for a long time, Georgie, and I know the score. There simply *isn't* anyone else. Unless you do something about it, the title will die with you.'

'It will have to,' George retorted. 'Father won't mind – he never wanted it in the first place.'

'I'll buy that,' Robert said. 'But what about your mother? *She* might have a few things to say.'

George was horrified. 'You're right,' he muttered.

They had to break off while a waitress cleared the accumulation of dirty crockery. When she had finally departed, Robert leaned across the table and said, 'There's nothing to worry about. Chaps like us *do* get married and have children.'

Dispiritedly, George nodded. By keeping his ears open and his face blank, he had learned a great deal at the War Office: the mess existed on talk of sexual misdemeanours and abnormalities.

'Something will be *arranged*,' Robert said. 'Blimey, for a chap with your prospects, finding a suitable woman should be a piece of cake. The aristocracy have been dealing with things like this for centuries.'

'And I'll still have you?' George asked desperately.

'Yes. And there's Oxford, remember. You won't be expected to marry until you've graduated.'

'Oxford!' The thought lifted George. 'It can't come soon enough. When's the war going to be over, Bobbie?'

Robert laughed. 'Haven't the big cheeses at the War Office told you?' Serious again, he said, 'It's going very well in France. There's talk of it all being over in a few months. We shall go to Oxford next year.'

There were times – particularly after the disastrous setback at Arnhem – when George cursed Robert for foolish optimism. Following the liberation of Paris at the end of August 1944, each week that passed made it brutally clear that the worst was yet to come, that Nazi Germany would fight to the last man. In addition to the desperate and prolonged fighting in Europe, the blitz on south-eastern England was renewed with V1 and V2 rockets, and calling them doodle-bugs did nothing to lessen their terror.

In 1918, the Great War had ended with not a single representative of the victorious nations standing on German soil. Annaliese, who had commented on this strange fact at the time, saw that things were to be very different in 1945. Three huge armies were advancing on Hitler's Third Reich and their ultimate target was Berlin. The Anglo-American force that had liberated France pressed on into Belgium and Holland. A new American contingent had landed in Southern France and was moving up the Rhône valley, picking up French recruits as it went. Finally, and most portentously, the Russians were bearing down from the east.

During the last February of the War, Celia listened to Edward's predictions on the consequences of allowing the Russians into Poland and East Germany. Although the men round the dinner-table were inclined to share Edward's views,

Celia was disinterested. Not only did she regard the forecasts as unduly dire, she was acutely conscious that her reign as mistress of Cadogan Square was drawing to its close.

She still had a tenuous grasp in the aftermath of VE Day, 8 May, largely because the immense relief at the end of the War produced chaos. The country indulged in an orgy of celebration during which no one cared what happened next and, mysteriously, Annaliese had shut herself away at Compton Allardyce, even refusing telephone calls. For three weeks, Celia was with Edward constantly, acting as hostess at Cadogan Square and accompanying him to other people's parties. After the nights, during which Celia openly shared in passion that had acquired a strangely valedictory quality, money was neither offered nor requested.

The bubble burst with the unexpectedly sudden resumption of domestic political hostility, shelved for the duration of the War. The Labour Party refused to continue the coalition until victory against Japan had been secured and a General Election was called for 5 July. Edward fretted throughout the campaign, fearing that the Conservatives were inexcusably complacent. That was certainly true of Churchill, who was far too busy with pressing international issues to bother with the squalid business of electioneering.

The outcome reduced Edward to ashen silence for two hours. Not only had the voters rejected Churchill, they had done so crushingly. The new Labour Government, headed by Attlee, had an overall Commons majority of 146. Much later, Edward came to understand the many complex forces that had boiled up to produce the result, but for several weeks after the event he remained numb. While he nursed his bitterness at the treachery of the British public and his removal from the Foreign Office, Celia took herself out of his life. Warmly welcomed back by Ursula as a permanent fixture at Putney Vale, she wasted no time in trying to make plans for the future.

'Edward thinks England's had it. According to him, Attlee and his crowd will succeed where the Kaiser and Hitler failed.'

Ursula chuckled indulgently. 'You can hardly regard that as an impartial assessment. Edward's views are somewhat right-wing.'

'He loathes Socialism,' Celia conceded, 'and he can be amazingly pigheaded. But, for all his faults, he's invariably right about these things.'

'So, what are you suggesting?' Ursula asked.

'I was wondering whether we ought to clear off out of it.'

'Where?'

'The South of France.' Briefly, Celia's eyes sparkled. 'The Côte d'Azur is *paradise*.' Remembering her wretched impediment, she added, 'Can you speak the language?'

'Yes – reasonably well, as a matter of fact.' Ursula was abstracted, gazing into space. 'Isn't France going to be an unhappy place?'

'Why?' Celia was baffled.

'My dear, an awful lot of them collaborated with the Nazis. I think that the first two or three years of peace will be quite trying – there must be an awful lot of scores to settle. Perhaps we could wait for a while to see what happens.'

Celia realised that Ursula had not given up all hope that Arabella was still alive and would turn up at Putney Vale in time for tea one day. 'We can make plans,' she said.

'Why not?' Ursula replied. 'I take it that you've finished with your "family"?'

'Yes – apart from Boothby's. If the Government is going to soak the rich the auction business will boom.'

'Don't you have enough money?' Ursula asked.

'You can *never* have enough,' Celia said, stung by the implied suggestion of avarice. 'I'm forty-two now. Yes, I know I look a lot younger with the sun behind me, but my fortieth birthday was one of the things that got lost in the bloody War. If I'm lucky, I've still got ten good years, then it's all downhill. I intend to have a very comfortable old age.'

George and Robert were demobbed at the end of August, spent a week hiking round the Lake District and the rest of September at the Castle. They saw very little of Annaliese and made their eager preparations for Oxford with the distinctly reluctant and frosty help of Baskerville.

'Your father's butler doesn't care for us,' Robert said after an especially fraught encounter.

'He thought the world of Douglas,' George replied. 'I expect he regards me as a poor second best.' While Robert was wondering whether to risk saying that he thought Baskerville's animosity had other, deeper roots, George added, 'Anyway, to hell with him. He's due to retire soon, so we shan't have to put up with it for much longer.'

Inwardly, Robert cringed at George's ill-natured attitude. He told himself that things would look up when they got to university and there was time to come to terms with the implications of Douglas's death.

There was talk of Edward accompanying them to Oxford, combining a trip down memory lane with showing them where everything was but, to George's great relief, the idea was crushed by a startling event. Desiring to talk to Edward in comfort and privacy, Winston Churchill invited himself to lunch at Cadogan Square.

After the preliminary courtesies, prolonged by the great man's courtly eloquence, they settled down to aperitifs and Churchill began to work towards the reason for his visit.

'I have it in mind to write an account of the War,' he growled. 'Do the job properly, you know, before the *historians* get at it.'

Smiling at the wealth of meaning heaped on the word

'historians', Edward said, 'That sounds like a splendid idea, sir.'

'It is, isn't it?' Churchill mulled it over, as though for the first time, and nodded approvingly. 'Added to which, it will keep me occupied. Being the Leader of His Majesty's Loyal Opposition is scarcely a full-time job.'

'Not after what you've been used to,' Edward murmured.

'Hmm.' Momentarily, Churchill was wistful, recalling the eighteen-hour days, the despair, elation, and final rejection. 'The thing is,' he said, 'the venture has acquired powerful stimulus. A publisher is interested — nay, clamouring. Money has been mentioned!' He grinned mischievously. 'It will be a huge undertaking, a veritable *magnum opus* — six or seven volumes, nearly two million words. I shall need help.'

Edward floundered around in the ensuing silence. 'Me, sir?' he said at last.

'Precisely.' Churchill looked pleased with himself. 'Lord Ismay and General Pownall have promised to marshal the facts and no doubt they will be recruiting others. I'm told there are five tons of papers to be scrutinised.'

'That doesn't surprise me.' Edward prayed that he was not destined to be a glorified filing-clerk.

'But I want someone to assist with the writing,' Churchill went on. 'Make sense of my drafts, set things straight, whip it into shape.' He raised a hand to quell Edward's astonished objection. 'You're an expert. That position paper you did on India was a masterpiece and it was no flash in the pan. My inquiries have revealed that your work has always been outstanding.'

'I'm honoured, sir,' Edward murmured.

'Never mind that, will you do it?'

Playing for time, Edward asked, 'Have you given any thought as to how it would be organised?'

'Of course I have.' Churchill was mildly offended by the

very idea that he had not. 'The operations centre will be my house, Chartwell, near Westerham, in Kent. I would hope, indeed, *expect* that you would spend time as my guest so that we can liaise closely.' The eyes boring into Edward's twinkled with slightly malicious amusement. 'Like me, you're at a loose end, with no gainful employment. My spies tell me that you continue to detest your ducal possessions and that you are not an unduly uxorious man. Am I not offering you a lifeline?'

'Yes, sir, you are.' Edward was all smiles. 'And I accept.'

'Good. You won't regret it. Now, can we eat? My belly is grumbling.'

Edward rang for the meal and they moved to the table.

'I was sorry to hear about your boy, Douglas,' Churchill said. 'A brave fellow, by all accounts.'

'Slightly foolhardy, though. It may have been his undoing.'

'Shame! They tell me the other one has brains.'

'Yes, George is very bright. He's gone up to Oxford today.'

Churchill, already preoccupied with soup, did not notice that Edward's pride in his surviving son rubbed shoulders with anxiety.

The whole of Annaliese's attention was fixed on one thing only.

Three weeks before VE Day, she had received a piece of news that made her seek an interview with the Princess Royal.

'I'd like to be released from my duties, ma'am. Immediately, I'm afraid. I wouldn't ask if it weren't very serious.'

'Annaliese, my dear, I understand that,' Princess Mary replied. 'Do you want to tell me about it? Can I help?'

'That's kind of you, but no, there's nothing anyone else can do.'

'Well, please go and attend to whatever it is. And thank you for all your splendid efforts.'

After Annaliese's departure, the Princess Royal was curious, wondering what had caused such desperation in the woman who seemed hardly to have noticed the death of her son.

For some months, John Brandon had been unwell, losing weight and enduring considerably more pain than he was prepared to admit. Now, a visit to a specialist at the hospital in Marlborough confirmed that he had stomach cancer. When he and Annaliese confronted the truth, it was decided not to risk surgery.

'It doesn't often do any good,' John said, 'and the doctor gave me the distinct impression that it could finish me off sooner.'

'I'm staying here to look after you,' Annaliese said. 'I shan't go away again.' She did not ask if any time limit had been put on what was left of his life.

'If possible, I don't want to be carted off to hospital,' John said.

'You certainly won't be,' Annaliese promised.

At the beginning of October, Edward's announcement that he would be working for Churchill and spending most of his time in Kent was a blessed relief.

9

1946
'...our own little piece of Austria'

John Brandon passed away on 13 February. Instead of coming like a thief in the night, death was benign and took him during the morning, when his bedroom was aglow with the bright sun of an unseasonably mild day. He was within a few weeks of his sixty-eighth birthday.

Shortly before he went, John drifted out of the drugged stupor that had made his last two weeks bearable. Blinking at the sun, he saw that they were all there, Gwen, Henrietta, the fifteen-year-old Athene, and Annaliese — the four who had seen him through.

'Serious, eh?' John whispered, smiling weakly.

'Whatever gives you that silly idea?' Annaliese took his hand.

'You've never been here *together* before.'

'Pure coincidence,' Annaliese said. 'Henrietta and I got our times mixed up.'

John, ignoring the white lie, lifted her fingers to his pinched, bloodless lips. 'Thank you,' he said. 'For everything.'

He closed his eyes and drifted away. Continuing to hold his hand, Annaliese was aware of the last moment. She turned to the others, nodded, and they filed out, leaving her alone with him.

Later, Gwen and Athene stayed at the house in Gainsborough Wood to wait for the doctor and undertaker while Henrietta walked back to the Castle with Annaliese. When they reached the Park's main, diagonal road, Annaliese paused to look round.

'What a shambles,' she said, referring to the mess left by the Army. 'John was going to put it right this year. He hated leaving it like this.'

Quietly, Henrietta said, 'What he hated most was leaving you.'

'Come along, there are things to do.' Annaliese was brisk, determined not to give way to tears until she was alone.

During his twenty years at Compton Allardyce, John Brandon had earned the respect of people far beyond the confines of the estate and village. Consequently, his funeral was extremely well-attended. The hardship and uncertainty of the times also had a bearing on the large turn-out; with hopes of a post-war miracle already scotched, it was a pleasure to celebrate the life of a man who had done so much good. Even Edward, without being asked to do so, tore himself away from Churchill's book for two days. The only notable absentee was Celia, her perfectly valid excuse being that she had to look after Boothby's in the absence of Beatrice, who had decided to spend a week in Wiltshire.

The potent symbolism of the occasion was not lost on Annaliese and Edward, both now parted from their lovers. What did the future hold? Every time they looked at each other, they turned away inconclusively, Edward continuing to mourn Douglas and regret Annaliese's inability to share his sadness.

After the ceremony in the village church, the congregation went to the Castle for the traditional gathering in the Long Gallery and a buffet that defied rationing.

Annaliese's first duty was an acute embarrassment: she had to offer proper condolences to Clementine Prideaux for the death of her husband – *twelve months ago!* When Hubert, the Seventh Duke of Laverstoke, had died early in 1945, Annaliese had been away on a ten-day morale-boosting tour of ATS units in Scotland. Other busy confusion had followed, then came the self-imposed exile of nursing John. Annaliese had scribbled a note of sympathy, but never spoken to Clementine – even though the Dowager Duchess, as she now was, often popped into Compton Allardyce to see Athene.

'Come with me,' Annaliese whispered, grabbing Edward's arm. 'She won't eat me alive if you're there.'

'Don't be silly,' Edward replied, welcoming a chance to be comfortably affectionate. 'Her bark's infinitely worse than her bite and she has a soft spot for you.'

'I am trying to believe that,' Annaliese said as they headed for the corner in which Clementine was holding forth to a group that included her eldest son and his wife, the new Duke and Duchess of Laverstoke.

'What ho, Annaliese,' Clementine said equably. 'You don't mind me rolling up, I hope?'

'Of course not. I . . .'

'Hell of a shame about John Brandon. He was a thoroughly good sort. I must say, you gave him a very decent send off.'

'Thank you. I . . .'

'You know my boy, Piers, and his wife, Rachel, I suppose?'

'Yes, we met at the coronation, didn't we?'

'Far too long ago,' Piers smiled. He was very like his father, handsome, urbane, and a gentleman to his fingertips.

Annaliese shook hands and Edward joined in the civilities, welcoming his fellow-duke. The hangers-on, overwhelmed by such a concentration of aristocracy, were fading away.

'Rachel was a Hawksworth before Piers grabbed her,' Clementine announced. 'She knows the Timberlakes.'

'Athene doesn't much care for them,' Edward said, proud of his surrogate daughter. 'Not that they want anything to do with her.'

'The feeling's mutual, though,' Piers chucked. 'My niece is quite rude about her distaff side.'

While Annaliese was curbing the urge to kick Piers, Edward's face was a picture. 'Your *niece*?' he said.

'Yes, she's brother Desmond's daughter.' It was Piers's turn to look flabbergasted. 'I say, didn't you know?'

Clementine clapped her hands in delight. 'That *is* impressive, damn me if it isn't. Honestly, Annaliese, when we agreed to keep mum, I never imagined you wouldn't even tell Edward. What a hoot.'

'Well – it slipped my mind,' Annaliese pleaded.

'No, it didn't,' Edward said, recovered from the shock and smiling. 'You imagined I'd disapprove. She always thinks the worst of me.' Lowering his voice, he asked, 'Does Athene know who her father is?'

'Of course,' Clementine said scornfully. 'Henrietta told her ages ago.'

'And what does Athene think about it?' Edward asked.

'Very little,' Clementine said in a way that showed her approval of the girl's point of view.

Nonplussed, Edward decided to take Piers away to canvass his views on the Government.

'What a good mood we're in at the moment,' Clementine said, softly and sweetly.

'That's what working for Churchill does for you,' Annaliese said and grabbed at her original purpose. 'Clem, I never told you how sorry I was about Hubert. I dread what you must think of me.'

Clementine shrugged. 'We've all been very busy – the War and everything. Don't worry.'

'How did it happen?' Annaliese asked diffidently.

'He keeled over after a good dinner,' Clementine said. 'Ticker packed in. There's no need to be upset, my dear, he was eighty-one and he'd had a sight more fun that most – *I* made sure of it.' Without pausing for breath, she skated to a different subject. 'The Park's in a *shocking* state. I hope the Government are paying for it to be put right?'

'They say so, but only after we've done the work.'

'Bloody typical,' Clementine snorted. 'How are you going to organise it?'

'I've no idea. You see, with John dying, I . . .' To her dismay, Annaliese was biting back tears.

Clementine took charge. 'Let's get away from this lot. Come on, no one will mind. Do your stuff, Rachel, create a diversion.'

The young Duchess of Laverstoke went into action like a seasoned campaigner, dropping a plate of sandwiches, breaking a glass, and simulating apologetic hysterics. People rushed to help. In the confusion, Annaliese and Clementine slipped away.

When they were hidden in the private sitting-room in the West Wing, Clementine said, 'You really were fond of our Major Brandon, weren't you?'

'Tremendously!' Annaliese said. 'I don't know what I'm going to do without him.'

'You'll be a fool if you try,' Clementine replied. 'Let's deal with the Park first. You aren't entertaining hopes of organising it yourself?'

'What alternative is there?'

'Find yourself a new estate manager, of course,' Clementine said as though talking to a simpleton. 'It isn't just the Park, is it? All your other properties will need attention. *You* can't do that. Not the way the Lincolnshires are endowed – you've got stuff all over the country.'

'How do I find the right man?' Annaliese asked. 'Advertise?'

'Only if you want to be inundated with incompetents,' Clementine replied. 'No, let Piers find you someone. He's got good contacts and he can spot a wrong 'un a mile off.'

'Very well,' Annaliese agreed. Feeling sorry for herself, she added, 'Edward should be looking after this, but he won't. He's less interested in the estate than when we arrived, twenty years ago.'

'I imagine that he lacks interest in other things, as well.' Clementine's hard stare made her meaning plain. Taking Annaliese's mortified silence as agreement, she pressed on. 'So, you'll need another man for *that*. I doubt you'll be able to combine the two again. Unwise to try.'

Annaliese was floundering for words. Eventually, laughing nervously, she managed, 'I don't think I need to bother with that, Clem, not at my age.'

'Stuff and absolute bloody nonsense!' It was an eruption of hilarity, not anger. At once, Clementine was earnest. 'If you're anything like me, my dear, you'll find that you've taken on a new lease of life at fifty – once you've finished with that ghastly ovulation business.'

Thoughtfully, remembering her visit to Portugal in 1925, Annaliese said, 'My mother told me that.'

'She was right. Hubert and I had tremendous fun. As a matter of fact, the poor old chap often said I was digging his grave. But he always came back for more and it's much the best way to go.'

'And where do I find this man?' Annaliese asked, treating it as a joke.

'Nancy Shenstone?'

'Why suggest her?' Annaliese was all innocence.

Clementine raised her eyebrows. 'Do you imagine I'm wet behind the ears? I'll lay you a hundred pounds to a penny that she introduced you to John Brandon.'

'Yes, you're right,' Annaliese admitted.

'She's here, isn't she?'

'Staying for a few nights,' Annaliese said.

'It's an ideal opportunity. Talk to her.'

'I'll see.' Annaliese was far from convinced. 'It's too soon after John.'

'Mourn by all means,' Clementine said. 'But don't overdo it. Those ravishing looks of yours need nurturing.' After pausing for effect, she added, 'You'll notice that I haven't mentioned Celia.'

'From what I can gather, she and Edward have gone their separate ways,' Annaliese replied.

'Splendid.' Clementine beamed approvingly. 'Not that anyone gave a damn during the War. Different now, though: peace and austerity seem to be breeding moral bigotry. Bear that in mind, my dear.'

Edward set out for Chartwell after lunch the following day, leaving Annaliese, Nancy, Beatrice and Charles Templeton in the West Wing's rather grand drawing-room.

Annaliese gazed out of the windows, despondent at the heavy rain that had started at dawn and showed no sign of easing. 'I wanted to go for a walk,' she said.

'Forget it,' Nancy replied. 'When I want pneumonia, I'll order it from Harrods.' Suddenly, her manner changed from brash confidence to nervousness. 'Actually, can we just ignore the weather and stay here? There's something I have to tell you and I guess this is as good a time as any.'

Assuming that it was not for his ears, the ever-tactful Charles stood up, murmuring excuses and hoping that Beatrice would support him. Nancy shook her head. 'No.

Please stay, Charles. I'm gonna need your help. Er – how about some more coffee?'

Beatrice busied herself with the jugs and Nancy went for a walk round the room, admiring ornaments and paintings, doing her utmost to avoid the subject she wanted to raise.

Tired of waiting, Annaliese said, 'Spit it out, Nancy.'

'Yes. Right.' Nancy resumed her seat and faced Annaliese. 'The fact is, I've had it with this country.'

'I don't understand.' Annaliese looked blank.

'It's turned into a hell-hole of misery. It's worse now than when the War was on, but at least there was a reason for it then. What's wrong with the Brits?'

'Nancy, I have no idea what you're talking about,' Annaliese insisted.

'Of course you don't. You haven't stirred from this place since last spring. You've been looking after John. That's great and I understand it, but you're in for a shock when you go to London. Honey, it is *terrible*.'

Puzzled, Annaliese looked at Beatrice and Charles. They both nodded. Beatrice said, 'I'm afraid Nancy's right.'

'Every last ounce of spirit has gone down the tubes,' Nancy went on. 'For instance, I and the other citizens of Belgravia haven't had our trash shifted for five weeks. Why? Because the dustmen are on strike – on *strike*, would you believe? Unless I'm very much mistaken, this happy state of affairs extends into Bond Street, to Boothby's, for Christ's sake.'

Again, Beatrice nodded.

'And to cap it all, there's that creep, Attlee.' Nancy was outraged now. 'Did you know that the Constitution of the United States has a clause that says the pursuit of human happiness is an OK thing? No, well, Attlee hasn't heard that one, either. Also, I am getting a teensy-weensy bit tired of his ideas on taxation, and finally, I am asking myself why England *enjoys* being so miserable!'

Still not understanding, Annaliese said, 'Nancy, what *are* you going on about?'

Nancy's anger evaporated and she took a deep breath. 'Honey, I'm packing up and going back to the States. Permanent!'

'Oh, no, you can't do that.' Annaliese spoke as if humouring a child. 'You've been here nearly forty years. I know you visited America a good deal before the War, but that doesn't mean anything. You don't know anyone over there.'

'Wrong,' Nancy said, realising that it was going to be difficult. 'I've kept all my old contacts and made friends with most of their kids. I'd be very welcome in all sorts of places. They want me in Washington.'

A vision of Nancy, happy as she manipulated a web of powerful men and women brought the truth home to Annaliese. 'What will you do with Martha's Vineyard?' she asked.

'Sell it.' Nancy shifted her gaze. 'That's where you come in, Charles. Would you advise me, please?'

'Yes, I can find you the right agent to handle such . . .' Charles hesitated '. . . an esoteric property.'

Nancy smiled. She remembered the time, nearly thirty years ago, when her unique type of hospitality had paved the way for Beatrice and Charles to become lovers.

'Oh, Nancy, are you sure of this?' Annaliese asked, a note of desperation entering her voice.

'Yes, I am.' Nancy was sad but resolute. 'Uncle Sam wants me back, honey, and I've gotta go. Hell, if I hang round here much longer, I'll be getting an old-age pension.'

'Rubbish.'

'Annaliese, I am fifty-nine years of age.' Nancy saw the admiration on Charles's face and laughed. 'I know, ain't I simply marvellous! But time's running out. If I blow this, they won't ask me again.'

Uneasily aware of Annaliese's mounting distress, Charles asked, 'What about the transfer of your funds to America, Nancy? May I be of assistance?'

'That's kind of you. It may not be too easy, huh?'

'Let's say *complicated*,' Charles replied. 'The Government's currency restrictions are a bit of a beast. Can I suggest that Nigel looks after it for you? He's made a study of the rules *and* he has good contacts in the States with Morgan's and Chase.'

'Sounds great,' Nancy said.

She had a soft spot for Charles's son, now thirty-five and re-establishing himself at Templeton's after spending the War as an RAF bomber pilot. He was expected to take control of the bank at any time: now that he was sixty, Charles's hints about his retirement were becoming increasingly frequent. Nigel, who had long since cast off the self-conscious timidity induced in childhood by his wayward mother, was one of London's most eligible bachelors.

'So, you won't be going tomorrow?' Annaliese asked peevishly.

Nancy laughed, trying to ease the tension. 'How can I? I'll be lucky to get out in under six months.'

'Well, *that's* something to be grateful for, I suppose,' Annaliese said.

On the pretext of needing a post-lunch nap, Beatrice and Charles excused themselves, leaving Annaliese to come to terms with the imminent loss of a good friend.

'One can't help feeling that Nancy's decision is unfortunate,' Charles said. 'Following John so closely, it must be a big blow to Annaliese.'

'Yes, I'm afraid so,' Beatrice replied. 'Is Nancy right about the mess we're in?'

'Yes, she is. Things look pretty bad.'

'And you don't believe that Attlee and company are the right people to sort things out?'

'I fear not,' Charles sighed. 'They're wasting far too much time on ideological claptrap and nineteenth-century sacred cows instead of tackling the issues that matter.'

'Gosh!' Beatrice was overawed by what was, for Charles, extraordinarily strong language. Then, after a few moments' thought, she added, 'Annaliese's in a funny mood these days.'

'Mmm.' Charles's seemingly noncommittal grunt was, Beatrice understood, agreement. 'She's out of touch, don't you think? Sort of drifting?'

'And what does that mean?'

'We tend to lose sight of the fact that she used to be a European and a Habsburg,' Charles replied. 'She's been awfully British for twenty years, but perhaps she's going back to her origins.'

'Why should that be?' Beatrice asked.

'Probably the War,' Charles said. 'We saw it as the Blitz, the Battle of Britain, El Alamein, and D-Day. Annaliese looked at things from a very different point of view.'

'She claimed to be bored by it.'

Charles laughed. 'That was an act, darling. You can bet your boots that Annaliese was interested in everything that happened.'

'Including Austria?' Beatrice suggested.

'*Especially* Austria,' Charles said.

In the eight months since the end of the War, Annaliese had been tormented by conflicting, wholly incompatible demands. Although she dared not leave John for longer than a day, she was impatient to visit her mother. There was no particular cause for concern, other than the passage of time. The regular flow of letters between 1939 and 1945, including those from Max, indicated that Elsa remained in good health. With Franco firmly in control, Spain was quiet, and Edward's predictions about Portugal's neutrality had proved accurate.

Given the facts about John's plight, Elsa wrote back with instructions not to worry about her. *You must stay with your dear friend until the matter is resolved. I am very patient.*

Well, the matter was 'resolved' now that John's suffering was over and Annaliese flew to Lisbon on 22 February. She travelled alone after informing Edward that she had no idea when she would return.

The contrast between a wretched, rain-shrouded Croydon and a colourfully verdant country enjoying weather that suggested an English May was a reminder of Nancy's criticisms: *did* the British enjoy wallowing in misery?

Neutrality had made Lisbon an important crossroads for international travel and the airport terminal buildings were far grander than the makeshift arrangements of 1938. Entering the arrivals area from Customs, Annaliese halted, momentarily bewildered and anxious; Elsa's letter had been vague as to who might meet her.

She spotted the man as he detached himself from the crowd and marched towards her. Tall, broad-shouldered, and extremely good-looking, he wore a grey suit and shoes that gleamed. The chauffeur's cap tucked under one arm was, Annaliese guessed, never worn: immaculate though he was, this man loathed anything that suggested a uniform.

Bowing stiffly, he spoke in German. 'Welcome, Your Imperial Highness. I trust you had a satisfactory journey?'

'I did.' Annaliese studied him closely, deciding that he might be thirty-five but could be ten years older than that. 'You are?'

'Kurt Schneider, Highness.'

She raked through her memories of Elsa's letters, trying to recall what had happened at the villa during the War. 'Ludwig's grandson?' she said.

'That is correct.' He relieved the porter of the trolley carrying Annaliese's luggage. 'This way, please, Highness.'

The car was a French Citroen, much more modest than the huge Mercedes favoured by Joseph and driven with such panache by Ludwig Schneider, one of the ex-Imperial Guards who had gone into exile with Annaliese's parents in 1919.

Annaliese sat in the front beside Kurt. 'When did you arrive in Portugal?' she asked.

'In the summer of 1944. I did not know it, but my grandfather had died the previous year. Her Highness, your mother, was gracious enough to offer me a position and a home. She is very kind.'

'What brought you here?' Annaliese asked.

As he negotiated the maze of streets that would bring them to the main road that led to Cascais, Kurt Schneider spoke of being uprooted from Salzburg, where he was working in the autumn of 1939, sent to Vienna and then Dresden to be conscripted into Hitler's *Wehrmacht*. He had taken part in the Ardennes offensive that had precipitated Dunkirk and the fall of France. Then, he was in the first wave of Operation Barbarossa, the attack on Russia in 1941. Annaliese's requests for details of the campaign were met with polite but implacable refusal. All that Kurt would say was that he considered himself incredibly lucky to have lived through nearly two years *and* been sent back to France to be part of a small garrison at Poitiers. It was a comfortable posting, one for a man who was forty-one and past his best, Kurt said with a flash of mordant, Austrian humour. Smiling politely at the quip, Annaliese was astonished to find herself calculating Kurt Schneider's age: he must be forty-four now, six years younger than herself.

One night, Kurt and his two comrades, also from Vienna and survivors of the Russian front, had stolen a staff car and deserted, driving south. Reaching the unoccupied sector of France, they gave themselves up to a Resistance unit. The leader, grateful for three authentic German uniforms and sets of documents, had escorted Kurt and his friends to the Pyrenees. They crossed into Spain and made their way to the isolated enclave of three villas on the hill above Cascais.

'I was hoping my grandfather would help us,' Kurt

While Annaliese was pondering this, Kurt added, 'My friends, Ernst Weber, and Joachim Hassler are in the service of His Highness, Maximilian, and Herr Kondrashin. We are all honoured.'

'Your father,' Annaliese said, 'what about him?'

For a few moments, Kurt was in two minds whether to answer the question. He did so only to avoid the unpardonable sin of insolence to an Archduchess. 'He was a Nazi. He became a senior party official.'

'So did my brother,' Annaliese said quietly.

Kurt made no comment and silence descended. Staring straight ahead, ignoring the lush countryside, Annaliese had the feeling that she was being drawn back to Vienna, as it was before the First World War. Compton Allardyce and her life as the Duchess of Lincolnshire ceased to exist and, for a few magical minutes, it was as if that last summer of 1914 had gone on forever. Closing her eyes, she imagined that Kurt was taking her to Schönbrunn and felt a happiness that touched her soul.

Waking from the fantasy, Annaliese found that they had arrived, were outside the villa. Kurt was gazing at her anxiously, summoning courage. 'I must tell you about Her Highness, your mother,' he said gently. 'She had a stroke in November – only a slight one. The recovery has been good, but you will see the effects.'

'She can walk? Speak?'

'Indeed, Highness. There is no great problem, but I thought you would like to be forewarned.'

She looked at his hands, resting on the steering-wheel.

They were big and strong, but expressively beautiful, hands such as Michaelangelo would have fashioned. Experiencing a strange compulsion to do so, Annaliese reached out to touch one of them. 'Thank you, Kurt,' she murmured. 'That was considerate of you.'

Quickly, relieving him of the obligation to attempt a response, she jumped out of the car.

The front door was open and she went in. The villa was cool and peaceful, perfumed by vases of flowers.

'In here, darling.' Elsa's voice from the lounge was unchanged, firm, clear, and much younger than her years. She was already standing when Annaliese dashed into the big, south-facing room and seemed to be using the walking-stick purely as an ornament.

'Mama!' Annaliese cried.

'Hello, my dearest.' Elsa laughed when Annaliese relaxed her fierce embrace. 'You'll break my poor old ribs.'

'How are you?'

'Pretty good. Did Kurt tell you about my little wobble?'

'Yes, he did. Sit down.' Over-solicitous, Annaliese helped Elsa back into the chair. 'It was very naughty of you not to let me know.'

'No it wasn't,' Elsa said flatly. 'Naughty would have been starting a panic that you couldn't do anything about. And don't be cross with Max. I know he was supposed to spy on me, but what *was* the poor man to do when you had enough problems of your own in England?'

'I must say, you don't look too bad.' Unwittingly, Annaliese sounded almost grudging.

'Thank you. What it is to have loved ones!'

'Oh, Mama, I'm sorry. Forgive me. You know what it's like when you've had a shock.'

'Of course.' Elsa put a finger to the left-hand corner of her mouth which was slightly lower than the right. 'I don't like this. It's improving all the time, though. I looked a terrible fright for the first two weeks. Don't gape, darling, sit down and tell me about the War. What was it like?'

Annaliese gave a scrappy, disjointed account of her work for the Princess Royal, what Edward had done, the shortages, and the blitz. Avoiding the issue of Douglas's death, Annaliese did not relax until Kurt appeared with coffee.

Noticing that Annaliese's eyes followed him when he left the room, Elsa said, 'He's a godsend. I don't know what would have become of me without him — Max and Vassily were in the same boat. Kurt and his friends arrived in the nick of time. All the men who came with us in 1920 were either dead or very ill.'

'Do you still keep other servants?' Annaliese asked.

'Not living-in,' Elsa replied. 'The three of us share two cleaning-women from the village and there's a cook four days a week. Kurt looks after everything. He taught himself Portuguese while he and his friends were walking here.'

As people will, they chatted as though they had never been apart, reviving gossip about people neither of them had seen or heard from for nearly thirty years. Then, at four o'clock, Elsa went to her room to lie down for a couple of hours. Annaliese unpacked, walked round the well-kept garden, and wandered into the kitchen where Kurt was helping the cook with dinner. In an apron and with his shirt sleeves rolled up, he contrived to look more powerfully masculine than ever.

'Yes, Highness?' Kurt asked pleasantly.

'Can I help?' Annaliese asked.

'Perhaps tomorrow when we are alone?' Kurt suggested. 'I don't think Your Highness should perform menial tasks in front of the locals. They do not understand these matters.'

Annaliese glanced at the dark-eyed woman from Cascais, who obviously did not speak a word of German. The cook smiled, curtsied, and carried on with her work. 'I shall observe the rules,' Annaliese said to Kurt.

Before she left the kitchen, the reborn Archduchess and the man who had risked his life to escape from the Nazis and enter the service of the Habsburgs exchanged knowing smiles.

On that first evening, Max and Vassily came to dinner. After greeting Annaliese, Vassily said, 'What a shame you did not bring your husband. Max and I are starved of informed opinion.'

Annaliese was taken aback by the realisation that it was little more than twelve hours since she had flown out of England, half a day in which she had forgotten everything she had left behind. Scraping a few ideas together, she said, 'Edward is very pessimistic about the future of Europe. He thinks that we shall see enormous changes – none of them for the better.'

'Wonderful. You see, Elsa, that's what I've been trying to tell you.' Vassily turned back to Annaliese. 'Your Mama believes that Europe has rid itself of all its devils and will become well-behaved and very dull.'

'Not if the Russians have anything to do with it,' Annaliese said.

'Just so.' Vassily beamed triumphantly. 'Hitler has bequeathed Russia to the world. What were they before he attacked them in 1941? A gang of half-baked Bolsheviks that no one took seriously. Now, they have captured Poland and nearly a third of Germany. Soon, they will have an atomic bomb.'

'Shut up, Vassily,' Elsa said affably. 'You'll spend what's left of your life here, so why worry about Europe? We're out of it.'

'Elsa, my darling, you know me. While pygmies fret over who is in bed with whom, I work out which country will go to war next.'

'It's fascinating, but Elsa's right,' Max laughed. 'We're well out of it, so let's forget it. Tell us about Douglas, Annaliese

— we were very sorry indeed to hear about him.'

With far more pride than she had been able to feel before, she gave details of Douglas's war record and what she knew of the action in which he had been killed. However, when asked about George, Annaliese was suddenly aware of the extent to which she had lost contact with her second son. For the first seventeen years of his life, he had been her favourite; now he was twenty-four and she knew practically nothing about him.

The following morning, when they were sitting in the garden, savouring the view across the estuary of the River Tagus, Elsa said, 'You never mentioned what George is studying at Oxford.'

Smiling ruefully, Annaliese said, 'I *think* it's history.'

Gazing studiously at a liner making its way up towards Lisbon, Elsa said, 'That tells me a great deal about how things were in the War.'

'The War is being blamed for a lot,' Annaliese replied. 'Too much. I'm beginning to see that I didn't do as well as I should.'

Elsa shrugged. 'Did anyone? What became of that nice boy, Robert Chappell? Is he all right?'

'Yes. He's at Oxford, too.'

'Good.'

Two more days passed before Annaliese was able to raise the subject of Leopold.

'According to Max, there's a chance that he escaped,' Elsa said. 'Argentina is a popular bolt-hole for Nazis — and Uruguay. Kurt believes there are two men in Lisbon who arranged for hundreds to get away.'

'Could Max be right?' Annaliese asked.

'I have no idea,' Elsa said, sounding bored. 'He claims to have contacts in Vienna who know when every sparrow in the Prater sneezes, but I suspect he makes most of it up. He's as bad as Vassily when it comes to intrigue. Personally, being dreadfully blunt, I regard Leopold as dead and hope he is.'

'Mmm . . . yes, so do I.'

And that was the end of it.

Tired and unwell though she was, Elsa saw that Annaliese was lost and suffering a form of depression. That was hardly surprising; the War had affected her more deeply than she knew, or was prepared to admit, and she was within a few months of her fiftieth birthday, a frightening milestone for most women. Patiently, Elsa waited for her daughter to rediscover herself.

Gradually, Annaliese began to talk more freely. As never before, she revealed what John Brandon had meant to her and how badly she missed him. Not prepared to allow self-pity to take hold, Elsa said, 'You will have to start a new life. There must be hundreds of things you could do.'

'Oh, there are and I shall have to find them. Edward's work on Churchill's book will tie him up for years, so I shall be free to please myself.'

'Wouldn't you have pleased yourself regardless of what Edward was doing?' Elsa inquired mildly.

'Yes.'

'Good.'

Annaliese frowned. 'The trouble is, Nancy Shenstone's decided to go back to America – to live there, if you please.'

'This is the end of the world?' Elsa asked.

'Well, no, I suppose not.' Annaliese sounded far from sure. 'But I shall miss her. She's been my best friend for twenty-five years.'

Elsa, who always felt that she knew Nancy intimately, smelt danger. 'There are millions and millions of people in Europe with far worse problems,' she said. 'Most of them don't have your considerable advantages and privileges.'

Correctly judging that she had been ordered to get a grip

on herself, Annaliese did her best to comply. Thereafter, the only sign of her deep-rooted discontent lay hidden in what failed to happen: as the days passed, turning into weeks, Annaliese showed not the slightest sign of wanting to return to England. It required a barrage of hints from Elsa to persuade her to go on 31 March, more than five weeks after her arrival.

At the last minute, when Annaliese had bade Max and Vassily farewell, and was bracing herself to say goodbye to her mother, Elsa sprang a surprise. 'I shall come and see you off. I've never seen an aeroplane. I'd like to while I still have the chance.'

Unable to frame a reply to the poignant implication of Elsa's statement, Annaliese saw that Kurt must have known: instead of the utilitarian Citroen, he had borrowed Vassily's pride and joy, a Packard sedan.

Elsa, bright and cheerful, chattered like a child all the way to Lisbon. At the airport, her fascination — even for such trivialities as the baggage check-in — was boundless. Snatching a few moments when Elsa was asking an official of Pan American Airways how long it took to fly to New York, Annaliese said to Kurt, 'You know my address and telephone number?'

'Yes, Highness.'

'I expect to be kept *fully* informed about my mother's health.'

Kurt nodded.

The final parting was tearful. They clung to each other for a long time, murmuring incoherent endearments, both wanting to reverse time and freeze it in a long-ago summer.

As the aircraft tore down the runway to take off, Annaliese stared out of her small window and saw that Elsa was on the balcony of the main terminal building. With Kurt towering protectively beside her, the seventy-six-year-old Archduchess,

born in Munich half a century before Adolf Hitler made the
city the springboard for his vile creed, was waving furiously.

Hoping against hope to be seen, Annaliese waved back.

After the cablegram to Matthew, finding Rigby at Croydon
Airport was an unpleasant surprise.

'Why isn't Matthew here?' Annaliese demanded. 'I told
him to meet me. Are you all stupid?' Initially annoyed by
Rigby's stunned incomprehension, she was embarrassed by
the realisation that she had spoken to him in German. It was
the first time she had ever made the mistake.

'He sends his apologies, Your Grace,' Rigby said after she
had corrected herself. 'He is suffering from a bad attack of
influenza.'

'Influenza?' Annaliese exploded. 'In this weather?' Freak-
ishly, it was a day that suggested summer rather than the
uncertainties of early spring.

'Until yesterday it was most inclement, Your Grace.'

Regarding him as a liar, Annaliese swept into the Rolls.
'Take me home,' she snapped.

At the end of the nerve-racking journey, Rigby was longing
for the cheery comfort of the servants' hall, a cup of tea, and
a chance to recount what a foul mood Her Grace was in.
Then, in the Park, only a few hundred yards away from his
goal, Annaliese wound down the partition to say, 'What's
going on over there? What *do* those men think they're doing?'

There were a dozen of them with a tractor, six magnificent
shire horses, harrows, and other pieces of agricultural tackle.
They were busy on a hundred-acre patch that had been
churned up and rutted by the Army. Already, the land looked
healthy and cared-for.

'They're starting to set things to rights, Your Grace.'
Rigby's tone betrayed his opinion that any fool could see that
for themselves.

'On whose authority?' Annaliese asked.

'I've no idea,' Rigby said, envying Baskerville and Mrs Pritchard who were, by all accounts, looking forward to their retirement.

'Drive on,' Annaliese ordered.

Gwen was waiting at the Castle's main door to explain Matthew's absence, but was unable to utter a word in the face of Annaliese's anger.

'Who told those men to start work?' she flared. 'Nothing was to be done until I'd carried out a thorough inspection of the damage.'

'We didn't know that,' Gwen replied. 'We're not mind-readers.' Then, sensing the enormity of Annaliese's fury, she abandoned truculence in favour of conciliation. 'We thought you'd like it. It's mostly Lord Laverstoke's idea – and Henry's, of course.'

'Henry? *Henry*?' If anything, Annaliese's mood was worsening. 'What does she think she's playing at? Where is she?'

At that moment, Henrietta came hurtling down the great staircase, grinning happily and crying, 'How lovely to see you. Did you have a super time?'

'What the devil are those men doing in the Park?' Annaliese shouted.

'Clearing it up, of course.' Henrietta looked mystified. 'Didn't you want it done?'

'I wanted it done *properly*!'

Henrietta was offended. 'I'll have you know that it *is* being done properly.'

'How can it be?' Annaliese retorted. 'Who's organising it?'

'Nicholas Hammond.' Henrietta was defiant.

'Nicholas Hammond?' Annaliese's reaction to the unknown name verged on the comical. Gwen was fighting laughter. 'Who's he?'

'A decidedly probable estate manager,' Henrietta said.

'Lord Laverstoke recommended him. Nicholas thought he'd make a start to show you how good he is. Actually, to be honest, I egged him on, so it's all my fault.'

Annaliese peered at Henrietta, hoping to discover why she looked so inordinately happy. Unable to divine the answer, she demanded, 'Where is this man?'

'In Keeper's Spinney, I think,' Henrietta replied. 'Deciding what to do next.'

'Do you think I could speak to him?' Annaliese asked, sarcastically polite. 'Would that be asking too much?'

Henrietta pranced off in search of a bicycle and three servants made themselves look tremendously busy with Annaliese's luggage before fading away to confirm Rigby's assessment of Her Grace's temper. Heading towards her sitting-room, Annaliese skewered Gwen with a look that said, 'Come with me. Tell me about it.'

Until the Royal Navy decided that his services were no longer required, Nicholas Hammond had been expecting to make it his career for life after entering Dartmouth in 1928, when he was eighteen. Now thirty-six, and with his wife and daughter killed in one of the air raids on Plymouth in 1941, he hated the thought of working in an office and was prepared to have a go at anything. Gwen stressed that the Duke of Laverstoke spoke highly of Nicholas and mentioned what sounded like a distinguished record on the Atlantic convoys. And, for a reason that Annaliese gave up trying to understand, Gwen drove home the point that Nicholas Hammond was six years younger than Henrietta.

When he finally turned up, shepherded into the room by an extraordinarily protective Henrietta, Nicholas Hammond was at a disadvantage. In addition to his mud-spattered workman's clothes, he had shed his wellington boots at one of the Castle's back doors and was shuffling around in thick, fisherman's socks, one of which had a huge hole in the toe.

Although the first impression was that of a scarecrow, Annaliese found herself being scrutinised by a pair of gentle, brown eyes set in a weather-beaten but sensitive face.

'How do you do, Commander Hammond,' Annaliese said.

'Hello, Your Grace. It's best not to shake hands – I'm pretty filthy.'

'So I see.' Examining him, Annaliese found that a determined effort was needed to preserve her bad mood. 'What are you playing at?'

'Well, the fact is, Lord Laverstoke thought you might set me on as your estate manager,' Nicholas Hammond said.

'So I've been told.' Annaliese glared at Gwen. 'Why have you taken the liberty of assuming that I will agree with Lord Laverstoke?'

'Oh, no, I haven't.' Nicholas rubbed a muddy hand through his light-brown hair and turned to Henrietta. She smiled encouragingly. 'You see, Lady Lincolnshire, I'm not qualified to do the job – don't know the first thing about it. But I'm willing to learn, so I took advantage of your absence to have a go, show you what I can do.'

'This is your idea?' Annaliese said to Henrietta.

'Absolutely. You should see what he's done. Parts of it are finished.'

'Where?'

'Gainsborough Wood.'

'Very well.' Annaliese remembered her mother's advice to get a grip. 'I *will* see. Organise a car, Henry.'

'Tomorrow will do just as well. You must be whacked after your journey. You haven't even had a cup of tea.'

'*Now*, Henry!'

The transformation of Gainsborough Wood was a revelation. By the end of the summer, when a season's growth had completed the healing process, only a keenly critical eye would detect that the Army had ever been there.

Refusing to comment directly, Annaliese said, 'There's more to the job than this, Commander Hammond. A knowledge of accountancy and law is needed to deal with our interests.'

'I know which books to read, Your Grace,' Nicholas replied. 'And when I'm a bit more presentable, folks tend to take notice of me.'

'He did wonders in the War,' Henrietta pointed out.

Apparently ignoring her, Annaliese said, 'Where are you living, Commander?'

'Miss Timberlake arranged digs in the village.'

For what seemed like an eternity, Annaliese was lost in thought. Then she pointed to the house in which she had known so much happiness and joy, the house from which John Brandon had been borne in a coffin six weeks ago. 'That's your new home,' she told Nicholas. 'I'm sure that Miss Timberlake will arrange things for you.'

While a stupefied Nicholas attempted to thank her, Gwen and Henrietta gaped at each other, recognising a fresh beginning.

The new era was not without its problems.

Baskerville and Mrs Pritchard retired at the end of June. Two days before they left for a cottage overlooking the sea at Brixham, they slipped into Marlborough and married at the Register Office, doing so without telling a soul at the Castle. Their obsessive desire for secrecy was taken as an unfavourable comment on what they were leaving behind. Below stairs, it was rumoured that Baskerville, increasingly disappointed by the Duke and Duchess, had given up hope when the rightful Marquess of Axholme was lost on D-Day.

It was common knowledge that there had been a serious disagreement over the appointment of a new butler and housekeeper. His Grace had wanted to transfer the couple who had been running Cadogan Square since 1938, but *she* — as often as not in a very funny mood these days — had put her foot down with a vengeance. Not that the outcome was unexpected: Gwen and Matthew had always been her favourites, unable to do a thing wrong. Gwen would be very effective — fearsomely so, some thought as they wondered about finding new jobs — but turning a glorified chauffeur into a butler went down badly.

Aware of the ill feeling, Annaliese let it be known that anyone who didn't like the new arrangements was welcome to leave. It was, she declared, time for a clear-out.

In May, Celia was made a fully-fledged partner of Boothby's and gave up The Chantry.

'I've hardly used it for two years,' she told Annaliese. 'And I don't see myself spending any time in the country in the future. I'm perfectly happy to live with Aunt Ursula.'

Annaliese promptly gave The Chantry to George. Delighted, he planned to spend most of the long summer vacation there with Robert Chappell. Learning of the arrangement during one of his brief periods away from Chartwell, Edward looked to be on the verge of protest, but thought better of it. Interested only in her mother's health and Nancy Shenstone's impending departure, Annaliese attributed Edward's unease to irritability at the demise of his relationship with Celia and dismissed the matter from her mind.

The sale of Martha's Vineyard had been organised with a speed that had dismayed Annaliese. A well-known industrialist with a notoriously flamboyant lifestyle, took one look at the amazing house, said it was just what he wanted and paid the asking price. In parallel with this, Nigel Templeton had cut through the red tape and transferred Nancy's funds to Chase Manhattan at least two months earlier than expected. She left Martha's Vineyard and London in early July and spent her final week in England with Annaliese at the Castle. They relived the highlights of their twenty-five-year friendship and were, by turn, ridiculously happy and desperately sad. At one stage, Nancy confessed that she viewed her future with trepidation.

'Don't go, then,' Annaliese urged. 'Stay here with me.'

'Better still, why don't you come with me? They'd *love* you in the States. You could open a branch of Boothby's in New York – Sotheby's have.'

Annaliese laughed. 'All right, I'll do that.'

They developed the knack of entertaining themselves with talk that was all fun and bravado, definitely not to be taken seriously. It was a charade to mask the bitter truth that, no matter what promises were made, there was every likelihood that they would never see each other again after Nancy had gone on board the *Queen Mary*.

On the last night, however, everything changed. As they ate supper from trays on their knees in Annaliese's private sitting-room, she told Nancy of the turmoil within her.

'It's as though I've lost my way and don't know who I am any more. When I was with Mama in Portugal, I wanted to forget all this and be *Austrian* again. How do you explain that?'

Nancy shrugged. 'I can't. I *could* say it's because you've lost John; maybe it's the War; maybe you're like me, just want to go home.'

'I can't,' Annaliese said. 'Every single member of my family is still banned from entering Austria.'

'So how did Leopold fix it?'

'He signed papers renouncing his claims to everything we ever stood for,' Annaliese said bitterly.

On impulse, Nancy reached for Annaliese's hands, turning them so that she could study the palms.

'What *are* you doing?' Annaliese asked.

'Looking at your future.'

Annaliese laughed nervously. 'How long have you been a fortune-teller?'

'Since I stayed with Grannie Hagen in Vermont when I was a kid.' Oblivious to Annaliese's surprise, Nancy concentrated. After a little while, she let out a long whistle.

'What is it?' Annaliese asked.

'I have *never* seen a life line like this beauty!' Nancy whispered.

'Is there anything wrong with it?'

'Not a thing.' Raising her eyes to Annaliese's, Nancy said, 'I take it you don't mind living forever?'

'I'm not sure it's something I'd look forward to.' Attempting to dismiss it, Annaliese said, 'You're making this up, Nancy.'

'No. See here.' Nancy traced out the bold line with a finger. 'Compare it to mine – see the difference?'

Annaliese did so. 'Yes, but what does it prove. This isn't reliable, surely?'

'It's never far wrong,' Nancy insisted. 'I've looked at hundreds of hands in my time and I doubt if more than five of them didn't tell the God's honest truth.'

Nancy returned to her study of Annaliese's palms. 'You can see what sort of life you've had,' Nancy said. 'Take a look at this lot.' She indicated a mass of fine lines criss-crossing the main lines of both hands. 'That was when you were young – eighteen to twenty-five, I guess.'

'What do they all mean?' Annaliese asked.

'Events. These are the hands of an archduchess who got mixed up in a world war, started a new life in England, became a duchess, had her marriage fall apart, and found a great love.'

'Poppycock!' Annaliese snorted. 'That's all hindsight.'

Nancy shook her head. 'Two things: one, take another look at mine.' Annaliese stared intently. 'Nothing like so busy, huh?' Grudgingly, Annaliese nodded. 'Second, back to yours again ... see this ... here, and here, and here again? Things are gonna keep on happening to you, right to the very end.'

'What sort of things?'

'Who knows? It's connected to this line.' Nancy pointed. 'I reckon that's the one that made the Duchess of Lincoln-shire, so you'll be kept busy.'

'These are future problems?' Annaliese asked.

'Yup!'

'Big ones, it seems,' Annaliese said, staring hard at the spot beneath Nancy's finger.

'I'd say so.' Drawing away, Nancy smiled cheekily and said, 'Want a bit of farewell advice?'

'I imagine it's compulsory.'

'It sure is. Honey, you've forgotten how to enjoy yourself. It's been going on for some time.'

'Eighteen months,' Annaliese sighed. 'When I began to suspect that John was seriously ill.'

'I sympathise one hundred and ten per cent, but it doesn't suit you. Rediscover fun.'

'Actually, I was intending to ask you to help me do that,' Annaliese admitted.

'Then I blew in and told you I was quitting. Hell!' Nancy was annoyed with herself. 'You'll have to do it yourself. Be positive.'

After a sleepless night and an early morning drive to Southampton, that battle-cry of 'Be positive,' was Nancy's parting shot from the promenade deck as the tugs eased the *Queen Mary* away from the quay. They waved and smiled like brave lunatics and Matthew looked on helplessly as the tears began to glisten in Annaliese's eyes.

Although she tried to make herself believe otherwise,

IN HER OWN RIGHT   243

Annaliese spent the rest of the summer on tenterhooks, waiting. Her mother's letters arrived every Tuesday and were full of cheerful gossip, yet Annaliese found herself developing a habit that rapidly became a debilitating constraint: she refused to stray far from the telephone.

Despite this and the difficulties of persuading anyone to carry out such tasks in post-war, Socialist Britain, Annaliese agreed to do one room for virtually nothing. Impressed by the result, Annaliese offered them what turned out to be a year's well-paid work which laid the foundations for a prosperous company.

'You'd better supervise it all,' Annaliese told Athene. 'I don't have the time and you seem to have them eating out of your hand.'

Relishing the responsibility, Athene waylaid Annaliese every afternoon to report progress and seek decisions on colour schemes. She looked for other ways of being useful and appointed herself chief purveyor of gossip, paying particular attention to the romantic attachment between her mother and Nicholas Hammond.

'They'll be married before the year's out,' Athene said one day. 'At least, I hope so.'

'Really?' Totally withdrawn from what was going on around her, Annaliese was startled.

'Definitely. They fell for each other on first sight – like a ton of bricks. He's younger than Ma.'

'So I believe,' Annaliese said, finally appreciating the significance of Gwen's harping on about Henrietta being six years older than Nicholas – exactly the same gap that existed between her and Kurt Schneider, Annaliese found herself thinking.

'I suppose some people might think that's ever-so-slightly wrong,' Athene continued. 'But I say good luck to them. They deserve to be happy and Nicholas is yummy.' She heaved a monumental sigh. 'Much as I adore him, though, my heart belongs to George.'

'*George?*' Annaliese's eyes opened wide.

Athene laughed. 'Don't worry, Aunt Annaliese, I know it's hopeless. Being illegitimate rather rules me out as a marchioness and prospective duchess, doesn't it?'

'George thinks a lot of you,' Annaliese said lamely. 'Always has done.'

'Not so much these days. He's very close to Robert Chappell.'

'I expect that's because of their studies at Oxford,' Annaliese replied. 'George is determined to get a very good degree. He wants to prove that he's more than just another member of the privileged classes.'

'That's a good idea.' Athene pretended to be convinced. She certainly had no intention of mentioning her two visits to The Chantry to see if there were any domestic chores that needed doing. George and Robert had behaved very oddly, not at all glad to see her and making no secret of their desire to be left in peace.

Perhaps feeling guilty, they came looking for Athene on the day before they returned to Oxford, apologising for ignoring her and suggesting a trip to Salisbury for lunch and a browse round the shops. 'We might go to a cinema,' George said. Smiling radiantly, Athene forgave him.

At about 4.00 pm that afternoon, Annaliese was chatting to the decorators and failed to hear the telephone bell. Several minutes elapsed before the breathless and incoherent maid tracked her down. One thing was clear: the German gentleman who wished to speak to Her Grace as a matter of great urgency could only be Kurt Schneider.

Snatching at the instrument, Annaliese said, 'Yes, Kurt, what's wrong?'

'Highness, your mother has suffered another stroke.'

'When?'

'This morning. Nine o'clock. I have been busy, of course.'

'How is she?'

'Poorly, but holding her own, I think. The doctor wishes to remove her to hospital, but Her Highness gave me strict orders against this.'

'Quite right.' Annaliese's mind was racing. 'I can't possibly get there today, but I'll be on the flight that arrives in Lisbon at two-thirty tomorrow.'

'Very well, Highness. I will see to it.'

'Don't leave her, Kurt,' Annaliese ordered. 'Get one of the others to meet me.'

'I understand.'

Max, accompanied by Ernst Weber, was waiting at the airport the following day. Elsa had enjoyed a comfortable night and was showing good signs of recovery, Max said.

They reached the villa to be greeted by a grim-faced Kurt with the news that the Archduchess Elsa von Habsburg had died at about the time Annaliese's flight as touching down at Lisbon.

The coffin was lowered into the grave first dug for Joseph, eight years ago, and Annaliese threw a handful of earth down. Stepping back, she found Kurt at her side, just as he had been for the past six days, organising, arranging for guests to be met and accommodated, taking care of everything. It was the most natural thing in the world for Annaliese to take Kurt's arm. He led her back to the car, through ranks of mourners, each of whom had a little smile or nod of sympathy for the handsome woman who remained inscrutable behind the black veil that covered her face.

Back at the villa, many of the guests took their drinks, food, and conversation into the garden, enjoying the balmy weather. It was, Annaliese thought, a bigger gathering than for her father. In addition to Habsburgs, there were representatives from most of the old German ruling families – Mecklenberg-Schwerins, Saxe-Altenbergs, and Elsa's own Wittelsbach nephews and nieces. Although many of them had spent their entire lives in exile, they were deeply ashamed of what their country had become under Hitler. As well as condolences for her mother, Annaliese, respected as British by marriage, received many murmured apologies for Germany's behaviour.

When they began to leave, Annaliese spared a thought for Compton Allardyce and enlisted Kurt's help in sending a cablegram to Gwen. After the bald statement that Elsa's funeral had taken place, Annaliese said that she had no idea how long she would stay in Portugal. The message was to be passed on to Edward.

'You do not wish to make personal contact with your husband?' Kurt asked. 'It is no trouble, Highness. I can make the telephone exchange do anything.'

'No, thank you, Kurt,' Annaliese said, smiling at his uncharacteristic boastfulness. 'There's no need.' Then, even as she willed herself not to, she added, 'We are no longer close.'

Giving no sign that he had heard her, Kurt set about sending the cable to Gwen.

In the days that followed, Annaliese sat in the garden, made several trips to the beach, and dined with Max and Vassily in the evenings. Kurt, systematically executing a list of orders left by Elsa, contacted her lawyer, who expressed a desire to see Annaliese.

'Ernst will fetch him from the airport,' Kurt announced.

'The airport?' Annaliese was surprised. 'Where's he coming from?'

'Zurich, Highness. There is no need to worry, he can come here and go back in a day quite easily.'

Franz Sussmeyer, a personable young man in his late

twenties, was the great-grandson, grandson, and son of men who had been looking after the private affairs of the Habsburgs since 1840. He apologised profusely for having to take the place of his father, who was recovering from an operation for appendicitis, offered sympathy for the loss of Elsa, and accepted lunch on the terrace in the warm, mid-October sun.

As they ate, he removed a single sheet of paper from his case. 'Your mother's will,' he explained. 'It is very simple. You are the sole beneficiary.'

'My brother?' Annaliese asked.

Franz Sussmeyer looked fierce and shook his head. 'Disinherited,' he said. 'Naturally, your mother drew this up *after* the death of His Highness, your father. She was *quite* clear about your brother.'

'He may not even be alive,' Annaliese murmured.

'Precisely.'

'So this is mine.' Annaliese waved a hand to encompass the villa and its grounds.

'Yes. You will keep it on?'

'I can't say yet,' Annaliese replied. 'I shall have to think about it.'

'Should Your Highness wish to dispose of it, we shall be happy to find a reliable man to act for you.' The lawyer allowed a flicker of disapproval to sully his cherubic face. 'Delightful though Portugal is in many ways, one has to be careful of the people one trusts with major transactions.'

'Of course,' Annaliese said, humouring him.

'Additionally, the funds that your mother had with Erbach-Bergmann now pass to you.'

'Good gracious!' Annaliese exclaimed. 'That's the bank my husband and I use. Fancy not knowing that Mama was a fellow-client.'

That, Franz Sussmeyer's eloquent look implied, was one of

the most respected features of the Swiss banking system. Aloud, he said, 'I have the honour to be a close friend of the younger Herr Bergmann. Should you have any instructions, I would be pleased to pass them on to him.'

'Again, that will require thought,' Annaliese replied.

'Quite. For your information, Highness, Erbach-Bergmann follow the practice of transacting amounts in United States dollars. This does not mean that the Swiss franc is anything other than *completely* stable — it's more a question of client preferences.'

'I see,' Annaliese said. She didn't, but wasn't interested.

'Perhaps you would care to know that at the close of business last Thursday, your mother's account balance stood at a fraction over fifteen million dollars. Interest is calculated on a daily basis and credited at the end of each month.'

Jolted out of wondering what to do about the villa, Annaliese gaped at Sussmeyer. Misunderstanding the expression on her face, he said, 'I suppose that's something like four millions in sterling — always contingent upon how the British Government feels about exchange rates today.'

No wonder he was prepared to fly from Zurich to Lisbon for a chat over lunch!

Although dazed, Annaliese heard herself saying, 'I won't have that account consolidated into my existing one, Herr Sussmeyer. It can stay separate and private.'

'I will see to it, Highness.' He produced a fountain pen and two more documents from his case. 'If you would sign here . . . and there . . . thank you.'

When Kurt drove the lawyer back to the airport half an hour later, Annaliese was still in a state of shock. Regularly, she had asked her parents if they had enough money: now she knew why her inquiries had been brushed aside with good-humoured disdain. Further reflection brought the conclusion that it wasn't all that great a sum for members of a family who had owned and ruled most of Central Europe for six centuries. However, it and the Falkenberg emeralds — still under the floorboards in her bedroom — probably made her one of the wealthiest women in England.

Over dinner with Max and Vassily that evening, she raised the question of the villa.

'We'd prefer you not to sell it,' Max said. 'If you do want to get rid of it, give us first refusal.'

Seeing Vassily nodding agreement, Annaliese asked, 'Why?'

'This is a special place,' Max said, unusually serious. 'It must remain so. I'm leaving my house to Franz, Karl's youngest boy, and Vassily has made a will in favour of our family.'

Responding to Annaliese's surprise, Vassily said, 'You Habsburgs have been good to me. When I escaped from the Bolsheviks, I never expected so many years of happiness.'

'Shut up, you sentimental old fool,' Max said fondly. Turning to Annaliese, he went on, 'The next generation may not wish to live here all the time, but it will be a safe haven if they ever need it.'

'Will it always be like this?' Annaliese asked.

'I don't see why not,' Max replied. 'If you look at the deeds, you'll find that, between us, we own the whole of the hill and all the land down to the beach.'

'They're using compulsory purchase of property in England,' Annaliese said. 'It's something to do with public works and improvements.'

'Pooh!' Vassily made an obscene gesture. 'That's democracy for you. Portugal has more sense. It's improved enough.'

'Very well, I take your point,' Annaliese told Max. 'I shall think it over.'

After a restful night's sleep, her mind was almost made up: there was only one more factor to be considered. When Kurt brought her mid-morning coffee to the terrace, Annaliese told him to join her.

'What would become of you if I decided to sell this place?' she asked.

Giving an impression of nonchalance, Kurt said, 'I would go somewhere else.'

'How easy would that be?'

'Not very — unless I could stay in Portugal,' Kurt smiled ruefully. 'Your Highness will appreciate that my nationality and status is — what shall we say? Dubious is the word, I think.'

'But if you stay here?'

'In three years they will make me a Portuguese citizen. Herr Kondrashin is arranging it.'

Annaliese nodded. 'In that case, I shall keep the villa. I can't have you wandering around Europe like a lost soul. I take it you don't want to go back to Austria?'

'No.' It was vehement and final.

'I shall come here often,' Annaliese said. 'Two or three times a year. Will there be enough to keep you busy?'

'The garden, Highness. With your permission, I would like to make improvements.'

'I look forward to hearing your plans. In the meantime, I must make arrangements for you to draw wages and household expenses. How do I do that?'

'Her Highness, your mother, used a bank in Cascais. I understand that money was transferred to it from Switzerland.'

'Excellent. You can take me there when we've finished our coffee.' Annaliese stretched contentedly, feeling that she was free of a great burden. 'Neither of us can go home, Kurt,' she said, 'but, by God, there's nothing to stop us creating our own little piece of Austria here.'

As a result of a strongly worded letter from Gwen, and for that reason alone, Annaliese flew back to England at the beginning of November. She was unhappy at being summoned and wasted no time in making her feelings known.

'Why can't a perfectly simple wedding take place without me? Don't I have enough to worry about?'

'Henrietta and Nicholas are important,' Gwen retorted. 'You owe them a lot. In any case, you've always been interested in weddings and things!'

It was true enough. Annaliese's involvement in the lives of the estate workers and villagers had helped to weld a community that respected her and cared deeply about each other. Sensing defeat, Annaliese stalked off.

The wedding, an oasis of jollity in the post-war gloom, was such a happy business that no one noticed Annaliese's failure to enter into the spirit of the festivities in the Long Gallery after the church service. To nearly everyone's surprise, it was Edward who stole the show. Absenting himself from Chartwell to give Henrietta away, he crowned the wedding breakfast with a speech that was both witty and touching. It was a splendid performance that he hoped made amends for his dog-in-the-manger attitude to Athene's christening.

Athene herself reduced nearly everyone to stitches when called upon to explain why she had refused Nicholas's offer to adopt her. 'I *adore* my stepfather, and it's terribly sweet of him to want to make me vaguely legitimate, but I'd like to carry on being called Timberlake. That way, I'll be a constant irritation to Ma's *ghastly* relatives.'

Only a few die-hard puritans and Annaliese, who was deep in faraway, disturbing thoughts, failed to laugh.

10

1948
'A dangerous age for a woman'

After breakfast on a wonderful May morning, Edward spent
ten minutes on the terrace that ran along the front of the
Castle. Looking round, he came to the conclusion that
Compton Allardyce *was* sublime after all. How ironic that
Annaliese, who had fallen in love with the place at first sight,
seemed to have become almost indifferent to it. A few days
ago, she had flown off to Portugal yet again. After the War,
1946 had brought three severe blows, the deaths of John
Brandon and Elsa, and Nancy Shenstone's departure: then, the
frightful winter of 1947 had depressed her profoundly. In
addition, Edward suspected that the menopause might have
something to do with the way Annaliese behaved these days.
Like most men, he knew nothing about this phase of a
woman's life – other than what he had deduced from snatches
of disgruntled conversation at his club. But he had made up his
mind that it was probably a factor. Though she looked
preposterously young, Annaliese would be fifty-two in a few
weeks and was bound to have undergone 'the change'.

Not that Edward minded her absence. On the contrary, given a week or two at home to work up Churchill's rough draft of the opening chapters of the second volume of the War History, he was glad to have the place to himself. He went up to the library and settled down to the pile of much-altered typescript. Barely had he done so, when the telephone rang. Edward answered it in the expectation that it would be Churchill's magnificently unflappable secretary. 'Hello, this is Edward Lincolnshire speaking.'

The voice at the other end was tormented. 'Edward, thank God I've got hold of you. It's Bernard Littlejohn here.'

Sir Bernard, one of the many Conservative MPs who had lost their seats in the 1945 Labour landslide, had been among Edward's closest political allies. Within weeks of the election, the bitterness of defeat was replaced by the fulfilment of a long-standing ambition: Littlejohn was offered the Wardenship of his old College at Oxford. By what they both regarded as a happy chance, it was also the College Edward had attended, the College at which George was an undergraduate.

'Bernard,' Edward said warmly. 'This is an unexpected pleasure.'

'I wish to God it was,' Littlejohn replied, beside himself with anxiety. 'I'm afraid we've got *the* most unholy mess on our hands, Edward. I'm going to have to send your boy down and it's got to be done damned quickly. Today.'

Sick with the fear that he already knew the answer, Edward asked, 'Why? What's he supposed to have done?'

'I hardly know how to break it to you.' Littlejohn sounded as though someone had a grip on his throat. 'And there's no *supposed* about it.'

'Well?' Edward snapped.

After a pause, Littlejohn said, 'One of the scouts found George in bed with another man this morning.'

Edward attempted to dismiss it. 'Slightly eccentric, I grant you, but hardly a sacking offence, Bernard. There must be a perfectly harmless explanation.'

'There isn't a hope in hell of it being construed that way.' Littlejohn's voice dropped to a frantic whisper. 'They weren't under the bedclothes – they were fully exposed, *doing* things to each other.'

'I'd better come over,' Edward said, his mood changing in response to the situation's gravity.

'I think so. If nothing else, you can take George away. The quicker the better.'

'I'll leave at once,' Edward said and slammed the receiver down.

After covering the forty miles from Compton Allardyce to Oxford in just under an hour, Edward left the Rolls with a porter and hurried through the inner quad to the Warden's Lodge. Littlejohn, waiting in his study, greeted Edward's forceful opening with wide-eyed disbelief.

'Look here, Bernard, you can't send George down, not now. Damn it, man, he's due to sit his finals in two weeks and you know he's in line for a first.'

'Edward, my dear fellow, you must, you simply *must* understand that I have no choice in the matter, none at all.' Littlejohn, always a tower of strength when demanding that Nazi war criminals should be brought to book, was a nervous wreck in the face of trouble on his own doorstep. 'This is an indictable offence – you do realise that, don't you? I should be handing this over to the police. As it is, I'm doing you a favour and risking my neck. The Vice Chancellor won't tolerate the slightest whiff of homosexuality.'

Edward's expression became hard and calculating. 'I hear that research is becoming very expensive, especially the fashionable stuff – nuclear physics, for example. Cambridge appear to have taken a lead: we can't have that, can we, Bernard?' Edward produced his cheque book, brandished it, and laid it on an occasional table in front of Littlejohn. 'Let's forget this, Bernard. You hush it up, I'll have a word with George, and no one need know a thing.'

Littlejohn had difficulty tearing his eyes away from the cheque book. Finally, he did so and erupted into speech. 'No, no, you simply don't understand. My own fault, I haven't tried to explain.' Sinking into a chair, Littlejohn waved at Edward to do the same. 'The scout who made this *frightful* discovery is a trouble-maker, a barrack-room lawyer. We should have got rid of him last year. There was an unsavoury incident, we had every right, but the fact is, we didn't. As far as I can make out, he has a grudge against George and I doubt if this morning was an accident – there's a suggestion that the wretched man has been spying on your boy for some time.'

'What are you expecting to happen?' Edward was fiercely sceptical, unwilling to concede that things were bad.

'Once George is out of the way, I hope we shall be in a position to cover our tracks.' The look on Edward's face unnerved the Warden. 'What alternative is there? If George goes, we *might* get away with it, if he doesn't, we stand no chance. And it's not only the College, Edward. Do *you* want a scandal?'

'No, I don't. So what will you do? Try to sweeten this scout you should have dismissed last year?'

'Yes.'

'How?'

'At the moment, I have no idea.'

'We're laying ourselves open to blackmail,' Edward growled, showing signs of intransigence.

'Do you imagine I don't realise that?' Littlejohn shouted. 'The only way I can be sure of avoiding blackmail is to send for the police. Is that what you want?'

Edward shook his head and raised his hands in a gesture of surrender. 'We'll do it your way, Bernard,' he said. 'You will keep me informed, won't you? If this bloody man refuses to co-operate, I want to know about it. At once!'

'Yes, I will, naturally.'

'I mean it,' Edward insisted. 'I won't have some bolshie blackening George's name. Is that clear?'

'Perfectly.' To his surprise, Littlejohn found that he was frightened by Edward's expression.

There was a brief silence. Reaching out to retrieve his cheque book, Edward saw the thwarted covetousness on the Warden's face and despised him. As calmly as possible, Edward said, 'Where is George?'

'I had him brought here. My dear wife will be looking after him – they've always got on well together.' Littlejohn cleared his throat. 'Er . . . he's packed, so you can take him away immediately.'

Ignoring the desire for indecent haste, Edward said, 'Who was the other man?'

'Chappell, Robert Chappell, from Keble.'

'Ah, yes. He and George have been friends since school.' Edward was loftily indifferent, at pains not to betray the faintest hint of prior knowledge. 'I suppose he's being sent down, too?'

'Most definitely.'

'He has no family,' Edward said. 'Only an uncle, in Northumberland, I think. Could you arrange for me to pick him up? I expect he could do with some help.'

It was apparent that Littlejohn found the request strange. However, the longing to be rid of an embarrassment was more compelling than his curiosity. 'Yes, yes, I'll see what I can do.' Littlejohn stood up, flapping fretfully. 'Shall we find George?'

Edward followed him into the hallway. The Warden called out, 'Cynthia, my dear, where are you?' several times and walked in agitated circles, unaware of how absurd he was. A door opened and a woman peered out. She had a brave, sensible face, was every undergraduate's ideal aunt, and seemed fully at ease. 'George, dear, your father,' she said over her shoulder and he emerged from the room.

While father and son faced each other, Lady Littlejohn flitted past them, caught her husband's sleeve, and drew him into the study.

For a reason that neither of them understood, Edward and George shook hands with great gravity.

'I'm sorry about this, Father,' George said. 'Very sorry.'

Fleetingly, there was an air of terrifying uncertainty between them as Edward made up his mind. George, who had been unable to contemplate this moment, braced himself. Then, Edward sighed and his shoulders sagged. 'Don't blame yourself,' he said. 'I should have given you stronger warnings – I tried, but I didn't go far enough, did I? The fact is, my boy, I didn't have the guts.'

'I wondered if you knew,' George whispered.

'Suspected,' Edward said. 'Strongly suspected. I think poor old Douglas had an inkling, but he never breathed a word – didn't know how to, I suppose.'

'Did you arrange for me to have that job in the War Office?' George asked. 'More or less out of harm's way.'

'I thought it best.'

Simultaneously, they embraced each other, Edward patting his son's back reassuringly. Through the Lodge's windows, wide-open on a beautiful, warm day, George heard a blackbird burst into impetuous, irrational song. Out in the quad, some exuberant soul made a fair job of whistling the opening bars of the first Rasumovsky Quartet. The unexpected solace of his father's sad love and the exquisite sounds entered George's soul. That blackbird and the efforts of a blithe, unthinking lover of Beethoven were to return and comfort him at the moment of his death.

Gruffly, Edward said, 'They won't hear of you taking your

finals. I'm to take you home at once.'

George nodded. 'Dare I mention Robert? I'm worried about him.'

'So am I,' Edward replied. 'I've asked Littlejohn to track him down. We'll take him with us.'

The Warden appeared from his study, hideously bright and cheerful, resolved to bustle his unwelcome guests out on a wave of *bonhomie*. 'Ah, there you are. It's all arranged, Edward. You'll find Chappell waiting outside Keble – I've had words in the right quarter. Now, George, where are your bags? I know, they must be in the porch. Yes, I thought so, here we are.' Two servants materialised, loaded George's bags on to a barrow, and set off along a little-used path to a side entrance of the College.

'The man on the gate must have moved my car,' Edward said.

'I don't think the Warden bothered to say goodbye,' George muttered. 'Should we feel sorry for him?'

'Pah!' Angrily, Edward waved the porters away, loading the luggage himself. He started the Rolls, achieved the almost impossible feat of stalling it, and turned the wrong way into Broad Street, heading for St Giles instead of Parks Road. George, painfully conscious of his father's mental state, wanted to weep.

Robert Chappell, looking crushed, was outside his College. He had only one suitcase.

'Where's the rest of your stuff?' George asked.

'They can send it on if they feel like it,' Robert replied. 'It doesn't much matter, does it?' He turned to Edward. 'I'm afraid this could involve you in a terrible scandal, sir. I don't know what to say.'

Edward smiled reassuringly. 'Don't worry about it, Robert. The people here have every reason to hush it up. The tragedy is, you're robbed of your finals.'

'It's extremely good of you to take that view, sir,' Robert said. 'I'm sorry – that's not meant to be as lame as it sounds.'

'Hurry up, Bobbie,' George said, anxious to have done with Oxford. 'Get in.'

'Yes, all right.' Rather reluctantly, Edward thought, Robert squeezed into the front seat to perch beside George. 'I could do with something to eat,' Robert said. 'There's a decent place in Hollybush Row, near the railway station.'

'Good idea.' Edward was cheerful, his control of himself and the car back to normal.

George was uneasy and sullen. He chose a corner table and sat with his back to the restaurant's other customers, picking at his food while Edward and Robert somehow contrived to indulge in meaningless small talk.

Eventually, George interrupted the chatter. 'There's one thing we can be thankful for, Bobbie, Allardyce is a marvellous place to lie low while we decide what we're going to do next.'

Robert shifted in his chair in order to face George squarely. 'I'm not coming with you, George,' he said, pale and tense. 'It's best if we don't see each other for a few weeks.'

'Don't be silly.' George was treating it as a joke. 'Of course you're coming to Allardyce. Where else *can* you go?'

Robert was desperately earnest. 'Look, George, we're in a serious pickle. If there is going to be trouble, I'm the last person you want hanging around the Castle. I'm nobody, so a scandal wouldn't affect me, whereas it could make your life a misery – impossible, even.' Robert turned to Edward. 'I'm right, aren't I, sir?'

Doing his best to be fair, Edward said, 'There *is* a slight risk, but we're nicely insulated and private.'

'Not as much as you were,' Robert said. 'Things have changed a good deal in the last three years.'

Edward frowned. 'In what way?'

'Most of the servants are newcomers with what you might call "post-war attitudes",' Robert replied. 'I wouldn't say they're disloyal, but a chap like me, an outsider, would be daft to rely on them. If the University can't suppress this story and the press were to start a witch-hunt . . .' Robert shrugged '. . . well, to be brutally frank, sir, I think some of your staff would shop me for a few pounds.'

Edward squirmed. Robert's assessment of the atmosphere created — albeit unintentionally — by Annaliese was too accurate for comfort.

Already resigned, George asked Robert, 'You've really made up your mind to do this?'

'Yes. It's the only way. We'll give the dust time to settle and meet up again in the autumn.'

'Do you think this is the best way, Father?' George asked, realising that it was.

'On balance, yes, I do.' Although willing to offer Robert sanctuary at the Castle, Edward decided to support his need to be away from George so that he could work out his future. 'Where are you going?'

'To my uncle in Northumberland,' Robert replied. 'He farms near a place called Wark.'

'You're going up there today?'

'Yes. There's a train at one-twenty. I change at Birmingham and get into Newcastle about ten. Uncle Jim will meet me.' Glancing nervously at George, Robert added, 'I telephoned him when I knew we were being sacked.'

'You'll write, won't you?' George said.

'You know I will. Here's my address.' Robert handed over a folded slip of paper.

Briskly, to spare George's feelings, Edward said, 'It's nearly one o'clock. Without wishing to cause a panic, shouldn't we be making a move?'

At the station, George wandered aimlessly, head bowed,

hands deep in his pockets, getting in people's way. Easing Robert aside from the booking-office window, Edward bought him a first-class ticket to Newcastle and pressed ten five-pound notes into his hand.

'I don't need that, sir,' the young man protested.

'I'll bet you do,' Edward replied. 'I was always skint when I was here. Don't create a fuss, Robert, just put it in a safe place.'

'Thank you. Thank you for everything.' Smiling thoughtfully, Robert said, 'I've never had proper parents, so I'm hardly qualified to judge, but they seem to be a sadly underestimated breed.'

Staring at him quizzically, Edward said, 'Explain.'

'George was categorically, dead-certain that you'd go mad over this business – chuck him out, cut him off without a penny – you know the sort of thing. I said you'd be sensible.'

Edward laughed. '*Sensible?* I don't know about that, but I'm touched by your confidence. Take care of yourself, Robert, and keep in touch. I'll expect you at the Castle soon.'

'Goodbye, sir.'

George, who had bought a platform ticket, looked up as Robert approached, smiling sadly. Overcome by sorrow, Edward watched them pass through the barrier, then headed for the Rolls to wait for George.

After dinner that evening, Edward and George went outdoors, strolling past the lake and into Keeper's Spinney where the dogs went joyously mad.

George, who had been asking a good many questions about Edward's work with Churchill, suddenly said, 'When will Mother be coming back?'

'I don't know. As a rule, she stays three or four weeks and she's only been gone since Monday.'

'Will you write to her about me?' George asked.

'Good God, no!' It was impossible to tell whether Edward was amused or horrified by the idea. 'We've got enough on our plate without looking for more trouble.'

'She's going to be angry?' Having assumed that Annaliese would be sympathetic, George was alarmed.

'You can bank on it.' Seeing the panic in his son's dark eyes, Edward hastened to allay his fears. 'With me, not you. She'll say it's all my fault.'

George was bemused. 'Fault? How can it be anyone's *fault*? In spite of what the law says, I won't blame myself or Robert, let alone anyone else.'

'Mmm. Yes.' Edward was relieved when one of the dogs tore up to him with a piece of wood in his mouth. Gaining possession of the stick and hurling it into a patch of dense undergrowth gave him a few moments to collect his thoughts. 'The thing is, George, your mother never wanted you to go away to school. She and I had words about it – there was a serious falling-out and I put my foot down.'

'Do you think that Moss Close and Winchester turned me into a queer?' George asked.

Edward winced. 'Don't use that word, there's a good chap,' he said tetchily. 'No, I wouldn't accept that, but your mother will and I shall cop it in the neck.'

'I'm sorry,' George said, both for the way things were and his rather infantile attempt to shock by using the word 'queer'. 'Will it be bad and will you take any notice of her?'

Edward made a rueful face. 'No, I don't expect I shall take all that much notice. If it gets unbearable, I shall stay at Chartwell until the worst blows over.'

Abruptly, George said, 'Mother never seems to mention Douglas.'

'No, she doesn't,' Edward agreed.

'Isn't that rather strange?'

'Moderately so.' Edward was uncomfortable. 'All sorts of

tricky forces at work, I imagine.'

They covered nearly a hundred yards in silence. George was longing to ask Edward why he and Annaliese didn't appear to mind that they had drifted so far apart. However, when George did speak, he took off in a new direction.

'What am I going to do with myself now?'

'You carry on as planned,' Edward replied. 'There's a job waiting for you at Boothby's. No reason to change, is there?'

'Not unless Aunt Bee objects to having me.'

'She won't,' Edward said confidently. 'Beatrice is a very modern, enlightened woman – always has been. There used to be a chap called Paul Marks at Boothby's: he was a homosexual and your Aunt Beatrice thought the world of him. He was her right-hand man.'

'I suppose she does have to know the truth?' George said.

'It's best. She'll wonder why you didn't sit your finals and we shouldn't lie to *her*.'

'What about everyone else?' George asked.

'Anyone in particular?' Edward asked shrewdly.

'Well . . .' George was embarrassed. 'Athene.'

'Ah, yes.' Edward understood. There had been no sign of Athene when they arrived from Oxford. Later, it had emerged that she had spent the day in Bath with Nicholas, helping him with estate business, but she was sure to find out that George was unexpectedly home. 'I'll concoct a good story,' Edward said. 'Some sort of illness should do the trick.'

'Thanks.' George decided to make a clean breast of it. 'As a matter of fact, Athene might know that I'm sort of different. Two years ago she caught Robert and me out a few times at The Chantry – we weren't actually doing anything, but it must have looked odd.'

'It hasn't stopped her thinking the world of you,' Edward said. 'No, leave it to me, I'll put everyone off the scent.' He paused to pat breathless, happy dogs and throw sticks. Then, smiling, he shook his head in a way that suggested self-deprecation. 'Beatrice might find this amusing. You see, I loathed that chap, Marks, simply because he was a homosexual. He never did anything to offend me and he was very good to your mother when she joined the firm.'

'Why did you hate him?' George asked, curious, not annoyed.

'This is strictly between ourselves,' Edward said, suddenly wary.

'Of course.'

'When I was at Winchester, I must have appealed to a certain type of chap. Even though I didn't give them a scrap of encouragement, some of them . . . well . . . they tried to force their attentions on me.'

George was horrified. 'Mother would play merry hell with you for sending Douglas and me there after *that*!'

Closing his mind to the possibility of Annaliese ever finding out, Edward went on. 'Then, in Vienna, before the First War, one of my contacts was a homosexual. He was a slimy individual who always looked as though he was going to touch me.'

'Robert and I came across them at Oxford,' George said. 'They make your flesh creep.'

'How did you deal with them?' Edward asked.

'Robert did. Very firmly.'

'Probably the only way.' Again, Edward broke off to humour the dogs. 'So, you see, Beatrice will have grounds for finding this a trifle ironic.'

'In that case, I shall look forward to letting her know how broad-minded you've become,' George said. 'Seriously, Father, you've been splendid. I was terrified of what you'd say or do.'

'Going off the deep end didn't seem like an intelligent way to behave.' Touched by George's affectionate compliment,

Edward added, 'Heaven knows what you must think of being robbed of a chance to get a good degree.'

'It's pretty awful,' George said quietly. Taking Edward's arm in a gesture of companionship, he asked, 'Do you think that Robert *will* come back in a few months?'

'Why shouldn't he?'

'I don't know. I have a feeling that he won't. He's been *damaged* by this. I wouldn't be surprised if he isn't hoping to start a completely new life in Northumberland.'

The same thought had occurred to Edward on Oxford railway station. He said, 'What will you do if that proves to be the case?'

'What *can* I do? Get over it.'

'Has Robert been the only one?' Edward asked gently.

'Yes.' This time it was George who busied himself with the dogs, using the delay to assemble his tormented thoughts into a semblance of order. 'I'd like to wait before I go to Boothby's – give myself time. At the risk of sounding ridiculous, is there a way I could hide for, say, a year?'

'But *doing* something,' Edward replied. 'You wouldn't want to be twiddling your thumbs.'

'I'd go mad if I did.'

Edward mulled it over as they walked. 'How about helping me, eh? I'm sure Winston wouldn't mind if I adopted you as my research assistant.'

'Could you?' For the first time that day, George was happy. 'That would be tremendous.'

'I'll arrange it tomorrow. I'll also have words with Beatrice. Better still, why don't you and I run up to Town to see her?'

'Thank you, Father.'

When they were back in the Castle, enjoying a glass of whisky in the library, George raised another of his worries, blurting it out impetuously. 'I shall have to marry, shan't I? This place needs an heir.'

'For pity's sake, George, let's cross one bridge at a time, shall we?' Ashamed of his exasperated outburst, Edward added, 'Marriage is a tricky business at the best of times, old chap. And I'm hardly the best person to advise you. But, since you raise the subject, yes, something will have to be worked out – your mother will be keen. Now, can we relax?'

Smiling, George nodded. Whatever else, the nightmare had finally brought him close to his father.

Annaliese had come to like Lisbon very much.

During the fiendish winter of 1947, she had cursed her adopted country for giving up the ghost. A two-day blizzard followed by five weeks of harsh frost produced chaos and misery on a scale that beggared belief. The British blended their obsession with the weather and grim prediliction for the downright bad into a joyful acceptance of power cuts that lasted for days and a total breakdown of the transport system. Extreme though the original conditions were, Annaliese was convinced that nationwide incompetence and lack of will made everything ten times worse. As soon as travel became possible, she fled to Portugal and stayed there for six weeks.

On subsequent visits in June and October, she began to spend days in Lisbon and found it very much to her taste, a far cry from London's pinched drabness. The comparison was grossly unfair: Lisbon had not been bombed and forced to act as the nerve-centre for the most punishing war in history. Annaliese knew this, but denied London any entitlement to special consideration and gave her heart to Lisbon.

Kurt, acting as guide, interpreter, and protector, was her constant companion. When Annaliese began buying clothes from the salon that Cristobal Balenciaga had opened on Rua Augusta, neither of them thought it strange that he should offer his judgement on which garments suited her best. That was how they spent the morning on which George was sent down from Oxford. At midday, Kurt drove back to the villa and, in the absence of the cook, who came in very rarely these days, prepared a salad which they ate together on the terrace.

Afterwards, leaving Kurt busy in the kitchen, Annaliese went to Max's house. Since it was her first visit of this particular trip, there was a great deal of news, mostly information from his contacts in Vienna. Generally, it was cheering. Having escaped the fate of inclusion in the Soviet bloc, Austria was making a good recovery from the War. The country was split into four zones, occupied by Britain, America, Russia, and France, who also exercised joint control over Vienna. The victors were using a light touch, exerting minimum influence on the freely elected Government. The contrast between this and what appeared to be happening behind the barrier that Churchill had called the Iron Curtain was stark.

'Three years after the War, and we have the first disaster already,' Vassily chuckled. 'That's democracy for you. It's never any good when it comes to the crunch.'

Laughing, Annaliese asked, 'What *do* you mean?'

Gleefully, Vassily expounded. 'The minute victory was proclaimed, the Americans went home. President Truman had promised it, so it happened – poof! Same with the British. Some idiot persuaded Churchill that he'd win the election if he got boys out of uniform double-quick. But the Red Army stayed. Three, maybe four million of them, all over Eastern Europe. Stalin isn't bothered about the democracy farce, you see. He has no homes for his soldiers and they can't cause trouble in Mother Russia if they're camped out in Poland, Germany, Hungary, and every other damned place. Very clever.'

Annaliese, realising that this was probably what Edward would have told her had she bothered to ask, admitted that Vassily had a point.

At around 5.00 pm, she returned to her own villa, changed into a swimsuit from the morning's shopping spree and found Kurt to tell him that she was going to the pool.

'What do you think?' she asked, posing. 'Does it look all right on me?'

'Excellent, Highness.' After a thorough inspection, Kurt added, 'Most flattering.' As ever, he was impeccably respectful, but they both realised that Annaliese was taking a further step along a new road. It had begun when she clasped his hand at the airport three days ago.

Before diving into the pool, Annaliese removed the new swimsuit. Kurt, who knew of her fondness for nude bathing, always kept well out of the way. After ten minutes of vigorous exercise, she climbed out of the water, dried off, and wriggled back into the swimsuit. Then, until dinner, which they took at the early hour of 7.00, Annaliese soaked up the warm evening sun.

Kurt was visibly surprised when she took her seat at the table on the terrace. Always, whatever the informality of the day, she dressed in the evening. Tonight, however, Annaliese simply slipped a cotton blouse over the swimsuit. She noticed Kurt's reaction and was pleased.

As they enjoyed a Wiener Schnitzel that matched the best of pre-1914 Vienna, Annaliese tried to draw Kurt out on the menace of Communism. 'It was inevitable,' he said dismissively. 'When Hitler failed to crush Russia, he unleashed the demon.'

'Better if Germany had conquered Russia?' Annaliese suggested.

'Who knows? No, on balance, I think not.'

They talked on, but it was obvious that Kurt was distracted by Annaliese's unconventional attire and faintly disturbing attitude. Although they both paid lip-service to the mistress-servant relationship, subtly adapted to their own use, she was inviting him to view her as a woman, rather than an archduchess. Half an hour passed and Kurt, recovering from his initial confusion was beginning to respond.

Annaliese chose what she prayed was the right moment. Allowing their conversation to peter out and recede into a short silence, she asked, 'Do you find me attractive, Kurt?'

'Yes, Highness, very much so.'

'I'm fifty-two next month. A dangerous age for a woman.'

'Dangerous?' Kurt frowned thoughtfully. 'No, I don't think so. Perhaps you mean *vulnerable*.'

Annaliese inclined her head in agreement. 'Perhaps.'

Kurt shrugged. 'And what is forty-six for a man? Very awkward, some would say. For me, it is contentment after my excursion to Leningrad with the Nineteenth *Panzer* Division.'

After studying him closely for a few moments, Annaliese said, 'We trust each other, you and me. Is it enough, I wonder?'

'Does it not seem so? We manage perfectly.'

'So we do.' Annaliese drained the last of her wine and placed the glass on the table with exaggerated care.

Resting his chin on his hand, Kurt stared thoughtfully into the deepening dusk across the garden, assessing the tension and promise of excitement that they were generating. 'You think this will make things troublesome?' he asked.

'It could. Lovers fall out. That's no good, is it? I can't afford to lose you.'

Kurt nodded. 'I understand. Who else could you rely on to look after this place?'

'Indeed.'

'We must have two, disconnected relationships,' Kurt said. 'One for the days and one for the nights. Different rules.'

'Are you giving me your word of honour on that? It would work?' Annaliese was tense as she awaited the answer.

'Yes, Highness, I am and it would.'

Suddenly, Annaliese lost the courage that had brought her this far. 'This won't be disagreeable for you, Kurt? Wouldn't you prefer a young woman – someone of, say, twenty-five?'

At once, Kurt was galvanised into action. Standing up, he lifted her from the chair before she knew what was happening. Instinctively, Annaliese put her arms round his neck and kissed him. 'I've been so lonely,' she murmured.

'I know, Highness. It has caused me great concern.'

Carrying her indoors, Kurt took Annaliese to her bedroom. A few minutes later, her cry of pleasure was the first of many that were to echo through the villa that night.

Normally, she woke no later than 7.00 am: the following morning it was nearly 10.30. Lying in the bath, sipping cool, fresh orange juice, Annaliese tried to remember what time Kurt had left her and returned to his own room. It must, she supposed, have been nearly 3.00 am.

They had behaved outrageously. Annaliese had experienced a torrent of sexual pleasure that obliterated all her previous memories. Moreover, her splendidly vigorous partner had been a man with whom Annaliese was not in love – or was she? Not that such niceties mattered: she felt wonderful and had no inclination whatsoever to indulge in soul-searching. Her mother, Nancy Shenstone, and Clementine had been right and Annaliese saluted them with a laugh of exuberant joy that came from the depths of her soul.

She dressed, discovered that she was alone in the villa, and wandered out to the terrace and garden. As if by magic, Kurt appeared at her side, dusting soil from his hands.

'Good morning, Highness. You slept well?'

'Yes, thank you, Kurt, very well.' In the nick of time, she stopped herself asking him the same question: they were working to daytime rules now.

'May I get you some breakfast, Highness?' Kurt asked.

'I'll wait for lunch,' Annaliese replied. 'I'd like us to go out to dinner this evening, Kurt. Can you suggest a place – good food, pleasant atmosphere, quiet?'

'The Cidadhe Velha at Sintra is supposed to be first-class. Expensive, though.' After Annaliese had waved the attempt at a veto aside, Kurt added, 'You promised to dine with His Highness, Maximilian, this evening.'

'That's easily settled,' Annaliese said. 'Telephone this place at Sintra for a booking.' She shot off to see Max before Kurt could think of another objection.

Not bothering to invent an excuse, Annaliese told Max that she would not be joining him for dinner. He was perfectly affable about it, but stared at her intently.

'Is something wrong?' Annaliese asked nervously.

'No. Far from it. You look especially lovely this morning, my dear.'

'Oh, thank you.' To her dismay, Annaliese felt herself blush.

'Yes, you're in magnificent form. I tell you what you remind me of. You're like your dear mother used to be after one of her little expeditions to Cascais. I believe she was friendly with the Italian chap who owned that hotel by the harbour.'

Annaliese laughed. 'Max, you're wicked!'

'I'll bet I'm right,' he called as she fled.

Following lunch, Annaliese decided that it was her turn to wash up. Turning to Kurt, who was incapable of accepting that she might like performing such chores, she said, 'What are you doing this afternoon?'

'I shall cut the lawns, Highness.'

'Don't bother,' Annaliese replied. 'Do them tomorrow morning before it gets too hot. Take a siesta instead. You need it. No.' She held up an imperious hand to silence him. 'There are times when the rules need to be flexible.

Just be sensible and rest, will you? With the mood I'm in, you'll be dead within three days if you don't take care of yourself.'

Kurt's handsome but impassive and often brooding face lit up with a brilliant smile. 'I shall obey orders, Highness,' he said and disappeared to his room. Ten minutes later, when Annaliese poked her head round the door, he was fast asleep. Very soon, so was she.

At 5.00 pm, when they were refreshed, Annaliese insisted that Kurt joined her for a swim. 'Get rid of those shorts!' she called after surfacing from her dive into the water. 'You look much better without them.'

She covered ten lengths of the long pool as fast as she could, then dog-paddled over to Kurt who was standing at the shallow end. Clasping his shoulders and exploiting buoyancy, she wrapped her legs round his hips. 'There's something I have to ask you, Kurt Schneider,' she said.

'Please do, Highness.' Recognising that the idea of a firm division between day and night was impossible, Kurt slid his hands round her buttocks, providing support.

'Before you, there were only two men in my life,' Annaliese said. 'But, I know enough to appreciate that you're a great expert.'

'I'm glad you think so, Highness.' Po-faced, Kurt was playing a game. He was also, Annaliese noticed happily, becoming aroused by their embrace.

'You're exceptionally virile,' she went on. 'Very skilful, too. You know tricks that I haven't come across before. Who taught you?'

'I have known other ladies.'

Annaliese looked at him quizzically, realised that he was hoping to avoid giving details, and decided not to let him. 'Tell me,' she said. 'And why were you in Salzburg when the War started?' Smiling wickedly, she made the request for information irresistible by the way she rocked against Kurt's hardness.

He was an only child, adored by his mother, regarded as an inconvenience by his father. When he was sixteen, Kurt had started work at the Altwienerhof, one of Vienna's best restaurants, systematically progressing from dishwashing to wine waiter. In 1926, when he was twenty-four, his mother had died, a victim of tuberculosis. Almost immediately, wanting nothing further to do with his father, Kurt accepted the offer of a post at *Schloss Hellbrunn*, Salzburg's most celebrated hotel. That, he attempted to imply, was the end of the story.

'Oh no, I don't think so,' Annaliese laughed. 'What happened? Did you meet a ravishing girl – marry, perhaps?'

'No, I have never been married,' Kurt replied. 'Not after seeing the unhappiness my mother endured.'

'There are successful marriages,' Annaliese pointed out. 'I've come across one or two.'

'I haven't. Many of the ladies who visited *Schloss Hellbrunn* were completely disillusioned.'

'And frustrated?' Annaliese asked.

'Yes.'

'So, you did your best to provide relief?'

'They insisted on it, Highness,' Kurt replied, fearsomely straight-faced.

'Yes, I see.' Annaliese gazed at him solemnly, as though they were discussing a great tragedy. 'This was hard work?'

'Many of them were very demanding.'

'But you put up with it?'

'It was a point of honour.'

'Yes, I suppose it must have been. Tell me ...' Annaliese ran the tip of a finger along the line of Kurt's fine chin '... what about after you came here?'

Rather sheepishly, Kurt said, 'There was a lady in Estoril, Highness.'

'Aha.' Annaliese smiled gleefully. '*Was*, you say, not *is*?'

'I gave her up after Her Highness, your mother, died and you decided to keep the villa.'

'Why?'

'Because I knew that, sooner or later, Your Highness would need me. I did not wish to be involved with anyone else when that happened.'

Annaliese gaped at him. 'You knew ...' Recovering her poise, she began again. 'You expected that I would want you?'

Kurt remained calm. 'I saw that you were disappointed and in need of consolation. Since I admired Your Highness, I hoped to be of service.'

'What do you mean by "admired"?' Annaliese asked teasingly.

'If you insist on knowing, I desired you,' Kurt replied, rather put out.

Annaliese chuckled. 'How lovely! No, Kurt, don't be annoyed. I'm very grateful to you – and all these women. They obviously taught you the tricks you showed me last night.'

'Yes.'

'God bless them!' Annaliese laughed. 'Are there more?'

'I think Your Highness will be pleasantly surprised.'

'Good. Let me tell you something,' Annaliese said. 'A long time ago – nearly twenty-five years – I was here, on holiday, with my husband. He was having lunch with Max and Vassily and I was down here, swimming. My mother was over there – where that sun bed is. I climbed out of the pool, naked, of course, and was frightened half to death by my husband, bawling at me. He'd crept down through the garden, was disgusted by the sight of my body, and was shouting that I should cover myself up. There was a shocking scene. Mama was terribly upset. Later that afternoon, my husband was notified that his father was very ill and he went back to

England. I stayed here and the quarrel was never repaired. It was the end for us.'

Annaliese turned away, looking at the trees surrounding the pool, then up at the clear, blue sky. Imagining that she had finished, Kurt said, 'A sad story, Highness. I'm sorry.'

Still gazing skywards, Annaliese said, 'Over the years, I've had a secret wish – a sort of ambition. I've imagined how nice it would be to do something utterly scandalous here, something to justify the poor opinion my husband had of me that day.' She smiled at her lover. 'At long last, the time has come. You're going to take me on that sun bed, Kurt. Let's see if you can perform even better than last night.'

Three weeks later, on 5 June, Annaliese tore herself away from the villa and returned to Compton Allardyce. As usual, Gwen had received a cable. Matthew was dispatched to London Airport and Edward was advised of the arrangements. Making his excuses at Chartwell, he drove to the Castle to be with George when Annaliese arrived.

Leaving Kurt had been a terrible wrench that had plunged Annaliese into the strangest of moods. She was abstracted, unable to concentrate on her surroundings, loathed the need to speak English, was dauntingly unapproachable, and longing for an excuse to be bad-tempered.

Tea was brought to the largest of the sitting-rooms in the West Wing and Edward set about explaining George's departure from Oxford. As a defence against Annaliese's mood, he made the sort of speech that would have gone down well at a Foreign Office briefing. Hardly daring to breathe as he watched his mother, George was astonished by her lack of reaction: she heard Edward out in withdrawn, unfathomable silence.

When Edward had finished, Annaliese looked directly at him for the first time and asked, '*Have* we avoided a scandal?'

'It seems so.' Edward relaxed. 'That very night – the day

it happened – the scout who was threatening to cause trouble was drowned.'

'*Drowned?*' Annaliese was incredulous.

'Yes. Apparently, Littlejohn had a word with him and made vague promises about money and a better job. He went to a pub in the evening and had a skinful. At closing time, he got mixed up in a brawl over a woman and fell into the canal, which is more or less directly outside the pub. He couldn't swim and no one was sober enough to get him out.'

'The police aren't treating the incident as suspicious?' Annaliese asked.

'No, the inquest returned a verdict of accidental death.'

'How very fortunate!' Annaliese said acidly. Then, turning to George, she demanded, 'Why didn't you have the sense to lock your door?'

'I . . .' Paralysed by nerves, George was unable to answer.

Unconcerned, Annaliese walked to a window and surveyed the Park, obviously finding nothing to interest or please her. She said, 'I hope you've got this homosexual fad out of your system, George. I know it's a phase that many young men seem to enjoy, but it's time you were thinking of marriage. Allardyce needs a son to follow you.'

Not waiting for a reply, she walked towards the door. While Edward and George were exchanging stunned looks, there was a parting shot. 'I shall be returning to the villa in July,' Annaliese said. 'The prospect of summer in Portugal is *tremendously* appealing.' Then she was gone.

Edward cleared his throat. 'I *think* that was worse than I'd feared,' he muttered.

'I can't believe it.' George was dazed, like a man dragged from an accident. 'What did she say?' He counted the points off on his fingers. 'Are we free of scandal? Why didn't I lock the door? I must marry and have a son. She never asked about Robert.'

'That surprised me,' Edward said. 'I thought she was fond of him.'

Petulantly, George asked, 'Why the devil did she bother coming back from Portugal? She'll be off again in five minutes.'

Edward shrugged and made no attempt to comment. 'Look, George, I'm due at Chartwell tomorrow, but I'll tell your mother what I've arranged for you before I go. If you're wise, you'll keep out of her way.'

'Don't worry, I will. I'll take that work you've given me up to The Chantry. I like it there.'

'Be patient with your mother,' Edward said. 'She'll come round in time. She's going through a tricky patch at the moment.'

'What's the trouble?' George asked.

'I haven't the faintest idea,' Edward sighed. 'That crack about young men going through a phase shook me. I had no idea she knew of such things. I'll bet that goes back to Vienna. She does that a lot nowadays. And, strictly between the two of us, I gather that Nancy Shenstone has let things slip – she doesn't write too often. However, as I say, give your mother time and she'll be as nice as pie again.'

'There's still the marriage thing,' George grumbled.

Edward rubbed his chin. 'Yes, we shall have to think of something.'

'I've got it!' In less than a second, George soared from despair to elation. 'What about Athene? She's a good sport – pretty, too.' Slightly unsure of whether it was the right thing to do, he added, 'I've told her everything – about Robert and Oxford.'

'*Have* you?' Edward was pleased. 'Yes, that was sensible. It helps her to understand – be your friend.'

'That's how I saw it,' George replied, much relieved.

'As to marriage, I'm afraid it's not on,' Edward continued.

'You're right about Athene, she is ideal – or would be if it weren't for the wretched illegitimacy business.'

'But she's a Laverstoke, Father,' George protested.

'You, I, and about half a dozen others know that, George, and it must stay that way.'

'Wasn't our First Duke a bastard?' George asked rebelliously.

'In more ways than one, from what I've read.' Seeing that his attempt at humour had failed, Edward became deadly serious. 'I'm sorry, George, you can't have an illegitimate duchess, especially in this glorious twentieth century of ours.'

Even though George saw very little of Annaliese over the ensuing ten days, it was clear that she remained unsympathetic. Worse still, George suspected that his mother had given the matter no further thought: she had stated her opinion and for her, that was the end of it. In the absence of Edward, who divided his time between Chartwell and Cadogan Square, George relied on Athene for companionship and moral support.

The Government's bureaucratic mania for asking stupid questions in triplicate meant that running the Duchy of Lincolnshire's affairs involved coping with an avalanche of paper. After Nicholas and Henrietta had been reduced to gibbering wrecks, it was discovered that Athene had a talent for deciphering the turgid utterances of pompous civil servants. That, and a photographic memory, made her a miracle-worker. Hidden away in a cubby-hole on the ground floor of the Castle's Central Wing, she dealt with the dreaded buff-coloured forms and everything else that others were unable to handle. Soon, she was revelling in the title of 'Estate Secretary' and demanding a bigger office. At 5.00 pm, when she cycled home to Gainsborough Wood, she invariably made a detour to call in at The Chantry to chat with George.

'Have you seen anything of Mother?' he asked at the end of a day that had seen his spirits sink to new depths.

'She went up to London yesterday evening,' Athene replied.

'What for?'

'Boothby's, I think.' Athene's green eyes lit up with mischief. 'She wants to make sure everyone's on the ball.'

George threw up his hands in despair. 'She hasn't been anywhere near the place for ages. Aunt Bee *will* be pleased.'

'What about your friend, the awful Dowager?' Athene asked. 'Doesn't *she* need watching?'

'*I* can't stand her, but that's only a personal thing,' George said. 'By all accounts, she does a splendid job at Boothby's.'

After a thoughtful pause, Athene said, 'Isn't it funny how things have changed? Your father used to be the villain and your mother thought the world of you. Now it's the other way round.'

'Confusing, isn't it?' George smiled ruefully.

'And this all started when you were chucked out of Oxford? There were no signs before?'

'It's difficult to say.' Perplexed, George ruffled his hair into a shambles that had Athene biting back laughter. 'I've come to the conclusion that things must have been changing for some time. The War stopped people noticing what was going on.' After staring intently into space for a few moments, George said, 'This Portugal caper bothers me. Why does she spend so much time over there?'

'Perhaps she just likes it,' Athene suggested. 'It must be more fun than England. These days, anywhere is.'

'Father has a theory that she's reverting to being a foreigner,' George said.

'True.' Athene was putting on an act, pretending to be terrifically wise and all-seeing. 'You can never really tell what's going on in that Viennese head of hers.' In response to

George's startled look, she grinned sheepishly and admitted, 'That's what Ma says.'

'Yes, I expect that's what it is,' George mused. 'All perfectly innocent.'

Athene's eyes opened saucer-wide. '*Innocent?* Of course it is. You surely don't think that there's hanky-pankies in the lush hills about Cascais?'

'Of course not,' George said angrily. 'And even if there were, how would a pervert like me be able to judge?'

Athene groaned. '*Do* stop it, George,' she begged. 'This self-pity's getting to be a trial.'

'I'm sorry,' he said huffily. 'I don't want to be a nuisance.'

'You'll have to try harder,' Athene said.

Annoyed, George retaliated, 'To save you the trouble of asking, no, I haven't heard from Robert yet. It's over two weeks since I wrote to him and he *still* hasn't replied.'

'I wasn't going to ask,' Athene stormed, working up to one of her melodramatic departures. 'I'm fed up of the way you act like a dead duck when I do. *If* I come tomorrow, I'll expect to find you in a better mood.'

Normally, when Athene pedalled the two miles from The Chantry to Gainsborough Wood, she was aware of the Park's beauty and her good fortune in having a mother who had found them such a wonderful home. Today, however, she was deep in thought, oblivious of her idyllic surroundings.

She knew that George dreaded marriage. Athene was almost eighteen and innocent of sexual experience: but her instincts whispered that George was terrified by the prospect of attempting sex with a woman. Apart from factors she made no pretence of comprehending, he probably feared that his efforts would earn ridicule.

Surely, Athene kept telling herself as she cycled home, surely there was something she could do to help George.

Annaliese was in a serenely good mood when she came back from a five-week stay in Portugal.

'I'd sell what's left of my soul for a tan like yours,' Clementine Laverstoke said over tea in the middle of August, a few days after Annaliese's return.

'I didn't do much besides swim and lie in the sun,' Annaliese replied.

'Rather more than that, I think,' Clementine said quietly.

'What *do* you mean? Don't stare at me like that, Clem, it's unnerving.'

'You've been more than unnerved in the last few weeks,' Clementine retorted. 'Am I not right in thinking that there's a replacement for poor John Brandon?'

'Well – yes,' Annaliese admitted.

'Want to tell me anything about him?'

'I'd better not.' Then, after a pause, Annaliese was unable to resist saying, 'I'm afraid it's the man who looks after the villa – he's a servant, really.'

'Is he, by God?' Clementine was vastly impressed. 'Well, he's doing you a power of good, my dear. You look disgustingly radiant. And you aren't in the least "afraid".'

'No, I'm not,' Annaliese said. As if simultaneously explaining and excusing everything, she added, 'He's Austrian.'

Clementine nodded understandingly. 'Something else, too,' she said. 'He's hidden away from prying eyes: remember what I told you about this country?'

'Yes, I do.' Smiling, Annaliese told the truth. 'But I didn't take that into account when I decided to throw myself at him.'

Robert Chappell's letter, which eventually turned up at the end of August, was an edgy combination of affection and calculated detachment. It was difficult to get away, Robert said, because of work on his uncle's farm. A list of all the tasks he was undertaking plunged George into despair. Nevertheless, doing his best to be cheerful, he wrote back at once.

The reply, in November, had been delayed by clearing up after the harvest, the autumn livestock fair at Hexham, and goodness knows how many other things. Rather too casually, Robert mentioned that he was thinking of a career in farming: his uncle was all in favour. There was also Mary, a local girl who helped out and was proving to be a good friend.

11

1951
'. . . she looked ready to pass out'

During supper at Putney Vale on an evening in July, Celia finally abandoned the idea of persuading Ursula to pack up and go abroad. Arabella, never mentioned, but now presumed to be dead, was no longer used as an excuse. Instead, Ursula had become adept at discovering the shortcomings of other countries. Her, 'No, I don't think so, my dear. Better the devil you know,' was the all-embracing excuse for staying put that Celia came to dread.

She had considered going it alone, only to be beaten by her bane, the language difficulty. For nearly twelve months during 1949 and 1950, she had taken French lessons with a retired schoolteacher in Wimbledon. After well over 200 hours of coaching on Monday and Thursday evenings, the certainty of the verdict had not lessened the angry humiliation it provoked.

'I'm sorry, Lady Lincolnshire, but you don't seem to have any aptitude for the language. You're not alone, by any means, so don't blame yourself. You *could* make yourself understood at a rudimentary level, but you'd have no idea what people were saying to you. The vocabulary gives you no end of trouble and your pronunciation will always let you down. It would be very wrong of me to carry on encouraging you – or taking your money.'

For a day or two, Celia's bitterness was magnified by the fact that, even if she could achieve perfect fluency, she probably lacked the courage to go to the Côte d'Azur on her own. She concentrated on how well she was doing at Boothby's and persuaded herself that she felt happier. She set a new goal: in 1958, when she was fifty-five – and still capable of turning men's heads if her allure at forty-seven were anything to go by – she would retire to a cliff-top house on the south coast and entertain a handful of lucky clients. It was a good thought.

'In any case, all our troubles will soon be over,' Ursula said on that summer Friday evening in 1951.

'Why do you think that?' Celia asked.

'There's going to be another election,' Ursula replied. 'Winston will be back and everything will come right.'

Although Labour had won the General Election of 1950, they had done so with a drastically reduced majority. Unable to rely on the support of Aneurin Bevan and his idealistic cronies, it was certain that Attlee would be forced to go to the country. It was almost equally certain that he would lose.

'That will be a good thing,' Celia agreed. 'Not that this government can be blamed for *everything*. A lot has been beyond their control.'

Ursula laughed. 'Where did you get that nonsense from?'

'Nigel Templeton.' Provocatively, Celia took her time over a mouthful of food before adding, 'We have lunch together every so often and he talks about economics.'

'Economics, my foot,' Ursula snorted. 'He's single, attractive, he controls a merchant bank, and you want me to believe that you talk about economics. How old is he now?'

'Forty.'

'Have you had a fling with him?'

'No, I haven't.' Celia, who regretted her inability to be anything more than a casual friend to Nigel, pulled a sour face. 'Actually, he's about to announce his engagement.'

'Who's the lucky woman?'

'Julia Christopherson.'

Ursula's eyebrows shot up. 'Part of *the* Christophersons?'

'Cedric's daughter, no less,' Celia said. 'Nigel claims to love her.'

'Don't be cynical,' Ursula scolded. 'Just because two banking families are getting together, you mustn't assume that the divine passion is absent.' After chuckling at Celia's scowl, Ursula asked, 'What sort of week has it been at Boothby's?'

'Quiet. Next week will be hectic. There are three big sales.'

'Have you had the benefit of the Duchess of Lincolnshire's invaluable assistance?' Ursula was sweetness personified.

'Yes, we have.' Celia was furious. 'She's been here, there and every-bloody-where. Yesterday, she decided that one of next week's catalogues ought to be reprinted.'

'Oh dear,' Ursula said, deeply insincere.

'Beatrice put her foot down,' Celia went on. 'She actually stood up to the interfering cow. The lovely thing is, Her Majesty won't even *be* there when the sales take place.'

'Off to sunny Portugal again?'

Celia glared and said, 'Whatever it is she gets out there, I'd like some of it.'

'Don't jump to conclusions,' Ursula said, very aunt-like. 'It's probably perfectly harmless. If you had a villa in Portugal, wouldn't you want to escape from miserable Mr Attlee and his austerity as often as possible?'

'Perfectly harmless be damned,' Celia said. 'Honestly,

Ursula, you should see her when she gets back from these holidays – the woman is getting herself screwed witless.'

'Really, my dear, do you *have* to use crude Americanisms?' Ursula's pretence at lofty distaste was so convincing that Celia was contrite. Then, after a pause, Ursula asked, 'Are you sure?'

'Positive. I, of all people, know the signs.' Celia's smile was self-mocking. 'And it's not only afterwards, when she's worn out and happy, it's before, when she's looking forward to it. That's what's been behind this week's performance.'

'Well, I wish her luck.' Pushing aside the pangs of nostalgia and longing for her prime, Ursula said, 'You miss Edward, don't you?'

'Yes, I suppose I do.' Hating the admission, Celia sighed heavily. 'Towards the end he was quite good at it, and I enjoyed talking to him. I used to like hearing his views on what the world was up to.'

'Perhaps you'll come together again,' Ursula suggested. 'How much longer will he be involved with this book of Churchill's?'

'They're nearly finished. I think they've started on volume six, which is the last one.'

'Let's hope they complete it before Winston becomes Prime Minister again,' Ursula said.

'I don't think it will make any difference to me.' Celia was petulant. 'Edward and I served each other's purpose, but we're finished.'

'Perhaps he's found someone else?'

'No.' Celia was confident. 'He might accept an offer if it fell into his lap, he'd never go looking for it.'

After leaving Celia alone with her thoughts for a few moments, Ursula asked, 'How are you getting on with George?'

'We manage,' Celia said. 'He doesn't like me.'

'Why?'

'He knows what Edward and I used to get up to – or suspects, which is virtually the same thing. He's always worshipped his mother, so that gives him a reason to detest me. *However*, Annaliese doesn't seem to care much for him lately. She flew off the handle today because Beatrice is letting him do one of next week's auctions.'

'You've said he's good at a sale.' Ursula smiled. 'Somewhat grudgingly, I recall.'

'He is. But for the last two years, Annaliese's had it in for him.'

'Curious.' Ursula was lost in thought. 'How old is George?'

'Twenty-nine.'

'Isn't it time he was married?'

'I've been wondering about that,' Celia replied.

'And what conclusions have you reached?'

'None. I simply cannot weigh him up.'

'Where does George find his pleasures?' Ursula asked.

'I *presume* it's Compton Allardyce,' Celia said. 'He goes there at lunch-time every Friday and doesn't show his face in Bond Street until Monday afternoon. He has The Chantry, so he can do as he likes.' Celia's face lit up. 'Like I used to.'

'But you aren't *totally* sure of this?' Ursula insisted. 'You *presume?*'

'Well, yes – but it seems likely, doesn't it?'

Ursula's eyes narrowed shrewdly. 'Possibly. I find it very interesting, though, that someone who knows as much about men as you do is reduced to making assumptions about the Marquess of Axholme. Is there a more eligible man in England?'

'I doubt it,' Celia said.

'Yet his name has never been linked to a woman,' Ursula murmured. 'Especially not to the four or five obvious candidates to be the next Duchess of Lincolnshire. Do you know, Celia, I could easily find that extremely strange.'

'What are you suggesting?'

'Eh?' Ursula looked mildly surprised. 'I don't know that I'm suggesting anything, my dear – except that your friend, George, is a bit of a puzzle.'

Late the following afternoon, a Saturday, George stood at a window of The Chantry, looking south across the Park. Not for the first time, the view of the Castle from this direction seemed unsatisfactory. The front elevation was superb and probably without equal in England, but the back, with its higgledy-piggledy assortment of outbuildings that were at odds with each other was far from pleasing. The two views – perfection from the south, an ugly hotchpotch from the north – struck the heir to it all as summing up himself.

'I don't want any of this,' George said. 'I'll renounce it.'

Taking her time, Athene asked, 'What would you do with it? Let the Government take it over? Assuming they could sell it, how many pairs of false teeth would it provide? Better still, they might get a couple of hospitals out of it.'

Ignoring her, George said, 'I wonder how close Father came to turning it down?'

'Not very,' Athene replied. 'Your dad is a *noblesse oblige* sort of bloke. Duty and all that.'

Choosing not to respond, George continued to stare out of the window.

Athene studied him, perplexed by the towel he had grabbed and wound round his waist. He had a gorgeous body, why was he so bashful? Firmly, Athene reminded herself that this was only the fourth time, and that George would soon relinquish his excruciating modesty. Mentioning it was out of the question: after the effort needed to get him this far, the thought of ruining it all made her cringe.

Becoming alarmed by the silence, Athene had another go at facetiousness. 'Don't you like the false teeth scheme? How much does a set cost? If you could raise the money for a million of them, they'd make you a national hero. Think of it – "The man who gave up his birthright so that the people could chomp!" It's terrific.'

George turned round, smiling broadly and handsomely. 'Athene, you are an idiot,' he said. 'Why can't you be serious?'

'I am being serious!' she squawked. 'It's a super idea, bang in line with your sympathies for poor old Attlee and his Welfare State.'

'Athene, much as I agree with the National Health Service, I don't think I should be expected to pay for it – not the whole thing.'

'Oho! Hypocrisy. My God, Axholme, you're a two-faced devil. Let me tell you ...' Athene stopped as she saw the change that had come over George. Her display of mock outrage seemed to have made him aware that she was sprawled stark naked on his bed. In a small, wistful voice, Athene said, 'I wish you'd look at me like that more often.'

'I've just realised how beautiful you are,' George told her, his voice wonderfully firm and confident.

'Thank you, kind sir. As a matter of fact, I must confess to finding you tolerably yummy.' Staring at him earnestly, Athene risked all. 'How did you find the fun and games before you decided you had to glare at your inheritance?'

'It was good – very good indeed.' George nodded vehemently, as if trying to convince himself. 'I ... er ... like being inside you. Robert and I never did that. It always struck us as distasteful – well, it would be, wouldn't it, up *there*?' As an anguished after-thought, George said, 'I don't think you enjoyed it all that much.'

Hanging on to her policy of total frankness, Athene said,

'I've no idea what it's *supposed* to be like — but it wasn't at all nasty. Look poppet, you've deflowered me, orgasms take longer, need more practice.'

Boggling, George asked, 'How do you know?'

'I've got a book.' Athene's eyes glowed with wickedness. 'I bought it when I went to London to see that poor soul at the Min of Ag about the farms in Devon. After I'd finished him off, I went to Greek Street and found this *fantastic* shop.' Pleased with herself, she added, 'And I still caught the three-fifteen.'

'Can I see it?' George asked, desperately eager.

'I'll bring it tomorrow.' Athene held out her beautiful arms. 'Come here. I'd like a cuddle and you need relieving of that ramrod you're hiding under that wretched towel.'

'I'm rather proud of that,' George said, lying down beside her.

'So am I, you toad,' Athene shrieked. 'It's my delectability wot caused it. You like my legs, don't you?' With graceful, lissome ease, she raised one of them until it was vertical. 'Lovely, ain't they?'

'They are,' George said enthusiastically.

Athene unravelled the towel round his waist. 'Shall I rub you, like Robert used to?' she asked.

'Yes, please,' George murmured, infinitely thankful for her patience and understanding.

'There are conditions,' Athene said, trying to sound dictatorial even though she was already obliging him.

'Go on.'

'First, I'm definitely to be allowed to watch you do your stuff at Boothby's on Wednesday?'

'Yes. But I'll have you thrown out if you start pulling faces at me. What else?'

'We need some more of those rubber thingeys. *You* get them this time! No, it's not a scrap of good looking like that,

Lord Axholme. I mustn't get pregnant, but I'm damned if I'm going into that place again.'

'What do I ask for?'

Athene mentioned a trade name that had become famous during the War.

'There aren't women serving in this shop?' George asked.

'That depends on your luck, matey. Get two dozen while you're at it.'

For a moment or two, George attempted to dissent, but Athene's exuberant efforts to induce his climax were too much for him.

*

The sale, which began at 11.00 am, consisted of eighty-odd paintings by the English water-colourists from the 1810–1840 period. About a dozen of the lots were highly desirable and there was a good turn-out. George, who could be a bit of a showman when he was on the auctioneer's rostrum, was in fine form and soon exceeding estimated prices by handsome margins. As usual when she watched a sale, Celia stood at the side of the room. For the first twenty minutes, she was preoccupied with the bidding, working out who was buying and for whom they might be acting. Absorbed by this, it was some time before she realised that, as each lot was knocked down, George glanced towards a particular point at the back of the room. Whatever he saw there produced a series of brief, private smiles and a boost to his confidence.

Celia had to edge several feet to her right in order to locate the source of George's support. Having done so, her eyes gleamed.

It was four years since her last sight of Athene. Then, the seventeen-year-old girl had been a potential beauty, but rather tomboyish, not quite knowing what to do with the mixture of her colt-like grace and awkwardness. Now, the problems had vanished and Athene was a most attractive young woman.

Moreover, she was deeply in love with George: she never took her eyes off him. Each time he looked at her, Athene smiled, wrinkled her nose, or pouted her lips into a childlike kiss.

When the sale ended at 12.30, and George was swamped by clients who had questions about payment and delivery of their purchases, Athene hung back. Soon, Beatrice joined her and they chatted animatedly. Drawn into conversation by two dealers, Celia reserved part of her attention for George. The moment he was free, he hurried to the back of the room where Athene congratulated him with a hug. By now unaware of what the dealers were saying to her, Celia heard Beatrice decline an invitation to join George and Athene for lunch.

They went off hand-in-hand, two people who were thrilled with each other. When George eventually returned to his office next to Celia's at a few minutes to four, she called out, 'What have you done with Athene?' making it sound like a friendly joke.

Pausing in the doorway, George said, 'I took her to Paddington for the train.' Looking very much as if he wanted to add, 'Not that it's any of *your* business,' he disappeared.

That evening, Celia told Ursula. 'This explains everything,' she concluded triumphantly. 'All is made clear.'

'Let me get this right,' Ursula said, anxious to clarify a point that Celia, in her excitement, had omitted. 'Athene is the girl without a father?'

'That's right, she's illegitimate. Therefore, no matter how much in love she and George are – and believe me, they *are* – marriage is out of the question.' Celia was struck by a thought. 'Actually, I'd put money on Desmond Prideaux being the father, which means that Athene has the breeding to be a marchioness. Sadly, she lacks the birth certificate.'

Disregarding Celia's merriment, Ursula frowned. 'George's parents must know what's going on,' she said, sounding aggrieved.

'They *ought* to,' Celia replied. 'It's happening under their noses.'

'Is it?' The question was thrown out like a challenge. 'You're always telling me how big that estate is, how easy it is to hide. You got away with blue murder at The Chantry, why shouldn't George? In any case, are his parents ever there? According to you, Edward virtually lives in Kent or Cadogan Square, and Annaliese thinks of nothing but Portugal. My guess is that they don't know what George has got himself into.'

Thoughtfully, Celia said, 'Yes, maybe you're right.'

'That pair are idiots!' Ursula was exasperated, as though the Duke and Duchess of Lincolnshire were close friends who pigheadedly refused to take her excellent advice. 'They should be scouring the country for the right daughter-in-law, not leaving George to his own daft devices.'

Athene subsequently turned up at Boothby's every two weeks or so, either to watch George conduct an auction, or to wait until he was ready to take her out to lunch. At the end of September, Annaliese witnessed their departing love-bird act and displayed outraged disbelief, thus confirming Ursula's theory. Later that day, Celia saw Annaliese stalk into George's office with a look on her face that would have cowed most people. Their argument lasted for nearly an hour and Annaliese seemed to be satisfied when she emerged.

A few days later, lunching at Whitaker's with a man who wanted Boothby's to sell his family silver, Celia spotted George and Athene tucked away in a corner. They looked very happy.

The General Election at the end of October duly returned the Conservatives to power, but by a narrower margin than expected. With a relatively slender majority of twenty-six, Churchill became Prime Minister again. As well as the unfinished business of post-war recovery, he had to deal with British involvement in the Korean conflict.

As luck would have it, most of the work on the final volume of the great history was finished: the one outstanding section, dealing with the intense fighting of March and April 1945, was being worked on by Churchill's team of military experts. Until they completed the draft in January, there was nothing more for Edward to do and he began to attend the House of Lords again.

Having taken herself off to Portugal to avoid the election and its campaign, Annaliese returned more full of beans than ever. Realising that it was time she displayed some interest in her home, she carried out a thorough inspection of the Castle, discovering curtains and carpets that needed replacing and a serious gap in the family history. Descending the main staircase one afternoon, Annaliese took more notice than usual of the paintings on the walls, the portraits of the first eight dukes. Not surprisingly, Ralph had never bothered to commission a picture of himself, but neither, after all this time, had Edward. The oversight must be rectified at once.

Expecting an argument, she was agreeably surprised.

'You're quite right, my dear,' Edward said, answering her telephone call at Cadogan Square. 'How do we set about it?'

'I imagine that it's perfectly straightforward. Artists must be queueing up to paint portraits. I'll talk to Beatrice, she knows the right people.'

Four days later, it was arranged. Edward had met Michael Taverner, liked him, and offered a fee that was nearly twice the going rate. Taking advantage of a November that was cold but clear and bright, thus providing an ideal studio light for five hours each day, work began immediately.

Taverner was thirty-two and a recent Royal Academician. Before the War, he had studied at the Academy's schools. Then, after serving with the Royal Navy, he had completed his training in Paris, returning to London in 1949. According to Beatrice's contacts, he was the man to watch.

When they settled down in the studio on the top floor of Michael's house in Chesham Place, one of the first things Edward said was, 'Forgive me for saying so, Mr Taverner, but you don't look like an artist. Of course, that stupid statement is based on my idea of what an artist *should* look like.'

'Not at all, Your Grace, most people say the same.' Michael's smile, though shy, lit up his powerful, craggy face.

Over six feet tall, he suggested a genteel, well-bred navvy, with massive shoulders and a body that was obviously muscular and powerful. By contrast, his hands were delicate and expressive, as were his brown eyes.

'I'm supposed to be the image of my grandfather,' Michael went on. 'He was *A Great Man*.'

Edward was intrigued by the subtle hint of mockery. 'What did he do?'

'He was an artist, too. Henry Algernon Taverner.' After intoning the name in a very grand manner, Michael looked up from the pad on which he was making a preliminary sketch. Realising that he must give more emphasis to Edward's jaw, he bowed his head again.

'Despite my links with Boothby's, I'm abysmally ignorant about art,' Edward said. 'Is your grandfather very famous?'

'Was,' Michael replied. 'Actually, notorious is probably a better word.'

Henry Algernon Taverner, who, Michael said, had liked to be known as HAT, with each letter enunciated separately, not dismissed as 'hat', had lived from 1838 to 1910. Throughout his adult life which, according to him, had begun at the age of sixteen, he had claimed to be a member of the Pre-Raphaelite Brotherhood. In fact, even his obscure and worthlessly sycophantic biographer of 1913 had been unable to unearth anything other than a tenuous link with Holman

Hunt and a single exchange of letters with Ford Madox Brown. That aside, HAT had produced a good many fine pictures and, in the 1880s, had succeeded in selling them to the municipal art galleries that a rush of competitive civic pride was creating in the cities of Northern England. Simultaneously, he developed a following in Chicago and Philadelphia.

Edward said, 'How interesting,' and Michael grunted. Apparently immersed in his work, he privately reviewed what else he knew about his grandfather.

HAT's other talent was as a womaniser. In 1891, he abandoned his wife and five children in order to establish an overtly Bohemian existence in a house on Hampstead Heath, bought with the proceeds of his American successes. Other artists, models, and hangers-on came and went, staying for a day or six months as the fancy took them, but two of HAT's associates were permanent fixtures. Maud Atkinson was his favourite model and mistress: there were over thirty known paintings of her, usually in an Etruscan setting with a soulful expression that was tantalisingly at odds with her lush, sensual beauty. The other immovable member of the household was a man who insisted that his name was Leonardo Gibbons, a couple of years younger than HAT and, supposedly, a fellow-artist. Contemporaries regarded Gibbons as an out-and-out charlatan, although there was substantial interest in something he said at a dinner-party in 1913.

In the summer of 1900, Gibbons claimed that HAT had rented a house in the hills between Florence and Siena. Accompanied by Maud and Gibbons, he had spent three months painting a series of pictures that would take the world by storm. Because Gibbons was drunk when he arrived at the party and grew worse as the evening progressed, such detail as could be extracted from him was garbled and far from convincing. The gist was that using Maud and three of the servants as models, HAT had executed a number of stunningly erotic canvases.

Exciting though the story sounded, no one gave it much credence. The pictures had been 'lost' for thirteen years; HAT was dead and his reputation, always dependent on a constant supply of scandal, was in rapid decline; and, six months after the Bloomsbury dinner, Leonardo Gibbons lost the battle against alcoholic poisoning. The disruption of the First World War put paid to the intriguing but implausible anecdote.

That, at any rate, was the public perception of the matter. Michael Taverner thought he knew differently.

His sole surviving relative, Aunt Muriel, one of the Great Man's two daughters, had told Michael that her father frequently spoke of the pictures. Muriel, seventy-eight and proud of the fact that she had never married, had been spectacularly promiscuous in her youth, earning HAT's approval and the bequest of the Hampstead House. Muriel Taverner relished the tale and was convinced that the pictures existed: in her considered opinion, they had gone to America.

Michael doubted it. One room of the house in Chesham Place that he had inherited from his mother was crammed with HAT's sketches, diaries, and papers. The diary for 1900 made no mention whatsoever of the sojourn in Italy: over four months were blank, a unique gap in HAT's generally verbose and self-congratulatory account of his life. And last year, Michael had stumbled across a letter to his grandfather from a man in Chicago who expressed a strong if coy interest in what were referred to as 'your epicurean masterpieces'. How, the writer wanted to know, could a viewing be arranged?

The letter was dated 9 October 1910, the day after HAT's death.

At their next sitting, Edward asked Michael Taverner about his parents.

'My father must have been a very remarkable man,' Michael said, not looking up from the sketch-pad. 'I never knew him – he was killed before I was born. In the First War. September 1918, when it was nearly over.'

'That was damned bad luck,' Edward murmured.

'Wasn't it, though? He'd been in France since the start and survived without a scratch to within six weeks of the end. Then a bloody great shell did for him.'

'What was he?' Edward asked. 'Infantry? Cavalry? Artillery?'

'He was a medical officer.' Michael looked up, smiling gently. 'That's why he was remarkable, you see. Despite having HAT for a father, he became a doctor – got himself into Guy's and worked like a demon.'

'That's an impressive achievement,' Edward agreed.

'Things were probably easier after the old man cleared off to Hampstead,' Michael said. 'It gave Grandmother a free hand with the children and she did well.' Nearly a minute passed, during which the pencil skimmed expertly across the pad. Shyly, Michael looked up to say, 'Would you care to see my father's Victoria Cross?'

'I'd be honoured,' Edward replied warmly.

'Give me a few minutes and we're finished for the day.'

They went downstairs and Michael left Edward with the medal while he made coffee. Edward noticed that there was only one decent cup: Michael used a chipped, badly stained mug.

'What about your mother?' Edward asked, offering his cigarette case.

'Also a doctor,' Michael said, leaning forward into the companionship of the lighter flame. 'She died four years ago in that terrible winter. Flu, bronchitis, turned to pneumonia overnight and she was gone.' Still missing her, Michael looked bleak. 'No one thought of sending for me.'

'Where were you?'

'Paris.'

Edward shuddered. 'That's an unhappy coincidence, Michael. I was in France when *my* mother died. Same damned thing, influenza – that dreadful epidemic in 1919.' As if attempting to exculpate himself, Edward added. 'I was on honeymoon – at St Malo, in January, if you please!'

Sensing his client's pain, even after all these years, Michael introduced a diversion. 'Lady Lincolnshire was a member of the Austrian Imperial Family, wasn't she?' Made nervous by Edward's sudden and surprisingly hard look, Michael added, 'I did some research. Nothing much, just a bit of background. I looked you up in *Debrett*.'

Relaxing, Edward nodded. 'Yes, she's a Habsburg. Wonderful woman. Between ourselves, Michael, I couldn't have coped without her. The title was thrust on me, you know.'

'Your cousin's murder,' Michael said quietly.

'Ghastly affair!' Edward straightened convulsively. 'Shall we be more cheerful?'

'Certainly. I'd like to show you where I'm up to.' Michael reached for the sheet of paper he had brought down from the studio.

Edward studied his likeness and was impressed. 'Well, I certainly look the part, don't I?' He held the sketch at arm's length, squinting at it through half-closed eyes. 'Hmm … Edward Boothby-Graffoe, Tenth Duke of Lincolnshire. It's very good. You've made me appear quite intelligent.'

'You are,' Michael said simply. 'One of the best brains in the House of Lords and a great loss to the Foreign Office.'

Edward laughed. 'What twaddle.' Secretly, he was immensely pleased. Handing the sheet of paper back to Michael, he asked, 'What happens next?'

'I transfer this outline to a canvas – scaling it up, of course. I'll do that this afternoon. Tomorrow morning we can start work on the real thing.'

'This is where you get cracking with oils and a palette?' Edward asked.

'Afraid not. I tend to mix colours on the top of that old table.' Michael pointed. 'And I use razor blades and knives as much as brushes.' He smiled. 'As you said, I'm not much like an artist.'

'You're good enough for me,' Edward declared. 'Do you think I could have that sketch when you've finished? It might go rather well in my library at Allardyce.'

Ten days later, when the portrait was almost complete, Edward took a morning off from the studio to attend a House of Commons Select Committee. Michael was glad of the opportunity to perform an errand. A friendly contact at the Royal Academy had told him that he had Lady Beatrice Templeton to thank for the desperately needed commission to paint her brother.

After buying a bunch of flowers from the barrow outside Bond Street Underground station, Michael presented himself at Boothby's and asked if Beatrice would spare him a few moments. Bored by one of the quietest mornings in months, she was delighted by the flowers and the gallant little speech that went with them.

'Now you're here, Mr Taverner, I wonder if we can be of assistance to each other,' Beatrice said. 'I understand that you're an authority on the Pre-Raphaelites.'

'Oh, no, that's putting it too strongly,' Michael replied. 'But I have made a special study of them – and I am the dreaded HAT's grandson.'

Beatrice laughed. 'I won't hold that against you.' Immediately serious, she said, 'I'm worried about the amount of rubbish coming on to the market.'

'You mean forgeries?' Michael asked. He had heard whispers.

'Yes, Mr Taverner, that's exactly what I mean. It's become a much sought-after period, especially with the Americans. We can't get enough of it. Even the minor, peripheral members of the school are fetching good prices.' Beatrice lowered her voice. 'About a month ago, we had two W H Deverell pictures – *everyone* we spoke to said they were genuine. The day before we put them on sale, Paul Mellon called in – he happened to be over on a visit and wondered if we had anything interesting.' Beatrice closed her eyes as if offering prayerful thanks. 'It was one of the luckiest things that's ever happened to Boothby's. Mr Mellon took one look at these so-called Deverells and said they were forgeries – almost certainly from Sweden, of all places!' Whispering now, Beatrice said, 'I have it on good authority that one of our competitors *did* sell a forgery, albeit in good faith, a few weeks ago.'

Michael grimaced. 'In those circumstances, there's no such thing as "good faith".'

'Quite. We can't afford to make mistakes. The consequences could be ruinous. Should the need arise, may I call on you for advice, Mr Taverner?'

'Of course. I'd be glad to help. But I don't claim to be infallible.'

'No one is. I'm working on the principle that the more we scrutinise, the less likely we are to be duped.'

'It's a good idea. Please call me at any time, Lady Beatrice.'

'Thank you, Mr Taverner.'

They shook hands and Michael made his way downstairs, blessing his good fortune. However small and infrequent the consultancy fees, they would be very welcome. Not looking where he was going, Michael collided with a woman in the awkward front doorway that Beatrice kept promising to modernise and improve.

Celia was on her way back from a chat with a client in a coffee-shop. Her initial reaction was to tell the hulking great oaf to take a great deal more care in future. The words died on her lips as she stepped back and appraised Michael.

Five seconds passed, a very long time for two strangers to stare at each other, transmitting quite extraordinary signals as they did so.

'Who are you?' Celia asked.

'Michael Taverner.'

'You're painting Edward's portrait?'

'Er . . . the Duke of Lincolnshire, yes.'

'I'm Celia, his predecessor's widow.'

Michael nodded, indicating that he knew the circumstances of her misfortune. Under the impression that he had regained control of himself, he said, 'I'd love to paint *you*, Lady Lincolnshire.'

'Why?'

'You're very beautiful,' Michael said. 'And interesting.'

'So are you.'

The truly amazing feature of what they were experiencing was that neither of them regarded it as out of the ordinary — except, perhaps, in respect of the immense good fortune that had befallen them on the pavement of a busy London street.

'Could we have dinner?' Michael asked.

'This evening?'

'I'd like that very much.'

'You live alone?' Celia asked.

'Yes.'

'Where?'

Michael told her.

'I shall be there at seven-thirty,' Celia said. 'I'll cook, you shop.'

'Are you sure?' Michael asked. 'You wouldn't like to go somewhere nice?'

Celia shrugged. 'Why waste time?'

They were loath to part, to destroy the spell. Before he finally moved aside to let her into Boothby's, Michael saw that Celia seemed breathless. When he forced himself to start walking, he found that his legs were shaking.

That afternoon, at the end of their deliberations on a catalogue, George asked Beatrice if Celia had complained of feeling unwell.

'No. Why, do you think she is?'

'When I saw her just after eleven this morning, she looked ready to pass out.'

'She's all right now,' Beatrice said. 'Or was, an hour ago. Actually, I thought how bright and cheerful she seemed.' Smiling and introducing mock envy, she added, 'And frightfully *young*.'

George shook his head. 'It must have been my jaundiced imagination.'

After dashing home to Putney Vale to inform Ursula of the morning's miraculous encounter, Celia arrived promptly at Michael's house in a taxi. He was surprised to see that she was carrying a holdall.

'I didn't know if you'd have one of these,' she said, producing a cook's apron. 'Where's the kitchen?' The holdall, hurriedly zipped up, was dumped casually at the foot of the stairs.

Michael's afternoon had been frantic. As well as stocking the larder, he had given parts of the uselessly big house their best cleaning in months, lit fires, scrubbed the kitchen, and prepared the vegetables. 'Lamb cutlets, mashed potatoes, and Brussels sprouts,' he informed Celia. 'Will that do?'

'Of course. Open that wine.' When the cooking was underway and she was able to sip at her drink, Celia said, 'Tell me about yourself.'

There was a brusque urgency in the request: obtaining the salient facts was a chore to be completed as rapidly as possible. Michael responded in that spirit. While keeping an eye on the progress of the meal, Celia listened intently, silent until he came to Heloise, the girl who had made such a mess of his life during what should have been the joyous, post-war period.

Leaning forward eagerly, Celia asked, 'You were in France?'

'Yes. I studied in Paris for nearly three years.'

'You speak the language?'

'Like a native, I'm told.' Michael smiled ruefully. 'It's the only thing I'm good at – apart from painting, of course.' Suddenly realising that it was a matter of life-or-death importance to Celia, he asked, 'Why?'

'Never mind. Forget the girl. Carry on.'

Less confident after the interruption, Michael continued, ending with an admission that his finances were precarious. The house, bought by his father, passed on to his mother, and inherited by him, cost more in upkeep than he could afford. Celia, dishing up the meal by now, was unconcerned.

They ate in the kitchen and she gave a skilfully condensed version of her story. She was, she admitted, a nobody, brought up by her Aunt Ursula, meeting Ralph while working as a receptionist for a doctor in Harley Street. Seeing that Michael was interested in Ralph's outrageous behaviour and grisly end, she provided details. After that, it was largely a matter of innuendo, hinting that, although Edward and Annaliese had not treated her too badly, they had not gone out of their way to help her. Celia implied that she was unhappy, looking for a new life.

The theme of dissatisfaction grew. They took their coffee into the sitting-room and Michael admitted his fears of ever earning a decent living in England. Even if he did, the grind of making money would stop him doing what he wanted, what he was best at.

'Which is?' Celia asked.

'Seascapes and coastal scenes.'

'Would the Côte d'Azur suit you?'

Michael laughed. 'Perfect! And completely beyond me.'

Celia allowed the conversation to drift into the mundane maze of everyday life. An eavesdropper, unable to see them, would have found it tedious and been bewildered by the perfunctory way it was conducted. In fact, by look and gesture, they were spurring each other towards a simmering sexual tension.

The moment chose itself. They moved simultaneously, impelled out of chairs on opposite sides of the hearth to meet in a savagely hungry embrace.

'Upstairs,' Celia whispered as Michael's hands roamed over her. 'This is going to take a bloody long time – we need comfort.'

Everything was ready, a blazing fire, a subtle table-lamp, clean linen on the bed. When they were both naked, Michael knelt at Celia's feet and gazed up at her svelte perfection in wonderment. 'Will you let me paint you like this?' he asked.

Reaching out to his massive shoulders, Celia murmured, 'Michael Taverner, you can do absolutely anything you like with me.'

Her reaction to his impetuous entry both astounded and delighted Michael. 'Oh, *yes!*' Celia said in a voice that welled up from deep within her. Screaming and laughing madly, she climaxed at once. 'Christ, I'd forgotten what it was like – I really had.' She glared at Michael who, watching her in bemused rapture, was perfectly still. 'What are you doing? Don't just lie there, damn you, get on with it!'

He did so, surpassing all Celia's previous experiences. Michael was an even more ferociously effective lover than Ralph. At some stage in the frenzied struggle for more and more pleasure, a thought pierced Celia's mind: *I wonder if*

Annaliese gets anything this good in Portugal? I'll bet she doesn't. The idea magnified itself obsessively, causing her to give voice to it. Michael, gripped by the whirlwind of his own orgasm, took the garbled ravings to be part of her ecstasy.

They were neither satisfied nor physically taxed by that first battle. While their eyes were still exchanging jubilant compliments, Celia said, 'I want you again,' and he was ready for her.

Celia stayed the night at Chesham Place and, since it was a Saturday, was in no hurry to leave the following morning. The holdall, ostensibly used for the cook's apron, also contained toiletries, lingerie, and a dress. In the same way that she had made no comment on the obviously special cleanliness of the bedroom, Michael took Celia's foresight for granted: after all, everything that mattered had been settled on the pavement outside Boothby's in the first five seconds.

After breakfast, Celia asked to see the portrait of Edward and Michael took her to the studio. Head cocked to one side, she spent a long time over her inspection, studying the painting from several angles. Now aged sixty-one, Edward's silver hair gave him a distinguished aura. To this, Michael had added profound intelligence and a suggestion of humane open-mindedness.

'He should be pleased with that,' Celia said.

'He is.'

As Michael moved to replace the dust-sheet, Celia said, 'Don't tell him about us. Not a word.'

'I wouldn't dream of it.'

Seeing that Michael was offended, Celia reached out to stroke his cheek. 'Don't take it to heart, my darling,' she murmured. 'You may be a savage in bed, but I suspect you're an innocent out of it. I can see that you've made friends with Edward – it's very easy to let something slip when your guard's down. I want us to be left alone to be happy.'

The implication of a future soothed Michael. However, the cold light of the November morning forced another difficulty into his mind. Hesitantly, he said, 'The difference in our ages.'

'What about it?'

'Does it bother you?'

Exploding into laughter, Celia surprised Michael by pushing her hand into the waistband of his trousers, rummaging until she found and grasped his penis. 'Do you expect me to be worried by *this*? And if you have any sense at all, you won't dare think of me as an old hag!'

'Certainly not,' Michael said. 'Not after last night.'

'Good. Two years from now, I shall be fifty – *fifty!* Would you like to know what happens then?' Michael nodded, in thrall to the arousal of her hand. 'Whenever a woman does it after she's fifty, I think she's always got the idea niggling away at the back of her mind that it could be the last time. Can you imagine the effect *that* has on her?'

'I think so.'

Drawing away from him, Celia chuckled at the disappointment on his face. 'Not now, Michael,' she purred. 'You can have your evil way with me the minute I get back. I shall be looking forward to it.'

'Where are you going?' he asked plaintively.

'Home to Aunt Ursula.' Celia allowed him to suffer for a few moments before adding, 'I have to fetch some clothes. I take it that you would like to have me here for most of the time?'

'Of course.'

'In that case, I need a wardrobe.'

'Can't it wait for half an hour?' Michael pleaded.

'No, it can't. Am I a manipulative, scheming bitch?'

'It seems so,' Michael said, perfectly happy.

'That's right.' Celia's smile conveyed a wealth of voluptuous promise. 'Let me assure you, my fine friend, you and I are going to be good for each other. Do you want to know *how* good?' Michael nodded eagerly. 'The past will cease to exist.'

Well-pleased with his portrait, Edward gave Michael a generous cheque and promised to recommend him to others. Beatrice sent a Boothby's van to collect the canvas for framing: there was a message suggesting that Michael might care to visit Allardyce Castle for the hanging, although no date was hinted at.

Celia and Michael made love incessantly, rejoicing in their insatiable hunger for each other. Michael assumed that a time would come when they would discuss the future, but was content to let the matter drift: he had no idea that Celia's plans were irrevocably settled.

Her only problem was Michael's Aunt Muriel in Hampstead. The old lady, whom Michael visited every Sunday afternoon, was in poor health. When, largely as an experiment, Celia suggested that they spend Christmas and New Year in Paris, Michael prevaricated, eventually saying that he preferred not to be out of touch with Aunt Muriel. He was, he confessed wretchedly, still suffering from his absence during his mother's final hours. Celia converted her exasperation into sexual energy.

On 20 December, Muriel Taverner fell down a flight of stairs and broke a hip. She was taken to the Royal Free Hospital where phlebitis and other complications soon set in. Her nephew was with her when she died, an hour before the bells rang out for the arrival of 1952.

12

1952

'Lots and lots of lovely news'

Five undertaker's men, Celia, Michael, and a clergyman were the only mourners when Muriel was laid to rest in St Marylebone Cemetery alongside HAT's grave, over which an immense marble angel towered. Afterwards, in response to Celia's amused curiosity, Michael told her that the extravagant memorial had been paid for by Leonardo Gibbons and was an idealised likeness of Maud Atkinson. Celia paid scant attention to the details which Michael provided to flesh out the names: she was preparing for what she assumed was going to be a tedious difference of opinion.

She attacked it head-on over supper by asking, 'Is there anything to keep you in England now, Michael?'

'Only earning a living.' He paused reflectively. 'Things are easier now, I suppose. Aunt Muriel's solicitor says that I'm the sole beneficiary. She must have had a few thousand and there's the house. It will make life easier for a while – perhaps give me a chance to drum up a reputation.'

Impatiently, so brisk that she sounded unfeeling, Celia said,

'Never mind that, come to the South of France with me. For good.'

Michael threw his hands up in despair. 'My love, I can't. No, *daren't*, that's the truth of the matter.'

'Why on earth not?'

'I'm not too smitten with my ability as an artist. At least I have a roof over my head and a trickle of work here. What would happen to us if we cleared off to France and the money ran out?'

'We won't run out of money.' Celia spoke softly, but with steely conviction.

Puzzled, Michael said, 'You sound very sure of that.'

'I am.'

They stared at each other in silence, Michael becoming mulish. 'How can you be so confident?' he asked eventually.

Celia reached into her handbag, extracting a sheet of paper. 'Because I have over one and a half million dollars deposited in a Swiss bank,' she said. She pushed the paper, the last statement she had received from Zurich, across the table. Michael gaped at it, tried to speak, but failed.

'Presumably, you don't feel able to live off a woman's money?' Celia sighed, laying the irritated boredom on with a trowel.

'Something like that, yes.'

'By the way, I would insist on marriage,' Celia said. 'That would make the money joint property. Is that any better?'

'Yes – it might be.'

The ensuing argument, which never quite flared into a full-blooded row, left Celia tense with suppressed anger and Michael so surly that she considered spending the night at Putney Vale. But they discovered that the disagreement had not reduced their sexual need for one another or the perfection of the way they quenched their desire.

'Wasn't that better than ever?' Celia gasped.

'I think it was.'

'Can you match it elsewhere?'

'Out of the question, I'd say.'

'The Côte d'Azur would improve it still more,' Celia said. 'I guarantee it.'

Michael obviously regarded this as food for thought.

He resisted for six days, gradually weakening. One evening, Celia returned from Boothby's to find him poring over *The Financial Times*.

'What's that in aid of?' she inquired.

'I'm trying to find out how many francs there are to the dollar,' Michael replied.

'Plenty,' Celia assured him. 'All you need to know is that a hundred thousand dollars would buy us a palace.' She made the arbitrary figure sound totally convincing.

'Aunt Muriel left twenty thousand,' Michael said. He had been to see the solicitor that morning. 'The house in Hampstead is worth six or seven thousand, this one might fetch four.'

'Thirty grand,' Celia said. 'Well over a hundred thousand dollars. A useful contribution, don't you think?'

'It's not bad,' Michael agreed.

Later, after they had made love, Michael propped himself up on an elbow to stare at Celia quizzically.

'Yes?' she asked.

'How did you come by all that money?'

'For heaven's sake, Michael, I *am* a dowager duchess,' Celia said grandly and they fell about laughing.

Later that night, Michael asked Celia to marry him. She accepted.

Aunt Muriel's house had to be cleared before an agent would sell it. Celia and Michael set aside a Sunday to search the place before letting the junk merchants loose.

Set well back in extensive grounds at a quiet corner of a private road on the southern edge of the Heath, the house needed attention. Several slates were skewed at dangerous-looking angles, paint was flaking, and the front door showed signs of rot. Inside, however, everything was neat and tidy, although most of the furniture was old and faded, and the patch of worn stair carpet that had caused Muriel's fatal fall was painfully obvious.

They had already agreed on a division of the work: Celia was to look for furniture that might be worth taking to Boothby's while Michael made an inventory of the silver. When they stopped to eat the sandwich lunch they had brought with them, nothing of any value had come to light.

There was a mild quarrel over the attic. Celia wanted to go back to Chesham Place, Michael insisted on inspecting it.

'I'll bet no one's been up there for years,' Celia grumbled.

'That's the whole point,' Michael said patiently. 'Who knows what we might find?'

He had brought a powerful flash-lamp with him. On the second-floor landing, Celia steadied the step-ladder while Michael climbed up and struggled to open the trapdoor.

'It's stuck,' he grunted. 'Been painted over — several times, by the feel of it.'

When the trap finally yielded to his heaving, it was with a crash and a shower of dust. More dirt descended as he clambered through the hole. Disgusted, Celia left Michael to it and went down to the first floor, hoping to find a clothes-brush in Aunt Muriel's bedroom.

Crouching in the attic, Michael was coming to terms with the space enclosed under the steeply pitched roof. Its sheer size made it difficult to assess. The beam from the lamp did not penetrate the furthest corners, especially when it was blocked by one or other of the three massive chimney ducts.

Crawling gingerly from joist to joist, Michael set off into the darkness.

Ten minutes later, Celia returned. 'What have you found?' she shouted.

'Two tea chests full of old magazines,' Michael replied, his voice eerily hollow. 'Worthless.'

'Anything else?'

'I don't think so. I'd better come down.'

Listening to the slow thumps of his progress, Celia glanced at her watch and decided that they could be back at Chesham Place and in bed by 3.00 pm. Absorbed in thoughts of Michael's strong, hard body, it was some time before she realised that the loft was silent.

'Are you all right?' she called.

There was no response. Michael was peering into the gap between two cisterns that he had missed on his way to the tea chests.

'Michael,' Celia cried anxiously. 'What's happening?'

'Don't worry,' he replied.

The sound of something fairly light being dragged from its hiding-place followed. Staring up at the blank aperture of the trapdoor, Celia saw the lamp beam swing as Michael examined whatever it was. He muttered, sounding disappointed.

'What *is* it?' Celia cried.

Instead of a reply, there was the sound of more dragging. Michael's whispered, 'Good God!' drifted down as clear as a bell.

'You've found something?' Celia said, starting up the steps.

'Yes.'

'What?'

'Hang on, I'll soon be there.'

There was a reckless haste in the way Michael made his way back to the trapdoor. His feet appeared, groping for the top of the steps. Celia grabbed an ankle and guided him to safety.

Michael descended until his shoulders were level with the ceiling, then reached for his discovery. Although wrapped in a sheet, it was obviously a painting, unframed, Celia thought, and measuring about six feet by four. Very carefully, Michael manoeuvred it lengthways through the opening. Reaching the floor, he laid the picture reverentially against the wall, choosing a position where it would get the best of the light. Grinning at Celia, he removed the sheet.

'Bloody hell!' she gasped, recoiling under the impact. 'Is that your grandfather's handiwork?'

'It is.'

'Who are they?' Celia whispered.

'The woman is Maud Atkinson. If the stories are to be believed, the young Hercules giving his all was a servant at the Tuscan villa that HAT rented in 1900.'

Maud was lying on her back on a crimson-draped divan. Both she and the man were stark naked. He was on top of her, between her thighs, thrusting: the musculature of his buttocks was graphic testimony to his efforts. Maud's knee, the one in the foreground, was raised, accentuating the lines of her flawless leg. The trick, which looked natural enough, obscured the genital areas, but there was no doubt whatsoever that the splendidly Junoesque Maud and her young, olive-skinned companion were indulging in sexual intercourse. Their faces suggested that they were close to orgasm. As fresh as at the time of its completion, the picture was vibrantly alive, shockingly exciting.

'That is *sensational*,' Celia breathed.

'I'm amazed at the quality of the workmanship,' Michael said calmly. 'Look at the sweat on the man's shoulders – and the background.'

'Rather fanciful,' Celia said.

'It's the courtyard of the archetypal Etruscan mansion.'

Tearing herself away from the rivetingly erotic image,

Celia asked, 'Is this the only one?'

'As far as I can see, there are seven others.'

'We'll get them down,' Celia said. 'Then you can tell me the story.'

She studied each one as it was passed through the trapdoor. Four involved Maud, the other three another woman, younger, slimmer, more abandoned. Even in the grip of passion, Maud had a slightly anguished air, as though feeling self-disgust for exhibiting herself in such a way *and* enjoying it; the younger woman had no such reservations. In all, there were three men, two Italians, and an older, Nordic type. The three pictures using the younger woman were completely explicit, with no cleverly raised, concealing knee.

They went downstairs. While Michael recounted the legend of the pictures, Celia unpacked the milk, sugar, and tea she had brought and boiled a kettle.

'I can't get over it,' Michael said after he had related all the myth and rumour. 'He must have brought them back from Italy, shoved them in the loft, and ignored them. He died just as that chap from Chicago was getting interested and nobody's ever bothered to go up there. Hardly credible, is it? On the other hand, he might have had them on display and . . .'

Celia cut Michael off before he ran away with himself. 'How much are those things worth?' she asked.

Puffing his cheeks out, Michael tilted his chair back and gazed up at the ceiling. 'A good HAT sells for five thousand these days. Assuming that there are collectors with minds as dirty as the old man's, I'd say these could fetch ten thousand apiece.'

'Eighty thousand pounds,' Celia mused. 'You're becoming a wealthy man. Does it make you feel better about us?'

'Yes, it does.' Michael tousled his hair. 'How do we sell them? Boothby's?'

'I shall have to think about that.' Celia smiled wickedly.

'They are rather *esoteric*, aren't they? A private sale might be best – we wouldn't want to embarrass the purchaser.'

They made plans for moving the pictures to Chesham Place the following day and prepared to leave. At the last moment, Michael decided to go back upstairs to replace the trapdoor.

'Actually, there's something else we ought to take out,' he said. 'There are four blank canvases up there.'

'What sort of canvases?' Celia sounded uninterested.

'Same as those.' Michael pointed to the pictures.

'Get them,' Celia said.

Michael did so and examined them carefully. 'Yes, they *are* the same – oak stretchers and look, there's the May and Hobbs mark.' He pointed to the maker's name, stamped in copperplate script on every piece of wood. 'They were the very best.'

'Were?' Celia asked.

'They went out of business in 1920.'

For the moment, Celia confined herself to saying, 'If I were you, I'd bring them home.'

After they had bathed to rid themselves of the day's grime, they went to a French restaurant in a quiet street off Knightsbridge, then dashed back to Chesham Place and hurled themselves into bed.

Michael laughed at Celia's wildness. 'Has Maud inspired you?'

'No, the other one,' Celia replied. 'She knew a thing or two. I wonder who she was?'

'Probably a local girl led astray by Leonardo Gibbons. He was the one with the gift of the gab.'

'She didn't need any persuading,' Celia laughed. 'Come on, let's see how badly you can lead *me* astray.'

When they had finally worn each other out, Celia floated the question across the warm afterglow of their contentment. 'Can you paint like your grandfather?'

'It's how I started,' Michael replied. 'Copying his stuff. I was quite good at it. I might have one or two of them lying round somewhere.'

Celia waited before asking, 'Could you do anything with those blank canvases? For example, could you make them worth, say, ten thousand pounds each – another forty thousand pounds?'

'Forgeries, you mean?' Michael asked.

'Yes,' Celia said, sweetly innocent.

Michael gazed into the far distance, giving the impression that he was trying to think of a polite way of telling her not to be so ridiculous. In fact, he was remembering his conversation with Beatrice, imagining the lengths to which collectors would go, and assessing an opportunity to prove himself worthy of Celia. 'There's a problem,' he said at last.

'Not the canvases,' she said. 'Surely, they authenticate themselves.'

'They do.' Michael nodded. 'No, it's those backgrounds. I don't have HAT's gift for that Etruscan business.'

'Can't we think of a convincing alternative?'

'I'm sure we can.' Michael drew Celia closer. 'Why do I have the feeling that you're looking forward to being the third woman in this terrible set of pictures?'

'Michael, I honestly cannot imagine,' Celia chuckled.

The eight paintings and four blank canvases were taken from Hampstead Heath to Chesham Place in great secrecy the following morning. By the end of the week, Aunt Muriel's house had been cleared and put up for sale at an asking price of £7,000. Almost at once, the London Borough of Islington, flush with ratepayers' money, snapped it up with the intention of turning it into flats. Michael was far too busy with other things to worry about the outrage of his late aunt's neighbours.

He dashed up to Manchester to spend an afternoon studying a large batch of his grandfather's works in the Whitworth Gallery. He was struck by two studies of Maud in which the Etruscan theme was restricted to the impression created by her dress and a Doric arch set against a monochrome expanse of pale blue. Michael returned to the paintings over and over again, convinced that they offered the perfect solution. Before hurrying off to catch the last train back to London, he made a note of the Doric arch's proportions and its exact setting in the composition.

The next two weeks were devoted to sketches. Since there was no hope of getting the studio warm enough, the sitting-room, blazing with extra lights, had to be used. Here, surrounded by mirrors – including a huge specimen from the front of a hideous old wardrobe – Celia and Michael posed naked and he drew them. There were many diversions. Love-making was a frequent necessity and Celia laughingly accused Michael of overestimating the size of his erection. She was happy to apologise when he demonstrated that the scale was correct: his penis, excited by her, did indeed amount to slightly over three-quarters of the distance from the point of his elbow to his wrist. Despite carnal and humorous distrac-tions, nine large drawings were produced and Celia chose the four she liked best.

'Now the interesting part,' Michael said. 'The faces.'

'Can you make me a really hard, sensuous bitch?' Celia said, smiling at Michael's expression. 'Even worse than I am. Dark eyes, lots of glossy hair, prominent cheek bones.'

'How about a pair of castanets and a rose in your teeth?' Michael joked.

The following evening, he had a series of drawings that showed ten different aspects of a cruelly beautiful, rapacious face. 'Very, very good,' Celia murmured after studying them for several minutes. 'I may not look anything like that, but it's how some people might see me, I suppose.'

'They should have a go at discovering what's underneath.'

'I wouldn't dream of letting them,' Celia said. 'What about the man – any ideas?'

Michael produced more sketches. Although of an older man, with an arrogant mouth and dissolute eyes, they bore a striking resemblance to himself.

'Isn't this a bit risky?' Celia asked.

'No, not in the least,' Michael replied. 'Those are copies of some self-portraits that HAT did at about the time he was enjoying himself in Italy. They're reproduced in the biography.'

Celia smiled and said, 'Clever!'

'I thought so.'

Next day, Michael set to work on the first painting.

The death of King George VI at the age of only fifty-six on 6 February came as a great shock. Although His Majesty had been ill during 1951, he was thought to be fully recovered – so much so, that Princess Elizabeth and her husband, Philip, Duke of Edinburgh, were abroad on a visit to Kenya.

Beatrice decided that Boothby's should be closed on 7 February, a sign of respect that was repeated over much of London. Although they re-opened on the 8th, business was non-existent; in the absence of George, who was visiting a potential client at Guildford, Beatrice and Celia spent most of the morning talking about the man who, never wanting to be King, had made such a splendid job of it.

When they had run out of things to say, Beatrice wondered what Annaliese would do, concluding that she ought to come home.

'Oh, do you think so?' Sad though the King's death was, Celia failed to see any need to break off a holiday in Portugal. 'The aristocracy don't have to turn out in force for a funeral, do they?'

'No, it isn't like a wedding or a coronation. Even so . . .'
Beatrice hesitated, aware that her argument was weak '. . . I
thought that *being* here would show sympathy.'

'She can do that just as well at the villa,' Celia suggested.
Then, seeing an opportunity, she began to exploit it. 'I can't
say that I blame Annaliese – this country *is* an everlasting trial,
Beatrice. As a matter of fact, I'm thinking of clearing off
myself.' She made it sound like a casual, spur-of-the-moment
whim.

Beatrice was shocked. 'Are you serious?'

'Mmm . . . yes. I'm afraid I am.'

'When were you thinking of going?'

'This year – summer, perhaps?' Celia gave the impression
that she was undecided.

'Oh, Lord, that's a blow,' Beatrice said. 'You'll be missed,
Celia. We rely on you for all sorts of things.'

'That's why I'm giving you as much warning as possible.'

'Yes, I see. Thank you.' Beatrice was thoughtful. 'This is
going to force the issue,' she muttered.

'What do you mean?' Celia was genuinely concerned.

'Anno Domini,' Beatrice sighed. 'Charles wants me to plan
for retirement – I am fifty-nine, after all. Annaliese's fifty-six
and *very* part-time, so we need new blood. Frankly, Celia, I'd
been assuming that you'd see us through for another ten
years.'

Gently mocking, Celia said, 'I shall be fifty next year –
hardly a good long-term prospect.'

'Quite – we should have realised that.' Beatrice fiddled
with a paper-knife. 'George thinks we should bring Athene
into the firm.'

'Athene?' Celia was amazed.

'Yes. She's very keen to have a go and she's more or less
one of us. I couldn't bear outsiders in senior positions here.'
Sensing what she imagined to be Celia's displeasure, Beatrice

was uneasy. 'Is there something wrong? Don't you approve?'

'Whether *I* approve or not hardly matters,' Celia replied. 'Have you spoken to Annaliese about it?'

'No, not yet. Might she object?'

'I'd say it was more than likely. Fond as she is of Athene, she doesn't want her and George thrown together.'

'Why not?' Beatrice was baffled.

'They're almost certainly having an affair,' Celia said.

'*Are* they?'

Watching closely, Celia thought it strange that Beatrice seemed relieved to hear that her nephew was involved with an unsuitable young woman.

'Athene's lovely, of course,' Celia said airily, 'but being illegitimate is a drawback. Between ourselves, I happen to know that Annaliese and George have had a row about it.'

'I can't see that affecting Athene's suitability for Booth-by's,' Beatrice said firmly. 'I'll talk to Annaliese – *when* she deigns to put in an appearance.'

Dear me, Celia thought, the saintly Beatrice stoops to sarcasm! It exposed the problems building up as a consequence of poor planning for the future: Beatrice, Annaliese, and George weren't talking to each other in the right way. No doubt they would claim that, since business went on increasing, the future was secure. Telling herself that she must be on the look-out for ways of manipulating the situation to her advantage, Celia realised that Beatrice was staring at her, expecting the answer to a question.

'I'm sorry. What did you say?'

'Where are you going to live?' Beatrice repeated.

'The South of France.'

'Isn't it very flashy and noisy?'

'Not if you choose the right spot,' Celia replied. 'Which is something I must attend to.' She took a diary from her handbag. 'We've nothing much scheduled for the week after next, so I'd like to go down there and start house-hunting.'

'Yes, all right,' Beatrice said, dimly aware that her permission was a formality that had been taken for granted.

On the flight from London, Celia drove home the point for the umpteenth time. 'We aren't just browsing, Michael, I intend to buy a house and I'm not leaving until I do. Is that clear?'

'Yes, my darling, absolutely crystal,' Michael laughed. 'I promise you, I won't be awkward and I'll do everything you tell me.'

Softening, Celia took his hand. 'I'm sorry to go on – it's very important to me.'

'To us,' Michael corrected.

An airport taxi took them to the palatial Hotel Negresco on the Promenade des Anglais where a suite had been booked. From the balcony of their lounge, Celia discovered that Nice had changed a good deal in the twenty-odd years since her last visit. It was busier, noisier, more brash.

'I hope the whole of the coast hasn't been spoiled like this,' she muttered anxiously.

'I'm sure we'll find a quiet spot,' Michael replied. 'Your ideas on price were way out, though.'

Celia turned to find him brandishing a sheaf of papers. 'What's that?' she asked.

'Details of houses. I contacted a couple of agents and asked them to give us something to chew over. They sent these.'

'Show me.' Celia snatched at the bundle and flicked through it, calculating as she went. 'Mmm – up to four hundred thousand dollars,' she mused.

'Can we afford it?' Michael asked.

'We can't *not* afford it,' she snapped.

On being told that Monsieur and Madame were willing to go to half a million dollars, one of the agents loaned them a car. Next morning, they drove east to Monte Carlo and

Menton. At their first stop, St. Jean-Cap-Ferrat, Celia's disappointment was crushing. The picturesque village of her memory was now a construction site. After wandering round in a daze for fifteen minutes, the final blow was the discovery that a block of flats was being built where Arabella's house had stood. Refusing to look at any of the properties suggested by the agent, Celia asked Michael to drive on. Everywhere else was even worse. That evening, Celia could only pick at the meal that was brought up to their suite and, for the first time since she and Michael had bumped into each other outside Boothby's, did not want to make love.

The following day, when they headed west to Juan-les-Pins, Cannes, and St Raphael was, if anything, a bigger disaster. The harsh truth was that the Côte d'Azur was now the playground of what Celia regarded as hordes of loud-mouthed riff-raff. Money was blatantly conspicuous.

'Where have they got it from?' she asked Michael.

'The War, I expect. A lot of people did well out of it.'

'And they've come here to flaunt it?'

'It would seem so.'

Grimly, Celia said, 'They needn't expect us to join them.'

After breakfast on the third morning, Michael felt slightly embarrassed as he told the agent that all his recommended properties were unsuitable. Celia, prowling morosely round the office, wondering what on earth she was going to do, suddenly spotted a brochure for a house at Preuilly, a village nine miles north of Nice in the foothills of the Alpes Maritime. After studying the details, she thrust it at Michael with a curt, 'Tell him I want to see this place!'

It turned out to be a dream set in paradise. The owner had died two weeks ago, leaving his servants, a married couple of about forty-five, fearfully expecting to be homeless. They were courteous and eager to please. Celia's intuition marked them as honest and dependable – *and* they spoke English. By lunch-time, their future was assured: Celia agreed to pay 325,000 dollars for the house and to provide Pierre and Marie Chaladon with jobs for as long as they chose.

Michael barely coped with the ensuing forty-eight hours. For the first time in her life, Celia had a clear idea of a future that was firmly and irrevocably under her control. The result was an explosion of organisational and sexual energy. Acting as her interpreter, Michael dealt with lawyers, set up a bank account, ordered furniture, bought a car, and handled countless other incidents. Whenever there was a lull, Celia dragged him back to the hotel for a frenzied half-hour in bed.

Not until they were flying over France on their way back to England was there time to discuss the pictures that Michael was painting.

'How long before they're finished?' Celia asked.

'Three weeks at the most. Have you thought of a way of selling them?'

'I've come to the conclusion that Boothby's should handle it,' Celia replied.

'You think they'd get the best price?'

'No, any of the leading houses would do just as well. Unless I'm very much mistaken, darling, Boothby's aren't in too good a shape at the moment – the left hand doesn't know what the right's doing. That will reduce the risk and work in our favour. The other big attraction will be afterwards, knowing that Boothby's have sold forgeries. That *really* appeals to me.'

Gazing at her admiringly, Michael said, 'You're a wicked bitch when you put your mind to it.'

'Is that a criticism or complaint?'

Michael laughed. 'Certainly not. I'm just glad you're on my side.'

'Oh, I am,' Celia told him. 'As long as you keep performing like you did last night, I'm on your side.' Serious again, she said, 'We have to make Boothby's *want* to sell those pictures.'

'How?'

'It depends on the way we break the news of this great find. It mustn't come from you, or not directly. We have to get the story into a newspaper.'

After a moment's thought, Michael said, 'I can do better than that. What about *Gallery Scrutiny*?'

'You could arrange that?' Celia's face lit up.

'I think so. I know Tony Austen-Cave reasonably well.'

Gallery Scrutiny was a monthly review, founded in 1849 by the Austen-Cave family, art-lovers, patrons, and critics. Although its sales figures were believed to be no more than 2,500, its influence was immense. Available on subscription only, *Scrutiny* was read by the world's most important dealers and collectors. Tony Austen-Cave, son of the present editor and owner, was twenty-eight and had a glittering future.

'Isn't Tony an authority on the Pre-Raphaelites?' Celia asked.

'Amongst other things, yes.'

'He sounds ideal,' Celia said. 'You can fix it?'

'I'm sure I can,' Michael replied.

'Remember, I have to keep out of the way,' Celia cautioned. 'It might be best if I left Boothby's at once.'

'You're the best judge of that,' Michael said. 'One other thing – now that we know where we shall be living, ought we to have another go at your Aunt Ursula?'

'Yes, definitely.'

That evening, Ursula examined the agent's brochure for the house at Preuilly while Celia and Michael waited like children hoping for a treat.

'It *is* beautiful,' Ursula agreed. 'And so big. How many bedrooms – six?'

'Seven,' Celia said. 'And at least two of everything else.'

Michael joined in. 'Twenty acres of garden. Close to the village, but very secluded. You'd think you were miles from anywhere.'

'There's a swimming-pool,' Celia said.

'And a summer-house,' Michael added.

'You should see the flowers – and smell them.'

'The Chaladons are very decent. They'll take good care of us.'

'All right, you've convinced me,' Ursula cried. 'Much as I love this old place, I'll put it up for sale tomorrow.'

'Ursula, I'm *so* glad,' Celia said, hugging the woman to whom she owed so much. 'We're going to be very, very happy.'

'Yes, I believe we are,' Ursula replied. 'See, I was right to make you wait.'

Although stunned by the apparently capricious change of heart that drove Celia to immediate resignation and departure, Beatrice was able to persude her to stay on at Boothby's for another two weeks. When, somewhat ungraciously, Celia had gone downstairs to check preparations for the following day's sale, Beatrice went into George's office to find that Annaliese, recently back from Portugal, was with him. The atmosphere between mother and son was uncomfortably tense, making Beatrice nervous as she announced Celia's decision.

'When is she going?' George asked.

'The end of next week.'

'*Where* is she going?' Annaliese wanted to know.

'The South of France.'

'Whereabouts?'

Beatrice struggled to remember the few details volunteered by Celia. 'Cap Ferrat. She's renting a flat – not all that big, but lovely views.'

'I hope she knows what she's doing,' Annaliese said,

implying that she thought it unlikely.

'That's neither here nor there,' George said. 'All that matters is that she's out of our hair. Thank God.'

'Oh, George,' Beatrice muttered unhappily.

'Why does everyone think so highly of her?' George protested. 'Didn't it *ever* matter that she had an affair with Father?'

'That will do, George,' Annaliese snapped. To Beatrice, she said, 'You want to bring Athene in?'

'I do. She's just what we need.'

In the blink of an eye, Annaliese's attitude veered from hostility to indifference. 'You're probably right.' She stood up and moved towards the door. 'Do *try* to be sensible about her, George.'

After she had gone, Beatrice and George exchanged rueful looks. 'I hate it when she washes her hands of problems,' Beatrice said.

'According to Father, it's because she's Viennese,' George replied. 'Good excuse, eh?'

Most unusually, Annaliese and Edward dined together at Cadogan Square that evening. Since George was at a concert, they were alone.

'Celia is leaving Boothby's and the country,' Annaliese announced over soup. 'She's going to live in the South of France.'

Having realised that Edward was not going to respond, Annaliese went on. 'Beatrice is bringing Athene into the firm. She'll probably be an asset, but she and George mustn't see any more of each other than necessary, so don't invite her to stay here.'

'What's the poor girl supposed to do?' Edward grumbled. 'Exist in some frightful bed-sit?'

'Beatrice and Charles have plenty of room at Upper Overs.' Annaliese made it sound cut and dried. 'Athene can read and learn on the train each morning – like I did.'

Edward considered trying to instigate a discussion about George, suggesting that it was high time they organised his marriage. On balance – or was it moral cowardice? – he decided that Annaliese was not in a receptive mood.

Michael Taverner telephoned Tony Austen-Cave at the beginning of April, two weeks after Celia left Boothby's.

'I've got something I'd like you to look at, Tony. Could you pop round?'

'Certainly. Do I get a clue?'

'I'd rather not,' Michael replied. 'I'm not prepared to commit myself without your advice – and we shall need the chaps from the Academy, as well.'

'Michael, you intrigue me,' Tony Austen-Cave gushed. 'Are you in this afternoon?'

'Whenever you like.'

'I'm lunching with that old bore, Fortescue, but I'll be with you as soon as poss thereafter.'

He arrived at 2.30 pm, a tall, well-built, almost indecently handsome man: wasting their time, women were inclined to become ga-ga over his superb features, limpid hazel eyes, and long, light-brown hair. After solemnly shaking hands with Michael, he said, 'Well, dear boy, here I am. Surprise me.'

'Come up to the studio,' Michael said.

The twelve paintings were arranged in a semicircle, propped against the backs of chairs. Any single one of them was sensational: together they were overwhelming. Tony Austen-Cave was stunned. He was also thrilled.

'Ye Gods, the stories *were* true!' he cried, recognising Maud Atkinson, and hence the artist, immediately. 'Where in the name of all that's bright and beautiful did you find them?'

'Aunt Muriel died recently, and I inherited the old house

in Hampstead.' Michael shrugged disarmingly. 'Believe it or not, this lot were in the attic.'

Tony roared with laughter. 'Can you think of a more *obvious* place? Isn't it just too, too typical? Well, well, well!' He stood back, surveying the pictures again. 'Shall I tell you what's always fascinated me?'

'Go on,' Michael said diffidently.

'In 1913, when the rumours were at their height, Maud was vilified. But she never stood up and denied that this . . .' Tony waved an expansive hand at the canvases '. . . had happened. Made no attempt to clear her name. She was done for and died in poverty. That's always struck me as *highly* significant and I was right, damn it.'

'I didn't know about Maud's miserable end,' Michael said. 'I found this in HAT's papers.' He gave Tony the letter from Chicago. 'And the diary is blank during the period when this was happening.' Tony reached for the leather-covered notebook. Satisfied, he began a close inspection of individual pictures. Looking on, apparently unconcerned, Michael felt relief: although Tony must have known when Muriel Taverner died, he had, as yet, failed to notice the delay in finding the pictures and his being invited to look at them. The chances were now tilted in favour of the oversight becoming permanent.

'I must say, Maud was splendid, wasn't she?' Smiling self-mockingly, Tony pointed to the young, sweating Italian. 'He's more to my taste, of course.' Having made the reference to his own proclivities – which had once necessitated a rebuff from Michael but produced no lasting ill feeling – Tony moved on, kneeling in front of a forgery. 'Now *that*, unless I'm badly adrift, is HAT himself, banging away like a good'un!'

'That worries me,' Michael said. 'I'm not convinced that a self-portrait like that is possible.'

Tony laughed. 'Of course it is – especially if someone else

did the working drawings. Remember, Leonardo Gibbons was part of this jamboree and he wasn't the incompetent he's made out to be. I know he wasn't much good with paint, but he was a superb draughtsman. I'd say he was perfectly capable of executing the sketches and HAT did the rest, God bless him. That's an interesting lady he's enjoying.'

'Hardly one of the servants,' Michael ventured. 'Not like the other girl.'

'Who cares?' Tony was using an eyeglass on the distinctive flourish with which HAT had signed his pictures. Satisfied, he said, 'She'll be someone Leonardo picked up along the way. Looks like an aristocrat of the old school, doesn't she? My word, didn't they live?'

After making approving noises about the Doric arch against the plain background, Tony settled down to his detailed examination of each picture. Half an hour later, he stepped back and said, 'Amazing. Truly amazing. Am I the first to see them?'

'Yes.'

'I'm grateful, Michael, very grateful indeed.'

'You think they're right?'

'Not a shred of doubt.' Seeing Michael's uncertainty, Tony said, 'I can organise second, third, and fourth opinions.'

'Yes, please.'

Tony pulled out a pad and began to make notes. 'What are you going to do with these beauties?' he asked.

'Sell them.' Michael was apologetic. 'Frankly, I need the money.'

'Who doesn't?' Tony moaned. 'How are you proposing to go about it?'

'I've no idea.' Grinning bashfully, Michael said, 'Between you and me, Tony, I find the wretched things embarrassing. They're pornographic.'

'Nonsense,' Tony hooted. 'This is erotic art, a fish of a totally different kettle.'

'Call them what you like,' Michael insisted, 'I can't see myself taking them to a dealer, or advertising them.'

'You don't have to,' Tony said. 'If you'd let me write an article, the world will beat a path to your door, cheque-books at the ready.'

'That would be wonderful,' Michael said. 'Could you put them in *Gallery Scrutiny*?'

'Most definitely.' Tony's manner became calculating. 'Actually, I'd like to do something else, too. I write a column for *The Sunday Times*.'

'I read it,' Michael said. 'Good stuff.'

'It isn't always easy to find the right subject,' Tony admitted. 'I'm stuck this week. Would you mind if I used this story?'

Michael pretended to think about it. 'It couldn't do any harm, could it?' he asked.

'Quite the contrary. It gets you off to a better start. The new issue of *Scrutiny* is at the printer's now, so you'll have to wait for up to five weeks for the next one.'

'You won't make it scandalous, will you?' Michael asked, his apparent uncertainty concealing his conviction that things were unfolding in a way that exceeded his wildest hopes.

'My dear chap, of course not. The editor will be tremendously chuffed by a scoop like this. You'll be doing me a big favour.'

'All right,' Michael said graciously.

'Thank you. I shan't forget this, Michael.' Tony was scribbling furiously. 'Let me make sure of the salient facts, right?'

As Michael was showing him out half an hour later, he asked Tony, 'What might they be worth? Fifty thousand?'

Tony's face went through a series of expressions as he weighed a multitude of factors. 'I can think of five men who might be prepared to kill for those pictures. If they decide to fight each other, you could be looking at one hundred and fifty of the best.'

This time, there was no need for Michael to feign surprise.

After watching Tony Austen-Cave stride off towards Belgrave Place, Michael closed the door and bounded upstairs to the bedroom where Celia had been dozing. One look at him was enough to bring a broad smile to her face. 'I'm going to enjoy hearing this, aren't I?'

'You are. Very much.'

Pushing back the covers to reveal her nakedness, Celia said, 'Come here and tell me.'

Tony's piece appeared in *The Sunday Times* four days later. By then, experts from the Royal Academy and a Cambridge art historian had professed themselves satisfied that the twelve paintings were the work of HAT.

Under the headline:

ATTIC YIELDS EROTIC MASTERPIECES

Tony created a graphic impression of the pictures without actually going into details. It was cleverly done, relying mostly on an examination of the relationship between HAT and Maud Atkinson.

The first telephone calls, four of them in the middle of Sunday afternoon, were from popular daily newspapers. As editors began work on Monday morning's editions, they were hungry for details of the pictures and the two 'mystery women' to whom Tony had made astutely titillating reference. Politely but firmly, Michael declined modest sums of money to co-operate in a story.

On Monday morning, the auction-houses were busy. Boothby's were first.

'I'm cross with you, Mr Taverner,' Beatrice chided. 'Why didn't you bring your grandfather's paintings straight to us?'

Much embarrassed, Michael said, 'They're indecent, Lady

Beatrice. I couldn't possibly inflict them on an establishment such as Boothby's.'

'I wish you'd let us be the judge of that, Mr Taverner. May I look at them?'

'There's no point, Lady Beatrice. I'm arranging for a private sale.'

'You have a buyer?'

'Not exactly,' Michael hedged. 'I'm considering offers.'

'Oh, I see.' Beatrice was disappointed. 'You will contact me if you change your mind, won't you?'

'Of course, Lady Beatrice.'

Five minutes later, Michael had a similar conversation with the managing director of Galbraiths. Sotheby's and Christie's followed as soon as the line was free.

Two dealers, acting for clients who wished to remain anonymous, turned up on Michael's doorstep on Tuesday morning. Michael allowed them to inspect the pictures and both men scuttled off in great excitement. An hour later, the bids came through, one for £90,000, the other for slightly more. Michael rejected them out of hand and refused to be drawn on the sort of figure he was looking for. Incredibly, the *Evening News* got hold of the story and telephoned for confirmation. Michael provided it and, starting to enjoy the game, let slip that he was thinking of giving Galbraith's the sale.

Wednesday morning saw Benjamin Galbraith and his two sons in Chesham Place, demanding to view the paintings. The old man's eyes gleamed when he saw Maud in all her glory, whereas his sons were unable to tear their eyes away from Celia's body. Largely to get rid of them, Michael gave a promise – verbal and, therefore, breakable – that Galbraith's would act for him.

The news produced near-panic at Boothby's. Copies of Tony Austen-Cave's *Sunday Times* article had reached New

York by Monday afternoon. Now, two of Beatrice's contacts had sent cables offering £120,000 for HAT's paintings, sight unseen. At 2.30 pm, Beatrice had a taxi waiting to take her to plead with Michael: George, however, was profoundly unsure.

'Aunt Bee, on Taverner's own admission, these pictures are obscene,' he said. '*Why* do we want them?'

'Don't be so obtuse, George.' Beatrice was extremely cross. 'There's no such thing as obscenity in great art. These pictures look like being the event of the year. Can't you understand the prestige involved?'

'I fail to see what prestige there can possibly be in the erotic daubings of a third-rate hack,' George grumbled. 'HAT wasn't a great artist.'

'No, but he was a very good one,' Beatrice said. 'Look, if you can't cope with ideas, what about the commission on at least one hundred and twenty thousand pounds? Isn't that worth having?'

George, at a loss to know what had come over his aunt, let her dash off. Hovering nearby, Athene was trying to work out whose side she was on.

There was a double celebration at Putney Vale that evening. At almost exactly the same time as a Boothby's van was collecting the now notorious pictures from Chesham Place, Ursula had received and accepted an offer for her house. Even better, the purchasers, two middle-aged lady teachers, wanted to move in as soon as possible and had expressed a strong interest in buying the contents.

'Leave tomorrow,' Celia urged.

'Where to?' Ursula shrieked.

'Why not go to Preuilly?' Michael suggested. 'It's about time we had the advance party in. Travel with Celia on Tuesday.'

Ursula made her mind up at once. 'Yes, please,' she said happily.

After studying Michael carefully, Celia said, 'There was a time when I wondered if you'd be able to carry this off. Instead of that, you're enjoying it, positively revelling in it, aren't you?'

'Blame yourself,' Michael grinned. 'Remember, this was your plan. It's a shame you weren't around this afternoon. Beatrice was prepared to offer me anything to get those paintings into her showroom. *Anything!* I'll swear she'd have gone down on her knees if I'd hung out any longer.'

'Yes, I would have liked to have seen that.' After looking and sounding disappointed, Celia became gleeful. 'What did Lady Beatrice think of the pictures?'

'She was very pink and flustered at first,' Michael replied. 'She said, "Good gracious," and "Dear me," quite a lot. Afterwards, when we were taking them to Bond Street, she acted as though they were a collection of flower arrangements.'

Clearing her throat loudly to gain attention, Ursula said, 'May I ask what may seem like an utterly daft question?'

Michael smiled encouragingly. 'Go on.'

'Now that Boothby's have fallen over themselves to take these masterpieces to their bosom, are you able to stop worrying about authentication? Will everyone believe that your efforts are the genuine article?'

'Yes!' Celia and Michael shouted in unison.

'In that case, let's open another bottle of bubbly,' Ursula said.

The paintings were placed in a small gallery on the rarely used second floor of Boothby's. Beatrice kept the one, solitary key to the room which was opened only to would-be purchasers whose bona fides were impeccable. At the end of the first week, six men and – to Beatrice's astonishment – two women had been allowed into the room. Of the four offers made, the best was £130,000.

Telephoning Celia, who was now installed at Preuilly with Ursula, Michael had to insist on patience. 'The Americans haven't started yet,' he said. 'Nigel Templeton thinks they'll go much higher.'

'What's *he* got to do with it?' Celia demanded, nervously suspicious.

'He's advising on finance and any export licence that might be needed,' Michael replied. 'Don't worry, darling, everything's under control.'

'How long is this going to take?' Celia asked.

'Only a few days.'

'Had I better come back?'

'Not unless there's anything here you particularly need.'

'You! I need you.' The little-girl voice that Celia used to convey her desire for him made Michael smile.

'Actually,' he said, teasingly offhand, 'I was thinking of clothes and things. What about all the stuff you've left at Chesham Place?'

'Throw them away,' Celia said. 'Ursula took me shopping in Nice yesterday, so I don't want that rubbish.'

'What about the house? Is everything all right?'

'It's heavenly,' Celia said. 'Ursula wishes we could have done this ten years ago. Michael darling, you will get this business over as soon as you can, won't you?'

'I'm as anxious as you are,' he assured her, discomforted by the erection that her sensual pleading had incited.

The auction took place three days later. Two men in Beatrice's office were to bid against two others at the end of telephone lines in New York.

At Beatrice's invitation, Michael arrived at Boothby's

before lunch, ready to deal with any last-minute problems. The first person he encountered was Edward.

'I've been trying to resist these dreadful pictures of yours,' Edward joked as they shook hands. 'All to no avail, as you can see.'

'What do you think of them?' Michael asked, playing the part of the innocent out of his depth.

'I haven't seen them yet – I'm to be taken up now. Perhaps you'd care to come with me and give me an expert opinion. Sorry, you haven't met my wife, have you?'

'How do you do, Your Grace?' Michael said, clasping the hand Annaliese offered. Taken aback by her youthfulness and golden beauty, he added, 'A great pleasure.'

'For me, too, Mr Taverner. My warmest congratulations on the portrait you did for us. It's quite excellent.'

Dazzled by her smile, Michael was only half-aware that Edward, impatient to view HAT's outrageous work, was trying to organise the departure to the second floor. Catching sight of someone, Edward called, 'Are you joining us, George?'

'No, thank you, Father,' was the curt reply. 'I've seen more than enough of them.'

Tearing his attention away from Annaliese, Michael caught a glimpse of George disappearing into his office. It seemed that the Marquess of Axholme was in a bad mood again: his demeanour on the day the canvases were brought to Boothby's had indicated deep-seated disapproval of his aunt's determination to handle them. Edward smiled bravely, Michael responded, and they shrugged the incident off.

Once on the second floor, Annaliese strode into the small gallery ahead of everyone else. The impact of the paintings, all standing on tables, stopped her dead. 'Good heavens,' she said weakly. 'How shocking.'

'I'm inclined to agree with Your Grace,' Michael said.

'Although my grandfather seems to have made me a rich man, I'm appalled by his lack of judgement and taste.'

'Oh, I don't think they're quite *that* bad, Mr Taverner.' Annaliese was fascinated by one of the genuine canvases, a study of the Italian girl and a man making love in a way which Kurt carried out to perfection. 'The execution is brilliant, don't you think?'

'They *are* tremendously vibrant,' Beatrice said earnestly.

'Very much so,' Annaliese agreed and began to study the exhibits individually.

Edward, keenly interested, but also bemused and embarrassed, shuffled along beside her, trying to convey the impression that he was hardly looking at the startling pictures. Then, a detail on one of the forgeries caught his attention. The woman was astride the man, her head thrown back in violent ecstasy. They were depicted from a viewpoint slightly below them, to the right of and behind the man, thus exposing every detail of the woman from the fork between her legs to the tip of her tilted chin. As if drawn by an irresistible force, Edward leaned towards the canvas, his eyes narrowing in concentration.

A chill instinct told Michael what had caught Edward's attention. Just above the triangle of the woman's luxuriant pubic hair, there were two small moles, painted with a lifelike accuracy that was, Michael now realised, totally stupid. For what seemed like an eternity, Edward stared at them.

Eventually, it was Annaliese who broke the trance-like silence. 'What *have* you found, Edward?' she asked in a voice charged with sardonic humour.

'Eh? What?' Edward straightened up, trying not to look foolish. 'Er – I was admiring the brushwork.'

'*Were* you?' For a moment or two, Annaliese's expression suggested that a barbed retaliation was imminent, but she changed her mind. 'Are you dashing off to the House of Lords, or can you have lunch with us?' she asked.

'Lunch,' Edward said.

'Lovely.' Annaliese turned to Michael. 'Will you join us, Mr Taverner?'

'I'd be delighted, Your Grace.'

As they waited for Beatrice to relock the door of the small gallery, Michael was conscious of Edward's quizzical stare. Meeting it, he was sure that the forgeries had been detected, yet Edward had no intention of saying anything. After that one disconcerting look, he was charmingly affable.

Even so, Michael did not enjoy lunch at Whitaker's. How, he asked himself repeatedly, had Edward spotted it? What could those two minor blemishes above the woman's pubis possibly have told him? To add to Michael's discomfort, Annaliese came to the conclusion that she would like him to paint her portrait. 'George, too,' she said. 'It's over a hundred years since anyone bothered with the heir.' Promising that he would be in touch to arrange sittings, Michael prayed for the meal to end. At long last it did; Edward took a taxi to the House of Lords, Annaliese, Beatrice, and Michael returned to Boothby's.

Almost at once, Michael realised that he was in the way. The representatives of the two British bidders for HAT's pictures were arguing with each other and George over procedure and the possibility of splitting the twelve canvases into two separate lots. There were problems with the telephone links to New York, causing secretaries to twitter, and Beatrice flew into a panic when told that Nigel Templeton had been delayed. Nodding understandingly at Athene, who was hopping about on the fringes of the chaos, Michael took himself off to browse round the store-room on the top floor.

It was a neglected jumble of worthless trash that held the promise of hidden treasure. Michael began to sift through it and soon found a small oil-painting that made him forget everything else. When Athene came charging up the stairs, he brandished it at her and said, 'This shouldn't be buried with this rubbish, it's a Stubbs. Look, it's beautiful.'

'Oh – right.' Breathless from excitement and exertion, Athene was disinterested. 'It's all over,' she gasped. 'Your pictures have been sold.'

'What, already?' After a glance at his watch, Michael smiled sheepishly. 'I'm sorry, I got carried away and lost track. Er – how much?'

'One hundred and ninety-five thousand guineas,' Athene shrieked. 'Isn't it marvellous?'

'Incredible,' Michael said, shocked into calmness. 'Who bought them?'

'Not the Americans, they couldn't stand the pace. Beyond that, I mustn't breathe a word.' Athene held out a hand. 'Come on, Beatrice is looking for you.' On the way down the stairs, Athene whispered, 'It's all very hush-hush, you see. The buyer can't be named.'

'I sympathise with him,' Michael said. 'If I'd paid a fortune for that stuff, I'd want it kept quiet.'

Athene giggled. 'They are naughty, aren't they? Jolly good, though.'

Outside the offices on the first floor, jubilant pandemonium reigned. Nigel Templeton and the man who had acted for the successful bidder had their heads together and were writing busily; Annaliese and Beatrice were surrounded by members of the staff, all laughing and congratulating each other; and George was talking to Tony Austen-Cave, who had promised to turn up if he could unload another engagement. Michael had the impression that, surprisingly in view of their closely related careers in the small world of fine art, George and Tony were meeting for the first time.

Everything was happening at once. Strangers were shaking Michael's hand, Nigel was trying to catch his eye, and Beatrice wanted to speak to him but was being swamped in the hubbub.

Just before Tony became aware of Michael's presence and tore himself away from George, there was an instant in which Michael disbelieved the evidence of his eyes. George's mood, so sour before lunch, had switched to pure enchantment: he and Tony were gazing at each other in a way that must, Michael supposed, resemble his first encounter with Celia. He was telling himself not to be so damned silly when Athene spoke. Staring directly at George, she said, 'Oh *dear!*' in a small, plaintive voice that only Michael heard. She put an immense wealth of meaning into the short, simple utterance.

The moment was swept away by Tony's ostentatious cordiality. 'Michael, my dear chap, what a *coup* for you. Well done.'

'Thank you – and for your help,' Michael said.

'Not at all. Mind you, there isn't much left for *Scrutiny* to say, is there, eh? Never mind, it's been a very useful exercise, especially now that I've made the acquaintance of Lord Axholme.' He broke off to look at George who responded with a smile that lit up the corridor.

'Well – good, I'm glad,' Michael said lamely.

Nigel Templeton moved in to tell Michael about the arrangements made by the purchaser's negotiator. 'I'm to give you a banker's draft,' Nigel said. 'That protects the buyer's identity. I take it you have no objections?'

'None whatsoever.' Michael could hardly believe his luck: it was as good as being handed cash. When endorsed, the draft could go straight into Celia's Swiss account.

'I'll have it sent round to your house before close of business,' Nigel promised.

'Can I ask a favour?' Michael said. 'Would you pay Boothby's commission direct to Lady Beatrice, please? Deduct it from what you send me.'

'With the greatest of pleasure,' Nigel replied warmly.

After thanking Beatrice for her efforts, Michael set about extricating himself. Patiently, he allowed Annaliese to remind him of her portrait and edged towards the exit. As he did so, he had to take evasive action to avoid George, returning exuberantly from a temporary farewell to Tony.

Seeing Athene, George caught her by the arm. 'I'm sorry, I shall have to cancel this evening,' he said. 'I'm having dinner with Mr Austen-Cave.'

Despairingly, Athene shook her head. 'You fool, George,' she whispered. 'You utter, bloody fool! Don't you know *anything*? Austen-Cave isn't like Robert Chappell – he's a menace.' Turning on her heel, she hurried off – but not before Michael had seen the tears in her eyes.

George and Michael stared at each other, George scowling defiantly. With a wry smile to acknowledge that it was none of his business, Michael walked away.

The following afternoon, having left the keys to his house in Chesham Place with an estate agent who was instructed to take the first decent offer, Michael flew to Nice. He went without so much as a toothbrush; Celia and Aunt Ursula assured him that everything he needed was waiting in the house at Preuilly.

Three months slipped by and Celia was all but forgotten. Annaliese, exasperated by the discovery that Michael Taverner seemed to have disappeared, steadfastly set her face against reading anything untoward into the growing entanglement between George and Tony Austen-Cave. Athene's frequently voiced anxieties about the friendship were brushed aside. The money from the sale of HAT's pictures vanished into the obsessive privacy of the Swiss banking system leaving no one, not even Nigel Templeton, with any clue of a link between Michael and Celia.

Then, on an oppressively warm evening in July, Beatrice got back to Upper Overs to find a letter from Celia.

'That is her handwriting, isn't it?' Charles said after studying the envelope yet again.

'Yes, it is. I expect she's gloating about having a wonderful time.'

'Aren't you going to open it?' Charles teased.

'Eventually, yes.' Beatrice was tired and irritable at the end of a stifling, difficult day in London.

After supper, while Charles was pottering round the roses in search of greenfly, she reached for the letter. When Charles came back fifteen minutes later, he was alarmed to see that Beatrice was as white as a sheet and incapable of moving.

'What's wrong, old thing?' he asked, hurrying to her side.

With an effort, Beatrice raised the hand in which she was clutching Celia's letter.

'Are you all right?' Charles said anxiously. 'You look ready to pass out – need a tot of something?'

Beatrice shook her head. 'Read it,' she whispered, offering the letter.

Lots and lots of lovely news, Celia had written. *First, I'm living in my own splendid house in the hills above Nice, not in a rented flea-pit on the coast. Aunt Ursula is with me, so is my husband, Michael Taverner. (We were married at the beginning of June and are extremely happy.) We do little except walk, swim, and enjoy sex at every available opportunity. Aunt Ursula complains about the noise we make – she is, of course, slightly jealous. Young, properly trained men are quite magnificent in bed. We're at it for hours on end. (Does Annaliese share my enthusiasm, I wonder? I can't help feeling that her 'friend' in Portugal might be even younger than my own, splendid Michael.)*

I'm delighted to tell you that four of the pictures you sold for Michael were forgeries. He painted them himself, although I claim credit for the idea. They were the ones against the Doric arch and the plain blue backdrop: the canvases were with the genuine articles in the attic at Hampstead and it seemed a shame to waste them. The models were Michael and me. The clever chap made sketches of us doing all those marvellous things and gave us new heads. (Didn't I look a bitch? Can you remember?) When he was painting my body, which he worships, Michael was terribly, punctiliously accurate. Without stopping to think what he was doing, he did me warts and all — or, to be precise, moles and all. There are two of them, just above my pubes. No harm in that, you might think: who was likely to recognise them — and, therefore, me?

Well, Edward did. It was when he looked at the pictures before lunch on the day of the sale. Michael was horrified! He knew what Edward was staring at, but not why: the poor lamb was baffled witless. (Naturally, I have now told him of how Edward came to have such an intimate knowledge of my body and Michael, being a man after my own heart, finds this very exciting!) Not surprisingly, Edward kept his mouth shut and allowed the sale to go ahead even though — and Michael swears that this is true — even though he knew that some of the paintings must have been forgeries.

Why am I doing this? Let me reveal all. A long time ago, when Greg McBane was offering me a new life in America, Edward frightened him off by informing him that I had been a prostitute. This was perfectly true. I was the woman in whose arms your Uncle William died. I met Ralph when he was clearing up and concealing the subsequent mess. Edward was aware of this when Ralph was murdered. (He had known the 'awful' truth for some time, but didn't confront me with it until the issue of him inheriting the title arose.)

If I had married McBane, I would probably have been a rich widow by now, queening it over Long Island. I evened the score with Edward by changing places with the whore he was using in the summer of 1933 — (a terrific piece of subterfuge!). Later, it must have been common knowledge that he and I were having an affair, but no one knew that he was paying for my services. During the War, we became quite friendly, but I made him suffer untold agonies of conscience before I allowed us to reach that happy state.

As things have worked out, I have enough money for the rest of my life and a young man who adores me more with every day that passes. So, in the end, I'm satisfied. Or nearly. After much thought, I came to the conclusion that I wanted you to know that Boothby's had sold forgeries. Don't worry, Beatrice, I shan't breathe a word to anyone else; to be honest, Michael isn't all that keen on me sending this letter and he would probably get very annoyed if I took it further. I wouldn't like that. Rest assured, therefore, that it will be our secret — but you may wish to share it with Edward and Annaliese.

One last, little thing. Michael wonders if George is homosexual. Apparently, the ravishing Mr Austen-Cave, who took a tremendous shine to him, is as queer as they come. If George is like that, no wonder everyone was content to let him have a fling with poor, illegitimate Athene!

Goodbye forever,

Celia.

In the stifling twilight at Upper Overs, Charles looked up to gaze at Beatrice in appalled silence.

13

1952–1955
'Don't worry, Mother, I'll do my best'

Celia's bombshell caused the only serious quarrel that Charles and Beatrice ever had. He wanted the letter destroyed and consigned to oblivion. Beatrice, while promising that she would never reveal its contents to a living soul, insisted on keeping it.

'Why, for pity's sake?' Charles demanded. 'There's nothing you can do about it now, my dear. Good God, it's only petty spite – she even admits that Taverner disapproved of what she was doing. You *must* forget it.'

'How can I forget a thing like that?' Beatrice wailed. 'You're being unreasonable to expect it of me.'

'You see?' Charles shouted. 'Look at the damage the bloody woman is doing – and that's before you show it to anyone else.'

'I shan't,' Beatrice screamed back. 'I've promised, haven't I?'

But only a week later, driven out of her mind with worry by the thought that Boothby's had sold forgeries, Beatrice smuggled the valedictory act of malice out of Upper Overs. Although abjectly conscious that she was doing precisely what Celia had counted on, Beatrice was unable to help herself. Possibly hoping to share the burden of guilt, she made Annaliese read the letter.

It took well over two years for the acrimony to subside. In the autumn of 1954, when it had all been swept under the carpet if not actually forgotten, Beatrice was left with one, relatively minor consolation: Celia could have no real idea of the trouble she had caused. She could guess, probably with spiteful accuracy, but was deprived of details.

After reading the letter, Annaliese insisted on involving George, giving him a summary of what Celia had said – albeit only about the forgeries: no mention was made of the reference to Annaliese's behaviour in Portugal, or to the sting in the tail concerning George's homosexuality. It was his initial reaction that influenced most of what followed.

Beginning by reminding his mother and aunt that he had always regarded Celia as unfit to work at Boothby's, George claimed that they would never have found themselves in such a mess if normal caution had been exercised. It was Beatrice, he stated flatly, who had rushed to handle HAT's pictures, doing so against his advice. Annaliese seized on the idea. Furious at the mention of herself in the letter and the discovery that Edward had paid to sleep with Celia, she was spoiling for a row and set about Beatrice mercilessly.

When it had been raging for ten minutes, Athene rushed into the office, and, having failed to stop the quarrel, banged on a desk to attract attention. In the consequent stunned silence she asked, 'Who is actually *in charge* of this place?'

Greeted by mystified silence, Athene said, 'Very well, let me put it another way. Who *owns* the company?'

'Well, as a matter of fact, I do,' Beatrice muttered.

'I see.' Athene's calmness evaporated. 'I must say, Aunt Annaliese, it's a bit steep. You only come here when you aren't in Portugal and you've nothing better to do. If you ever did know what was going on, or take a share of the responsibility, it was a long time ago. I don't think you have the right to blame Beatrice, especially on *his* say so.' The full force of Athene's incandescent anger was turned on George. 'He's having an affair with the man who started all the fuss over those blasted pictures. In case anyone has forgotten, it was Tony Austen-Cave who said they were genuine and brought in experts from far and wide to agree with him.'

Stunned by the unexpected onslaught, Annaliese stormed off the premises. Left looking foolish, George went back to his own office and Beatrice smiled weakly at her rescuer. 'Thank you, my dear,' she said. 'That was very brave of you. I hope you don't live to regret it, though. Annaliese's a good friend, but a terrible enemy.'

'I'm not frightened of her,' Athene said. 'Now, let me see the repellent Celia's letter.'

'Oh, no, I couldn't possibly do that,' Beatrice said.

'Do you want me on your side or don't you?' Athene demanded.

'Well, naturally – but you see, my dear, I promised Charles . . .'

'Hand it over,' Athene ordered.

Meekly, Beatrice did so.

As she read, Athene's face was a picture. She also let out strangled cries of, 'Oh, I say,' and, barely able to keep a straight face, did a lot of tut-tutting. When she finally folded it up and gave it back to Beatrice, her eyes were sparkling. 'I'd say I'm in the clear for a while,' she said. 'Before Aunt Annaliese comes gunning for me, she's got to deal with poor old Uncle Edward, and that could take quite some time – pardner.'

The confrontation, delayed for several days by an elusiveness on Edward's part that Annaliese came to believe was deliberate, began on the steps of Allardyce Castle. Edward chose an unfortunate moment to arrive: his car drew up just as Annaliese, enraged by his failure to respond to the telephone messages she had left everywhere, was setting out to London to look for him.

Heedless of the fact that half a dozen transfixed servants were hanging on her every word, Annaliese told Edward of Celia's letter and its contents. When he refused to respond in front of a goggling audience, Annaliese's temper spiralled out of control. Paralysed by the verbal flogging, Edward turned into a stuffed dummy, open-mouthed, rooted to the spot. Not until Gwen appeared, grimly disapproving, to take Annaliese unceremoniously by the arm, did the flood of invective stop. Gwen said something to Annaliese, who, with ostentatiously bad grace, did as she was told and headed for the library. Edward followed her and Gwen set about the servants.

'Well, how much of this is true?' Annaliese demanded when they were alone.

Taking her by surprise, Edward said, 'All of it.'

'*All* of it?'

'Yes.'

'You actually *knew* that Celia had been a prostitute when you inherited the title?'

'Yes.'

'Why in God's name didn't you say so?' Annaliese shouted. 'We should have got rid of her.'

'You will recall that I wanted to,' Edward said, far too composed for Annaliese's present taste. 'I hope that you also recall that you obstructed me at every turn. In the end, I bowed to the need to avoid scandal.'

'Scandal!' Annaliese looked at him in mocking disbelief.

'We were up to our necks in scandal when we came here, *but none of it concerned us*. By blaming it on Ralph — and Celia was certainly his fault — we could have got away with *anything*. Instead of which, you let it ride and we've become tainted by association.'

'I made the wrong decision,' Edward admitted.

After a deep breath, Annaliese lowered her voice, sounding even more dangerous. 'And you gave her money for sex? You actually *paid* her?'

'Yes, I'm afraid I did.'

'Why?'

'It was tantamount to blackmail. I was already seeing another girl and Celia threatened to expose me.' Edward was painfully aware that now, years after that first, incredible night at Rashleigh's house, it sounded like an excuse, not a reason — an extremely weak excuse. To his horror, he found himself saying, 'And I suppose it became a habit.'

'A habit.' Annaliese shook her head incredulously. 'How much did you pay her?'

Edward shrugged. 'Over the years, it must have come to a tidy sum.'

'Enough to afford the South of France?'

'Maybe.' Edward pretended to think about it. 'If she invested it sensibly, yes, she'd be well-off.'

'Why, Edward?' Annaliese asked, almost pleading. '*Why* did you allow yourself to be so silly?'

'In the end, I think it was to protect you.'

Something snapped. 'Protect me?' Annaliese stormed, lividly angry. 'What on earth do you mean?'

'I imagined that you'd be upset if you found out what Celia was.'

'You idiot. You absolute, utter *idiot*!'

The insult was delivered with all the force and venom of a violent slap across the face. Edward blinked, appeared upset, then pulled his shoulders back resolutely. Giving Annaliese no time to realise what he was doing, he strode out of the library. By the time she caught up with him, he was halfway down the main stairs and calling for his chauffeur. Conscious of Gwen's watchful presence in the shadows, Annaliese stood by as Edward asked a bewildered Rigby to take him straight back to London.

Bringing afternoon tea into the small sitting-room, Gwen did not mince words. 'You made a right mess of that.'

'Don't you think I had every provocation?' Annaliese cried. 'That letter from Celia was poison, pure poison. Let me tell you . . .'

'You already have done,' Gwen said. 'Me and some of the biggest blabber-mouths in the county. Bill Perkins got a lovely earful. After he's been in the pub tonight, it'll be all over Marlborough.'

Flaring up, Annaliese said, 'If that's the case, I shall dismiss him.'

'That,' said Gwen heading for the door, 'will improve things no end.'

Conscious that she had behaved foolishly, thus dancing to Celia's tune, Annaliese stayed in Wiltshire for a week. Going out of her way to be nice to Henrietta and Nicholas Hammond, with whom she spent a great deal of time on estate business, she persuaded herself that she had regained her poise and self-assurance. The feeling vanished when a tense, pale-faced Beatrice greeted her return to Boothby's by saying, 'What now, Annaliese? If you've come to cause more trouble, be warned that I won't put up with it. Not any more. If you can't be pleasant, keep away. Failing that, Charles thinks I should sell.'

'*Sell?*' Suspecting a joke, Annaliese almost laughed. 'Don't be silly, Beatrice, you can't sell Boothby's.'

'Oh yes I can – and I am not being silly,' Beatrice retorted.

'Charles is in favour and Nigel is standing by to handle the negotiations.'

'With whom?' Annaliese asked, considerably less confident than a moment ago.

'For the last twenty years, Sotheby's have taken me out to lunch during the first week in June and made an offer,' Beatrice said, the thrill of revealing the secret making her imposing. 'It's been quite a tradition, and I hope it continues. Now, since the Taverner pictures, I am also being wooed by Benjamin Galbraith. Oh, and one other thing – I've *almost* stopped fretting about the forgeries. Athene, bless her, has persuaded me that we have no reason to reproach ourselves – the buyer was far more interested in the content than the artist and has no cause for complaint.'

Badly shaken by Beatrice's uncharacteristic pugnacity, Annaliese made herself scarce, doing odd jobs for George and avoiding Athene.

But at Cadogan Square that evening, she boiled over again and spent an hour berating Edward for his long, weak-willed relationship with Celia. There was also his failure to voice his doubts about the forgeries. 'You needn't have made a fuss about it,' Annaliese concluded. 'A word or two in Beatrice's ear and she could have told Taverner that she'd changed her mind.'

'You think it would have been that easy?' Edward asked, speaking for the first time.

'Yes, I do. Beatrice respects your opinion.'

'Whereas you don't?'

'No, Edward, I don't. How *can* I?'

Unconcerned, he got up, crossed to the sideboard for more whisky and lit a cigarette. Punctiliously, aware that he was irritating Annaliese by doing so, he searched for an ashtray. At last, he said, 'I liked Taverner, you know. Still do.'

'You would,' Annaliese snapped. 'The man was a complete

scoundrel. Sex-crazed, too, if Celia is to be believed.'

'No harm in that,' Edward said mildly. 'He was a first-class painter. That portrait he did for me was good. Where is it, by the way?'

'You surely didn't expect me to give it houseroom after the way he behaved,' Annaliese said. She was unwilling to admit that she had overseen the destruction of the painting and watched the remains being fed into the furnace that provided the Castle's hot water.

Edward grunted and took a studious interest in his cigarette. 'Do you know, I think I'd like a divorce,' he said, chillingly matter-of-fact.

Taken by surprise, Annaliese's voice rose alarmingly as she said, 'Divorce? Have you gone mad?'

'I don't think so.' Edward considered the point. 'On the contrary, that could be the most sensible thing I've said in ages.'

'No it isn't. We can't possibly divorce. It's out of the question. A ridiculous idea.' Believing that she had a right to attack and unable to come to terms with defence, Annaliese was floundering.

'Why not?' Edward drew deeply on his cigarette. 'The facts are staring us in the face. I've made quite a few mistakes in this marriage – big ones, that I regret. I'm very sorry. I would have liked to put things right – I wanted a daughter. Did you know that?'

'No,' Annaliese lied.

Edward shrugged. 'All water under the bridge now, anyway. As I say, I'm sorry, but there's nothing I can do – especially since you seem to be taking it into your head to become a harridan, a shrewish dictator.' Shocked, Annaliese felt the colour drain from her face. 'I'm not prepared to have what's left of my life turned into a misery,' Edward went on. 'I'm disgusted with myself over Celia, but your ranting and raving makes it a hundred times worse. I'll give you the grounds and you can divorce me.'

'Grounds?' Annaliese was at a loss. 'What do you mean?'

'I'll find a woman and you can sue me for adultery. That would leave you free to live in Portugal.'

'I didn't realise . . .' Badly shaken, Annaliese got up and began to pace the room agitatedly. 'I didn't mean to. I don't want to make your life a misery – in some ways you've been very good to me . . .' Touched by her penitence, Edward made a move to embrace her, only to find that she flinched away. 'No, there's no need for that,' she said wildly. 'I'm going to telephone Matthew.'

'What for?'

'I want to go back to Allardyce. Tonight.'

'Annaliese, it's eight o'clock,' Edward protested. 'If nothing else, think of Matthew. What's wrong with tomorrow morning?'

'I shall be on my way to Lisbon tomorrow morning,' Annaliese replied and Edward despaired.

Two hours later, as she was getting into the car, he said, 'What are we going to do about George?'

'I neither know nor care,' Annaliese snapped.

'We must talk about it.'

'I don't think so, Edward. I'd hate to sound like a harridan!'

That night, Edward was furious, with himself and Annaliese. Yet again, she had walked away from a problem.

Huddled in the back of the Rolls on the way to Wiltshire, Annaliese found herself thinking that Edward never stopped being a gentleman. Even when confronted with all his misdemeanours and goaded into talking of divorce, he had not mentioned John Brandon.

'Oh dear,' Annaliese sighed.

Matthew, normally her most solicitous admirer, did not respond.

Annaliese stayed in Portugal for three months.

From time to time she wondered about the sentence in Celia's letter that she had not repeated to Edward in any of her diatribes. *I can't help feeling that her 'friend' in Portugal might be even younger than my own, splendid Michael.* The mistaken assumption about Kurt's age was small comfort compared to Celia's deadly accuracy in sensing that Annaliese had a lover. Would Beatrice tell Edward? It was unlikely – particularly in the prevailing mood of tension, where everyone was pretending that Celia didn't exist. In any case, as the weeks passed, Annaliese came to the conclusion that she didn't care.

Towards the end of a day that had been devoted entirely to unhurried love-making, she told Kurt that she was considering taking up permanent residence at the villa.

'Why is that?' he asked.

'Because I'm sick to death of England and all the people in it.'

'*All* of them, Highness?'

'*All* of them, Kurt. And I want to be with you.'

'Is that wise?'

'Why shouldn't it be?'

Drawing her to him, Kurt looked troubled. His apprehension changed to wonder as, apparently unaware of what he was doing, he used her Christian name for the first time. 'Annaliese, you must be careful.'

'Why?' she whispered, awestruck by his tenderness and courage.

'You and I are from different worlds.'

'Initially, yes. What of it?'

'We are not suitable for one another.'

For the first time in months, Annaliese shook with uninhibited laughter. 'Kurt, you are a fool,' she spluttered. 'What do you think we've been doing for the last few years?

Playing games? Indulging our lust?'

'Some of that, I think.'

'Possibly – but what else? Don't you think we're a little in love?' Chuckling at the expression on his face, Annaliese said, 'Only a *very* little, of course. You wouldn't allow yourself to fall *completely* in love with an Archduchess, would you?'

'Definitely not.' Kurt was sharing her good humour. 'But, yes, I do love Your Highness a little.'

'Annaliese,' she said. 'When we're alone, call me Annaliese.'

'I will if you remember your obligations.'

'Obligations?' Annaliese frowned. 'What do you mean?'

'You are an Archduchess and an English duchess, Annaliese. That means you have duties to your class. Obligations. You must not neglect them and you can never turn your back on them, not permanently.'

'I see. Is that the end of the lecture?'

Kurt smiled lovingly. 'For the moment.'

After that, they never talked about her staying forever – but neither was going back to England mentioned. Eventually, Annaliese's curiosity was aroused by a note from Gwen informing her that Edward was in the Government yet again and rumoured to be having a fling with a girl who was young enough to be his granddaughter.

Much to her jaundiced amusement, Annaliese discovered that the story about romantic attachment was groundless. Edward *did* see rather a lot of a young woman who worked in an obscure niche of the Foreign Office, but the timing and nature of their trysts made it plain that the association was purely platonic. It was, Annaliese finally concluded, another attempt on Edward's part to find a surrogate daughter.

Three months was far too long an absence, Annaliese discovered. It had given people time to adjust and decide where their loyalties lay.

A subtle but powerful change was underway at Boothby's. Beatrice was formal and Athene disapproving. The impression was that they were vaguely glad to see her, but would Annaliese kindly mind her own business and go away quickly. George, ashamed of his relationship with Tony Austen-Cave, but unable to help himself, was evasive.

At Compton Allardyce, Gwen was more truculent than ever and Matthew had acquired a talent for radiating disapproval. Whether in Wiltshire or London, Edward was affable but alert, an unnerving combination that suggested he hadn't given up the idea of divorce. Only Nicholas and Henrietta, deeply in love with each other and Compton Allardyce and disregarding what Athene said about Annaliese, behaved normally towards her.

Powerless to change the situation, Annaliese loathed the new atmosphere at Boothby's. As a consequence of the forgery débâcle, Beatrice had become obsessive about checking the provenance of every item that was offered. George was given more than his fair share of this tedious work and regarded it as a punishment for his disloyal reaction to Celia's letter. Now secure in her alliance with Beatrice, Athene let him see that she enjoyed his discomfort.

During 1953 and 1954, Annaliese felt useful only twice; ironically, these were the occasions on which she organised the funerals of her two old friends, Max and Vassily. Max died in the summer of 1953, while Annaliese was in Portugal. Just over twelve months later, Kurt telephoned to say that Vassily was very ill and fading fast.

Ownership of the dead men's villas was transferred to their nominated beneficiaries, both of whom were Habsburgs of the generation made up of Annaliese's nephews and nieces. Max's property went to Franz, who was a successful architect in Geneva and married to a very beautiful Swiss girl; Sophie, the recipient of Vassily's house, was the wife of a German industrialist, a young man belonging to one of the great Ruhr dynasties. Both couples were delighted with their new possessions, but said they would be able to use them rarely – possibly for part of the summer holidays. To Kurt's great satisfaction, his friends, Ernst Weber and Joachim Hassler, were re-engaged as live-in caretakers.

'You three will have a marvellous time when I'm not here,' Annaliese said to Kurt.

'It will be pleasant,' he agreed. 'Not marvellous, though. That's when you *are* here.'

Laughing, Annaliese asked, 'Do Ernst and Joachim have women friends?'

'Yes, from the village.' After a reflective pause, Kurt's face cracked with one of his rare smiles. 'They poke fun at me for not bothering. You are the only secret I have from them.'

'So I should hope!' Annaliese cried.

'You see,' Kurt said, 'there *is* a difference between us.' He looked pleased with himself. 'Deep down, you're ashamed of a common fellow like me.'

'Kurt, it's not my status that bothers me,' Annaliese replied. 'It's my age.'

'You think I should find young girls, like Ernst and Joachim?'

'Don't *you* ever think that?'

'Young girls know nothing,' Kurt said dismissively. 'What use would a silly virgin be to a man who is accustomed to you?'

'Are you sure?' Annaliese was teasing, fishing for compliments and reassurance.

Picking her up, Kurt carried her from the terrace to her bedroom and set about proving his point. As usual these days, there were two voices in Annaliese's head, one telling her that this was surely madness, the other insisting that she was perfectly sane and had every right to her pleasure. Not surprisingly, the second voice won. It always did.

In October 1955, another death and funeral — one that she had missed — gave Annaliese considerable pause for thought. Arriving home after six weeks at the villa with Kurt, and more reluctant than ever to begin speaking English again, she was greeted with the news that her old friend, Clementine Laverstoke had passed away and been buried during her absence.

'Oh, Gwen,' Annaliese moaned. 'Why, oh why didn't you send for me?'

'Would it have made any difference?'

'Of course it would,' Annaliese retorted angrily. 'What exactly are you implying?'

'Nothing, I'm sure,' Gwen said, using pugnacity to cover her retreat. 'We were represented at the funeral, so it didn't look too bad.'

'Edward?' Annaliese asked meekly.

Gwen nodded. 'He took Athene with him.'

The following morning, Annaliese went to Eaton Mandeville and apologised profusely to Piers.

'My dear Annaliese, don't upset yourself,' he said. 'Mother understood.'

'Did she?'

'Yes. It was all very sudden. She was taken ill on a Tuesday and died on Thursday. On Wednesday, she asked for you and I telephoned Allardyce.'

'And I was away,' Annaliese muttered.

'So your housekeeper informed us. When I told Mother you were in Portugal, she gave strict instructions that you weren't to be disturbed. She thought you were probably acting on her advice.'

'As a matter of fact, I was,' Annaliese said, praying that Piers had no idea what that advice had been. 'That doesn't help me feel less guilty, though. If you remember, I wasn't anywhere to be found when your father died.'

'You mustn't worry,' Piers replied. 'I was ordered to tell you – and I'm quoting Mother, you understand – not to be so damned self-indulgent.'

Annaliese nodded. 'Typical Clem, and very true.'

'She was in quite a hurry to be off,' Piers went on. 'Reunion with Father, you see.'

'Oh!' Annaliese was unable to contain her surprise.

'She believed very strongly,' Piers explained.

'I would never have thought it,' Annaliese admitted.

'You weren't meant to. She left a note for you.' Piers glanced at his wife, Rachel. 'Where did you put it, darling?'

'Here it is.' Rachel took the envelope from a drawer and handed it to Annaliese who looked at it apprehensively. 'Go on, it won't bite you,' Rachel urged.

It was short and to the point.

Annaliese, my dear,

I've overstayed my welcome – I am 82, you know. So I'm off to join my darling Hubert. I expect the silly old fool will be glad to see me. If you must mourn and be downright bloody miserable, get it out of your system as soon as possible, then carry on enjoying yourself. One last piece of advice: FIX GEORGE. It's long overdue.

All my love,

Clementine.

Blinking away tears, Annaliese passed the note to Piers. 'Ah!' he said when he reached the end. 'George. Yes.'

'Well?' Baffled, Annaliese looked anxiously at Piers and Rachel, both of whom were suddenly uneasy.

'Mother suspected problems,' Piers said. 'You know what those instincts of hers were like.'

'I do indeed.' Annaliese hesitated, realised that the time had come, and took the plunge. 'The fact is, George has homosexual tendencies. Strictly between ourselves, of course, he was sent down from Oxford because of an unfortunate incident with another man.'

Piers heaved a sigh of relief. 'Good, now we know where we are. The fact is, Mother was worried about George long before the innuendoes started.'

'What innuendoes?' Annaliese asked sharply.

'Mostly in the *Daily Sketch*,' Rachel replied. She produced a week-old edition of the popular newspaper from a rack that was stuffed with copies of *Country Life* and *The Times*. 'It has a gossip-column written by someone they call "Jackdaw". Look at that item.'

Annaliese read it aloud. '"London's brightest and finest were out in force last night for the opening of a Turner exhibition at the Tate Gallery. The ceremony was performed by the celebrated art connoisseur and critic, Tony Austen-Cave. Tony's very good friend, the Marquess of Axholme, a leading light at Boothby's of Bond Street, was in his usual close attendance. Lady Honor Corbishley, escorted by Major Claude Dalrymple, was wearing a stunning dress . ."' Annaliese's voice tailed off.

'Tony Austen-Cave is somewhat suspect,' Piers said gently.

Unwilling to tolerate such a mealy-mouthed description, Rachel said, 'He's a homosexual.'

Piers, who considered that the law was repressive in this respect, winced. Suddenly struck by the fact that the Taverner pictures had brought George and Tony into contact, and remembering her reaction to the Robert Chappell affair, Annaliese gained her first nebulous insight into how much her indifference might have contributed to what was beginning to look like an unholy mess.

Mistaking the reason for Annaliese's obvious abstraction, Rachel drove the point home. 'These little digs by Jackdaw have been going on for at least a year.'

Tactfully, Piers asked, 'How old is George, Annaliese?'

'Thirty-three. Yes, all right, he should have been married years ago.'

'Does George know any girls – apart from Athene?' Rachel said.

Annaliese drew breath to answer, changed her mind, and shook her head dejectedly. 'I have no idea,' she said. 'What an admission, eh?'

'George has never socialised.' Piers was robustly cheerful, determined to find a solution. 'A chap with his position and prospects should be able to pick and choose from the very best.'

'Just like you did,' Rachel chuckled, fondly recalling the days when she had fought her way through scores of debutantes to win the future Duke of Laverstoke.

'I have no idea how to set about this,' Annaliese confessed. 'Beyond belief, isn't it?'

'I suppose George *is* vaguely amenable to women?' Rachel asked. 'He doesn't cringe away from them?'

'He didn't with Athene,' Annaliese replied.

Piers nodded. 'I'm pretty sure they had a fling. Poor Athene was livid when Austen-Cave turned up.'

Painfully aware that she should have noticed this – and, no doubt, many other danger signs – Annaliese said, 'Athene really won't do, will she?'

'Frankly, no.' Piers was unhappy with the judgement. 'It's a damnable shame. You won't do better than Athene if you scour the whole country.'

'Not that I have the faintest idea how to set about *that*,' Annaliese grumbled. 'I've lost touch with the people who might have helped.' The best ones had died, she realised. In addition to Clementine, the redoubtable Lavinia Torksey would have gone through the fortune- and title-hunters like an avenging angel.

'Shall we keep our ears to the ground?' Rachel asked.

'Yes, please,' Annaliese replied. 'In the meantime, I must talk to George.'

It was clear that she was not looking forward to it.

Appreciating the enormity of her task and the potentially ruinous consequences of failure, Annaliese approached it with great care. She rejected the idea of involving Edward. Two people who were so cruelly at odds with each other would not help George. There was also the insurmountable barrier of her pride: even though she knew that he would not wish to take advantage of it, Annaliese refused to let Edward see that she now accepted she had been wrong about George.

Pretending that it was no more than a casual call, she went to Boothby's. Slipping unnoticed into George's office, she found him disconsolate.

'What's wrong?' Annaliese asked.

'Oh, it's just one of those days,' George sighed. 'Aunt Bee got out of bed on the wrong side this morning and there's been a reign of terror.'

'Is it bad?'

'Fairly, She's still threatening to sell out. Don't worry, it usually blows over fairly quickly.' Smiling weakly, George asked, 'To what do I owe the pleasure?'

'I wondered if you were coming to Allardyce this weekend,' Annaliese said.

'Er – yes, I was planning to.'

Guessing at the cause of George's wariness, Annaliese asked, 'Alone?'

'I've invited Tony to join me.'

Going to immense trouble to keep her voice level and quiet, Annaliese said, 'I'd like you to put him off. You and I must have a long talk.'

George gazed at his mother sombrely. 'It's about Tony, isn't it?'

'Yes, it is,' Annaliese admitted. 'But I don't want to get drawn into anything now. This is very important – probably the biggest thing we've had to deal with since Edward succeeded to the title. That means we have to be very calm and honest. If we start shouting at each other, we shall ruin everything.'

'Will Father be down there this weekend?' George asked.

'No, he's intending to stay in London. There's a dinner at the Carlton Club on Saturday evening.' Annaliese studied George, seeking out his thoughts. 'Would you like your father to be with us?'

After an agonising moment or two of indecision, George relaxed: it was as if the dormant embers of his childhood love for Annaliese were flickering back into life. 'No, Mother,' he said. 'Just the two of us together.'

'Good.' Annaliese walked round the desk to kiss him. 'Saturday afternoon, then?'

'Can we have a slap-up dinner afterwards? At The Chantry?'

Annaliese smiled. 'Certainly, darling. I'll tell Gwen to arrange it.'

After spending an idle Saturday morning at the Castle, Annaliese and George took advantage of a perfect, golden October afternoon to walk to The Chantry. Every few hundred yards, Annaliese paused to look round, marvelling at the autumn colours of the woods, waiting for the dogs to stop exploring and catch up.

'Are you falling back in love with it all?' George asked, breaking half an hour's companionable silence.

'Mmm.' Annaliese took his arm. 'That's very astute of you,' she murmured. 'Perhaps it's the first step, something I have to do.'

'To be at ease with yourself again – like you always were?'

'Perhaps.'

Long before they reached The Chantry, Annaliese knew what she had to say to George, but she waited until they were settled with tea, scones, and the fires lit against what promised to be a chilly evening.

'Darling, the first thing I must do is apologise,' Annaliese said. 'When you left Oxford, I turned my back on you. That wasn't because of what you'd done, it was what was happening to me.'

'In Portugal?' George asked gently. 'After the War and Grandmama Elsa – and Nancy Shenstone going to America?'

'Yes.' Annaliese paused to collect her thoughts, reviewing the long telephone conversation with Kurt the previous evening. 'I'm making changes. They aren't particularly big ones, but they will enable me to deal with what a dear friend has called my *obligations*.'

'Is that what I am, an obligation?' To show that he wasn't about to take offence, George was smiling.

'You're my son and it's time I helped you.'

'To do my duty?'

'Well, frankly, that *is* what it comes down to, George. Look, to save beating about the bush, let me tell you what I want. I'd like you to marry and produce your heir. I'm sorry to be so blunt, but there it is.'

George stood up and wandered round the room, turning on a pair of table-lamps and drawing the curtains to shut out the misty dusk. Returning to his seat, he had a bewildered expression on his face, reminding Annaliese of how he was as a child when working out his response to Douglas's latest outrageous suggestion.

'It's a relief to be away from Tony for a while,' George said at last.

'Why is that?' Annaliese asked, gently disinterested.

'No one who isn't close to him would believe it, but he's

desperately insecure. He always wants approval and admiration. For instance, he airs his knowledge *ad nauseam*. If a picture can be summed up in thirty seconds, he'll take five minutes over it and expect a round of applause. And he's terribly vain – every hour, on the hour, one has to admire his looks.'

'Irritating,' Annaliese said mildly, thinking that George sounded like a complaining wife. 'What about other things?'

'He's very demanding.' In spite of her best efforts, Annaliese's eyebrows rose. Embarrassed, George added, 'I mean, *emotionally*. He went mad when I told him I wanted to be alone here this weekend.'

Annaliese waited, sensing that there was more to come. 'The wretched thing is that he has someone else,' George said.

'Is this a recent development?'

'No, the other man pre-dates me. I imagine his attraction is that he allows Tony to do the things I won't. Robert and I agreed not to and – well – that's the way I am.'

'What exactly are you saying, George?' Annaliese asked.

Bravely, he replied, 'I won't let Tony bugger me – nor will I do it to him. Is that a relief to you?'

'No, it isn't, my dear, for the simple reason that I'm not sitting in judgement on you. It might interest you to know that I've made myself aware of the attempts that are being made to decriminalise what consenting men get up to in private and I think it's high time it happened.' After a slight pause, Annaliese said, 'If I may, I'd like to ask you about Athene.'

'Yes.' George found it necessary to take a deep breath.

'Did you and she ever make love – have sex like men and women are supposed to?'

'Yes, we did. Lots of times.' Strangely relaxed and confident, George was eager to substantiate the claim. 'Athene taught me how to do it – here, in this house. She had no more idea than me what was supposed to happen, but she got a book that explained it all. We had great fun. She kept me on the straight and narrow until Tony turned up out of the blue. If only I *could* marry her.'

Annaliese sighed. 'It's out of the question, I'm afraid.'

'That's what Athene always said.'

A thought occurred to Annaliese. 'There's something else. Even if we did risk Athene, the press would go mad. They'd leave no stone unturned to discover her father. That would be horrible for Henry and Nicholas.'

'Not much fun for the Laverstokes, either,' George added.

Inclining her head to acknowledge the point, Annaliese asked, 'How attached are you to Tony Austen-Cave?'

George attempted an objective analysis of his emotions. 'I'm afraid he has some sort of compulsive hold over me.'

'He seems to have qualities you don't like,' Annaliese pointed out. 'And he's unfaithful.'

'Yes. Actually, he isn't a very nice person – not at all like Robert.' Briefly, George's face registered pain and loss. Then, just as quickly, he perked up. 'Unfortunately, that doesn't stop me being besotted.'

The whimsical way in which George said it was the greatest test of Annaliese's resolve to conduct the discussion in a spirit of loving and constructive harmony. Fleetingly, she had the urge to box George's ears, then give him a good shaking in an attempt to impose her perception of sense and reason on him. After winning the battle Annaliese said, 'Infatuations are supposed to burn themselves out.'

'I've never imagined that my involvement with Tony would last indefinitely,' George replied. 'We're both aware that I have to marry.'

'You've talked about it?'

'Oh yes.'

'Do you consider yourself capable of living with a woman?'

Annaliese asked. 'Leading what most people refer to as a "normal" life?' Feeling that fairness required her to do so, she added, 'Even if it is like your father and me?'

'I don't see why I can't have a go,' George said. 'Robert has married.'

'*Has* he?' Suddenly, Annaliese's eyes registered the fondness she had once felt for Robert. 'You keep in touch?'

'Not any more,' George said. 'He wrote about eighteen months ago to say that his wife was pregnant. I did my best to congratulate him and that was that.' Pulling himself together, George was resolute. 'I'm prepared to give it a try, even if I can't guarantee success.'

'It's a risk we have to take,' Annaliese said. '*Anything* is preferable to having the title die with you.'

'That matters, does it?' George's voice was strained.

'Yes, it does.' Annaliese was weary but adamant.

After staring at her for a long time, George asked, 'What if the marriage is miserable? Is that acceptable?'

With an effort, Annaliese said, 'Yes, darling, it is.'

Understanding, George nodded. 'Don't worry, Mother, I'll do my best,' he said.

'Thank you, my dear.' Annaliese's relief was overwhelming. 'I'll help you, of course.'

'There is one thing you could advise me on,' George said.

'Yes, what is it?'

'*Who* am I going to marry?'

Annaliese burst into peals of laughter. 'Darling, I have absolutely no idea,' she gasped. 'I decided that I had to talk to you first, then find the lady. At the moment, I'm reduced to saying that I shall be keeping my eyes and ears open.'

'Perhaps we should organise parties,' George suggested. 'Here, I mean, not in London — we don't want to attract the wrong sort, do we?'

Responding in kind to his po-faced gravity, Annaliese said,

'We most certainly do not, George, my dear!'

Tony Austen-Cave allowed George to begin detaching himself from their relationship, understanding what lay behind his need for freedom. Superficially, it was a calm, civilised process: however, behind the pretence, George suffered endless emotional pain during the following three months. Although he no longer visited Tony's flat, they had lunch together at least once a week on the pretext of discussing business. But no matter how absorbing the latest gossip from the sale-rooms happened to be, Tony invariably created an opportunity to mention his other lover – the man who, devoid of fastidious inhibitions, apparently relished anal intercourse. George's jealousy grew by the day, nurturing insidious forces that threatened his resolve.

In the first week of 1956, after a wretched Christmas, George's willpower was in a parlous state. When he met Olivia de Vere Lawson-Grey, he was on the brink of attempting to reverse the break with Tony.

14

1956
'Being very blunt, she's a tramp'

The message from the would-be client via an intermediary was unequivocal: either Annaliese handled the business, or it would go elsewhere. Digging as deeply as she dared, Beatrice discovered that the demand for her sister-in-law's involvement was based on recommendations that went back thirty years, to a time when, for many people, Annaliese epitomised Boothby's.

In essence the Duke of Dorchester wished to realise about £200,000 from the sale of pictures. The transaction was to be handled with the utmost discretion in order to stifle speculation as to why so much cash was needed in a hurry.

Reluctantly, for their relationship was still scarred by the aftermath of Celia's letter, Beatrice gave Annaliese the details and arrangements were made to visit Widney Cheyne, the Dorchester seat near Hungerford, during the second week of January. Conscious that she was out of touch with the business and needed help, Annaliese took George with her.

Aubrey de Vere Lawson-Grey, Eleventh Duke of Dorchester, was in his mid-fifties. Annaliese thought that, behind the tension that made him inexplicably aggressive, he was probably rather ineffectual. Caroline, his wife, a few years younger, had a coldly insincere sort of beauty; the smile that showed off her flawlessly maintained teeth went nowhere near her eyes, suggesting that she was as hard as nails.

After coffee, served in a dowdy, draughty drawing-room and punctuated by the Duchess's peevish observations that Widney Cheyne was not *quite* as grand as Allardyce Castle, the Duke took Annaliese and George to see the pictures. They were in an unfurnished barn of a room at a remote corner of the house. For most of the time it must have been gloomy, but the windows were ablaze with reflections of the sun off the previous night's snow.

George scanned the walls, dismissing most of what he saw as mediocre. However a group of four paintings – a Madonna, two Venuses, and a triptych portraying biblical scenes – made him gasp in wonder.

'I would have to seek other opinions, of course,' George said, 'but I think they're by Titian.'

Aubrey Dorchester nodded morosely. 'That's what we've always believed. They've been around for donkey's years. One of my ancestors is supposed to have taken them in settlement of a debt.'

George, now close enough to the Madonna to be almost certain of its provenance, pulled out his notebook. 'There are scores of collectors and institutions who would give their souls for any one of these.' He was trembling with excitement.

'Good.' Aubrey Dorchester was both pleased and bored. 'I'll leave you to it.'

After he had gone, Annaliese said, 'Ho hum!'

'Decidedly odd,' George agreed.

Perching on a window-seat, he began to make notes. Annaliese stared out at the grounds for a while, then prowled round the room, pretending to examine pictures.

'Presumably, he'll raise what he wants for this lot?' she said.

'He'll get it for one of the Titians,' George replied. 'This is a tremendous find.'

'*Total* confidentiality, remember,' Annaliese said.

George recognised a warning: there was to be no currying favour with Tony Austen-Cave by providing material for *Gallery Scrutiny*. 'Message received and understood,' George murmured.

Shuffling restlessly, Annaliese said, 'Can I leave you to it?' George, busy with his notebook, nodded absently. 'I'm nosy, I'd like to know what's wrong with the Dorchesters.'

George immersed himself in composing descriptions of the four magnificent pictures. As he wrote, his mind was whirling round the question of authentication, trying to anticipate what would be needed to satisfy the stringent conditions imposed by Beatrice after the Taverner fraud. The sound of high-heeled footsteps – though not Annaliese's – advancing along the stone floor of the corridor was an unwelcome distraction. Irritably, George stopped work and glared at the door, ready to rebuff the intruder.

Instead, he was utterly disarmed the instant she strode into the room. The first things he noticed were the outward similarities to Annaliese – the golden hair, the pale blue eyes, and proudly upright bearing: this was a young woman intent on making the very most of her five feet nine inches and splendid legs.

Laughing at George's naively unconcealed wonderment, she said, 'Hello. I'm Olivia, the daughter.'

'George Axholme.'

'The big cheese from Boothby's, eh? Hello, George.'

He toyed with the idea of shaking hands, made an irresolute move, but changed his mind.

Counteracting his ineptitude with a glorious smile, Olivia asked, 'What do you think? *Are* they by Titian?'

'Yes – well, almost certainly.'

'Glory be!'

Olivia had a blithe *joie de vivre* which dissolved the reserve that George instinctively used as a shield against women. As though they were friends of long-standing, he said, 'Is it such a big relief?'

'George, you have no idea.' Olivia rolled her eyes and swayed, emphasising the clean, firm curves of her body. She had a way of using herself – completely natural, it seemed, like a dancer – that showed her to breath-taking effect. 'Would you like to know?' she asked. 'Can you keep a secret?'

'Absolutely. I'm the soul of discretion. Really.'

Olivia looked long and hard at George, made up her mind and moved closer to him. Light-headed at the scent of her lustrous hair, George was dimly conscious that she was forging a bond between them. He felt privileged.

'It's my brother, Monty,' Olivia said. 'He's only twenty-seven – which is three years older than me, by the way – but he's got himself into the sort of trouble that took Uncle Joe until he was fifty-odd – and Uncle Joe was a *very* determined wastrel!' Making her voice sepulchral, Olivia intoned, 'Gambling and drugs. He owes a fortune and all sorts of totally unpleasant people are making threatening noises.'

'Oh dear.' George looked distressed.

'Well, yes, that's one way of putting it,' Olivia conceded. 'Father takes a somewhat grimmer view. Monty has been banished to Australia until further notice.'

'Good gracious.' George was moved to attempt a joke. 'I had no idea that it was still taking our cast-offs.'

'Don't be silly,' Olivia said, punching George's chest. 'We have distant relatives out there – well, twelve thousand miles is distant, isn't it? They've got a sheep station – or maybe it's a mine – at a place called Boorawoola – or something like that.' When George had finished laughing, Olivia said, 'So, we shall soon be able to breathe again?'

'I think there's a fortune hanging on that wall,' George said, pointing at the Titians. 'Your father will receive a substantial sum from any one of those paintings.'

'Goodie.' Plunging into a sudden, desperate seriousness, Olivia said, 'It's Mother, you see. We simply must find a way of cheering her up.' Just as quickly, her spirits soared. 'Don't you think that would be an awfully bright idea?'

George was enchanted. This astonishingly lovely girl, with her slightly naughty, tomboyish attitude, was surely a sister under the skin to Athene. The affinities appeared convincing, the differences lay beyond George's experience and knowledge of the female sex. Nor were they obvious to Annaliese, who, returning from a stiltedly uninformative encounter with the Dorchesters, discovered George and a stunning young beauty enthralled by each other.

Olivia grasped the moment with a skill that passed itself off as artless enthusiasm. 'Lady Lincolnshire, what a pleasure. I'm Olivia, Aubrey and Caroline's daughter. Thank you for saving our bacon.'

Annaliese was moved to produce her most radiant smile as she said, 'Hello, my dear.' Watching as the two golden women shook hands, George saw that Olivia had made an excellent first impression.

'Don't count any chickens yet,' Annaliese told Olivia. 'I'm sure George is right, but we shall have to get the experts in to swear that these marvellous pictures *are* by Titian. You see, strictly between ourselves, my sister-in-law, Beatrice, is a fearful stickler for authentication.' It seemed that Olivia beguiled everyone into an immediate desire for close, conspiratorial friendship.

'I understand,' Olivia said. 'Have you been trying to pump Father?'

'I'm afraid so,' Annaliese replied. 'It didn't do me a scrap of good.'

'It's my brother,' Olivia whispered. 'Monty's landed himself and us in terrible trouble. I told George all about it.' She bathed him in a resplendent smile.

'I see.' Annaliese nodded gravely. 'Don't worry, Olivia, we shall do our very best for you.'

After ten days of hectic activity, Annaliese offered Aubrey Dorchester £275,000 for the Titian triptych. It was to be a private sale that would transfer the masterpiece to Allardyce Castle.

In response to the Duke of Dorchester's blank amazement, Annaliese was happy to explain herself. 'The experts reckon that it will fetch a quarter of a million at auction – possibly a shade more. Try it, if you like. If you do it my way, you have a copper-bottomed guarantee of confidentiality.'

'Yes, I see that.' Impressed but indecisive, Aubrey Dorchester turned to his wife. 'What do you think, m'dear?'

Caroline Dorchester bent over backwards to appear happily bemused and uncertain. 'That seems *very* fair,' she said. 'I'm no judge of these things – but bearing in mind all the problems, yes, I think we should accept that.'

'Right. Well, there you are.' Aubrey Dorchester stuck his hands into the pockets of his trousers, jingled some non-existent change, and forced a smile. 'Thank you ... er ... Annaliese. That's deuced good of you. Much appreciated.'

'Not at all,' Annaliese said. 'I'm glad to be able to help out.' By now, Aubrey had told her of the problems created by his son. 'It will be seven days before I can let you have a cheque, the money has to come from Switzerland, you see.'

'That's perfectly all right.' Aubrey Dorchester was unable

to mask a brief flicker of envy at the hint of a Swiss account.

'And don't worry about Boothby's,' Annaliese went on. 'I'll pay the commission they would have earned for selling the picture at that price.'

'How kind!' Caroline Dorchester gushed. She was never to discover that Beatrice, deciding that it was high time to finish patching up the quarrel caused by Celia's letter, had already refused the offer.

'I shall hang the triptych in the Long Gallery,' Annaliese said. 'All on its own, in magnificent isolation. For some reason or other, no one's ever used it for pictures.'

'I believe it's an amazing room,' Caroline replied.

'You must see it,' Annaliese said. 'Come to lunch one day next week.' She added an enticing titbit. 'Perhaps you'll get there before Olivia.'

After exchanging puzzled looks with her husband, Caroline said, 'I'm sorry, I don't understand.'

'Oh, have I put my foot in it?' Annaliese was deliberately arch. 'Well, I know it's early days, but I *think* there's a whiff of romance in the air.'

'You mean between your boy, George, and Olivia?' Aubrey asked.

'Yes. Didn't you realise? They've already met *four* times. It was dinner in London last Friday.'

'Ah – I see.' Aubrey nodded.

'So that's why she stayed overnight in Town with Joanna,' Caroline said, happy to have the answer to a mystery.

'As I understand it, an invitation to Compton Allardyce is imminent,' Annaliese said. 'George seems very taken with her.'

Caroline's eyes were narrowed in thought. 'Yes, Olivia was rather excited when she came back on Saturday,' she said.

'I can never tell,' Aubrey grumbled. 'She's always in a state when she's been in that blasted car.' Turning to Annaliese, he explained. 'I was forced to buy her an Austin-Healey for her twenty-first birthday. She drives it like a maniac.'

'She's awfully good,' Caroline said. 'I feel safer with Olivia at eighty miles an hour than with you at thirty, Aubrey.' While the Duke was glowering at this accurate assessment of his driving skills, Caroline's expression became calculating.

Reading her mind, Annaliese said, 'Shall we put our cards on the table?'

'Why not?' Caroline replied.

'It's time George was married.'

'Olivia, too.' Caroline raised an eyebrow at her husband. He grunted what seemed to be agreement.

'I certainly wouldn't disapprove,' Annaliese said. 'Quite the contrary.'

'A union made in *Debrett* if not in heaven,' Caroline said.

Annaliese disregarded the cynicism. 'For the moment, it's up to them. I shall mind my own business – for a month or two, at least.'

'I'll do likewise,' Caroline promised.

After Annaliese's departure, the Dorchesters considered the change in their fortunes.

'Annaliese Lincolnshire appears to be solving all our problems,' Aubrey said.

'What about Monty?' Caroline asked. 'Is there any chance of him coming back to spoil everything?'

'I wouldn't have thought so.' Aubrey was evasive.

'Don't you *know*?' Caroline demanded.

'No, I damned well don't!' Briefly, Aubrey Dorchester was assertive. 'You know perfectly well what he's like. No son of mine would . . .'

'Aubrey, we *never* mention that,' Caroline said, her voice charged with menace. 'It's in neither of our interests. I don't expect to have to remind you again.'

'All right, all right.' Beaten, Aubrey Dorchester looked at

his watch, planning an escape. 'Before you start laying the law down, no, I won't let the Lincolnshires see how profoundly glad I shall be to get rid of Olivia.'

'I should hope not,' Caroline said. 'That's up to them. It's a case of *caveat emptor* – let the buyer beware, and something tells me that they won't look too closely.'

'Why is that?'

'Never mind, Aubrey,' Caroline replied. 'Leave it to me. In the meantime, I suggest you make contact with George's father and butter him up. Can I trust you with that *simple* task?'

Annaliese's inquiries about Olivia revealed nothing to her disadvantage. The only slightly curious fact to emerge was Olivia's desire to obtain a pilot's licence. She was, and had been for two years, a member of a flying club based at Lulsgate Airport, near Bristol. For someone who drove a high-performance sports car with considerable skill and *élan*, aviation was not an unusual hobby.

Olivia saw Allardyce Castle, was bowled over by it, and became a frequent visitor. When, as soon happened, she stayed the night, she gently insisted on a bedroom in the West Wing while George slept at The Chantry. Pretending to approve, Annaliese prayed that virtue would not be taken to excessive lengths.

Olivia and George were seen together in London, dining at the Savoy, attending concerts at the Royal Festival and Wigmore Halls. George took it for granted that Olivia would share his taste in music and, much to her surprise, she found that she did. Her preoccupation with flying was mentioned, but failed to interest George. 'I hope you won't expect me to go up with you,' was his response. Shrugging off his condescension good-naturedly, Olivia visited the club at Lulsgate once a week, choosing days when George was exceptionally busy at Boothby's and unable to see her. Generally, she spent the night in Somerset, claiming that she stayed with friends at Cheddar.

In the background, the couple's parents became friends and visited each other's houses. Edward, as dedicated as ever to the intrigues of Westminster and Whitehall, found an appreciative listener in Aubrey Dorchester. Delighted at the rapport they struck up, Annaliese failed to notice that Edward had not been won over by Olivia. He treated her cordially enough, but there were occasional displays of over-polite formality; with Edward that was a sure sign of unease, of mistrust, perhaps. In fact, even if Annaliese had spotted the signs, she would have ignored them – as she did with Gwen's sniffs of disapproval whenever Olivia was mentioned.

By the middle of April, Caroline Dorchester told Annaliese that Olivia spoke of George constantly and had mentioned the possibility of marriage. Satisfied that she could leave things to look after themselves for a short time, Annaliese flew to Portugal. After a wonderful week with Kurt, she returned to find George on the verge of proposing to Olivia.

'Am I doing the right thing?' he asked.

'*I* think so, darling,' Annaliese replied. 'She's an awfully nice girl. What do *you* think?'

'Well, I'm very fond of her, of course.' George was fretful, wondering whether this was enough.

'And I'm sure the feeling is mutual,' Annaliese said. 'The important thing is that Olivia is one of *us*. She's been brought up to appreciate how the aristocracy functions.'

'Should I tell her about Tony and Robert Chappell?' George asked, sounding as though he would like to.

Ordering herself to be calm, Annaliese said, 'No, I don't think that's necessary. Get married, then iron out the difficulties. I'm sure that's the best way.'

Dutifully, George drove the twenty-odd miles to Widney

Cheyne and observed the old-fashioned niceties. In a private meeting with Aubrey Dorchester, he sought permission to ask for Olivia's hand. It was given enthusiastically. Five minutes later, Olivia said yes. Excitedly, all four – George, Olivia, and her parents – rushed to Compton Allardyce to give Annaliese the news.

She was overjoyed. Edward, who was spending a few days away from London, created the impression that he shared Annaliese's sentiments. Champagne was sent for and plans hatched. It was decided to make the official announcement in two weeks' time and there was talk of a big dinner-party. Primed by Annaliese, Edward took Aubrey Dorchester to one side for a tactful word about the costs of the engagement and the wedding itself.

'Look here, old man, we were wondering whether we could chip in,' Edward said. 'I don't want to be invidious, but I expect you could do with some help in that direction. You'd be amazed at how many fellows in the House of Lords are feeling the pinch these days – and you had Monty's problems, of course.'

'That's damned handsome of you, Edward,' Aubrey Dorchester replied. 'I have to admit that we aren't well-placed at the moment. My father's death duties nearly did for us, you know.'

'Good, that's settled.' Far from being annoyed by the indecent haste of Aubrey's capitulation, Edward was relieved to have an embarrassment out of the way. 'Perhaps you'd like to tell Olivia that she only has to ask for anything she needs.'

Winking, Aubrey said, 'I'll get Caroline to do it.'

Edward laughed. 'That's the way.' Airily unconcerned, he said, 'Is there any chance that we shall be seeing Monty?'

Immediately, Aubrey was grim. 'Not if I have anything to do with it. He's in Australia, you know.'

'Yes, George mentioned it.'

'Believe me, Edward, with a wedding coming up, the last thing we need is my blasted son. If the press got hold of him . . .'

As he was meant to, Edward saw the implications in the eloquently unfinished sentence. Later, however, as he was getting ready for bed, he wondered what the Dorchesters were hiding. Together with his reservations about Olivia, the thought preyed on his mind, so much so that he considered going to Annaliese's bedroom to discuss it. He soon abandoned the idea: the point of no return had been passed and nothing would be allowed to interfere with the wedding.

A few days before the engagement was made public, George had dinner with Tony Austen-Cave and gave him advance warning of the notices that were to appear in the newspapers.

Tony was dismissive. 'Don't worry about it. You've got to do your duty, George. I understand. *Who* did you say the bride-to-be is?'

'Lady Olivia de Vere Lawson-Grey, the Duke of Dorchester's daughter.'

'Heavens! Do I detect the "Wedding of the Year"?'

'I hope not,' George muttered.

'The gossip-writers won't agree with you, dear boy.' Tony thought it was a huge joke.

For him, that was the end of the matter. Totally uninterested in hearing anything about Olivia, Tony launched into an account of disreputable goings-on at Galbraith's. Despite himself, George was fascinated, wondering if Beatrice knew of the machinations of the organisation to whom she had considered selling Boothby's. The close fellowship of scandal was treacherous. George had no idea of the extent to which he had been drawn back into the web of Tony's magnetism until they were outside the restaurant, hovering between awkward farewells and the search for taxis.

'I'm alone tonight,' Tony said, easy and confident. 'Why don't you come to my place? I promise to be good – we'll only do what you like.' Detecting George's indecision, he said, 'Will *she* look after you as well as I do?'

'I don't know,' George admitted. 'We haven't . . . well . . . you know.'

'Only too well, dear friend. I've been watching you for a couple of hours. I know exactly what you need.'

A cab drew up and George followed Tony into it.

Earlier that day, Olivia had driven to Bristol Airport. She spent the afternoon in and around the flying club on the western edge of the airfield, chatting to friends, laughing at their suggestions that, just this once, she might take a lesson.

'How long is it since you went up, Ollie? Six months?'

'Nearer a year, surely?' someone else said.

'Let me take you aloft,' a gorgeous man offered. 'I'll give you a navigation refresher course. If you can find the Severn Estuary in less than fifteen minutes, you qualify for a prize.'

'What *can* he have in mind?' a girl shrieked.

'I'm saving myself,' Olivia said with mock dignity.

'And we all know who the lucky devil is!'

He arrived soon after 3.30 pm, piloting a Dakota carrying Channel Island tomatoes. Olivia watched the reliable old aircraft land and trundle across to the makeshift freight terminal, then drove round the perimeter track.

Simon Faulkener was an ex-RAF pilot who, unwilling to accept the routine and discipline of BEA or BOAC – both of whom had offered him jobs – preferred the distinctly cowboy B & L Airways, a two-aircraft outfit that did remarkably well ferrying market-garden produce from Jersey and the south of Ireland. He was thirty-one, tall, dark-haired and, Olivia thought as he waved and hurried towards her, far too bloody good-looking for his own or anyone else's good.

The flippant casualness of their greeting was deceptive. Briefly, as Olivia paused before driving across the main Bristol to Exeter road, their eyes clashed in an expression of desire that was savage. There were times when neither of them particularly liked the other, but the sexual bond, which had flared into life within an hour of their first meeting just over two years ago, was an inexorable force.

Simon rented a bungalow three miles from the airfield. As usual, it was a shambles. Olivia added to the chaos by throwing her clothes on the floor. Simon did the same and they attacked each other, expertly athletic, knowing everything about their lusts and the way to relieve them.

After an hour of almost brutal pleasure, they were temporarily exhausted and paused to rest.

'That was good,' Olivia said. 'I got the distinct impression that you haven't had your leg over anything else since our last get-together.'

'As if I would,' Simon protested, his air of injured innocence grossly overdone.

'Spare me the crap, darling,' Olivia said, no longer pleasant. 'What's to drink?'

'The usual range of duty-frees.'

'Get me a Bacardi and Coke.'

Simon fetched the drinks and sat on the edge of the bed, sipping whisky, admiring Olivia's body, and waiting. 'So, what's new?' he said at last.

'George and I are engaged,' Olivia said. 'The world is being informed on Saturday.'

'Congratulations.' Simon raised his glass in a derisory salute. 'Marchioness of Axholme, eh?'

'Yes.'

'When's the happy day?'

'September the first looks likely.'

'Why the rush?'

Olivia shrugged. 'Why wait?'

Simon's pretence at cheerfulness faded. 'I still don't see why we couldn't make a go of it,' he said sulkily.

'Oh, God, not again,' Olivia whispered to herself. She drained her glass and held it out to Simon. Dutifully, he fetched a refill. With laboured patience, Olivia said, 'You're broke, Simon, and always will be. So are my parents and always have been. I need money. The Lincolnshires have got hundreds of tons of the stuff. Is that clear?'

'Wonderful,' Simon said bitterly. 'As icing on the cake, there's a nice title to go with the loot.'

'Very gratifying,' Olivia agreed. 'It also guarantees my future. I shall be the wife of the Eleventh Duke of Lincolnshire and the mother of the Twelfth. Excellent long-term prospects, wouldn't you say?'

'What's he like, this George?' Simon asked, not particularly interested.

'He's a nice chap – thirty-four, decent-looking. Oh, and he's a queer.'

Simon gaped at her. 'You're joking!'

'It's hardly a joking matter, is it?' Olivia was resentful.

'How do you know?' Simon spluttered. 'Has he told you?'

'*Do* try to be vaguely sensible,' Olivia replied. 'No, it's perfectly simple – George has been very thick with a man called Austen-Cave who's a notorious poofter. That isn't *totally* conclusive, but dear Mummy, who has been reminding some of her friends in high places of the favours they owe her, has discovered that my intended was sent down from Oxford after being caught in bed with another man.'

Simon was appalled. 'What does your father think of this?'

Contemptuously, Olivia said, 'Mummy and I gave up involving him in things a long time ago. I thought I'd told you that.'

'But . . .' Simon floundered for words. 'If George *is* bent, why does he want to get married?'

'To get an heir, you berk.' Olivia shook her head, as if sympathising with herself at having to humour a simpleton. 'For someone like George, a son is vital – otherwise one of the country's premier titles expires when he does.' After a reflective pause, she added, 'I could easily feel sorry for the poor sod.'

'Why?'

'George used to have an elder brother. Unfortunately he got the chop in the War, so the responsibility of siring the next Duke but one passed to my affianced.'

Cautiously, Simon asked, 'Have you tried him out yet?'

'Not yet. That treat awaits him.'

'What if he can't or won't perform?'

'He will.'

'How can you be so sure?'

Olivia grinned wickedly. 'Mummy knows of three noble lords who've done the business despite being as bent as sin.'

'This may not be much fun for you,' Simon said.

Olivia's face clouded. 'I'm expecting it to be *hell*. Never mind, when I've delivered the goods, I shall rush back to you.'

'Not before *then*?' Simon was horrified.

'Of course not.'

'Why?'

'Don't you know *anything*?' Olivia screamed.

'No, at least, not as far as the aristocracy's concerned,' Simon shouted. 'I'm an ignoramus – and, do you know something? I think I like it that way.'

'Look, Simon . . .' Olivia held out a hand in a conciliatory gesture. 'I know it's difficult for you – it is for me, too. Until I've produced a son, I must behave myself. One false step and my future mother-in-law would be demanding blood tests on anything I produce.'

'Really?'

'Definitely. Behind the lovey-dovey exterior, she's an utter bitch.'

Simon whistled. 'Coming from you, my precious, that is praise indeed.'

'Yes, but listen to me.' Olivia was anxious to make him understand. 'After I've had a son, I shall be able to do whatever I like, when I like – no one will care. It's how the system works.'

'All right, I believe you.' Simon scratched his head. 'When does this ban come into force?'

'Tomorrow morning, I'm afraid. I'm sorry, darling, but once the engagement is announced, I have to be as pure as the driven snow.' She rose up to kneel beside him. 'So let's make it a night to remember, eh?'

Sourly, Simon asked, 'What am I supposed to do while you're trying to get pregnant by a queer?'

'Amuse yourself, you fool. What about that little popsy who looks after your paperwork in Jersey? Hey, I know.' Suddenly struck by a brilliant idea, Olivia put an arm round Simon's shoulders; her other hand snaked into his crotch. 'Why don't you marry Emma Meakin? She's crazy about you *and* her father left her that super house at Blagdon.'

'Quite a bit of money, too,' Simon mused.

'Even better,' Olivia cried. 'She's passable in bed, I suppose?'

'Not bad,' Simon admitted.

'As good as me?'

'*No one* is as good as you,' Simon said, quiet and intense.

'Is that what this is about?' Olivia asked, squeezing the erection that had sprung up remarkably quickly. 'Or are you thinking of the fair Emma?'

'It's for you,' Simon said, his voice hard with desire. 'You know it is.'

Putting her lips close to his ear, Olivia whispered, 'I hope so, darling. I'd hate to think I was losing my grip.'

Violently, Simon pushed her back on to the bed, struggling to part her legs.

'Will you take me to eat after this?' Olivia said, resisting.

'Yes, damn you!'

'The Country Club at Burrington – you're going to need one of their mixed grills – for energy.'

'Anything you like,' Simon snarled, overpowering and penetrating her. Then, in an inexplicable moment of tranquil tenderness, he was sad. '*Will* you will come back to me?' he asked.

'Yes.'

'How can I be sure?'

Olivia's blue eyes burned with an intense, selfish lust. 'Because you're the best fuck I've ever had. And *that*, Simon Faulkener, is the voice of experience. Did I ever tell you that I started when I was fifteen? No? Well, it was with one of Monty's school chums. He wasn't much good, but his father was much better – so was Mummy's current "gentleman friend". There were a lot of others, but you're the best yet.'

Eight hours later, in the middle of the night, Olivia asked, 'Do you think you will marry Emma Meakin?'

'It's a distinct possibility,' Simon replied. He was breathless and sweating, preoccupied by the effort of prolonging their struggle in an outlandishly demanding position.

'Make sure *you* don't forget *me*,' Olivia said, her voice broken into staccato gasps by his lunging. 'Always remember what it's like to have my legs round your neck and your cock stuck up me.'

Olivia saw that she had created an image that would haunt Simon's mind for a very long time.

The dinner-party to celebrate the engagement was a great

success. George, placidly resigned to being a minor part in the proceedings, fortified himself with drink and basked in congratulations. Demure and apparently overawed by her good fortune, not the least part of which was a stunning diamond and sapphire ring, Olivia was enchanting.

Edward refused to fall under her spell. For him, the evening was ruined from the start. Someone — it must have been Annaliese, whose boundless enthusiasm for the occasion was impervious to tact — had invited Athene. Perversely ignoring Edward's advice, she dressed herself up to the nines and went to Widney Cheyne, travelling with Piers and Rachel Laverstoke.

Meeting Olivia for the first time, Athene was venomous. Only Edward noticed the brief explosion of hostility: Olivia, wondering why on earth a trainee member of Boothby's staff was at her engagement party, moved away to more interesting guests the moment George's awkward introductions were completed.

Soon after dinner, when people were dispersed over three, interconnected rooms, Edward was almost certain that Athene had disappeared. When, half an hour later, he was sure, he button-holed Piers Laverstoke.

'I can't see Athene anywhere. I'm worried. Do you know what's happened to her?'

'She's gone,' Piers replied.

'Gone?' Edward was baffled and alarmed. 'Where?'

'London. Said she was clearing off to her flat.' Piers was untroubled.

'How's she getting there at this time of night?' Edward asked anxiously.

'Apparently, someone even less enchanted than she by this function offered her a lift.' Piers was faintly amused.

'A young man,' Rachel added helpfully. 'Very pleasant from what I saw of him.'

'I hope he's trustworthy,' Edward muttered, glancing at his watch, considering setting off in pursuit.

'He looked all right to me,' Rachel said assuringly. 'In any case, give her credit, Athene can take care of herself.'

Edward was forced to suppose so. Nevertheless, he remained uneasy. It was while he was prowling, hoping to find Aubrey Dorchester and slip off for an hour of political gossip that Edward saw something that struck him as profoundly disturbing. Olivia was with George and three other men; at the other end of the large room, Caroline was in a group that included her two sisters-in-law. As George turned away from his fiancée to greet a new arrival, Olivia and Caroline locked eyes. Their cynically self-satisfied smiles and air of complicity startled Edward, who was the sole observer of the moment. There could, he thought, be only one explanation for such cunning.

On the way back to Compton Allardyce, Edward told Annaliese of his concern.

'What are you trying to say?' Annaliese asked, irritable after spending a long time trying to make sense of Edward's less than coherent misgivings.

'They were like conspirators, damn it,' Edward said. 'I believe we've been duped. I think Olivia's a bad lot, that she's marrying George for unworthy motives.'

'Don't be silly,' Annaliese snapped. 'She's devoted to him, anyone can see that.'

'I don't think so,' Edward said, fighting to make his point. 'I haven't been able to put my finger on it until this evening, then the penny dropped. She's like Celia.'

Even in the dim light inside the Rolls, Edward could see Annaliese's anger as she said, 'Ah, Celia – a subject on which you have immense knowledge.'

'Enough to recognise a replica,' Edward retorted, determined not to be put at a disadvantage. 'I don't think that

Olivia would stand up to scrutiny.'

Annaliese responded with imperious contempt. 'What do you propose? A private investigator?' She laughed derisively.

'That might not be a bad idea,' Edward muttered, wondering how it might be organised.

'I forbid it.' Annaliese was furious. 'Absolutely and utterly. What *would* Olivia and Caroline think if they found out we'd been playing such imbecilic tricks?'

'How could they find out?' Edward noticed that Aubrey was not worth consideration.

'It's a small world,' Annaliese said. 'How would you like people prying into *our* lives? Olivia is a lovely girl and George is marrying her on the first of September. Is that clear?'

Defeated, Edward slumped back into his corner of the Rolls and cursed his self-inflicted lack of authority.

Three weeks after the engagement party, Olivia had a long weekend at Allardyce Castle. On Saturday evening, she told George that she was spending the night with him at The Chantry.

Olivia took charge, steering George through the preliminaries to love-making with an artless spontaneity that dispelled his fears and persuaded him to believe that good fortune had sent him another Athene. Afterwards, having feigned a climax to coincide with his own, Olivia told George that he was wonderful.

'Do you *really* think so?' He wavered between disbelief and being ridiculously proud of himself.

Olivia hesitated coyly. 'George, darling, I expect you noticed that I wasn't a virgin. You see, there have been other men – two, actually. Are you angry?'

'Good gracious, no.' George smiled ruefully. 'To be honest, I'm glad you've had experience. I'm a bit of a duffer.'

'You aren't,' Olivia whispered. 'The fact that I've had other men means that I know how good you are.'

George was flattered. He had also fallen under the spell of Olivia's physical beauty, especially her long, perfect legs. Prepared to accept anything she did or told him, he said, 'You were marvellous, Olivia. I liked the way you took control.'

'Thank you, darling. We're going to be so happy.' Olivia congratulated herself on a masterly performance, one that had required her to conceal most of her sexual skills.

At some time during the following day, George gave Annaliese at least a hint of what had happened at The Chantry. Olivia thought that it was probably done as they stood around outside the village church after morning service. George was alone with his mother while Olivia mingled with the locals who had come to gawp at her. Without looking at Annaliese, and doing his best to emulate a ventriloquist, George spoke, uttering no more than two short sentences. Staring straight ahead, Annaliese kept her face blank. Later, over lunch, she was more agreeable than ever until George, wondering about the honeymoon, suggested that he and Olivia might go to the villa at Cascais.

'Oh, no.' Annaliese was rather sharp. 'That won't be possible, my dear.'

'Why not?' George asked, aggrieved.

'Because I shall be there during those three weeks,' Annaliese replied. Banteringly over-bright, she went on, 'Don't you think that I shall deserve a holiday when it's all over?'

When she returned to Widney Cheyne and told her mother about it, Olivia was contemptuous. 'She's been spending up to six months a year in Portugal. Now, apart from that week in April, she daren't turn her back until George and me are safely spliced.'

'Where shall you go on honeymoon?' Caroline asked.

'I've told George to book us on a cruise.'

'Where to?'

'I'm not bothered,' Olivia said. 'Apparently, most of the good ships are tremendous fun – plenty of things to do.'

'Is that essential?' Caroline inquired.

'Well, it will help, won't it?'

Caroline studied her daughter for a few moments. 'What *is* George like in bed?' she asked.

'Hopeless,' Olivia said. 'Not a scrap of use to me.' Then, after a pause, she added, 'But he wasn't completely inept. I think he *has* been to bed with a woman – not that it did him much good.'

'What about Simon Faulkener?' Caroline asked.

'Ditched,' Olivia replied. 'Until I've produced a son and heir.'

Caroline nodded approvingly.

As the summer unfolded and preparations for the wedding kept Annaliese fully occupied, Edward became drawn into a series of events that had the menacing stamp of international crisis. Under Colonel Nasser, Egypt was emerging as the leading Arab state and Britain, with its strategic interest in the Middle East, was at pains to cultivate good relations with Cairo. All was going well until Nasser began to seek aid for his dream, the Aswan High Dam. Britain and the United States offered a 70-million-dollar package. But stories of a Russian bid began to circulate and Nasser declined to buy American armaments, preferring to place a huge order with Czechoslovakia, a Kremlin satellite. At once, the American Secretary of State, John Foster Dulles, let it be known that he doubted whether US aid should go to such an ungrateful nation.

Edward was in the Foreign Office, evaluating the possible repercussions of Dulles's trenchant statement, when a call came through on his personal line. It was Athene.

'Uncle Edward, can I see you? Soon, please.'

Responding to her urgency, he said, 'How about this evening?'

'Lovely. Come to supper. Eight o'clock.'

'I will.'

When he arrived at Athene's flat near Sloane Square, Edward found himself being introduced to a personable man in his late twenties. 'This is David Naismith,' Athene said. 'He's the chap who spirited me away from the horrors of that engagement *thing* at Widney Cheyne. The food's ready if you are.'

Over the meal, Edward learned that David was a solicitor, an outstandingly brilliant one, Athene insisted, already a partner with one of London's most respected firms. Deducing that Athene and David were lovers, Edward thought they were normally a happy couple; this evening, they were tense, waiting for an appropriate moment to broach a difficult subject.

It came when they moved away from the table with coffee and, for Edward, a generous measure of fine brandy. Perched on the edge of her chair, Athene said, 'David knows Monty Dorchester. They went to school together.'

Smiling nervously at Edward, David said, 'It's over three years since I spoke to Monty, but I must have been in an out-of-date address book, which is why I was invited to that party.'

'I was a mistake, too,' Athene chortled.

'Go on, David,' Edward prompted.

'Well, about Monty . . .' David shuffled uncomfortably. 'I don't know what to think about this gambling and drugs story.'

After gazing shrewdly at the young man for a few moments, Edward said, 'Neither do I.'

'Monty simply wasn't that sort,' David said. 'At Eton, he had a reputation for being a prig – very righteous, full of principles.

He's one of the last chaps I'd expect to go off the rails.'

'People change,' Edward murmured. 'However, I take your point.'

There was an awkward pause. Unperturbed, Edward waited for the evening's main issue to emerge.

'Go on, sweetie-pie, spit it out,' Athene urged.

'Monty's sister, Olivia.' David cleared his throat. 'I wonder how much you know about her, sir?'

'Tell me,' Edward said.

'Being very blunt, she's a tramp. Monty always said that it would be a miracle if a decent man ever took the risk of marrying her.'

Responding to Edward's quizzical look, Athene said, 'No, this is *not* sour grapes. I always knew there was no hope for me and George.' Giving David a dazzling smile, she added, 'And I'm glad.'

Shifting into a more relaxed position, Edward said, 'What do you know, David?'

'A friend of mine had a big crush on Olivia. They went steady for nearly a year and her parents seemed to approve — there was talk of an engagement. Ian had started looking at rings when he found out that she'd been two-timing him. That's an understatement, actually — there were three or four others, all at the same time.'

'Did your friend have money?' Edward asked.

'A fair amount,' David replied. 'Not enough, though, according to Lady Olivia. The silly fool tried to kill himself. Nearly succeeded, too.'

Edward was thoughtful, staring into his brandy glass. 'This doesn't surprise me,' he said at last. 'There's something about Olivia that I find very worrying. Tell me, David, did your friend say anything about her interest in flying?'

'At that place near Bristol? Yes, she had a regular man down there.'

'Fellow by the name of Simon Faulkener?'

'That rings a bell,' David agreed.

Athene was gaping at Edward. 'What *have* you been up to?' she asked.

'Oh, stumbling across a few things,' was the airy reply.

'Aunt Annaliese will kill you.'

'It's a possibility I wouldn't rule out,' Edward replied. 'I appreciate your concern, David. You see, we have a delicate problem on our hands; my daughter-in-law needs to be an especially sensitive and loyal girl.'

After a quick glance at Athene, David nodded. 'I doubt if Olivia knows the meaning of either word, sir.'

'She is, however, an astonishingly good actress,' Edward said bitterly.

'What are you going to do?' Athene asked.

'I shall go to Wiltshire tomorrow,' Edward replied.

Annaliese heard him out in silence. When it came, her response was scornful. 'According to *The Times*, the Government is up to its neck in problems over Egypt, yet you have nothing better to do than dash down here full of tittle-tattle.'

'This is a damned sight more than tittle-tattle,' Edward said, more angrily than he had intended. 'David Naismith is a good man. He isn't grinding an axe, he simply wants to protect us from embarrassment. And the link between Olivia and Faulkener is confirmed by other sources.'

Annaliese stared at Edward levelly, knowing what he was implying, but seeing no advantage in an exchange of recriminations. Very calmly, she said, 'It's possible that Olivia *does* have something of a past. It hasn't escaped my notice that Aubrey sometimes appears glad to be getting rid of her. But Olivia has enough sense to know that her life must change when she marries George.'

'You don't think we ought to talk to him?' Edward asked.

'Certainly not. Have you considered the likely outcome if

you did stop George marrying Olivia?' Annaliese paused, giving Edward time to respond. 'No? Well, let me tell you. In less than a week, a grubby journalist would be digging up George's friendship with that Austen-Cave creature. What would that look like *after* a broken engagement?'

Edward went back to London. In all honesty, he intended it to be nothing more than a temporary break in an argument that would resume when he had gathered more information. But two days later, on 26 July, Nasser nationalised the Suez Canal. It was a flagrant breach of international law that plunged the British, French, and American Governments into crisis and left Edward no time for anything outside the Foreign Office.

The wedding, at which the Bishop of Salisbury officiated, took place in the Chapel at Allardyce Castle. A handful of the 800 guests – only 200 of whom were able to witness the service – thought it slightly odd that the ceremony was not being held at the bride's home, but Olivia had bowed to Annaliese's request without a hint of dissent. After all, she who was paying the piper was entitled to call the tune.

Olivia was a glorious, glowingly beautiful focus of attention. Her dress, designed by Norman Hartnell and made from over thirty yards of white silk organza, drew gasps of admiration when she appeared on her father's arm. Behind Annaliese's warmly approving smile lay the knowledge of what it had cost to deck out Olivia, her six bridesmaids, and four pages. It was a little over £20,000, roughly half the day's expenditure but worth every penny.

Curiously, although Olivia was justly the cynosure of all eyes, it was George who warmed hearts. Painfully shy and nervous when he and Piers Laverstoke, his best man, took their places, his first glimpse of Olivia filled him with tenderness and pride. Throughout the service, and especially when they went to the tiny vestry to sign the register, George's concern for his ravishing wife was evident and touching.

Afterwards, the guests split into two groups. About 500 sat down to lunch in the Long Gallery – from which the Titian triptych had been removed to avoid the risk of embarrassing Olivia's parents. These were peers, their wives, and eldest sons, men and women who would wish George and Olivia well, then fade away to big houses in the shires to watch their progress from afar. In years to come, there would be nods and courteous banalities when their paths crossed at other weddings and funerals.

Younger sons and their sisters, together with friends from all walks of life, went to the marquee by the lake. The lavish buffet was supplemented by champagne, lashings of Pimms, and barrels of beer. There was dancing to a jazz band and, after an hour, when the main purpose of the day was forgotten, riotous stupidity took a firm hold. At 4.30 that afternoon, an Earl's daughter climbed on to a table and began to perform a striptease, two men joined her and not a soul knew or cared that the bride and groom had left the Castle. Ten minutes later, they were followed by the woman whose will had brought the day to fruition. Matthew was driving Annaliese to London for an evening flight to Lisbon and three weeks with Kurt.

The Cunard liner, *Carmania*, called at Gibraltar, Casablanca, Santa Cruz de Tenerife, Funchal, and Vigo, spending two days in each port. George and Olivia went ashore only twice: there was a hurried sightseeing trip round Gibraltar, and lunch in Reid's Hotel at Funchal on the beautiful island of Madeira. For the rest of the time, Olivia lazed in the sun, swam, and did her damnedest to become pregnant.

Blithely unaware of the fact, George was subjected to

constant guile and manipulation. Olivia mixed intercourse with treats of the type she assumed her husband had enjoyed with Tony Austen-Cave, episodes that required him to do no more than lie back, close his eyes, and wallow in pleasure. Pathetically grateful for these favours, George was increasingly eager to indulge in normal love-making. Always falling well short of orgasm as she acted out a pantomime of ecstasy, Olivia wondered if George imagined that he was 'doing his duty'. The thought was so funny that she sometimes found herself on the verge of laughter.

Their magnificent accommodation on the top desk of the ship was an ideal bridal suite, luxurious and hedonistic. There was also a small private sun-deck, screened from crew and other passengers, but not from a good vantage point on shore. As George pounded away between her thighs after the rushed inspection of Gibraltar, Olivia saw the flash of reflected sunlight from the lenses of binoculars high up on the Rock. The certainty that someone was watching, probably becoming aroused at the sight of her convincing writhing, gave Olivia the only thrill of the entire three-week, 3,500 mile voyage.

Her cynical sense of humour was unexpectedly titillated over lunch at Reid's Hotel. The waiter, a too-beautiful German boy, whose blond hair needed attention at the roots, was attracted to George. Fascinated, Olivia waited to see what, if anything, happened: how would George respond to the young man's inviting allure? His embarrassment proved that he had recognised the youth's sexual interest and availability. Recounting the incident to her mother a week after the cruise had ended, Olivia said, 'Most men wouldn't have realised what the waiter was doing, but George did. God, he was in a state. He practically raped me when we got back to the ship.'

'Wasn't *that* enjoyable?' Caroline asked.

'No, it bloody wasn't!' Olivia said sullenly.

Her ill humour had two causes. Since returning from honeymoon, she had discovered that life at The Chantry was tedious in the extreme. And, two days after *Carmania* docked, the onset of her period had shown that she was not pregnant.

Britain, France, and Israel commenced military action against Egypt on 29 October. By 6 November, the Israelis had won a crushing victory to the east of the Canal Zone yet, far from being humiliated, Nasser secured a diplomatic triumph against Britain and France, who were denounced as aggressors. The abrupt and ignominious end to the operation soured relations between Britain and France and left the Suez Canal firmly in Egyptian hands, albeit blocked by sunken ships. During November, Britain's gold reserves fell by a crippling 300 million dollars.

After leaving no stone unturned in his efforts to avert the fiasco, Edward resigned from the Government on 29 October, the first of three ministers to do so. Bitterly disappointed, he told Annaliese that this was the end of his association with the Foreign Office and politics.

Worried by his exhaustion and lack of appetite, Annaliese knew that he needed a good, long holiday. 'Why don't we go away together?' she said.

For a few moments, they stared at each other in dumbfounded silence, astounded by the suggestion. Eventually, Edward asked, 'Do you mean that?'

'Yes, I do.' Having surprised herself, Annalise laughed nervously.

'Where shall we go?'

On impulse, Annaliese said, 'Torquay.'

Edward smiled. 'Why there?'

'I've heard people talk about it.'

'I only know it by reputation,' Edward said. 'It sounds ideal for a pair of old crocks like us – well, me, at any rate.'

They spent a fortnight at the Imperial Hotel. When the weather was fine, they walked in the gardens or took to the promenade. At other times, they sat in front of blazing fires, rebuilding friendship but not risking intimacy and remaining isolated in separate bedrooms. Although they talked at length about the great events of the past forty years, there was a tacit agreement to steer well clear of their own lives, so separate after a beginning of immense promise. Despite this, Annaliese found it a curiously comforting time and it worked wonders for Edward: he ate like a horse, put on much-needed weight, and cast off the grey pallor caused by the strain of the Suez crisis.

On their last evening at the Imperial, Annaliese asked the question that had niggled away at the back of her mind throughout the holiday.

'If you *are* giving up politics . . .'

Edward interrupted. 'I am. Wild horses wouldn't drag me back after this. In any case, I'm past retiring age.' His sad smile made him look ludicrously young.

'So what will you do?' Annaliese asked. 'How will you pass your time?'

'I was wondering whether I ought to take more interest in the estate.' Seeing Annaliese's dismay, Edward was quick to offer reassurance. 'No, I'm not going to start interfering at Compton Allardyce. That's your department. It's all the other stuff. You got rid of a fair bit to pay death duties for Uncle William and Ralph, but we've still got property all over the place. For example, did you know that we own part of Felixstowe docks?'

Annaliese shook her head. Since 1925, she had never taken the slightest interest in anything beyond the Park and village.

'Nicholas Hammond gave me a complete list,' Edward went on. 'It's amazing. I dread to think how the family acquired some of it. Anyway, I'm going to go through it all and decide what needs doing.'

'You'll sell?' Annaliese asked.

'I expect so, in some cases. There might be areas where investment is called for.'

'You'll continue to live in London?'

'No, I've had enough of the place.' Annaliese was taken aback by Edward's vehemence. 'I'm going to make Cadogan Square over to George, a belated wedding present – like my father did with us. Do you remember?'

'Don't be silly, of course I do.' Annaliese recalled the mixed feelings evoked by the gift. Although it had been a heartfelt and loving gesture by Lord Douglas, she had always found the house unfriendly.

'George and Olivia need somewhere decent in Town,' Edward said. 'Aubrey's place in Eaton Terrace is dreadfully run-down.'

'So, after all these years, you're going to live at the Castle?' Annaliese said.

'When I'm not visiting our far-flung possessions, yes.' Edward smiled affectionately. 'There's no reason why we shouldn't rub along, is there? I promise not to get in the way.'

'There's plenty of room,' Annaliese said. 'I might be glad of the chance to keep an eye on you.'

'Why? I'm not doing anything disgraceful.'

'That isn't what I meant.' Annaliese took his hand. 'It's your health, Edward. That Suez business nearly did for you.'

'Stuff and nonsense,' he retorted. Then, more calmly, he said, 'I was worried about Eden, you see. I wanted to stop him making a pig's breakfast of it. He's such a good man, but he has this unreasoning hatred of anything that smacks of appeasement and he thought Nasser was another Hitler. He'll have to resign, you know. It's the end of him.'

Edward drew back, reclaiming his hand. He was, Annaliese saw, deeply upset, close to tears. It occurred to her that

Edward thought that the consequences of Suez would finish Britain's pretensions to be a respected, world-class power. Having watched her own country suffer a similar fate, Annaliese felt a rush of sympathy. 'It will be nice having you at the Castle,' she said.

'Good.' Edward recovered his composure. 'We shan't have much of a chance to get on each other's nerves. As I said, I expect to be travelling, and you'll be off to Portugal.'

'Oh yes.' Annaliese smiled confidently. During the summer, her sixtieth birthday had been quietly pushed to one side. She was proud — excessively so, she sometimes admitted to herself — of her continuing ability to excite Kurt and revel in his lovemaking. Moreover, Annaliese had no intention of giving up sexual pleasure until the step was forced on her. Happily, she had no idea when that would be.

Edward nodded. 'I think we should do pretty well,' he said. Annaliese, certain that he knew what she did at the villa, smiled in warm agreement, glad that he had forgotten that silly idea about divorce.

Returning to the Castle in a benignly relaxed frame of mind, Annaliese was greeted by a bolt from the blue. Making no effort to prepare the ground, Gwen said, 'Matthew and me are leaving.'

'Leaving?' Annaliese was aghast. 'You can't. You don't retire for ages — it must be ten years yet.'

'We're not retiring,' Gwen retorted defiantly. 'We're going elsewhere.'

'Where?' Annaliese demanded.

'Lady Beatrice and Mr Charles want us to go and look after them. It's been on the cards for nearly two years.'

Matthew, standing by uncomfortably, felt that a placatory contribution from him wouldn't go amiss. 'It's all to do with Upper Overs, Your Grace. That house, and the area, mean a lot to Gwen and I. We were ever so happy there when we were young.'

Annaliese knew that. She was also keenly aware of the implications that Matthew and Gwen had not enjoyed their thirty-one years at Compton Allardyce. One of the most eloquent of Gwen's looks suggested that recent times had been especially disappointing.

The ensuing silence was charged with danger. Seeing that Annaliese was ready to fly off the handle, accusing Beatrice of poaching staff and goodness knows what else, Edward pushed himself forward, speaking earnestly to Matthew and Gwen. 'We understand,' he said. 'To be honest, I've always had a soft spot for Upper Overs – I haven't been there for years, but it's where I grew up. When would you like to leave?'

'To suit Your Graces,' Matthew said quickly, not giving Gwen a chance to mess things up. 'We couldn't go before you find replacements.'

Annaliese broke free from Edward's diplomatic restraint. 'Heaven alone knows how we do that,' she cried. 'There isn't anyone here who's remotely suitable.'

'We shall have to look further afield,' Edward said calmly. 'Now, my dear, perhaps we should go to our rooms, it's been a long day.' Taking Annaliese by the arm, he led her towards the stairs. Then, with his foot on the first step, Edward turned. Wanting only the privacy of her sitting-room so that she could give vent to her anger, Annaliese left him.

'I'd like to thank you for everything you've done for us over the years,' Edward said to Matthew and Gwen. 'I know I haven't shown it, but I've always been grateful to you. I should have said something to you, Gwen, about the way you brought my sons up. Douglas was a credit to you – and so is George, in his way. He's a good boy. As to recent developments . . .' Edward raised his hands to signify helplessness '. . . we can only hope and pray that his wife will be worthy of him.'

Matthew and Gwen stayed rooted to the spot as Edward went slowly and wearily up the stairs.

After he had disappeared into the West Wing, Gwen shuffled and sniffed. In a small, tremulous voice, she said, 'You know, Matty, I think I've misjudged him.'

'To tell you the God's honest truth, my sweet, I've always thought so,' Matthew replied, quite stern.

Realising that Annaliese had turned her back on the problem, Edward shouldered the responsibility of finding a new butler and housekeeper. Eventually, and helped by Piers Laverstoke and Nigel Templeton, Edward selected a comparatively young couple who had been in charge of the directors' dining-room at the head office of a big clearing bank. Although aged only thirty, Peter and Tess Osbourne had the experience and moral authority to take charge of Allardyce Castle's forty-odd servants. And, after what they must have heard over lunches and dinners for the last five years, their respect for confidentiality was self-evident. Unnecessarily and rather severely, Edward thought, they insisted on telling him that they did not intend to have children.

The Osbournes moved to Wiltshire on the last day of 1956. A week later, Matthew and Gwen left. The sadness of a miserably damp, cold day was sharpened by Annaliese's attitude: unforgiving to the end, she could barely bring herself to thank the couple who had done so much for her. She was also annoyed at what she regarded as a stupid piece of play-acting on Edward's part. He drove Matthew and Gwen, together with their possessions, to Upper Overs in the newest Rolls-Royce. After lunch with Beatrice and Charles, Edward set off to return to Compton Allardyce, but not before he had given Matthew an envelope containing 'a little something' as a sign of his appreciation. Forgetting about it in the emotional chaos of saying goodbye and adjusting to Upper Overs,

Matthew opened it that evening and discovered a cheque for £10,000. The attached note said: *For your retirement — when it comes! Many thanks for your loyalty. Edward.* Gwen wept for two hours.

Under the Osbournes, the staff at the Castle had to adapt to a stricter, more efficient regime. However, Edward saw that the new butler and housekeeper gained immediate respect and, within the limits of what they were prepared to allow, became well-liked.

There was one glaring exception.

The Osbournes took an instant dislike to Olivia. Naturally, they concealed their antipathy. Only Edward, who had quickly established a rapport with his new butler, was aware that the Marchioness of Axholme was regarded with pained disfavour; she was not what Peter and Tess Osbourne had expected when they entered the service of the nobility.

Edward decided that there was no point in telling Annaliese, or in attempting to explain that the faithful Gwen had finally been driven to leave because of Olivia.

15

1957

'Start looking forward to next year'

On a morning in late May, Olivia was filling in time until her mid-afternoon departure from London.

She got out of bed soon after George left for Boothby's at 8.30 and spent a narcissistic hour and a half over her bath, hair, and make-up. Gratified with the results, she had herself driven to Harrods, where she bought several dresses and some lingerie, asked for the goods to be delivered to Cadogan Square, and went to Bond Street, arriving shortly before noon.

It amused Olivia to give the impression that she was interested in Boothby's. George was immensely pleased, Beatrice politely cautious, and Athene downright hostile, suspecting that 'the adventuress' was trying to inveigle her way into the firm. Thinking what idiots people were, Olivia barged into George's office, as usual, without knocking.

He was desperately glad to see her. Behind her façade of affection, Olivia cringed as she kissed him. Then she saw the pile of silver cutlery lying on his desk. 'They're rather nice,' she said, meaning it.

'Aren't they?' George held up one of the knives. It was an elegant piece, long, heavy, but perfectly balanced. 'As right as rain. Jeremiah Cornysh, 1780. The very best. This is part of a hundred-piece set. It should fetch over three thousand – maybe more.'

'Super,' Olivia agreed, running a caressing finger over the knife. 'Have you been clever again? Did you find this stuff on a junk heap?'

'Not quite, although the owners had no idea how good it was.'

'Well done you,' Olivia said warmly. Then, hoping to catch George unawares, 'Where did they come from?'

'A client,' he replied blandly, putting the shutters down.

Secretly, Olivia fumed. It was the only thing George was capable of denying her. Once in a while, it would be fun to know who was in enough trouble to flog the family silver – like the Titian that had paid for Monty's foibles. But George refused to play, always hiding behind that urbane civility that was the hallmark of his Boothby's persona.

Nettled, Olivia said, 'Athene is in a foul mood today.'

'She's going through a difficult time at the moment,' George replied. 'She can't make up her mind about marrying David Naismith.'

Later, as she drove to Chippenham, Olivia was proud of the careless way she had asked, 'Who's David Naismith?'

'Oh, he's a chap Athene's been seeing a lot of,' George said. 'I think they sort of live together.'

Olivia had to make a snap judgement. Was George being extraordinarily devious, or did he know nothing about David Naismith and, more to the point, his friend, Ian Brown?

'Anything wrong, darling?' George asked, troubled by the calculation she had allowed to show in her eyes.

'No, I was racking my brains, that's all – wondering if I'd ever come across this Naismith.'

'I doubt it,' George said, unaware that David had been an accidental guest at their engagement party. 'He's a lawyer, I believe. Now, am I taking you to lunch?'

'Lovely.' Favouring him with one of her broadest, brightest smiles, Olivia came close to pitying her husband; he was turning out to be a bigger fool than she had imagined.

After the meal at Whitaker's, George put Olivia into a taxi to Cadogan Square, promising to hurry down to Wiltshire the following evening, a Friday. He believed that Olivia was going to Widney Cheyne to visit her mother, who was recovering from a minor operation. Olivia had said that she would probably spend the night with her parents and go to Compton Allardyce after breakfast. In fact, George would discover that his dutiful wife had changed her mind and arrived at The Chantry late on Thursday night.

The nearest Olivia went to her mother was a signpost that said, 'Widney Cheyne 5 miles'; she passed it at 85 mph as she tore along the main A4 road between Hungerford and Marlborough. She paused at a garage near Froxfield to fill the Austin-Healey's petrol tank, then drove on, thinking about yesterday's visit to the Harley Street gynaecologist.

It had been her third consultation in as many weeks and had yielded the results of tests carried out in the small, exclusive private hospital which Mr Cazenove graced with his presence for a few hours each week. What it boiled down to was that Olivia was perfectly capable of conceiving. With the simple facts out of the way, Mr Cazenove had launched into a suavely tactful patter.

'These are early days, Lady Axholme. You have been married for nine months, yes? There really is no need for disquiet so soon in a marriage.'

'How long is it going to take?' Olivia had demanded.

'Lady Axholme, there are no rules. How I wish there

were! Assuming that you and your husband are having intercourse frequently and at the appropriate times, I can assure you that we do not need to be concerned for at least another year.'

Olivia had been horrified. Apart from the enormity of the time-scale, what the hell was an 'appropriate time' – especially with a man like George? Masking her feelings, she said, 'Our circumstances *are* unusual, Mr Cazenove. We are seeking an heir for an illustrious inheritance. The family has suffered great loss and tragedy, you know. My husband's elder brother died in the War, George and I didn't find each other until he was thirty-four, and my mother-in-law is anxious.'

It was plausible and heartfelt. Mr Cazenove, who knew of the formidable Annaliese, Duchess of Lincolnshire, plunged in with sympathy. 'Lady Axholme, I understand *perfectly*. Please don't concern yourself on that account – you have my full support. May I suggest that you visit me at, shall we say, three-monthly intervals?'

'Certainly, Mr Cazenove.' Olivia hesitated, gathering herself for the unthinkable. 'What shall we do if the fault lies with my husband?'

'Approach the matter very cautiously, Lady Axholme, very cautiously indeed. Do you wish me to tell his lordship that he *might* be sterile, or have a deficient sperm-count?'

'Of course not, Mr Cazenove.'

'In that case, Lady Axholme, we must wait and see.'

Olivia reached the Angel Hotel in Chippenham at 5.00 pm. Leaving the Austin-Healey in the area that had once been the stables of the old coaching inn, she entered through a back door. After pausing to listen to the hotel's soporific, late-afternoon stillness, checking for the unexpected like an animal sniffing at potential danger, Olivia strolled into a maze of corridors and small rooms. She found Simon Faulkener tucked away in a corner of what, by virtue of two dilapidated desks, passed as the 'writing-room'.

Their meetings – strictly forbidden in Olivia's original plan – occurred at intervals of approximately two months and always began in an atmosphere of acid animosity. Making no attempt to get up from his comfortable seat, Simon nodded at Olivia: she stared at him in apparent distaste before settling in an armchair facing him. A casual observer would have concluded that they hated the sight of one another.

'Nice honeymoon?' Olivia asked, her voice and manner disagreeable.

Shaking his head, Simon stood up to draw his chair closer. When he sat down again, their hands joined in a clasp that whitened the knuckles. 'It wasn't bad,' Simon said. 'All things considered.'

Since their last encounter in March, he had taken Olivia's advice and married Emma Meakin.

'And you're settling down nicely?' Olivia's tone was brittle, threatening danger.

'I'm managing. How about you?'

'Still not pregnant!' Olivia hissed.

'Oh.' Simon was at a loss.

'It isn't my fault. I've had tests done – bloody unpleasant they were too. Christ, you've no idea the things they do.'

'I'm sorry,' Simon said lamely. 'Don't they say that it's usually the woman's fault?'

'Yes, that is what *they* say,' Olivia snapped. 'But it isn't true in this case. I'm all right.' Suddenly, the venom drained away and she looked like a frightened rag doll. 'What the hell am I to do, Simon? If there *is* something wrong with George, how do I get it out in the open?'

'That's tricky,' Simon said, recognising that it could take years. 'Perhaps it's a little early to be panicking,' he suggested.

'No, it isn't,' Olivia replied wearily. 'To coin a phrase, no stone has been left unturned.' Simon's hangdog expression amused her. 'Let's face it, lover, we're both doing things we hate – at least, I am. How's Emma?'

'Nowhere near as good as you,' Simon said miserably.

'We knew *that*,' Olivia retorted. Leaning towards him and pulling Simon's hand to her breast, she said, 'Isn't she improving with training and practice? How often do you screw her?'

'Nearly every night.' Realising that he had been lured into what seemed like an damning admission, Simon added, 'She expects it. You must do the same.'

'Of course I do. Twice, most nights. Poor George!' Olivia shook her head, smiling sadly. 'Sometimes, I'll swear he enjoys it.'

'Of course he enjoys it!' Simon exploded. Looking round, fearful of having been overheard, he dropped his voice to a pleading whisper. 'I miss you like hell, Olivia. How long is the silly game going to last?'

Irritated by his tone and disturbed by his physical allure, Olivia drew away abruptly; Simon's fingers had found and taunted her erect nipples. 'For as long as it takes. I told you that – it's part of the bargain.'

'There's no bargain, I'm just doing as I'm told. And suffering. Can you look me in the eye and say you *aren't*?'

Olivia shook her head wretchedly. 'No, I can't do that,' she muttered. 'I'm *aching* for you.'

'So why don't we do something about it?' Simon urged. 'Shall I see if this place has a vacant room for tonight?' He was coiled to spring out of the chair.

'No, darling, we mustn't,' Olivia said. 'Give it until the end of the year. If nothing's happened by then, I'll start dropping hints that George has a check-up.'

Simon glared at her bleakly. 'That means at least twelve months.'

'Nearer eighteen, in all probability,' Olivia said, falsely cheerful. 'Why don't you go and find a menu. I know it's early, but deciding what to have for dinner might take your mind off sex.'

Until the moment they parted, nearly five hours later at 10.15 pm, Simon both hoped and expected that Olivia would change her mind and spend the night with him. The fact that she remained resolute annoyed him very much.

Subsequently, he found it easier to stay away from Olivia and her compelling but unattainable body. Simon replied to her letters, with trumped-up excuses. Every time she wrote proposing a meeting, he claimed to be booked for a flight on the day she suggested. Eventually, however, the strain became too much for him and, on a Wednesday afternoon at the beginning of September, Simon arrived at their usual rendez-vous and went to ground in a bar that was only used for special occasions, such as Rotary Club functions and dances in aid of worthy causes.

Because she was considerably later than arranged, he was in a foul mood. She, on the other hand, was elated, smiling radiantly and tossing her head with the exuberance of a thoroughbred. To set the seal on the impression of high spirits, Olivia perched on the arm of the sofa and gave Simon an opulent kiss.

'What's got into you?' he asked, still sour despite the probing of her tongue.

Olivia laughed gaily. 'Good question,' she said. 'Very aptly put – not that you intended it. What a mood you're in! Look, shall I go out, walk round for five minutes, then come back to see if you can have a bash at being nice to me?'

'I'm sorry,' Simon said, not sounding it. 'Why are you so bleeding cheerful?'

Grinning wickedly, Olivia said, 'George got into me, that's

what. We're in business, dear heart. I'm preggers.'

'I say, that's wonderful.' Standing up, Simon embraced Olivia. After they had kissed, he asked, 'Are you sure?'

'Confirmed three weeks ago.'

'When's it due?'

'Middle of March.' Saving Simon the trouble of mental arithmetic, Olivia added, 'Conceived between the seventh and tenth of June, according to know-all Mr Cazenove. That's soon after we were here last. Make of that what you will.'

Simon sat, drawing Olivia down beside him on the sofa. 'What does George think?' he asked.

'*Grotesquely* pleased with himself. Insufferable. You can't imagine it. He sees it as an earth-shaking achievement.'

'I suppose it is for someone like him,' Simon said.

'He is also immensely relieved,' Olivia went on. '*Entre nous*, the Marquess has been running out of steam on the old heterosexual caper — gritted teeth and other signs of desperation. However, sex is banned during pregnancy.'

Simon frowned. 'Is it?' Although totally ignorant on the subject, he was sceptical.

'Absolutely. Dangerous for the child, don't you know?' Olivia's eyes rolled mischievously. 'Well, George believes it is and that's all that matters.' She stretched luxuriously, admiring her legs. 'So, no more struggling and grappling. *Ever!*' Mockingly, she fluttered her long eyelashes at Simon. 'That goes for you, too, no nookie while I am with child.'

Scandalised at the suggestion, Simon said, 'Are your parents-in-law pleased?'

Olivia took her time answering. 'Her Grace, the Archbitch, is in seventh heaven,' she said at last. 'The poor love nearly cried when I passed on the glad tidings. Bear in mind that she knows all about George and has been wetting her knickers in anticipation of the happy announcement — or lack of it.'

'What about the Duke?' Simon asked.

'Very pleased.' After the rapidly automatic response, Olivia stared up at the ceiling, apparently fascinated by the elaborate cornice. 'He's always terrifically nice, but he doesn't like me very much. Little voices in my head whisper that the Duke of Lincolnshire has *seen through me*.' She used a dramatically hollow voice for the last three words. 'Poor old Edward thinks I'm a bad lot.'

'But his wife doesn't?'

'Oh, who can tell what Annaliese thinks?' Olivia's gaiety was disfigured by cynicism. 'I'm sure Edward has had his say, but he's been told to keep his opinions to himself. She rules the roost – has done since they inherited the title.'

'So she's on your side?' Simon asked, bemused.

'Only because I'm a worthy child-bearer,' Olivia retorted. 'Other than that, I wouldn't like to say.'

'But now they're going to get an heir . . .'

Olivia finished it for him. 'Everything in the garden is splendid and we shall be able to get back to normal.' On reflection, Olivia found that her use of the word 'normal' to describe what they had in mind was hilarious.

The mood of the evening became gleeful. Some of the more staid occupants of the dining-room were moved to glower at the immoderate laughter streaming from the table in the corner. One group were almost told to mind their own business; preparing to let rip, Olivia remembered that she must not draw attention to herself in circumstances like these and gave the offenders a smile of matchless acidity.

Mocking her 'condition', Olivia left much earlier than usual, claiming that she needed to be tucked up in bed no later than 10.00 pm. 'I don't want to worry the servants,' she said. 'Ever since the great news broke, they fuss like mother hens – it's pathetic.'

Setting off on his forty-mile drive to Somerset, Simon was unconcerned by the abrupt end to the evening. He would be home before Emma fell asleep, which meant love-making, an activity at which she was becoming quite expert; these days, if he worked hard at imagining Olivia, it wasn't at all bad. The sense of euphoria lasted until Simon reached the outskirts of Bath. Feeling an utter idiot for not having spotted it before, he realised that everything he and Olivia had said over dinner – including the suggestion that they would spend whole weeks together next summer – was based on the tacit assumption that her baby would be a boy.

Swearing to himself as he thought of what would follow the birth of a girl, Simon slowed down and began to look for a pub. The desire to get home to Emma had vanished.

Five weeks later, on an overcast October afternoon, Simon saw the distinctive red Austin-Healey as he made his final approach to Bristol after a flight from Shannon. Olivia was waiting for him in the ramshackle hut that served as the head office of B & L Airways. She had, Simon saw at once, thoroughly antagonised Mrs Gill, the ex-WRAF sergeant, who did everything at B & L except fly the two venerable aircraft.

'Hello, darling.' Olivia inclined her head at the special, bewitching angle that invited a kiss. Doing his best to disregard Mrs Gill's censure, Simon obliged, noticing that Olivia now had a lustre that made her more desirable than ever.

'Er – would you like some tea?' Simon asked.

'That would be nice.'

In response to Simon's mute appeal, Mrs Gill wrenched herself away from her typewriter and clumped off to the adjoining hut.

'What are you doing here?' Simon burst out angrily. 'It's a miracle Emma hasn't come to meet me – she often does.'

'How am I supposed to know the details of your blissful

life?' Olivia retorted, displaying a willingness to be downright unpleasant if she considered it necessary. 'Am I to take it that you and Emma are living happily ever after? Do you want me to leave you to get on with it?'

'No, of course I don't.' Simon was abject. 'I'm sorry I bit your head off, but how would you feel if I suddenly turned up at a place where George might see us?'

'Yes, all right, I won't do it again.' Olivia was as contrite as she was ever likely to be. 'This is because I have some *rather* splendid tidings.'

'Yes?' Simon was eager.

'It's almost certain that I'm carrying twins. Three doctors say so, the fourth is *nearly* convinced. Aren't I a clever girl?'

Dazzled by her smile, Simon struggled to draw conclusions from the surprising news.

'You aren't getting the message, are you?' Olivia chided. 'Let me spell it out for you. I don't know exactly what they are, but the odds on me having a son have improved no end. Start looking forward to next year.'

16

'We shall both be very, very discreet'

The final tests and calculations indicated that the twins would be born on 12 March. Annaliese and Caroline Dorchester arrived at Cadogan Square on the 7th and proceeded to make everyone's life unbearable by pretending to be dreadfully calm. Olivia was immensely relieved when, soon after breakfast on 10 March, it became apparent that the birth was destined to be slightly early; her removal, by a brave but white-faced George to Mr Cazenove's exclusive hospital, transferred her to a world of ethereal peace.

The pretty, surprisingly young matron put herself in charge of Olivia, making sure that all was well and revealing an amusing piece of information. 'Your mother-in-law is expecting two boys, Lady Axholme.'

'How do you know that?' Olivia asked, glad of the chance to talk to a pleasant, competent stranger.

'We have the *strictest* instructions to make sure that your first born is clearly identified,' the matron said. 'We were wondering whether we should tie a luggage label round the poor little soul's ankle.'

'It *is* important,' Olivia replied. 'Whoever's first will be the Duke of Lincolnshire one day.'

'Don't worry, we understand. It's bad luck on the one who comes second, isn't it? What happens to him when he grows up?'

'He fends for himself,' Olivia said. 'The aristocracy doesn't have much time for younger sons, although they come in useful sometimes – my husband, for example.' She frowned nervously. 'This doesn't feel too bad at the moment, when will it get gruesome?'

'We're here to make sure that it doesn't,' the matron said.

In the event, Olivia's worst enemies were fear and impatience. By the time the first baby arrived at 11.35 that night, she had worked herself into a state and suffered accordingly during the birth. A serenely detached voice said, 'It's a girl, Lady Axholme. She's very beautiful.' The infant bawled lustily and Olivia slipped into a state of semi-consciousness.

Above and beyond her, there was talk, mostly medical jargon. No one seemed concerned and Olivia, floating, forgetting that she had another life within her, wanted to sleep.

'Don't let her drop off,' someone muttered. There was a trace of anxiety.

'Come along, Olivia,' the wonderful matron said. 'A little co-operation, there's a dear. At this rate, they're going to have different birthdays.'

As the delivery of the second child began, Olivia opened her eyes and understood. The clock on the wall said five minutes to midnight.

Annaliese had spent weeks deciding the names that would be given to *the* son. For the first time since the birth of Ralph in 1890, a little boy obviously destined to be Duke of Lincolnshire was entering the world. Therefore, the tradition that had, perforce, lapsed with Edward and her two sons must be reinstated. Heirs always had three Christian names, the last of which was a town or village in the county that had provided the family with both its titles, Axholme and Lincolnshire.

After hours in the library, poring over the family archives, Annaliese consulted Edward, forcing him to devote an afternoon and evening to help her reach the final decision. What began with indifference and floundered into argument, ended with happy accord.

'Is that it, then?' Extravagantly relieved, Edward leaned back in his chair and threw the rubbish on to the carpet for one of the Labradors to snuffle at. 'We're agreed, are we?'

'Yes.' Annaliese smiled contentedly and stared at the piece of paper that mattered, the one that had the name which she had favoured all along. 'John Arthur Wainfleet Boothby-Graffoe. It has the right ring, don't you think?'

'Definitely.' A thought struck Edward. 'Will George approve?'

Annaliese stared at him in wide-eyed amazement. 'Of course he will,' she said forcefully.

'And Olivia?' Edward inquired mildly.

'Naturally.' Annaliese's disdainful smile was an evocation of a bygone era and a ruling class that still existed – if only in its own imagination.

'And the other son?' Edward asked, pandering to Annaliese's belief in two boys.

'Edward Douglas Joseph,' Annaliese replied, firing back the answer with the assurance of someone who has considered every possibility.

'I can't argue with that,' Edward said gruffly. 'Any views on girl's names?'

'No, not really.' Annaliese had lost interest. 'We can leave that to Olivia.'

John Arthur Wainfleet came into being so effortlessly and gave Olivia such an overwhelming sense of achievement that, for the first hour of his life, she felt something akin to maternal love. When, washed and wrapped in a towel, he was placed in her arms, Olivia's smile was pure joy. He, amazingly pretty, regarded her in a way that was uncanny: although some experts claimed that new-born babies lacked faculties, John peered at Olivia with a mixture of bemusement and dog-like devotion that mirrored George to a T.

The moment passed, drowned in the racket from the other twin. The obvious assumption was that the girl wanted her mother and, sure enough, as soon as she was on Olivia's breast, happy silence descended. The matron, shooing the nurses and midwife out of the delivery room, had other ideas. During the interval between the births, the baby girl had been waiting for her brother, looking round with myopic anxiety, fretting, and gurgling with delight when he appeared. Secretly, the matron half-admitted that her theories of what could happen inside the womb were a little fanciful. That didn't stop her believing that the tiny Lady Boothby-Graffoe had stopped screaming the instant she was able to clutch her brother's hand, not on account of any maternal comfort.

At about 1.30 am, when Olivia and the twins were back in her private room, one visitor was admitted. George, allowed to present a mere fraction of the masses of flowers he had brought with him, came to the bedside to gaze wonderingly at his wife and children.

'Everyone says you were magnificent,' he whispered, overawed, afraid to speak normally.

'Breeding will out,' Olivia replied, drowsy and tender. 'And, talking of breeding, what do you think of this pair?'

'Well . . .' George looked at the little faces, still slightly red from the effort and shock of birth and puckered in recuperative sleep. 'They're gorgeous — I think. Are you any good at spotting family likenesses, darling? It's the first thing our mothers will ask.'

'I've no idea,' Olivia yawned. 'But the matron, God bless her, is an expert. She says they're going to have blue eyes, blond hair and very fair skins. Typical Boothby-Graffoe, with help from me.'

'But not me,' George said ruefully, still, at the age of thirty-six, apt to be self-conscious about his dark hair and colouring. 'I'm a throwback to Father's Spanish grand-mother.'

'Like the dreaded Ralph?' Olivia managed a mischievous grin. She had familiarised herself with the history of the Lincolnshires, studying all the available photographs of Edward's notorious cousin. The arrogant, ruthlessly selfish, probably cruel, and diabolically handsome Ninth Duke of Lincolnshire would, Olivia knew instinctively, have been an ideal match for her. With a man like Ralph, there would have been no need for Simon Faulkener; and Ralph wouldn't have got his silly head blown off messing around with another woman. Married to Olivia, he would have had neither the time nor the inclination to play with anyone else.

Looking at the babies with bewildered love, George said, 'Which is which?'

'This is John Arthur Wainfleet,' Olivia said, smiling at the child cradled on her left breast.

'And the other?'

'Valerie.'

'Valerie Boothby-Graffoe,' George mused. 'Mmm . . . yes, that sounds right. Only one name?'

'One's good enough for your mother and Aunt Beatrice,' Olivia pointed out. 'Me, too.'

'Why did you choose Valerie?' George asked.

'I like it.' Although half-asleep, Olivia was determinedly

obtuse, defying George to question her judgement. He had no intention of doing so: in any case, the matron came in to say that it was time everybody settled down for what was left of the night.

Outside, waiting in the corridor, George found Miss Barclay. A formidable individual who went to great trouble to appear much older than her age of about forty, Miss Barclay was the nanny selected by Annaliese to look after the twins for their first three years.

'They all seem to be extremely well,' George said nervously: the wretched woman terrified him.

'I'm sure they are, Lord Axholme,' she said, implying that he knew nothing about such matters. 'Go home and get some rest, you look quite done-in.'

Four weeks to the day after they were born, John and Valerie were christened in the Chapel at Allardyce Castle. It was a sparkling April day of azure skies and cotton-wool clouds that rode on a strong south-westerly breeze, a day when the buds on the Park's thousands of trees brought tentative signs of life to the skeletons of winter.

Valerie, first to receive the holy water, threatened to scream the roof off until George intervened. Stepping out of the circle gathered round the font, he approached the Bishop of Salisbury, who had been persuaded to carry out the baptisms, and said, 'If you could do them both together, sir, we shall be spared the racket.' Smiling and confident, George took John from an outraged Miss Barclay and placed him alongside Valerie in the bend of the Bishop's left arm. 'Don't worry,' George whispered, as he helped to support the infants, 'they won't fall.'

Valerie sought for and found her brother's hand, where-upon she stopped screaming and smiled. Olivia, jolted out of her decorative complacency, was astounded. From what little she had seen of them, her children *did* appear to have a strong affinity that defied Miss Barclay's efforts to break it. And here was stupid, ineffectual George demonstrating that he knew all about the bond between the twins. A quelling look from her mother was needed to ensure that Olivia's jealous anger was converted into a theatrically sweet smile.

After blinking her way through the ordeal of baptism, Valerie stared at her brother as the Bishop's mellifluous voice pronounced, 'John Arthur Wainfleet, I baptise thee in the name of the Father, and of the Son, and of the Holy Ghost. Amen.' Lord John took not the slightest notice of the water trickling down his back and gazed with solemn curiosity into the Bishop's eyes, perfectly aware that something of great importance was afoot.

Then the godparents came forward. In keeping with tradition, there were six pairs, three from each side of the family. In addition to the Laverstokes and another aristocratic couple who were Annaliese's nominees, George had come up with a rather surprising choice. In the face of mild opposition from his mother, he had insisted that Athene and David Naismith, who had married in February, should be among those who vowed to look after the children's spiritual well-being.

The main justification for Athene and David was incontestable. George hoped that Valerie and, to a lesser extent, John, would grow up to take an active interest in Boothby's: since Athene was likely to be in day-to-day control of the firm by the time the twins were adults, she was an ideal godmother. David was included for the simple reason that, as Athene's husband, he couldn't very well be excluded.

Olivia's instincts made her look for other motives. Was George up to something – possibly taking the first tentative step in some clever, long-term game? Eventually, she decided that she was crediting her husband with a deviousness worthy of herself, an attribute he clearly lacked. Unconcerned, Olivia settled down to enjoy a glass or two of champagne and watch the interesting undercurrents among the guests: when they went to the Long Gallery after the Chapel, she amused herself by trying to spot who was illicitly involved with whom.

*

Beatrice had come alone to the christening, leaving Charles at Upper Overs. Now seventy-four and suffering from angina, he was under doctor's orders to avoid all unnecessary exertion. Although Beatrice was anxious to be on her way back to him, she also felt duty-bound to spend time being pleasant to Annaliese. The two women did not meet often these days and Beatrice hated the thought that her sister-in-law continued to blame her for the 'theft' of Gwen and Matthew.

In the event, Annaliese was at pains to make her peace so that she could take Beatrice to one side and ask a question that came as something of a shock. 'Well, what are we to make of Olivia *now*?'

'I'm sorry, I don't understand,' Beatrice said.

'Doesn't she strike you as somehow . . .' Annaliese had to search for the right word '. . . *uninvolved*? She couldn't care less about what's happening today.'

'I'm still not with you,' Beatrice replied, pretending to be slow on the uptake in order to get at the whole truth.

Annaliese hesitated, wondering whether to go further. 'Look, Beatrice,' she said, deciding she had to risk it, 'the fact is, Edward doesn't care for Olivia. He didn't want George to marry her.'

'Oh, I see.' Beatrice blinked and collected her thoughts. 'Well, I know that Edward has been known to get things dreadfully wrong, but in this instance, I suspect he's right.' After what was, for her, a bravely outspoken statement, Beatrice smiled self-deprecatingly. 'However, I fail to see that my opinion matters.'

'You think Olivia's a bad lot?' Annaliese asked.

'*Think* is very much the operative word,' Beatrice insisted. 'I haven't a shred of evidence, but if that young woman led a blameless life before she met George, I'll eat my hat. Frankly, I'd guess that she was exceptionally *un*blameless.'

'I arranged that marriage,' Annaliese admitted. 'Insisted on it, actually. Edward unearthed some disturbing information which may or may not be true, but I overruled him.' As a hopeful after-thought, she said, 'She's behaved well so far.'

Staring hard at Annaliese, Beatrice took a long time to respond. 'Let's hope that your grandson justifies the risk.'

'We can't let the title die out,' Annaliese retorted.

'That is a point of view.' Beatrice clearly had reservations. 'I think that George probably deserves a medal for getting *this* far with someone like Olivia. If I were you, I'd watch her closely.'

'You think we're in for trouble?' Annaliese was worried.

'Who can tell? It depends on a number of things.' After a pause, Beatrice asked, 'Does she know the truth about George?'

Wincing, Annaliese said, 'I've asked myself that a thousand times.'

'And your conclusion?'

'I don't know. Perhaps not.'

Beatrice cleared her throat in a way that suggested polite scepticism. 'You're right about her lack of involvement,' she said. 'She's playing the part of the mother to perfection, but she doesn't give a fig for the twins – never will.'

'That doesn't necessarily count against her,' Annaliese said. 'The female members of the aristocracy aren't famous for their maternal instincts and abilities.' Wishing that she had never started the conversation, she added, 'And I know of nothing to suggest that Olivia and George aren't perfectly happy.'

'Good.' Uncharacteristically tenacious, Beatrice said, 'Do

you want to know how she's struck me today?'

'Go on.'

'She's biding her time. Looking innocent and absolutely gorgeous, but biding her time.'

'For what?' Annaliese asked.

'I have no idea,' was Beatrice's unhelpful reply. 'Now, I must be off. Will you come and say hello to Matthew?'

'Is he here?' Annaliese cried, at once pleased and nervous.

'You don't imagine that I drove myself, do you?'

'Yes, I'd love to see him,' Annaliese said.

'Right, come along. Let's go down the back stairs so that I can escape without saying goodbye to everybody.'

Anticipating Beatrice's departure, Matthew was in the yard behind the Castle, waiting beside Charles's Daimler. Seeing Annaliese, he stiffened respectfully, but there was also apprehension.

Ashamed to be the cause of fear, Annaliese held out both hands in a warm greeting. 'Matthew, how lovely to see you. My word, you are looking well.'

'So are you, if I may say so, Your Grace.' Matthew, seeming hardly a day older than when he used to drive Annaliese to Crowborough to catch the London train in 1920, smiled broadly.

'And Gwen? How is she?'

'Same as ever, obstreperous and lovable. Er . . . she and I are very happy for you. We wish Your Grace's grandchildren every happiness.'

'Thank you, Matthew. You won't believe this, but I don't feel like a grandmother.'

'Well, you'd never think it to look at you,' Matthew said. 'We – Gwen and me, that is – often hope you might come and see us.'

'I . . .' Annaliese stopped short, looking at Beatrice for guidance.

'You'd be very welcome,' Beatrice said at once. 'Charles would love to see you.'

Annaliese thought quickly. As a young bride, thirty-nine years ago, she had been confronted by the death of Edward's mother at Upper Overs. Her status as the brand-new Mrs Boothby-Graffoe, a naturalised British refugee from the catastrophe and confusion of the Great War, had seemed in peril on that grim January day in 1919. But when she recalled the happy times with Edward's father, Annaliese felt a surge of nostalgia for the cosy, rambling old house in the Ashdown Forest.

'Yes, I'd love to come,' she said.

'Perhaps you'll telephone me?' Beatrice suggested.

'Of course. Now make haste back to Charles and give him my love.'

Annaliese and Beatrice kissed warmly.

Athene and David stayed overnight with her mother and stepfather at the house in Gainsborough Wood. After supper, they settled down to go over the events of the day, especially, of course, the christening. Everyone agreed with Henrietta, that it was a happy occasion that augured well for the future of Compton Allardyce.

'We've got two dukes in reserve now,' Nicholas said. 'That should keep us going for at least seventy years.'

'By which time, none of us will be around to care,' Henrietta said wistfully.

As if to cheer her up, Nicholas asked, 'Does anyone know how long Annaliese's been dyeing her hair?'

While Henrietta was gaping at her husband's unwonted perception and roguish effrontery, Athene was vastly amused. 'Fancy you noticing that, Nicholas. It's called "tinting". I first noticed it just before George's wedding.'

'It looks jolly good,' Nicholas said.

'My hunch is that it's only a temporary measure,' Athene went on. 'Eventually, her hair will turn silver and be lovely. It's this in-between stage with odd bits of grey that she hates.'

'Good luck to her,' Nicholas replied. 'We're all entitled to a bit of help to disguise the ravages of time.'

Without thinking, Henrietta said, 'One gets the impression that some people believe they'll never need anything but their own divine beauty.'

In a deliberately mild response to her sudden bitterness, Nicholas asked, 'Whom had you in mind, my dear?'

'Olivia. Did you see the way she was acting today?'

Eventually, Nicholas broke the uncomfortable silence. 'She and George seem to get on reasonably well.'

'You're doing your devil's advocate act, aren't you?' Athene accused. Before Nicholas had time to deny it, she went on. 'If it's any consolation, I think George is waking up to her.'

'Do you?' Henrietta perked up. 'Why?'

'Because he asked us to be godparents.'

Failing to see any great significance in this, Henrietta frowned. 'George has always been fond of you, darling. Isn't it as simple as that?'

'Yes, partly,' Athene conceded. 'I also happen to be married to the brightest, sharpest solicitor in the world. All the best barristers are queuing up for his instructions.'

Henrietta laughed. '*We* know that, but it won't mean anything to George.'

Conscious that she was on weak ground, Athene was working herself up to bluster her way out of it when David came to her rescue. 'As a matter of fact, George *has* been pushing business my way from Boothby's. It started three months ago.'

'What sort of business?' Athene demanded.

'Complicated and highly confidential,' David replied,

tempering the refusal with a smile and sparkling eyes.

'Well, there you are, that proves it,' Athene said triumphantly.

'I hope you're right,' Henrietta muttered, dithering between concern for George and the hope that Olivia's potential as a menace had somehow got itself exaggerated.

Nicholas was silent. Although he would never dream of saying so, not even during the intimate moments that he shared with his beloved Henrietta, Commander Hammond thought that Olivia, Marchioness of Axholme, was an out-and-out, five-star, ocean-going bitch. And he doubted whether George had the gumption to do a damned thing about it – let alone hatch up whatever elaborate plot Athene was suggesting.

That spring was even more capricious than usual. On 27 April, a rain shower at lunch-time turned into a blizzard that lasted for the rest of the day and paralysed most of southern England. From the window of her sitting-room in the West Wing, Annaliese gazed out at the white wilderness, worrying about Edward, who was in Suffolk with Nicholas, inspecting yet another obscure part of the Lincolnshire estates.

Deciding that two sensible men were perfectly capable of keeping themselves out of trouble, Annaliese became fretful over the twins, permanently resident at The Chantry even though George and Olivia spent most of their time in London. Annaliese liked to see John and Valerie every day: when would the road through the Park be passable?

Following a spectacularly rapid thaw during the night as the temperature soared to a normal, late-April level, one of the chauffeurs was able to drive Annaliese to her grandchildren the very next morning. As usual, the infants were delighted to see her and their nanny was effusively respectful.

Secretly, Annaliese was already doubting the wisdom of

selecting Miss Barclay from the dozens of competent women who had applied for the post. Left with a free hand, Miss Barclay was shamelessly exploiting Olivia's complete lack of interest in the children, aspiring to the role of mother. Furthermore, to judge by the attitude of the servants, every one of them hand-picked from the Castle's staff when George and Olivia had set up home after their wedding, Miss Barclay was giving herself airs and graces, acting as if she were mistress of The Chantry.

Something should be done, Annaliese realised.

However, she fell into the old trap of turning away from the problem, tempted by attractive diversions. Back at the Castle, Annaliese telephoned Beatrice and arranged a week-long visit to Upper Overs. With the beginning of May taken care of, she consulted her diary and pencilled in a date for the next flight to Lisbon.

As the weeks passed, Olivia knew that two men were waiting for her to make a move in their direction. One was beside himself with desire and frustration, the other was fearful.

Simon Faulkener, who had seen the announcements of the twins' birth and christening in the newspapers, wondered why Olivia had not been in touch with him, not even to confirm that she had received his letters. Perhaps they had been intercepted by her husband, or a servant acting on his behalf? There was, Simon supposed, the possibility that Olivia was still suffering from the after-effects of giving birth to twins. Finally, and most destructively, the fear that she had found someone else to satisfy her voracious needs turned into a recurrent nightmare. Even when persuading himself that he was in love with her, Simon recognised that Olivia was selfishly disloyal and would always take the easiest route to her own pleasure.

In fact, none of Simon's assumptions and fears were true;

the delay was caused by Olivia's wish to behave in a way that was, for her, considerate and altruistic. She had Mr Cazenove's blessing to resume 'marital relations', had received Simon's letters, and was longing to be with him. All that was holding her back was the need to have things straight with George; amicable coexistence would be much easier if he were spared undue distress or reason for anger. That was the theory, but finding the right opportunity to broach the subject was proving impossible.

By what seemed to be a combination of accident and design, they had adopted a life-style that was busy but bland, forcing their relationship into the background, making it something that was to be taken for granted and not examined too closely. George worked excessively long hours at Boothby's – far more than necessary, Olivia suspected – and was happy to join at least six other people for dinner each evening. Olivia's talent was for organising these gatherings, whether at Cadogan Square, or at a fashionable restaurant after a visit to the theatre. There was always at least one man unable to keep hungrily speculative eyes off her and, as a consequence, a wife who was badly upset. Olivia noticed that George, sometimes drinking rather more than was good for him, remained oblivious to these signs of wishful lust and jealousy.

At the end of an evening, usually about 11.30 pm, George and Olivia would go upstairs, exchange vaguely affectionate kisses, and go to separate bedrooms. Weekends at Compton Allardyce were no different. Olivia came to the conclusion that George was making sure there was never time to talk; behind his drinking and manic insistence on being busy, he was a bundle of nerves.

Growing afraid of her own impatience, Olivia was eventually able to engineer an evening alone with George. As a special treat for him, she acquired tickets for a Beethoven concert at the Royal Festival Hall on 29 May. Overjoyed at being able to see the great conductor, Otto Klemperer, in action, George was relaxed and unsuspecting.

When they returned to Cadogan Square, Olivia headed George off as he was making for the whisky decanter. 'Give it a miss, darling,' she said, putting her arms round him. 'Wouldn't you like to sleep in my bed tonight? I'm fully recovered from the twins and I'm dying to make love again.'

George was unable to disguise his immediate reaction: for a moment, his face registered sheer horror. Then, pulling himself together, and much to Olivia's surprise, he said, 'Yes, of course. Let's go straight up, shall we?'

Strangely, once they were in bed, George seemed to have recovered from his initial terror. But Olivia was quick to realise that, no matter what she did to him, he would not achieve an erection. Having used every trick she knew, she secretly rejoiced as she felt black desperation tighten its grip on George. All that Olivia had to do was to feign dismay and bewilderment when he finally gave up, broke away from her, and rolled out of bed to snatch at a dressing-gown.

'It's nothing to worry about, darling,' she said, oozing sympathy. 'All men have this problem from time to time – I'm sure they do.'

George, his back to her, shook his head violently. 'No, it isn't that,' he said, emotional turmoil making his voice unrecognisable. 'It isn't that simple.'

'What *are* you talking about? Don't upset yourself, darling. Here, come back to bed. Let me help.'

'You can't.' It was a strangled whisper, the sound of a man in terrible torment.

Moving with lithe agility, Olivia was at his side, arms comforting, eyes wide with concern. 'I've worried about this,' she murmured. 'You've been overdoing it, working far too hard. Come along.' George allowed himself to be guided back to the bed. Tense, like a frightened rabbit, he perched uncomfortably on the edge of the mattress. Olivia knelt at his feet, clasping his knees. 'This isn't right,' she said gently. 'At the very least, you must take a holiday. How about a cruise? You enjoyed those three weeks on *Carmania*, didn't you? And it might be an idea to have a chat with Doctor Murdoch.'

George's vague, distant expression gradually focused into a wild look that suggested derangement. 'That wouldn't do the blindest bit of good,' he said harshly.

'Oh, no, I'm sure you're wrong, darling.' Olivia's tone was silky and persuasive. 'You're run-down, but it's easily put right.'

'Yes, I probably am run-down,' George agreed. 'It isn't what you think, though, my dear. No.' He shook his head, as if convincing himself. 'It isn't overwork.'

'Well, what is it, then? Tell me.' Olivia was earnest.

She waited, anxiously patient, while George completed the struggle with his conscience. At last, he forced it out. 'Olivia, I have a dreadful confession to make. I've been living a lie — with you. The fact is, I don't much care for women. I'm afraid that I'm a homosexual.'

Olivia's disbelief took her ability as an actress to new heights. Gazing at her in dread, expecting a torrent of hysterical anger, George was completely taken in.

After a carefully calculated pause, Olivia said. 'No. I don't believe you, George. Why are you saying such silly things?'

'You'll have to believe me, it's the God's honest truth,' he replied. 'I've had affairs with men. One of them got me slung out of Oxford. I never took my degree.'

'But I . . .' Olivia floundered, at a loss. 'I had no idea. I mean, we always seemed so well-suited in that respect.'

Deciding to say nothing of the misery he had suffered while making love to her, George shrugged wretchedly.

'You're not making this up?' Olivia asked. 'You prefer sex with men?'

'Yes!' George shouted. 'Yes, yes, yes! How many more times do I have to tell you?'

Perfectly calm, Olivia said, 'All right, don't let the whole Square know. Are you seeing anyone at the moment?'

'No.' George shook his head vigorously. 'Not since before we were married.'

After making him stew in silence for a few seconds, Olivia said, 'One thing puzzles me. Why are you telling me this now?'

'Because it's over,' George replied. 'Our marriage. I was relieved when you got pregnant and we had to stop doing it. What do you think of that, eh? Very flattering, isn't it? And I've been dreading the thought of starting again – I knew I wouldn't be able to do it. I was right.' Self-pity was creeping in.

'Do you intend taking up with a man?'

George let out an explosion of bitter laughter. 'I have no immediate plans, if that's what you mean. However . . .' He left the rest to Olivia's imagination. Ashamed, he added, 'You'll want a divorce, I expect?'

'Divorce?' Olivia's eyes expressed astonishment. 'Why? On what grounds?'

'Oh, I don't know – we can cook something up.'

'I hardly think so, darling.' Olivia was whispering and, for the first time, introducing a hint of intimidation. 'The scandal would be *appalling*. It would be unbearable for our parents – and the children, for heaven's sake. You must think of them, George, especially John. After all, he's the reason you forced yourself to marry me, isn't he?'

George, his face paler than ever tonight, seemed almost relieved to jump into the trap. 'Yes, I'm afraid he is. Olivia, I can't tell you how sorry I am about this – it was wrong to marry you – grossly unfair. My mother . . .' He stopped abruptly, shocked by what he had been about to say.

'Go on,' Olivia coaxed. 'What about your mother?'

'Well, she was very keen on our marriage. If I'd wanted to have second thoughts — which I didn't — I don't think it would have been allowed.'

'I understand perfectly,' Olivia said. 'Remember, I'm from the aristocracy, too. My family is no stranger to problems. We have Monty.'

Overwhelmed by her compassion, George took a while to collect his thoughts. 'What *are* we going to do?' he asked at last.

'*Do?*' Olivia was mystified. 'About what, darling?'

'*Us.*' George was becoming distraught. 'This marriage.'

'Apart from carrying on as though everything is perfect, I don't see that we need to do anything.'

'Yes, but . . .' George squirmed. 'What about your physical needs? They can be quite . . . er . . . powerful.' Hastily, he added, 'I suppose that's a compliment.'

'I shall certainly take it that way,' Olivia said. 'There's a simple answer, darling. Like you, I shall find myself a man.' She smiled craftily. 'We shall both be very, very discreet — especially you. If you were found out, we should be in the mire up to our ears. Both of us.'

Olivia had expected George to agonise his way towards a grudging acceptance of her suggestion; she had not bargained for instantaneous enthusiasm. 'Do you think that would work?'

'Why not? If we're photographed together, smiling all over our silly faces, say, every two weeks or so, there's no reason why we couldn't get away with blue murder. There must be dozens of people in the same boat as us, and I'll bet that's what they do. Our parents mustn't know, of course, and we shan't be able to afford the luxury of personal recriminations.'

Frowning, George said, 'Sorry, my dear, I'm not with you.'

'You go your way and I go mine,' Olivia replied. 'We keep it strictly between ourselves and we ask no questions – none of that "Where the hell were you last night?" nonsense.'

'Yes, I see.' George thought about it. 'There's no reason why it shouldn't work.'

'None whatsoever,' Olivia agreed, as though it had been his idea in the first place.

George thought of a problem. 'How will you find a suitable man?'

'Neither your mother, nor mine has ever experienced difficulty in that respect,' Olivia said. Taking advantage of George's mild shock, she chose a name at random from their social circle. 'What about Leo Hammerwich? He's always giving me the eye.'

George laughed. 'Sarah will turn bright green if you pinch him.'

'I can't think why,' Olivia said sweetly. 'She obviously doesn't have the faintest idea what to do with him. In any case, I shan't steal, just borrow.'

Unthinkingly, hypnotised by the web of alluring possibilities that Olivia had spun, George blundered off in an astounding direction. 'Hector Abercrombie might be a good bet. He's a devil for women and it could be useful if you were involved with him.'

Olivia, to whom the name meant nothing, asked, 'How come?' She was only slightly interested.

'He messes about with racehorses at Cannings Norton, you know, just outside Marlborough. His house is full of pictures, including twelve Canalettos. *Twelve!* To the best of our knowledge, that's the largest number under one roof – other than the Royal collection, of course. They've been in his family for years. The silly fool refuses to sell.'

'Perhaps he likes them,' Olivia said reasonably.

'Rubbish. The man's a Philistine, doesn't give a damn about

art.' George was becoming heated. 'You should hear Athene on the subject – she's had several goes at persuading him to sell.'

'So he doesn't want to,' Olivia said.

'Yes, but he *should*. It's an open secret that he's been near to bankruptcy for the last five years. Those Canalettos would put him in the clear for the rest of his life. If we could get him to Boothby's, the opposition would be sick, especially Galbraith's. They're always after him.'

'I'll think about it,' Olivia murmured. 'I'd like to help.'

Hiding her triumph was the most difficult thing that Olivia had ever accomplished. George was so intoxicated by her solution to the problem of his homosexuality that he was denying every principle he held dear. Boothby's regarded itself as the purest, most unselfish of auction-houses, unsullied by base commercial considerations, yet here was the man who virtually ran the firm suggesting that his wife might care to go whoring for business.

Professing interest, Olivia asked, 'What did you say this man's name was?'

'Hector Abercrombie.'

'And he trains racehorses?'

George sneered. 'Pretends to. I hear he's a failure.'

'Mmm. Interesting.' Purely to preserve the balance of their pact, Olivia asked, 'What about you? How will you find a man?'

'I expect I shall look up an old friend.'

'They're usually the best,' Olivia murmured.

She was still kneeling at his feet. Looking for a fitting conclusion to the bizarre episode, she obeyed her instinct and slid a hand inside George's dressing-gown. She was right: what had so humiliatingly eluded him twenty minutes ago was now tangible reality. George was powerfully erect.

'There, it's all sorted out.' Olivia's eyes were glowing

enticingly. 'What shall we do about *this*? Will you see to it yourself? Or would you let me help you?'

George offered no resistance as she pressed against his shoulders, persuading him to fall back on to the bed. Parting the dressing-gown, Olivia knelt astride him, caressing and teasing his hardness.

'You don't mind, do you?' she whispered. 'I like doing this to you. Perhaps you'll still let me from time to time, if you're lonely and I happen to be around.'

George, a prisoner of exquisite pleasure, mumbled agreement.

'Good. We can always be friends, you see.' Olivia was silent for a few moments, giving the rampant penis her full, expert attention. Once she was sure that nothing would divert George from the need to climax, she said, 'You've shaken me tonight, darling. I had no idea that you didn't like having sex with me.'

'I didn't dislike it,' George said.

'No, but you always seemed so – oh, I don't know – *capable*. You knew what you were doing.'

'There was another girl,' George heard himself say. 'She taught me to go through the motions.'

Olivia chuckled. 'How lovely. Anyone I know?'

'Actually, it was Athene.'

Eyes closed, his mind transfixed by what Olivia was doing to him, George missed her first genuine display of surprise. Immediately, however, she was telling herself that she should have known: Athene's hostility had always been blatant, particularly at the engagement party and christening. Had the silly creature seen herself as rather more than a tart whose function was to prepare his queer lordship for the horrors of marriage?

'Come along, darling, let me see what you can do,' Olivia urged, masturbating George savagely. She watched the final disintegration of his intellect and personality with avid curiosity. Exerting this power over a man – particularly one she despised – had always given Olivia a deeply satisfying, malicious thrill.

She was careful not to send George packing too quickly. It was he, fearful of circumstances which threatened embarrassment, who was eager to escape to his own room.

Left alone, Olivia stood in front of a full-length mirror, admiring herself and smiling jubilantly. Never doubting her ability to run rings round George, she had not expected that victory on such a scale would come so easily. Providing a modicum of care was exercised, she had *carte blanche* and Annaliese would be none the wiser. Soon, Simon Faulkener would be performing prodigies on her body, which, after the twins, looked better than ever.

And George's unforeseen willingness to reveal his proclivities had brought an added bonus, the resolution of a slightly worrying mystery. Once the awful truth was out, he had been expecting a divorce, assuming that she would demand it. Looking beyond the spectre of scandal and disgrace, George, doubtless spurred on by his mother, would be seeking custody of the children. Attributing normal maternal instincts to Olivia, they would anticipate a hard, dirty fight. That was why David Naismith, one of the sharpest solicitors in London with influential friends in Lincoln's Inn, had been insinuated into the family circle.

Olivia laughed. 'Totally unnecessary, my darlings,' she said to her reflection in the mirror. She flexed a leg to emphasise her carnal beauty and thrust her pelvis out. 'The matter will never arise. Ollie has Georgie by the balls, so there isn't going to be a divorce!'

Breaking the habit of not emerging from her bedroom until he had gone to Boothby's, Olivia joined George for breakfast. He was wary, unsure whether to accept that the events of the previous evening had really taken place.

Reading his mind, Olivia said, 'I meant it, darling.'

'You're sure?'

'Positive. Let's get on with our lives, eh? Just remember, be careful.'

As if seeking to demonstrate their ability to act circumspectly, they waited. A week passed before George manufactured an excuse to meet Tony Austen-Cave; sensing that he had done so, Olivia waited another two days before she left a message for Simon Faulkener with Mrs Gill, the ogre of B & L Airways.

17

1961
'My wife is a law unto herself'

Long before their third birthday, John and Valerie had shown themselves to be exceptional characters with a singular attitude to life. The most distinctive feature was their mutual love; they hated being apart or even out of sight of each other for more than ten minutes. Although John, a philosophically imperturbable little chap whose seriousness often seemed comical, was prepared to suffer longer separations in stoical silence, Valerie always bawled for her brother.

Beyond themselves, their greatest love was for George, who, since they were about six months old, had been the perfect father. They were very fond of Annaliese and Edward, but not of their Dorchester grandparents, whom they hardly knew. Valerie, able to give the impression that she was uncannily wise and shrewd, had a most unnerving way of staring at Aubrey and Caroline. It was as if she were thinking, 'What a hopeless pair of frauds you two are. And pretty damned miserable together, I'd say.' These disturbing moments led to fewer, less frequent visits by the Dorchesters and more indifference from the children. Caroline had an additional reason for staying away; there was something faintly embarrassing about meeting the twins in their mother's absence, and Caroline was well-aware that Olivia's whereabouts were unpredictable.

John and Valerie regarded Henrietta, Athene, and their husbands as great chums and favoured them with their most boisterous behaviour. Even John, normally so restrained, was exuberant with Athene.

At the other end of the scale was Miss Barclay, politely but comprehensively detested. Her defects were an insistence on discipline for its own sake and a doltish refusal to come to terms with the fact that her charges would *not* be separated. On their first visit to Cadogan Square, when they were eighteen months old, Miss Barclay's inexplicably pigheaded attempt to put them in different bedrooms had produced tantrums cataclysmic enough to disrupt a dinner-party. Now that George had made it plain that Miss Barclay's services would not be required for much longer, she had given up in disgust and, inadvertently, become almost pleasant.

Finally, there was Olivia.

George thought that the children's attitude to their mother was a consequence of the selfishly headstrong way Olivia was exploiting the bargain they had struck over their private lives. John and Valerie cared neither one way nor the other for Olivia for the simple reason that they had no idea what to make of her. Mystification had bred an apathy that contained elements of distrust.

Olivia was dutiful in that she spent most weekends at Compton Allardyce. She saw this as an essential part of persuading Annaliese – and, to a lesser extent, Edward – that all was well between her and George. As it happened, Simon Faulkener was unable to escape from his wife at weekends, a failing that was tolerable only because it fitted in with Olivia's notion of normality. She turned up at The Chantry every Friday, usually several hours ahead of George, sometimes after spending the morning in bed with Simon at a country club near Axbridge in Somerset.

Once she was there, confronted by two sceptical children, Olivia's behaviour tended to be frenetic. Her attitude was, 'Well, here I am, my darlings, aren't we going to have fun? What shall we do first? How about a fishing trip to the lake? Daddy used to love that when he was your age.'

Having ruined a perfectly good game which John and Valerie had invented, Olivia would drag them off somewhere, only to lose interest immediately. If it wasn't her nails, or concern for her stockings, she would wander away, aching with sexual melancholy and renewed hunger, leaving the children to their own devices. Once, an alert and devoted Labrador dragged a near-drowning John from the lake after he had stumbled, gone under, and panicked. Olivia's grudging regard for her son rose temporarily when, despite Valerie's challenging look, he steadfastly declined to tell George the complete truth about the incident.

Olivia's hectic moods in Wiltshire stemmed from what had been happening during the week. She saw Simon at every possible opportunity. Tuesday nights in Bath were the centre-piece of the affair, always planned well in advance. Invariably, however, there was another chance to be grabbed, often at chaotically short notice. For these afternoons, evenings, or whole nights, Olivia tore off in the E-Type Jaguar that had replaced her Austin-Healey. Dinners at Cadogan Square were reorganised or cancelled, leaving guests pretending not to mind.

George, who carefully restricted his meetings with Tony Austen-Cave to Tuesday evenings and was always home by midnight, was thoroughly annoyed by Olivia's cavalier atti-tude. He never imagined that he could curb her activities, but he was determined to make sure that John and Valerie were shielded from them.

In the third week of March, soon after the party to celebrate the twins' third birthday, Annaliese went to Upper Overs for a few days. Beatrice, a widow since the previous April, was glad of her company.

Charles's death, after a long and trying illness, had been a blessed release, but Beatrice missed him sorely and, Gwen whispered to Annaliese, always would until they were together again. Laid to rest in the old Boothby-Graffoe family plot at Hatchetts Green, Charles had asked to go alongside Archie Shackleton, Beatrice's fiancé who had died in 1917.

On Annaliese's first complete day in the Ashdown Forest, she and Beatrice took flowers to the graves, including Edward and Beatrice's parents, Lord Douglas and Lady Alice, in their tribute. It turned out to be one of those treacherous afternoons that promised spring, only to deliver flurries of snow in a stinging, north-east wind. Gwen put her foot down and insisted that they returned to the comfort of Upper Overs, where she served crumpets and tea with a tot of whisky in the sitting-room.

Finding that it eased the pain of her grief, Beatrice began to talk about Charles, recalling their early years when they had been forced to flout convention and live in sin because the objectionable and weird first Mrs Templeton had refused to countenance divorce.

'That was so silly,' Beatrice said. 'We worried ourselves sick over that, but no one ever turned a hair.'

'Except Edward,' Annaliese pointed out. The years had mellowed her opinion of the upsetting episode; now, a mildly sardonic smile replaced the white-hot fury of 1925. 'Of course, you met Charles at Martha's Vineyard, didn't you?'

Beatrice blushed like a schoolgirl. 'Can you believe it? *I* can't. I was there, doing frightfully wicked things before you became a regular.'

'If you recall, it was through you that I met Nancy Shenstone,' Annaliese said.

Made bold by the whisky-laced tea, Beatrice asked, 'How naughty were you in those days? Charles always thought you weren't.'

'No, I did nothing at Nancy's – not until John came along. And that didn't start until after Edward and I had moved to Allardyce.' Feeling a strange need to justify herself, Annaliese added, 'That was after the two big quarrels – the one over you and Charles, and that *frightful* business at the villa when I was swimming in the nude.'

'It's a miracle that you and Edward have stayed together,' Beatrice said. 'Has that been for the sake of the title and estate?'

'More or less,' Annaliese sighed. 'Actually, between you and I, there was a time when he did talk about divorce.'

'No!' Astonished, Beatrice clapped a hand to her mouth. Noticing that Annaliese looked rather shaken by the memory, she asked, 'When was this?' in a hushed voice.

'About five years ago.' Annaliese scowled ferociously. 'It was all to do with that letter from Celia.'

'Charles was *so* cross with me for showing you that,' Beatrice moaned. 'It was the only time we ever fell out.'

'It might have been best if I hadn't seen it,' Annaliese said. 'The fact is, I suppose I *was* rather harsh to Edward. He called me a harridan and told me that if I was going to make his life a misery, I'd better clear off.'

Full of admiration for her brother, Beatrice replied, 'But you got over it.'

'Mmm. Yes, we did.' Annaliese's expression was inscrutable.

Changing the subject, Beatrice asked, 'Do you still hear from Nancy?'

'No, I'm afraid we lost touch,' Annaliese said sadly. 'There was talk of her moving to California some years ago, but I've no idea what happened.'

'I suppose she's all right,' Beatrice mused.

'I'm sure she is. Nancy wouldn't put up with anything less.'

'Assuming she isn't dead,' Beatrice murmured.

Annaliese made no attempt to respond and the ensuing silence was made more uneasy by Beatrice, shuffling as she examined her courage. 'May I ask you a very personal question?' she said at last.

'Go on.'

Beatrice opened her mouth, shut it again and smiled nervously. 'You'll either think I'm mad, or bite my head off.'

Smiling, Annaliese said, 'I could do both. Let's see.'

Beatrice gabbled it out in a rush of bravado. 'Charles and I often wondered if you had a lover in Portugal. He was sure you had, I didn't think so.'

Looking dreadfully serious, Annaliese said, 'Charles was right – again! There is someone.'

'*Is?*' Beatrice squeaked. 'You mean you're . . .?'

'Why on earth not?' Annaliese gaze was studiously bland, implying that she couldn't imagine what Beatrice was driving at.

'Well . . .' Wishing that she'd never started, Beatrice was at a loss. Looking hot and bothered, she let out a pathetic little sigh and gave up.

'It's my age, I suppose?' Annaliese said, very matter-of-fact. 'I'm going to be sixty-five in June, and I don't feel anything like that.'

Smiling weakly, Beatrice asked, 'How old is your . . . er . . . friend?'

'A little younger than me – fifty-nine, I think.'

'Who is he?' Beatrice dared to inquire.

'His name is Kurt Schneider. He looks after the villa.'

'A *servant*?' Beatrice gasped.

'Isn't it dreadful?' Annaliese said, po-faced.

'Surely, he didn't have the gall to make a pass at you?' a horrified Beatrice asked.

'No, of course not. I had to encourage him.' Laughing at the expression on Beatrice's face, Annaliese said, 'Aren't I a shameless, scandalous creature? You and Edward were convinced that Olivia was the one to watch.'

'How is she?' Beatrice asked, grabbing at a chance to escape from a subject that was threatening to embarrass her to death.

'Very well indeed,' Annaliese replied cheerfully. 'She isn't much use to John and Valerie, but I wasn't a brilliant mother, so I can hardly complain.'

'Behaving herself?'

'To the best of my knowledge, yes. She and George appear to live it up in London and he probably works too hard.'

Beatrice, now fully retired from Boothby's and trying to keep her nose out of the firm's business affairs, had heard as much from Athene. However, that was the only slight concern in a rosy picture; 1960/61 promised to be another record-breaking year.

Even so, Beatrice was suspicious. 'Olivia isn't having affairs?'

'No, certainly not.' After a slight pause, Annaliese diluted her conviction. 'Well, let me put it this way – if she is, she's being extremely discreet about it, which is the next best thing.'

'And George is keeping to the straight and narrow?' Beatrice said, unhappy with Viennese logic. 'No men?'

'Good gracious, no. Not since he and Olivia became engaged – probably longer.' Annaliese showed a flash of irritation. 'I'm sure everything is as it should be. There's no need to look for problems that don't exist.'

'I'm sorry,' Beatrice said meekly. 'What about the loathsome Miss Barclay?'

'Aha, yes.' This was much more to Annaliese's liking. 'She's going. George is looking for a woman who can take care of the twins *and* teach them.'

'Will he find one?' Beatrice asked, wondering if such multi-talented paragons existed nowadays.

'I'm sure he will. George has a list of names and he's having a week's holiday to interview them all.'

'I defy him to do worse than Miss Barclay,' Beatrice said in what was, for her, a grim tone.

'Actually, you mustn't blame George over that.' Annaliese smiled sheepishly. 'I'm afraid that Miss Barclay was my idea.'

Beatrice tried to look severe. 'Annaliese, you do make things difficult when you barge in.'

'I know.' She pretended to be sorry. 'I've promised George not to interfere again. These days, I'm too busy. I've been dragged into all sorts of charity work.'

'Oh, how interesting,' Beatrice said, giving no indication that Athene had already told her a great deal about this. 'What are you up to?'

'I was descended upon by a deputation,' Annaliese announced grandly. 'They came to inform me, in the nicest possible way, that I wasn't pulling my weight.'

'Gosh!' Beatrice marvelled at the deputation's nerve.

'Apparently, there's an old tradition that the Duchess of Lincolnshire takes an interest in Salisbury,' Annaliese went on. 'I ask you! Uncle William's wife died in 1910, Celia never did a stroke, and it's taken them thirty-five years to track me down. Old tradition, my foot!'

'What does it involve?' Beatrice asked.

'Hospitals, schools, and two diocesan committees. As a matter of fact, it's quite important and useful work – busy, though, I'm doing things for them nearly every day.'

At that moment, Gwen came in to see to the fire and ask if they wanted more tea. Beatrice took advantage of the interruption to equate what Annaliese had said with Athene's more hard-headed version. What it boiled down to was that Annaliese was enjoying being an aristocratic celebrity, had seen very little of Compton Allardyce – particularly during the short hours of winter daylight – and had no real idea what George and Olivia were up to.

When Matthew had brought a fresh pot of tea and guided the fussy Gwen out of the sitting-room, Annaliese said, 'All this work *could* stop me going to Portugal. Naturally, I shan't let that happen.'

Although disapproving, Beatrice found herself charmed into acquiescence. Especially with that smile, Annaliese looked ridiculously young and beguiling.

George spent two days interviewing prospective nanny-cum-teachers. Fourteen of them presented themselves at Cadogan Square, thirteen were unsuitable. Rather than being a true reflection on their abilities, this was caused by the excellence of the fourteenth applicant. George offered her the post as she was leaving after their two-hour chat, a spirited exchange that had lasted twice as long as planned and was to throw the rest of the afternoon into confusion.

During the interview in the drawing-room, her eyes had appeared to be the same cornflower-blue as his mother's. When she reprimanded him for his premature offer, they changed to that perplexing grey that often accompanied Annaliese's displeasure.

'I'm sorry, Lord Axholme, but I couldn't possibly accept until I've met your children. They might not like me – that is important, you know.'

Rebuffed and impressed, George collected his thoughts.

The best he could think of was, 'I'll have them brought up to Town.'

'You'll do no such thing,' she said, deeply shocked. 'They aren't *objects* that you can move around according to demand. I shall go to them. They'll be much happier in their normal surroundings.'

'Yes, you're quite right,' George said hastily. 'When do you think you could get down to Wiltshire?'

'Tomorrow?'

'Would you like me to drive you?'

'It's essential that you should be present, Lord Axholme, so that would be ideal.'

'Good. What time shall we set out?'

'Whenever you like.'

'How about eight-thirty? Fine. Where shall I pick you up?'

'I'm at the YWCA in Great Russell Street.' In response to George's astonished expression, she said, 'If you recall, Lord Axholme, I told you that I left my last job rather abruptly because of the children's new stepfather. That made me homeless.'

'Yes, of course, I *do* remember.' Flustered, George added, 'That must be awful for you.'

'Slightly inconvenient,' she said, not keen on drama. 'I'll see you tomorrow morning, Lord Axholme.'

In the event, they were both five minutes early. There was one surprise which George was apparently expected to take in his stride and duly did. Beside Kate Trenchard on the pavement outside the YWCA were two suitcases, almost certainly containing everything she owned. Making no comment and keeping a straight face, George placed them in the boot of his Lagonda and they set off. Neither of them spoke for the first few miles, but once clear of Brentford and the worst of the traffic, Kate insisted on telling George all about herself. Understanding that her purpose was to give him the information he needed to make a balanced final decision, George was silently attentive.

Kate, who was tall and serenely lovely, was the youngest of a senior civil servant's three daughters. Educated at Cheltenham Ladies' College, she had gone on to Birmingham University to read English. This had been her first departure from the path dictated by her parents, both of whom had studied at Cambridge and wanted Kate, like her two sisters, to do the same. Neither did her choice of subject find favour: the Trenchard girls were expected to read Classics, like their father, or Mathematics, as their mother, a lecturer at London University, had done. In fact, it soon became even worse: at the end of her first year, Kate switched to History, then had a go at Music. Not surprisingly, she failed to obtain a degree.

Catastrophe followed. A year later, when her parents remained tediously insufferable on the subject of Kate's wasted chances, her affair with a married man came to its inevitable, traumatic end. It was the final straw for everyone. Mr and Mrs Trenchard made it plain that they had no further time for their lamentably disappointing offspring and Kate, thoroughly sick of their autocratic snobbery, found herself a job in the wilds of Essex, looking after three young children whose father had been killed in an air disaster.

For two years, everything had been perfect. Then, out of the blue, the children's mother, thirty-two, attractive, and made wealthy by the insurance settlements, married a man who had, until a few days before the hurriedly arranged wedding, been invisible. Fortunately, the children took to their stepfather and were, therefore, not as upset as they might otherwise have been when Kate walked out after the man's umpteenth attempt to drag her into bed.

'I'm appalled,' George said. 'Didn't you talk to your original employer – the lady – when this nuisance started?'

'Mmm . . . yes, I did.' Kate gave George a sidelong glance,

wondering how much she could tell him. He was, she had concluded, a supreme gentleman, possibly too naive and easily shocked for his own good. 'I spoke to her several times,' Kate said. 'She told me that I was being silly, behaving like a Victorian virgin.'

'Dear, dear!' For half a mile or so, George considered the matter. Much to Kate's relief, he let it drop: the thought of being cajoled into telling him what the bloody woman had suggested made her toes curl.

After twenty minutes of less than comfortable silence, they neared the end of their journey and George was able to launch into an enthusiastic commentary on the surroundings.

'This is Compton Allardyce village. My mother has had most of it rebuilt since we came here in 1925. You wouldn't think it, would you? It was like a huge jigsaw puzzle. They took each house apart, brick by brick, then put it back together, looking exactly as it was, but with all sorts of improvements. Now, look at this.' George slowed down to give Kate time to appreciate the grandeur of the south-eastern entrance.

'Very nice,' she said drily as they drifted past the wrought-iron gates with their heraldic crests. 'These trees are a surprise. You can't see a thing through them.'

'Wait a moment,' George said smugly. He stabbed his foot on the accelerator, making the Lagonda surge through the tunnel of beeches and oaks. As they burst out into the broad acres of the Park, Kate saw the Castle, luminescent and ethereally graceful in the brave, late-March sunshine. Determined to remain in control of her emotions, she said nothing.

After they had breasted the rise to the centre of the Park, Kate coughed politely, interrupting George's enthusiastic description of the Castle. 'Tell me about Miss Barclay,' she said.

'She's been very good,' George replied, far too quickly.

'In that case, why do you want to replace her?'

'She was never meant to be with us for more than three years,' George said. 'That was a strict condition when she came. I want someone who can *educate* John and Valerie, as well as look after them. They're very talented.'

Kate took her time, admiring the pleasing folds of the land and staring into the woods. 'And how long is Miss Barclay's successor expected to last?' she asked.

'Henrietta Timberlake, who looked after my brother and me, has been here for thirty-five years,' George said. 'When we went away to school, she helped my mother, then she married Nicholas Hammond, the estate manager.'

'I'm impressed,' Kate admitted.

'As a rule, we take good care of the people who work for us,' George continued. 'Most of them seem to appreciate it.'

'Let's hope that Miss Barclay doesn't dislike me *too* much.' For once, Kate sounded nervous.

Looking pleased with himself, George said, 'There's no question of that. Miss Barclay left last week.'

After smiling at each other, George and Kate were conscious of a growing rapport as they covered the last few hundred yards to The Chantry.

At the sound of the car on the gravel in front of the house, the door opened and the children appeared. Valerie was eager to greet her father and inspect the newcomer, John hung back, frowning. The young maid who had been given the responsibility of looking after the twins until Miss Barclay's replacement turned up peered anxiously through a window.

Kate was stunned by the children: they were hypnotically beautiful, not simply pretty, like many youngsters. A second, longer glance provided the answer. John and Valerie did not have snub noses, chubby cheeks, or rose-bud mouths; every one of their features was a miniature of adult perfection. Perhaps the brilliance of the flaxen hair and blue eyes would fade slightly as they grew up, but Lord John Arthur Wainfleet and Lady Valerie Boothby-Graffoe were surely destined to be the most dazzling exemplars of a famously good-looking family.

Valerie ran round the front of the Lagonda and, after George had opened the door, launched herself on to his lap, all ankle socks and knicker frills. After planting a wet kiss on his nose, she said, 'Hello, Daddy, how are you today?'

'Very well, thank you, sweetheart. And you?'

'Not so bad.' A huge sigh. 'Emily can't cope with us.'

'Who says so, you or Emily?'

'Emily!' Valerie groaned. She turned to Kate, her eyes surprisingly disconcerting for one so young. 'Who's she? The new dragon?'

'Valerie, darling, this is Miss Trenchard,' George said, with affectionate patience.

Valerie turned back to Kate and they stared at each other. Just as Kate was beginning to wonder why she had bothered coming to Compton Allardyce, Valerie struggled free of George's embrace, leaned across the gap between the opulent leather seats, and kissed Kate full on the lips.

George's laugh as he gathered Valerie back into his arms was an expression of joyous relief. Neither Kate nor George took any notice of the nervous tapping at the metal work on Kate's side of the car until Valerie shouted, 'It's John!'

Unable to see him and fearful of knocking him over, Kate eased the door open an inch at a time. She was met by a bashful smile.

'Hello, John,' Kate said.

'What's your name?' he asked, terribly earnest.

'Kate.'

Satisfied, he clambered into the Lagonda to stand close to Kate, supporting himself against her shoulder. After a moment's indecision, she gathered him into her arms. He snuggled down and smiled at Valerie, who let out a merry chuckle.

Above the children's heads, George and Kate glanced at each other quizzically. 'We'll go inside shortly,' George said. 'Have some lunch and let you look round.'

'That will be nice,' Kate said softly.

Not for a while, though. John, who was not nearly so grown-up as he sometimes liked to think, lay with his head against Kate's breast, contentedly sucking his thumb.

A few hours later, George and Kate strolled through the woods that covered 300 acres in the north-western corner of the Park. Ahead of them, warmly muffled against the March wind, John and Valerie romped with their dogs.

Halting, Kate looked round and said, 'This place is extraordinary. I've never seen anything like it.'

'It will be even better in a few weeks, when the leaves are out,' George said. 'What did you think of the house?'

'Nice. Very nice indeed.' Kate walked on. Falling into step beside her, George tried to work out what was going on behind the eyes which had been grey for a worryingly long time. At the same time, he did his best not to think of her suitcases, still in the boot of the Lagonda.

Briskly, Kate asked, 'What do you want for John and Valerie, Lord Axholme?'

'They must be happy,' was the unhesitating reply.

'Nothing else?'

'What else is there?' George asked. 'They can have anything they want. Look at it.' He waved an all-encompassing arm. 'Allardyce is the most obvious thing that we own, but there's plenty more hidden away – and there's the money I earn from Boothby's. I can guarantee the children everything – except happiness.'

'You expect me to arrange that?'

George responded robustly to the challenging question. 'Up to a point, yes, I do. It's perfectly possible – you've seen how they react to you. Look at them now. I can't remember them being so happy.'

'John and Valerie are the most important part of their happiness,' Kate said. 'They don't like being apart.'

'That's very perceptive of you, Miss Trenchard.'

Kate shrugged the compliment away. 'Common sense, more like. Will you try to keep them together when they go to school?'

'I shall do my best,' George said, his vehemence surprising Kate. 'There's no question of John going to Moss Close and Winchester. Even my father has accepted that.'

'Moss Close?'

'A prep school,' George replied. 'Home from home for Boothby-Graffoe boys since God knows when.'

'Not a good place?' Kate said, sensing the carefully concealed bitterness.

'My brother and lots of other chaps enjoyed it,' George said, cheering up in response to Kate's encouraging smile. 'But John goes there over my dead body. Really and truly, Miss Trenchard, I'd be pleased if they didn't go to school at all, if we did the job ourselves. Is that possible, do you think?'

Kate pulled a face and kicked at a tuft of grass. 'I could get them through a few "O" levels, I suppose.'

'That sounds good enough.'

'Wouldn't you like them to go to university?'

'What on earth for?' George said. 'I was at Oxford and it didn't do me the blindest bit of good. No, you teach them the basics and they can pick up the rest as they go along. I have an idea that John has a talent for music.'

They walked several paces in silence, Kate staring intently at the ground. 'Forgive me mentioning this,' she said eventually, 'but doesn't your wife have any say in how the children are educated?' Grasping her courage in both hands, Kate added, 'By the way, where *is* Lady Axholme? Doesn't she want to look me over?'

'Yes, those are good questions,' George muttered. 'You're entitled to ask.' Having said that, he seemed reluctant to provide the answer. Kate watched him struggle with the problem of how much to tell her and decide on candour. 'My wife isn't much bothered about John and Valerie,' he said.

'Oh.' Disconcerted, Kate hoped that George would explain. He did.

'The fact is, Miss Trenchard, my wife and I lead pretty separate lives. We sleep under the same roof sometimes, but she's away a good deal.'

'I see.'

'I want to be sure that you do,' George said, staring at Kate with an intensity that was disconcerting. 'You're very intelligent and sensitive, Miss Trenchard, and I feel I can trust you, so I'm going to be absolutely frank. To all intents and purposes, mine was a marriage of convenience. It's certainly turned out that way. The purpose of the exercise was to produce John — you understand the importance of that for a man in my position?' Kate nodded. 'Valerie was a wonderful bonus,' George went on. 'Now that she has provided an heir, my wife is a law unto herself. You won't see much of her and you'll have a free hand with the children. Apart from all the other considerations, I don't think Olivia could be *bothered* to interfere.'

Kate thought about it. She looked towards the twins who were rolling in a drift of last year's leaves with the dogs. 'In other words, that pair need a nanny, a nurse, a teacher, *and* a mother?'

'Yes, Miss Trenchard, that's about the size of it,' George agreed.

Both fearful, they gazed at each other.

Suddenly, Valerie, who was now riding on the back of the wise old Labrador who had dragged John from the lake, came closer. 'Kate, are you going to stay with us?' she called.

After a moment of agonising suspense, Kate shouted, 'Yes, I am!' Although it was an impulsive, split-second decision, it had come from the bottom of her heart.

Beside herself with joy, Valerie fell off the dog. John ran to help her up. They whispered in some secret code and burst into peals of happy laughter. Carried away by gratitude, George grabbed Kate's hand, kissed it, blushed to the roots of his hair, and stammered, 'Do please forgive me, Miss Trenchard, I forgot myself. I promise you that nothing like that will *ever* happen again.'

Believing him, Kate smiled weakly, overawed by what she had done. She knew that, on the spur of a moment that already seemed mad, she had made the decision that would govern the rest of her life.

'When?' Valerie wanted to know. 'When are you coming to live with us?'

'Straight away?' Kate suggested. Looking at George for approval, she said, 'I don't have to go back to London. I checked out of the YWCA.'

'Have you got a toothbrush and a nightie?' Valerie asked. Solemnly, and to the intense discomfort of George and John, she went on, 'And knickers. Did you bring any knickers? You can borrow some of mine, if you like.'

Doing her level best to be serious, Kate said, 'Don't worry, Valerie, I *do* have a few useful things with me.'

John, who had been hanging back, darted towards Kate and hugged her knees. Bending, she scooped him into her arms where he settled contentedly.

'It's going to be a long way home,' George said, crouching so that Valerie could climb up for a piggyback. Wagging their tails furiously, the dogs fell in behind, adoring Valerie but glad to have her taken care of for fifteen minutes.

Later, in the dusk, while the twins had tea with Emily, George removed the suitcases from the boot of the Lagonda and carried them upstairs to what was now Kate's bedroom.

'I can't tell you how pleased I am about this, Miss Trenchard,' he said. 'I hope you'll be very happy here.'

'I'm sure I shall. Lord Axholme, do you think we could dispense with the formality now? I'd prefer to be called Kate, rather than Miss Trenchard.'

To her utter astonishment, George seemed shocked. 'I don't know about that,' he replied, backing out of the room. 'As a rule, one only uses Christian names for *junior* members of the staff, and you're hardly in that category, Miss Trenchard.'

Baffled by his confusion, Kate allowed George to escape and set about unpacking her cases. Minor though the incident was, it struck her as bizarre.

Two days later, she realised that 'bizarre' was a silly overstatement. For one thing, using it to describe George's harmless pomposity robbed Kate of an accurate description of her first encounter with the Marchioness of Axholme.

It was one of Olivia's hectic Fridays after a night in Somerset with Simon Faulkener. She arrived at midday, lustrous, radiating sex, complaining of starvation, and demanding to be fed. George, normally in London when the phenomenon of his wife in this mood descended on The Chantry, rapidly became exasperated and edgy. He attempted to calm Olivia down while Kate and the children kept out of the way.

The mere fact of their mother's presence in the house had a remarkable effect on the twins. In forty-eight hours, Kate had learned that Valerie was the boisterous, recklessly brave half of the partnership, while John followed her lead and, in his reserved, self-effacing way, exerted a calming influence. Now, as Olivia filled the house with narcissistic anarchy,

Valerie was tense and sullen, looking to John for support.

When she finally condescended to visit the group of rooms that made up the nursery suite, Olivia's ostentatiously high spirits were crushing rather than uplifting. George, trailing behind like a fish out of water, introduced Kate.

'Lovely!' Olivia said, ignoring the respectful greeting and outstretched hand. 'This *is* nice. I can see that we're all going to get on *splendidly*. How are you, my darlings?'

'Very well, thank you, Mama,' John replied. Valerie, clutching his arm, was tight-lipped. In an instant that scorched itself on to her memory, Kate saw that the normally bold little girl was frightened of her mother. John, on the other hand, was regarding her with detached contempt.

'I believe you've worked wonders already, Miss Trenchard,' Olivia gushed. 'That poor girl – Emily, is it? – has nothing but praise for you. Ask for whatever you need, but don't hesitate to use your initiative. That really is frightfully important. Do you think you can manage that?'

Taking Kate's nonplussed disbelief for agreement, Olivia switched on a smile that might have dazzled and enchanted had it reached her eyes. Then she was gone.

George and Kate stared at each other. 'Well, there you are,' he said. 'As predicted, no interference.'

'It seems that I have a free hand,' Kate said.

'I'd say so.' With a broad grin, George jettisoned his reserve in a way that was clearly intended to set him apart from his wife. 'How do you feel about that, *Kate*? Will you be all right?'

'I think so.'

Downstairs, Olivia's voice rang out as she informed anyone who might be interested that she was off to visit her mother. Doors slammed, the engine of the E-Type Jaguar roared into life and was revved up flamboyantly. Valerie gave a little skip and began to laugh again.

During her first month at Compton Allardyce, Kate had half a dozen encounters with Annaliese. The children's boundless joy at the sight of their grandmother should have put Kate at her ease: however, the careful inquiries she made to discover the background of the people for whom she was working had left her painfully in awe of the woman who had started her life as a member of Europe's oldest and most celebrated royal house. Fully aware that she acted like a tongue-tied nincompoop whenever the Duchess of Lincolnshire appeared, Kate was unable to help herself.

A miraculous transformation occurred at about 9.30 on an evening in April when George and Olivia were away in London.

It began inauspiciously. Kate, at ease in her sitting-room, was not aware that Annaliese had arrived at The Chantry. There was a light tap on the door. Thinking that it was Emily or the cook, Kate called, 'Come in,' and there she was.

'Please don't alarm yourself, my dear,' Annaliese said. 'I happened to be passing on my way back from Marlborough and I had this sudden urge to see the little ones asleep.' With a wry smile, she added, 'I've started chasing my youth – I used to look in on George and his brother every night.'

Nervously, Kate took Annaliese to the room in which the twins lay, their angelic expressions suggesting sweet dreams. Soon satisfied, Annaliese turned away. 'Beautiful,' she whispered. 'Aren't they wonderful? Very good-looking.'

'Gorgeous,' Kate agreed. Chancing her arm, she said, 'So fair, though. Not like Lord Axholme.'

Annaliese's eyes sparkled with mischief. 'Most of the Boothby-Graffoes resemble Scandinavian gods – but there was a Spanish duchess – she was my husband's grandmother. She seems to have asserted herself in George. The ghastly Ralph was just the same.'

'Oh, I see.' Kate, who wasn't sure that she did, guided Annaliese out of the children's bedroom.

There was a moment's awkward hesitation, then, heading towards the sitting-room, Annaliese said, 'Can we have a little chat, my dear? I loved to gossip with Gwen and Henry in the old days.'

Making herself comfortable in an armchair, Annaliese reached for the book that Kate had left open and face-down on the coffee-table. 'What are you reading?' Annaliese looked at the cover. 'Goodness me – "*The Habsburgs: The Last Hundred Years*".' Her eyes sparkled. 'I haven't seen this one. Will you lend it to me when you've finished?'

'The author doesn't seem to be terribly sympathetic, Your Grace,' Kate said, praying for the ground to open and swallow her.

Annaliese chuckled. 'Not many of them are. Do sit down, my dear.' She was flicking through the book, searching for anything of special interest. 'Oh, my word, listen to this,' she said, her attention caught by something at the end of a paragraph. 'It says, "Throughout history, most dynasties have constituted a few chapters to the history of a people. For the Habsburgs, the people were an occasional complication or slight irritation in the history of a dynasty".'

'It isn't a very good book,' Kate mumbled.

'What he says is absolutely right,' Annaliese replied. 'The Habsburgs spent over seven hundred years looking after themselves. As things turned out, that was usually good for Austria, but it was always self-interest first and foremost.' Seeing the astonishment on Kate's face, she said, 'Since I grew old and wise and began studying books, I've come to the conclusion that we only survived for such a long time because all the alternatives were ten times worse than us.' After a sad pause, she added, 'The last forty-odd years have proved that.'

Kate leaned forward, her face shining. 'Your mother was a

Wittelsbach, from Bavaria, I believe?'

'Yes, she was.'

'Please, tell me about her,' Kate said.

'Why?' Annaliese was charmed by the interest.

'I read somewhere that they were a much nicer bunch than the Habsburgs.'

Annaliese laughed. 'I don't know that Ludwig the First was very nice – he was the chap who became involved with Wagner and went mad. I've always thought that there was a connection.'

'Didn't Ludwig build those fairy-tale castles perched on the sides of mountains?' Kate asked.

'Yes. When she was a little girl, Mama used to go to Neuschwanstein for the summer holidays.'

'Is that the very famous one?'

'It's certainly the most extraordinary,' Annaliese replied. 'The walls of the dining-room are covered with huge murals of scenes from *Tristan, Lohengrin*, and *Parsifal*.'

Responding to Kate's wide-eyed interest, Annaliese settled down to talk about her mother's family.

Fortunately for the chauffeur who was driving Annaliese, Emily realised what was happening upstairs and invited him into the kitchen for some supper. At midnight, when he finally took Annaliese home, she was full of apologies for keeping him waiting so long and promised to be quicker in future. In fact, when her thrice-weekly visits to The Chantry on Tuesday, Thursday, and Sunday were established ritual, the chauffeur's romance with Emily flourished. As it did so, Annaliese and Kate became the closest of friends.

The weeks passed and Kate revelled in her first summer at Compton Allardyce.

Throughout June and July, the pattern of Olivia's comings and goings gradually altered. Firstly, she began to disappear at

weekends. As she watched the subtle changes unfold, certain
that she was the only person to notice what was happening,
Kate saw the cunning in the way it was carried out. It started
as a few hours here and there; whole afternoons imperceptibly
stretched into the evening; by the end of July, Olivia was often
away all night. A month later, she rarely spent more than two
hours at The Chantry between Friday afternoon and Sunday
evening.

One day, apparently waking up to what was going on,
George volunteered the information that his wife now
preferred to be in London at weekends, cultivating friendships
that he claimed were useful to Boothby's. Smiling politely,
Kate pretended to believe him. Although the Marquess and
Marchioness of Axholme were often pictured together in the
glossy magazines, didn't everyone who mattered go to the
country on Fridays? How, therefore, could they be 'cultivated'
in London? In any case, George's explanation was undermined
by the other variation in Olivia's behaviour.

She began to appear at The Chantry during the week. These
were flying visits, usually occurring at either 11.00 am or
4.00 pm and lasting about three hours: the precision was
uncanny. Avoiding the children whenever possible, Olivia
flitted silently round the house, had a bath, and, according to
Emily, left with a case of clean clothes. Kate became intrigued
by what looked very much like breaks in a journey:
improbable though it seemed, she found herself suspecting
that Lady Axholme was using The Chantry as a stopping-off
point between lovers.

On a Wednesday towards the end of August, she arrived at
the unusual time of 1.45 pm. Kate, who was enjoying a day
off while the twins were in Bristol with Annaliese and
Edward, kept well out of her way – at least, she did until a
few minutes past three o'clock. She was taking a cup of tea
upstairs to her sitting-room when she noticed that the door of

the Olivia's bedroom was half-open. Her attempts to tiptoe past were defeated by the old, creaking floor-boards on the broad landing.

'Is that you, Miss Trenchard?' Olivia called out.

'Yes, my lady.'

'*Do* come and talk to me.'

Silently cursing her bad luck, Kate went into the room.

Olivia was sitting on the bed, brushing her hair. She wore only a bra and tiny briefs; shocked, Kate understood at once that Lady Axholme was showing off.

Deciding that her hair was perfect, Olivia smiled in a way that verged on sincerity. 'We never get a chance to speak,' she said. 'How are you? Are you completely settled in?'

'Yes, thank you, my lady,' Kate mumbled. She must not, she told herself, stare at the bloody woman, at least, not in *that* way. All right, she had a superb body, but there was no need to pander to her narcissistic conceit. Resolutely, Kate said, 'I love it here.'

'*Do* you?' Olivia's expression implied that this was a somewhat eccentric view to take of Compton Allardyce. 'You don't find it too *isolated*? Do you manage to get out and buy things? Clothes? Don't I remember my husband saying that you didn't bring much with you? Where on earth do you go?'

Questions were Olivia's speciality, Kate saw. It was a technique designed to keep the other person on the defensive. 'I manage very well, thank you. Lady Lincolnshire has taken me shopping a few times.'

'Oh, yes, of course!' Olivia's eyes were expressively round. 'How are you getting on with the old dear? Don't you find her ever so slightly forbidding?'

'Not in the least,' Kate replied. 'She's kind to me.'

'Good,' Olivia snapped dismissively. 'What about your social life? Do you have a boy-friend?'

'Not any more, my lady.'

'Do I detect a trace of bitterness there, Miss Trenchard?'

'No. I'm perfectly happy as I am.'

'Really?' Olivia was mocking. Then, taking Kate by surprise, she sprang from the bed and walked to the dressing-table, sensually graceful, calculating every movement. Good though her own legs were, Kate envied Olivia's, and was disturbed to realise that the semi-transparent briefs did little to conceal her beautiful bush of pubic hair. Olivia toyed with a perfume bottle, decided against it and sat on the stool to face Kate. Arrogant and reckless, she said, 'I suppose you're wondering what the hell George and I are up to?'

'It's none of my business, Lady Axholme,' Kate said. Determined not to feel inferior, she began to sip at the cup of tea.

Olivia laughed unpleasantly. 'That doesn't stop you noticing, though, does it? You aren't going to stand there and tell me that you don't think we're unusual – sort of odd?'

'I repeat, it's none of my business,' Kate said doggedly.

'Has George said anything to you?' Olivia asked. 'Told you about us, perhaps?'

'No, Lady Axholme, he has not. Nor would I expect him to do so.' Kate began to doubt her ability to keep calm.

'Mmm.' Briefly, Olivia seemed sceptical, inclined to fire off more questions. Instead, she reached for the perfume and set about applying liberal amounts to her thighs. Smiling at Kate's amazement, she said, 'I find this helps enormously. I'm glad we had this little chat, Miss Trenchard. You may go now.'

After that, Olivia stayed away from The Chantry for two weeks. When she returned, she was – to Kate's relief – briskly offhand.

In her absence, life had carried on in its own sweet way. At weekends, when George was with the children constantly, he and Kate discussed Olivia. They did so by means of eloquent looks, using a system that was devised telepathically as they went along. The exchanges, which took place rapidly when the children were preoccupied, always ended with George signalling, 'Don't worry, Kate. Everything is under control. I've no idea where she is, but we're better off without her.'

Although it was mildly reassuring, Kate came close to telling Annaliese about her misgivings. There were enough opportunities. In addition to their evening talks, Annaliese made room in her busy 'Salisbury schedule' to spend one afternoon a week with Kate and the twins. If the weather was fine, they rambled round the Park, with Kate paying careful attention to all that Annaliese had learned about this glorious piece of England during her thirty-six years as its chatelaine and custodian. When it rained, they went off to Bath or Salisbury in Rolls-Royce splendour.

In their comfortable, private moments, Kate often wanted to say, 'Annaliese, Your Grace, what are we going to do about that bitch, Olivia?'

But she never did. Her courage always failed and there was George's comforting, 'We're better off without her.'

18

1964

'... the day you and he escaped from Berlin'

On 23 June, Edward and Nicholas Hammond went to London to complete the disposal of a large part of the Lincolnshire holdings in East Anglia.

Because Edward had grown weary of the worsening traffic congestion on the approaches to the capital, the greater part of the journey was by train. Nicholas drove to Pewsey, where they left the car at the station and caught the 9.35 to Paddington. A taxi delivered them to Templeton's in Angel Court off Throgmorton Street at 11.30 and they were shown into the elegant oak-panelled office that Nigel had taken over from his father, Charles. The chairman and finance director of the development company to which Edward was selling a processed-food factory, three farms, and several hundred houses in the centre of Norwich had already arrived and they got straight down to business. In under an hour, the final details were agreed, all the documents signed, and a banker's draft for more than £1.6 million was handed over to Edward. Declining an invitation to take lunch in the directors' dining-room, the property men shook hands and hurried away.

'I suppose they can't wait to start the asset-stripping and demolition,' Edward grumbled, giving the impression that he was regretting the sale.

Smiling urbanely, Nigel picked up the draft. 'I'm sure you'll feel better when this is safely ensconced in Switzerland,' he said. 'Give me a couple of minutes to send it on its way and we'll eat.'

Over the meal, which they shared with two of Nigel's senior colleagues, Edward was in good form, commenting with mordant humour on the fortunes of the Conservative Government. Harold Macmillan had resigned the previous autumn on the grounds of poor health. In reality, his departure was so obviously linked to the Profumo affair that it was impossible to accept illness as the sole reason. A General Election was imminent and Edward gave Macmillan's somewhat improbable successor, Sir Alec Douglas-Home, rather less than a snowball's chance in hell of winning it. Enjoying himself, Edward warned Templeton's to prepare for Socialism, making it sound like the end of civilisation.

On the way to Paddington for the 3.15 train, Edward suddenly felt very tired and considered contacting George to ask if he could stay at Cadogan Square instead of going back to Wiltshire. In the end, Annaliese was the deciding factor: she was returning from a two-week holiday in Portugal that afternoon and would expect him to be waiting for her. Much more importantly, while she had been away, Piers Laverstoke had warned Edward that Olivia was causing tongues to wag. Incredibly, she was believed to be involved with at least two and possibly three men. It was time for some straight talking and action.

Comfortable in a first-class compartment, which he and Nicholas had to themselves, Edward felt much better once the train was under way and speeding past Old Oak Common.

However, as they ran through Sonning, the feeling of lethargy returned, accompanied by stomach pains.

'Can't think what's come over me,' Edward muttered. 'Must be that lunch. I seem to get dyspepsia these days.'

'Do you need help?' Nicholas looked out of the window anxiously, judging how close they were to the first stop at Reading.

'Don't be so damned silly,' Edward growled. 'This will do the trick.' Producing a hip-flask, he took two swigs. 'Brandy. Can't beat it.' He shook himself and grinned jauntily. 'Don't look like that, Nicholas, the world isn't going to come to an end.'

To Nicholas's immense relief, he was right. By the time the train pulled away from Reading, there was no sign that anything had been wrong. Indeed, Edward's mind was as sharp as ever. 'I enjoyed putting the fear of God up those fellows at Templeton's,' he said, 'but it's no joke. Any ideas as to how Harold Wilson and his gang are likely to affect us?'

Nicholas, who shared Edward's political views and had been keeping a close watch on developments, was prepared for the question. The discussion that ensued carried on as they left the train at Pewsey, crossed the bridge to the car-park, and set off towards Compton Allardyce. They paused in the village so that Edward, finally at ease with the status and title he had hated for so long, could chat to a group of his tenants who were waiting for opening time at the pub. Afterwards, as Nicholas drove through the Park, Edward was thinking aloud about an ambitious tree-planting scheme. 'Tax allowances,' he said, nodding sagaciously. 'I tell you, Nicholas, it's what Annaliese will want. She *detests* the very thought of being fleeced to pay for Socialist profligacy.' They drew up at the Castle's main entrance and Osbourne, the butler, came down the steps to greet Edward.

As the door was opened for him to get out, Edward patted

Nicholas's arm. 'It's been a good day. Thank you for your help. Why don't you bring Henrietta to dinner tomorrow evening? Afterwards, you and I can hide in the library and plan an anti-Wilson campaign.'

'Good idea,' Nicholas agreed.

'I'll talk to Annaliese and confirm,' Edward said, easing himself out of the car.

The moment he straightened up, he said, 'Oh dear!' in a strange voice.

Urgently, Osbourne cried, 'Your Grace, what is it?' Edward staggered, recovered, but clutched at his butler's shoulder for support. He turned in bewilderment as Nicholas rushed to help.

'Bit of a rum do,' Edward said.

'Come along inside,' Nicholas replied, putting one of Edward's arms round his shoulders. Osbourne did the same and they made a start up the steps.

Believing himself to be recovering, Edward fumed, 'This is ridiculous.'

'No, it isn't,' Nicholas said placatingly. 'Let's get you settled, with your feet up, and I'll call Doctor Harrison.'

'To hell with him,' Edward snapped. 'Fetch me a glass of brandy. Is my wife back yet, Osbourne?'

'No, my lord. We're expecting Her Grace in about an hour.'

They reached the top of the steps, passed through the oak doors, and entered the vast entrance-hall, cool after the heat of the June afternoon. Osbourne exchanged glances and nods with Nicholas and hurried away to use the telephone in his pantry. Mrs Osbourne and a footman had taken up positions at the foot of the staircase; they were apprehensive, awaiting instructions.

Freeing himself from Nicholas's support, Edward braced his shoulders back. 'Thank you,' he said huffily. 'There's no need for any of this fuss, I'm perfectly all right. It's only a touch of . . .'

Racked by a crucifying pain, he dropped the old document-case that he had used constantly since his early days at the Foreign Office fifty years ago. Clutching at his chest, eyes tightly closed, Edward sank to his knees. Looking on in horror, Mrs Osbourne and the footman were to remember how gracefully he fell.

Crouching beside him, Nicholas was trying to think of something sensible to say when Edward pre-empted him with a vice-like grip on his wrist. They spoke – about what, Mrs Osbourne and her terrified companion had no idea.

There was another wave of dreadful pain, a choking sob, and he was gone. After struggling to make the final stage of the collapse as dignified as the first, Nicholas stared blindly at Mrs Osbourne.

Edward Boothby-Graffoe, Tenth Duke of Lincolnshire, had fallen victim to a heart attack. He was in his seventy-fourth year. As Nicholas edged away from his lifeless form, Allardyce Castle's multitude of clocks began to strike six. Until that moment, no one had ever realised what an eerie din the thirty-odd sets of disparate chimes made.

Edward's body had been moved by the time Annaliese arrived at ten minutes past seven. She found Nicholas, Henrietta, and Doctor Harrison waiting on the threshold. One look at their faces was enough.

After Nicholas had recited the bare, appalling facts, Annaliese insisted on seeing Edward. He was lying on his bed. When she took his hand, vestiges of warmth remained. But the agony of the final terrifying seconds was already seeping away from him, relaxing his face into an older, very distinguished-looking version of the earnest young man who had, despite his peculiarly fuddy-duddy ways, added magic to that golden Viennese summer of 1914. The first coherent thought that flashed through Annaliese's mind was that they had never commissioned another portrait to replace the one by Michael Taverner.

Telling herself not to be so ridiculous, she turned to Nicholas and asked, 'Were you with him all the time?'

'Since nine o'clock this morning.'

'Did he suffer?'

'I don't think so.' Not sure of the extent to which he was lying, Nicholas noticed that Doctor Harrison made a funny little throat-clearing noise and shuffled uneasily.

Annaliese sat on the edge of the bed, placing a hand on Edward's breast. 'This is absolutely awful,' she whispered.

Seeing that she was close to tears, Henrietta bustled to her side, embracing her and murmuring words of comfort.

'No, no, you don't understand,' Annaliese said petulantly. 'I am *never* in England when the people who matter die. Edward's mother – his father – Ralph – and now Edward. I'm *always* away . . . usually in Portugal. It must be some sort of curse.'

'What time did your flight land at London?' Henrietta asked.

'At a quarter to five, I think.'

'Then you *were* in England when he died,' Henrietta said firmly, prepared to be stronger if the need arose.

'You're splitting hairs, Henry,' Annaliese retorted dangerously. The fires of rebellion flared in the extraordinary blue eyes, then subsided as Annaliese pulled herself together, repulsing the threat of tears. 'What do we need to do about this?' she asked.

'I took the liberty of telephoning George,' Nicholas said.

'What time will he be here?' Annaliese asked.

'Ten o'clock was his best estimate. He had things to look into and I wasn't as quick off the mark as I should have been – shock, I'm afraid.'

Annaliese raised a hand to convey understanding. 'The Chantry? Have you told Kate?'

'No, I thought you or George would want to do that.'

What an astonishing place the Park was, Annaliese thought. Two miles away, the six-year-old John was blithely unaware that, as a result of his grandfather's death, he was now the Marquess of Axholme. 'Quite right,' Annaliese said to Nicholas. 'What else? Are there any problems with my husband?'

Doctor Harrison woke up to the fact that this was his question. 'Is Your Grace thinking, perhaps, of the need for a post-mortem examination?' he asked nervously.

'Something like that, yes.'

'There is no reason why I can't sign a death certificate,' Harrison said. The surprise that greeted the remark confirmed his suspicions. 'The fact is, Lady Lincolnshire, your husband had been unwell for three years.'

'And consulting you?' Annaliese asked.

'Indeed. Since he found my advice so unpalatable, he took a second opinion, a London man by the name of Murdoch. From what I was able to glean, his view was the same as mine – His Grace should have rested more, given up smoking, and taken the medicine we both prescribed.'

'I see.' Annaliese turned to look at Edward, shook her head sadly, and said, 'Thank you, Doctor Harrison.' Correctly interpreting this as a polite dismissal, he left the room.

'I *had* wondered whether he'd seen Harrison or Murdoch,' Nicholas admitted. 'He wasn't too good on the train coming home. He had a funny turn last month when we went to Exeter – and there were others.'

'What did he do?' Annaliese asked gently. 'Guzzle brandy?'

Nicholas nodded.

'Well, there we are,' Annaliese said and patted one of Edward's hands.

'Er . . . he asked me to tell you a couple of things,' Nicholas said.

'When was this?' Annaliese inquired.

'Down there, in the hall, after he'd collapsed.'

'Go on,' Annaliese said, her voice quavering.

'He said you had to be strong. I was to remind you that when you first came here, everyone thought you were entitled to be a duchess in your own right. Act accordingly, were his words.'

'I see.' Annaliese had a shrewd idea what had been in Edward's mind. 'And the other thing?'

'He said that he was thinking of the day you and he escaped from Berlin.' Gravely, Nicholas added, 'He got it out as he died. Does that make sense?'

'Yes,' Annaliese whispered. 'I understand.' She let the tears come, weeping for the hopes of 1919, the failure of the years that followed, and for Edward, who had probably tried too hard to be a good man.

When George reached the Castle two hours later, she was in control of herself once more. Mother and son embraced, clung to each other; and Annaliese asked, 'Would you like to see him?'

Unnerved, George shook his head. 'No, I don't think so. I'll remember him as he was.'

Impassively, Annaliese summoned the butler. 'Osbourne, will you tell the undertaker that he can take my husband's body away,' she said.

'Very well, Your Grace.'

It was left to George to voice Osbourne's thoughts. 'You're being very efficient, Mother.'

'One has to be at a time like this,' was the crisp reply. 'I've been in touch with the lawyers and they'll be here tomorrow morning. Unless you have any objection, I think the funeral should be delayed until next Thursday – an awful lot of people will want to come and we need time to make the plans and contact them all.'

Puzzled, George asked, 'Why should I object?'

Annaliese's manner softened. 'Because, my darling, *you* are now the Duke of Lincolnshire. Your word is as strong as the law in Compton Allardyce and everyone must comply with your wishes.' With a brave attempt at a cheerful smile, she added, 'That includes me.'

George rubbed his chin, eyed the decanters on the sideboard and helped himself to a treble whisky. 'It's going to take me a long time to get used to it,' he said shakily.

'That's perfectly understandable,' Annaliese assured him. 'To be honest, I don't think your father *ever* accepted it. Oh, I know he seemed at ease over the last ten years, but I'm sure he wouldn't have minded being rid of it all.'

'It was thrust on him,' George mused. 'At a few days' notice.'

'Whereas you've had twenty years to prepare yourself.' Annaliese was alluding to the time that had elapsed since Douglas's death in Normandy.

'I'm not sure it's done much good,' George said unhappily. 'You'll help, won't you?'

'Naturally.'

'I say . . .' George hesitated, then plunged in. 'Would you like to carry on running this place?'

'Very much,' Annaliese replied, her eyes glowing at the prospect. 'Are you really not interested?'

'Interest hardly enters into it,' George replied. 'I'm not *competent* to do one-tenth of the things you deal with.'

'It's no good denying it, I'm glad.' Annaliese said. 'I'd dread having nothing to occupy me.' A new thought struck her. 'What about the House of Lords? Will you take your seat?'

'I don't *have* to, do I?' George asked. 'Politics isn't for me.'

'As far as I know, you can ignore it,' Annaliese said. 'Piers seems to. I'll check. So, you'll stick to Boothby's?'

'I'm very happy there,' George said. 'And, no matter what she thinks, Athene isn't *quite* ready to take over yet – she needs a few more years.'

'Darling, you must do whatever makes you feel good and comfortable,' Annaliese replied. 'Now, listen to me, if everything has gone according to plan – and God help those involved if it hasn't – news of your father's death won't have reached The Chantry. I thought it best if you told the children.'

'Thank you, that's a good idea. I'll talk to them after breakfast.'

'And Kate, too,' Annaliese said.

'Of course.' Startled by Annaliese's sudden dismay, George asked, 'What's wrong?'

'I should have thought of it before,' Annaliese moaned. 'What if Olivia lets the cat out of the bag? I assume she went straight to The Chantry, which was considerate of her.'

George's face turned crimson. 'Actually, Mother, Olivia didn't come with me,' he said.

'*She didn't come with you?*' Annaliese was incredulous. 'Why not?'

'She's away – visiting friends.'

'What friends? Where?'

'I don't know,' George admitted wretchedly.

As Annaliese stared at him, wondering what sort of madhouse she had been plunged into, her disbelief turned to anger. 'Is this a regular occurrence?' she demanded. 'Not knowing where your wife is?'

'Er . . . no. A bit of a special event, that's all. It won't happen again. I'm sure she'll be here tomorrow.'

'I *do* hope so!' Annaliese retorted icily.

After that, there was nothing for George to do except finish his drink and go. Driving slowly towards The Chantry through the balmy summer night, he doubted if he had ever seen his mother so annoyed. But who could blame her? Entering the house like a thief so as not to wake up the twins or Kate, he crept up to his bedroom and spent a long time on the telephone. His frantic inquiries, mixed with professions of unconcern and weak excuses, yielded nothing. No one had the faintest idea of where Olivia was.

At the Castle, Annaliese sipped a little whisky and told herself to calm down. Was it likely that, with Edward barely cold, his misgivings about Olivia would be proved correct? No, of course not!

Treating herself to a spot more whisky, Annaliese went to the sitting-room that had always served as an office and began to write to Kurt Schneider. After a baldly factual statement of what she had found when she returned from her two weeks with him, Annaliese gave a long account of how she had come to meet and marry the man who was, out of the blue and against his will, to become the Duke of Lincolnshire. She spent over two hours at the desk and, when it was done, realised that she had passed through a form of catharsis.

It was not until 5.30 on the following afternoon that Olivia reached The Chantry, the radio of the E-Type blaring raucously. She had stayed on the Isle of Wight rather longer than intended, but Adrian Mayhew had been worth every second of it. An even finer sexual athlete than dear Simon, he had the advantage of wealth – which meant that he knew how to live – and an utter disregard for his wife, an area in which Simon was becoming excessively painful.

Olivia was astonished to see George charging out of the house like a lunatic. He intended to vent his feelings, taking advantage of the fact that John and Valerie were safely out of the way, visiting the Castle with Kate.

'Where the hell have you been?' George shouted. 'And turn that bloody noise off!'

In her own good time, Olivia reached out to the radio. With what she thought was superb acidity, she said, 'I've been living my life, darling, as we agreed. Do you remember?'

Calming down, George said, 'Did you call in at Cadogan Square?'

'No, I came straight here.'

'You didn't get *any* of my messages?'

'Sorry, darling, I didn't.' Olivia went through the motions of looking conscience-stricken, saw that it was having no effect and said, 'What's wrong? Has something *happened*?'

George opened the door of the Jaguar. 'Please get out,' he said, grinding his teeth with the effort to be reasonable. Olivia did so, making sure that her mini-dress rode up to show most of her thighs.

'Is there some sort of drama in progress?' she inquired, affecting monumental boredom.

Shaking with rage, George replied, 'I suppose you could put it that way. My father died yesterday evening.'

Olivia gasped and stepped back, bumping into the car. What sort of mess had her absence landed her in? Did this mean that Sunday night with Simon was in jeopardy? More to the point, what about Adrian on Tuesday? Belatedly and weakly, she said, 'I'm sorry – very sorry.'

'Spare me the hypocrisy,' George snarled. 'Have you the faintest idea of how much you've embarrassed me? My mother is furious. Do you think you could use your apology for a mind to decide what you're going to do about it, how you might make amends?'

Incensed by the reference to her intellectual mediocrity, a subject that George had tactfully avoided until now, Olivia lashed out, striking his face with all the violent strength she could summon. It hurt and amazed him. Olivia's first reaction was vindictive satisfaction: she had been longing to do something like that for at least two years. Then, she realised that they were no longer alone. The Morris Minor estate car, in which Kate drove the children round the Park and on outings to Marlborough, had cruised to a halt only feet away.

Quietly, both subdued, John and Valerie got out. John, disgusted by what he had seen, walked purposefully towards the house and disappeared inside. Valerie, precociously grown-up at six and no longer afraid of Olivia, gave her a withering look. '*We've* been to the Chapel,' she announced. 'We saw them bring Grandpapa back in his coffin. It was very nice. Grandmama and Great Aunt Beatrice had a little cry. Why weren't you there, Mother?'

Not waiting for a reply, Lady Valerie stomped after her brother.

Inexplicably distressed by her daughter's obvious hatred, Olivia reached for George, appreciating the necessity to beg his forgiveness and make a temporary peace. He had gone, walking towards Kate.

'Valerie mentioned Beatrice,' George said. 'When did she arrive?'

'In time for lunch,' Kate replied. 'Matthew brought her.'

'How is she?'

Kate pulled a face. 'Shocked. Very upset. She was fond of your father.'

'Oh.' George shook his head. 'I was under the impression that they'd drifted apart.'

Once in a while, Kate experienced Annaliese's desire to shake some common sense into George. Restraining herself, she said, 'They had a very happy childhood together. Bonds like that never break, no matter what happens in later life.'

'Did Beatrice tell you that?' George asked.

'More or less.' Kate looked at him in a way that somehow contrived to be both affectionate and mocking. 'That was quite a humdinger she gave you, George. The skin's broken.'

Resisting the urge to dab at his face, George muttered something about the bathroom and hurried indoors, leaving Kate and Olivia staring at each other. For once, Olivia was out of her depth, awkwardly unsure of herself. There was no hope of her being subdued for more than a few hours, Kate thought. The bitch had landed herself in such a heap of cow plop that the full significance of Edward's death hadn't dawned on her. It wouldn't take long.

In the days leading up to the funeral, George kept himself extremely busy, helping Annaliese with the arrangements and avoiding Olivia. She was given ample opportunity to make telephone calls to Simon Faulkener and Adrian Mayhew, informing them of the crisis that prevented her seeing them for a few days, but became alarmed at not being able to engineer a few minutes alone with George. Eventually, she was left with only one possible chance. On the night before the funeral, having waited for the house to fall silent, Olivia padded along the landing to George's bedroom.

She went in to find him emerging from the *en suite* bathroom, a towel draped across his shoulders. Otherwise, he was naked and, to Olivia's amused surprise, his penis was fully erect. Amazingly, however, he was unabashed and combative, snapping, 'What the devil do you want?'

'I wanted to say how sorry I am, darling,' Olivia replied. 'Sorry for being away *and* for flying off the handle when I did get back. It won't happen again.'

'Of course it won't,' George snapped. 'The situation was unique. My father can only die once.'

Olivia was alarmed. Two months ago, Adrian Mayhew had warned her to be more careful. 'Even if your husband *is* the complete idiot you make him out to be, worms can turn, you know, and they're often surprisingly nasty when they do. A bitch like you could goad a lap-dog into acting like a tiger.' The opinion of Mayhew, who was an utter bastard and virtuoso exploiter of human nature, carried a great deal of weight with Olivia.

'I don't blame you for being cross,' she said. 'What I meant was, I'll be more careful in future.'

'I'm sure we shall all be suitably grateful,' George said. Tossing the towel into the bathroom, he walked towards the bed, where he pulled back the blankets and top sheet. Glaring at Olivia, he said, 'Is that it? Do I get some peace now?'

Intrigued by his continuing arousal, Olivia gambled. 'Is there anything I can do for you?'

George glared at her, apparently unmoved. Shrugging, Olivia said, 'As you wish – if you think you can make a better job of it than I would, carry on. That *is* what you intended doing, I presume?' She turned away, making for the door.

'No, don't go.' George's manner had changed dramatically; suddenly, he was pleading.

'It *is* a long time since you had a treat,' Olivia said, crossing to the bed. 'You should let me do this more often, darling. I like it.'

'You're never around when I need you,' George grumbled.

'Well, I am now. Get yourself nice and comfortable.'

George moaned as her fingers closed expertly round his hardness. Part of him knew that he was making a fool of himself; Olivia's eyes confirmed it. But he was helpless.

'Relax,' Olivia murmured. 'You've had a terrible few days. I'll make you feel better, mmm?' Bending over him, she whispered into his ear. 'Who does this best, I wonder – me, or your friend, Tony. Are you thinking of him now?'

George's mind played a strange trick on him. As he

succumbed to Olivia's cunning manipulation, it was Athene who slipped into his thoughts. Athene: the girl who would have been Duchess of Lincolnshire now but for that damnable blank space on her birth certificate.

The day of Edward's funeral was fine and bright, but rather chilly. This pleased Annaliese, who had feared that some of the older guests might suffer if the heatwave continued.

Nearly a thousand came. The aristocracy turned out in force to express solidarity and sympathy, to see and be seen, and to witness the moving spectacle of a senior peer being buried in his own private vault at the centre of 8,000 incomparable acres. The Foreign Office and Government had sent representatives, as had the Conservative Party and Edward's club, Fisk's. Every good cause supported by Compton Allardyce had rallied, and so, of course, had tenants and estate workers. Nigel Templeton brought nearly thirty friends from the City of London, prompting Annaliese to wonder what Edward might have been up to since the Suez fiasco had given him time to extend his brilliant mind into other fields. Finally, although Edward had played no part in the firm, the Boothby's contingent was strong.

Steeling herself to behave exceptionally well, Olivia chivvied George into driving to the Castle half an hour earlier than the time stipulated in the plan. Demure in a black dress that was almost frumpishly long and shapeless, Olivia was able to talk to Annaliese, begging forgiveness for her tardiness in reaching Compton Allardyce after Edward's death. The excuse she offered, though over-elaborate, was convincing enough and Annaliese, her mind on other things, was inclined to accept it. Later, taking advantage of a few minutes alone with Annaliese to express her condolences, Caroline Dorchester let slip a few comments that were calculated to corroborate her daughter's story. 'Olivia was desperately upset about it,' Caroline said in the manner of one betraying a confidence. 'When she telephoned with the news about poor Edward, she was *terrified* of what you might think of her.'

'It's all forgotten and forgiven,' Annaliese replied. 'To be honest, Caroline, I wonder if George wasn't slightly at fault. He can be so absent-minded sometimes. Come along, my dear, it's time we went into the Chapel.'

The sombre ceremony had an enchanting feature that came as a surprise to everyone except George and Kate. The choir, a mixture of boys and men from the village and a church in Pewsey, included the twins. Valerie made no attempt to sing; the sole reason for her presence was that she had categorically refused to be anywhere other than at John's side. His contribution, made in a voice of sublime purity and great strength for one so young, aroused considerable interest. Accompanied by Valerie, John was one of the small group that followed Edward's coffin down into the vault for the final part of the liturgy. When he sang the five verses of Psalm 103 that were prescribed for the burial service, the 200-odd people in the Chapel were touched by the unearthly beauty of the sound that floated up the stone stairs and tunnel-like passages.

Afterwards, as Olivia and George were walking towards the Long Gallery and the traditional buffet, she said, 'I had no idea that John had such a lovely voice.'

In the nick of time, George stifled the automatic response which, though true, would probably have unleashed a bitter argument. 'He's quite good, isn't he? He sang for Father several times, so I thought it would be appropriate if he joined in today.'

'He was *so* sure of himself,' Olivia said enthusiastically.

'He's learned a lot from Kate,' George replied.

'And he plays the piano?'

'Very well. So does Valerie. They're fed up of waiting for their hands to grow bigger so that they can tackle more difficult pieces.' George was the proud father.

Smiling sweetly, Olivia said nothing, conscious that the merest slip would catapult her into the potentially dangerous territory of how little she knew about her children. And, after his performance with the choir, Olivia was surprised to find that she was jealous of her own son. It wouldn't do to betray that! She applied herself to the task of displaying the right attitude to the hawk-eyed crowd in the Long Gallery. So far, being the Duchess of Lincolnshire was proving to be an unexpected strain.

Annaliese was, of course, the centre of attraction. She sat at a table in one of the lofty, mullioned windows that gave superb views of the Park and guests queued up to offer sympathy and every sort of help. The tributes to Edward were not gushing or effusive, but warm and deeply felt; everyone considered the late Duke to have been a man who had served his country well and steered Compton Allardyce away from the scandalous horrors of 1925. In effect, he had been a safe pair of hands with a strong sense of duty. He would have been satisfied.

Two hours passed and the crowd was thinning out as the mourners, particularly those with long journeys, began to leave. Although they had no distance at all to travel, Aubrey and Caroline Dorchester – he looking more than usually unhappy – made their excuses and went. Beatrice escaped to her bedroom to rest. She was staying one more night at the Castle, then taking Annaliese to Upper Overs, removing her face from the scene of sudden death and offering the new Duke and Duchess a chance to find their feet.

No sooner was Annaliese finally alone than the twins appeared, deserting Kate to glide eel-like through the remaining guests to be with their adored grandmother.

'John, my darling, what a wonderful surprise you were,' Annaliese said, hugging him. 'You sang beautifully.'

'He's not bad,' Valerie said proprietorially. 'I think he should join a *proper* choir. So does Kate, by the way.'

'What sort of choir?' Annaliese asked, sensing that Compton Allardyce, Pewsey, and Marlborough had been weighed in the scales and found sadly lacking.

'We shall have to wait and see,' Valerie declared, terribly self-important.

Annaliese laughed. 'Do you have any views on this, John?'

'It's a good idea,' he said thoughtfully. 'I love singing.'

'That was very obvious,' Annaliese assured him. 'I was proud of you.'

Moving close to Annaliese so that she could whisper directly into her ear, Valerie began to give her unflattering opinions of some of the guests. Despite protestations that he did not care for his sister's scurrilous prattle, John pressed his face to his grandmother's other cheek, hoping to pick up a gem or two. Shaking with repressed laughter, Annaliese scanned the vast chamber, seeking out the objects of Valerie's scorn. Through a sudden parting in the crowd, which still numbered over two hundred, Annaliese caught sight of Olivia.

She was at a far corner of the Gallery, near the door that led to the West Wing and main stairs. Believing that she had done more than enough to create the required impression, and that the proceedings had reached the final, informal stage, Olivia had allowed herself the treat of a flirtatious interlude with a fascinatingly attractive man. One of Nigel Templeton's City friends and heir to a huge fortune, he was slightly Latin-looking, dark, with wicked eyes.

Since John and Valerie were deeply preoccupied, their faces pressed against hers, Annaliese took time to study the man. He looked thirty-five, was probably older, and gave off sexual energy like a furnace. His every gesture, outwardly spontaneous and impulsive, was contrived to show his companion what a tremendous fellow he was in bed. Such poseurs were as old as the hills; it was Olivia who galvanised Annaliese's interest.

No woman, let alone one wearing such an unbecoming dress, should have been capable of indulging in such a blatant exchange of carnal signals. Wishfully, weaving her supple body to and fro, Olivia was having imaginary intercourse with the wretched man. Then, Annaliese's outrage was replaced by a cold, creeping sense that she was witnessing an echo of the past. Something very like this had happened before, here, in the Long Gallery. What was it?

A movement of people hid Olivia and her would-be lover. Annaliese straightened up and Valerie drew back, offended. 'What is it, Grandmama?' she asked. 'Aren't you interested anymore?'

'I'm sorry, darling,' Annaliese said. 'Do you know, I think I must be getting old.'

A spate of departures caused the crowd to shift again, revealing that Olivia and the man had disappeared. For a few moments, Annaliese was appalled by the possibilities that suggested themselves. Then, to her immense relief, George and Olivia emerged from the centre of a closely packed group. They were holding hands and wearing brave, end-of-funeral smiles.

'Come on, you two,' George said to the twins. 'Let's leave Grandmama in peace. She must be longing to put her feet up.'

Annaliese protested – but not too strongly. The occasion had tired her rather more than she cared to admit and the prospect of leaving the stragglers to get on with it was attractive. As George shepherded John and Valerie away, Olivia kissed Annaliese and whispered a confession.

'I shan't be sorry to lie down. I'm afraid I've had too much wine and not enough food.'

She *was* flushed, Annaliese realised. Although the gathering had been for a sad purpose, some of the guests were the worse for drink, and, as they always did, were starting to behave badly. Did this explain Olivia's sensuous posturing with the swarthy Casanova? Emotionally drained and weary, Annaliese decided to accept that it did.

Edward's will was a simple document, barely altered since the death of Douglas in 1944. Under the terms of the Royal Charter that had created the dukedom in 1670, the eldest — or only — son inherited everything. There were a string of minor bequests of money from Edward's personal nest egg and a non-material codicil added as recently as 1962.

It is my hope that, unless she expressly wishes to do otherwise, my beloved wife, Annaliese, will continue to occupy the rooms in the West Wing of Allardyce Castle that have been her home since 1925. I trust that my son and heir, George, will honour this request.

Annaliese was touched by the clause and, since she had never envisaged moving, slightly amused. She raised the matter with George when he paid a mid-week visit to the Castle soon after her return from Upper Overs.

'You don't mind, do you, darling?'

'Of course not,' George replied. 'To be honest, though, I'm surprised that Father was so . . .' He searched for the right word '. . . sensitive.'

'Mmm.' Annaliese was owlishly non-committal, her smile faintly mischievous.

'Anyway, don't worry,' George said unnecessarily. 'There's plenty for us to choose from in the East Wing.'

'I hope Olivia understands,' Annaliese said.

'Oh, absolutely.' George's artificially whole-hearted response concealed the fact that he had yet to raise the issue with his wife. After two weeks at Cadogan Square, demonstrating what an accomplished hostess the new Duchess of

Lincolnshire was, Olivia had dashed off to spend three days with Adrian Mayhew at a borrowed cottage in the New Forest. After that, Simon Faulkener was being treated to a couple of days in Jersey.

Not in the least concerned as to whether her daughter-in-law liked the East Wing or not, Annaliese turned to far more important business. 'Death duties,' she said. 'Has a start been made on working out the likely damage?'

'Nigel's doing it,' George said. 'He and I are having a preliminary meeting with the Inland Revenue next month.' He smiled ruefully. 'It seems that Father spirited a million and a half out of the country on the day he died.'

'Well done!' Annaliese clapped her hands. But, after thinking about it for a moment, she was not so sure. 'I suppose it's doubtful if we shall be able to get away with that?'

'Nigel thinks we should try,' George replied.

'You don't?'

'It could be risky. That money came from the sale of several properties. The details of the transaction must be recorded in several places, so the Revenue will want to know what became of the proceeds. Nigel says he can do conjuring tricks on our London accounts and I've told him to have a go. But I shall surrender if it looks like getting awkward.'

'Why?' Annaliese challenged.

'I don't want to give some over-zealous tax inspector a pointer to Switzerland.'

'Ah, I see.' Annaliese, fearful that George was suffering from a chronic increase in his sense of social conscience, relaxed and smiled. This was good, old-fashioned *realpolitik*, reminiscent of her Vienna.

'What about Glengrantach?' George asked. 'Do you think we should get rid of it? You've never liked it.'

'I never went there!' Annaliese laughed. 'It's always *sounded* such a dire place. Incredible though it may seem, I have no idea what it looks like, where it is, or how many servants we employ there.' Serious again, she shook her head. 'But I don't think we should sell it. In the first place, your father loved it.' She fell into wistful contemplation of Edward's two or three weeks in Scotland almost every year.

'And in the second place?' George prompted gently.

'It's making a fortune.' Firmly back in the present, Annaliese fixed George with a determined stare. 'Nicholas is letting the shooting rights to all sorts of strange people.'

'Americans?' George suggested.

'Oh, they're the least of the problems,' Annaliese said. 'Nicholas talks about haulage contractors and estate agents clamouring to hire guns.' She threw up her hands, looked extremely Habsburg, and calmed down. 'When the death duties have been agreed, perhaps you'll tell me what's needed. If necessary, I'll help.'

'You?' George was flummoxed. When the right moment arrived – together with the requisite courage – he had been intending to broach the delicate subject of an allowance. He wasn't having Annaliese turning into one of the penniless aristocratic widows who were meat and drink to the popular press.

'George, my dear, let me tell you a secret.' To emphasise the strict confidentiality of what she was about to say, Annaliese leaned forward to tap his knee. 'There are *two* accounts in Zurich, the one that now belongs to you, and the one that I've had since 1946. I set it up with the money my mother left me.'

'Yes. I see.' George nodded. 'How much have you got?'

'Enough to see you and your children through almost anything you can think of,' Annaliese replied, wondering why she was disinclined to tell George the plain truth. In twenty years, the original £4 million had, with the accumulated interest, grown to over £10 million.

Laughing indulgently, George said, 'All right, if I'm strapped for a few hundred, I know where to get it. Seriously, though, Mother, do you need an allowance?'

'Can you set me against tax?' Annaliese asked.

'Yes, especially if you carry on running the estate.'

'In that case, I'll have fifteen thousand a year.'

'Is that enough?' George asked.

'I shall manage,' Annaliese sighed, playing the martyr but let down by the twinkle in her eyes. 'So, you think we shan't suffer too badly with death duties?'

'Nigel seems optimistic,' George said. 'The important thing is that Father died before Harold Wilson and his cronies could get their grubby hands on the tax system.'

Annaliese smiled warmly, convinced that Edward would be enjoying that thought. Leaning back in her chair, she was content as she realised that there was no question of the proverbial rainy day, the sort of financial catastrophe that could bring a great family down before anyone knew what was happening. The Falkenberg emeralds would continue to nestle under the floor-boards beside her bed.

Reminded of her greatest asset, Annaliese understood the reason for her reticence over the money in Zurich. Despite George's repeated assurances that all was well with his marriage, Annaliese had a growing mistrust of Olivia: and, because of his wife, poor George was vaguely suspect, somehow unreliable.

When it was eventually put to her, the idea of living in the East Wing infuriated Olivia.

At odd times during the eight years since she had married George, she had made it her business to explore every inch of Allardyce Castle. As a result of her prowling and snooping, Olivia knew the East Wing and disliked it intensely. For her, the atmosphere was badly wrong, drawing attention to the fact that it was over sixty years since this part of the building had been used as anything other than a fading showcase. Hoping that she had found a powerful negotiating lever, she pointed out that it would cost a fortune to make even the ground floor truly habitable.

'I appreciate that,' George said. 'It will also take a longish time, so I've asked the decorators to start next Monday.'

Olivia paraded a stream of other objections, including the distance of the East Wing from the kitchens and its lack of sun, except during the early part of the morning in midsummer. Blithely ignoring her and the possible consequences of his high-handedness, George pressed on.

However, when the twins were shown the rooms that had been earmarked for them, Valerie was disgusted. For the first – and, as things were to turn out, only time in her life – she agreed with Olivia. 'This isn't a bit nice,' she informed George. After another look, she went further. 'It's *nasty*.'

'You're seeing it at a very bad time, sweetheart,' George replied. 'Perhaps I should have waited until everything's finished.'

Valerie wrinkled her nose. 'That won't make any difference.' She turned to John, who nodded. The gesture, barely perceptible and devoid of emotion was, nevertheless, damning.

'Well, what am I to do?' George asked, painfully aware that he was close to pleading.

For once, it was John who took the lead. 'We're settled at The Chantry, Papa. Why can't *we* carry on living there with Kate?'

'Yes,' Valerie said, 'that's best.'

Since George felt obliged to make some sort of a stand, there was an argument that rumbled on for a week. In the end, it was John's pained silence as much as Valerie's tantrums that carried the day. To Kate's amazement, George caved in.

Apparently without the faintest idea of the damage he was doing to his last hopes of enjoying anything remotely resembling a normal family life, he agreed that the twins and Kate, together with a cook and two maids, should continue to live at The Chantry. He, fully involved with Boothby's from Monday to Friday, would stay in the East Wing at weekends, dividing the time between the children and his obligations as Duke of Lincolnshire.

In response to a tentative question from Kate, Annaliese was flippantly dismissive. 'My dear, we've always been unconventional. Do you know, when Douglas and George were at Winchester, we had to deliver and collect them *separately*? In two different cars, if you please!'

'Why?'

'Douglas was such a toff that he couldn't be seen associating with a younger brother. One gets used to these things.'

The ludicrous arrangement presented Olivia with fresh, unlimited licence to do whatever she liked whenever the mood took her. She became craftily adept at creating the illusion that she spent far more time at Compton Allardyce than the brief, twice-weekly visits that were a very small part of her feverish routine. Annaliese, who was busier than ever now that she had assumed responsibility for the whole of the Lincolnshire estates on top of her other commitments, was always profoundly glad to see the back of Olivia. She failed to appreciate that her daughter-in-law's exuberant interruptions, usually involving requests for trivial information or offers of worthless help, were calculated to produce relief at her departure.

When Kate was alone with Annaliese, she often wondered if she ought to sound warnings about George and Olivia's strange way of life. Largely because she enjoyed having the children to herself at The Chantry, she never did.

One crisp November afternoon, Annaliese insisted on

walking all the way to Gainsborough Wood to inspect progress on her latest pet project, yet another new drainage and replanting scheme. Managing to break into the flood of enthusiastic description of the work and its benefits, Kate said, 'You're really enjoying yourself these days, aren't you? Being the Dowager Duchess really suits you.'

Immediately, Annaliese's smile was replaced by a petulant scowl. 'No it doesn't,' she grumbled. 'I hate it. Dowager, indeed. Pah!'

'Actually, most people still think of you as *the* Duchess,' Kate said, immediately wondering if she had gone too far.

'Well, they would, wouldn't they?' Annaliese snapped. Then, in one of those mercurial changes of mood that often left Kate open-mouthed, her eyes lit up and she was smiling again. Unfastening the top buttons of her long sheepskin coat, Annaliese parted the lapels to show off the brooch on her left breast. It had once belonged to the Empress Maria Theresa and depicted the Habsburg double-headed eagle, jet-black on a white, enamel background.

'Never mind the Dowager nonsense,' Annaliese said. 'I'm still an Archduchess of Austria. That's much more important.'

19

1966
'It was a close-run thing, wasn't it?'

Cornelius Goss, Director of Music and composer of church anthems, was a man who concealed discerning sensitivity and a readiness to be moved to tears behind the autocratic façade of a martinet.

As Organist and Master of the Choristers at Salisbury Cathedral, he was constantly looking for young boys to replace those whose voices were about to break. Quite often, this meant enduring auditions that were painful: most of the applicants were untalented screechers with tone-deaf parents who had an infinite capacity for self-delusion. Very, *very* occasionally, however, and invariably when least expected, a jewel would appear and Cornelius Goss's jaundiced opinion of the human race was replaced by a short period of euphoria.

On a Thursday afternoon in May, choirs from all over Wiltshire travelled to Salisbury to give a concert in the Cathedral. It was an annual event to reward the efforts of parishes, parents, and legions of loyal helpers by giving them a taste of glory in the mother church of the diocese. Invariably,

Cornelius Goss sat hidden in the South Transept while his deputy played the organ. During performances that he deemed unbearably bad, Goss would disappear into the Cloisters.

That afternoon, he spent longer than usual pacing the well-worn flagstones. At 4.15, when the programme was almost over, Goss was thinking of going across the Close for a cup of tea with his good friend Mrs Darley-Stevenson when the Cathedral's best tenor came to tell him that the last choir, a composite group from churches in the Marlborough area, were about to tackle Thomas Tallis's monumental forty-part motet, *Spem in Alium*. Might it not be interesting? Not at all sure why he did so – for the risks of failure with such a complex piece were high, even for trained professionals – Goss went back into the Cathedral.

Soon, he was creeping along the South Choir Aisle, hoping to catch a glimpse of the boy who was singing the exacting first treble part. As luck would have it, he was in the stalls on the north side and visible through the screen in front of the Mompesson Monument.

Goss was transfixed. The boy soared and billowed above Tallis's fine web of polyphony, producing an effortless flow of heart-piercing, liquid silver sound. It was one of the most sublime voices that Goss had ever heard, so spellbinding that several minutes passed before he spotted an oddity. Standing beside the boy was a girl, virtually identical, just as fascinatingly beautiful. She did not sing and spent most of the time staring at the boy, apparently peering into his ear. He ignored her until the last chords finally faded into the airy vastness of the great church, then they exchanged brief smiles.

It was beneath Cornelius Goss's dignity to go anywhere near the mêlée of reunions and scrambling for front seats on homeward-bound coaches that followed the event. Next morning, one telephone call told him what he wanted to know: the boy was John Boothby-Graffoe, the eight-year-old Marquess of Axholme. For what the information was worth, the girl was Lady Valerie, his twin sister. Goss went to see his ally, the Dean.

The idea of having young Lord Axholme in the Cathedral Choir was appealing. Although the old Duke of Lincolnshire had shown precious little interest in the diocese, his successor was known to be much more favourably disposed – if only because the Bishop had officiated at his wedding and the baptism of the twins.

'You've got your sights set on that new roof for the Chapter House,' Goss said.

The Dean dismissed the distastefully mercenary suggestion with a fastidious wave of his hand. 'As it happens, Cornelius, I shall be seeing the boy's grandmother, the Dowager Duchess, next Tuesday. We sit on a committee together. Do you wish me to raise the matter?'

'I must have that boy in my choir,' Goss said. 'I *must*.'

Annaliese was delighted by the Dean's suggestion and arranged for Cornelius Goss to talk to John. The meeting took place at The Chantry and was, Goss thought, a success but for the distinctly unnerving presence of Valerie, silent and wary. She was, Annaliese later explained to Cornelius Goss, assessing whether he was in charge of a 'proper' choir.

A formal letter followed, offering John a place at Salisbury Cathedral Choir School in September. Choristers, it was stressed, were required to be boarders and available at all times. By return of post, John sent an impeccably written rejection.

Cornelius Goss had the wit to contact George at Boothby's.

'I'm sorry John turned you down,' George said. 'I hope he was polite about it.'

'Extremely so, Your Grace.'

'You see, Doctor Goss, John has been promised that he will be educated at home. I can't see him warming to the idea of school, especially one where he has to stay all the time. There's also his sister to be considered – they tend to be inseparable.'

'I believe I've seen evidence of that,' Goss said drily.

There was a pause while both men considered possible solutions.

'I would like John to be in the Cathedral Choir,' George said at last.

'In that case, we have common cause,' Goss replied. 'For a boy as talented as your son, I might be able to make concessions – bend the rules somewhat.'

Reaching for his diary, George said, 'Let's arrange to get together and chat.'

What happened during the next three weeks would, Annaliese said, have delighted Edward. 'I've never seen anything like it,' she told George. 'This must be how they negotiate international treaties. Your father would have wanted to join in.'

'I wonder if he could have done anything about Valerie?' George muttered. 'That young lady is asking to have her neck wrung.'

'You'll find that she knows exactly how far she can go,' Annaliese chuckled. 'It will be judged to a nicety.'

She was right. The following day, after Cornelius Goss's fourth letter, Valerie graciously accepted the revised terms.

John was to be a day boy at the Cathedral School. As if that concession weren't enough, his only compulsory activities were to be music lessons and duties with the Choir. However, since Compton Allardyce was twenty miles from Salisbury, a distance considered too great to be covered up to four times a day, Cornelius Goss insisted that John should live in Salisbury.

To the amazement of Olivia, who had taken a passing interest in the proceedings, George declared his intention of solving this final problem by buying a house in Salisbury. Olivia told Adrian Mayhew about it as they recovered from an afternoon of love-making at the cottage in the New Forest.

'You're joking,' was his amused response.

'I am not.' For a moment or two, Olivia was furiously straight-faced, then she shrieked with laughter. 'We shall be a four-home family. It's true – count them. Cadogan Square, the Castle, The Chantry, and now this new place in Salisbury. Have you ever heard of anything so absolutely bloody ridiculous in all your life?'

'You won't catch me complaining.' Propped up against the pillows, Mayhew studied Olivia's body. She was thirty-four and, he judged, at her physical peak. None of the others were quite as classy as Olivia, or had her single-minded addiction to sexual pleasure. Despite her selfish unpredictability, she was worth the effort for another twelve months or so. 'Won't an extra house mean that your loving husband will take even less interest in you?' Mayhew asked.

The shrug of the shoulders with which Olivia displayed her utter indifference produced a thrilling movement of her breasts.

The house-hunting party, consisting of George, Kate and the twins struck it lucky at the first attempt, less than half an hour after arriving in Salisbury. The property, an elegant Edwardian villa in Shady Bower at the top of Milford Hill, had vacant possession. Its owner, the widow of a surgeon, had tired of a place that was far too big for her and moved to a modern bungalow in Bournemouth. The house was given the thumbs up by Valerie, John nodded, Kate reckoned that she could learn to like it, and George went back to the agent to make an offer that was accepted without quibble.

At the end of August, after four frantic weeks of buying furniture – including a concert grand piano – and arranging for carpets and curtains to be fitted, John, Valerie, and Kate, with a cook and one of the maids from The Chantry moved in. Until John's voice broke, the house in Shady Bower was to be their home. He thought he would like to go back to Compton Allardyce occasionally, but happily accepted that holidays would be short and infrequent – none at Christmas and Easter, and only three weeks in summer. For the honour of singing in Salisbury Cathedral and the gift of Cornelius Goss's guidance and approval, John would cheerfully have done without a single day off until his voice deserted him – something he was already starting to dread.

A routine was soon established. On weekdays, John's singing lessons began at 8.00 each morning. After delivering him to the Cathedral, Kate went back to Shady Bower and taught Valerie for two hours. Tremendously proud of John, his twin adapted to his absence far better than Kate had feared. At 10.15, they drove to the Close, collected John, and had more lessons until lunch at 12.15. Work began again half an hour later and continued until 3.00, when John was taken back to the Cathedral to sing in Choral Evensong. Kate and Valerie listened to the service from seats reserved for them in the New Sanctuary which gave the twins a good view of each other. Afterwards, at about 4.15, they returned to the house and more lessons, or, if it was one of her days for a Salisbury committee meeting, tea with Annaliese.

Saturdays were quieter, Sundays very busy. Apart from the extra services, beginning with a sung Eucharist at 7.30 am, it was George's day for visiting. Keeping unobtrusively in the background on Sundays, Kate was always touched by George's love for the children and theirs for him.

Olivia never came to Salisbury. As autumn advanced to the point where dusk was falling as Kate urged the Morris Minor up Milford Hill after Choral Evensong, it seemed that the twins' natural mother had ceased to exist.

George allowed himself to drift into the same delusion.

Consequently, when he returned to Cadogan Square at midnight on a Tuesday in mid-November, it came as an unpleasant surprise to find Olivia waiting for him. Pale and drawn, she dashed into the entrance-hall when she heard the front door. After a long day and an exhausting evening with Tony Austen-Cave, George made no attempt to conceal his irritation with a nuisance that threatened to keep him from his bed.

'What are you doing here?' he demanded. 'I thought you were away all week.'

'Yes, that *was* the plan.' Olivia was subdued and taking care not to rise to the provocation of George's exasperation. 'I'm afraid that something has sort of cropped up.'

Unlikely though it was that Olivia could possibly be the bearer of such news, George asked, 'It's not the children? There's nothing wrong?'

'No, they're all right – well, as far as I know, of course.' Olivia looked wretched.

Briefly tempted to reply with sarcasm, George let it pass. 'What, then?' he asked.

Looking round furtively, imagining a servant lurking within earshot, Olivia moved towards the sitting-room door. 'In here,' she said, hurriedly adding, '*Please.*'

She perched on the arm of the sofa, George remained standing, his back against the door. 'Well?' he said when Olivia showed no inclination to speak.

'Er . . . something has cropped up.'

'So you said. What is it, for heaven's sake?'

Jumping up like a startled animal, Olivia rushed to the sideboard for a drink. With her back to George, she said, 'I'm going to be named as a co-respondent in a divorce.'

Dismayed by the silence, Olivia took a gulp of brandy and turned. George had moved away from the door and was resting his hands on the back of a chair, staring into space. His expression, apparently a mixture of bewilderment and calculation was unfathomable.

'We agreed to be discreet,' he said at last. 'You hammered the point home endlessly.'

'Damn it, I *was*!' Olivia's feelings, pent-up for eight hours, exploded into an anger that brought an unflattering colour to her face. 'We were so careful, it was like the bloody secret service. How was I to know that his wife was having us watched by a private detective? Imagine it, some oik in a greasy mac was spying on us! How low can you get, for Christ's sake?'

Slowly and carefully, George took off his overcoat, folded it with painstaking precision, and placed it on the chair against which he had been supporting himself. The over-elaborate pantomime was designed to keep him calm. Wandering to the sideboard, he filled a glass from the soda siphon, hoping that the gassy water would dispel the aftermath of the cheap, raw wine that Tony had sworn was a château-bottled claret.

George drank deeply, breathed in and belched spectacularly.

'Is that your considered opinion?' Olivia shouted.

'No, it isn't. Please forgive me.' George raised his empty glass in a gesture of mock apology.

'So what *do* you think?'

'What do *I* think?' George was amused by the question. 'Well, my dear, the first thing that occurs to me is that you will be dragged through the dirt.'

'*Really*?' Olivia was panic-stricken. 'I *have* been worrying about that.'

'Since when?' George said mildly. 'When did you find out?'

'I met him this afternoon.' Olivia needed more brandy. 'His wife sprang it on him this morning, as he was leaving.'

'To meet you?'

'Yes.'

George savoured the entertaining nuances of the assignation that had obviously gone horribly wrong. It was more than likely that the man had expected to drop his bombshell – in a casual sort of way – laugh it off, and continue with the planned four days.

'Will there be a lot of publicity?' Olivia asked.

'I would have thought so,' George replied. 'You *are* something of a celebrity – very glamorous. The press will be on to it like vultures.'

'God!' Olivia buried her head in her hands.

'Actually, it isn't the press that worries me,' George said, still bland. 'We have something far, far worse to consider.'

'What?' Olivia shrieked, her eyes dilated by fear.

'My mother.' George was studying the bottles on the sideboard, wondering whether a tot of whisky would finally settle his stomach. He turned round to find Olivia gaping at him, wide-eyed, aghast.

Seeing that she was incapable of speech, George explained. 'It won't be your name that ends up in the gutter, it will be mine – Boothby-Graffoe and Lincolnshire. Mother isn't going to care for that.'

There was a whiff of deceitful flippancy about the last part of George's statement which alerted Olivia to an imminent change of mood. She waited.

Deciding against whisky, George continued. 'We must talk to my mother. Soon.'

'What for?' Olivia screamed. 'Why does she need to know?'

'She's the head of the family that you're going to disgrace.'

'No, she isn't, you are.' Olivia's attempt at defiance

emerged as a petulantly childish squeal.

'Only in name,' George replied. 'Mother's far better at it than me.'

'I thought we could sort something out between ourselves,' Olivia protested. 'Surely, we must be able to?'

'No.' George shook his head vigorously. 'Frankly, I wouldn't know where to start. This is all beyond me. I shall telephone Mother in the morning and arrange to see her.' The last remnants of his mild manner disappeared and a steely anger that was quite unlike anything he had ever shown before took over. 'We shall, of course, go together, you and I. In the meantime, you will stay inside this house and wait to hear from me. Is that clear?'

In a voice that neither of them recognised, Olivia said, 'Yes, all right.'

Nastily, George pressed the point, making another implied reference to the lack of brain power that was usually concealed by her selfish cunning. 'You are *capable* of understanding that simple instruction, I take it?'

Olivia nodded.

After glaring at her for an uncomfortably long time, George left the room. Rushing for more brandy, Olivia realised that he hadn't bothered to ask for details of the man whose wife was threatening trouble – not even his name.

They went to Compton Allardyce the following afternoon. Irritated by George's alarmingly cryptic telephone call, Annaliese had promised him an hour before she went to Eaton Mandeville to dine with Piers and Rachel Laverstoke.

'Well, what's this about?' Annaliese asked. Installed behind the desk in the sitting-room she used as an office, she looked like an imposing but benign headmistress. 'Why the mystery and fuss?'

George, who had driven all the way from London in

silence, wanted no truck with preliminaries. 'Olivia tells me that she is to be named as the co-respondent in a divorce case,' he said, completely shut off from the woman to whom he was referring.

'Goodness me!' Annaliese became a mildly startled head-mistress, assimilating news that might prove to be amusing when she got used to it. Turning to Olivia, she said, 'Is this true? George hasn't gone off his head?'

'It's true, I'm afraid,' Olivia said meekly.

'This is a wife who thinks you've been having an affair with her husband?' Annaliese asked.

'Yes.'

'Now, be honest with me, my dear,' Annaliese said, 'is the accusation true, or false?'

'True, but . . .'

'Let's not worry about the "buts" at the moment,' Annaliese cut in. She reached for the telephone. 'I'd better let Piers know that I shan't be able to see him this evening – such a pity, I was looking forward to it. Olivia, would I be right in thinking that you need a drink? Will you see to that, please, George. Oh, and tell Osbourne that I shall want dinner. You, too, I expect.'

Olivia sat through the next two minutes in a trance. The call to Eaton Mandeville was made with poised, apologetic charm. George returned with a tray of drinks and Olivia grabbed at a tumbler half full of neat brandy, hoping that, if nothing else, it would ease her hangover.

After sipping at orange juice, Annaliese reached for a pencil. 'The man's name?' she asked.

'Adrian Mayhew,' Olivia replied.

Before writing the name down, Annaliese noticed that it meant nothing to George. 'His address?' she said.

Olivia gave it, together with a telephone number.

'The name of his wife?'

'Susan.'

'Their ages?'

'He's thirty-eight, she's about twenty-seven.'

'How long have they been married?'

'Six years.'

'Do they have children?'

'No.'

Gazing steadily at Olivia, Annaliese asked, 'When did your affair with Mayhew start?'

'Four years ago.'

Briefly, Annaliese turned to George. Neither of them spoke and her face remained impassive. 'What does Mrs Mayhew know?' Annaliese asked Olivia.

'She's been using a private investigator to follow her husband. From what he told me, she has a list of dates and places when we were supposed to be together.'

'Is it accurate?'

'Apparently so.' Feeling slightly better now that the brandy was getting to work and reassured by Annaliese's relaxed objectivity, Olivia gained confidence. 'They had a huge row yesterday morning and she told him what she was planning. To make him feel bad, she gave him a copy of the snooper's report. The wretch seems to have followed us nearly everywhere.'

'Oh dear,' Annaliese murmured. 'How does your friend, Mayhew, occupy himself when he isn't with you or his wife?'

Olivia shrugged. 'Sails and fools around with racing cars.'

'No, I mean what's his profession?' Annaliese said with an indulgent little smile.

Olivia was amused. 'He doesn't have to bother with anything as sordid as *that*. His father and two uncles left him a fortune. A big one.'

'I see.' Purely for effect, Annaliese studied her notes. 'Do you want to marry this man?'

'*Marry* him? Olivia's eyes opened wide in disbelief. 'No, I don't. Absolutely not!'

'You sound awfully sure.' Annaliese seemed puzzled.

'I'm married to George,' Olivia said. 'In any case, I couldn't trust Adrian any further than I could throw him.'

'And you believe that trust is important in a marriage?' Annaliese said softly.

Lured into making a fool of herself, Olivia was stung. 'Did you?' she retorted. 'Was your behaviour always snow-white?'

From the corner of her eye, Annaliese saw George stiffen with shock. Willing him to keep calm, she gave Olivia a sardonic smile. 'You don't seem to understand why we are here,' Annaliese said, perfectly unruffled. 'Whatever else you have or haven't done, you, my dear Olivia, have committed the cardinal sin of being found out. *That* is the crucial issue, not what you and Mayhew got up to in bed.'

Well and truly put in her place, Olivia was sullen, waiting for Annaliese's thought processes to reach a conclusion. The silence was oppressive.

Eventually, Annaliese asked, 'You said that Mrs Mayhew told her husband about the action she intended to take?'

'That's right.'

'She hasn't started proceedings yet?'

'I don't think so.' Olivia was struggling to be reasonable again.

Annaliese raised her eyebrows in a question to George. He had the answer ready. 'David Naismith says it would be at least six months before the case reached a court.'

'And until then, the details remain strictly private?' Annaliese asked.

'Yes. They're locked up in the legal system.'

'Which we're expected to trust?' Annaliese said.

George shrugged his acceptance of her point: a corruptible secretary or clerk *was* a threat.

The disclosure that George had already talked to a solicitor – and David Naismith, of all people – frightened Olivia. It was some time before she saw that Annaliese and George were looking at each other in a speculative way that suggested telepathy.

'Any suggestions?' George asked. 'What ought we to do?'

Eyes raised to the ceiling, Annaliese was miles away. When it came, her response was a surprise. 'I'm wondering whether we need to bother. It may be best to do nothing.'

'How would that help?' George asked.

'If Mrs Mayhew gets her divorce, your wife is a proven adulteress,' Annaliese replied. 'By the way, Olivia, is your friend proposing to defend the case?'

Olivia was so taken aback that she gave an honest reply. 'He was talking of it – if only to reduce the alimony.'

'I see.' Annaliese's attention went back to George. 'That means lots of dirty washing, which will be unpleasant. The newspapers have become utterly disgraceful since that Profumo business – it seems to have given them a new sort of power.' Annaliese sighed, remembering the old days when a spot of scandal was the exclusive property of a small, select circle and did not ruin reputations or careers. 'But, at the end of the week, or however long it takes, the uproar will die down, everyone will forget it, and you have grounds for your own divorce. I'd say you could be rid of her pretty quickly.'

George nodded. David Naismith had hinted at this.

Olivia's gasp of outrage was delayed by the momentary paralysis that Annaliese's ruthless view of the situation had induced. The power of speech returned in the form of a strident shriek. 'What the hell are you talking about? I *won't* be dumped!'

Impetuously, Olivia stood up, snatched at her glass and stalked to the table on which George had left the drinks tray. As she tossed back a mouthful of brandy with flamboyant insolence, Annaliese tensed. The brilliance of her blue eyes turned to cold grey as the arching line of Olivia's pliant body in its clinging dress brought back that disquieting sense of *déjà vu* at Edward's funeral, when Olivia had been flirting with the dark, flashily attractive man. Edward had been wrong when he said that Olivia reminded him of Celia: it was another, infinitely more dangerous woman.

'Blanche Hamilton!' Annaliese spat the words out with a venomous force that astonished George and froze Olivia in the middle of another gesture of defiance.

'*That's* who you bring to mind,' Annaliese went on. 'For your information, Blanche was the wife of the estate manager, the creature who was murdered with Ralph. You've heard of her, I take it?'

Rooted to the spot, Olivia nodded.

'The only thing that counted for anything with Blanche Hamilton was pleasure,' Annaliese said. 'The sort she got flat on her back. She was an utter slut and you are exactly like her.'

'Don't try dragging me into your unsavoury history,' Olivia screamed. 'Not that it did *you* any harm. Where would you have been now if Ralph hadn't been murdered? Tell me that, you arrogant old bitch!'

Springing out of his chair, George grabbed Olivia and shook her savagely. 'If you ever speak to my mother like that again, I'll kill you!' he hissed, his face contorted by fury.

Frightened, Olivia believed him. Then, as the madness drained out of them, they felt foolish, stranded in the wreckage of a farce.

'Sit down, the pair of you,' Annaliese snapped. They did so, like badly behaved children, sulking in the face of implacable resolution.

Beneath the cover of the desk, Annaliese clasped her hands together, hoping that they would stop shaking. She was thinking of Edward, of how right he had been about Olivia. 'Divorce is the best thing,' she said.

'I would contest it,' Olivia said quietly. Suddenly, she was menacing.

'Oh?' Annaliese sat bolt-upright in her chair. 'On what grounds?'

'That George knew what was happening and condoned it.' Olivia's voice grew with the confidence that came from Annaliese's slightly worried frown. 'Allow me to tell *you* something, Mother-in-law, dear. After the children were born, I discovered that my husband couldn't face sleeping with me again. We had a very nice, civilised talk and decided to preserve the marriage, but go our separate ways. I was allowed to look for someone who *would* satisfy me, George went back to Tony Austen-Cave.'

Pretending to ignore her own fears and George's obvious discomfort, Annaliese said, 'I'm sorry, Olivia, but I haven't the faintest idea what you're suggesting.'

After a slight pause to gather her strength, Olivia said, 'Your precious son is a homosexual – a queer! As we've proved, he *can* perform with a woman when he puts his mind to it, but he much prefers men.'

Annaliese shook with fury. 'Where on earth did you get that preposterous notion from?'

'George,' Olivia said in a sweet voice. 'He told me.'

'Is this true?' Annaliese snapped at George.

Unable to meet her eyes, he nodded.

'And this has been going on since the twins were born, for the last *eight* years?' Annaliese's voice rose in distress and disbelief.

Another abject nod.

As she grasped the full enormity of it, saw the results of her complacent lack of interest, Annaliese was appalled. Smiling to herself, Olivia went for yet more brandy. 'I can see we understand each other,' she said.

'What do you mean?' Annaliese asked.

'I like being the Duchess of Lincolnshire,' Olivia replied. 'If you try to get rid of me, I'll give the press a story that will keep them going for weeks.'

'About George?'

'Yes.'

'As I understand it, Parliament is on the verge of passing legislation to de-criminalise homosexuality,' Annaliese said.

'So they are.' Drink and a mounting sense of power made Olivia affable. 'But that isn't going to make it *acceptable*, is it? The social stigma will stick. There's another thing, too. I wonder how much you knew about George's tendencies when you encouraged him to marry me to get your precious grandson.'

'This is becoming ridiculous,' Annaliese said angrily.

'*I* knew,' Olivia retorted. 'At least, I had a fairly good idea, so I'm damned sure you must have done.' She smiled at the expression of horrified disbelief that was spreading across George's face. 'I'd heard about your little contretemps at Oxford – although I have to admit that I enjoyed your touching confession.'

Annaliese saw the hopelessness of the immediate situation. 'George and I must talk about this,' she said. 'In private.'

'Suits me.' Olivia put her glass down rather more heavily than she intended. 'I want to see my mother – I need to borrow a car. Mine's in London.'

Later, in the cold, grey light of the following morning when she was sober, she would have been dismayed to learn how close she came to having her request granted. In the full knowledge that Olivia was too drunk to drive, Annaliese very nearly reached for the house telephone to order that a car be put at her disposal. It was only a last-minute concern for other motorists that made Annaliese say, 'I won't hear of you driving yourself, Olivia. Come along, we'll find someone to take you.'

Shepherded out of the room, Olivia saw that George was looking at her with a hatred whose intensity came as an unpleasant surprise. Perhaps she had said too much; telling him that she had always known he was a homosexual might prove to have been a mistake. It had been fun, though.

Having summoned a car and chauffeur, Annaliese waited with Olivia at the front door.

'What about this divorce?' Olivia asked.

'I shall make every attempt to keep your name out of it,' Annaliese replied.

'How?'

'I've no idea yet. Inquiries will be made and I'll see what I can do. It's in both our interests to suppress it.'

Olivia nodded. 'Look, I'm sorry I . . .'

'Don't.' Annaliese's interruption was brusque. 'There's no point in apologising. It's essential that you stop seeing Mayhew.'

'I've already finished with him,' Olivia replied.

Annaliese believed her. But as she watched Olivia walk unsteadily down the steps to the car that had arrived, she doubted if it would be long before another man was considering himself the luckiest fellow alive.

Returning, slightly breathless, to her sitting-room, Annaliese found George still slumped morosely in the chair.

'Did you hear what she said?' he complained. 'She knew about me all along.'

In a flash of sympathy for her son, Annaliese wondered whether she should tell him of Edward's deep mistrust of Olivia and her own insistence on the marriage. No, it would increase George's self-pity and make him intransigent. She needed his co-operation to help her make amends for shackling him to such a dreadful wife.

'We're going to be busy,' Annaliese said briskly. 'I've told Olivia that I'm going to look for a way of keeping her out of this Mayhew divorce. But there's something you and I must agree on. We have to get rid of her. I remember telling you that I didn't mind your marriage being miserable, however, this is beyond endurance. It won't be easy or quick, but she has to go.'

'You're right.' George's surliness gave way to a smile that was uncharacteristically sly. 'You very nearly tried tonight, didn't you? I saw you working out whether to let her have a car, hoping that she'd save us a load of trouble. It was a close-run thing, wasn't it?'

'Don't be so fanciful,' Annaliese scolded. Caught out by George's shrewd observation, she switched rapidly to attack. 'Have you ever seen anything like that woman's nerve? She has the mind of a child and the morals of an alley cat, yet she expects to dictate terms – to *me*!'

'Her position isn't what you could call weak,' George pointed out. 'To be honest, I more or less offered her a divorce after the twins were born and she turned it down flat.'

'Your honesty is a mixed blessing, George,' Annaliese said acidly. 'Since you mention them, the children are very important. Tomorrow morning, you must go to Salisbury and talk to Kate. Olivia isn't to be allowed anywhere near John and Valerie.'

'I have to go back to London,' George said petulantly. 'There's no need to worry, Olivia never goes near them.'

'George, darling, be a good boy and do as you're told,' Annaliese said. 'What Olivia's been doing may not be worth a fig now. The children, especially John, are one of the two holds she has over us. They must be protected.'

Agreeing reluctantly, George said, 'Kate's the woman to do it.'

'Of course she is,' Annaliese said, irritated by his slowness. 'Kate can be trusted, so tell her the full story – or as much as your self-esteem will bear. One other thing, we need a good solicitor, someone *fresh*. Is David Naismith up to it?'

'It depends on what you have in mind,' George said.

'Our survival,' Annaliese replied spiritedly. 'Is David sharp? I don't just mean up here . . .' She tapped her forehead '. . . can he bend the rules if the occasion demands it?'

'I'd say so.'

'Then get in touch with him. *Now*. Ask him to forget all his other business and come to see me. Tell him to bring Athene for the weekend.'

'Oh, all right.' George was unenthusiastic.

Annaliese laughed at him. '*Now*, darling, do it now. Go to your rooms, contact David, soak in a bath for half an hour, and dine with me at eight.'

To speed her bewildered son on his way, she gave him a warm embrace and kiss. George went, grateful that Tony Austen-Cave had not been mentioned, unaware that it was Annaliese's remorse for Olivia that had saved him from a barrage of searching questions.

Having savoured the delight of being alone, Annaliese picked up the telephone and dialled the international operator.

After only a few minutes, much quicker than usual, she was through to the villa. 'Kurt, my dear, darling friend,' she said in German, 'it is Annaliese.'

'Highness, what a pleasure. How are you?'

'I need your arms around me.'

Catching the hint of strain in her voice, Kurt asked, 'What's wrong, my love?'

Annaliese told him. 'So now, I have to discover if anything can be done to prevent a scandal,' she concluded.

'Can it?'

'I haven't the faintest idea, Kurt,' Annaliese said wearily. 'Investigations will have to be carried out. For what it's worth, my instinct tells me that there *is* a way out.'

'Your instinct is infallible,' Kurt replied. 'Or so you've always told me.' They laughed and he asked, 'Am I to expect you soon?'

'Oh, how I'd love to see you,' Annaliese sighed. 'But I must attend to the mess here – I'm afraid it's mostly my fault. It will be next year, probably spring, before I can get away.'

They talked for another five minutes, then, after exchanging their special endearments, ended the call. Later, when George came back to join her for dinner, he was struck by her serene composure.

Shortly after 9.00 the following morning, Caroline Dorchester took a cup of strong, black coffee to Olivia's bedroom at Widney Cheyne.

'You look terrible,' Caroline said as her daughter, groaning and wincing, struggled to sit up.

'Do you *have* to sound so pleased about it?' Olivia mumbled.

'Why not? It isn't every day I get this sort of excitement. Life here is usually rather boring – when it isn't downright dreadful.'

Olivia tasted the coffee, grimaced, and slumped back on the pillows. 'I think I'm in a mess.'

'Curiously enough, that thought had occurred to me,' Caroline replied. 'And I'm afraid your father is frightfully pissed-off with you. He's talking of going over to Compton Allardyce.'

'What for?' Olivia screamed, aggravating a wicked headache.

'It's difficult to be sure,' Caroline said. 'He'd like to tell Annaliese what a frightful cow you are – but she knows that already. More usefully, he has some vague notion of asking her to go easy on you.'

'Why should the old fool want to do that?' Olivia demanded. 'In any case, the boot's on the other foot. He should be asking me to go easy on her.'

'Oh dear.' Caroline gazed in the general direction of heaven, hoping for patience and inspiration. 'Do you think I might be allowed to enlighten you, my precious?' she said. 'Last evening, you were overwrought and well-oiled, so you didn't make a great deal of sense. However, we did get the distinct impression that you had – how shall I put it – *threatened* Annaliese. Is that right?'

'Yes!' Olivia was proud of herself.

'Sweetness, one does not threaten people like Annaliese Lincolnshire. Apart from the fact that she's one of the hardest bitches you'll ever come across, she's a Habsburg. They ran most of central Europe for seven hundred years and that, I can tell you, requires certain attitudes of mind. I would guess that one of them is a refusal to be dictated to by a jumped-up tart – even one with legs as divine as yours.'

'What can she do?' Olivia asked.

'Again, I must guess,' Caroline said. 'If she chose, she could employ fifty times more private eyes than Adrian's wife could even dream of affording. And what would she find? How many men have you had since the children were born?'

Olivia grinned. 'Two or three.'

Caroline hooted derisively. 'You've smuggled half a dozen of the bastards into this place – and I presume that they were only the one-night stands, the fanciable hunks of impulse that you couldn't plan for. As to the rest, the serious stuff . . .' Caroline pulled an eloquent face.

'You're a fine one to talk,' Olivia said sulkily. 'My most vivid childhood memory is of finding you in that shed with one of the gardeners.'

'And very nice he was,' Caroline replied. 'So were most of the others. But, while I was going without knickers and spreading happiness, I never had anyone like Annaliese Lincolnshire after my blood. If she gets the merest whiff of the extent to which you've been cuckolding George, you'll be finished.'

'George and I had an arrangement,' Olivia protested.

'Which the divorce court and the newspapers will respect,' Caroline said. Biting sarcasm announced the end of her forebearance.

Showing signs of alarm, Olivia asked, 'What shall I do?'

'Stay here and behave yourself,' Caroline replied. 'I shall let Annaliese know where you are and do a spot of grovelling on your behalf.'

'If Father goes dashing off to Allardyce, he'll ruin it.'

'He won't go,' Caroline assured Olivia. 'It's all bluster. He hasn't got the guts to face Annaliese. Hell's teeth, the mood she must be in, I doubt if *I* have.'

'What about Adrian's foul wife and the divorce?' Olivia asked. 'Do you think Annaliese will be able to do anything?'

'If she can't, it will definitely not be for the want of trying,' Caroline said. 'Providing you're sensible, this will all be over and done with in six months and you'll be back to normal. Believe me, darling, being stuck with an idiot like George earns you my deepest sympathy. I suppose he must be even worse at it than your father.' Caroline shuddered in mock horror.

Athene and David arrived at the Castle on Friday afternoon, just as the November dusk was falling over the Park. Osbourne, the butler, took David straight up to Annaliese's office while Athene went to the house in Gainsborough Wood and a warm welcome from Henrietta and Nicholas.

'This sounds rather fraught,' Athene said, fishing for information.

'It seems that way,' Nicholas replied, pretending to know nothing. 'Something big, I'd say.'

Unable to contain herself, Henrietta gave the game away. 'Olivia has got herself dragged into a divorce case. A wronged wife is citing her as co-respondent.'

Bouncing with glee, Athene begged for details. After exhausting the few facts that were known, they indulged in speculation until nearly 8.00 pm when David was delivered from the Castle in a Rolls-Royce.

'Tell all!' Athene screamed, tugging at her husband's coat as he kissed Henrietta and shook hands with Nicholas. 'Let's hear the squalid, sleazy details.'

'Hey, steady on,' Nicholas said. 'I expect the poor chap's been sworn to secrecy.'

'Have you?' Athene asked David.

'No, not really.' David rubbed his chin thoughtfully. 'That's only because Annaliese probably didn't think it was necessary. You don't expect your solicitor to go shouting his mouth off to all and sundry, do you?'

'We're not "all and sundry", you toad.' Athene pummelled David's chest with her fists. 'We knew this place's dark secrets *years* before you turned up. Annaliese trusts us.'

David was persuaded. Over a supper of steak and kidney pie, he described what had happened and outlined the plan that he and Annaliese hoped would yield the desired result.

'All that to save Olivia's reputation?' Athene said, disappointed and disgusted.

'No, not really,' David replied. 'Her standing doesn't matter a jot – Annaliese made that very clear. We have to protect George.'

'And the twins,' Henrietta said quietly.

'All right.' Athene was placated. After a few moments of intense, glowering thought, she asked David, 'Do you think the frightful Olivia would expose poor old George?'

'Annaliese does,' David said. 'At the moment, hers is the only opinion that matters.' He shot a wry look at Nicholas, who smiled and nodded, appreciating the ferocity of the argument that had taken place at the Castle. 'Ultimately,' David went on, 'Olivia is to be dumped.'

'How?' Athene demanded.

'Money, I expect.'

'Buy her off?'

'Her parents are likely to be interested,' David said. 'Otherwise her brother will inherit nothing but debts.'

'Are things that bad?' Nicholas asked.

In his confidential, lawyer's voice, David said, 'Widney Cheyne is mortgaged. A few years ago, everyone swallowed the story that Monty was the cause of all the problems, but things have got far worse since he went to Australia.'

'They've got three Titians in that house,' Athene said. 'Boothby's could solve all their problems tomorrow.'

David shook his head. 'Those pictures are included in the bank's security for the second part of the mortgage.'

'The *second* part?' Athene's eyes were popping out of her head.

'Forty per cent of Widney Cheyne was mortgaged eleven years ago,' David explained. 'That was *before* Monty's so-called disgrace and departure.' He paused to underline the possible significance of this. 'Then, two years ago, the other sixty per cent *and* the Titians went the same way. I'd be surprised if either Olivia or her mother are aware of this. Those who matter regard Aubrey Dorchester as a devious devil who keeps the cards extremely close to his chest.'

Athene stared at David with affectionate respect. 'Did you just happen to have these facts at your fingertips?'

'Yes.'

'Any particular reason?'

David cleared his throat. 'Suffice it to say that your "Aunt"

Annaliese is not the only person with a close interest in the Dorchesters.'

'And *that* is as much as you're going to get out of him,' Henrietta told Athene.

She was right.

On 23 December, his last day in the office before the Christmas holiday, David telephoned Annaliese with news that the investigation into the Mayhews had yielded its first fruits.

'Adrian hasn't been near Olivia as far as we can tell, but he is seeing two other women.'

'Sleeping with them?' Annaliese asked.

'Almost certainly. Give me another month and we'll have enough evidence to satisfy ten courts.' David paused for effect. 'Mrs Mayhew also has a lover.'

'Ah.' Annaliese's broad smile transmitted itself across the telephone connection.

'The impression is that it's rather more than a tit-for-tat fling,' David went on. 'Last Thursday evening, over dinner at a restaurant near Romsey, Mrs Mayhew and her beau were overheard discussing marriage plans.'

Again, Annaliese said, 'Ah.'

'It promises well for the New Year.' David allowed himself the luxury of self-satisfaction.

'Indeed. Will you be at Allardyce for Christmas?'

'Yes. We're looking forward to it enormously.'

'Come to lunch on Boxing Day with Henrietta and Nicholas,' Annaliese said. 'I'd ask you for Christmas Day, but George and I are going to Salisbury to see the twins.'

'You'll have a marvellous time,' David said.

They did, even though it meant leaving the Castle at 6.00 am so that George was in time for first Communion in the Cathedral at 8.00. In between Morning Service and the Carols at 3.00 pm, a huge turkey dinner was demolished and

Valerie played Beethoven's *Waldstein* Sonata, reading almost faultlessly from the music that had been part of George's present. Despite the season, no one mentioned Olivia.

20

1967
'At your very earliest convenience, Ollie'

David was so meticulous that Annaliese became exasperated. Although the evidence obtained during the first two weeks of January seemed more than adequate, he insisted on prolonging the investigation. Eventually, at the end of the month, the final piece of the jigsaw emerged and it was pure gold. When she heard about it Annaliese's expression was, in David's subsequent account to Athene, 'Absolute, Machiavellian bliss.'

It was time to talk to Susan Mayhew, the wronged wife.

Initially believing that a letter was not the way to go about it, David telephoned the house near Chandler's Ford in Hampshire. When Susan herself answered, he imagined that he was in luck and launched into a carefully prepared explanation of his business with her. Susan Mayhew slammed her receiver down almost immediately. Subsequently, she ignored the two short, discreetly worded letters that David sent.

'This is no use to me,' Annaliese fumed. 'Give me all the documents.'

'What are you plotting?' an alarmed David asked.

Annaliese, who had gone to the trouble of travelling to London so that she could nail him in his office, became icily calm. 'Hand over your files,' she ordered.

David, who had never realised that Annaliese could be so tall, did so. 'Er . . . what are you planning to use them for?' he asked, purely as a matter of form.

'Don't be silly, my dear,' Annaliese replied and, picking up the two manila folders, shoved them into Edward's old case, and marched out of the office. As she went, David saw that an extra inch or two of intimidating height was the result of the very high heels that did wonders for her ankles and calves.

On 28 February, Susan Mayhew slept late. It was nearly 11.00 am before, finally bathed and dressed, she sat at the kitchen table, enjoying her first cup of tea and remembering the previous night with Stephen.

Her jubilation faded at the prospect of the empty hours ahead. The stress and unpleasantness of recent months had left Susan fearful of solitude. The sound of the doorbell was a blessing and she hurried to respond, hoping for Fiona and a trip to Southampton. Instead, she found a regally handsome woman who might have been fifty-five, but was probably, on closer examination, over seventy. Her mink coat and matching fur hat – which was set at a slightly rakish angle – had cost a fortune. To complete the aura of story-book unreality, there was no sign of a car. Surely, she hadn't walked all the way from the centre of the village to the end of this remote lane?

Stupefied, Susan said, 'Oh – I thought it might be my sister.'

'Never mind, you'll find me much better company.' The incredibly confident statement was accompanied by a glowing smile. 'You *are* Susan Mayhew?'

'Yes.'

'I'm Annaliese Lincolnshire. How do you do?'

Susan was bewitched into shaking hands. 'Er . . . should I know you?' she asked.

'I'm the Duke of Lincolnshire's mother. Your husband has been having an affair with my daughter-in-law.'

'Oh!' Susan recoiled, horrified. 'I don't want to talk to you. I mustn't.'

'Who says so?'

'My solicitor.'

'The man's an ass,' Annaliese said pleasantly. 'Believe me, my dear, you can't afford *not* to speak to me. Not on the doorstep, though. I see that your neighbours aren't too close, but one never knows, does one?'

Taking advantage of Susan's numbed inability to stop her, Annaliese crossed the threshold, appraising her surroundings as she did so. The old farmhouse had been taken apart and rebuilt to Adrian Mayhew's own design. 'Charming,' Annaliese said, making it obvious that she thought the whole thing was dreadfully tasteless. 'Where were you? Ah, yes, in the kitchen.' She led the way.

'This is all wrong,' Susan said, trotting to keep up. 'We have nothing to say to each other.' She was confused, trying to recall anything she might have been told about this amazing woman. Wasn't she some sort of Austrian princess?

'You're mistaken,' Annaliese said gently. 'By the way, *are* you expecting your sister?'

'No, not really. She sometimes pops round – we go to Southampton and look at the shops.' Susan was making nervous, fluttering gestures with her hands.

'Good. I don't want us to be disturbed.' Annaliese removed her hat and coat, piling them on a work surface near the washing machine. Her austerely straight black skirt and simple, white blouse were timelessly elegant. Susan's attention focused on the brooch.

'It belonged to Maria Theresa,' Annaliese said. 'May I have a cup of coffee, please? Fairly strong, with a dash of cream if you have it.'

Mesmerised into obeying, Susan set to work, praying that her hands would stop shaking. Annaliese chatted, commenting on what she had seen of the village, especially the amount of building going on. Wasn't it going to spoil things? Susan, stammering responses when appropriate, knew that she was being scrutinised.

Annaliese thought that the young woman's hair would benefit from more skilful cutting and styling, but she was pretty and had a mouth that hinted at sensuality. A baggy Aran sweater and dark-green corduroy slacks disguised a body that was almost certainly firm and shapely. She undervalued herself and, for that reason alone, was no match for Olivia and her husband's other mistresses.

'Thank you.' Annaliese took a sip of coffee and smiled. 'Yes, that's lovely.' Reaching down beside her chair, she lifted the well-worn document case that she had dropped on the floor, placing it on the pine table. 'This belonged to my late husband,' she said in response to Susan's apprehensive look. 'He took it everywhere.' Unfastening the zip, Annaliese put a hand inside, drawing out a cheque-book and an ancient fountain pen. Placing them beside the case, she shook her head at Susan's hostility. 'No, my dear, this isn't going to be straightforward bribery. Hear me out, there's a good girl.'

Curiosity won. Susan nodded.

'My daughter-in-law and your husband have been involved with each other for even longer than you realise,' Annaliese began. 'She admits to four years, but I think it could be as much as seven – in which case, I'm afraid it pre-dates your marriage.'

'I *have* wondered,' Susan admitted. 'It doesn't say much for me, does it?'

Annaliese was dismissive. 'Some men are uncontrollable idiots – and you seem to have chosen a particularly wretched specimen. The point I want to make is that I don't dispute your allegations. You are perfectly entitled to cite my daughter-in-law. But I don't want you to. You see, there's every chance that it would set off a scandal that would ruin my son.'

'Yes, I can understand that ... er ...' Susan paused, disconcerted. 'I'm sorry, what do I call you?'

'Annaliese.'

'It's a lovely name.'

'Isn't it? Go on, Susan.'

'Well, I don't want to cause trouble for your son, or you, Annaliese, but I simply *must* divorce Adrian. Our marriage has been a terrible disaster. I'm only staying in his frightful house because the solicitor said I had to.'

Annaliese was shocked. 'What on earth for?'

'It's got something to do with giving Adrian grounds for a cross petition based on desertion. It might slow things down and I couldn't bear that.'

Making a mental note to return to the question of Susan's solicitor, Annaliese pressed on. 'From what I've been able to discover, you began to employ a private detective last July. On his first outing, he stumbled across your husband and Olivia having lunch together at a place in Lymington that's popular with the yachting set. Afterwards, they went to a hotel in Beaulieu and shut themselves in a bedroom until the following morning. About ten days later, your man discovered the cottage near Lyndhurst that someone called Toby Squires had made available.'

Badly shaken by the accuracy of Annaliese's information, Susan said, 'Yes, that's correct.'

'Your detective was so pleased with himself that he didn't bother digging deeper,' Annaliese continued. 'Why should he?

He'd found what he wanted. You couldn't afford to pay him for his exclusive, full-time services, so he had to consider other clients. He devised a way of knowing when our love-birds were at the cottage – that was probably a talkative barmaid in The Hutton Arms at East Perrywood, by the way – and all he had to do was confirm what she told him.'

'What are you suggesting?' Susan was wary.

'That your investigator missed at least two other women.'

'No!'

'It's true, Susan, I promise you.' Annaliese paused. 'One of the reasons why I descended on you today is that I knew your husband wouldn't be here. He's at that blasted cottage with a girl called Gillian Bellingham, who describes herself as an actress and dancer.'

Susan shook her head in disbelief.

'Miss Bellingham isn't new,' Annaliese said. 'Nor is Veronica Ibbotson, with whom he spent last weekend at Brackley – which is near the race-track at Silverstone. Here are the details of his activities with both women during the last six weeks.' Annaliese extracted several sheets of paper from the document case and passed them across the table.

Pretending to read, Susan said, 'You want me to name one of these women instead of your daughter-in-law?'

'Yes, please. Gillian Bellingham, for preference. She isn't married and may actually enjoy the publicity. Mrs Ibbotson's husband is much older than her and suffers from a heart condition.'

Susan was gnawing at her lower lip. 'I'd better talk to my solicitor,' she said. 'Perhaps it isn't possible to change tactics at this stage.'

Smiling apologetically, Annaliese said, 'You'll find that your petition isn't over the first hurdle yet. Yes, I *have* been poking around, haven't I?'

Susan nodded.

'I understand that your husband is disgustingly wealthy,' Annaliese went on. 'I expect you'll relieve him of some of it and I'm prepared to supplement your good fortune.' She stared at the cheque-book. 'What about a hundred thousand pounds?'

Susan blinked. '*A hundred thousand?*' she whispered.

'Yes.' Annaliese peered quizzically across the table. 'Isn't it enough?'

'It's amazing. Unbelievable. Are you sure?'

'Perfectly. It's a fair price for one's good name.' Casually, Annaliese added, 'That amount should set you and Doctor Richardson up very nicely.'

Susan was unnaturally still, every vestige of colour drained from her face.

'I am right, aren't I?' Annaliese inquired mildly. 'He *is* the gentleman you wish to marry?'

'Yes, he is.'

'I hope you'll be happy. Have you chosen better this time?'

'Stephen's a good man,' Susan said fiercely. 'We're going to have children.'

'Splendid.' Annaliese's eyes underwent that baffling change to grey as, with apparent innocence, she said, 'His first wife died tragically young – leukaemia, I believe?'

'Yes.' Susan looked almost panic-stricken as she stood up and backed away from the table. 'I'll ring my solicitor.'

'Is he a local man?'

'Swaythling – that's part of Southampton.' Without knowing why, Susan went on to say, 'He isn't keen on divorce. I think he prefers selling houses.'

'Susan, my dear, may I make a suggestion?' Annaliese said. 'And do sit down for a moment, you look rather agitated.' Susan sat and Annaliese patted her hand. 'Tell your solicitor to withdraw your petition and pay him off. I'll put a *proper* firm on the case, the people who did all my dirty work.

Wouldn't you like to have them on your side? They'll skin your husband for a lump-sum settlement and you won't pay a penny in legal fees.'

'*And* a cheque for a hundred thousand?' Susan asked.

'Yes. Post-dated two weeks from today so that I can be sure you're doing what I want.'

Susan looked doubtful. 'Is that long enough? This man in Swaythling didn't do anything for ages.'

'My people aren't like that,' Annaliese said, supremely confident. 'They'll take your breath away.'

As Susan thought about it, the tight, worried lines of her face began to relax into a smile. 'All right, Annaliese,' she said. 'You've got yourself a deal.' Solemnly, they shook hands. 'I'll make that call.'

Annaliese wrote the cheque, then eavesdropped on a conversation that was clearly heavy going for Susan. She came back boot-faced, only to burst out laughing when she saw the mischief in Annaliese's eyes, now brilliant blue once more.

'What about your friend, Stephen?' Annaliese said. 'Do you want to consult him? Perhaps he'd like to have lunch with us.' She glanced at her watch. 'My car will be here in seven minutes.'

'Lunch?' Susan was distraught. 'It would take me ages to get ready. I can't possibly go out looking like this.'

'Yes, you can,' Annaliese said equably. 'You'll be with me, so no one would even dream of criticising you. In any case, I'd rather like to go to one of these Berni places – my grandchildren assure me that they're frightfully good, but not all that posh, I believe?'

Susan dithered for a moment. 'Why not?' she cried. 'Let's have some fun.'

'I've always found it's much the best idea,' Annaliese said.

Shortly afterwards, while Susan was talking to Stephen Richardson on the telephone, trying to calm him after her over-excited revelations, Annaliese opened the front door and hurried outside to have words with the man who was reversing the Rolls-Royce into the drive. Then, after Stephen had been cut off with orders to be outside his house in ten minutes, Annaliese was introducing Nicholas Hammond to Susan.

'You can see that he isn't really a chauffeur,' Annaliese said. 'For a caper like this I had to have someone who was totally trustworthy. Much to her disgust, Nicholas probably won't even tell his wife about today. Actually, he's my estate manager – been with me twenty years. Now, can we get on? I'm ravenous.'

Smiling nervously at each other, Susan and Nicholas did as they were told.

At 2.45 pm, Susan Mayhew and Stephen Richardson stood outside his house, waving as Annaliese and Nicholas set off for Compton Allardyce.

'Are you *sure* you're all right, darling?' Susan asked, guiding her lover away from the pavement and the risk of being recognised by someone in one of the cars that were hurrying along the busy main road.

Stephen, a bashfully unassuming man of forty, had been bowled over by Annaliese, and was struggling to recover from the goodbye kiss she had given him. 'I shall be fine,' he said, finding his keys and letting them indoors.

'What's your considered opinion of the Dowager Duchess of Lincolnshire, alias Her Imperial and Royal Highness the Archduchess Annaliese von Habsburg of Austria?' Susan asked.

'Phew!' Stephen sat down on the stairs, shaking his head in dazed admiration. 'I suppose that's what people mean by "style".'

'In superabundance, I'd say.'

'What did you do when she arrived at the house?'

'Nearly died,' Susan laughed.

Stephen shook his head wonderingly. 'Did you see the way she tackled that steak and chips? Has she ever eaten food like that before?'

'Only recently, with her grandchildren.' Susan assumed an air of mock suspicion. 'What was going on when I came back from the loo? Why the whispering?'

'She was explaining why she'd made the cheque out to me,' Stephen said.

'*Did* she?' Susan delved into her handbag and retrieved the slip of paper. 'Heavens, yes, she did. How strange.'

'As a matter of fact, it isn't,' Stephen said. 'You still have the joint account with your husband. She didn't want him getting his filthy hands on it.'

'Lord, I'd forgotten that,' Susan muttered. 'But fancy *her* knowing.'

'Was there anything she didn't know?' Stephen asked.

'About us, you mean?'

'Yes.'

Susan cast her mind back to the conversation in the kitchen. 'No,' she said quietly, 'I reckon she knew everything.'

'But never mentioned it?'

'No.' Susan thought again. 'There was no need – I agreed to do what she wanted. I wonder if she would have put the screws on?'

'You can bet that hundred thousand on it,' Stephen replied. 'Lady Lincolnshire is an extremely ruthless woman. I wonder what will become of the errant daughter-in-law?'

'Doesn't she sound an absolute bitch?' Susan said forcefully. 'I hope she burns in hell-fire.'

'Mmm.' Stephen, who usually had no interest in other people's personal problems, looked wistful. 'Unfortunately, we shall never find out.'

'Why?'

'Because we shall have no further contact with them,' Stephen said. 'The other thing that your friend, Annaliese, whispered was that today never happened and may God have mercy on our souls if we ever breathe a word to the contrary.'

Nicholas, with Annaliese beside him in the front of the Rolls, drove fast, enjoying the splendid machine. Also, he was glad to be putting distance between himself and what he was sure had been a questionable piece of business.

By unspoken mutual consent, neither of them said a word until they were through Salisbury. Naturally, in order to avoid awkward questions, they did not call on Kate and the twins at Shady Bower. But once the lovely old city was behind them and they were heading towards Amesbury, Annaliese came to life.

'Well, Nicholas, what did you think of Stephen Richardson?'

'He's a good chap,' was the warm reply. 'Seems to have had a lot of bad luck.'

'Like you, in the War,' Annaliese said quietly.

'Long forgotten,' Nicholas said. 'Henrietta and everything.'

'Which brings me to Mrs Mayhew,' Annaliese replied. 'What about her?'

'Very nice.' Nicholas was slightly cagey, not wishing to go overboard about an attractive young woman.

'Brainy, too,' Annaliese said. 'She got a very good degree at Bristol University.'

'That would seem to make her marriage to a man like Mayhew even more of a mystery,' Nicholas mused.

'You mean what did she see in him?' Annaliese asked.

'Yes.'

'Oh, I think that's easily explained,' Annaliese said. 'We haven't had the pleasure of meeting the deplorable Mr Mayhew, but he's obviously a very attractive individual. Susan became sexually obsessed.' After enjoying Nicholas's blushing discomfort, Annaliese added, 'And who knows, she may have been influenced by his money. No, the *real* question is what did he see in her? Why did he marry a decent girl instead of one of the flashy tarts that flock round him?'

'He wanted her to be the mother of his children?' Nicholas suggested.

Annaliese nodded approvingly. 'Very good. Unfortunately, he found out he was incapable of producing them.'

'How do you know?' Nicholas was bold enough to ask.

'I don't,' Annaliese admitted. 'But Susan said that she and her doctor *were* going to have children. She was adamant. That suggests that Adrian Mayhew is sterile.'

Nicholas grunted in agreement and they fell into a companionable silence. Eventually, the sight of Stonehenge reminded Nicholas of what Annaliese had said as they were passing the ancient site five hours ago, on their way to find Susan. Rehearsing her campaign, a grimly determined Annaliese had stated that if common sense failed, she would resort to intimidation.

'You didn't have to threaten Mrs Mayhew, then?' Nicholas said offhandedly.

'Dear me, no,' Annaliese replied. 'She was far too sensible for that.'

Nodding sagely, Nicholas waited before asking, 'What has she done wrong?'

'It isn't her that's at risk,' Annaliese said. 'It's Stephen Richardson. Susan was his patient when they became lovers. After two months, they realised the danger and she found another doctor, but the British Medical Association would take a very dim view of it.'

'He'd be struck off,' Nicholas said. 'Banned from practising.'

'Quite.' Annaliese turned away to gaze out of her window.

'*Would* you have gone that far?' Nicholas ventured.

'The question didn't arise. Susan decided to co-operate.' Annaliese's smile was enigmatic.

Mulling it over afterwards, Nicholas was in no doubt what would have confronted Susan Mayhew if she had failed to grasp the 'sensible' option. Whatever differences they may have had while he was alive, Annaliese seemed to be taking Edward's last piece of advice to heart with a vengeance.

A little over two weeks later, Nigel Templeton telephoned Annaliese. 'Stephen Richardson has presented your cheque at his bank in Eastleigh. Am I to honour it?'

The previous day, David Naismith had made an encouraging report on the progress of Susan's revitalised divorce petition in which the actress, Gillian Bellingham, was now cited as the guilty party. Pushed hard by David's prestigious firm, the case was likely to come before a court rather sooner than Adrian Mayhew would like. He had made the mistake of moving into Miss Bellingham's London flat after Susan, acting on new legal advice, had kicked him out of the house at Chandler's Ford and put it up for sale.

'Pay it,' Annaliese told Nigel.

Somewhat capriciously, she had deprived George of information – apart from a vague statement ten weeks ago that she was looking into the matter. It was time to put him out of the misery he had worked so hard to conceal and she rang him at Boothby's.

'Olivia is no longer involved in the Mayhew divorce,' she said, wishing that she could see her son's face.

'Mother, that's wonderful news.' Relief made George sound very young and happy. 'How did you do it?'

'Me?' Annaliese was all innocence. 'What makes you think that *I* had anything to do with it?'

'You must have done. Athene says that you and David have been hatching up all manner of dire plots.'

'Does she, indeed?' Annaliese said, feigning annoyance. 'Well, she's wrong.'

'Of course,' George said, sounding deadly serious even though he was smiling to himself. 'Anyway, thank you very much – for the news, that is.'

'Are you in touch with Olivia?' Annaliese asked.

'We talk occasionally.' Hesitating, George added, 'Actually, I was thinking I might look into Widney Cheyne on the way down to Allardyce on Friday evening.'

'You might pass the news on to her.'

'I will. She'll be pleased.'

Annaliese sniffed disdainfully. 'Much as I dislike saying this, George, I believe you need to consider some sort of reconciliation.'

'Why?' George was guarded.

'It seems that practically everything is used to generate rumour these days,' Annaliese said. 'Living apart looks bad.'

'I suppose you're right,' said George grudgingly.

'I know I am,' Annaliese retorted. 'What I'm suggesting is purely a temporary measure, but you are not to let Olivia know that. You'll need to be careful – she's craftier than a wagon-load of monkeys, so watch what you say. It will probably suit her mother's convenience to back you up.'

'How do you know that?' George asked.

'I've spoken to Caroline,' Annaliese replied. 'She's contacted me several times, claiming to be on our side.'

'All right, I'll see what I can do.'

Unconcerned by George's painfully obvious reluctance, Annaliese changed abruptly. 'I may not be here when you arrive for the weekend,' she announced cheerfully. 'I'm off to

Portugal as soon as I can arrange a flight. I need a rest.'

'After all this plotting you *haven't* been doing?'

'Goodbye, George,' Annaliese said firmly.

Three months later, in June, although George and Olivia had spent a few evenings together, they continued to live apart.

Caroline Dorchester was becoming increasingly worried. 'Hasn't he said anything about wanting you back?' she asked Olivia.

'There's been the odd hint.' Olivia pulled a sour face. 'He isn't exactly enthusiastic. I think he hates my guts.'

'Some people might sympathise with him,' Caroline said. 'Your father does. My big concern is that you're losing your hold over him. This separation is getting to the stage where it could be turned against you.'

'What can I do?' Olivia asked peevishly. 'There are dozens and dozens of men out there who want me, but George isn't one of them.'

Caroline went away to think about it.

That same evening, Tony Austen-Cave felt compelled to raise the issue when he and George returned to his flat after a recital at the Wigmore Hall.

'The whispers are starting about you and the fair Olivia.'

'What sort of whispers?' George demanded, ready to lose his temper.

'Hey, calm down.' Tony made a series of placatory gestures. 'This is your best friend talking, right?'

'Yes, I'm sorry.' George sank into a chair. 'What are they saying?'

'That you and the bitch have split up. No, hold hard, George, you *have* done. It's six months now. You're lucky to have got away with it for so long. The big trouble is, no one's seen her. Now she's lying low, people miss her. They're bound to – she's decorative and exciting, the genuine article. Men like feasting their greedy eyes on the body beautiful and women adore loathing her.'

George took the point. 'My mother thinks we should be together again,' he admitted.

'So, what's stopping you? Isn't she interested?'

'Oh, she's interested,' George said bitterly. 'Her latest idea is that she should do something at Boothby's. I ask you! What would Athene have to say?'

'She could be an asset,' Tony said. 'Her sexy curiosity value would attract customers. Why do you think Galbraith's have given Angela Maitland a job? She knows not the blindest thing about art, for God's sake, but she's slept with at least half the men they'd like as clients.'

Suspecting that there was another motive behind Tony's advice, George asked, 'Anything else?'

'Well, there is something you need to know,' Tony replied, preparing the ground.

'Go on.'

'Now that Olivia has been out of circulation for so long, I'm being asked questions about you – how are you, have I seen you lately – you know the sort of thing.'

'Who's doing this?' George said nervously.

'That creep Willis,' Tony replied. 'And Randolph Turner waylaid me this morning outside Sotheby's.'

'They both sell dirt to the press,' George muttered, disgusted and apprehensive. 'Are you telling me that I need Olivia as a sort of . . .' He hesitated, at first unwilling to use the word that sprang to mind. '. . . *protection?*'

Decriminalisation meant nothing to Tony, who had always been intractably proud of his homosexuality. But he knew that George suffered permanent agonies of conscience and fear that would not be dispelled by an Act of Parliament.

'Yes, I think you do,' Tony said quietly. 'I know how much

you detest her, especially after the way she threatened you, but she does have her uses. She'll soon be up to her old tricks, so you won't have to spend much time together – just as long as you're *seen*. Even better if she were at Boothby's. You can leave the rest to folks' imagination.'

To George's horror, it made sense. What a damning indictment of his life: he needed the veneer of respectability that only Olivia could create.

Misinterpreting the chaos of emotions that chased across George's face, Tony said, 'Or do you want to pack this in?'

'No!' George shouted. When he paused to consider his reflex response, he realised that it was right, was what he wanted. For the last eighteen months, Tony had not been involved with anyone else and George, free of nagging jealousy, had experienced happiness of a kind that had eluded him since the idyllic days at Oxford with Robert Chappell. The idea of ending it was unthinkable.

More calmly, George said, 'No, I don't want us to break up. I'd go mad without you.'

Taking his arm, Tony moved towards the bedroom. 'That's good to hear,' he said. 'You know I feel exactly the same. Promise me you'll take my advice about Olivia.'

George nodded.

What appeared to be a reconciliation took place early in August. Olivia moved back into Cadogan Square and began spending two days a week 'helping out' at Boothby's. George loathed the arrangement and found it difficult to be anything other than indifferent towards his wife.

Resenting George's attitude, Olivia immediately renewed her authority to do as she pleased. She avoided Adrian Mayhew, whose divorce was due to be heard in September, and Simon Faulkener, who was too far away and not worth the effort. It seemed prudent to start afresh, so Olivia dumped all her other lovers and turned to some of the men who had hitherto been forced to admire and desire her from afar. She raised an eyebrow and they came running.

The entertainment was restricted to the period between Mondays and lunch-time on Fridays. Throughout August and September, Olivia's weekends were ostentatiously blameless. She was at Widney Cheyne for most of the time, but made occasional visits to Compton Allardyce in an attempt to court Annaliese's forgiveness. Olivia was encouraged to think that she was making good progress in that respect.

Fully aware of what was going on in London, Caroline Dorchester expressed concern.

'London can be a frighteningly small place, darling. Are you sure it's wise to be associating with all those men?'

'What about George and Austen-Cave?' Olivia retorted. 'It looks as though they're at it *every* night now.'

'And no doubt they cover their tracks very well,' Caroline replied. 'It's easy for them in a permanent hide-out. You must be dashing around all over the place, but in a very small area. What is it – half a mile square?'

'Probably less than that,' Olivia conceded. 'Yes, it *is* a problem. The worst part of it is that none of them are any good! I'd give anything for a man who was half as useful in bed as Adrian.'

'Preferably out of London,' Caroline said. 'I do think that's awfully important. Meanwhile, what sort of an idiot are you making of yourself at Boothby's?'

'I'll have you know that I'm doing rather well,' Olivia replied, preening herself. 'Thanks to me, we got the Pagnell Hall sale last week.'

'Good gracious.' Caroline was amazed. 'What did you do?'

'Turned on the charm at the right time.' Proud of the achievement, Olivia became cynical. 'Blessington couldn't make up his mind between us and Galbraith's, so I humoured him. The silly old fool thinks I'm going to let him get his leg over.'

Wondering what sort of disruption her daughter was creating, Caroline asked, 'How do your colleagues treat you?'

'They couldn't be kinder or more helpful,' Olivia enthused. 'Apart from George, of course. He's very peevish.'

George was baffled by Olivia's popularity. Bringing news of Lord Blessington's decision to allow Boothby's the pick of Pagnell Hall's treasures, Athene was fulsome in her approval of Olivia's efforts. 'The awkward old devil had no intention of making up his mind until Olivia went to work on him. She was *brilliant*.'

'Oh, good,' George said weakly.

'I'm thinking of letting her have a go at Dermot Slattery — you know, that Anglo-Irish lunatic in County Kildare with no roof and about five tons of very early Wedgwood in the cellar. We've been after him for years.'

Bemused, George said, 'It might be worth a try, I suppose.'

'Leave it with me,' Athene said and hurried away.

Seeking the sanctuary of his office, George fretted. What *was* going on? Bringing Olivia to Boothby's had been an expedient, a measure that was bound to fail, he thought. Instead, Athene, potentially the most scathing of Olivia's critics, was singing her praises and suggesting that she be given greater responsibility. The prospect of Olivia becoming a permanent fixture at his beloved auction-house filled George with horror.

Distracted by the obsessive, time-consuming necessity to conduct his personal life on a makeshift, day-to-day basis, George had forgotten Annaliese's determination to get rid of Olivia — not that he had ever taken the idea too seriously in the first place. Therefore, the thought that Annaliese had given Athene strict instructions to pamper Olivia never occurred to him.

Tickled pink by the scheme, Athene saw to it that other members of the staff went out of their way to help and flatter Boothby's newest recruit. While Annaliese devised her removal, Olivia was to be charmed into thinking that she was a valued member of the family. Athene saw another possibility: given enough rope, Olivia might hang herself.

What looked like a chance for her to do so arose on 11 October.

It was a Wednesday and George was in Norfolk to conduct a sale at the house of a client near Thetford. Olivia, working the second of her days that week, was in her husband's office, checking the printer's proofs of the catalogues for November and December. Until 11.15, it was a quiet, uneventful morning, then, just as Olivia was feeling the onset of boredom, there was a flurry of activity. One of the front-office staff came upstairs with a would-be client who had turned up out of the blue, demanding to talk to whoever was in charge and refusing to be put off. Going into the corridor to see what all the fuss was about, Olivia found herself looking at one of the most magnetic men she had ever seen.

Tall, with opulent, light-brown hair, he was extravagantly good-looking. Naturally, he knew it. Everything about him – the walk, the set of his shoulders, the twist of his mouth – spoke of self-approval and amused contempt for mere mortals. At the sight of Olivia, however, his arrogant insouciance evaporated; fleetingly, he was a sexual freebooter who had spied a uniquely worthy adversary. Lips slightly apart, eyes blazing with acknowledgement of his interest, Olivia matched his stare. The moment passed and he walked on, guided toward's Athene's office by the girl from reception. Very significantly, Olivia realised, she and the man made no attempt to speak: there was no point in a banal 'Good morning' after what their eyes had said.

Olivia remained in the corridor, hoping to learn something about the unexpected caller from Athene's greeting. As he was shown into her office, she laughed and said, 'Mr Abercrombie, what a nice surprise. Are you taking my advice – *at last*?'

The receptionist closed the door, cutting off the reply. 'Is that Hector Abercrombie, the man who trains racehorses at Cannings Norton?' Olivia asked.

'Yes, I think so. He says he wants to sell *twelve* Canalettos.' The girl, who seemed immune to Abercrombie's magnetism, was sceptical.

Muttering her thanks, Olivia shut herself in George's office. She was shaking, not quite able to believe what was happening. On the memorable evening that he had confessed his homosexuality and agreed to an open marriage, George had suggested that she have an affair with Abercrombie in the hope of persuading him to let Boothby's sell his pictures. Olivia telephoned her mother.

'Hector Abercrombie,' she said, brushing aside Caroline's wish to chat. 'What about him?'

'Oho!'

'What does that mean?' Olivia snapped.

'My word, did we get out of bed on the wrong side this morning?' Caroline cooed. 'What brings the magnificent Hector to mind?'

'He's here, at Boothby's,' Olivia said. 'Walked in about ten minutes ago. Athene is talking to him about some pictures he wants to sell.'

'Ah, it's come to that, has it?' Caroline was smug, enjoying confirmation of someone else's financial difficulty. 'Actually, darling, Hector would be ideal for you. His place at Cannings Norton is *beautifully* situated 'twixt Compton Allardyce and us.'

'Is he married?' Olivia asked.

'No, and never likely to be. Hector wouldn't tolerate anything that cramped his style.'

'What about style?' Olivia asked. 'You called him "magnificent".'

'Oh, he is. Leonora Gibson swears that he is supreme between the sheets, totally and utterly the best ever. I've often thought that if I were a few years younger . . .'

Olivia let her mother prattle to a wistful standstill and terminated the call.

The ensuing half-hour was agony. What *was* she to do? Hang about, waiting for him to leave? Absurd. Barge into Athene's office and offer to help? Aware of her limitations, Olivia was at a loss to know how she could justify the claim. Nevertheless, she was on the verge of doing something along those lines when there was a tap on the door and Athene appeared.

'Olivia, may I introduce you to Mr Abercrombie?' To Olivia's astonishment, he had the unmitigated gall to make a timid, hesitant entrance. 'You won't know this, Olivia,' Athene continued, 'but we've wanted this chap as a client for longer than I can remember. He has *twelve* Canalettos. I've tried everything, all to no avail. Now, he walks in and surrenders. He's going to sell – through us. Hector, this is Olivia Lincolnshire, the wife of our chairman.'

They shook hands, exchanged unnaturally polite smiles and said, 'How do you do?'

Athene bustled on. 'Hector's pictures are bound to be next year's most important and talked-about sale. Because of that, he thinks we should take him out to lunch. Unfortunately, I promised to go to the Tate to see Godfrey Hall and I daren't put him off. Olivia, could I ask you to do the honours?'

'It will be a pleasure,' Olivia said quietly.

'Lovely.' Athene smiled happily. 'Go to Whitaker's. Use our table. All you have to do is sign the bill and they'll add it to our account. *Bon appétit!*'

Athene tore herself away, leaving a man and a woman who were having the most disturbing effects on each other to find their way out of the building and into Bond Street. Crossing to the corner that led to Cork Street, they fell into step and clasped hands.

'Hello, Lady Lincolnshire,' Abercrombie said softly.

'Olivia,' she replied. 'And I like my *real* friends to call me Ollie.'

'Fine. One observation to be going on with, Ollie.'

'Yes?'

'It's difficult to be sure at this stage, but I suspect that your legs might be the finest I've ever seen.'

She chuckled and squeezed his hand.

As an article of faith, Whitaker's kept their best table reserved for Boothby's. It was in the furthermost corner of the downstairs dining-room, set apart from the others and screened by head-high panelling. Adopting an air of conniving intimacy, they ordered and stared at each other expectantly.

'What do I need to know about you?' Olivia asked.

'I train racehorses,' he replied.

'Why?'

Abercrombie explained that he had never given serious consideration to anything else, having inherited the stable and a love of horses from his father. The only snag, he said wryly, was that he lacked his father's luck and the last, elusive spark of talent necessary to make things work properly, to put the icing on the cake. It was a relatively small stable, there was little margin for error, the bad seasons outnumbered the good ones, and the time had come to sell the Canalettos.

The question of how he had come to acquire the immensely valuable paintings never crossed Olivia's mind. 'Are you involved with anyone?' she asked. 'Another woman?'

'Only on a casual basis.'

'I shall want all of you,' Olivia said.

'But you're happy to carry on being the Duchess of Lincolnshire?' Abercrombie said, his face calculating.

'Yes.'

The waiter brought the first course. With studied non-chalance, they waited until the man had completed his task and left them alone. Olivia leaned across the table, fixing Hector Abercrombie with a gaze of blazing intensity. 'I haven't had a good fuck for nearly a year,' she whispered.

'I thought not,' he replied, every bit as arrogantly calm as she had expected. 'I intend rectifying that deplorable state of affairs.'

'When?'

'At your very earliest convenience, Ollie.'

Her mind raced. 'I only work two days a week,' she said. 'At six o'clock, I'm finished until Monday.'

'With no other commitments?'

'None that matter.' Thinking aloud, Olivia added, 'I spend a lot of time at my parents' place – they're not far from you.'

'So I believe.' Abercrombie was vague, more interested in stroking Olivia's thigh.

'Are you going back this afternoon?' she asked.

'Three-forty from Paddington.'

Calculating how long it would take her to grab a change of clothes from Cadogan Square and drive down to Wiltshire, Olivia said, 'Expect me at nine-fifteen.'

Abercrombie drew a map of the route to his house on the back of the menu. Handing it to her, he said, 'By the time you arrive, there won't be any other involvements – not even casual ones.'

In her office at Boothby's, Athene finished her sandwiches and polished off *The Times* crossword. Her appointment with Godfrey Hall at the Tate Gallery was not until tomorrow.

The sale in Norfolk occupied George for longer than he had anticipated and he did not reach London until 8.00 pm. He took a taxi from Liverpool Street station to Tony Austen-

Cave's flat. While Tony prepared omelettes for supper, George, as he always did after a day out of the office, telephoned Athene. She told him of Hector Abercrombie's visit and his decision to dispose of the Canalettos.

'That will be a tremendous event,' George said, sounding thrilled.

'Absolutely,' Athene agreed. 'How's Olivia?'

Completely thrown, George fumbled for words. 'I don't know. Actually, I haven't been home yet. I called in to see a friend. Why do you ask?'

Athene chortled. 'Olivia and Mr Abercrombie seemed entranced by each other. I couldn't take him to lunch, so I palmed him off on your good lady and she came back looking rather dazed. I wondered if she'd recovered.'

At that moment, George had only the dimmest recollection of mentioning Abercrombie to Olivia and no idea whatsoever of the circumstances in which the name had cropped up. He laughed at what Athene was implying. 'Hector has that effect on thousands of women,' he said. 'He must get tired of them falling at his feet.'

An awkward silence followed. There was nothing more to be said, yet neither of them knew how to end the call. Suddenly, his voice and manner different, George said, 'Could I have a word with David, please?'

'Sorry, he isn't home yet,' Athene replied. 'He's gone to Surbiton to see a special client. Shall I get him to call you when he arrives?'

'No, don't bother, I'll contact him at the office tomorrow morning.' Almost as an irrelevance, George added, 'I want to arrange a meeting. There's something I *must* straighten out.'

After her first night with Hector Abercrombie, Olivia reached Widney Cheyne in time for lunch. Her make-up lacked its usual perfection, her hair wasn't right, she was exhausted –

and she looked far better than she had done for at least twelve months.

'Well, well!' Caroline Dorchester crowed. 'It's started already, has it?'

'It has, by God!' Olivia was pleased and proud.

'You look *revoltingly* good,' Caroline grumbled. 'He's certainly brought the roses back to your cheeks. Drink?' She was helping herself to a gin and tonic.

'No thanks, I'm on the wagon. As from now, I want razor-sharp senses so that I can appreciate Hector.'

'Tell me . . .' Caroline took a bracingly large gulp at her drink '. . . Leonora Gibson swears that he's fearsomely well-endowed. Can you confirm?'

Olivia laughed, clapping her hands jubilantly. 'I can, Mother dear, I definitely can. The master of Saxon Lodge Stables has the most stupendous cock I've ever come across. He is *huge!* And he knows how to use it.'

'High praise from one who knows,' Caroline muttered.

Olivia frowned petulantly. 'What's this? Not sour grapes, surely?'

'No, of course not, darling.' Caroline shook herself. 'Abercrombie will be good for you. He's made a difference already. But yesterday, on the phone, I should have mentioned that he and your father are sort of acquainted.'

'What do you mean, "acquainted"?' Olivia was suspicious.

'It's a business relationship – I think you'd call it that.'

'You mean gambling?' Olivia said bluntly.

'Yes, I suppose so.'

'Is that where the money goes?' Gradually, over the last few years, a few unassailable facts had permeated the shell of Olivia's selfishness. She now realised that, far from improving, the Dorchesters' financial position had deteriorated since her brother's disappearance to Australia and Annaliese's purchase of the Titian.

'Curiously enough, the bets on Abercrombie's horses always appear to win,' Caroline said. 'The others – well – it's awful.'

Stirred to compassion for her mother, Olivia said, 'Why do you put up with it?'

Caroline gaped at her in utter astonishment. 'Because I have no alternative, you twerp. You're not casting me in the role of the perfect wife, are you? Good grief, Hector Abercrombie's rotting your brains. Aubrey would dance for joy if I left him. Apart from anything else, it would probably save him a fortune.'

'How?'

'He must spend tens of thousands a year on his sort of sex in London – he likes to be tied up and beaten. If I were out of his way, he'd move one of his fancy women in and promise to marry her.'

After a stunned pause, Olivia said, 'Do you know, I think I will have that drink after all.'

Caroline attended to it, replenishing her own glass at the same time.

'What a bloody mess,' Olivia said savagely.

'We're no different to the others,' Caroline said. 'I doubt if there's a big house in the country that isn't riddled with exactly the same problem.'

'Why does Monty hate us?' Olivia cried. 'He didn't even answer my letter.'

Caroline was surprised. 'You wrote to him?'

'About eighteen months ago. Monty can't stand the sight of us. Why?'

Ironic amusement lit up Caroline's face as she formulated her reply. 'Let's deal with the easy one first,' she said. 'Monty thinks that I'm an out-and-out whore.' Caroline paused to sip at her drink. 'A harsh judgement, but accurate – though sadly out-of-date. As to your father, Monty started off by being quite affectionate and sympathetic. I think he understood the dreadful damage that foul old Grandfather Dorchester did to your father when he was a boy. But, in the fullness of time, Monty decided that Aubrey was nothing more than a self-pitying, weak-willed crook. So he walked out. *After* he'd gone, he was accused of being responsible for the great disaster of 1956.'

'Which was really caused by Father's gambling?'

'Something like that,' Caroline sighed.

Flabbergasted, Olivia asked, 'How come I knew nothing about this?'

'You were terribly, terribly busy,' Caroline said sweetly. 'You were trapping George, having fun with Simon Faulkener – and there was that other chap whose name I forget. And be honest, darling, even if you hadn't been fully occupied, you still wouldn't have given a damn.'

Olivia glowered. 'What's Monty got against *me*?'

'He was never particularly fond of you,' Caroline replied. 'If pressed, I'd say that he finally turned after you drove his best friend to commit suicide.'

'I did no such thing,' Olivia flared. 'In any case, they saved the fool.'

'Only by the skin of several people's teeth,' Caroline pointed out. 'Including, may I remind you, David Naismith.'

'There's no need to drag him into it,' Olivia snapped. 'It's all in the past and done with. Let's deal with the present – are you suggesting that I should keep away from Hector Aber-crombie?'

'If I said yes, would you be able to?' Caroline asked.

'No, not after last night.'

Caroline lapsed into thought. 'Hector obviously didn't mention your father,' she said at last.

'No.'

'I imagine it's in his interests not to. I'm certain that

whatever it is they do isn't entirely legal.' Caroline spread her hands in a gesture of despair. 'There's nothing I can advise. You're going to have an affair with him whatever I say, so get on with it and enjoy yourself. However, I have misgivings.'

Feigning shock, Olivia said, 'You aren't starting to suffer from moral scruples, are you?'

'Certainly not.' Caroline resented the accusation. 'I'm being practical. I have a feeling that your association with Abercrombie will cause something bad.'

Reverting to normal as only she knew how, Olivia treated it as a huge joke. 'Doom, doom, doom!' she shouted. 'The end of the world is nigh. For heaven's sake, Mother, cheer up. And I'm starving, so can we please have lunch? Then, I *must* sleep.'

Hector Abercrombie was an arrogant, generally disagreeable individual whose one saving grace was that he treated horses and whoever happened to be his current mistress with a degree of consideration. To the limited extent that he considered Olivia's personal qualities, he judged her to be unprincipled and more selfish than himself – a serious defect.

But the fact that they were incapable of liking each other was neither here nor there in the face of the sexual obsession that obliterated all else. Perfectly matched and insatiable, they continually generated a delirious excitement that acted on them like a drug.

The only restraint on their pleasure was Olivia's rapidly mounting aversion to the atmosphere at Saxon Lodge. The stable lads were a coarse, inferior bunch, paid substandard wages and living under the permanent threat of arbitrary dismissal. When it proved impossible for Olivia to get in or out of the place without being the object of their brazenly prurient curiosity, her temper boiled over.

'Can you imagine what these bloody oiks must say about

me,' she screamed at Abercrombie.

'Vividly.' He thought it funny. 'They're jealous, that's all.'

Calmly, because she was prepared to forgive him anything in return for his sexual prowess, Olivia said, 'No, Hector, I'm not coming here again. I have a house where we can enjoy privacy.'

'Is that wise? I mean, is it *safe*?'

'Perfectly.' Not bothering to consider the point, Olivia was supremely confident.

For a variety of reasons, Hector Abercrombie was tempted to argue. He had always preferred to indulge his propensity for adultery in the comfort and security of his own home: somehow, allowing the mistress to choose the venue often gave her the idea that the relationship would put an end to his constant search for new conquests. However, until he had banked the money for the Canalettos and was ready to abandon Wiltshire in favour of somewhere far more exotic, Abercrombie decided that Olivia was worth a small sacrifice.

Having inspected her house, he had no qualms. The Chantry, less than fifteen minutes' driving time from Saxon Lodge, seemed ideal. Just inside the Park's north-western gate, it could, especially during winter's long hours of darkness, be reached without risk of being seen. The only slight problem was the maid who lived there in splendid isolation, ready to be at Olivia's beck and call on visits that had, since the Mayhew affair, been few and far between. The girl was ordered to return to the Castle. She could, she was graciously informed, clean The Chantry on Tuesdays and Wednesdays while the Duchess of Lincolnshire was away in London.

Travelling to Compton Allardyce one Friday evening, Athene was thinking of Hector Abercrombie as she mulled over the experts' valuations of his pictures. With her mind leaping from pillar to post in a way that seemed perfectly logical, she remembered the evening George had telephoned after his day in Norfolk.

Out of the blue, she asked David, '*Did* you see George?'

'Eh?' David, concentrating on driving, was baffled. 'Was I supposed to?'

'He was asking for you – that time you were in Surbiton with what's-his-name.'

'Oh, *then*.' There was a slight pause while David overtook a lorry. 'Yes, we had a get-together.'

'George said it was important,' Athene hinted.

'Pretty much so,' David said. Staring fixedly at the road ahead, he could feel Athene's eyes boring into him. 'Am I going to get any peace if I don't tell you?' he asked.

'No.'

'He wanted to make his will – and before you jump to conclusions, that's perfectly normal. He should have done it when he succeeded to the title.'

Considering the point, Athene agreed. 'Fancy asking *you*, though, instead of the other lot – you know, the people Edward used. Isn't that a feather in your cap?'

'I suppose it is,' David said mildly, glad that Athene had found something to keep her preoccupied and happy.

21

1968

'You don't think you should wait for her opinion?'

St Valentine's Day, Wednesday 14 February, was bitterly cold with snow showers driven by a piercing east wind. Soon after dusk, the sky cleared, the winds dropped, and a hard frost set in.

At 8.00 pm, two cars converged in a rarely used lane on the southern edge of Savernake Forest, seven miles from Compton Allardyce. Nicholas Hammond, who had driven the Rolls-Royce, left the virtually silent engine idling to provide heat as he got out and walked towards the nondescript family saloon in which the Duke of Dorchester had travelled alone from Widney Cheyne. The two men passed without a word.

Annaliese, muffled in rugs, nodded a cursory greeting as Aubrey Dorchester joined her in the back seat of the Rolls. Twenty yards away, Nicholas made himself comfortable in the Ford and hoped they wouldn't be too long: there was a TV programme at 9.30 that he particularly wanted to see.

'Damn me if this isn't a new car,' Aubrey said, examining

the luxurious interior in the dim glow of the light behind his shoulder.

'It's the latest Silver Cloud,' Annaliese replied. 'Bodywork by Mulliner's, of course. Rather nice.'

'You do yourself well.'

'I have money, you need some of it,' Annaliese said, retaliating and reminding him of the harsh facts behind their association.

But Aubrey Dorchester wanted to air another grievance. 'Do we have to play this silly game? Why can't we go somewhere decent and have dinner? We'd be all right in The Bear at Hungerford.'

Annaliese's sigh of exasperation was slightly louder than she intended. On this, their fourth such meeting, she had hoped to be spared the peevish preliminaries. 'No, Aubrey,' she said firmly. 'If you imagine that we can risk being seen together in public and avoid recognition and speculation, you're an even bigger fool than I took you for.'

The mild, almost craven response to the deliberate insult intrigued Annaliese. Squirming, Aubrey Dorchester said, 'This is difficult – devilishly so.'

Beneath the rugs, Annaliese's hands clenched in irritation. When she spoke, she was ominously calm. 'Let me remind you of what we are trying to achieve. George will divorce Olivia on whatever grounds David Naismith deems appropriate. Naturally, we shall be granted custody of John and Valerie, who will be fully protected from the proceedings. You will take Olivia under your wing and ensure that she remains silent. In return I shall pay you two million pounds over five years. The instalments are conditional upon Olivia's behaviour.'

'It's a good offer,' Aubrey muttered. 'I appreciate that.'

Patiently, Annaliese asked, 'Have you found a way of keeping Olivia quiet?'

'I envisage using a form of blackmail. I'll give her an allowance from what you pay me *and* threaten her with the past.'

'There's ammunition there, I take it?'

'More than enough,' Aubrey said grimly. 'You have no idea. I should never have allowed George to be saddled with her.'

'As a matter of fact, we were warned,' Annaliese replied. 'I chose to ignore it. We required an heir. In that respect, at least, Olivia has done us proud.'

'You must pray that Valerie hasn't picked up her bad blood,' Aubrey said. 'Olivia takes after Caroline, you know. That woman has made my life a misery.'

In no mood to indulge her companion's desire for sympathy, Annaliese said, 'Don't worry about Valerie, she's splendid. Why are you finding this so difficult?'

'It's Abercrombie,' Aubrey grumbled. 'Olivia taking up with him is a confounded nuisance.'

'Why?' The question was like a gunshot.

'I have what you might call a partnership with Abercrombie.'

'What sort of partnership?' Annaliese demanded. 'Horses? Gambling?'

'Something along those lines.' It was plain that Aubrey Dorchester was unwilling to go further.

Annaliese let out a snort of displeasure. 'Are you telling me that this appalling man is in a position to make trouble for you?'

'Yes,' was the abject response.

'Without incriminating himself?'

'Well – I'd have to think about that.' There was grudging respect for the shrewdness of the question.

'What does this mean?' Annaliese asked. 'Won't you be able to control Olivia as long as she's associating with Abercrombie?'

'I don't know. I shall have to study the options.'

'So shall I,' Annaliese snapped.

'What have you in mind?' He was anxious.

'*One possibility* . . .' Annaliese stressed the words '. . . is that we act without your so-called help. That would mean filing for divorce and letting Olivia do her worst. We could expect a week of muck-raking in the press, but then what? They'd find a new sensation, we'd be forgotten, and I would have saved two million.'

'You might not get away with it that easily,' Aubrey Dorchester said, trying to sound calm. In reality, the prospect of losing the money made him feel sick.

'All right, the pandemonium could last *two* weeks,' Annaliese conceded. 'Three if Olivia carried out her threat to expose George. I'm prepared to ride that out if you can't – or won't – help.'

Nervously, Aubrey said, 'You implied that you think there are other avenues open to you.'

'Yes.' Annaliese paused, clearly wondering whether to show her hand. 'I could try something that doesn't seem to have occurred to you. Caroline has influence with Olivia: why haven't you enlisted her?'

Aubrey laughed derisively. 'She'd never co-operate.'

'Not even if I persuaded the bank to foreclose the mortgage on Widney Cheyne?' Annaliese said quietly.

'Damn it, do you know *everything*?' Aubrey snarled.

'I'm not sure,' Annaliese murmured. 'I wasn't aware you had links with Abercrombie and I'm not *au fait* with the whole of Olivia's chequered past. However, I certainly know about your financial affairs. All it needs is a word from Nigel Templeton and the bankers would be after your blood. I can't see Caroline liking that.'

Aubrey thought for a few moments before saying, 'I'll talk to her – but don't raise your hopes. She's an awkward bitch.'

'I've never doubted it,' Annaliese replied. 'She may change her tune when she finds out just how bad things are, that you're living from hand to mouth on borrowed money which you have no hope of repaying.' After a pause, she said, 'I understand Monty is doing very well in Australia.'

They stared at each other, eyes suddenly intense in the dim light. Annaliese watched Aubrey Dorchester's defiance give way to a hunted look. 'You've been in touch with him?' he whispered.

'David Naismith has.'

'And?'

Annaliese took her time. 'One of the things that's consistently baffled me, Aubrey, is that you've never seemed to care about what will happen to you after you've gone. People of our class usually spend their entire lives building for a future they won't see, worrying how much their son will inherit, looking for ways of augmenting the family's wealth. But you've frittered it away – on horses, roulette, and women wielding canes. I have been well and truly amazed! Ten days ago, I was given the answer.' In a softer, even more frightening voice, Annaliese said, 'David Naismith and Monty were close at Eton. It seems that the friendship remains intact.'

The Duke of Dorchester was silent, gazing bleakly at his clenched hands, stunned by the appalling extent of his adversary's knowledge.

Understanding his state of mind, Annaliese realised that there was no point in going any further at the moment. 'You have four weeks to produce a plan that will convince me,' she said.

'That isn't long enough. Give me two months – preferably three.'

'Out of the question. Your daughter becomes more of a menace with each day that passes, Aubrey, and I want rid of her before she drags us into something that could be ten times worse than betraying George.'

'She's sorry about saying that, you know.'

'She threatened me,' Annaliese said. 'No one does that with impunity. Go away and think. Unless I hear from you in the meantime, I shall be here four weeks from tonight. That will be your last chance.'

Realising that argument was futile, Aubrey Dorchester grunted a churlish attempt at 'Good night' and went. Anticipating the end of the meeting, Nicholas was already out of the Ford. Again, the two men passed without a sign of acknowledgement.

Nimbly, Annaliese transferred to the front of the Rolls to sit beside Nicholas. They watched the other car leave, then set off towards Compton Allardyce.

There was silence until Annaliese decided to say, 'This isn't going to work. I now discover that Dorchester is involved with Abercrombie in something shady.'

'And is scared of him?' Nicholas suggested.

'Apparently so,' Annaliese said curtly.

'The Jockey Club have been watching Abercrombie for at least two years,' Nicholas said. 'He isn't expected to last much longer.'

'He won't mind,' Annaliese replied. 'When his pictures are sold, he can run if things get awkward. Come to think of it, that was probably his intention from the start.'

'When is the sale?'

Annaliese pulled a face. 'Not before April. Both George and Athene want plenty of time for publicity. It's one of the biggest things that Boothby's have ever done.'

They fell silent, Nicholas sensing that Annaliese was in turmoil, weighing pros and cons, looking for a better solution. Eventually, she unburdened herself. 'You see, Nicholas, it isn't as though I can trust Dorchester. There's every chance that he'd disappear the minute I gave him the first instalment. Four hundred thousand would take him a long way.'

'I might be tempted if I had *her* for a wife,' Nicholas said.

'Mmm.' Annaliese nodded. 'There's more to it than that.'

'Do you want to tell me?' Nicholas asked.

'Yes, I think I do. But you'd better stop for a moment.'

Mystified, Nicholas pulled up.

Facing him squarely, Annaliese said, 'The absent Monty — who appears to be a fine man, contrary to what we've been told — is Olivia's *half* brother. They share a mother, but Monty's father was someone other than Aubrey Dorchester. This came to light when Monty was about fifteen. Caroline had always known, of course. Aubrey suspected.'

Stupefied, Nicholas understood why he had been told to stop: otherwise, there was every chance that they would have ended up in the ditch. Clearing his throat, he said, 'Was the Duchess of Dorchester pregnant when she married the Duke?'

'No. Monty was born fourteen months later.'

'So . . .' Nicholas was struggling to come to terms with the enormity of the revelation and its implications. 'The Duchess behaved extremely badly immediately after her marriage?'

'It would seem so.' Annaliese smiled at the expression on Nicholas's face as an appalling thought took root in his mind. 'Don't worry,' she said, patting his arm reassuringly. 'Olivia didn't. I'm sure of it.'

'Really?'

'Yes. Thanks to my Wittelsbach ancestors, George has a very rare blood group. Olivia's isn't all that common and both John and Valerie are exactly as they should be given that combination. The chances of another man producing that are millions and millions to one.'

Shaking his head in amazement, Nicholas asked, 'Is anyone aware that you had that check carried out?'

'Don't be silly!' Annaliese chided. They both grinned, fellow-conspirators glad of a chance to relieve the tension

'The Dorchester mess is no concern of mine,' Annaliese said. 'In the normal course of events, I wouldn't give it a second thought. But things seem to be coming to a head and I can't predict what they'll do. Therefore, they're untrustworthy. Even if Aubrey says he'll keep Olivia quiet, I can't rely on him doing so.'

Diffidently, Nicholas asked the question that had nagged at him for weeks. 'You haven't told George that you're talking to Dorchester?'

Annaliese shook her head furiously. 'He's too honest. He'd let Olivia know – especially now. He hates her, you see, so it's getting very tricky.'

Nicholas nodded. On the verge of coming to terms with it all, he was struck by a new thought. 'Does Olivia know that Monty isn't her full brother?'

'We think not,' Annaliese replied.

'This is the very devil,' Nicholas muttered.

'Isn't it, though? Are you in a fit state to drive now?'

When the Rolls was underway, Annaliese said, 'Go round to the north-west gate. I want to be nosy.'

Ten minutes later, Nicholas brought the limousine to a gentle halt at the entrance to The Chantry's short drive. Initially, the house appeared unoccupied and lifeless. Then Annaliese said, 'The curtains are drawn. The maid wouldn't have left them like that.' Lowering the window, she caught the faint but distinctive smell of wood smoke. 'There's a fire going,' she whispered, drawing back and pressing the button to close the window.

'No sign of a car,' Nicholas said.

'She's started putting it in the garage,' Annaliese replied. 'So does he.'

Annaliese's mind was inside the ostensibly empty house, where she was certain that Olivia and Hector Abercrombie were revelling in sex. 'It's Wednesday,' she mused. 'That means Olivia was at Boothby's until five-thirty or six o'clock.'

'Wasted no time getting here,' Nicholas commented drily.

'No.' Annaliese bit her lip, thinking furiously hard. 'I'll let it go another month,' she said at last. 'It can't do any harm and Aubrey might come up trumps. If he doesn't, we'll do it the hard way.' She threw up her hands to signify that she had reached the final decision and it was time to relax. 'Let's get on. If we go to your house, Nicholas, you'll be in time to watch that programme about the Battle of the Atlantic. I'll gossip to Henry, and you can take me home afterwards.'

'That's very thoughtful of you,' Nicholas said.

'I can be a charmer when the mood takes me.' Apparently without a care in the world, she smiled in that special way that always made Nicholas think that most of the twentieth century and the two terrible wars had never happened.

Looking forward to a long weekend, George left Boothby's early in the afternoon of Thursday, 22 February. It was to be four days of rest and self-appraisal, an attempt to come to terms with the discovery that Tony Austen-Cave had reverted to wanting more than one lover. The most hurtful aspect of the previous evening's row had been Tony's inability to take demands for faithfulness seriously. 'Good God, we aren't *married*,' he had laughed. 'Don't be such a wet blanket, George. You can't beat us, so why not join us? Clive would sell his soul for a threesome. We could educate you – show you what you've been missing.'

Horrified, both by the suggestion and the flippant way in which it was made, George had reacted angrily. 'That's a monstrous idea. Why do you have to put me through this after what we've been to each other? Don't you appreciate the risks I run on your account? It's a nightmare.'

Tony's good humour had vanished in an instant. 'It's

beyond me why you bother,' he had shouted, unpleasantly angry. 'I suggest you take a look at yourself and decide once and for all just what you want. You've never committed yourself to me. Do you know how many times I've had to listen to you blethering on about how utterly brilliant your bloody wife is at masturbation? That's what it boils down to, isn't it? You only need someone to toss you off. Well, I'm sick of it. Lord Lincolnshire, you and I have had it. We're finished, washed-up, done for!'

Although shaking with rage, George left the flat with a passable attempt at dignity. Tony had rushed after him, but in the thirty seconds that had elapsed before remorse took a grip George was able to jump into a taxi which, in light traffic, promptly disappeared round the nearest corner. As he headed towards Wiltshire on that Thursday afternoon, still upset as he tried to enjoy the brand-new Rover 2000, George forced himself to accept that his relationship with Tony was finally and irrevocably over.

That evening, when he accompanied Annaliese to Eaton Mandeville to dine with the Laverstokes and two other friends, George was in a far better mood, acting as though finally relieved of a crushing burden. Having come to the conclusion that he would be celibate in future, he was looking forward to his forty-sixth birthday on Monday. There was to be a party at the house in Shady Bower; part of the Cathedral Choir were expected to sing a special arrangement of 'Happy Birthday' followed by what John described as 'A suitable piece by Vivaldi'.

Later, however, while preparing for bed in the remoteness of the Castle's East Wing, George felt tension beginning to grip him and knew that he was in for a bad night. Desperate for oblivion, he searched for the tablets Dr Murdoch had prescribed at the height of the Mayhew crisis. After swallowing twice the recommended dose, he slept until nearly

10.00 am the following morning when Osbourne brought him a tray.

'I hope I'm doing the right thing, Your Grace,' the butler said. 'Mrs Osbourne thought you'd want to be up and about. I'm afraid she's inclined to *worry*, if you get my meaning.'

'I'm grateful to you, Osbourne.' Struggling to wake up, George asked, 'Have you seen my mother, this morning?'

'Indeed I have, sir. Her Grace breakfasted early and has gone to Sherborne for one of her diocesan functions. She's opening two bring-and-buy sales, addressing the Mother's Union, and presenting swimming certificates at the school.' Osbourne, who worshipped Annaliese, provided the information with a flourish of pride. 'She asked me to tell you that she will return no later than four o'clock.'

'What about my wife?' George asked. 'Any idea of her whereabouts?'

Osbourne had learned to conceal his intense dislike of Olivia. His manner was perfectly neutral as he said, 'Her maid informs me that Lady Lincolnshire is spending the weekend with her parents at Widney Cheyne.'

Smiling, George said, 'Thank you, Osbourne.'

Fortified by coffee and toast, George bathed, shaved and dressed. Then, on his way to the West Wing, he paused in the Long Gallery. It was a fine day, and the sun was streaming in through the windows that made up virtually the whole of one wall. Shading his eyes against the glare, George gazed out. Strong though the sun seemed in the clear, azure sky, it was unlikely to make much impression on last night's deep frost. Beyond the frozen lake, the grass was brilliantly white, each blade glittering with a thousand tiny crystals of ice. It was one of the most beautiful views in England and George looked forward to the time, only a few weeks away, when it would be vibrant with the life of a new spring.

On his way to the old stables at the back of the Castle,

George popped into the butler's pantry.

'I'm going to take the Rover out for a spin, get used to it and blow a few cobwebs away.'

'Very well, Your Grace.' Osbourne interrupted his polishing of a silver salver to stare at George with po-faced gravity. 'How do you find the Rover, sir? According to the motoring magazines, it's an excellent machine, but somewhat *sedate*, shall we say?'

George laughed. 'You're quite right, Osbourne. "Sluggish" is the word you're looking for. But it behaved itself coming down from London yesterday and I *have* to like it – it's a premature birthday present from my mother. According to the report she read, it's a very safe vehicle.'

'Ah, I see, sir.' Osbourne smiled sympathetically. 'Well, do your best with it.'

George was turning to leave when the butler remembered something. 'Miss Trenchard telephoned from Salisbury.' He dug into a drawer for the piece of paper on which he had made notes. 'It seems that Lady Valerie left a book at The Chantry when she was there for those few days last summer. If Your Grace would be so kind, you are to retrieve it and take it to Shady Bower on Monday.'

'Of course, what is it?'

'Piano music by Brahms.' Osbourne gave George the paper.

'Ah, yes – she was moaning about that a couple of weeks ago. I'll collect it now so that it doesn't get forgotten.' George looked at the board on which dozens of key rings were hanging. 'Have you got a set for The Chantry there, Osbourne? It will save me traipsing back to my rooms.'

'I have, sir. Here you are.'

'Thanks.' George slipped them into the pocket of his short motoring coat. 'I'll be about two hours, I expect. Is there any chance of one of your wife's steak pies for lunch?'

'*Every* chance, Your Grace,' Osbourne replied.

George cruised up the road towards the north-western entrance to the Park, his window open, enjoying the invigorating, champagne-like air. Stopping the Rover within feet of The Chantry's front door, he took the keys from his pocket, turned the well-oiled mortise and the equally quiet Yale lock, and went in.

One of Bach's *Brandenburg Concertos* had been running through his carefree mind. As George closed the door and took stock of his surroundings, the joyful music stopped abruptly.

Very deliberately and carefully, George thought, *No, this isn't right*.

The house was not empty. It was warmer than he'd expected. Edging closer to one of the electric radiators in the entrance-hall, George discovered that it was pouring out heat. He caught a whiff of grilled bacon. Above all, there was the noise.

Stealthily, hardly daring to breathe, he tiptoed towards the kitchen, unable to resist the terrible, fascinating sounds of lust.

Olivia and Hector Abercrombie had woken late and treated their lack of desire for each other as a joke.

'You excelled yourself last night,' Olivia said. 'You've ruined us.'

'Don't you be so sure,' Abercrombie replied, running his hands over her. 'Give me a good breakfast and I'll show you how ruined I am.'

'A good breakfast?' Olivia hooted. 'Where does that come from? I'll have you know that cooking was one of the eleven subjects I failed abysmally.'

'And you've never tried to rectify that?'

'Of course I haven't, you fool. I'm a duchess, for Christ's sake!'

After they had both enjoyed the joke, Abercrombie said, 'Is there food in the house?'

'I'll crucify that maid if there isn't.'

Grandly, Abercrombie announced, 'I can cook.'

'I *am* hungry,' Olivia admitted. 'Faint and wan through lack of nourishment.'

They went to the bathroom, laughed at each other's use of the lavatory, cleaned their teeth, grabbed dressing-gowns, and padded downstairs. While Abercrombie delved into the larder and fridge, Olivia turned on the electric heaters and boosted the oil-fired kitchen range that provided hot water as well as cooking. Somewhat to her surprise, she began to make coffee. Having found bacon, eggs, sausages, and mushrooms, Abercrombie set to work with grill and frying-pan. Expertly, he produced a meal that Olivia devoured ravenously.

'How do you feel now?' Abercrombie asked when they had finished.

'Better. Ready for anything.'

Reaching for the coffee-pot to refill his cup, Hector Abercrombie wondered if any other woman could possibly have a smile like Olivia's – certainly, he had never seen anything so lustrously insolent, a combination of carnal invitation and challenge.

'Are you up to it?' she asked, reading his thoughts.

'Whenever you like,' Abercrombie said. To prove it, he parted the dressing-gown.

'You're a horny bastard,' Olivia said, feasting her eyes.

'Uniquely so, I've always believed.'

'Could be. You do a good line in egotism, too.'

'Why bother with modesty? *You* don't.'

'I'm the best,' Olivia said happily. 'You've said so.'

'I don't deny it.' Standing up, Abercrombie caught her wrist, intending to take her back to the bedroom.

'No, here,' Olivia said, resisting. 'Let's do it here.'

Shrugging out of her robe, she flaunted her nakedness, then turned away from Abercrombie and bent across the old-fashioned, scrubbed-top table. 'How does this strike you?' she asked, glancing over her shoulder.

Abercrombie's face tautened with desire as he studied her perfect legs and buttocks. Motionless, he savoured the sight. 'What's wrong?' Olivia said. 'Too much for you? Can't you handle it? I'm ready if you are.'

Closing the gap between them, Abercrombie lunged straight into her, his exultant shout of 'Bitch!' mingling with the scream of her sudden, sharp ecstasy.

Brutal though he was, she found it inadequate. 'Harder . . . go on, harder,' Olivia panted. 'This is fabulous . . . more!'

The table shook under Abercrombie's assault. One of the breakfast plates danced its way to the edge and fell to the stone floor, shattering. The noise of the breakage and Olivia's laughter wiped out what slender chance the demented pair had of hearing the quiet locks on the front door.

'It's been too quick,' Olivia moaned.

'What the hell do you mean?'

'I'm coming, damn you, I'm coming . . .'

'So am I – soon.'

Olivia climaxed first. Hector Abercrombie needed another fifteen seconds of crazed lunging before he erupted into orgasm. As he leaned forward to gasp obscene compliments into Olivia's ear, the door opened and George appeared.

They were facing each other, separated only by the table.

Several moments passed before Abercrombie, then Olivia realised they were being gaped at.

Minds refused to function. George was befuddled, wondering if the delayed after-effects of two sleeping tablets were playing tricks on him. Olivia and Abercrombie, enmeshed and slumped across the table, gasped for breath and waited for rationality to return.

Olivia was first. Contemptuously calm, she said, 'Good morning, darling. To what do we owe the pleasure?'

To George's subsequent astonishment, he gave an equally composed reply. 'I came to collect some music for Valerie. She left it behind last summer.'

'Ah. I see.'

No one had moved so much as a finger.

George, suddenly aware of Abercrombie's sneering amusement, said, 'What *are* you doing?'

It was as if Olivia had spent the last twelve years waiting for the half-witted question. 'This is what's known as heterosexual intercourse, darling – a pastime you never quite got the hang of. My friend, Hector, is something of a specialist. I think he could win prizes for it. My only regret is that I didn't take your advice sooner.'

'What advice?' George seemed genuinely curious.

'Don't you remember when we had our little chat and decided to go our separate ways? You suggested that I might like to screw Hector so that he'd let you handle his pictures. Well, it happened the other way round – he decided to sell, then we screwed – repeatedly!' Olivia laughed. 'He's good, not a bit worried by you blundering in here. Shall I tell you how I know? It's because he's still got his cock inside me and it's as hard as iron – even though he came just before you popped in. I think he's going to fuck me again.'

Slightly giddy, feeling that the kitchen floor was tilting under his feet, George said, 'I'll go – I'll look for Valerie's music.'

'Why don't you do that?' Olivia purred.

George went, leaving the door open. Although he knew where the book of Brahms Rhapsodies and Intermezzi was, he blundered round the drawing-room like a drunkard, bumping into furniture, upsetting a magazine rack, and breaking a vase. Picking up the music, he wandered back into the hall and stood indecisively at the front door. He had made up his mind to go when Olivia called out, ''Bye, darling.'

Looking into the kitchen, he saw that she was still sprawled across the table. Behind her, standing upright now, Hector Abercrombie was rocking gently backwards and forwards. Goerge took a few paces towards them, halting in the doorway.

Olivia's mood changed. 'Do you want to watch?' she demanded nastily. 'See how it's done? What a waste that would be! Piss off, George. Go and play with yourself. Or find a pretty, young boy. Did you know there's a club in Swindon for perverts like you?'

Wondering why he hadn't done so before, George saw the smashed plate and realised that one of the dressing-gowns on the floor belonged to him. Quietly, but with the beginnings of a terrible anger, George said, 'You vile creature! Is this what Ian Brown had to put up with? You know who I mean — Monty's friend, the chap who slashed his wrists.'

Leaving the house as if pursued by demons, George was unaware that he had ruined Olivia's morning.

George drove back to the Castle, left the car at the main entrance and charged upstairs to the library. Ten minutes later, Osbourne received news that His Grace was back already and in a filthy mood. 'Looked fit to kill, he did,' the footman said.

'Where is he?' Osbourne asked.

'Somewhere in the West Wing, I think.'

Snatching at the telephone, George misdialled several times before getting through to David's office in London and disappointment.

'I'm terribly sorry, Your Grace, Mr Naismith is out,' the secretary said.

'When's he due back?' George snapped.

'He's at Horseferry Road Magistrate's Court,' the girl replied. 'He was expecting the case to be finished before lunch.'

'Will you ask him to ring me the minute he gets in.' Swallowing hard and attempting to be more pleasant, George added, 'Please tell him that it's very, very urgent.'

'Yes, Lord Lincolnshire, I will.'

Slumped in the chair behind his father's old desk, George gradually became aware of his surroundings, saw the decanter of whisky in its time-honoured place on top of the filing cabinet that had once held Foreign Office secrets. Grimacing as the neat spirit scorched his throat, George promptly felt better. His hands stopped shaking, the floor no longer slanted away from him. In control, he poured a second drink. There was a tap at the door and Osbourne appeared. Two Labradors sidled into the room, snuffled welcomingly round George and collapsed in front of the fire.

'I heard you were back, sir,' Osbourne said. 'Is anything wrong?'

'Wrong? Why should anything be wrong?' George blustered. 'No, I'm fine, thanks, Osbourne.'

'Very well, Your Grace.' Hiding his scepticism, Osbourne said, 'Would you like lunch now, or shall you wait?'

'Now,' George replied. 'Sandwiches, I think.'

'You were thinking of steak pie, sir.'

'Never mind that,' George snapped. 'I want sandwiches. Bring them here, I'm waiting for a call.'

George ate one small ham sandwich and fiddled with the others, looking at his watch every minute. David's call came through at 12.50.

'George, what can I do for you?'

'I must see you as soon as possible.'

'Fine. What's the problem?' David was calmly proficient.

'I want to divorce Olivia. The sooner the better.'

'Fair enough.' After the merest pause to gather his thoughts, David asked, 'What's brought this on?'

George needed a sip of whisky. 'I went to The Chantry this morning to get something for Valerie. I was expecting the place to be empty. *She* was in the kitchen with Abercrombie. They were having sex – Olivia was draped across the table.'

'You actually caught them at it?'

'Yes.'

'Good God,' David said quietly. 'I'm very sorry, George. I can see that this must be the last straw.'

'Oh, it is, believe me.' George's voice was heavy with emotion. 'When can I see you?'

'Monday?' David suggested.

'That's no good, I need to get things moving.' George was shaking again. 'I'm a bit of a coward, David, you know that. If I spend too long thinking, I'll start inventing excuses to forget it. But I won't. Not this time!' Slightly calmer, he said, 'What about tomorrow? I know it's Saturday, but it's desperately important.'

'Sorry, George, tomorrow's a big day. It's the annual Law Society golf jamboree at Wentworth. I'm playing and Athene wouldn't let me opt out – it's her only chance of hearing some of the legal profession's dark secrets.' Thinking quickly, David said, 'How about today? Can you come up to Town?'

'Yes!' George said eagerly.

'I shall be tied up all afternoon,' David said. 'But if you call in at six, we could have a chat, draw up a plan, then join Athene for dinner.'

'That's good of you, David. I'm very grateful.'

'Er . . . there is one thing. Have you spoken to your mother about this?'

'No. She's out. I doubt if she'll be back before I leave. She's hardly likely to disapprove, is she?'

'Oh, I wouldn't think so,' David said airily. 'Quite the contrary, I imagine.' He paused, wondering whether it would be best if George knew about the negotiations with Aubrey Dorchester. 'You don't think you should wait for her opinion?'

'Don't be silly,' George said. 'We can take that for granted.'

Accepting that Annaliese would have a chance to express her views before the first formal steps were taken on Monday or Tuesday, David said, 'Right, see you at six.'

Replacing the receiver, George was struck by a thought that gave him a moment or two of ironic amusement. David, his rescuer, was married to the one woman who, but for the accidental unworthiness of her birth, could have altered the entire course of the last twelve years. Aloud, George said, 'Athene, Duchess of Lincolnshire. Mmm . . . yes. It sounds good.' Realising that he had attracted the interest and curiosity of the dogs, he continued, addressing them. 'Imagine, no Olivia! We probably wouldn't even have heard of her. On the other hand, what about John and Valerie, eh? They wouldn't exist, so it hasn't been a *total* disaster.'

The dogs grunted what seemed to be agreement and George reached for another sandwich. Changing his mind, he poured the whisky and began to compose a note to Annaliese, telling her why he had decided to dash off to London.

After George's departure from The Chantry, Olivia found that she had lost her appetite for sex and sent Hector Abercrombie packing. Having dressed and tidied the kitchen, she drove to Widney Cheyne. Arriving soon after 1.00 pm, she found her parents picking at lunch in an atmosphere of venomous hostility.

Dragging Caroline away from the dining-room, Olivia told

her of the morning's events at Compton Allardyce.

'And he mentioned Ian Brown?' a surprisingly disinterested Caroline asked.

'Plus the wrist-slashing,' Olivia said. 'He knows everything.'

Caroline let out a shriek of bitter, humourless laughter. 'I doubt if poor George does know everything. *That* is the prerogative of his mother, the all-seeing Annaliese!'

Setting her own worries aside to take more notice of Caroline, Olivia realised that she was in a strange, wild mood. 'Mummy, what is it?' she asked.

'There's something you simply must do,' Caroline said.

'Yes?'

'Let me explain – and *please*, Olivia, darling, don't interrupt. This morning, while you were in the trough with Abercrombie, your father has been acquainting me with the facts of life. They are as follows.' Caroline held up her right hand, ready to emphasise her points by counting on her fingers. 'This house and the Titians are mortgaged – have been for three years. Effectively, we're penniless, muddling along on credit that's running out. Annaliese wants rid of you and is prepared to pay two million if you go quietly, creating no scandal over George. Unless I use my best endeavours to persuade you in that direction, your father proposes telling the world that Monty is not his son. Monty, by the way, has known this since he was fifteen. I have no idea what Aubrey expects to gain by baring his soul, but I think he means to do it and to hell with the consequences.'

There was no risk of Olivia interrupting; she was ashen-faced and dumb with shock.

'Two million pounds will just about save us,' Caroline went on. '*If* we get it, Aubrey has promised to mend his ways and attempt a reconciliation with Monty. He said he'll go to Australia and talk to him, do his best to reach an understanding. If we don't get that money from Annaliese, we're finished and heading for utter disgrace. Now, listen carefully, darling. I want you to go back to Allardyce and beg George's forgiveness – if necessary, on your bended knees with tears in your eyes. Then, very politely and humbly, you will say that you won't contest a divorce or create the tiniest bit of trouble. Afterwards, I shall see Annaliese and make her believe that your father and I have worked a miracle and please can we have our two million pounds. It's all quite simple, isn't it?'

George lost track of time while writing to Annaliese. The note turned into eleven pages and he broke off frequently to prowl round the library, fingering the spines of books, looking out of the windows, and petting the slumbering dogs. It was almost 3.00 when he rang for Osbourne.

Handing over the bulging envelope, he said, 'I have to go to London on urgent business. Will you see that my mother gets this when she comes back from Sherborne.'

'Of course, Your Grace. How are you travelling?'

'By car. I'll drive myself.'

Noticing the level in the decanter and the uneaten sandwiches, Osbourne said, 'Might not the train be best, sir? The four thirty-five from Pewsey is very good. Jenkins will take you to the station.'

'I haven't got time for that,' George said irritably. 'I'll tell you what Jenkins can do, though. Ask him to put the Rover away and bring the Lagonda to the front door. I don't want to be sedate or sluggish on this trip.'

Osbourne attempted to stand his ground.

'Well, what are you waiting for?' George demanded. A craftiness came over him, making his eyes glitter. 'This is good news, Osbourne. You've never liked her, have you?'

'I beg your pardon, sir?'

'My wife. The greatest bitch in Christendom. You hate her. Well, so do I, Osbourne, so do I. I am going to London to start divorce proceedings. Right?'

Osbourne forgot himself. Smiling broadly, he said, 'Yes, Your Grace, well done!' Joyfully, he hurried off.

Fifteen minutes later, George strode out of the Castle to find the Lagonda waiting, its engine ticking over sweetly. A final thought occurred to him. 'Osbourne, be a good chap and ring Cadogan Square, will you? Tell them to expect me – probably late, I'm dining with Mr and Mrs Naismith.'

'They will appreciate the warning, Your Grace,' Osbourne replied with a knowing smile.

George drove off, turning left on to the main road through the Park. He breathed in deeply and looked round, elated by a new sense of freedom. Soon, he would be able to enjoy his inheritance without the constant, debilitating humiliation of a wife against whom he really should have been warned. Jabbing his foot on the accelerator, George started to sing – *Di quella pira* from *Il Trovatore*.

Entering the last four hundred tree-lined yards before the south-eastern gate, the Lagonda was travelling very fast indeed. George saw the squirrel about to dart across the road, swore affectionately and, without thinking, stamped on the brake.

Although bare of foliage, the trees had prevented the sun from making any impact on ice that had been accumulating over three days. Euphoric at the thought of permanent happiness and with his reflexes reduced to jelly by whisky, George was fascinated by the way the car veered inexorably and uncontrollably towards a two-hundred-year-old oak tree.

The noise of the calamitous impact was heard at the Castle and in the village. After the steering-wheel had crushed George's face, the column burst into his chest. Very soon, the frightful pain ebbed and he was drawn to the golden, welcoming light at the end of the dark tunnel that had been his life. As he went, George heard the sounds that had floated in from the quad on his last, wretched day at Oxford: the sweet song of a blackbird rose above that exceptionally gifted whistling of the first Rasumovsky Quartet.

When George died at precisely 3.17, Olivia was approaching the north-western gate, delayed and rendered distraught by the vicious row with her parents that had followed the revelation concerning Monty.

Annaliese, pleased to have completed the day's engagements with time to spare, was well on her way home, three miles and seven minutes away from total catastrophe.

And in Salisbury, Kate Trenchard and Valerie were taking their places in the Cathedral for Evensong. Neither they, nor the ten-year-old boy who was waiting in the Cloisters, fretting over the fact that his surplice was back to front, knew that John Arthur Wainfleet Boothby-Graffoe had just become the Twelfth Duke of Lincolnshire.

THE DANGEROUS FLOOD
Derek Nicholls

British Embassy official Edward Boothby-Graffoe assumed his passion for the beautiful Archduchess Annaliese von Habsburg would, inevitably, be unrequited. But, approved by the Imperial Family and made more piquant by the turbulent times, their love flourished in the weeks leading up to the Great War.

With the continent in turmoil, however, their marriage would have to wait; and even when their new life together eventually gets under way, it heralds further intrigue as the Boothby-Graffoes wrestle with forces that threaten to tear them apart. . . .

Set against the troubled backdrop of pre- and post-war Europe, *The Dangerous Flood* brilliantly captures the hypocrisy and rigidity of the ruling classes — while exposing their murky underworld of scandal, sex, and even murder. ‒

FICTION
0 7515 1309 1

THE JERICHO ROSE
Olive Etchells

1864: Keen to escape an unhappy past, Matthew Raike travels north from Devon to Lancashire. He soon sets his heart on employment at Jericho Mills.

The Schofields, a prominent local family, seem blessed with health, wealth and happiness – but misfortunes are waiting in the wings. Troubles are also on the way for Tizzie Ridings, the clever, flame-haired eldest daughter of local pawnbroker. Her longing to escape her background will lead her into dangerous territory ...

Trying to survive as best he can on the little work there is to be found, Matthew meets Martha Spencer. Though he had never thought to find love, Martha breaches his defences – but deep in Matthew's past lies a secret he cannot bear to reveal ...

FICTION
0 7515 0071 2

THE JERICHO TRUMPET
Olive Etchells

In 1876, Saltley is a flourishing mill-town at the heart of the Lancashire cotton trade. Jericho Mills is the town's lifeblood and the pride of its owner Joshua Schofield, an honest working man revered for his integrity and fair dealing. Work is plentiful, with the lean years of recent times mere distant memories.

Yet events are soon to disturb the peace, events which will resurrect the past and cloud the future for local people in hitherto unforeseen ways. For Matthew Raike, head gardener of the Schofield estate, it is a chance illicit encounter which reawakens youthful passions; for ambitious Tizzie Ridings, the family tragedy and malicious gossip that threatens her business reputation; for Sam Schofield, the one instinctive act of devotion which ends his wasted years.

But under the greatest threat of all could be Jericho Mills – and the danger, long dormant, comes from within, from the ranks of the Schofield family itself …

FICTION
0 7515 1032 7

VIKTORIA
Jenny Glanfield

Two great loves rule Viktoria Jochum-Kraus's life. One is the Hotel Quadriga, built by her father, opened on the day she was born and, in January 1933, the most luxurious hotel in Berlin.

The other is her son, Stefan. Only Viktoria knows that Stefan is the result of a youthful infatuation with her husband Benno's cousin, Count Peter von Biederstein. After a long absence abroad, Peter returns to Berlin – to the Berlin of a new political era, that of Hitler's Third Reich.

Terrified that her carefully guarded secret will be discovered, Viktoria soon realises that she no longer controls her own destiny. Not only is she forced to relinquish her hold over the Hotel Quadriga, but Stefan embarks upon a fateful love affair which she alone knows must have a tragic ending.

And as Stefan's affair reaches its climax and Germany moves irrevocably towards war, Viktoria is forced to make the most dreadful decision of her life ...

FICTION
0 7515 0996 5

The Dangerous Flood	Derek Nicholls	£5.99
The Jericho Rose	Olive Etchells	£5.99
The Jericho Trumpet	Olive Etchells	£5.99
Hotel Quadriga	Jenny Glanfield	£5.99
Viktoria	Jenny Glanfield	£5.99
Children of Their Time	Jenny Glanfield	£5.99

Warner Books now offers an exciting range of quality titles by both
established and new authors which can be ordered from the following
address:

    Little, Brown & Company (UK),
    P.O. Box 11,
    Falmouth,
    Cornwall TR10 9EN.
Alternatively you may fax your order to the above address.
Fax No. 01326 317444.

Payments can be made as follows: cheque, postal order (payable to Little,
Brown and Company) or by credit cards, Visa/Access. Do not send cash or
currency. UK customers and B.F.P.O. please allow £1.00 for postage and
packing for the first book, plus 50p for the second book, plus 30p for each
additional book up to a maximum charge of £3.00 (7 books plus). Overseas
customers including Ireland, please allow £2.00 for the first book plus £1.00
for the second book, plus 50p for each additional book.

NAME (Block Letters) _____

ADDRESS _____

_____

☐ I enclose my remittance for £ _____
☐ I wish to pay by Access/Visa Card

Number | | | | | | | | | | | | | | | | | |

Card Expiry Date _____